The novels of R. F. Delderfield, available from Hodder

A HORSEMAN RIDING BY
Long Summer Day
Post of Honour
The Green Gauntlet

Diana
To Serve Them All Our Days
Cheap Day Return

About the author

R. F. Delderfield was born in South London in 1912.
He was a journalist, playwright and a highly successful
novelist, renowned for brilliantly portraying slices of
English life. With the publication of his first saga, *A
Horseman Riding By*, he became one of Britain's most
popular and enduring authors. His novels were
international bestsellers and many were adapted for
television. He died in 1972.

R. F. DELDERFIELD

Post of Honour

HODDER

Copyright © 1968 by R. F. Delderfield

First published in Great Britain in 1968 by Hodder and Stoughton
A division of Hodder Headline

This paperback edition published in 2007

The right of R. F. Delderfield to be identified as the Author
of the Work has been asserted by him in accordance with the
Copyright, Designs and Patents Act 1988.

A Hodder paperback

I

A CIP catalogue record for this title
is available from the British Library

ISBN 978 0340 92292 7

Typeset by Hewer Text UK Ltd, Edinburgh

Printed and bound in Great Britain by
Mackays of Chatham Plc, Chatham, Kent

Hodder Headline's policy is to use papers that are natural, renewable
and recyclable products and made from wood grown in sustainable
forests. The logging and manufacturing processes are expected to
conform to the environmental regulations of the country of origin.

Hodder and Stoughton Ltd
A division of Hodder Headline
338 Euston Road
London NW1 3BH

For Deirdre Gibbens
and
Sir Geoffrey Harmsworth,
both old friends, with a genuine
love for the Westcountry.

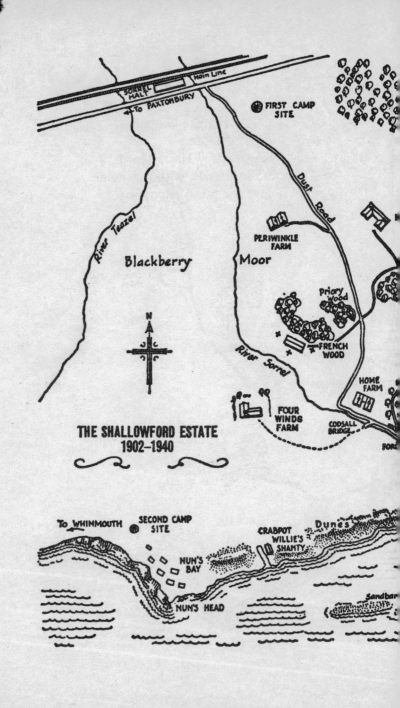

THE SHALLOWFORD ESTATE
1902–1940

At Shallowford House   Paul Craddock = (1) Grace Lovell (m. 1903)

                            Simon (1904)

                            (2) Claire Derwent (m. 1907)

Stephen and Andrew (The Pair, 1908)	Mary (1910)	Karen ("Whiz") (1913)	Claire (1918)	John (1934)

Ikey Palfrey (adopted 1902)

At Four Winds   Martin Codsall = Arabella (until 1904)

                     Will   Sydney

               Norman Eveleigh = Marian (until 1932)

Gilbert	Deborah	Rachel	Harold	Robbie	Esther	Mavis	Susan

               Harold Eveleigh = Connie (after 1932)

At Hermitage Farm   Arthur Pitts = Martha

                     Henry = Gloria

                  David   Prudence

At Periwinkle Farm   Will Codsall = Elinor Willoughby (until 1931)

                 Mark   Queenie   Floss   Richard

              Rumble Patrick Palfrey = Mary Craddock (1934 onwards)

                     Jerry

At High Coombe   Edward Derwent = Liz (second wife)

             Hugh   Rose   Claire (all by first wife)

At Deepdene Farm   Edwin Willoughby
                              Francis   Elinor

At Low Coombe   Tamer = Meg

    Sam = Joannie Smut = Marie   Hazel = Ikey

         Cissie = Brissot   Violet = Jumbo
                              Bellchamber

                            Pansy = (1) Walt Pascoe
                                  (2) Dandy Timberlake
                                  (3) Reg Willis

At Home Farm   Old Honeyman
                      Nelson = Prudence Pitts

Estate Workers (1902-40)   John Rudd, agent = Maureen O'Keefe, lady-doctor
                      Horace Handcock, gardener = Ada Handcock
                                        (housekeeper)
                      Thirza Tremlett, parlourmaid and nurse
                      Chivers, groom
                      Matt and Luke, shepherds
                      The Timberlake family, sawyers
                      Gappy Saunders, gardener's boy

At Coombe Bay   Parson Bull
                      Parson Horsey
                      Keith Horsey = Rachel Eveleigh
                      Abe Tozer, smith
                      Ephraim Morgan, builder
                      Tom Williams, fisherman
                      James Grenfell, M.P.
                      Walt Pascoe, labourer
                      Professor Scholtzer
                      Bruce and Celia Lovell
                      Aaron Stokes, reed-cutter
                      Willis, wheelwright

Chapter One

I

They were Squire Craddock's vintage years, the brief, crowded period beginning immediately after the fillip given to the Sorrel Valley by the 1911 Coronation Jubilee, and moving on into the blazing summer of 1914 that, on looking back a little later, seemed as remote as the Middle Ages.

Some guide as to what occurred in and around the Shallowford Big House and its seven farms during these thirty-six months could by found in the Bible-bound estate record kept up to date by Squire's wife Claire – 'the Derwent Maid' as many Shallowfordians continued to call her, notwithstanding the fact that she had been Squire's second wife for four years and had already presented him with three children and sometimes by Paul Craddock himself, particularly when he felt more than ordinarily complacent.

Into that great book, once used as a pornographic photographic album by Craddock's predecessor, poured the trivia of the years, a tumultuous hotchpotch of births, deaths, marriages, crop records, boundary adjustments, structural alterations, floods, frosts, droughts and occasional unrehearsed farces, like Craddock's short-lived addiction to the internal combustion engine. It was much more than an estate diary, for Paul Craddock did not see himself as a landlord to most of the hundred-odd people who lived between Blackberry Moor and the Sorrel outfall at Coombe Bay but as a kind of self-appointed tribal headman, part reeve, part mayor, part father-figure and friend. Nobody in the Valley contested this claim or would have wished to contest it, for not only did he perform the office efficiently but brought to it the thoughtful zest of a junior officer commanding his first platoon in the field. He grumbled a good deal and frequently cursed the responsibilities he had laid upon himself when he bought the estate back in '02, but for all that he was so jealous of them that he begrudged his agent John Rudd a small share of the packload.

John would have told you that Paul Craddock made his own decisions and Claire, Paul's plump, pretty and practical wife would have added that he enjoyed making them and even derived a certain gloomy satisfaction from his failures. Either one of these prejudiced witnesses could have told you everything worth knowing about this eccentric, generous, dedicated, self-opinionated young man, who had ploughed a fortune into the remote thirteen-hundred-acre estate between the main line and the sea but they would have preferred you to settle downalong and find out for yourself, the way everyone else had done in the years between the two coronations. For all the signposts were there, pointing across the river to Four Winds, down the river-road to Home Farm, over the shoulder of the hill to where the Pitts' family farmed Hermitage, and across the great belt of old woods to the three Coombe Farms and the steep, cobbled street of Coombe Bay. He knew and he loved every tile and every sprig of yellow gorse hereabouts. He could tell you how many Friesians Norman Eveleigh of Four Winds numbered in his herd, how many pigs Henry Pitts of Hermitage marketed last year, how the half-gypsy Potter tribe were faring over at Low Coombe now that old Tamer had died a hero, and how many of his tenants' wives were pregnant at any one time. He missed very little (unless it occurred under his nose on his own hearthstone) and because of this Claire found him far easier to manage than she had anticipated in view of his first and dolorous marriage to Grace Lovell. Two things only he demanded of her – identification with the Valley, which was his lifework, and a regular access to her ripe and blessedly complaisant body. Both demands were readily, not to say gaily fulfilled. Why not? She was Valley-born, deeming those born elsewhere deprived and luckless wights, and she had desired him as bedmate and helpmate ever since he had ridden into her father's rickyard as a city greenhorn within a month of her nineteenth birthday. And by now, like every other Shallowfordian, she had come to terms with his first disastrous marriage even though it had cost her five frustrating years of her youth. After all, every dog in the Valley was forgiven a first bite even when they bit Quality and at least he had emerged from the unlucky encounter with a ready-made stepson who was easy to love.

Typical of the entries written into the estate record by Claire during this three-year halcyon period was one dated February 12th, 1912. It read: *'Today. Doctor Maureen Rudd, M.D. wife of John Rudd, agent of Shallowford, delighted and astonished Sorrel Valley by presenting her husband with a bouncing boy! It was her first and she is, we think, more surprised than any of us, for she declares her age to be 39 although privately we think she is 37'.*

Whether or not Maureen Rudd was indulging in a little blarney about her age Claire was not exaggerating when she wrote that 'Lady Doctor' (as her patients continued to call her) was quite astounded to discover that she was pregnant. She had dashed up and down the Valley inviting all and sundry to witness the miracle, and would say, when they hastened to congratulate her, 'It's the air in this damned Valley, so it is! It's a forcing-house for women! Every woman, married or single, this side of the Teazel calls me out in the middle of the night sooner or later! And now who the Devil can attend me?' They all laughed with her and reassured her, for she was one of the most popular figures in the Valley and the initial prejudice against her sex had long since disappeared, banished by her explosive laughter and her habit of cutting the cackle and coming straight to the point but John Rudd, who loved her dearly, had never quite recovered from the shock of having his diffident proposal accepted, voiced his anxiety to Paul after Maureen had returned from seeing a specialist in Paxtonbury.

'She says Clifford Goreham has assured her everything will be all right,' he said, 'but it's obviously a risk for a woman to have her first child at that age. If anything happened to her I'd never forgive myself.'

'For God's sake don't say that to her,' Paul told him, 'or
she'll throw something heavy at you, John! It's the kind of
remark that would infuriate her if I know Maureen.'

'Oh, it's well enough for you,' John grumbled, 'Claire is only
twenty-nine and she's already had three children, but damn it
I just couldn't believe it when Maureen told me and, strictly
between ourselves I feel a bit of a fool! After all my son Roddy
is thirty and I'm not far off sixty!'

'Obviously a young sixty,' Paul joked, having been warned
by Claire to laugh John out of his anxieties. 'As for Maureen,
she's as fit as a fiddle, whether she's thirty-nine or, as I'm
inclined to believe, thirty-seven for it's just like her to make
the most of a situation like this! Believe me, John, everything
is going to be all right, so let's wet the baby's head in
advance.'

And so it proved when Maureen's baby was born in a
Paxtonbury nursing home 'on the anniversary of Abraham
Lincoln's birthday', as the almost incoherent father informed
Paul and Claire by telephone. Maureen had had a stiffish time,
he said, and was very tired, but Goreham who was attending
her was pleased with her on the whole. The baby weighed
seven pounds and they were going to christen him Paul, after
his godfather!

'How many godchildren have I got around here?' Paul asked
Claire, after he had passed the news to the anxious kitchen
staff and Claire, after consulting the record, told him seven,
four girls and three boys, and she would have to make a
special entry in the back of the book so that he did not
overlook anyone's birthday. She kept her promise the next
day and read the list to him over the luncheon table. The
first, Sam Potter's eldest daughter, was now nine and between
Pauline Potter and Paul Rudd came one of Will Codsall's
boys, Eveleigh's youngest daughter, a son of Henry Pitts,
a child of Honeyman's foreman at the Home Farm, and
the daughter of a cottager employed by Edward Derwent,
whose wife had died in labour.

'Well, it's enough,' he said, 'we'll have to call a halt to this
nonsense. How can I be responsible for seven children learning

their catechism when I'm going bald and putting on weight? Maureen's right about this Valley. Every woman who sets foot in it finds herself in the family way sooner or later.'

'If they didn't you'd be the first to complain about diminishing returns,' Claire told him. 'Who knows, I might have some interesting news for you myself in the spring.'

He looked at her so sharply that she laughed and said, 'It's all right, I'm only teasing but don't look as if I could go about it without your enthusiastic co-operation! Sometimes I'm surprised we haven't got as many as the Eveleighs! I do hope they've finished or we shall be saddled with the expense of extending Four Winds.'

Maureen returned to the Valley in early April and Thirza, who had been Simon's nurse, was flattered to be taken on in like capacity at the Lodge, her place as parlourmaid-nanny being filled by a pert fourteen-year-old called Joy, the daughter of the eldest Timberlake girl.

Another entry in the record, dated '*March 1st, 1912*' told of Paul's acceptance of the mastership of the combined Teazel Vale and Downland Farmers' Hunt, on condition that he was not expected to hunt more than three days a fortnight and could hand over to Rose Derwent on alternate hunting days. The invitation originated from Lord Gilroy, who, despite their political rivalry, flatly refused to perpetuate his father's feud and took little or no interest in country activities.

The Teazel Vale pack was sadly run down but the Downland farmers, who hunted the country east of High Coombe where the Shallowford boundary ran inland from the sea, were only too anxious to halve their expenses by bringing in new hounds and combining the two hunts, renamed the Sorrel Vale Hunt and housed in kennels built on to some old outbuildings belonging to the Hermitage. Gilroy provided his own huntsmen and Eveleigh's eldest boy was engaged as whipper-in and kennel-man, so that after a shaky start the new hunt settled down to a lively season in the autumn of 1912.

To see the motley field move off on a fine autumn morning and draw one of the Hermitage coverts, or cross the moor in a north-easterly direction to the rough country behind

Shallowford Woods, was like watching a column of moss-troopers embark on a border foray. It was by no means a fashionable hunt for Paul was no stickler for etiquette and most of the followers wore corduroys, leggings and hard, low-crowned hats. Only Rose Derwent and one or two of the wealthier freeholders were well-mounted but there was an easy familiarity about a company where most of the field addressed one another by Christian name and once they were in full cry over the open country there was often some hard riding and a good deal of rivalry to be in at the death. Paul, who considered himself no more than a competent horseman, was outclassed by the small group of thrusters to whom a day in the saddle was the breath of life. Always up with the leaders, and usually in advance of them, was Rose Derwent, who would ride straight at the most formidable fence; not far behind whenever he was home on furlough, was Ikey, with young Gilbert Eveleigh, Gottfried Scholtzer, the son of the German historian, little Pauline Potter, Sam's eldest daughter (who was Rose Derwent's chief apprentice), and two or three others. Paul himself, Chivers his groom, Henry Pitts, Edward Derwent and Eveleigh when he could spare the time, usually followed in a pounding bunch, with stragglers sometimes as much as a quarter-mile in the rear, those who turned out for the exercise like John Rudd, old Arthur Pitts and even, on occasion, the German professor himself, who splashed along on a barrel-chested cob, his Teutonic passion for tidiness requiring him to see the last of the cavalcade out of a field and make sure every gate was shut and fastened. Rose Derwent had taught every child in the Valley to ride, accepting fees from no more than half of them but relying on their services as stable-hands during school holidays and week ends. Claire came out occasionally but, unlike Rose, who shocked some of the older members of the hunt, preferred to ride side-saddle. Whenever she appeared at a meet Paul noticed the sad, proud look in her father's eye and guessed that he was comparing her with her mother, who had died in a gully across the Teazel more than twenty years before. Although he did not take his mastership very seriously (it was difficult to think

of the Sorrel Vale and Southdown Farmers' in terms of the
Quorn or Pytchley) he always enjoyed himself and felt better
for the day out. He liked best, however, the long treks home
to Shallowford when the deep goyles intersecting the moor
were bowls of blue dusk and the smell of wet leaves came
out of the woods. Sometimes he would ride partway home
with Eveleigh, or Henry Pitts, and they would discuss the
day's run, chuckling over John Rudd parting from his cob at
a jump or telling each other that young Gilbert Eveleigh and
little Pauline Potter would make first-class steeplechasers in
the years ahead. For there always seemed to be so many
years ahead and whenever he was alone on the final stage
along the river road or crossing the shoulder of the Bluff, Paul
was aware of the timelessness of the Valley, and the rhythm
of its seasons that seemed unrelated to the passage of time
elsewhere. When Claire was with him they would sometimes
talk of the future and speculate on the probable careers of
Simon, the twins, Andy and Steve, and their daughter Mary,
but secretly, and sometimes a little guiltily, Paul preferred
to make these homeward journeys in solitude, for then he
could kick his legs free of the stirrups and let his thoughts
range back across the years to the days when he first ambled
over this familiar ground, surely the greenest and possibly
the luckiest landowner in the Westcountry.

II

Old Willoughby died in the new year, the direct result according to his boy Francis, of travelling to Whinmouth in foul
weather to conduct a service and riding home the same night.
It was partially true, inasmuch as he died only a week later of
pneumonia but Willoughby was nearly seventy and had never
enjoyed the robust health of the other tenants although, for
some years now – ever since his Road-to-Damascus conversion
at a Methodist camp-meeting – he had driven himself hard,
sometimes making a journey of forty miles to witness The
Truth. At his funeral in the tiny Nonconformist burial ground

adjoining the Methodist Chapel in Coombe Bay Paul noticed
that the Valley was as well represented as it had been at old
Tamer's funeral, when the whole countryside had turned out
to pay tribute to such an unlikely hero. The centuries-old
feud between church and chapelgoers was finally buried with
Willoughby, for Parson Horsey attended, standing a little apart
from the dry-eyed Elinor Codsall and her hulking husband
Will, who looked clownish in his blue serge suit. Paul said
to Francis Willoughby, as they walked back to the lych-gate,
'He was a good man, Francis, and I shall never forget how
well he behaved on the night of the wreck. He didn't have an
enemy in the Valley, did he?', and Francis said no, not now
that Parson Bull had gone but that the old man had been
inclined to let Deepdene take second place to his preaching
and the place was now in bad heart.

'You'll be carrying on, I hope,' Paul said and Francis replied
that it depended on how much money his father had left for
there was very little profit in poultry now that Elinor had gone
and for some time the farm had been badly understocked. 'I
always wanted him to go in for beef,' he added, 'but he never
would, for he couldn't stomach the idea of fattening animals
for the slaughter-house. He ought to have been a vet instead
of a farmer, he was clever with a sick beast.'

Paul said, 'Look here, Frank, if you think you can make
a success of beef go ahead and chance your luck! I'll ask
Honeyman to see what he can do to give you a start and
you know that I'm all for specialisation. It's certainly worked
over at Four Winds, and at your sister's little place. You don't
have to show a profit for a year or two for I shouldn't press
you,' and Francis, a young man of few words where his father
had had so many murmured his thanks but little else, so Paul
sought out Elinor who agreed that it was a sound notion
and told Francis so on the spot.

The upshot of the conversation was that Francis Willoughby
sold his poultry to his sister, his pigs to Henry Pitts and
thereafter concentrated on beef cattle and Paul noticed that
he seemed to flower within weeks of his father's death, as
though, for the first time in his life, he could farm instead of

deputising for a man who preferred the pulpit to the strawyard. He had always been a very reserved young man, small and neat like Elinor but lacking the stamina she had shown from the day Will Codsall carried her as a bride to the half-ruined holding at Periwinkle. Paul first noticed the dramatic change in Francis while crossing a Deepdene meadow on his way home from the last meet of the season. He saw him driving a bunch of steers into a kale field and at first he thought the lad must be having trouble for he darted this way and that, waving his jacket and uttering sharp, staccato shouts but after watching a moment he realised that Francis was only amusing himself by pretending to be a matador so he rode on without advertising himself, realising that the new master of Deepdene would be very embarrassed if he thought his charade was overlooked. He thought, 'Well, that's another little problem sorted out but it's a pity the old man had to die first! That's the way it seems to be, however; Martin Codsall goes crazy and Eveleigh steps in to make a go of Four Winds; Tamer Potter gets drowned and his two daughters take up with a tireless clodhopper who succeeds in revitalising the Dell; and now Frank Willoughby plays at bullfighting in his own meadow and that within a month of his father being laid in the earth!', and he rode on down to the Ford musing and feeling that, although the Valley seemed always to stand still, this was really a delusion and that its blood was circulating all the time as new approaches were made to old problems and new hands laid on old tools.

III

Ikey Palfrey passed out of Woolwich with creditable marks in the late summer of 1912 and came home on furlough for a month before joining his battery in India. Claire thought he had changed a good deal during the last two or three years and Paul admitted that he had, at least outwardly, for he was now a shade short of six feet and had also filled out, losing the lean, rakish build of his cross-country days. Yet to Paul he was still the Ikey Palfrey plucked from the scrapyard ten years ago, a waif with an impudent way of looking seniors in the eye as if, whilst prepared to be lectured now and again, he reserved the right to treat scoldings as so much pi-jaw without much significance.

Claire had never felt wholly at ease with Ikey and, without in the least knowing why, went out of her way to maintain the slightly impersonal relationship that grew up between them. In the early days of her marriage, when Ikey was only a boy and away at school most of the time, it had been easy to patronise him but later on, when he was about eighteen, she began to suspect that, more often than not, and in the kindest possible way, he was laughing at her and this led her to discard patronage in favour of propitiation, although she could think of no reason at all why she should adopt such an attitude. It might, she sometimes thought, have something to do with that curious letter he had written her all those years ago, the one urging her to visit the injured Squire after he had called out for her in a fever. She had never mentioned this letter to anyone, not even to Paul, yet here again she could find no adequate reason for keeping it a secret, for she had never once doubted its substance. Ikey was always very polite to her and she did not think it likely that he still regarded himself as the agent who brought man and wife together, reasoning that he had probably forgotten the letter by now and yet, every now and again when their eyes met over the table, or she found herself alone with him, his knowing air put her at a disadvantage. He still addressed her as 'Ma'am', as though she was a queen to whom he owed an indirect allegiance, and this slightly uncomfortable relationship had not been eased by a recent exchange over Simon, occurring soon after her discussion with Grace concerning the boy.

Claire took her duties as stepmother very seriously and had gone out of her way to avoid discriminating between Simon and her own children, often to the latters' disadvantage. Simon was a difficult child to know and inclined to walk alone but she had persisted and was confident that he had a genuine affection for her. She had thought a good deal before taking Grace's advice, and discussing with Ikey the possibility of telling Simon some form of disguised truth about his mother. She would have preferred to leave things as they were and let him grow up thinking of himself as her child but she remembered that the Valley relishèd scandal of every kind and with Simon approaching his eighth birthday it was likely that he would soon learn the truth from an outside source which it was surely her duty to anticipate. So, in the end, she told Ikey the gist of her conversation with Grace in the hotel bedroom after the suffragette scuffle and as always he listened gravely and politely to what she had to say. When, however, she told him that Grace had advised her to employ him as her agent, he smiled his rather irritating smile and said, 'I'm afraid it's too late, Ma'am. Simon already knows all there is to know.' She said, shocked by this news, 'He does? Who told him?' and without a blush he admitted having told Simon himself more than a year ago, after the child had made an appeal to him for information on the subject.

At first she was furiously angry but then common sense warned her that she was being unjust and that Simon must have got an inkling from one of the tenants or estate workers before approaching Ikey in the first place. She said crisply, 'He *came* to you? After hearing gossip from somebody else?'

'I couldn't say,' he replied calmly, 'I didn't ask him.'

'Why didn't you ask him?'

He lifted his shoulders, refusing to be rattled. 'I don't know, perhaps because it seemed to me to be prying. He had probably been eavesdropping and heard something he wasn't meant to hear. He asked me about his mother so I told him.'

'Wouldn't it have been wiser to have sent him to me or his father?'

'I don't think so, Ma'am. If he had wanted that he would have gone to you or Squire instead of me.'

She bit her lip and at that moment she could cheerfully have boxed his ears but behind her resentment she could not help admiring his grasp of essentials. She said rather sharply, 'Well, how did he take it? Was it a shock to him?'

'No,' he said, 'I don't think it was a shock. I cushioned it as well as I could, and I got the impression he had always

known there was a difference between him and the twins
and Mary. How can we be sure he didn't get a hint years
ago, a chance remark made by any one of us when we
thought him too young to notice?'

She considered this and the pause gave her a chance to
master her temper and make an honest effort to put herself in
Ikey's place. After all, he was quite possibly right, for adults
often make this mistake and in any case it was done now
and her relationship with Simon had improved rather than
deteriorated in the last year. She said with a shrug, 'Well, I'm
glad it's over and done with but I shall have to tell Squire what
happened and I daresay he'll want to hear more details.'

Ikey nodded, absently she thought and said, 'I did what
I thought best at the time, I'm sorry if I put my foot in
it. It seemed to me that, by making an issue of it Simon
might have been more confused than he was. That was why
I made light of it, Mrs Craddock.'

Devil take the boy, she thought, he's infallible! It occurred
to her then how odd it was that Grace should have singled
out Ikey for a mission already accomplished and with this
thought came another, more disquieting one for it seemed to
her that Ikey's loyalty was to Grace rather than to her and
it distressed her to think this for until then it had always
seemed that all trace of Grace Lovell had been banished
from the house whereas it was now evident that something
of Grace lingered. The uncertainty caused by this reflection
must have shown in her face for, with his strange faculty for
reading thoughts, he said, gently, 'I wouldn't worry about
it any more, Ma'am. Simon looks on you as his mother
and why shouldn't he? You haven't failed him in that respect and I'm sure you never will.'

Suddenly, and shamefully, she wanted to cry and he must
have seen this too, for he turned away and lounged off,
hands deep in his pockets while she stood there feeling
more unsure of herself than at any time since her return
to the Valley. But she was Edward Derwent's daughter and
had emotional reserves at her disposal, so presently she blew
her nose, threw up her head and marched off along the

terrace to the rose garden where she remained until she
had regained control of herself.

She found a way of telling Paul without making an issue of
it, throwing the information into a general conversation about
her talk with Grace at the hotel and saying, with a casualness
that deceived him, 'Grace wondered if Simon knew I was his
stepmother; I told her that Ikey had explained it to him long
ago,' and all Paul replied was, 'Ikey did? Well, good for him!
It was something I should have put off indefinitely.'

And that, so far as Claire was concerned, would have been
that had not a new development involving Ikey and Simon
taken place during Ikey's embarkation leave, a year later.
This time Claire found herself in uneasy alliance with Ikey,
siding with him at the risk of engaging in her first serious
quarrel with the man she adored.

It happened at lunchtime, on a day towards the end of
October after Paul and Simon had come in from a morning's cubbing in the woods. Paul seemed very put out about
something and Simon, after kicking off his little boots and
throwing down his hard hat and riding switch, disappeared
upstairs, remaining there in spite of being called for lunch.
The twins and Mary were in the nursery and the only other
person at table was Ikey, who had seemed very preoccupied
this leave, a circumstance Claire attributed to the imminence
of his first tour overseas. Claire said, as Mrs Handcock
appeared with the vegetables, 'I'll see to that! Go up and
get Simon, I've aleady called him three times!' but Paul
said, unexpectedly, 'Leave him to work out his sulks!' and
Mrs Handcock departed, buttoning her lip as she always did
when there was an atmosphere at table.

'Did anything happen this morning?' Claire asked and
Paul grunted that sometimes he couldn't get to the bottom
of 'that boy', and that it was time Simon went to school
to get sense knocked into him.

Ikey perked up at this, winking at Claire who at once
demanded to know what had happened. It was something
very trivial, he told her – Gilbert Eveleigh, as whipper-in,
had posted Simon on his pony in the north run while most

of the others stood back from the covert. The boy had been told to holler back as soon as the fox in the thick undergrowth crossed the ride towards a known earth north of the mere. The fox went in that direction – Gilbert and others would swear to that – but no holler came from Simon, and when they had all dashed round to his side of the wood he was seen walking his pony down a ride nearly a mile from the spot where he had been stationed. The fox got clean away and when Paul demanded to know whether Simon had seen it he admitted that he had but had turned away rather than holler.

'Why ever did he do that?' asked Claire much surprised, and Paul said that on the way home Simon had told him he did not want to go hunting again and that he thought hunting 'wasn't really a gentleman's sport!'

This was too much for Ikey who let out a loud guffaw and even Claire smiled but Paul, whose sense of humour was unpredictable, said, 'What's funny about it? I felt a damned ass I can tell you! And as for him feeling squeamish about hunting we don't want the boy to develop into a milksop, do we?'

'He'll not do that,' Ikey said and with so much emphasis that Claire saw he no longer treated the incident as a joke. 'If the kid really feels that way,' he went on, 'then jolly good luck to him! He's probably right anyway!'

'Now what the devil am I to make of that?' demanded Paul angrily and Claire said they were both making too much of the matter, and that if he took Simon at his word, and left him behind next time, the boy would probably be disappointed.

'I wouldn't bank on that,' Ikey said, quietly, and when they both looked at him, he added, 'He's got a natural sympathy for the fox. He always has given me the impression he's signed on with the hunted!'

'Sometimes, Ikey,' Paul said, gruffly, 'I wish to God you would stop favouring us with undergraduate drivel when you're at home! It doesn't suit you and it damned well irritates me!'

It was the first time Claire had ever heard him address Ikey sharply and she suddenly was aware that the clash between them went beyond Simon's quixotic sympathy for a hunted fox. She said hastily, 'All right, all right! Don't let's quarrel about it, it isn't that important.'

'It might be,' Ikey said, ignoring her cautionary glance, 'if the Gov'nor is determined to warp Simon into being the kind of person he isn't, and never will be!'

'Well he isn't likely to do that,' snapped Claire, feeling annoyed with both of them but she could not help noticing that Paul winced at Ikey's remark as he said, sharply, 'Look here, Ikey, I happen to think young Simon made an exhibition of himself turning his back on the field the way he did! I daresay the incident seems trivial to both of you but to my mind it was a blatant piece of showing off! If he really felt that way he could easily have made some kind of excuse.'

'What kind of excuse?' Ikey asked, and Paul replied, irritably, 'Any kind! He could have pretended he wasn't looking, or that he had just taken a toss!'

'Yes,' said Ikey, still quietly, 'he could have done that and revealed himself as a liar and a coward when he's neither.'

'Oh do let's get Simon down and forget it,' said Claire but Paul said, 'No, I'm damned if I will for I'll not have Ikey trying to teach me how to bring up my own son! I tell you the boy was showing off and nothing more!' whereupon Ikey growled, 'That isn't true and you know it, Gov'nor! It's a damned pompous attitude and I'm hanged if I'll sit here and listen to it! The kid was perfectly justified in doing what he did and as his father you ought to sympathise with him instead of bullying him!' and he got up, nodded to Claire and strode towards the door.

He was stopped by Claire who shot out her arm as he passed and caught him by the wrist. She said, in a way that made them both feel slightly ashamed of themselves, 'You can't walk out on this now, Ikey! And neither can you, Paul! You've both said too much for my peace of mind and it's quite wrong to begin an argument like this and then turn your backs on it!'

'I wasn't turning my back on it,' Paul said, although he had in fact half risen. 'All the same I can't see any sense in prolonging it and upsetting everybody. You'd better go,

Ikey, and I hope you mind your manners better than this in
the mess!'

'Stop it, Paul!' Claire almost shouted, 'just stop it and let
me say something!'

They both looked at her then, Paul settling back in his
chair, Ikey standing irresolutely by the door.

'Now then,' she said, trying hard to get her voice under control, 'this is something we must have out here and now if only
because I happen to be concerned. Very much concerned!'

'I don't see how,' Paul grumbled but in a more reasonable
tone. 'What are you driving at, Claire?'

Claire looked at Ikey, realising that he was very well
aware what she was driving at and went on, 'Ikey is implying that Simon is . . . well, is his mother all over again!
That's what you meant, isn't it?'

'Yes, it is, Ma'am,' he said, 'and I'm sorry.'

'You needn't be sorry but for heaven's sake do stop calling
me "Ma'am", as if I was someone who had usurped Queen
Victoria!' she snapped and a ghost of a grin plucked at the
corners of his mouth and then vanished as he saw thunder
in Paul's glance.

'I've never heard such damned nonsense in my life,' Paul
said but Claire, turning on him, said that it wasn't nonsense
and if he would have the patience to think about it he
would see that it wasn't. Paul said, helplessly, 'But hang
it, woman, Grace hunted twice a week! She was one of the
best riders to hounds in the country.'

'It isn't simply a matter of hounds and foxes, Gov'nor,' Ikey
said, patiently, 'it's an attitude to life, an inherited attitude
maybe. That's what you meant, wasn't it – Claire?'

Colour came back into her cheeks and through the fog of
the issue that had them snapping at one another she saw
that, for the first time since they had sat around this table
together, they were of a single generation, no longer a man,
his wife and a boy but three adults, each equally involved.
She said, more calmly, 'Yes, Ikey, that was exactly what I
meant, and because of it I entirely agree with you! It would
be quite wrong of Paul to bully Simon into hunting against

his will, or looking on him as a ninny because he wouldn't! I don't like saying this, Paul, but you can be very stupid about some things and you're being stupid now, because your pride as the local M.F.H. is involved.'

Ikey looked at her admiringly and for a moment nobody spoke. Then, when Paul moved as though to get up, and they both made sure he was going to storm out of the room, the door opened and Simon came in, silently taking his place and helping himself to vegetables. Claire said, gently, 'You really must come when I call, Simon, we've all been waiting for you,' and the boy, looking slightly startled, said, 'I'm sorry, Mother, I was changing,' and began to eat with catlike deliberation.

It was the strangest meal they had ever sat through but any prospect of further discussion was averted by Ikey's tact for he talked to Simon about one thing and another and occasionally included both Paul and Claire in the conversation so that Claire, whose heart was still beating an uncertain rhythm, had cause to be grateful to him but wondered bleakly what Paul would say to her when they were alone.

After about twenty minutes Paul rose, saying, 'Run along and give Chivers a hand rubbing down, Simon, he's on his own this afternoon,' and the boy slipped off, glad to be out of it so cheaply.

'Well, I'm not exactly climbing down,' Paul said, as soon as he had gone, 'but there might be something in what you say. It's worth thinking over at all events because if it is so then it will need tackling one way or another! To have Simon go Grace's way wouldn't bring him much joy, would it? Or us either?' and with that he stumped out. Ikey said, 'I'm sorry I let you in for that, Claire. If I had to open my big mouth I shouldn't have done it in your presence!'

'It's just as well you did,' she told him, 'for there's little enough you could have done on your own, Ikey. Paul is hard to drive but I do flatter myself I've learned how to lead him.'

'Yes,' he said, with a grin, 'I'm quite sure you have!' and he thought, 'Grace certainly knew her business when she urged me to write that letter, for Claire understands him better than any of us, yet he can manage her when

he wouldn't have managed Grace in a thousand years!' He
moved across to the window, looking across the paddock
under its green and gold autumn mantle.

'Are you depressed by the prospect of exchanging this for
India?' she asked him suddenly but he said no, on the contrary
he was relieved but he did not add why. She said, after a pause,
'Well, if ever you want to talk, Ikey, I'll listen and do anything I
can to help. We've at least made that much progress today.'

He came back to her then, holding his head slightly to
one side as though considering. And then he did something
he had never done in the ten years she had known him. He
bent and brushed her cheek with his lips and was gone before
she could decide what had prompted the gesture. When she
thought of him afterwards, however, it was not as the brash,
affable young man of whom she had once been so wary, but
rather of a youth as confused and uncertain as any of them,
despite a convincing show of self-containment.

IV

Claire was learning about him. The shifts of his life had taught
him how to deceive most people, to cod them into believing
that he had all the self-confidence necessary to make a place
for himself wherever he went, but he had stopped deceiving
himself long ago, soon after finding himself in a straitjacket
tighter than any he had worn at High Wood or Shallowford.
Yet he still might have worn it comfortably had it not been for
Hazel Potter who stood squarely between past and future and
was always there, clutching her rags and freedom no matter
how many new friends he made, how many cadet sprees he
embarked upon, how enthusiastically he threw himself into
the business of learning to be a gunner. He would see her in
his mind's eye at odd times of the day and night, when his
thoughts should have been engaged elsewhere and it was not
only his body that yearned for her. She had the power to make
everything he did seem profitless, sometimes almost fatuous,
as if she alone was the one substantial force in his world and

everything else – the ritual of mess life, the airs and opinions of instructors and fellow cadets, the menace of the great tools he was learning to use, were toys in a nursery of men and women clinging to the fantasies of childhood. Yet he did not accept this duality without a bitter, inward struggle for he sensed, somehow, that it would bring him down in the end whichever way he turned and he was still tormented by the demands of loyalty to the Squire, the man who, from the kindest of motives, had turned him loose in this desert. But it was Hazel Potter who triumphed. Only a day or two after he had returned home for his first leave his good intentions were forgotten. Shedding his fashionable clothes with his army drawl he slipped off into the woods to find her and here, so long as they were alone, he was happy again, his tensions miraculously eased.

They did not become lovers again, or not on that first occasion, for as long as their association remained innocent he could hold the door on the other world ajar but when he came home again in the spring the temptation to slam that door and go to Heaven or hell with a flower in his mouth was too strong for him; and having once recrossed into her world he had no regrets, although he sometimes wondered what would become of them both and how loud the crash would be when it came.

He no longer felt shame or fear when he parted from her but he took great pains to ensure, as far as possible, that the woods kept their secret, riding out on his chestnut mare, Bella, and unsaddling and haltering her below the hill where Hazel kept her little house. As long as he went out mounted Paul and everyone else would assume him to be riding for exercise and sometimes on his return he would describe the imaginary route he had taken. Chivers might have noticed that Bella always looked fresh when he stabled her but Chivers was an unimaginative soul and would have found it difficult to believe that horse and rider had gone no further than the north side of the mere, there to part company for an hour or longer.

Hazel received him gladly but without excitement. She was aware of the obligations he owed the world beyond the screen of the woods and had long grown accustomed to his erratic

comings and goings at odd times of the year. Whenever she
saw him emerge from the rhododendrons and begin to climb
the hill she would slip down from her rock, mend the fire
and, after propping the polished tin lid on a niche, shake
out her hair, crooning softly to herself and admiring her
reflection in the surface. Then she would fill her battered
kettle at the spring and put it to boil, for he always liked
her strong bitter tea and the honey she gathered to spread
on bread baked in her Dutch oven.

There was nothing urgent or impetuous about these occasions. Sometimes, after they had kissed in greeting, they
would sit together and look out over the Valley and she would
tell him of her trivial encounters since he was last here, of
lumbering badgers visiting one another's sets on the slope, or
another attempt of the stoats to rob the woodpecker's nest and
the struggle that followed. There were always fresh flowers in
a jam jar on her 'table', not only the more homely flowers of the
woods, bluebells, harebells, primroses, foxgloves and campion,
but much shyer plants that she alone knew where to find and
had gathered to give brief splendour to the cave. Then, when
they had talked and sipped their tea, he would sometimes
stroke her hair, caressing it with a gentle, unhurried touch and
looking at her as if he never ceased to wonder at the texture of
her skin, the lights in her hair, or the suppleness of her limbs
tanned nut-brown by sun and wind. Whenever he spoke to
her he used her familiar burr but without selfconsciousness,
for it seemed to him an affront to talk to her as he talked
to the cadets and the people up at the Big House. He would
say, stroking her breasts, 'Youm beautiful, Hazel! Youm the
prettiest creature yerabouts, that you be! An' I loves touching
'ee, do'ee know that?' and she would smile a gratified, vacant
smile and shiver under his hand or lift her own to trace a
path down the side of his face with a forefinger, as though
to assure herself that he was real. Then, without explanation,
he would be gone again and she would busy herself renewing
the bracken on the floor, or scouring her battered pots, or
would resume her aimless movements about the Valley. She
was always happiest in the hour when he had gone for then

her memory of what passed between them was fresh and
she could compose one of her long, rambling prose poems in
which they ranged the woods and river valley together but
soon she would half forget him until some sixth sense told
her he was home again and it was time to resume her vigil
on the rock. They had tried to coax her back to the Dell or
to take service with one of the farmers but she resisted their
persuasions, disappearing completely for days at a stretch so
that, short of locking her up, there was no way of stopping
her wandering. Meg saw her and talked to her from time to
time, but Meg did not join the crusade to tame her; she alone,
with the single exception of Ikey, understood what freedom
of movement meant to the only true gypsy in the family and
would do nothing to threaten it.

Two or three days after the dispute about Simon, Ikey set
out across the woods on foot in the dusk of a dry autumn
day. He did not hurry for he was depressed at not having
had the courage to tell her that he would be gone in the
morning, this time for at least three years. He knew that
she took little heed of time and that even if he told her the
truth she would not be much concerned but the finality of
the occasion weighted on his mind nevertheless. It was almost
dark when he threaded his way through the rhododendrons
but she heard twigs crackle under his feet and lit a candle to
guide him to the screen of the gorse at the mouth of the cave.
He was a long time coming up and the kettle, which had been
simmering, was boiling when he reached her little house.

'Will 'ee tak' tea now?' she said, as though she had been
a polite hostess welcoming a guest and he said he would
and squatted on a truss of bracken, balancing himself on his
heels. Sitting in that posture, with the candlelight flickering
over his dark hair and strong features he looked a little like
an Arab pondering a purchase and she said, handing him tea,
'Youm sad, Ikey boy; be 'ee off outalong tomorrow?' He said
this was so and that he would be outalong much longer than
usual for they were sending him across the sea. This did not
frighten her but it must have astonished her for she uttered
the low hissing sound she used to express surprise.

'Across the sea?' she repeated. 'Baint 'ee scared?'

'No,' he said, 'I baint scared but I'm mumpish, mumpish to be leavin' 'ee so long.'

'Aw giddon,' she said, carelessly, 'you'll be back zoon enough, dornee mope along o' that!' and she sidled up to him and tweaked his ear. He seized her then with an urgency he had never used, not even when he was drunk on his mother's hedgerow wine, throwing her across his knees and covering her face with kisses so that she laughed and pretended to resist and they rolled sideways into the bracken, their shadows dancing a crazy pattern on the wall. Then, breathlessly, she freed herself and said, 'Wait on, boy! Dornee rush zo! Tiz dark now, so why dornee stay the night zince youm going? Tiz mild too and us'll be snug if I mends the fire!'

He said, for once not using the brogue, 'I can't stay, Hazel; it's my last night and they'll expect me to dinner,' but he made no effort to go and she was puzzled by his sudden listlessness. 'I don't like leaving you and that's a fact,' he added and she smiled for he had never previously committed himself so deeply, 'I don't like to think what might happen to you up here alone with me thousands of miles away. Dammit, you can't even read a letter I could write! Why the devil won't you go and live in the Dell, at least until I get back again?'

He had suggested this many times, just as he had urged her to return to Miss Willoughby's school and learn to read and write, but tonight she saw that he meant it and his sudden concern baffled her.

'Now whyfore should harm come to me up yer?' she demanded. ''Er never has, has 'er?'

'No,' he admitted, 'it never has, and I suppose you can look after yourself for if you can't, who can?'

'I likes it yer,' she said, doggedly, 'so yer I stay 'till I dies!'

'*Why* do you like it so much, Hazel? Tell me, if you can.'

'Because I can zee what goes on,' she said, but then he saw that she was teasing him and that this was not the real reason, and said, 'That isn't why! I don't mind about you being here by day, it's sleeping out that matters.'

'Aye,' she said, now looking at him slyly, 'but mebbe I stay on because 'o you!'

'Because of me? But I only get up here once in a blue moon!'

'Ah,' she said, 'that's zo but when I'm yer *youm* always along o' me in a manner o' speakin'. Do 'ee mind that, now?'

He minded it well enough and it filled him with a tenderness that no words, in or out of the brogue, could convey. He put his arm round her and drew her close so that they sat there with their backs to the shelving wall, her head on his breast as he stroked her tumbling mass of hair. They sat thus for so long that he thought she was asleep and presently the candle guttered and went out but as though to replace it a sliver of moonlight crept into the cave. Time passed and neither of them moved but when, shifting slightly to glance at his luminous watch, he saw that it was already long past dinner-time, she stirred and said, plaintively, 'Youm turrible mumpish tonight, Ikey! Dornee want me no more?' and he took her face between his hands and said, 'I'll always want you, Hazel, wherever I am and I'll always come back to you, don't ever forget that! I'll always come back!' It seemed to satisfy her for she brightened up at once, saying cheerfully, 'Well then yer us be an' tomorrow you'll be outalong zo tiz no use frettin', be it? Us best make the most of it, Ikey-boy!'

Her philosophy, thus expressed, boosted his spirits for he thought, 'They all call her "mazed" but she's more sense than any one of us! She doesn't live by the week or the day but by the hour, so that's how I'll think of her, always!' and he pulled her down and would have taken possession of her with the impatience he usually displayed when time was short, but tonight a subtle difference entered into their relationship; after the first moment or so it was she who led, as though she realised he was the one standing in need of comfort.

It was after ten o'clock when he kissed her for the last time and, taking his lantern, went out along the track to the north end of the mere and home by the long but less overgrown route, approaching Shallowford from the east. He slipped in by the yard door and up the backstairs to change his clothes and when he came down to the library he found Paul and Claire waiting up but they did not ask him where he had been, or why he was so late, remembering that he was almost twenty-one and might well have some private good-byes to say in the Valley. In fact they had laid a wager on the subject, over dinner, Paul betting that Ikey was mildly interested in the eldest Eveleigh girl, Claire wagering that Deborah Eveleigh was not Ikey's type and suggesting that his fancy had strayed over the county border during his summer furlough and fixed on the daughter of a retired cavalry major called Ella Stokes, who lived at Brandon Chase or the next village on.

'It's a damned long walk in the dark,' Paul said, when ten o'clock struck, 'so you've lost your money, old girl!'

'Not so long at his age, and with the prospect of three years pig-sticking and polo playing in the company of men,' she said. 'In any case, don't you dare question him unless he volunteers information!'

'Not me,' he told her chuckling, 'I know that much about Ikey!'

He apologised for missing dinner when he came at last but he did not explain where he had been, except to say, off-handedly, that he had lost track of time. Claire, kissing him good night, noticed that he still looked a little wan and decided that the bet would be null and void, for he had almost certainly been mooching around in his own company all evening and this did not surprise her. If she had been exchanging Shallowford for India it was what she might have done.

Chapter Two

I

Keith Horsey's wooing of Rachel Eveleigh was progressing but at such a pedestrian pace that sometimes Rachel would lie awake for hours wondering how to bring him to the boil. It was almost two years since she had correctly assessed the worth of Sydney Codsall and, miraculously it seemed at the time, switched to Keith who had undoubted possibilities as a swain but whose technique was even more cumbersome than Sydney's, although for very different reasons. Sydney had held off because he had no intention of committing himself, whereas Keith was clearly enslaved but was so humble about it that it had taken him nearly twelve months (spaced by absences at Oxford) to reach the hand-holding stage. Now that the fine weather had arrived, and they could take long walks together in the cool of the evening, she had managed to apply the spur once or twice but the entries in the diary she kept recorded only three kisses and two of them were hardly more than pecks in the region of the right ear. It was depressing to compare her recent experience with those of her pre-Sydney period, when, in the company of Debbie, her sister, she had attended harvest suppers and an occasional hop in the Coombe Bay Village Institute. Here she had had the greatest difficulty in extricating herself from bucolic embraces without crossing the line that might have led to a thrashing from father, endless nagging from mother, a shotgun wedding and a life-sentence in a tied cottage behind one of the farms. Faced, however, with Keith's abject humility Rachel sometimes wished that the Devil his father was always preaching about would take fleeting residence in his son, just long enough to enable her to turn temptation to permanent advantage.

It was not to be, however. Keith must have imbibed so many warnings against the lusts of the flesh that he was more or less inoculated against the Devil's wiles, for even when their fingers touched he trembled and began to stutter, and once, when he was helping her over a stile and her dress had caught on a briar to expose about two inches of shin, he had blushed the colour of a ripe plum and they walked all the way home unlinked.

Reviewing the situation as it was when he came home for the summer vacation in June, 1913, Rachel concluded that she could only hope for an appreciable advance if something dramatic occurred during one of their silent evening rambles, something calculated to galvanise him into action and precipitate his suit by involuntary personal contact. She visualised a number of bizarre situations – Keith throwing his arms about her to shield her from a falling bough, Keith clasping her to him in defiance of Honeyman's prize bull, or, better still, Keith lifting her dripping wet from Sorrel and attempting artificial respiration on the bank. In the event she was not required to set the stage for any of these occurrences.

It happened on a warm June evening as they were moving round the shoulder of the great escarpment north-west of the mere, using the overgrown path above the hill where the Shallowford badgers had their sets. Their walk had been even more uneventful than usual for the ground was rough over most of the route and for the last two miles they had been walking in Indian file, with Keith ahead, beating a passage through the brambles. Like most countrybred girls Rachel took the glories of nature for granted. Woods, ferns, wildflowers and brambles were to her little more than a growth on what might be converted into arable land and she was sorry now that she had agreed to turn off the sunken lane that ran a half-circle behind the Big House. Since he had returned home a few days earlier she had been growing desperate. Stile after stile had been negotiated and she had seen any number of available logs to sit upon but he had passed every spot where, on such an evening as this, and under a bronze and heliotrope sunset, lovers might have been tempted to linger. She finally made up

her mind to try the simplest of all, a stumble and a sprained
ankle, that would encourage him to stop and perhaps try a
little gentle massage, for by now Rachel was convinced that
only close physical contact would give her a sporting chance
of casting a net from which he, as a parson's son, could hardly
escape with honour. She did not expect miracles but a miracle
was unnecessary, a little patting and probing would do the
trick and a proposal would almost certainly follow, particularly
if she prescribed the areas where the patting was done. And
then, just as she was looking for a suitable briar to entrap her
foot, the Valley mating gods took a hand and a low, choked
cry issued from a gorse thicket within a few yards of the path.
They both stopped, surprised, and a little alarmed to hear such
a sound in such a place, and he said, seeking corroboration,
'That was human! Somebody is hurt in there!' and although
the cry had sounded human common sense told her that it
was far more likely to be the moan of an animal caught in a
trap and she said as much. 'Squire has forbidden the use of
steel traps on the estate,' he said. 'I'll push through and see!'
and he barged through the gorse that grew close against the
summit of a large, flat-topped rock on the crest of the slope.

She did not follow for the gorse was dense and she was
wearing her Sunday stockings. She sensed, however, that
a crisis in their relationship had arrived, or was on the
point of arriving and was therefore partially prepared for his
re-emergence within a matter of seconds with an expression
of terror on his face. She had never seen so much horror in a
man's eyes, or a face more tense and blanched and cried, 'What
is it, Keith? What's in there?' and he gibbered, 'It's . . . it's a
woman, a gggirl! She's . . . she's . . . there's a bbbaby coming!'
and for a moment she thought he was going to faint. Then a
second cry came from the base of the rock and another and
another, each louder and more pitiful than the other, so that
Rachel rushed past him and dived through the gorse to find
that it screened a small, shallow cave, evidently the hideout
of a tramp or gypsy, for there was a burned-out fire and a
few trumpery utensils scattered about. Beyond the fire, close
against the wall was a girl, her knees drawn up and her single

garment, a faded dress, rucked up level with her breasts. Her
matted hair tumbled as she heaved and when her mouth was
not open in a yell her teeth were clamped over her lip.

Rachel recognised her at once as Hazel Potter, the half-
crazed postscript of the Potter tribe and a glance told her
that Keith, unbelievably, was right and that the poor little
wretch was indeed giving birth to a child, for the baby's
head was already showing and it seemed to Rachel, who
had witnessed the birth of innumerable foals and calves, that
labour was about half-way through and progressing rapidly
before her eyes. She had inherited courage from her father and
any amount of common sense from her mother, so that even
before the shock had receded she knew what she must do and
also what Keith must do if he could keep his nerve. She dived
back through the bushes and seizing him by the shoulders
shook him as though he had been a troublesome child.

'Listen!' she shouted, 'listen, and then do exactly what I
say! Are you listening? *Are* you?' and when he nodded, his
head wobbling on his long, thin neck, she went on, 'It's Hazel
Potter and she *is* having a baby! I'll have to stay and help
but you must go for the lady doctor as fast as you can. Don't
go the shortest way but across the stream to Sam Potter's
cottage and send his wife here to help me – tell her to bring
towels and a sheet and . . . and string and scissors, can you
remember? Then take Sam's pony, ride on to the Lodge and
guide the lady doctor back here.'

She was agreeably surprised to see that he pulled himself
together at once and repeated her instructions like a recitation.
Then he set off at a long, loping run, disappearing round the
bend in the track while she ran back through the bushes
and flung herself on her knees beside the girl, looking wildly
around for something approximate to a bed and rejecting the
pile of sacks in favour of a great truss of freshly-cut bracken
bundled against the wall. She saw the kettle beside the almost
extinct fire and would have crawled across to revive it by
blowing on the embers had not Hazel, at that moment, clutched
her with both hands as her mouth opened in another fearful
yell. Then she understood that everything else would have to

wait, that her immediate presence as someone to cling to for as long as the ordeal lasted, was more important than water or bedding or linen, so she wriggled in a half-circle that brought her in a position where Hazel's head could rest on her lap and Hazel's hands could retain their grip on her wrists and in this way she rode out the girl's successive heaves, pouring out such words of comfort as she could invent while the climax mounted and mounted until there was no interval between the spasms that touched off the girl's cries.

She was never able to recall how long they were alone before Joannie Potter arrived. It might have been twenty minutes, or an hour, or even longer before Rachel saw the child lying there and Hazel's grip on her wrists relaxed, so that she was able to shift her position and spill the truss of lean bracken across the floor, dragging some of it under the girl's shoulders, then scrambling round to revive the fire. The water in the iron kettle was still warm and in one of the cave's recesses she found the deep earthenware bowl that Hazel used for baking. She cleaned it as best she could, using strips torn from her petticoat and half-resting the squirming little creature on her knee sponged it from head to foot with her best cotton blouse. She had no means of separating mother and child, for although there was a large wooden-handled knife among the utensils its blade was rusted and she remembered that Jamieson, the Valley vet, had impressed upon them the importance of using clean instruments. It did occur to her to hold the blade in the fire but she shrank from this and anyway it did not seem to matter for the terrible urgency had ceased with the girl's cries. She was still making sounds of distress, long, whistling gasps, like a cider-sodden harvester asleep in the hay but her big brown eyes followed Rachel's every movement and noting this Rachel said, softly, 'It's a boy, Hazel! I think he's all right!' The girl twisted herself to look at the child but even this small effort exhausted her and she slumped back on the bracken while Rachel, now using the hem of her petticoat, tied the cord tightly in two places about twelve inches apart as she had seen Jamieson do in the byre at Four Winds. When the water had been changed and the baby sponged again it looked,

Rachel thought, more like a baby and less like a slimy pink monkey. It let out a single yell and its tiny feet pressed feebly against Rachel's knee, so that she forgot her terrible anxiety in a surge of achievement, wondering again whether or not to use the knife to cut the cord but again rejecting the idea from motives of hygiene. Instead she cradled the baby against her soiled skirt and with her left hand tore off another strip of material from her petticoat, using it to wash Hazel's face and the lower parts of her body. The girl spoke, suddenly, her voice seeming hardly to belong to her after all those cries:

'Where's 'er tu?' she demanded. 'Where's The Boy?' and Rachel, surprised that she should have remembered Keith's fleeting appearance in the cave, said that he had gone for Joannie Potter, who would be here any moment and also the lady doctor, who would come as soon as Keith Horsey guided her here. Hazel received this information thoughtfully, lying back with her eyes fixed on the roof of the cave and Rachel noticed that her breathing was slowly returning to normal and that she seemed, miraculously, little the worse for the ordeal. Then, as the light in the cave waned, they heard someone call from the path and Rachel shouted, 'In here – through the bushes under the rock!' and Joannie Potter appeared clutching an armful of bedding and towelling and with barely a glance at the baby began to make a couch at the back of the cave, spreading the sacks as a base for heaped-up bracken. The little cave seemed very crowded now and Rachel realised that Joannie was very much out of breath, so much so that it was minutes before she could gasp, 'You've washed the mite? 'Twas warmish, I 'ope?' and Rachel told her the kettle had contained lukewarm water and that the baby, a boy, had cried out within a moment or two of birth. Joannie paused in her work of doubling the blankets. ''Er baint crying now an' her should be! Turn un over, an' give un a smack or two!' and Rachel, smiling now, began to turn the child face down and then remembered that the cord was uncut.

'I tied the cord but couldn't cut it, Mrs Potter!' she said and Joannie, without a word, poked her head under Rachel's elbow and bit so that the cord parted and Rachel was able to administer a smack on the child's tiny behind. The baby opened his mouth as wide as it would go and roared its resentment, the volume of his yells astonishing Rachel almost as much as the mother's unaided scramble on to the bed. The baby continued to bawl so loudly that Joannie said, grimly, "Er'll do! Just 'ark to un! Still, 'twas lucky you was by, with nought but a few dirty sacks to hand!' and she sighed as though the birth of a child in these circumstances was a bit of a nuisance but otherwise unremarkable.

'Be 'ee gonner tell 'em whose tacker tiz?' she asked carelessly but Hazel replied, sharply, 'Tiz mine! Dornee pester me, Joannie!' whereupon Joannie sighed again, grumbling that Sam would want to know and so, probably, would the lady doctor but implied by her tone that the identity of the father was not very important.

'Be 'ee strong enough to give un the breast, child?' she said and Hazel, in answer, reached out for the baby and Rachel, a little regretfully, placed him carefully in her arms while Joannie pulled the crumpled dress over the mother's shoulders and busied herself tucking the blankets around her. The baby's outcry ceased so suddenly that the silence inside the cave seemed uncanny. Joannie said, dispassionately, 'You'd better go an' watch for 'em. That boy was so scared I woulden wonder if 'er dorn taake lady doctor to Hermitage! I'll bide 'till they come, for Sam's with the children, young Barby bein' sick abed!'

Rachel went out into the open, surprised to find it was now almost dark. In the glimmer of light over the Bluff she saw the foliage stir down by the north corner of the mere and presently, where the trees fell away around the stream, she caught a glimpse of two figures on horseback moving at a trot and yelled at the top of her voice in case, as Joannie had suggested, Keith had difficulty in locating the spot. Somebody answered her and they came on at a canter, the ponies' hooves chinking on the stones of the ascent like bottles in a basket. Keith appeared first, rolling from the saddle of Sam Potter's chestnut pony and shouting the moment he saw her, 'Are you all right, Rachel?' and Rachel said, 'Of course I'm all right! It

wasn't me who had the baby, stupid!' but then she understood
why he had asked for she was blouseless and her hair was
falling over her bare shoulders so that for once it was she who
blushed and was glad to answer the bark of Doctor Maureen,
who climbed out of the saddle holding her bag, demanding to
be shown the way to the patient.

They left Keith with the horses and pushed through the
gorse, guided by the gleam of a lantern Joannie had lit but
Rachel, acutely conscious of her dishevelled appearance, and
feeling suddenly helpless in the presence of a professional,
was glad to wash her face, hands and neck in what remained
of the water before despatching Keith to the stream for more.
While he was gone she hitched up her skirt, tore away the
trailing edge of her petticoat hem and tried to tidy her
hair by rearranging pins but she could do nothing about
her bare neck and shoulders until Joannie said, 'Taake my
jumper, child, and go along home! Us can manage now and
you can ride Sam's pony backalong, and Passon's boy can
return un in the mornin'.' Gratefully Rachel slipped on the
soiled jumper that hung about her like a cloak, tucking it
into the waistband of her skirt and giving a final, fascinated
glance at Hazel, as she sat propped against the rear wall of
the cave, the child at her breast. Then she went out to find
Keith and said, apologising for her appearance, 'It's Joannie
Potter's jumper! I . . . I had to use my blouse in there,' but she
didn't mention her petticoat thinking that the poor boy had
had a surfeit of embarrassments that evening. It was when
he helped her climb up behind him and she clasped him round
the waist, that she began to feel happier and more serene than
she had felt in twelve months for somehow, after all that had
happened back there in the cave, his angular body was a
source of comfort and what had occurred seemed, perversely,
to have given him more confidence, for he said as they crossed
over Codsall Bridge, 'You were wonderful, Rachel! I was proud
of you, and some time . . . some time I'd like to . . . to speak to
Mr Eveleigh about you, Rachel.'

It was not the proposal she had daydreamed about either
before and since the entry of Keith Horsey into her life, but

it was valid she supposed and she hugged him in silence. There was really nothing she could reply to such a delightfully old-fashioned statement of his intentions. When they reached the yard and got down, unbridling the pony and turning him loose in the duck field, Keith found an excuse to linger by the gate. She could have wished that he had sought an elbow-rest further from her own kitchen door for she could hear the clatter of dishes and the voices of the children, any one of whom might appear bawling, 'It's Rachel, Mum!' for it was late enough to merit explanations. She said, therefore, 'I must go in now, Keith dear. It's late and Dad's very strict about time,' and then, without the slightest prompting on her part, he seized her by the shoulders and kissed her on the mouth, and she kissed him back and ran swiftly across the cobbles towards the oblong of light in the kitchen yard. As she ran she giggled, partly with excitement but also with relish at the thought that it had taken Hazel Potter's bastard child, born in a cave in Shallowford Woods, to convert him from a possible into a certainty.

II

There was less speculation in the Valley as to the identity of the man responsible for bringing Hazel Potter to bed than there was comment regarding her reply to every enquiry, a sullen, reiterated, 'Tiz mine an' my man's, baint it?' to which she would sometimes add the admonition directed at Joannie Potter at the time – 'Dornee pester me!' as though requests for enlightenment on the subject were not merely impertinent but frivolous. Her sisters, who were shocked by the event, came up with a list of probables that included a half-witted crowstarver employed on the Heronslea estate and all three of the Timberlake boys. Fathers were canvassed in Coombe Bay and among the labouring population on the western side of the estate, the Potter girls reasoning that if Hazel's lover had lived on the eastern side they would have been sure to have seen him coming and going about his shameful business.

Meg, for her part, did not seek information, realising that one might as well ask a vixen to name the dog-fox that had crossed into Shallowford country when she was last in season. She was, moreover, resigned to the arrival of babies without fathers and in any case did not consider it her business. In her view any grown woman could renew herself if she felt so inclined and with whom she went about it was a personal matter. Doctor Maureen, however, had other views and after making no headway at all with Hazel consulted her husband, declaring that the father of the child should be sought out, encouraged to marry the girl or if he was disinclined, compelled to contribute towards its upkeep but John told her not to waste time and shoe leather. 'That child has lived rough in the woods for years,' he said, 'and I'm surprised it hasn't happened before! It might be any one of a score of men and no one is likely to own to it.'

'If that child is promiscuous I'm Boadicea!' Maureen declared. 'It wouldn't surprise me to learn that she'd been raped and threatened and that's why she's holding her tongue!' but John said, wearily, 'Why do we have to put such a dramatic construction on a Potter producing a bastard? They were doing it when I came here!'

'The circumstances are different,' his wife said, 'very different and not on account of the child being born in a cave. That Hazel Potter is fey for how else did she conceal her pregnancy all the time?'

'With the help of the Great God Pan I wouldn't wonder,' John said, grinning and resumed his attempt to teach his seventeen-month-old son to walk a straight line across the carpet.

So Maureen turned elsewhere, questioning patients up and down the Valley but adding nothing to her knowledge. Few recalled having seen Hazel Potter during the last few months and those who had declared she was always alone. She persisted, however, and it was while casting about for some means of providing for the child's future that she was approached by Keith Horsey, the son of the rector, whom she recalled as being a friend of the absent Ikey. Keith came to her with a practical suggestion. If Hazel would domicile herself within walking distance of Coombe Bay, he said, the rector was prepared to pay her a small weekly sum out of parish funds for cleaning the church and helping Marlowe, the sexton, keep the graveyard free of weeds. She thanked him and recalling that it was he who had summoned her the night the child was born asked if he or Ikey had any knowledge of the company Hazel kept. He was on the defensive at once.

'Certainly not,' he said, stiffly, 'why should I have? Or Ikey either for that matter!'

'Oh come, lad,' she chaffed. 'I'm not suggesting it was either one of you but you and that lass you're courting walk the woods of an evening whereas Ikey, whenever he was home, was through them on horseback often enough. He's sharp enough to have noticed and remembered if he did see her with anyone. Will you mention it when you write?'

The boy turned aside and it seemed to her that he found the subject distasteful. Then she realised why, recalling that he had burst into the cave and seen the girl in labour and it had probably been a considerable shock to a person as shy and withdrawn as Keith Horsey. He said, finally, 'I'll write and ask Ikey but I don't think he'll know anything. Won't the girl say?'

'No,' said Maureen, 'she won't but for your information that isn't at all unusual in these cases.'

'Why?' he asked, genuinely surprised. 'Why should that be so?'

'All manner of reasons – fear, a bribe perhaps, or even mistaken loyalty. Sometimes they break down when they are faced with angry parents but this won't happen in Hazel's case, for that gypsy mother of hers thinks no more of a bastard than a litter of kittens under the stairs.'

He flushed and she was sorry she hadn't chosen her words more carefully but after repeating his father's offer he left abruptly and she tackled her husband again, this time on the subject of accommodation for Hazel.

'There's a half-ruined cottage near the old mill a mile or so along the river road,' she said. 'Do you think Paul would do it up and let the girl have it on a peppercorn rent?'

'I daresay he would,' John said, 'he's soft enough, but why can't she and the child move into that harlot's nest in the Dell?'

'Because, if she does, she'll be in the family way again within six months,' she told him, shortly. 'I wouldn't put it past that great lump of a Jem adding another to his harem!'

'Ah,' said John, chuckling, 'you've got something there, old girl! I'll have a word with Paul,' and he did with the result that Hazel and her baby moved into Mill Cottage adjoining the long abandoned water-wheel, at the junction of the Sorrel and the stream that ran down from Deepdene goyle. Surprisingly she soon made herself at home, cultivating the vegetable patch and keeping a few goats in the water meadows and every weekday morning she carried her baby along the river road to the parish church where she scoured and polished for nine shillings a week, with a bonus of sixpence an hour for helping in the churchyard. Motherhood had sobered her somewhat, inasmuch as she did not wander so far afield but in other respects she was the same half-wild creature who had lived rough in the woods and Maureen, Irish enough to have faith in the Little People, thought of her as one and often passed to Hazel some of the payments in kind given her by cottagers for medical attention. She also took a keen interest in the baby, standing in as godmother when, at her suggestion, he was christened Patrick. As Maureen explained to her patients, saints had lived in caves all over Ireland when the English were still painting themselves blue, so why shouldn't a broth of a boy be born in one on the Shallowford estate?

As soon as Hazel had settled in the doctor ceased her random enquiries regarding the child's paternity, quite forgetting that she had advised Keith to write to Ikey on the subject. She never did learn how close she came to discovering the truth then, for Keith had few doubts on the subject but remained silent for reasons so complex that, notwithstanding his familiarity with Greek, Latin and Hebrew, he would have found it difficult to set down. Alone in the valley Keith had strong suspicions regarding the paternity of Hazel Potter's child and they stemmed from a single word uttered by the mother at the moment he had burst through the screen of gorse to find her lying up in agony beside the half-dead fire. She had seen him through a haze of pain, standing agape with his back to the evening light, and in the moment before he had turned and rushed back to Rachel, she had confused him with the tall young man who had come here so often and cried out, in desperation and perhaps relief, 'Ikey-boy!', clearly and distinctly, thus telling Keith when he had time to reflect, all he needed to know. He was aware, of course, of his duty even if he found it very hard to believe that his one time champion had seduced this girl and left her to face the consequences alone. It was clearly obligatory on his part to write to Quetta, asking Ikey to confirm or deny but he did not write, regarding the child or anything else. The chain-reaction that would almost certainly follow Ikey's admission would be shattering and result in so much trouble for everyone that he did not possess enough resolution to light such a fuse. Whatever happened it was he, Keith, who would suffer most, for if Ikey admitted paternity there would be legal claims that would broadcast the facts up and down the Valley and surely Ikey would find it hard to forgive the Judas who had so invoked the wrath of the Squire and Mrs Craddock and the contempt of rustics like Sam and Smut Potter and everyone else who sympathised with the girl. Yet if Ikey denied the fact, as he probably would, the accusation would destroy their relationship for life and it was a relationship that Keith prized almost as highly as his love for Rachel Eveleigh. The more he considered putting what he knew on paper the more profitless it looked and so, in the end, he kept his counsel, persuading himself that if the girl was determined to keep her secret then he was entitled to do likewise. It did not satisfy his conscience completely but it helped and because, at that time, his head was full of dreams involving Rachel, and the rosy future they would share when he had his degree, he was able to put the secret into cold-storage and even half-persuade

himself that Hazel Potter's agonised cry qualified as a kind
of audible hallucination on his part.

In September of that year, 1913, Squire Craddock, that
resolute hater of motors, confounded his friends by buying
one. He made the gesture on the occasion of his wife presenting
him with another daughter and the Valley was never to forget
the unlikely association of baby girl and horseless carriage, for
it was perpetuated by a quip of that inveterate Valley joker
Henry Pitts. On hearing of the simultaneous arrivals at the
Big House, he exclaimed, 'He give 'is missis a bliddy motor?
For coming up with another maid? Well damme, I suppose
he knows what he's at, but it sounds to me as daft as namin'
the baby Whiz-bang!' This comment soon reached the Big
House where Paul, having been told by Maureen that the
child's arrival was the quickest on local record, said, 'Well,
maybe Henry's hit on something! Let's call her "Whiz", since
she obliged her mother and me to that extent!' and from then
on his second daughter (officially named 'Karen') embarked on
life as 'Whiz', or 'Whizzo', just as the twins were known as
'The Pair', and Simon as 'Si'; only Mary, now almost three and
as pretty as a Devon violet, enjoyed the dignity of having her
Christian name put into general use.

Claire had been very relieved by the child's safe arrival,
for the previous year she had had another miscarriage, her
second in five years. Her tendency to miscarry worried her
much more than it need have done. There were plenty of
wives in the Valley (Maria Eveleigh for one) who welcomed an
accident of this kind but Claire derived the deepest satisfaction
from her ability to produce healthy, good-looking children and
her joy in doing so was closely linked to her consciousness of
intellectual inferiority to Grace. She always thought of herself
as rather a 'goose', with no pretentions towards intellectual
tastes and pursuits. She could play the piano by ear but
that was the nearest she ever came to the arts. She seldom
read anything but the country newspaper or the lightest of
romances and thought Holman Hunt's *Light of the World* as
the last word in masterpieces. She could strum any number
of ballads on the old upright piano but the thunder of Wagner,

the phrasing of Mozart and Mendelssohn, meant far less to her than, say, a waltz by Johann Strauss, and although Paul was by no means artistic he had a very lively appreciation of current political issues and was a wide if undisciplined reader, particularly of eighteenth-century classics and modern history. He had also cultivated a taste for period furniture, English porcelain and pictures and over the years had gradually transformed the reception rooms, getting rid of most of the pieces he bought when he first came to Shallowford and replacing them with furniture in the Chippendale and Sheraton periods and beginning a modest collection of Rockingham, Worcester and Swansea china. What he did not know about these things he was prepared to find out so that Claire now thought of him as an intellectual which he was not and never would be but because it was important to him to stand well in her eyes he encouraged the fiction, pretending to an erudition that he did not in fact possess. Grace would have rumbled him in an hour but Claire was not Grace and thanked her stars that she was not. She was a woman who knew her limitations and cherished them, her vanity resting in her children and her face and figure, which she regarded as her dowry as far as Paul was concerned.

She had ample excuse for this. Her placidity, that concealed a strong vein of obstinacy, occasionally irritated him but physically he was more in love with her than he had ever been. He still thought of her as an exceptionally beautiful woman and told her so, several times a week, which possibly helped to explain why, at the age of thirty, she still looked twenty. A pedant would have described her as fresh, and perhaps pretty rather than beautiful; she still had her pink and white complexion, unremarkable blue eyes, a very ripe mouth with its rather sensual underlip, and her small, determined chin. She worried about putting on weight but her fears were largely imaginary. Despite four children in six years she retained a surprisingly neat waist and a high, shapely bust but by far her most remarkable feature was her high piled corn-coloured hair, of which she was as vain as the late Empress of Austria. When it was unpinned it reached as far

as her buttocks and under lamplight it glowed like a river of
gold. He was always encouraging her to display it and no
miser derived more satisfaction from a hoard of guineas than
Paul Craddock on one of these semi-ceremonial occasions. He
would gaze at it and stroke it with boyish wonder and
she would sit smiling a little self-consciously but basking
in his admiration, telling him that they were really too old for
this kind of nonsense, yet he was always immensely gratified
by her complaisance, telling her at the time, or in retrospect,
that she made herself available to him so often in order to
flatter his masculinity and although this was said as a joke
between them it was really no more than the truth, for at
moments like this neither of them forgot the scars left on his
pride by his first marriage. She had, however, developed a
sure instinct about him. If things were going well an act of
love between them was a celebration; but if things went awry
her generous body was an instrument of solace. She may not
have been as clever as Grace but she was much wiser and far
better versed in the art of giving; her mind was uncluttered
with theories and the sores of humanity and concentrated, in
the main, upon enlarging him as a person.

There was little or no rhythm about their love making.
He would be stirred by any number of tiny, inconsequential
things, a cluster of stray tendrils on her neck that caught a
gleam of winter sunshine, the slow ripple of her breasts as she
reached up to put something in place and what was singular
about her in this respect was that she never used the excuse
of a task or appointment to bridle or postpone his demands
but would say, with a frankness that amused him, 'Now?
Well really . . . !' and would cease whatever she was doing
and accommodate him, initially with an almost complaisant
air but soon with a cordiality that began to manifest itself
the moment he laid hands on her. In this respect, as in others,
they remained lovers and were seldom conventional as regards
time and place. If the impulse touched him after the children
and servants had gone to bed and they were together in the
library of a winter evening, they would sometimes repeat their
impromptu encounter of Hermitage Hallowe'en night before

the fire and whenever this happened the process assumed a kind of lighthearted, unselfconscious ritual, beginning with his leisurely undressing of her and praising of each part of her, as though to prolong the occasion as long as possible. There was a stage, however, beyond which she would show impatience and then, when they were still, she would pretend to a modesty and delicacy that she did not possess and never had possessed, and he would tease her unmercifully but secretly he was immensely vain of his ability to awake such unthinking response in her. Intimate moments such as these brought her a disproportionate satisfaction, for she too had her vanities and they concerned, as well as his delight in her body, his virility, a virility that seemed somehow to spring from the valley around him, as though he were able, by some acquired magic practised over the years to catch and distil the fecundity of the countryside, storing it in his loins to bestow upon her as proof of his achievement. This enormous gusto in him, this bonus bounty of the fields and woods he loved, was something she prized even above her children, for she was persuaded that it was something rare that neither Grace Lovell nor any woman in the Valley could have conjured from him. It was partly this naïve pride in his masculinity that invested her with the power to match and surpass his easily aroused passion. She sensed that he possessed her not only as a woman but as the consuming instrument of his lust for life in the place he had made for himself in this gentle wilderness. She was a woman not much given to extravagant fancies but in this realm the wildness of her imagination had few limits. She saw herself then not as Claire Derwent, a farmer's daughter married to a man who had purchased his place among them with pounds, shillings and pence, but as consort to an almost godlike being who used her flesh as an altar to express his strange obsession with the fruitfulness and timelessness of the Valley, with every flower and cornstalk that grew in it, and every human or animal who lived and multiplied hereabouts, and it was acute awareness of this that made her reckless of giving, so that she felt at times that she could never absorb enough of him or demonstrate how dedicated she was to the gratification of his senses. Eagerness to convey this, communicating itself as it did to every nerve in her body as she enfolded and enclosed him sometimes half-stupefied him with delight.

And yet, in more mundane spheres, there were times when she called the tune, when an issue arose that encouraged her to make a stand and whenever this happened, when she once made it clear that she was determined to have her way, she could usually influence him without much trouble. This had been so in the case of Simon's renunciation of hunting and like matters but perhaps her most signal victory was in respect of the car he brought home on the occasion of the birth of 'Whiz'.

It was a 1911 Belsize, a great, square, brass-snouted monster, purchased second-hand from a Paxtonbury draper who had lost his nerve on the second outing and left it unused in his coach-house for almost two years. Paul decided to buy it after hearing Claire say it was a pity the family could never travel far afield as a group and after getting Frisby, the Paxtonbury coach builder, to service it and give him a few lessons in driving he piloted it home across the moor in dashing if somewhat erratic style, deriving unexpected pleasure out of his mastery of the brute and causing Eveleigh's foreman, who saw him come bouncing down from the water-shed, to run up the hedge in alarm, scarcely able to believe his eyes when he recognised the driver.

About a fortnight after Claire had come downstairs he suggested a family expedition into Paxtonbury and after some hesitation Claire got the elder children ready, veiled herself in a beekeeper's bonnet and they set off, little Mary sitting between Paul and Simon in the front, Claire and the exuberant twins in the back. Simon, holding Mary's hand to give her confidence, looked very solemn but the Pair squealed in unison when Paul clashed the gears at the foot of the drive and wedged the lever into its tortuous gate, so that the Belsize (christened The Juggernaut by Claire) leaped forward like a steeplechaser and came to a shuddering halt between the stone pillars.

'Are you sure you can manage it, Paul?' Claire asked anxiously and he said huffily that he certainly could for how else could he have driven the fifteen miles from Paxtonbury? He got out and swung the heavy starting-handle and soon they were moving at a steady twenty miles an hour along the river road, past the Home Farm, where one of the biblical shepherds swung his hat and cheered, past Codsall Bridge, where Eveleigh's cows turned tail and stampeded across the water meadow, then hard right up the unsurfaced incline to the moor where, long ago, Martin Codsall had taken his wife Arabella on a John Gilpin's ride to prevent her intervening at her son's wedding. And here, almost at the top of the hill, the engine coughed and fell silent, so that they were poised on a gradient of one-in-six, with no room to turn and no hope of breasting the hill.

He climbed out again, assured them of his confidence in himself as an engineer and swung the startling-handle until the sweat ran down his face but nothing happened and Mary's faith in her father's infallibility faltered so that she began to cry. Simon did his best to comfort her, declaring that Father would soon have them on the move again, while the twins shrieked offers of help from the back but Claire held them back, privately regretting her share in sponsoring the expedition and reflecting that, apart from the baby safe in her cot, all her eggs were now wedged in a single, unpredictable basket. Paul said there was nothing for it but a careful reverse back to the river road, where, if necessary, Simon could run and borrow ropes and a pair of Eveleigh's cart-horses.

He pretended to treat the matter as a great joke and had she been alone with him she might have humoured him but the safety of her brood was no laughing matter to Claire and she said, very sharply, 'Wait then, while we all get out!' and when the twins clamoured to remain she gave each a smart box on the ear that sent them scrambling on to the road, after which she opened the nearside front door and ordered Simon to bring Mary out and wait with the twins on the safe side of the hill.

'Look here,' Paul protested, 'if I get her started I shan't be able to stop again without the engine dying. Why can't you stay put and wait for her to spark when I slam her in reverse?' but Claire said firmly that her duty was to look after the children, and what he did with The Juggernaut was his business, so after telling her she was making an unnecessary fuss he released the brake, missed his gear again and zigzagged all the way down the hill backwards, his steering made wildly erratic by the pressure he was obliged to apply to the handbrake.

He got safely down and they followed him in a cautious group, finding his temper had not improved for he was using language that made the twins and Simon giggle and Mary glance fearfully at her mother. Claire said then that she would walk the children home and send Honeyman out with two cart-horses and ropes but Paul, declaring that such mass desertion would make him the laughing stock of the Valley, ordered them to remain, saying that all he needed was a shove along the flat. An open quarrel was narrowly averted by the timely arrival of Tod Glover, an engaging nineteen-year-old who was Old Honeyman's nephew and had recently forsaken the land to work for a Whinmouth hackney-carriage proprietor owning an eighteen-seater charabanc. Tod, cycling back from the Whinmouth direction, at once offered his services, inspecting the Belsize with the respect his ancestors would have reserved for its owner. As the only man within artillery range with the rudiments of a mechanical training Tod was regarded as the Valley witchdoctor and Paul welcomed him as the one person capable of rescuing his dignity. The lad had the bonnet cover off in a trice and after tinkering for some moments, and giving the handle a swing or two, he said, with a grin, 'All she needs is a drink, Squire! When did you last fill her up?'

'I haven't put any petrol in since I brought her home,' Paul admitted ruefully and the insertion of a twig showed that the tank was bone dry.

'How about that can on the running board?' asked Tod, trying not to look superior when Paul admitted that he thought the can contained water and after a sniff to make sure Tod made a funnel of paper and within minutes the

Belsize was climbing the hill again, Paul maintaining a discreet silence all the way to Paxtonbury.

'Well,' said Claire, after an uneventful journey home, and insistence upon the entire family taking a bath to rid themselves of layers of white dust, 'it was nice of you to buy a motor for us, but I can't help thinking we should be much cleaner and far safer without one! It would be promising, I think, if you had a mechanical bent like young Tod but you haven't and never will have, so why not admit it, and stick to horse and trap?'

'That's a ridiculous stand to take simply because I ran out of petrol,' he said. 'It's high time we got used to motors and I'll master this if it's the last thing I do!'

It almost was; a day or so later, having refused to engage Tod as a chauffeur, he came bumbling down the steep drive, clashed his gears at the gate and shot across ten yards of soft ground straight into the Sorrel, carrying ten yards of paling with him. There had been some heavy rainfall and the water above the ford was five feet deep. The Belsize plunged in nose down, looking like a primeval monster maddened by thirst and only the fact that he had managed to unlatch the door whilst ploughing through the iris bed enabled Paul to free himself before the heavy vehicle sank into the soft mud of the river bed.

Help came from all directions. Matt, one of the shepherd twins, hauled him ashore and Honeyman and Henry Pitts, summoned from the lodge where they were conferring with John Rudd, managed to get a rope under the rear wheels just before they disappeared from view. When Claire was summoned she found the river bank seething with activity as Home Farm horses struggled with the hopeless task of hauling the Belsize clear. What astounded her was the fact that Paul did not seem cured of his obsession. Instead of going back to the house to change he remained on the bank to supervise salvage operations, snarling at everybody who advised him to get into dry clothes. He was there for an hour or more during which time no progress was made, apart from the motor being anchored by ropes to saplings and the following day, to nobody's surprise, he had a heavy cold which did not improve his temper.

Claire said, as she dosed him with whisky and water, 'What do you intend to do with The Juggernaut if you ever do get it out?' and he said, grumpily, 'clean it up, get young Tod to service it and have another go.'

She said, with unexpected firmness, 'You'll leave it right where it is!' and when he exclaimed in protest, arguing that it was she who prompted him to buy, she went on, 'That was before I realised you haven't the temperament essential to anyone setting out to master one of those things! I admire you for trying and I shouldn't have to remind you that I usually back you to the hilt when you set your mind on doing something, but this is different; the children are involved and I'm obliged to make a stand.'

'Now how the devil are the children involved in my driving a motor?' he demanded. 'I'm not likely to let them play with it, am I?'

'Sooner or later you'll expect them to ride in it,' she said. 'It's only by chance that Simon wasn't beside you yesterday and if he had been he would have been drowned! Did you think of that while you were prancing about on the bank in wet clothes, catching this cold and working off your bad temper on people who were trying to help you?'

He had not thought of it but he knew it was true. Up to the last minute Simon had intended to accompany him but Paul, impatient to be off, had made a trial run down the drive whilst Simon slipped inside for coat and scarf. He said, reflecting how specially protective Claire always felt about Grace's child, 'You're right. If anything had happened to him you would have found it hard to forgive me, wouldn't you?'

'I should have found it impossible, Paul,' she said, calmly, 'even though indirectly, it would have been my fault! As it is, we were lucky and I mean to profit by the lesson, even if you won't! I can't stop you amusing yourself with your new toy but I won't have you take any of the children out ever again and that's final!'

It was an edict and he accepted it as such but for all that her attitude still piqued him, perhaps because, for the first time since their marriage he had failed to impress her.

'Suppose we retired old Chivers and signed on Tod as a chauffeur?' he suggested. 'He could give me lessons and I can't be such a damned fool as to fail to get the hang of it in time.'

'Paul,' she said, more gently, 'I know you better than anyone and a lot better than you know yourself! You'll never make a motor-driver because you haven't got that kind of patience. You're a bull-at-a-gate person and machines need a light touch. You are entitled to risk your own neck but you're not risking my children's! I don't often oppose you but in this I'm adamant and I'm not saying this because of what happened yesterday but because your prejudice against gadgets is so great that you ought never to be trusted with one as lethal as that motor!' She smiled, for the first time since the subject had been raised. 'Shall I tell you what my advice is? Leave The Juggernaut as a local landmark and go back to horses!'

And this, after a good deal of grumbling about wasted money was what he did. All that winter, when the river was high, the Belsize was the plaything of otters and water voles but when the floods receded part of the wreck was revealed, a permanent testimony to the Squire's short-lived attempt to adapt himself to the twentieth century. From then on the mechanisation of the valley proceeded without him. Soon the German professor appeared in Coombe Bay High Street in his new Humber, driven by his son, Gottfried, and then Eveleigh hired a traction engine to haul away the trunks of elms felled on his western boundary. Now and again, in that final glow of the Edwardian afternoon, an occasional motor was seen on the river road and occasionally, very occasionally, power-driven engines were used to harrow stubborn ground that had long lain fallow. But for the most part the horse continued to flourish and Claire consolidated her victory and in the main the people of the Valley were at one with her. It was Henry Pitts, watching the hired traction-engine pull roots as easily as a dentist extracts teeth, who voiced the opinion of witnesses when he said, with one of his slow, rubbery grins, 'Tiz quicker an' neater than us can do it wi' chains an' plough horses but somehow it baint real farmin', be it?'

Chapter Three

I

Looking back on the last summer of the old world Paul was always struck by two features of that time; the weather and the focus of attention on Irish affairs to the exclusion of everything else, including Germany.

The weather he remembered as being the most pleasant of any comparable season he had spent in the Valley, warm and consistently sunny by day, with gentle rain at night so that crops ripened early and even the habitual pessimist Eveleigh, spoke guardedly of excellent harvest prospects. In some ways it resembled his first summer at Shallowford when there seemed to have been blazing sunshine for weeks on end but there was no accompanying drought, as there had been in 1902, and under a temperate sky the Valley burgeoned with promise and fruitfulness so that people went gaily about their work and only a few local wiseacres like Eph Morgan expressed doubts about what was likely to happen when the Irish were given their precious Home Rule and began civil war.

James Grenfell was down in early June and Paul invited him to dine with Professor Scholtzer with whom he was now on cordial terms. James liked the old German on sight and it was over their port that night that Paul took part in his first discussion on the dangers inherent in the rivalry Germany, France, Russia and Great Britain had been practising for more than a decade. He was mildly surprised when the Professor put forward a theory that, without justifying the Kaiser's antics in the diplomatic field, at least shed a little light on them for he declared that, rightly or wrongly, fear of encirclement was very real to many Germans, even intelligent Germans. The Junkers, he told them in his expansive but guttural English, were anxious to come to some agreement with Great Britain and their fear of France and Russia was not merely a ruse to compel politicians into granting more and more money for military purposes. They saw Russia as a steam-roller driven by barbarians and France as an irresponsible nationalist mob determined to avenge the defeat of 1870. 'I am not excusing them, my friends,' he went on earnestly, when James Grenfell pointed out that sooner or later Germany would be obliged to restore the provinces of Alsace-Lorraine, 'I try to make you look at Europe through German eyes. Only if you British do that can we stop this Gadarene rush to destruction.' James said, with a smile. 'Oh, I don't question your thesis, Professor, but surely it is generally accepted that war, even on the scale of 1870, is an impossibility? Threats and border incidents yes – we'll always have those, but civilised nations, grinding one another to pieces? That's a very different matter, if only on account of cost!'

'Guns,' said the Professor sadly, 'have a vay of going off by themselves and vonce they bang there are always plenty of people to profit from refilling cartridge pouches! That has been my reading of history; it remains my greatest fear! Not a vor started by the Emperors or by the politicians or even the Junkers but those who profit by conflict!'

Neither Paul nor James took the Professor's warnings very seriously, James because he was too deeply imbued by Westminster's views that no power could afford to fight a modern war, Paul because he found it difficult to believe that anyone, even a crass idiot like the Kaiser, would, when it came to the touch, challenge the British Empire. He did not say this; it would have seemed to him a breach of good manners but he mentioned it to James after the Professor had gone home and they were smoking their last cigars in the library. James dismissed the Saxon's fears as the result of studying the past at the expense of the present. 'Even if the guns did go off by themselves, you can take it from me, Paul, that we should stay clear of it and I have that on the best authority – Asquith's, Morley's and even Grey's! For your peace of mind we couldn't get in even if we wanted to.

The pacifist group in the Cabinet would resign in a body and we should lose the backing of the Labour Party. That would mean an election and by the time we had gone to the country it would be all over bar the shouting! So in case we don't run our full term I advise you to concentrate on the Ulster question. That's real enough and they mean to fight if they have to! A good many Tory MPs are egging them on and you can imagine how I feel when I see suffragettes sent to prison for long terms on charges of conspiracy when idiots like Carson are openly advocating armed rebellion!'

When at length he went to bed it was not of German aggression and Russian steamrollers that Paul thought but of women like Grace, Annie Kenney and the girl Davison, who had died under the hooves of a Derby horse the previous summer. James' parting remarks robbed him of sleep for an hour or so, or it might have been the heavy meal and all the cigars they had smoked, for he lay awake beside Claire for a long time, wondering what had become of the woman who had entered and left his life so abruptly, so long ago it seemed that it might have happened in childhood. He thought, recalling the scenes they had witnessed outside the Houses of Parliament, 'It's their staying power that astonishes – that and their sense of dedication! But they don't seem to be getting anywhere, poor devils, and now this Irish business has edged them out of the spotlight!' When at last he fell asleep he had one of his meaningless dreams about her, a prolonged waiting in all manner of improbable places for Grace to keep a muddled rendezvous. If ever he did dream of Grace it was always along these lines.

In the decade after the Great War historians made play of the general anxiety caused by the shooting of Franz Ferdinand by a tubercular youth in Sarajevo that June but Paul, knowing the Valley and its people so well, never subscribed to this fiction. News of the Archduke's death came and went but hardly anyone in the Sorrel district remembered the incident until it was thrust under their noses a month later and even then they looked on it as no more than a scuffle in a far-away country where the crack of the pistol and the roar of a home-made bomb were commonplace occurrences. Few in the Valley bought any newspaper but the *County Press* and although this publication carried a small section devoted to foreign news, its local readers did no more than glance at it before turning to the market section or columns dealing with county cricket.

There was one man, however, apart from the German professor, who was very much aware of the open door of the European powder magazine. Horace Handcock's hatred of Germans dated from the day their Kaiser decided to compete with the British Navy and build himself a clutch of dreadnoughts. From then on Horace had waged a one-man campaign in the Valley, aimed at alerting his neighbours to the menace of Potsdam, and his warnings were so stark, and so original, that he was always able to enlist an audience in the Shallowford kitchen or the sawdust bar of The Raven. Horace appeared as a Solomon Eagle, preaching of wrath to come, and the regulars in the bar, seeking diversion, would sometimes encourage him to pronounce upon the latest forms of frightfulness Potsdam had in pickle for their British cousins. Nobody had ever discovered the source of Horace Handcock's information, which was so extensive and so detailed, that the simple-minded among his listeners might have been forgiven for supposing him to have had access to the Wilhelmstrasse wastepaper baskets. He would talk of bombs disguised as mangolds dropped over agricultural districts by Zeppelins, of bags of poisoned sweets for unwary children delivered by the same agency and of giant howitzers planted as far away as the Baltic coast and capable of destroying half London. He was obsessed by the presence of cohorts of spies, landed nightly by submarine, to rendezvous a night or so later at deserted coves like Tamer Potter's, east of the Bluff. To Horace every foreigner (Italian ice-cream vendors excepted) was in the pay of Von Moltke and quite aside from the personnel of German bands (spies to a man), he knew of at least two resident agents in the Valley, the mild-looking professor and his gentlemanly son, Gottfried. It was useless to point out to Horace that the professor himself was hostile to German militarists, or that he was on visiting terms with the Squire, Horace declared these instances typical examples of Teutonic guile and that they would not see the professor and his son in their true colours until the Kaiser's fleet out-numbered the British by two ships to one. Then, one awful morning, they would find the German's Coombe Bay house silent and shuttered, the occupants having been taken off by submarine the previous night in order to be spared the terrible naval bombardment that would follow and the sack of Paxtonbury and Whinmouth by field-grey hordes landed by fast torpedo boats, of which the Kaiser already had several thousand, with more building.

The only person agitated by these dire prophecies was Mrs Handcock, who was obliged to listen to them after everybody else had gone home to bed, and because she had always entertained a great respect for her husband's erudition she had long since convinced herself that a German invasion of the coastal strip between Coombe Bay and Whinmouth was a virtual certainty. Fortunately for her, however, she was optimistic by nature and had made up her mind that the balance of naval power was unlikely to be tipped during her life-time, so there was really no point in worrying about it, especially as they were childless. And yet, in the end, Horace was caught on the hop just like everybody else for like a fool, he allowed the Mutiny at the Curragh to distract his attention during the critical months leading up to August, 1914. It was only when he learned of the Austrian ultimatum to Servia, in late July, that he saw that events had overtaken him and by then it was too late to rouse the countryside.

The task would have been beyond him in any case for during the last few days of July, with hot weather continuing and the harvest upon them, the men of the Valley did not even pause to read the *County Press*. While the telegraph systems of Europe quivered under a ceaseless exchange of threats, proposals, counter-proposals, accusations, denials and politely-phrased disclaimers, the respective masters of Four Winds and Hermitage were bargaining over a Jersey bull, and Smut Potter was working sixteen hours a day in his greenhouses. Nearby his two sisters, burned almost black by the sun, were digging an irrigation channel across the cliff field under the threat of the Bideford Goliath's hazel switch and all over the estate men and women were discussing such things as the fruit crop, water shortage, field pests and the likely price of cow fodder in the autumn. On the very day that the Tsar of All the Russias was posting his ukase to the remotest villages in his vast domains, Sam Potter was blazing the next belt of firs to be felled in the plantation behind his cottage and Sydney Codsall was taking a posy to old Mrs Earnshaw, who was ninety-eight and making a new will at the expense of a niece in New South Wales. Sydney was one of the few who was half-aware of a crisis but it did not seem to him anything like so important as the transfer of Mrs Earnshaw's ropewalk to a company known as Coombe Bay Enterprises Ltd., who were offering hard cash for an enterprise that had failed even before Mr Earnshaw was drowned at sea in the eighteen-eighties.

In only one kitchen in the Valley did the distant roll of kettle-drum cause dismay and this was at Periwinkle, on the edge of the moor, where hostilities had already begun in a sharp engagement between Will Codsall and his wife, Elinor. Like the bigger conflict over the sea the dispute had its origin in a scrap of paper, not a treaty exactly but a printed summons ordering Will to present himself at the Devon Yeomanry barracks within forty-eight hours, on pain of arrest.

The arrival of the summons stupefied Elinor. Until then she had looked upon Will's territorial activities as a silly male game, for which, however (and she also considered this ridiculous), he had been paid a regular quarterly sum, ever since he had signed on the day of the Coronation Fête, in 1911. Will had been won over by the Yeomanry's smart turnout on that occasion and in the refreshment tent after the tug-of-war he had got into conversation with a troop sergeant, who had pointed out the advantages of a Territorial engagement which required of a volunteer no more than one drill a week and a fortnight's camp each summer. Will signed on the spot and had never regretted his impulsive act. He had enjoyed the drills and found the money useful for new stock, whereas the period

in camp had been a welcome change from farm chores. It had
never occurred to him that he might, at some time, be required
under the terms of his engagement to fire a rifle in anger, and
if anybody had told him there was the remotest possibility
of his being transported across the seas he would have paid
his solicitor brother to extricate him from such a menacing
situation. Elinor, once the meaning of the summons was made
known to her, flew into a temper that gave Will a foretaste of
the drum-fire and box barrages he was soon to encounter near
Armentières. She stormed and raved for an hour, likening him
to various vegetables of the coarser kind, and using phrases
that would have stunned her lay-preaching father, mercifully
at rest in the churchyard. Will reasoned and pleaded, pointing
out that all Territorial units were earmarked for home service,
for guarding viaducts and suchlike and that even if there was
a war it was unlikely to last more than a month and that he
would be paid for his time with the colours, just as he had
for his periods in camp, but Elinor's wrath continued to break
over him in waves until at length he fled to the privy in the
garden and locked the door against her. When it was dark he
stole out and foraged around for his kit. It took him back a
few years to be moving about a house with stealth as though,
at any moment, he would hear the shrill voice of his mother,
Arabella, but when Elinor found him packing in the kitchen
he saw that her rage was spent, that her eyes were red and at
once felt small, mean and wretched. He said, dismally, 'You'll
get the separation allowance, Ellen, and I daresay tiz all a lot
of ole nonsense and us'll be 'ome be weekend,' and he put his
arms round her and kissed her as she wailed, 'How be I goin'
to manage with harvest almost on us? What's to become of
everything we built up yerabouts if youm gone for months?
Was 'ee mazed Will Codsall, to put us in this kind o' fix for
a few shillings?' He admitted glumly that he must have been,
as mazed as a March hare, adding that there was a possibility
of him getting temporary exemption until the harvest was in,
and after that he would see Squire and anyone else who could
pull strings to prolong his deferment indefinitely. She cheered
up a little at this and cooked his supper and afterwards, in the

evening haze, they walked the boundaries of their eighty-acre holding and he issued his final instructions in case exemption took time to arrange. That night, while he slept, Elinor lay awake and her mind went back to the first night they had spent in this room after their wedding at the little chapel in Coombe Bay. They had, or so it seemed to her, achieved a great deal since then, enlarging what had been a ruined patch into a real farm, very small but prosperous. Then they had nothing but a few hens but now they had the biggest egg yield in the Valley, besides a cow, ducks, turkeys, pigs, and several acres of former heathland under the plough. Was this to be sacrificed because Will, almost an illiterate, had signed a paper he didn't understand? It was a monstrous price to pay for a small mistake and what kind of soldier would he make anyway, despite a hulking frame and hardened muscles? He had never been able to bring himself to wring a fowl's neck and all the killing was done by her. Perhaps they would find this out and send him back; perhaps, but somehow she thought it unlikely.

II

Will Codsall's summons was the plucking of the first brick from the parochial wall. News that he had been hustled away overnight sobered the Valley and sent some of the more thoughtful to the foreign news section of the *County Press*. Henry Pitts, of Hermitage, was not among this minority, giving it as his opinion that the German Kaiser, long recognised as mad, had now degenerated into a homicidal maniac and that Will was fortunate in finding himself among those charged with hunting the lunatic down and packing him off to St Helena, which Henry regarded as the traditional lock-up of all unsuccessful challengers of British naval supremacy. It was an extravagant theory, and Henry's father Arthur said there was surely more to it than that, for the British Army must have been very hard-pressed indeed to need the services of an amiable chap like Will. He was more inclined to think that the Yeomanry was being called out to replace regulars who had refused to bear arms against Ulster. Eveleigh, at Four Winds, being a more serious-minded man than either of the Pitts, was one of those who sought an answer in back numbers of the *County Press*, there to make what he could of newsletters published under such headings as 'Austria Threatens Servia!' 'Tsar Pledges Aid to Slavs', and 'Where Britain stands in Balkan Dispute', but he soon lost his way in a maze of despatches from St Petersburg, Vienna, Berlin, Paris and Belgrade, suspending judgment until he could consult Horace Handcock, the Valley oracle on foreign affairs. Eveleigh was a practical man and found it very difficult to connect the sudden disappearance of one of his neighbours with revolver shots fired at a bulging-eyed foreigner in a town of which he had never heard.

When he entered the sawdust bar of The Raven about seven o'clock that evening he was amazed to find more than a score of the Valley men already assembled and all, it appeared, in search of the answers to the questions he had sought in vain in the newspapers. Rumours, some of them too absurd to be credited, converted the usually peaceful atmosphere of the bar into a Tower of Babel. Churchill, they said, was calling out the fleet; the King had written a strong letter to his crazy German cousin ordering him to back down at once; Kitchener had been recalled from Egypt and was standing by to land the Army on the Continent whereas Horace Handcock, his face the colour of a ripe cider apple proved quite unequal to the task of sieving through these rumours, having been so generously plied with brown ale that he could only babble incoherently of spies, Zeppelins and lethal mangolds. About eight o'clock Eveleigh left in disgust, none the wiser save for confirmation that Will Codsall had left the Valley in uniform.

He should have waited a little longer. About eight-thirty Smut Potter looked in on his way back from Sorrel Halt and in his pocket was a special edition of a London newspaper, thrown from the window of a through express. It told of troop movements all over Europe, of Germany's pledge to support Austria against Russia, and of France's pledge to back Russia and Servia against Germany and Austria. There was no mention of England's involvement and this was a source of disappointment to those present, so much so that, as the evening progressed, and after a labourer who could actually vouch for Will Codsall's departure arrived, Will's stock declined, for it was thought discreditable on his part to have slunk away without a word to anyone, as though resolved to fight the Kaiser single-handed. Then, to everybody's relief word was circulated that Squire was in the bar parlour with John Rudd and Sam Potter asked the landlord if he would convey their respects to Mr Craddock and ask for enlightenment. A moment or two later Paul appeared and damped everybody's spirits by announcing that Mr Grenfell, who was surely in a position to know, had told him over the telephone earlier in the day that Great Britain was almost certain to remain neutral if war broke out but that he, personally, did not think it would because the latest news in London was that the President of the United States and the Pope had offered their services as mediators. This information fell upon the heated company like a cold douche and Smut pinpointed the only consolatory crumb by saying, 'Well, that'll bring old Will home with his tail down, for it dorn zeem as if any of us'll get a crack at 'em!' a remark that indicated to those who had known Smut in the old days that the poacher was not exorcised after all. Soon the forum broke up and the Valley men, their belligerence mellowed by beer and cider, dispersed, all but Horace Handcock who had progressed beyond the jovial stage and had to be forcibly restrained from staggering up the hill to denounce the German professor as a spy.

Paul was silent during the ride home and it was not until they were approaching the ford that he said, 'Do you suppose I'm right, John? Are those idiots really disappointed with the prospect of us keeping clear of it?' and John said that this was more than probable, for there wasn't a man in the Valley apart from themselves who had ever been involved in a war. Paul digested this in silence but when they reached the end of the tow-path, said, suddenly, 'It doesn't make sense, John! What the devil would any of them get from war but death or wounds? And what would happen here if only the half of them rushed into uniform?'

'I can't answer that,' John said philosophically, 'but I can tell you this; there wasn't a man among them who wasn't damned envious of Will Codsall and that's ironic, if you like, for he's probably the only one in the Valley who would prefer to be ordered about by his wife than by a sergeant-major!'

'But they always seemed contented enough,' Paul argued. 'Why should they want to go off and get shot at?'

'You did it yourself once, didn't you?' John reminded him, 'but this time it's more than high spirits and boredom, I fancy. For a century or more we've been telling everyone we're top nation and now we look like having to prove it.'

Paul said, 'Come, John, you heard what Grenfell said; there's no chance of us being involved, except as mediators. Do you honestly believe there's a likelihood of us siding with France and Russia?'

'Yes I do,' John replied and Paul noticed that there was an edge to his voice. 'Politicians like Jimmy Grenfell think they know better than most people but the fact is it must be difficult to see the wood for the trees in Westminster. I've been watching this damned naval race for a long time and I've thought about it too, more often than I cared to. If it doesn't come now it'll come next year or the year after, so maybe it's as well to get it over and done with while we still have the pretence of naval superiority. At all events that's what the Navy thinks!'

As John said this Paul had a vision of Roddy Rudd, the fresh-faced, motor-mad boy who had been dazzled by Grace and had once incurred his jealousy. 'Where is Roddy now?' he asked, and John said somewhere in the South Atlantic, serving as gunnery officer on the cruiser *Good Hope*. 'And damned well out of it, I hope, at least for the time being,' he added, 'for don't run away with the notion that the German Navy won't fight or that, ship for ship, it isn't a damned sight more up-to-date than ours!'

'Good God, you can't mean that, John,' Paul said, for having grown up in the belief that one British-manned ship was worth

ten of any other nation's he found his agent's disparagement
unpalatable.

'I do mean it and I have it on excellent authority,' John said,
'although it isn't the kind of thing one should noise abroad.
They've got better range-finders and thicker armour-plating
and many of them can show a better turn of speed! And now,
to more practical issues: Will you do anything to give Elinor
Codsall a harvest hand at Periwinkle?'

'Certainly I will, providing Will doesn't come back looking
sheepish the day after tomorrow. I'll tell you what, John, I'll
lay you two to one in half-crowns that he will!'

'You're on,' said John, 'for if we're to have everything turned
upside down for the rest of our lives I don't see why I should
miss a chance of making five shillings out of it!'

Paul knew that he had lost his bet some time before the
crowds began to gather outside the *County Press* offices in
Paxtonbury awaiting the appearance of the latest posters,
and before packets of newspapers screaming 'War!' were
flung among excited newsagents' boys when the Cornish
Riviera made its three-minute stop at the cathedral town.
He knew it even before the sombre Foreign Secretary, Grey,
had made his prolix but unequivocal speech to the House on
that tense Monday afternoon, for his telephone, still one of
three in the Valley, linked him with a man whose sources
of information were just as good as those of Grenfell's and
whose interpretation was more expert.

At about 2 a.m., on the night that Paul deflated the Valley
jingoes in the bar of The Raven, he awoke to hear his
telephone-bell shrilling in the hall, where it stood in an alcove
under the stair well out of sight of Mrs Handcock who still
regarded the instrument as a direct link with the Devil. And
in a way, on that close August night, it was. When Paul went
downstairs to answer it the voice at the end of the wire had
the fruitiness of Satan who had just succeeded, against all
probabilities, in winning over half Christendom.

Paul said, a little breathlessly, 'Who is it? What's happened?' and through a soft chuckle Uncle Franz replied,
'Now who would it be my dear boy? Who else, among

your bucolic friends, would be awake and abroad at this hour?'

'What the devil is the point of ringing me at this time of night?' Paul demanded, although he felt relieved. 'Is it about Grace?'

'Not specially,' the old man replied, enjoying his advantage, 'although I do have news of Grace. The Glorious Cause has come to terms with their Tormentors. I understand Holloway is to be emptied of the dear old ladies on condition they wave Union Jacks in a day or so!'

'Oh, get to the point, Uncle Franz,' Paul growled, 'I'm standing here practically naked and it's gone two o'clock! It's a miracle I heard the bell at all.'

'Well,' said Franz, slowly, 'there isn't a point, not really, particularly as you are not a man of affairs looking for a profit motive. I just thought you might like to know that I've leased the scrapyard for almost exactly the sum that you inherited from your father back in 1902! *Leased* it mark you, not sold it! It reverts to us again after five years!'

'Good God!' Paul exclaimed, 'who is the tenant? The Tsar of Russia?'

'Only indirectly,' Franz said, 'but I won't bother you with details now. I rang because papers will arrive for you to sign in a day or so, and you won't be under an obligation to read them! You have my word for it that they are . . . well . . . advantageous, shall we say?'

'Did you ring to tell me that or for some other reason?' Paul asked, suddenly seeing a chink of daylight through the old Croat's smokescreen and Franz replied, blandly, 'I suppose I really rang to stop you ringing *me* when the documents arrive for I won't be available; I shall be on the move as soon as the balloon goes up!'

Paul said breathlessly, 'You really think it will?' and there was a pause before the old man replied, as though he was choosing his words very carefully. Finally, he went on, in a slightly more serious voice: 'I don't imagine it will affect you much one way but if you do have emergency measures in mind take them now! Don't even wait for the morning papers.

Germany, France and Austria have mobilised and Austria is over the frontier into Servia. Germany will declare war on France tomorrow, if she hasn't already done so. As for us, we shall be in by Tuesday at the latest!'

'How can you be so sure?' Paul demanded. 'Grenfell rang two days ago and said it depended upon half-a-dozen unknown factors, any one of which might result in us standing aside.'

Franz said, 'My dear boy, the politicians are the clowns who provide the curtain raiser, an entirely different cast act the play! If I thought you would follow my advice I could put you in the way of making another fortune between now and next Sunday but you have always had your nose too deep in the dirt to do that and, in a way, I admire you for it! At least you know yourself, don't have self-doubts about your destiny, and have hit on the secret of real success, which is living one's life the way one wants to live it! Judged that way you're a very spectacular success indeed! Good night my boy! Sleep well . . .' but Paul cried, '*Wait*, Uncle Franz! You've hauled me from bed to say this much so you can tell me a little more! What'll be the outcome of this madness on everybody's part?'

'A very long war,' Franz said, 'so don't be taken in by the Kaiser's promise of Home-before-the-Leaves-Fall! Most of the poor devils won't come home at all and those who do will never be the same again. Kitchener's view is three years, although everybody is laughing at him right now. Personally I think he's an optimist!'

'Three years!' Paul exclaimed, 'but Great God, that would bankrupt everybody wouldn't it?'

'It will bankrupt a good many,' Franz said, fruitiness re-entering his voice, 'but I am reasonably confident that neither you nor I will be among that number. I'll give you one piece of advice that you may be inclined to take. Put every acre you've got under plough while you still have the chawbacons to do it! Who knows? You may come out of it better than I!' and he rang off, leaving Paul holding the receiver and conscious, despite his half-nakedness, of sweat pouring from under his arms and striking cold in the draught from the big door. He reached beyond the telephone and slipped on an old hunting coat, too agitated to go back to bed and disinclined to wake Claire who had not heard the bell. He went through the library and out on to the terrace where the heat of the day still lingered and the cloying, old-world scent of wallflowers hung on the air like the perfume of meandering ghosts. There was a waning moon low in the sky over the Home Farm meadows and the night was so still that the whisper of the avenue chestnuts reached him across the paddock. He thought, grimly, 'All over Europe men are shuffling along in the dark with their packs and weapons, and I daresay, by now, every main road in Germany is noisy with the rattle of wagons. Almost everyone here and there thinks of war as I thought of it, during the voyage to Table Bay fifteen years ago, but it didn't take me long to discover that war is a boring, bloody muddle, punctuated by moments of fear and disgust!' And suddenly his memory turned on a peepshow that he would have thought forgotten, of smoke rising from a burned-out Boer farm, of sun-bonneted women and snivelling children standing behind the wire of a waterless concentration camp, of a private of the King's Royal Rifles with a Mauser bullet in his belly calling on his mates to put another through his head. 'It was bad enough then,' he said half-aloud, 'but that was a piffling affair by today's standards! I don't suppose a hundred thousand ever met on one field and now there are millions, and fighting will occur in densely-populated areas! Who the hell is to blame for misery on that scale? The Kaiser? The Tsar? Those tricky French politicians or the starchy British ones, like Asquith, Grey and that Jack-in-a-Box Lloyd George?' He moved along the terrace to Grace's sunken garden and when the perfume of roses she had planted reached him he thought of her again, and how pitiful The Glorious Cause looked measured against a European war. What, precisely, had that cynical old rascal Franz meant when he implied there were men behind the politicians and generals pulling strings? Did he mean merchants like himself, who made a profit on war as his father had done years before? Or rabble-rousers, high and low, obsessed by the cult of nationalism who used their influence to convert happy-go-lucky chaps like Smut Potter and Horace Handcock into blood-thirsty patriots? And how did he himself view the prospect of war against the Kaiser's Germany? He had never considered it a serious possibility, not really, in spite of all the years of newspaper talk and even now found it difficult to whip up rage or resentment against the Germans. The only two personally known to him, the professor and his son Gottfried, were amiable, intelligent chaps. What he did feel, however, pressing like a girdle about his ribs, was a sadness at the finality of the occasion, and the sensation reminded him of the time he had lost Grace and fled from the sleazy lodging of the prostitute near the Turkish baths. It was a profound certainty that the way of life that was his he was about to lose and with it the promise the future had offered, for if Grenfell's predictions proved right it would be a savage, bloody business, no matter how long or short it proved, and if it did drag on, as Franz seemed to think, then nothing could ever be the same again for any of them. He wondered, objectively, if he would involve himself in it; if, before it was over, he would find himself alongside men like Will Codsall and some of the others who seemed eager to show their mettle but decided against, remembering that he was now thirty-five, with a wife and family to consider and that war was a young man's business.

The perfume of the roses from the sunken garden seemed to drench this end of the terrace so that when he heard a step on the flagstones and a voice calling him, he thought once more of Grace, whom he always associated with this garden. Then he saw a blur of white in the doorway and called, 'I'm out here, Claire!' and she came along the terrace towards him, her hair tumbling over the pink shawl he had given her last Christmas. She said, anxiously, 'I wondered where on earth you were! What's happened? Is it anything serious?'

'Serious enough,' he told her and repeated the gist of Franz's conversation over the telephone. He was amazed to note that she seemed relieved rather than startled, as though the clash of armies had nothing to do with themselves or the people of the Valley. She said, 'Well, all I can say is I'm glad you're too old and the children are too young!' and he thought the remark very typical of her and envied her ability to view catastrophe in such a personal light. He said, however, 'It will make nonsense of all we've been trying to do down here, Claire. You realise that I suppose?'

'I don't see why it should,' she argued, 'James told you it couldn't possibly last more than a month or so, didn't he?'

'I'd sooner take Uncle Franz's word than Grenfell's on an issue like this,' he said. 'If there are people around prepared to pay that much money for a five-year lease on a scrapyard they must have a good idea what's likely to happen! Those kind of people, Uncle Franz's kind, don't make mistakes that cost money, not their money!'

'Oh well,' she said, cheerfully, 'there's nothing we can do about it is there? I suppose they must fight it out and then go home and pick up where they left off!'

He smiled, putting his arm around her and kissing the top of her head. It would be a shame, he thought, to try and explain to her what a conflict on this scale could do even to a place as remote as this, or to a woman with a civilian husband and children in rompers. She would soon find out if Uncle Franz's gloomy prophecy came true. Then he thought how differently Grace would have reacted to the news and remembered that it was here, on this spot, that he proposed marriage on the night of the Coronation soirée. It was disturbing but also significant, he reflected, that Grace should seem so close tonight and the sharpness of his memories seemed almost an affront to Claire standing with her head on his shoulder inhaling the sweetness of the night air so he said shortly, 'Come on, there's no sense standing here, let's go back to bed!' and they went in and up the broad, shallow stairs. She curled up and was asleep almost at once and again he envied her narrow world. 'There's Ikey,' he thought. 'He'll have to go but she never bothered much with Ikey. He always seemed to belong to the era of Grace and anyway, he's a professional and might even welcome war as offering prospects of promotion.' Then, as it began to grow light, he borrowed something of Claire's complacency, thinking, 'Dammit, maybe she's right! There's no sense in losing sleep over something that can't be helped or altered!

I'll do my worrying when I have to!' and was sorry then that she had gone to sleep for the scent of the roses seemed to linger about her, and it occurred to him that casual access to the woman beside him was a more exciting prospect than storming every citadel in Europe.

III

In the first week of November a persistent north-easterly, showering Channel spray and needles of sleet across the Valley, drove the yellow-eyed gulls from their fishing grounds on the sandbanks and launched them on one of their periodical circuits across the shoulder of the Bluff, west to the upper reaches of the Sorrel then back across the shorn fields of Four Winds.

The gulls knew the features of the Valley better than any earthbound creature and as they hovered over the woods and streams, peering down for unconsidered trifles, they must have been aware of some of the changes that had taken place there in the last few weeks. They no longer had to contend with the wild cries of Eveleigh's crow-starver, or the ill-aimed pellets of Henry Pitts, because, at these two points of flight, they maintained height and swooped upon easier pickings behind the field kitchens of the vast tented camp that covered the moor between Periwinkle Farm and the Paxtonbury road. There was always food to be found here and nobody minded when they helped themselves from the bins ranged along the hedge that bordered the camp to the north. Thousands of men were living there but were either clumping about in cohorts, encouraged by bellowing figures out on the flanks, or cowering in their sopping tents, sheltering from wind and rain. So the gulls dived on the offal and hunks of bread scattered all around and flew off gorged to Coombe Bay, where the more observant might have noted other changes in and about the village, the absence of Tom Williams and his fishing team for instance, or the stillness of the house and garden where the old German professor had lived above the dunes, a man who had

always welcomed them and encouraged them to take bread
and bacon rinds he saved for them. This house, a favourite
port of call for storm-driven gulls, was unoccupied now, its
windows open to the rain and there were slivers of shattered
glass lying on the lawns back and front, reflecting the pale
gleam of the sun on the rare occasions it penetrated the low
cloud. This, perhaps, was the most significant change of all,
for there had been territorial camps on Blackberry Moor in
years gone by but never a scene like the one enacted outside
the old German's house one warm evening in late August.

It began with an advance up the hill of a knot of Coombe Bay
men, including Eph Morgan, the Welsh builder, Walt Pascoe,
Tom Williams shortly before he joined the Naval Reserve and
others, women and children as well as men. If the local posse
could have been said to have had leadership it was vested in
Horace Handcock, the Shallowford gardener. He it was who
had preached the crusade in the bar of The Raven but he
was too old and too drunk to take his place at their head
when they stormed up the hill to register their disapproval
of the Kaiser's rape of Belgium.

The professor was at his desk when the clamour reached
him and he got up to look out of his window. The first
stone, flung by Walt Pascoe, smashed the glass and grazed
his head, causing blood to flow. A moment later stones or
clods had shattered every window at the front of the house.
The professor remained downstairs long enough to bundle up
his manuscripts but while he was doing this a fragment of
glass struck his chin, inflicting another small wound. He went
upstairs and locked himself in Gottfried's bedroom overlooking
the garden but soon this window was shattered and he saw
that people had made their way round the house and were
cavorting about his flower beds, pulling up plants and shrubs
and howling like dervishes. Then Eph Morgan remembered
the German had a motor and at once linked it in his mind
to the Squire's derelict Belsize, still embedded in Sorrel mud.
It seemed to Morgan a good idea that there should be two
derelict cars in the district so, with the help of many willing
hands, he trundled it out of the coach-house and on to a rose

bed where, with the tools taken from the shed, it was soon reduced to a wreck. More people continued to arrive from the village and as it was nearly dusk someone suggested a bonfire so Pascoe punctured the petrol tank with a garden fork and soon there was a very good bonfire indeed, one that could be seen a great way off. Paul saw it as he crossed the ford and set off at a gallop for the village, making the journey in the record time of eleven minutes, for he was riding a mettlesome four-year-old that Rose had sold him just before the outbreak of war. He had been warned of the riot by Pansy Pascoe who had the forethought to use The Raven's telephone and she urged him to come quickly before murder was done. Pansy was probably the only person in the village who disapproved of the riot. She had been employed by the professor as a daily help and he had treated her with kindness and generosity. She realised, however, that it was useless to argue with her husband Walt in his present mood, for he was full of beer, having enlisted that very day at Whinmouth and was due to depart the following morning. She said, on the telephone, 'Do 'ee come quick, Squire! They'm murderin' the poor old toad!' and Paul had set off at once shouting to Chivers to send John Rudd after him and during his wild ride along the river bank he thought savagely of the strange madness that had seized people since newspapers had begun calling Germans 'Huns' and printing stories of crucified Belgian babies that no man in his sense could believe.

They would not have gone as far as to lay hands on the German. He could see that as soon as he flung himself from his horse and rushed round behind the house, where it seemed as though the entire population of the village was dancing round the blazing wreck of the Humber. The house, with all its windows shattered, looked empty but someone said the old professor was inside, hiding under a bed probably. Paul's informant seemed to assume that the Squire had arrived to share in the fun and was astounded when Paul grabbed him by the lapels of his jacket and shouted, 'What the hell do you think you're doing? Has everybody gone stark, staring mad? *Who* started this business? *Who* began it? Do you realise you could all go to prison for this?' and he punched his way into the centre of the ring.

His words had immediate effect. For a long time now they had been content to have him do most of their thinking. Tom Williams said, a little shamefacedly, 'I told 'em they was goin' a bit far, Squire. Breaking the old devil's windows would ha' been enough to frighten the ole bastard out o' the Valley!' but he too had a shock when Paul spun round on him, shouting, 'You bloody idiot, Tom! What harm has the old fellow ever done any of us, and how the hell can he be responsible for the Kaiser's doings? He's a fugitive from the Junkers himself! He only came here to get a bit of peace!' Then, having cleared a ring and seeing people beginning to slip away round to the front of the house, he shouted, 'The next person to throw a stone or touch anything here will be reported by me to the Whinmouth police, do you hear?'

They heard, those who were not already gone, and within a few moments Paul had the garden to himself, except for some wide-eyed children who should have been in bed. He said, sharply, 'Get on home. The policeman will be here in a moment!' and they fled so that he was left to wonder whether, when John Rudd arrived, they should round up the rioters and make them extinguish the blazing car with water taken from the rain butt. He decided not to bother for the motor was all but destroyed and there was no danger of flames spreading to the rear of the house. He stood in the centre of the lawn and called, 'Herr Scholtzer! Professor! It's me, Squire Craddock! They've gone now, you've nothing to fear!'

There was no answer so he tried the back door and finding it open went in. On the first landing, holding a lamp above his head, he saw the old man looking down and seeing the blood on his face, Paul said, 'I'll send one of those fools to telephone for the doctor!' but the German said, briefly, 'No! Please! It is nothing, Mr Craddock!' and came down to the hall where glass from the coloured panes in the front door crunched underfoot.

They went into the library, Scholtzer dabbing his head with a towel and in here was the same litter of broken glass and pages of manuscript blown to the floor. The room had always looked scrupulously tidy for the professor was a very methodical man and somehow, to Paul, the disorder emphasised the sheer idiocy of the assault. He said, grimly, 'You must let me deal with this, professor. I'll have every one of them in court for this night's work!' but the old man lifted his hand and said, 'No, Mr Craddock, it was goot of you to come quickly but please, you will not make the case of it! That would do no goot for you and I have plans to leave very soon. The police were here with my papers this morning,' and he began gathering up manuscript from the floor and sorting it into little piles.

'You don't have to leave on this account,' Paul said, 'they'll not bother you again. Get a few things together and come back to the house with me. We can clear up in the morning and I can guarantee you plenty of assistance!'

The old man made no immediate reply but having finished collecting his papers he poured two glasses of gin and handed one to Paul. He seemed, Paul thought, very calm and resigned, as though a frenzied assault upon his property and person by people he had regarded as friends brought sadness but neither rancour nor fear. He said, finally, 'You must not blame them so much, Mr Craddock! It will be happening all over Europe. It is kind that you should ask me to your house but it would not be wise, I think, to go. They would remember it against you as long as the fighting lasts. It would be different if my boy was here but there is nothing they can do to me. It is your glass that has been broken.'

'And your motor that has been burned,' growled Paul. 'Where is Gottfried? I heard he had gone abroad earlier in the summer.'

'He is in Germany,' the old man said. 'He went to Italy for a music examination in June. Then the foolish boy went tramping in the Dolomites and I have since heard that the authorities refused to allow him to leave. Perhaps, by now, he is in uniform. After all, he is German born, with German parents, and your Government would not consider him eligible for exchange. Perhaps his whereabouts are known and that is why your people come here to break windows.'

'I'm sure that had nothing to do with it,' Paul said but the fact that the shy young German was possibly serving in the Kaiser's Army astounded him almost as much as the demonstration on the lawn. Gottfried had grown up in the Valley and seemed to Paul almost as much a part of it as Eveleigh's children or Sam Potter's daughter, Pauline. He said, 'Can they compel him to serve in the Army?' and the professor replied, with a shrug, 'It will be a choice between the Army or prison. If I had foreseen such a thing I would have applied for his naturalisation papers when he was a child but one cannot blame oneself for not foreseeing what is happening in the world today.'

'You say the police were here? Is it likely that you will be sent to an Aliens Camp?'

'No,' said the old man, 'I have been given permission to go to the United States. My publishers and certain Oxford gentlemen were kind enough to vouch for me. It is a pity that Gottfried cannot change places with me, for even the Junkers could not use me as a soldier.'

There seemed nothing more to say and Paul felt trapped in a mesh of circumstances almost as frustrating and bizarre as those encompassing the German and his son. It was as though the entire structure of the estate and its way of life was crumbling and all one could do was to stand around wringing one's hands and making fatuous comments on each new development. Will Codsall had disappeared, then Gottfried, now the old professor, whom he had always thought of as popular in the Valley, and others would be going soon, among them some of those who had created this mess on the floor. He supposed that he would get used to what was happening in time but the rhythm of the Valley had been so smooth and settled, and the process of readjustment was not easy, for he was unable to subscribe to the strident patriotism that had been surging down the Valley ever since Bank Holiday; so much of it seemed as shrill and childish as the recent behaviour of sober men like Tom Williams and Ephraim Morgan.

He said, as a valediction, 'You were happy here, Professor, you won't forget us easily?'

The old man smiled, drawing a mottled hand across his great walrus moustache. 'No, Mr Craddock, I shall remember Shallowford with gratitude. I found what I sought here, the chance to live and work among kindly people and a single night's stone-throwing cannot erase the memory of more than ten years' peace!'

They shook hands and Paul left him, letting himself out of the shattered front door and crossing the road to the spot where his bay was tethered. The street was empty, so empty that Paul wondered if everyone had gone into hiding, but outside The Raven Pansy Pascoe came out of the shadows, calling softly, 'Is 'un all right? Did they 'arm the poor ole toad?' and Paul told her that the professor had escaped with a few cuts but that the police would be making enquiries in the morning.

'Well,' she said, philosophically, 'I daresay that'll put the fear o' God into some o' the gurt fools but it won't bother Walt! He's off first light an' dam' good riddance to 'un! Us 'aven't 'ad a word o' zense out of 'un zince it started!'

He wondered how she would manage on the meagre separation allowance and a house full of half-grown children but then he remembered that she was a Potter and that the Potters always managed somehow. He thanked her for telephoning and rode off up the empty street. Glancing over his shoulder he could still see the orange glow of the burning motor on the hillside; it looked, he thought, like a beacon warning the coast of invasion from the sea.

IV

There were changes that the sharp-eyed gulls did not see as they made their circuits waiting for the wind to change and enable them to return to their fishing grounds on the banks. By early November the Dell was beginning to assume its once familiar look of neglect and near-squalor, with tools and faggots scattered around, and rubbish accumulating behind the sheds and byres. Jem, the Bideford Goliath, who had reigned here ever since he quit his job at the fair and imposed his genial discipline upon the two Potter girls, had followed Will Codsall into the Army soon after the Miracle of the Marne, and although he was over thirty his giant frame had ensured acceptance by the fast-talking recruiting sergeant at the Paxtonbury Territorial centre. Jem had been followed, almost at once, by Smut, who had abandoned his greenhouses to the younger Eveleigh boy and gone gladly enough, as though, in soldiering, he saw an opportunity to recapture the excitement of a poacher's life. John Rudd warned him that his prison record might result in rejection but John was wrong for when Smut admitted that he had served a term of imprisonment for belting a gamekeeper over the head with a gun butt the recruiting sergeant was delighted, saying this was precisely the type of recruit needed. Smut's musketry instructor was equally impressed. At the initial five-round shoot-off Smut scored four bulls and an inner and that with a type of rifle he had never before fired. On the strength of this plus a pint or two of beer, the instructor withdrew him from the awkward squad and sent him on a sharpshooters' course. It was astonishing how rapidly Smut reverted to type, how quickly and completely he forgot his patiently acquired horticultural skills and became, in effect, a poacher again. He found that he could still move across country quickly and noiselessly at night and interpret and locate the sounds made by blundering adversaries opposed to him in training exercises and with the rediscovery of his skills he sloughed off the new personality he had acquired after his release from gaol, progressing rapidly in his new profession. After Will Codsall he was the first of the Valley men to cross to France and move into the soggy ditches that already reached from Switzerland to the sea, and here he adapted himself far more easily than did most of the men of his battalion. Alone among them, save for a tramp or two lured into the recruiting office by the promise of beer and the leonine glare of Kitchener, Smut could spend successive nights lying out in the open in all weathers and he did not find a five-day spell of front-line duty very different from life as a boy in the Dell in Tamer's time, or as a young man subsisting on what he could trap and kill between the Sorrel and the Whin. He had no personal quarrel with the Germans but he was more fatal to them than many of those who regarded all Germans as unspeakable swine. To Smut they were simply the equivalent of the hares, bucks and pheasants he had stalked in the past, and the techniques he employed against them were much the same. He would lie behind the parados for hours disguised as a roll of wet sacking on a pile of rubble, as still and patient as a famished cat at a mousehole. Whenever he caught a fleeting glimpse of a moving cap or a hunched shoulder in the trenches opposite, he would wheeze with satisfaction and gently squeeze the trigger of his specially-sighted rifle. Sometimes, if the weather was good, he would take a chance after making a kill and wait for a second victim but more often he would be inside his trench within seconds of his quarry hitting the ground. Then, after carefully notching his rifle, he would meander along to another sector, pick a fresh vantage point and begin another vigil. He would fire at almost anything that stirred but the mark that excited him most was a sun-reflecting *pickelhaube*, for this meant the passage of an officer and therefore a slightly longer notch on his scoreboard. He was held in high esteem by his officers not because of his sniping but because he was now a fully-licensed poacher and an enormous asset to men short of almost everything that made life bearable under conditions of constant danger and appalling discomfort. He never hurried and never acted impulsively. Before making a swoop he would study the routes of ration parties, just as he had marked out the rabbit-runs in Heronslea coverts and sometimes, when his platoon was desperately short of firewood, duckboards, sandbags, wiring stakes, plum and apple jam, bully beef and even the almost unobtainable navy rum, Smut would be permitted to lay aside his rifle and drift back towards brigade headquarters on some spurious errand. Here he would make a careful reconnaissance, and after selecting three or four of the more robust of his mates, return after dark to the areas he had memorised. Sometimes one or two of his carriers would be caught and mercilessly punished but Smut was never among this minority, for he never carried anything himself and could always melt into the darkness and try again the following night. They soon made him a corporal and he could have risen higher but he was content with two stripes, explaining that a third would cramp his style. The night he appeared at the entrance of his officer's dugout with a case of Scotch whisky his Company commander swore that he would recommend Potter for the D.C.M., declaring that men had been decorated for far less but Smut talked him out of it. One of the very earliest lessons he had learned as a poacher was to remain inconspicuous and after some discussion he settled for ten shillings which he sent home to Meg, telling her that more would be coming for he was now doing a brisk trade in the sale of souvenirs.

Smut was not the only member of the Potter clan to find release in war. All three of his elder sisters had their burdens appreciably lightened when their men marched out of the Valley whistling 'Tipperary'. Pansy let her cottage at an advantageous rent to a major at the camp on Blackberry Moor and moved herself and family into the farmhouse at the Dell and here, restored at last to the congenial company of the recently liberated Cissie and Violet, she began her war work.

The Potter girls were the first women in the Valley to make war show a credit balance. Although past their prime (Cissie and Pansy were on the wrong side of thirty and Violet was twenty-eight), they were still strong, vigorous, handsome, healthy women and the Lancashire Fusiliers, occupying the tented camp on the moor, were a jolly set of boys, all far from home and unfastidious. Often, of a winter evening, the Dell farmhouse erupted with song and laughter and even a man as formidable as the Bideford Goliath would have found it impossible to defend the fort as he had defended it against the raids of the Timberlake boys. The girls still thought of Jem affectionately and sometimes sent him parcels and money to eke out his rations and pay in the dismal Welsh camp, where he was learning to disembowel Germans with bayonet and Mills bomb but they did not wish him back, telling one another that war had opened their eyes to the pitiful state of servitude into which they had lapsed. Such work as was done on the farm was now performed by volunteers and paid for in kind, and whereas Jem laid the mark of his despotism on the fat posteriors of his handmaidens if they so much as winked at another man they now had a battalion of men at their disposal, with no question of any one man, or even two, claiming proprietorial rights over them. Meg, as usual, kept to herself and Hazel rarely appeared in the Dell. One way and another the Potter girls were set fair to enjoy the war, for when the Lancashire Fusiliers moved out the Shropshires moved in and the pleasant rhythm of life in the Dell hardly faltered.

In the last week of November there was a flare-up in the kitchen of Four Winds, where domestic scenes had once been commonplace but had been unknown since the Eveleighs had replaced the Codsalls. The cause of the only serious dispute that had ever broken out between the black moustached Norman Eveleigh and his wife Marian was Gilbert, their eldest boy, who had been whipper-in to the Sorrel Vale Farmers' Hunt ever since Squire Craddock had reorganised it, in 1911. Gilbert was now nearly eighteen, a slim, serious-minded boy, whose appearance favoured his mother but whose character was more like his father's. He was withdrawn and sparing with words but known in the Valley as a conscientious boy and the best rider to hounds for miles around. Squire Craddock liked and trusted him and the hounds, each of whom he could identify at a glance, adored him. The demands of the Government Remount Department, however, cost Gilbert his job. By early October there was hardly a horse left in the Valley, apart from those reserved for the plough and all prospects of hunting ended. Without consulting anyone Gilbert walked into Paxtonbury, added a year to his age and joined up, and this folly on his part disrupted a very united family for Mrs Eveleigh, who prized her eldest boy above all the rest of the brood, said she would disclose Gilbert's correct age and get him discharged at once. To her dismay Eveleigh told her to hold her silly tongue, saying that he, for his part, was proud of the boy. Periwinkle Farm had contributed a man to Kitchener's Army and the contemptible

Dell had sent two; if Gilbert wanted to rescue the honour of
Four Winds who were they to deny him?

All the children were present during this dispute and
what astonished them more than their father's stand was
their mother's obstinacy. Never, so far as any of them could
remember, had Marian Eveleigh contradicted her husband
but here she was actually screaming abuse at him, with the
white-faced Gilbert trying to reason with both and although
the matter seemed to end when Eveleigh also lost his temper
and threatened to strike her, it was Marian who carried the
day, for she flung herself out of the house, walked into Coombe
Bay and telephoned the military depot at Paxtonbury so that
Gilbert's enlistment was declared void.

After that, although tempers gradually cooled, things were
never quite the same between man and wife. It was as though
the ghost of Four Winds had not been banished after all but
was still lurking in one of the attics awaiting an opportunity
to sidle into the bedrooms and kitchen and foment trouble
between man, wife and children. In the event all that Marian's
defiance achieved was four months' deferment, for Gilbert
re-enlisted on his eighteenth birthday and the controversy
seemed likely to flare up again for there were two more
boys, aged sixteen and twelve, and by the time Gilbert had
gone nobody could say if the war would last three years, ten
years, or the remainder of everybody's life.

It was not long before the Eveleighs, man and wife, were
at one another's throats again and the dispute on this occasion
centred round their second daughter Rachel. Rachel Eveleigh
had been going steady with Keith Horsey ever since the
Coronation summer but it was only after they had been
instrumental in bringing help to the crazy gypsy-child, Hazel
Potter, that the Valley showed any interest in the association.
Now it was generally understood that Keith would marry the
farmer's daughter as soon as he passed his finals at Oxford and
was assured a good teaching post and Eveleigh was thought to
look upon the match with satisfaction, for a parson's son with
a university degree was a rare catch for the daughter of a man
who had begun as Codsall's hired hand.

Keith Horsey, luckier than most young men that cata-strophic summer, sat for his finals in June and the result, a double first gave him a choice of several careers. The couple had planned to marry in early spring but the war was rushing along at a speed that bewildered all but the very young and in mid-October Rachel informed the family that the wedding was being put forward to the last week in November.

The Valley was still apt to look suspiciously upon hurried weddings and none more so than the dour Eveleigh, whose unexpected opposition to the changed date was reinforced, it seemed, by sudden and inexplicable second thoughts re-garding the groom. Challenged by Rachel and her mother to explain them he said that he had been told that Keith Horsey was associated with a group of students dedicated to the ideal of international brotherhood. Rachel looked blank at this but Marian laughed in her husband's face, something else she had never done in more than twenty years of married life.

'You can't be serious, Norman!' she protested, 'what can it matter to us what Keith thinks about politics? He's a nice, well-mannered boy, capable of earning a good living independent of his father's money and in any case he's head over heels in love with our girl! I say the sooner they're wed the better!'

'Well I say different!' snapped Eveleigh, 'and seeing she isn't twenty-one until next summer she'll have to get my permission before she ties herself up to that snivelling little pro-German!'

At this Rachel burst into tears and rushed away but Marian stood her ground, for it occurred to her that this was her husband's way of punishing her for intervening in the matter of Gilbert's enlistment. Then another somewhat darker thought struck her and she came out with it at once. 'Have you got it into your silly head that our girl has got to get married?' she demanded and Eveleigh, to her amazement, replied, 'It wouldn't surprise me none, not with a boy of his type! Have ye not heard it said he's agin the war?'

'No, I haven't heard it,' said the wife stubbornly, 'but if I had it wouldn't cause me to think less of him! Anyone in their zenses is against the war I should think and the zooner more of them make it known the sooner this wicked slaughter among Christians'll stop!'

Now when Eveleigh had begun this conversation he had had no serious intention of withholding his permission but had merely sought to express disapproval of his future son-in-law's unpatriotic views. To a simple man like Norman Eveleigh lack of enthusiasm for the war amounted almost to treason. He had never given a thought to European politics before August 1914 but newspaper accounts of German atrocities in Belgium had stirred his anger so that he was among the most belligerent men in the Valley, growling that the world would never be safe until the Kaiser was put away, the German generals backed up against the wall and German towns given over to sack on the scale of Louvain. He was a man who had always driven himself remorselessly but he considered himself just and the German advance across France and Belgium surely called for retribution without mercy. The discovery that his own wife, the mother of his children, wanted the war stopped before justice had been done shocked him and hardened his resolve to make an issue of his daughter's marriage to a pacifist. He said, flatly, 'Lookit here, Marian! If she marries that milksop she'll do it without my blessing! I'll have no part in it, you understand? I'll not show at the wedding, and if she won't abide until she's of age then she can run off for all I care!' and having delivered this ultimatum he stamped off and took it out on a frisky bullock who had unwisely chosen this moment to break out of the pen behind the barn and career up the lane towards Codsall bridge.

Rachel, watching him belabouring the animal, said, 'He's mad! He must be! It's this place! This farm! Everybody who lives here ends up going off their heads, like old Martin Codsall and Arabella!' Then, drying her tears, 'Well, I'm not going to let *his* silly notions ruin *my* life, Mam, and you can tell him so for I shan't have another word to say to him! If he tries to stop us I'll go before the magistrates and get permission! They'll give it me and why shouldn't they? I'll be twenty-one in less than a year and Keith's father will stand by us!'

In the event this proved unnecessary, for although Eveleigh
persisted in his opposition he was persuaded by Paul to sign
the papers on the grounds that, if he did not, the couple would
marry in any case, war-time courts having little patience with
parental opposition to weddings. Every day girls younger
than Rachel were marrying soldiers, often after courtships of
less than a month. All the same, the new quarrels deepened
the unpleasant atmosphere at Four Winds and the ghost of
Arabella had reason to be pleased. After Rachel had married
and settled in Leeds, where Keith took a university post, the
Eveleigh family sat through a succession of silent meals and
when Gilbert re-enlisted Marian Eveleigh fastened on her old
grievance, going so far as to tell her husband that he had
driven the boy to his death! So many things were happening
so quickly in the Valley, however, that it was some time
before Paul was aware that strife had returned to Four
Winds after a lapse of ten years. He was usually alive to most
happenings in the Valley but at that season he had other and
more personal matters on his mind, notably an unexpectedly
violent dispute with his own wife. The disagreement centred
on another war-time marriage.

V

Late in November, less than a week before Keith Horsey and
Rachel Eveleigh were married in Coombe Bay parish church,
Ikey Palfrey reappeared in the Valley, home with his unit from
India after an absence of more than two years and destined,
in a matter of days, for France.

There was no time to warn anyone of his approach for he
was granted but seventy-two hours' leave and travelled west
on a night train that did not stop at Sorrel Halt. He arrived
very early in the morning, driving a hired car of uncertain
vintage and came into the kitchen just as Mrs Handcock
was brewing her ritual cup of tea. She let out a squawk
of joy as he came bounding up the yard steps, pouncing on
her, kissing her on both cheeks and declaring that she had

put on ten stone since he had seen her last. He had always
been her favourite and she bustled about frying him eggs,
bacon and potatoes, bubbling that she would 'share un wi'
no one, not even Squire, 'till 'e 'ad summat hot in his belly
and thawed-out-like!' She told him that he was 'as chock full
of 'is praper ole nonsense as ever, the gurt varmint!' adding,
with satisfaction, that he had 'villed out summat' and 'looked
more like a nigger than a Christian!' He had indeed broadened
so that his height was less noticeable and the Indian sun had
burned his face and hands berry-brown, but already his tan
was fading and looked, she told him 'more like grime than
zunburn!' While he ate she gave him the news, or such of it
as she could recall, for there had been so much in the last few
months, although, prior to that, little enough save for the birth
of the Squire's second daughter Whiz, 'the prettiest li'l maid
you ever did zee!' She told him Will Codsall had gone for a
soldier as soon as war started and that his wife, Elinor, had
been in a rare ole tizzy but had now got a good hand working
for her, the son of Tom Williams (now minesweeping), who
had a dread of the sea, having witnessed, as a child, the rescue
of the German sailors in the cove. 'And a praper zet o' bliddy
vools us maade of ourselves that day!' she added, 'for, like
as not, they us dragged ashore are vighting for that varmint
Little Willie!' She told him that Smut Potter had enlisted and
was said to have already killed hundreds of Germans and that
Jem, Dandy Timberlake and Walt Pascoe had gone after him,
leaving Walt's slut of a wife to move in with her sisters at the
Dell, there to earn more money on their backs, the hussies,
than they were ever likely to earn standing upright! She also
mentioned the rumour that Farmer Eveleigh was opposed to
his daughter's marriage to Keith, scheduled for next Saturday,
and this seemed to interest him most for he questioned her as
to the reasons for Eveleigh's opposition but she could supply
no satisfactory answer beyond saying, 'Tiz rumoured about
yer that Passon's son be one o' they preaching agin the war
and that's enough to turn any man sour, baint it?'

He surprised her by saying that before long a great many
people would be preaching against the war, for it now seemed

certain that it would not be over by Christmas or the Christmas after that and that he expected to be in France himself within days which was a pity for he would have liked to have attended Keith's wedding on Saturday. Mrs Handcock was dismayed that he would only be home for days after an absence of more than two years and at once recalled her duty to notify Squire and Mrs Craddock of his arrival. Ikey made the brazen suggestion that he should carry in their early morning tea but Mrs Handcock would have none of this for it would mean him seeing man and wife in bed together and this outraged her notion of propriety. She entered into a conspiracy, however, to tell Squire that someone had called on urgent business, bidding Ikey to wait at the top of the stairs so that she could watch the fun. Soon Paul came hurrying out, struggling into his dressing gown and his shout brought Claire on to the landing without a dressing gown for she interpreted Paul's bellow as an accident involving somebody's tumble downstairs.

They were delighted to see him and touched by the presents he had for them in his valise, a cashmere shawl for Claire, a pair of silver-mounted Mahratta pistols for the library wall and a cunningly-made Indian toy for each of the children. Mary, three and a half now, blushed with pleasure when he gave her a doll dressed in exquisitely worked embroidery closely sewn with amber and ruby-coloured beads.

News of his return ran down the Valley like a heath fire and all that morning tenants and Valley craftsmen made excuses to call and shake his hand, for he was the only professional soldier among them and Mons had raised the standing of a professional soldier in public esteem.

Among the last to arrive was Keith Horsey, who came into the yard as Ikey was saddling Paul's ageing Snowdrop for an amble round the estate before dusk. His greeting seemed so restrained that Ikey put it down to the nervousness regarding his imminent marriage. It was when Keith curtly declined the loan of the stable's sole remaining hack and an invitation to accompany him that Ikey noticed there was a reticence about him reminiscent of the nervous, shambling youth who had been the butt of High Wood during his first school year. He told

Chivers to exercise Snowdrop and walked Keith up the orchard as far as the sunken lane and here, exercising the privilege of an old friend, he said, 'Are you scared about getting married, Keith?' but Keith looked at him defiantly and replied, quietly, 'No, Ikey. I'm not a bit scared about Saturday. Rachel and I will be very happy once we get away from here.'

'I heard that your prospective father-in-law was flag-flapping,' said Ikey, 'but I'm damned if I'd let that bother me.'

'It isn't that either,' Keith said, stubbornly, 'in fact, it isn't anything much to do with me really. I suppose I should have written but it wasn't the kind of thing one could put to paper, at least, I couldn't!' and when Ikey raised his eyebrows, very puzzled by the other's embarrassment, he went on, 'It's . . . about you, Ikey, but before I make an idiot of myself will you tell me something?'

'Anything?'

'Well, before you left here, how . . . how well did you know Hazel Potter?'

Ikey, still bewildered, said, 'What the devil are you driving at? If you've anything on your mind, Keith, for God's sake stop drivelling and come out with it.'

'Very well, I will,' said Keith primly. 'I don't suppose anyone here wrote to tell you for there was no reason why they should but Hazel Potter – she had a child about eighteen months ago and I've always believed it was yours!'

It took Ikey thirty seconds to get a grip on himself while Keith, his eyes directed to the ground, stood with shoulders hunched and hands clenched like a man expecting a blow. At last Ikey said, quietly, 'If Hazel had a child it would be mine, Keith. Whose child do they think it is?'

'They don't think anything about it now,' Keith said, 'she wouldn't say and nobody cared much so after a bit they gave up guessing.'

'Where is she now?'

'She's living in the cottage beside the old mill on the river road. Doctor Rudd got her fixed up there and I found her a job, cleaning the church,' and when Ikey made no reply he described how he and Rachel had found the girl in labour and how, when he had burst into the cave, she had shouted Ikey's name. 'No one knows that,' Keith added, 'not even Rachel, for naturally I didn't say anything. I couldn't be sure anyway, not until the child began to grow but then, somehow, I knew! Well, it's off my conscience and I'm glad. I did what I could for her, Ikey, and she seems happy enough down there, happier than any of us I imagine.'

Ikey lowered himself slowly to the step of the stile while Keith continued to hover, seemingly more embarrassed than ever. They remained like that for a moment, neither speaking nor moving, until finally Ikey said, 'It was damned decent of you, Keith, decent to say nothing but even more so to take care of her. However, I'd sooner have known! Do you believe that?'

'Yes,' Keith said, 'I believe it now.'

'You could have told Doctor Maureen. She would have written and maybe she would have understood too.'

Keith said, wretchedly, 'I almost did but I couldn't be sure, not absolutely sure and it seemed . . . well, so disloyal I suppose. How could I forget all I owed you? Oh, it wasn't just watching out for me at school but everything, including Rachel. I suppose you've forgotten it was you who brought us together?'

'Yes, I had forgotten,' Ikey said but he remembered now, and a picture returned to him of a gawky, stammering youth shaking hands with the pert farmer's daughter against a background of swirling couples and the blare of a brass band.

He said, 'You're sure nobody knows?' and when Keith reassured him, 'It seems incredible that nobody saw us, not once. Maybe her mother Meg does know but she'd never say anything, she doesn't waste many words.' He got up, passing a hand over his hair. 'That old ruin beside the water-mill you say?'

'It isn't a ruin now, Squire had it done up for her.'

'She stays in it all the year round?'

'Why yes,' Keith said, 'why shouldn't she?'

'Ah,' said Ikey, 'that's something you wouldn't know, Keith. Well, I'll go there right away.'

'Would you like me to come?'

Ikey smiled. 'No, we had no witnesses in the old days so there's no point in enlisting one now. You could do something, though; tell Mrs Handcock to tell Squire I'll be in to dinner but that I would prefer it wasn't a celebration, I believe the Gov was planning one. There's something else you can do too, if you will. I've only got three clear days, and God knows if I'll ever be back. Would your father marry us if I got a special licence?'

Keith opened his mouth and closed it again, perhaps knowing his man better than anyone in the Valley. He said, 'I expect Father will help, if he can,' and hoisting himself over the stile walked down the orchard path towards the house.

The cottage stood on a low bank on the left of the road, a squat, three-roomed dwelling, built of cob with a pantile roof and around it a quarter-acre of vegetable garden hedged about with a criss-cross of angled beanpoles.

The setting sun over Nun's Head was a narrow sliver of orange, turning the small, deep-set windows to flame and when he climbed the winding path and looked inside he could see them both in the light of a log fire, Hazel squatting on the floor, with her back to him and the child, facing the window, on the point of tottering across the floor into her outstretched arms. It was a set-piece, like a woodcut illustration of a sentimental magazine serial, yet curiously moving in its banality. He stood watching as the child staggered the distance on chubby, bowed legs and the mother caught him round the waist and tossed him the length of her arms. What awed him was not the child's likeness to himself, which seemed to him so striking that he was astonished she had kept her secret so well but the domesticity etched on her and the room, as though the single act of giving birth to a child had changed her as no other pressures had been able to change her, drawing out her wild blood like wine from a cask and replacing it with the blood of a cottager's wife, who slept in a bed under a roof, cooked regular meals and worked to a domestic timetable from sunrise to sunset. The evidence was all there before his eyes, not only in the playfulness between them but in the clean hearth, the shining pans suspended from the whitewashed walls, the patchwork rug neatly spread beside the scoured table where lay a pile of ironed linen and two bowls and spoons set before a high and a low chair. He thought, 'It's like looking into the cottage of the Three Bears and I wouldn't wonder if she wasn't pretending to be a bear,' and suddenly a rush of tenderness choked him and he felt his eyes pricking and for a moment was a child again himself but one shut out of the simple delights of childhood looking in upon security and certainty he had never enjoyed. He stood back from the window making a great effort to collect himself and in a little he succeeded, so that he was able to pass the window and reach for the gargoyle knocker; yet he was unable to rattle it, thinking desperately, 'God help me, she has to know and there isn't much time! Maybe Dr Maureen or the parson can sort it out somehow but it's for me to make the first move,' and he thumped the knocker hard, hearing her steps scrape on the slate slabs and the slow creak of the heavy door being dragged open.

He had expected her to whoop, or scream, or make some kind of outcry but the only sound she uttered was a kind of prolonged hiss, expressing no more than a mild and pleasurable surprise and then she smiled, almost absently and stood back, waving him into the cosy room as though he had been a casual visitor calling with the parish magazine or a parcel of groceries. Then he remembered that she was endowed with the priceless gift of reckoning time by her own clock and calendar, and that her months had always been days and her days minutes or seconds. Yet erosion of this bastion must have started for she said, carelessly, 'You been gone longer'n I recall; *zeems* longer any ways! Will 'ee mind the tacker while I maake broth?'

He could think of nothing adequate to reply to this and so compelling was her bland acceptance of his presence that there was no necessity to say anything, or to begin the grotesque

task of convincing her that more than two years had passed
since he had climbed the long slope to her little house and
that within that period her womb had yielded up his child,
the fat youngster now perched on his knee and gurgling
with delight at this unlooked for variation in its routine. He
said, as she bustled between hob and table, 'He's a proper
li'l tacker. What do 'ee call un, midear?'

'Well, 'er's christened Patrick along o' the lady doctor,' she
said, 'but I dorn call un that, 'cept to plaise 'er when 'er's
about! I calls un anything as comes to mind and 'ee answers
to most. When us is yer alone tiz 'Rumble' on account o' the
noise that comes out of un! He's lively enough, mind, and us
never has to worry over 'un but he do zeem to have a man's
share o' the wind! Give un a pat and judge for yourself!' and
as if to support her claim the baby belched, a long, rumbling,
almost dutiful belch so that Ikey shouted with laughter and
Hazel smiled too as she poured soup into the two bowls and
then, using a piece of muslin as a strainer, a third portion
into another bowl she had taken from the dresser.

They sat and ate supper, slowly and ceremoniously, Hazel
lifting the spoon to the baby's mouth and turning aside every
now and again to help herself. It was as though they had
sat there through eternity, a man, a woman, and a child,
snug and smug between four thick walls, warmed by the
fire and their own complacency and it was only when he
had watched her put the baby to bed in a cot made from
a lidless coffer of ecclesiastical design that he was able to
escape from the cocoon of fantasy that she and the child had
spun around him from the moment of entering the cottage.
Then, as she coiled herself like a housecat on the rag mat
and leaned her thin shoulders against his knee, he realised
that, whether he willed it or not, he would have to coax her
a few steps towards reality and said, still using her brogue,
'I'm a real sojjer now, midear, and theym sending me to the
war in a day or zo. Suppose us goes down to the church an'
marries, same as Rachel Eveleigh an' Passons's son be doing
this week? Would 'ee marry me, an' zet up house here for me
so as to have a cosy plaace to come back tu?'

She turned and stared up at him and at first he thought the movement was one of protest but she looked no more than mildly surprised and said, chuckling, 'Now why ever should 'ee live yer along o' me? Us all knows you bides wi' the Squire, at the Big House.'

'Ah,' he said, 'that's zo but tiz a draughty ole barn of a plaace an' I've a mind to zet up with a plaace o' me own. Seein' as that tacker o' yours be mine tu I dorn need to look no further, do I?'

His logic appealed to her but she had reservations. 'Well, 'twould suit me well enough,' she said, 'seein' youm comin' an' goin' most o' the time but will the Squire let 'ee? Worn 'er fly in a tizzy at you leavin' 'un?'

'Lookit yer,' he said, 'I'm a grown man, baint I? And I can live where I plaise, so hold your chatter woman and give us a kiss!' and after kissing her he went on, 'I like the notion so well, I'll zet about it right away! I'll see Squire, then I'll have a word with Mother Meg for she'll have to give 'ee away, seein' Tamer's dead an' buried. You bide on yer an' I'll come to 'ee in the mornin', and us'll be married same as your sister Pansy, for that way us'll get money from the Army for 'ee so long as I'm away.'

It was as simple as that and after a peep at the sleeping child he went down the bank and along the river road into the dusk and it was here, by pure chance, that he met Meg returning from one of her autumn hedge sallies, with pannier baskets full of roots slung across her shoulders.

She stopped in her stately swaying walk and greeted him with customary civility and although she made no direct reference to Hazel he was aware that she knew where he had been. Meg knew everything that happened in the Valley and therefore showed no surprise at all when he told her that the child was his and he had only known of its existence that same afternoon. When he said he was determined to marry Hazel by special licence, however, a shade of doubt crossed her face and she said, clicking her teeth, 'Ah, you've no call to do that! 'Er's well enough as she be, an' Squire won't favour it. You baint our sort and never could be, not now!'

'I'm not gentry either,' Ikey told her, 'and everyone about here knows that well enough. Hazel, she knows how to care for the child as well as any woman in the Valley and at least the baby has stopped her wandering.'

'Aye,' said Meg, thoughtfully, 'it has that and I'm glad on that account, for the Valley baint safe for a maid to wander the way it once was,' and she jerked her head to the north where lay the camp beyond the hump of the moor. 'Still,' she went on reflectively, 'they won't take kindly to a man from the Big House marrying a Potter and come to think on it that makes no sense either, for youm better blood stock than the Quality! One can look into the baby's hand for that!' and casually she reached out and peered attentively at his hand, drawing her dark brows together as though resigned to what she read there. She said, suddenly, 'Will you be doing this to give the boy a name?' and he told her no; but he was doing it because he should have done it long since, before he went away, before he finally crossed over into the gentry's world by taking the King's commission. It had been a bad mistake and he admitted it for now he belonged to neither world. Only with Hazel did he feel rooted and at peace. If he survived the war, he went on, he would resign his commission and live out his life in the Dell or on some other holding. By then people all over the world would have seen the folly of money-grubbing, flag-waving and airs and graces and many would go back to agriculture, the family unit and simple basic things.

She nodded, as though disposed to agree with him and promised that if he sent a message to the Dell she would attend the ceremony and afterwards she watched him wade the ford and pass between the great stone pillars of the gate; they had never exchanged more than a few moments' conversation, yet she felt closer to him than to any of her own kin for somehow she recognised him as a spirit attuned to the rhythm of the seasons and privy to some of the earth's secrets that were no longer secrets to her. Now, having read his palm, she knew something of his future too and was glad that he had spawned a son in whose veins ran the oldest blood in the Valley. What the Squire said or thought about legalising the union was not important. Marriages performed in the church down on the shore were no more than a ritual not much older than some of the oaks in the Shallowford woods. She supposed that the mumbling of a priest and the signing of papers had significance for some but not for such as her, whose ancestors had hunted about here before the first church was built. She hitched her baskets on to her shoulders and set off again down the river road, walking like a queen bringing gifts to gods older than the sad-faced Jew they called Jesus.

VI

News that the Squire's protégé was to marry the half-witted postscript of old Tamer Potter and Gipsy Meg created a sensation in the Valley comparable to that of the Codsall murder or the wreck of the German merchantman in the cove. For a week or so, as talking-point, it ousted the war but then news of the Valley's first casualty was broadcast and it was half-forgotten by the Eveleighs, the Pitts, the Derwents and the Willoughbys. The topic lingered, however, in the kitchen and sculleries of the Big House, for here it was recognised as a flash-point of a tremendous family row, a long, rumbling affair leading to weeks of the monosyllabic conversation at table, to sudden outbursts of temper by the complacent Squire's wife and – this was the thing the servants noticed – a stricken look on the face of the Squire that reminded some of them of the dismal interval that had followed the flight of his first wife.

They were not far off the mark; in the days after Ikey had gone to France and Hazel Potter had become Hazel Palfrey, Paul was almost as miserable as in the months leading up to the wreck and his second marriage. He had enough to depress him in all conscience and without the added irritation of a semi-permanent quarrel with Claire. In four months he had watched the patient work of twelve years crash under the demands of war, with men leaving the Valley in ones and twos, impossible demands being made upon the Valley livestock and all the dislocations attendant upon the presence of the huge tented camp over the hill. Added to this were the constant appeals made to him for help from the bereft womenfolk, as well as personal embroilment in other people's brawls, like the sour quarrel at Four Winds. He could have managed and perhaps, at a pinch, extracted a measure of satisfaction from tackling these problems, had he been able to share in the general enthusiasm for the war and view the slaughter across the Channel in the unequivocal terms of newspaper leader articles but to a man of his essential tolerance and slow habits of thought this was not easy. He had always regarded Germans (the professor and his son excepted) as noisy ridiculous people, with their posturing Kaiser and childish preoccupation with military display but he could not, at a bound, subscribe to the popular view that they were a race of sadistic monsters, hell-bent on rape and plunder with homicidal tendencies reaching down from the All-Highest to the humblest private soldier in the field. Nor could he, as an unrepentant provincial recognising his own limitations, convince himself that Britain's involvement had been inevitable. For these reasons, and for others he sensed but could not put into words, he was depressed, frustrated and dismayed, without the compensating intoxication that the wine of patriotism seemed to produce in his neighbours.

Then Ikey arrived and Paul looked to him for reassurance and perhaps professional enlightenment but within hours of his return he calmly announced that he had fathered the Valley half-wit's bastard and was determined to advertise the fact by marrying her! This was depressing enough; what was far worse, from Paul's standpoint, was Claire's hysterical efforts to stop the marriage and, when she failed, her inclination to saddle him with the blame as a man who had side-stepped his responsibilities. Her attitude, he felt, was as illogical as Grace's had been all those years ago, for both instances proclaimed the maddening unpredictability of women and their brutish obstinacy in defending indefensible positions. He recognised at once that Ikey would have to make his own decision, no matter what any of them said or did and although he was hurt and baffled by the boy's gesture he understood, or thought he understood, the chivalrous impulse that prompted it. Moreover, as temporal leader of the Valley (a position he had always taken very seriously) he felt he had a duty to the child and questioned whether he had the right to dictate to a man of twenty-three, for although still in receipt of a modest allowance Ikey was no longer dependent on Paul's money and would not benefit by Paul's will. At his own instance, shortly before leaving for India, Ikey had insisted that his name was removed from the list of beneficiaries, declaring that Paul had already done more than enough for him and that any money or property he left should go to the children. Only thus, he told him with a grin, could he hope to remain in Claire's good graces for the rest of his life.

For all his reservations, however, Paul found it hard to look upon the marriage as anything but a madcap decision, pointing out that all the Potter girls were promiscuous and that even if Hazel was of different clay she was unlikely to prove a suitable wife for an officer, even in the middle of a war fought on behalf of democracy.

Ikey's reply to this counsel had astounded him and yet, in a way, half-convinced him. Declaring that no man other than himself had ever had access to the girl he said it was his intention, at the earliest opportunity, to resign from the Army and take a small holding on the estate, perhaps the Dell if it was vacant. As for the generally-held opinion that Hazel was dotty he would not subscribe to this and neither would Paul if he spent an hour in the company of the girl.

Paul then tried another approach, pledging responsibility for mother and child and promising Hazel a life tenancy of Mill Cottage, rent free. Ikey listened to him politely and when he had talked himself out said, quietly, 'I suppose you find it impossible to believe I want Hazel for herself? For what she has been and is in my life?'

'Yes, I do,' Paul grunted. 'I find that quite impossible to believe!'

'Well, it's true anyway,' Ikey said, 'and I realised it soon after I went overseas. Every woman I've met since is a bore or a harpy, especially the eligible ones! I suppose that's what comes from being a changeling, Gov'nor?'

'Damn it, you're not a changeling!' Paul yelled at him, 'you've got a better brain than any of us and I've always been damned proud of you!'

'Yes, I know that, Gov,' Ikey said, 'but the difference between you and me is that, although both of us started from the scrapyard you never worked there! Ever since I came down here as a kid I've had an affinity with Hazel Potter, a far closer one than I ever had with any of the jolly old Empire builders I met at school or since. In the ordinary course of events I don't suppose I should have had the guts to turn back and appear to throw everything you've done for me in your face, but now it's different! The whole damned lot of us are slithering down the slope and if I have the luck to come through, which seems to me pretty unlikely, then I'm done with pretence for good! All I shall want is a cottage, a bit of land, Hazel Potter and Hazel Potter's kids!'

After that Paul gave up and went grumbling to Claire and she listened with impatience as he recapitulated all that Ikey had said and when he told her that he supposed they would go ahead no matter what anyone advised she snapped, 'Nonsense! You must stop it, Paul! I won't have Ikey marrying that trollop, I *won't*, do you hear?'

He said despairingly, 'But I've just explained, he'll marry her no matter what we say! He's twenty-three, independent, and he'll be in the trenches this time next week!'

'I don't care,' she said stubbornly, 'you mustn't allow it! You must think of a way to stop it at once!'

'Maybe you can think of some way,' he said grimly and she replied, 'Yes, I can! You can tell him that if he goes ahead with this ridiculous marriage you'll turn the entire Potter family off their land and evict that girl from the cottage!'

'Good God!' he said, appalled, 'you can't mean that! It would be damnably unfair on Tamer's widow and the girls, to say nothing of Jem, who's away fighting for us!'

She said, with calculated emphasis, 'You've always been a sentimental idiot, Paul, and mostly I haven't minded because none of the issues were important enough to quarrel about. But this one is! I won't have you and I made a laughing stock from here to Paxtonbury!'

'Now how the devil are you involved?' he demanded and she said that they were both deeply involved for he had sponsored the boy when he was a waif of ten or eleven and she was his wife. Marriage to a half-witted slut would hold the estate up to ridicule.

'I don't agree with you for a moment,' he said, 'but even if I did I'm damned if I'd take it out on the girl or the girl's family! This isn't like you, Claire! You aren't a vindictive woman, but you're talking just like Arabella Codsall when she came bleating to me about Will marrying the Willoughby girl all those years ago!'

'I'm not apologising for that,' Claire said, 'for maybe Arabella Codsall had a point of view after all! You have always given everyone here far too much rope and let them impose upon you. Now it's time I stepped in and cracked the whip a little for if I don't I wouldn't like to think what might happen when our own children grow old enough to get themselves into this kind of situation, providing they are stupid enough that is! And that isn't all, either! The tenants are taking shameless advantage of you in all kinds of ways. They come down on us for everything nowadays and some of them are coining money out of that camp! As to this Ikey nonsense, I'll settle that in two minutes, if you'll back me up!'

'I certainly won't back you up to the extent of turning the Potters adrift!' he retorted. 'You can talk to Ikey if you like but you might as well understand he's genuinely attached to the girl!'

She looked at him steadily, no longer pale and tight-lipped but with a bright pink flush on her smooth, oval face. 'You actually believe that rubbish? Attached to a girl who won him in a ditch, a technique she probably learned from her sisters in the Dell?'

It occurred to him then that there had been a time, long years ago, when she herself had come very close to winning a man in a ditch but he knew that to remind her of the encounter beside the mere would only make a bad matter worse, so he shrugged and said:

'You argue with Ikey. I've had my say and as far as I'm concerned Hazel stays in Mill Cottage, married or single! I'm damned if I'll put her out to flatter your snobbery!' and he stalked off, leaving her trembling with rage.

He never discovered whether or not she made a direct appeal to Ikey for no one from the Big House attended the ceremony in the parish church three days later. It was held at 8 a.m. and Ikey was gone from the Valley by afternoon. Paul heard that a number of the curious had gathered at the church, among them Henry Pitts' big, rawboned wife and the kindhearted Mary Willoughby, who had once tried so hard to teach the bride the alphabet. Others watched the couple leave by the lych gate and drive off somewhere in Ikey's hired motor and one of them, Rachel Eveleigh, herself due to marry in the same church that following day, told Mrs Handcock that she had never realised how beautiful Hazel Potter was and how serene she had looked as she sat smiling down at them while the bridegroom cranked the car. Ikey came in to say good-bye to Paul before driving off across the moor to catch his train but neither made a direct reference to the wedding. Ikey said, shaking hands, 'I don't suppose I'll be back for at least six months, Gov'nor; if at all, that is,' and Paul growled, 'I wish to God the women of this Valley would be less bloody-minded and the men a bit more optimistic!' but he wrung the boy's hand and wished him luck.

Outside, as Ikey humped his kit into the little motor, he added, 'I'll keep an eye on her, Ikey!' and Ikey replied, 'I didn't have to ask, Gov!' That was all and Paul watched him swing round the bend of the drive to reappear again for a moment between the leafless chestnuts as he shot the gate. He thought, 'What the devil does it matter anyway seeing that he's heading for all that slush and slaughter. Somebody ought to remind Claire that she was young herself once, and a neighbour of the Potters but I'm damned if it's going to be me! In her present mood she'd probably sulk for an extra month!' and he went into the library and poured himself a stiff whisky.

He was standing there, his back to the fire, when Maureen came in from the terrace. She seemed very breathless, as though she had climbed the drive too quickly and she had a worried expression that looked odd on her broad, humorous face.

'Could you go down to John?' she said, quickly, 'he'll need you for an hour or so. It's Roddy, his boy. He had a telegram about an hour ago,' and as Paul exclaimed she said, 'Oh, you don't need to worry to that extent, Paul, he's taken it on the chin, but Roddy was all he had left of his youth and a wife who died young. I think you could give him more than me. I was a latecomer in his life.'

'Tell Claire,' Paul said, savagely, 'but don't have her come fussing! She's been damned difficult over this Ikey business,' and slipping a bottle of his best Scotch in his pocket he hurried across the paddock to the lodge.

John was sitting in his old leather armchair beside an untended fire, the last light of the short winter's day excluded by the closely latticed panes of the little window. He did not look grief-stricken, only small and a little shrivelled, an unlit pipe in one hand and the buff telegram form in the other.

He said, as Paul came in, 'It was that affair off the Falklands. Our squadron was outgunned, just as I said they would be. There'll be more naval shocks before it's all over, mark my words. You can't win a war by singing "Rule Britannia", Paul!' and he handed over the telegram containing the flat, impersonal expression of royal regret on the snuffing out of a life in its prime. Paul was to see and handle many of these telegrams in the next two years but because this was the first he read it carefully twice before laying it down.

'I do wish you hadn't taken Roddy's bit of nonsense with Grace so much to heart, John,' he said. 'There was never anything in it, and I knew that, even at the time. We ought to have laughed him out of it and encouraged him to spend another leave here. Was he married?'

'No, and I've got my own theory on that. It doesn't matter a damn now, so I suppose I can tell you. The truth is he never really got Grace out of his mind. Does that surprise you?'

'Yes, it does,' Paul said, 'for Grace never regarded him as anything more than an engaging boy. Did they meet after he left here that time?'

'Oh yes,' John said, 'after the divorce they met often but you're right, she never took him seriously. They used to dine and visit a theatre whenever he was in town or whenever he could catch her between spells in Holloway. Would you mind if I let her know about this?'

'Not in the least,' Paul said, 'why should I?' and he took glasses from the cupboard and half-filled them with his special brand of 'Loch Leven'. 'Here,' he said, 'I need one badly myself,' and with the object of giving John something else to think about he told him of his quarrel with Claire over Ikey's marriage.

'She's wrong and the boy's right,' John said, when he had finished, 'for here's another who never thought of Hazel Potter as dotty. Fey but not dotty. Anyway, who are any of us to talk about half-wittedness, when we've all got ourselves into this kind of mess? As for Claire, wanting to take it out on the Potter clan, I suppose I can understand that in a way.'

'I'm damned if I can,' said Paul, 'it came as a shock to me that she even suggested it.'

'It's odd,' John mused, sipping slowly, 'the Valley always clung to its class distinction, even in the Lovell days. There were the Derwents and the Codsalls on either border, the workaday Pitts and Willoughbys in the middle and finally the Potters. Claire was brought up to regard the Potters as scum and I suppose they are in a way, all except Meg, who comes closer to ancient royalty than any of us. Marrying into the Big House was a triumph for High Coombe and I don't think old Edward Derwent has ever stopped congratulating himself. The prospect of his grandsons inheriting High Coombe and every other farm in the Valley is a very unlooked for bonus and I daresay he'll side with his daughter on this issue. Still, I ought to have a fellow feeling for him today I suppose,' and when Paul asked why John said Roddy's death had stirred in him memories of the boy's mother that he thought he had forgotten and that Derwent too had lost a wife when she was about Myra's age. 'They were a bit alike,' he added, 'both pretty, dashing and maybe a little showy like poor old Roddy. It's funny, but that kind usually burn themselves out before their time. It's the plodders like you and me who die a little every day.'

Paul said, suddenly, 'How do you see this war, John? As a crusade, the way most people seem to? Or more as I see it, an appalling, stupid waste, without a shred of glory about it? It hasn't anything in common with the wars you and I fought in, you against those poor devils of savages, me against a few thousand Boers. They were incidents but this is genocide or will be if fought to a finish. Dammit, the way things are going, we shan't have an able-bodied man left in the Valley by this time next year!'

John Rudd lit his pipe and puffed it stolidly and Paul thought he looked much as he had that summer evening he first sat there after their ride from Sorrel Halt. He took his time answering, it was not often that anyone extracted a snap judgement from John Rudd.

He said at length, 'I happened to have professional tips from Roddy and some of his shipmates on which I based my opinion of the Navy's unpreparedness. That doesn't make me a wise-acre.'

'But you were the only one who was sure they wouldn't capture Paris,' Paul reminded him and John said: 'I'll be sixty next year; apart from the Zulu campaign I've lived all those sixty years in Britain. A man ought to learn something about his own people in more than half a century. He'd be a damned dull dog if he didn't!'

'What did you learn that makes you so cocksure, John? For you are cocksure, aren't you?'

'About the outcome? Yes, I am. We'll win all right though I don't know that it will do us much good in the end. I suppose I've seemed to you to take the war in my stride because I've been anticipating it so long and there isn't much point in arguing the rights and wrongs of an inevitability. The line-up started round about the time you settled here and if it hadn't been poor little Belgium this year, it would have been poor old Turkey next year, or hands off India the year after that! Now it's here the only thing left is to hold on and the British do that much better than most of them!'

'It looks to me as if it's all that's left to us,' Paul said, 'so what makes you confident about us getting anything better than a stalemate or a compromise peace?'

'Ah no,' John said quickly, 'you can rule that out! A nation that achieves all this one has in a century has to have special qualities and I don't say that in the spirit of somebody paid to write for the popular press, it's just a feeling, down here,' and he tapped his paunch with his pipe-stem.

'Then all I can say is I wish to God I had it,' Paul said emphatically. 'It seems to me we rushed into the business without a thought as to what was at stake and these people here, the Walt Pascoes and the Smut Potters, are amateurs. We all know what happens when an amateur takes on a professional!'

'They'll stay amateurs for a bit,' John said, 'but that's what I'm driving at. When they get desperate enough they'll knock hell out of everybody. Go up to that camp and watch those cotton-spinners at bayonet practice.'

'Not me,' Paul told him, 'I've no stomach for the business and I still think we were damned stupid to get drawn into it.'

'Well,' John said, 'I can understand that, knowing you. For too long now you've been giving your attention to what happens in your own backyard but when you realise that backyard is at stake you'll outdo the rest of them! That'll be when your Puritan streak shows. Puritans only show fight when they've convinced themselves their way of life is threatened. After that there isn't many who can stand up to them for long.' He got up and knocked out his pipe. 'Will you tell Maureen not to wait supper? I think I'll take a turn along the river road.'

'Do you want company?'

'No,' John said, smiling, 'but if I did I should prefers yours to anyone's. Thanks for coming down and thanks for getting my brain working on an abstract issue. I don't know whether it was intentional but it worked!' and he took his hat and stick and went out abruptly leaving Paul to contemplate two framed portraits on the mantelshelf, one of Roddy in his rakishly tilted naval cap, the other of the fat surprise packet Maureen had produced not so long ago, now asleep in the little room over the porch where Paul had spent his first night in the Valley. He thought, as he lit the lamp, 'I wish those bloody fools who had poor old John Rudd drummed out of the Army on account of that Prince Imperial incident could have shared the half-hour I've just spent with him! Could I show that much dignity if I'd just had a telegram telling me Simon or one of the twins had been blown to bits in somebody else's quarrel thousands of miles away?' He sat finishing his whisky, having heard the girl whom Maureen employed as a maid clank off into the dusk on her bicycle. Presently Maureen came back and he gave her the message. 'Well, that's John's way,' she said, 'he always is greedy with his troubles. Can't bear to share 'em with any of us, but maybe you've noticed?'

'Yes,' Paul told her, 'it was something I learned about him very early on. Did you see Claire?'

'Yes and made a point of not telling her about Roddy, tho' I rather wish I had. She almost bit my head off and the twins came in for a slap apiece. Is she that much upset about Ikey marrying the Potter girl?'

'About as upset as I've seen her.'

Maureen said, as though to herself, 'I find that very odd!' and then, turning to face him, 'Top up your drink, Paul, for you're going to need it!' and when he protested that he had already had too much whisky she took the decanter and half-filled his glass. 'I'll tell you something I've never told anyone, not even John, and you can please yourself whether you make use of it or not! If it wasn't for Ikey, Claire Craddock would almost certainly still be Claire Derwent. At all events, she wouldn't be mistress of Shallowford tucking your children into bed!'

Paul said, 'What the devil did Ikey have to do with me marrying Claire?' and Maureen, trying but not altogether succeeding to keep the chuckle out of her voice, replied, 'It was a letter written by him saying you were calling for her, that got her down here that time you were laid up after the wreck. And that's not all either, not by a long chalk! He wrote to Claire at the instance of Grace. The letter was written in her rooms that time he ran off to London.'

Said like that, bluntly and factually, it did not make an immediate impact on him. After a pause, while she waited for it to sink in, he said, 'How do you know that? How long have you known it?'

'I've known it ever since I came here.'

'*He* told you? Ikey told you?'

'He did that, down by Codsall bridge a week or two after it happened.'

'You believed him?'

'Of course I believed him. Would a boy of his age manufacture a story like that? Besides, Ikey was never a liar.'

The implications of her story began to register. He said, wonderingly, 'But he was only a kid! Claire came home on chance and finding me laid up volunteered as a nurse. If I remember rightly you engaged her.'

'Claire never mentioned that letter to you? The one telling her you had been calling for her when you were running a high temperature?'

'Never! I didn't know there was a letter!'

'Well boyo, there was! You can depend upon it and there isn't much doubt that the girl took it at face value, believing what she wanted to believe. Knowing that, I'm sorry I blabbed. She probably had good reasons for forgetting. Still, I've told you now so it's up to you if you jog her memory or not. The fact is she owes Ikey Palfrey her happiness, but come to think of it, so do you, for this silly business will blow over soon enough and taken all round you and Claire are as well-matched a pair as I've ever doctored!'

He said nothing for a moment so that presently she picked up his glass and pushed it into his hand. 'Get it down, lad,'

she said, 'it's not Irish whiskey but it'll serve!' and after he had
swallowed the measure and still remained silent, she cocked
her head on one side and said, humouring him, 'There now,
it's not worth brooding on. What began as a hoax turned out
well enough for all of us, didn't it?'

'In the light of what you've told me,' he said, slowly, 'her
present attitude to Ikey is impossibly arrogant! Ought she to
be reminded of what she owes him?' and it was Maureen's
turn to consider.

'No,' she said at length, 'I don't suppose it would help in
the least, it would probably harden her against him. How
many of us enjoy coming face to face with a generous
creditor after a lapse of ten years?'

For the first time since he had heard of Ikey's intention
to marry Hazel Potter Paul was able to smile. 'You were in
attendance as doctor at the time so will you tell me one thing
more? *Did* I cry out for Claire?'

'If you did I didn't hear you,' she said, 'but you have to
give that boy full marks for originality!'

He went out and up the drive feeling a good deal less
despondent than when he had descended it. He found that
his memories, jogged by Maureen's story, were sharp enough
when he summoned them. He could recall waking up after
they had set his bones on the kitchen table and seeing Claire
over by the window, looking as if she had always been there
and would always remain there, and he could also recall his
sense of relief at her presence, as though the excitement and
terrors of the wreck had, in half-battering the life out of
him, filled a vacuum left by Grace and given a new twist
to his life. He thought, a little smugly, 'Let her sulk! Let
her indulge her damned Derwent pride, for that's all it is
now I can get a close look at it! I could puncture it by
telling her what I know but Maureen's right – it would
only drive a permanent wedge between her and the boy, for
what woman likes to be reminded of the tricks she played
to get what she wanted? And she must have wanted me
pretty desperately and Shallowford too I daresay, although
I don't blame her for that. She's been a good wife and

mother and she cares for this place as much as I do, so
what have I got to complain about?'

He took a long sniff at the damp evening air and went
in to begin his penance. He might have dragged his step
a little if he had suspected that it would see him through
Christmas and well into the New Year.

Chapter Four

I

By early spring, 1915, the people of the Valley were dispersed as they had not been for two-and-a-half centuries. The last exodus on this scale had occurred as long ago as July 1685, when the Duke of Monmouth came recruiting and some of the Sorrel men had been rash enough to volunteer for a shorter war that had ended, for most of them, on the field of Sedgmoor or in transportation to the sugar plantations of Barbados.

Will Codsall, Dandy Timberlake, Walt Pascoe, Jem Pollock, Smut Potter, Gilbert Eveleigh, Tremlett the huntsman and Tod Glover, the mechanic, were already in khaki, the first three overseas, the others in training camps up and down the country. Others were on the point of going, including the sons of Eph Morgan, the Coombe Bay builder, and Abe Tozer, the Coombe Bay smith, and Willis, son of the Shallowford wheelwright. Tom Williams, who was a naval reservist, and his nephew Daniel had been at sea for months, minesweeping on the same vessel off Rosyth and by the time primroses were fading in the river road hedgerows one or two of the women had left, among them Rose Derwent, of High Coombe.

The war had given Rose's life a painful jolt but it happened that the enforced closing down of her riding school brought compensations. By May, 1915, she was married and mistress of an estate larger and more impressive in every way than that of her sister Claire, so that Edward Derwent, who had once dreamed of being freeholder of three hundred acres, now had prospects of seeing his grandchildren (providing thirty-four-year-old Rose bestirred herself) inherit two appreciable slices of the English countryside. It was an astonishing turn of fortune for the glum, taciturn man who, only a decade before, had resigned himself to dying a tenant farmer and sometimes he found it difficult that both his daughters had, against all probability, made brilliant matches. Yet it was so, for Rose married Major Barclay-Jones, DSO, on the first of May, 1915, and whilst Edward Derwent could claim no credit for getting Claire off his hands he played a vital role in disposing of the amiable horse-faced Rose, whom everyone declared would die an old maid and that in spite of inheriting her mother's seat on a horse.

There had been little to occupy Rose after the Government had emptied her stables in the hectic days when the High Command still had visions of cavalry charges over open country. Almost every hunter in the Valley had been bought and carted away and Hugh, her brother, ran High Coombe very efficiently with the help of his father, a hired hand too old to enlist and a couple of boys. For a time she mooched about in the dairy and then, at her father's instance, volunteered to serve in the YMCA canteen at the camp on the heath where she found herself the only woman among several thousand men. This would have been gratifying to most spinsters of thirty-four but it caused hardly a flutter in Rose's heart. She had always preferred horses to men and easily parried the passes made at her by homesick middle-aged men and even a few younger ones desperate for feminine society. She made friends with some of the senior officers, however, among them the stoutish, loud-voiced Major Barclay-Jones, who, as a former hussar, bitterly resented his enforced association with sweaty infantrymen and stinking motors. The Major, a rather explosive little man of five and fifty, had been blown out of retirement by the trumpet blast of August 4th and it was not long before the frequency of his visits to High Coombe put a thoughtful look on Edward Derwent's face. Unlike everyone else in the Valley he had never quite despaired of getting his elder daughter off his hands. He made a few discreet inquiries and was encouraged to learn that Major Barclay-Jones was a widower, owned a large estate in Gloucestershire, had two sons serving with the Army overseas and had been joint master of a famous hunt up to the time of rejoining the colours. It was this last piece of information that stimulated Derwent for he was a man who struck bargains with the minimum of sales talk, his method being to concentrate upon the most obvious selling point of the merchandise. Claire's selling points had been numerous, among them her pretty face and what Grace would have called her 'ripeness', but Rose's selling point if she could be said to possess one, was limited to her seat on a horse, a factor hardly likely to be overlooked by a man who had served thirty years in the 11th Hussars and had been master of a fashionable hunt.

In a matter as important as this Derwent could curb his pride. He approached his daughter, expressed a mild liking for the major and asked her bluntly, 'If the man had said anything as yet?' Rose, who could be obtuse, replied, 'Said anything about what, Father?' whereupon Edward, with a grunt of exasperation, took himself off to Shallowford and came riding home on Snowdrop, one of the two hunters left in the Valley, the other being Rose's mettlesome four-year-old Prince, the horse she had once hoped to school into a national steeplechaser.

To give Rose any real chance at all, Edward decided, it would be necessary for the major to see her mounted on a good horse and also to watch her handle an animal that even the grasping Government Commissioners had left behind as too spirited for their requirements. By this time Derwent had taken Claire into his confidence and on her advice left nothing to chance. There being no hunting anywhere within hacking distance he arranged to borrow Snowdrop for a week and offer the major an hour's pleasant exercise in the saddle on the afternoons he was free. Once he saw Rose in the saddle, once they were alone in the woods, Derwent decided, it seemed likely that Rose's selling-point would become apparent to him. If nothing resulted what had any of them got to lose?

It succeeded with a speed that astonished him. On his return from their third excursion Major Barclay-Jones was so full of admiration for Rose that he stayed on for supper, drinking nearly a bottle of Edward's sloe gin and pronouncing 'The Gel', as he called her, 'the possessor of a spanking seat and

the neatest pair o' hands in the business!' Encouraged by
Derwent and another noggin of gin, he went even further:
'Watched a lot o' good nagsmen in my time,' he added, after
Derwent had murmured modestly that Rose was reckoned
the best horsewoman west of Melton Mowbray, 'but she
tops 'em, Derwent! Tops 'em by inches! Dammit man, I
watched her put that temperamental joker at a five-bar on
the far side of the wood! Nothin' rotten mind you – good
solid timbah, by God! *Flew it!* Flew it with a foot in hand
at full gallop! Joy to watch! Lovely action! Dam' sorry I
couldn't follow but the old grey is past it, like me, since I
tied in with those blasted foot-sloggers!'

A day or so later, however, the major showed that he was
not quite past it and put the seventeen-year-old Snowdrop
at the bole of a fallen elm which he cleared with less than
an inch in hand. He was so delighted with himself that he
proposed on the spot and Rose, too astounded to accept or
refuse, stuttered that he had 'better talk to Father', Providing,
of course, 'that he wasn't joking'. He laughed all the way home
at this but he was not joking. He was among the dwindling
number of optimists who still believed that as soon as better
weather set in the two-million-strong German Army dug in
across north-eastern France would be herded back across the
frontiers by a few regiments of British cavalry, waiting with
drawn sabres to exploit a gap torn in the enemy's lines by
Sir John French's Territorial drafts. It therefore followed that
my midsummer he would be back at Lavington Court with
all his commandeered horses restored to him and a new pack
of hounds in the kennels. The mere prospect of sharing life
with a gel of Rose Derwent's calibre persuaded him that he
was good for another twenty years in the saddle.

So Rose travelled to Gloucester to meet his elderly half-
sister (fortunately for everyone the possessor of yet another
spanking seat) and because it was war-time, and everybody's
movements were uncertain, the wedding took place almost at
once, a colourful little ceremony in Coombe Bay church with
the groom in full regimentals and an arch of swords provided
by officers from the camp. It was the first military wedding

that had taken place there since the days of the South African war and the Valley was delighted. There were no bridesmaids, Claire acting as Matron of Honour, but the little church and yard was crammed, boys scrambling on to the granite obelisk of Tamer Potter's grave in order to get a better view. Nobody in the Valley remembered Tamer that sunny May morning, but by macabre coincidence, Tamer was remembered vividly elsewhere that very same night.

All day on May 1st, 1915, the German U-boat that had been lurking off the Firth of Forth for a week or more stalked the minesweeper *Venturer*, butting north towards Scapa Flow and the *Venturer* had two Sorrel Valley men in her crew. One was Tom Williams the leader of the fishing fraternity in Coombe Bay and the other was Tom's nephew Dan, who had been his uncle's crewman up to the time they left the Valley together. Dan was not a naval reservist like his uncle but had decided to share his active service because he was attached to him by ties stronger than blood. During a severe squall off Nun's Head in the winter of 1910, when Dan was an inexperienced lad of seventeen, Tom had put life and boat in jeopardy to rescue the boy swept overboard in a heavy sea and ever since they had been inseparables. The boy had a great respect for his uncle's seamanship whereas Tom was now linked to Dan by one of the strongest superstitions of the sea; having saved a soul from drowning he must abide by him for the rest of his natural life. At 2 a.m. sharp, on the morning of May 2nd, the U-boat fired two torpedoes, striking the *Venturer* aft and amidships and folding her like a hinge. She sank in six minutes and as there had been no chance to launch boats the nine survivors, including Tom and Dan, climbed aboard the only means of escape, a venerable life-raft that looked about as seaworthy as a soup-plate. Luckily the sea was no more than choppy but as they had but one paddle, and were all half choked with oil, their chances of making landfall seemed slim. Then, to their dismay, the U-boat surfaced, an officer addressing them by loud-hailer and speaking, to Tom's amazement, what he would have called 'Gentry English'.

'How many are you?' he asked and when Tom replied 'Nine!'
the sleek, grey shape manoeuvred alongside and someone
lowered a jar of rum and a bag of ship's biscuits. The officer
then gave Tom his position but when Tom told him that they
had no means of making way, and that their only chance
was to be picked up by daylight, a tow-rope was thrown
aboard. For more than two hours the strange convoy moved
westward, travelling at a speed designed to prevent the men
on the raft being washed clear. When the U-boat cast off
as the first streaks of dawn showed in the sky Tom saw
that the Scottish coast was not more than five or six miles
distant. It was difficult, he felt, to thank the man who had just
sent his ship and most of his crew to the bottom but clearly
some kind of acknowledgement was required, so he climbed
unsteadily to his feet and bowed and the U-boat captain,
standing on the conning tower, waved his hand and shouted,
'Witness, gentlemen, we are not barbarians! Good luck!' and
went below. Within minutes the vessel had submerged and
Dan Williams, drunk with excitement and several draughts
of German naval rum, said, 'Well, sod me? If that don't beat
all!' but his uncle sternly admonished him for profanity and
set about trimming the raft and distributing biscuits while
the second mate, having fetched up what he hoped was the
last of the oil in his stomach, set off the first distress flare.

It was not until they were being counted aboard a destroyer's
launch three hours later that Tom remembered another ship-
wreck, one that had occurred more than five hundred miles
south-west of their present position, an occasion when, so
to speak, the boot was on the other foot and roughly the
same number of Germans had been hauled ashore half dead
in Tamer Potter's Cove and ferried to Coombe Bay as soon as
the tide-race permitted. He did not see these two rescues as a
coincidence but as an exercise in Divine book-keeping. There
were nine German survivors out on that rock and there was
enormous significance in the number. He thought about it all
the next day when they were being fed, cosseted and fitted
out at the Sailors' Rest in Aberdeen and when, a day or so
later, he and Daniel boarded the train for a nine-day survivors'

leave, he said to the young man, 'Daniel! There's zummat us'll do the minute us gets to the Valley, zummat as *calls* for doin', I reckon!' Daniel could think of several things that he would like to do but since they included petting Eph Morgan's daughter and sinking a quart of homebrew at The Raven, and since he was aware that his uncle would frown on both indulgences, he merely said, 'Arr, an' what'll it be, Uncle Tom?'

'Us'll pay our respects to Tamer's grave, boy,' said Williams, 'and us'll lay some flowers there mebbe, for come to think on it Tamer shares that grave wi' the Germans us fished ashore dade time o' the wreck and I dorn reckon anyone's give a thought to any one of 'em zince!'

Daniel followed his uncle's reasoning although privately he thought him sentimental. Everybody knew there were a few good Germans and a lot of bad Germans and that they had been fortunate in encountering one of the few good Germans with a punctilious sense of honour. He was ready to admit that they owed their lives to the tow and the rum but he did not see how laying flowers on the graves of Germans drowned when he was a boy had any bearing upon their recent experience. As usual, however, he was prepared to defer to Uncle Tom in all matters affecting the sea and said, 'Arr, Uncle Tom, us'll do what you say! Come to think on it, I dorn reckon anyone has given old Tamer a thought for years never mind they Germans along of him!'

He was probably right although, at that precise moment, two men of the Valley were thinking of Tamer's kin in the person of his daughter Pansy, wife of Walt Pascoe.

Four months guarding the Sweetwater Canal, the victim of sandstorms, suffocating heat, sand-dusted bully beef, thirst, flies, scorpions, boils and the whining importunities of Egyptian hucksters had encouraged Walt Pascoe to regret the impulse that had led him to exchange corduroys for khaki and the Sorrel Valley for the Sinai Peninsula so that when his unit was hustled off to Alexandria to embark for Gallipoli he went with alacrity, happy to leave the riddle of the Sphinx unsolved. On the troopship he had the luck to encounter an old friend, one who helped to ameliorate the pangs of homesickness that Walt had endured ever since he ate tinned Christmas dinner in a temperature of 105 degrees in the shade. He was trying to find bedspace on the overcrowded deck when he heard his name shouted from among a group of soldiers wedged in the bows and he recognised Dandy Timberlake at a glance, for Dandy still wore his four-inch waxed moustaches that had given him a quasi-military look even in peace-time. The two greeted one another boisterously and teamed up for the voyage, celebrating their reunion with several bottles of warm, weak beer.

All day and much of the night as the troopship ploughed its way across the eastern Mediterranean they beguiled the hours with nostalgic talk of the Valley and Valley personalities and had she been able to hear them exchanging confidences and Wild Woodbines Pansy Pascoe's sense of humour might have been tickled, for she would have recalled an occasion, shortly before her marriage when Walt had blacked Dandy's eye for slipping his hand down her neck in Codsall's stubble field, and another, years later, when Dandy had walked her home through the violent thunderstorm that concluded Squire Craddock's Coronation Fête. Neither occasion was referred to during the endless flow of reminiscence but Walt remembered the fight in the stubble field and Dandy remembered the night of the Coronation Fête and both felt guilty for behaving so churlishly towards a comrade-in-arms, now bound for the same battlefield. Walt hoped that Dandy had forgotten the cornfield squabble and Dandy derived some consolation from the fact that, even if the fourth of Pansy's children did look more of a Timberlake than a Pascoe, he had been the means of contributing, albeit anonymously, to Pansy's separation allowance. They parted temporarily at Mudros but met again under even more cramped conditions in a gully under Achi Baba, about a month later. From then on they were inseparables until a Turkish sniper shot Dandy through the lung and Walt, his concern for the wounded man overcoming his caution, was cut down by a burst of machine-gun fire at less than two hundred yards range. Dandy was not mortally wounded, but his long convalescence, first at Mudros and later at Alexandria, was not made easier by reflecting how and why Walt had died. He thought about it a long time and it made him feel mean, small and treacherous. When he was well enough to sit up he composed a long letter to the widow which puzzled her a good deal for as well as recounting how Walt died the letter hinted that he was prepared to wait in the wings indefinitely as a possible replacement and she never thought of Dandy Timberlake as the marrying kind. In her fashion Pansy had loved Walt, and in the lighthearted way of the Potters she regretted him, but she had plenty of reminders of him under her feet and life was very hectic in the Dell just then, so she did not read into Dandy's letter all she might have done. In any case it would have seemed to her ridiculous that Dandy's conscience should trouble him on Walt's account, or on account of Timothy, her youngest boy. After all, Walt had been blind drunk that particular night and one could not reasonably expect a bachelor to walk three miles in pouring rain pushing a pram-load of another man's children without receiving some kind of reward for his chivalry.

Spring, 1915, found Smut at the celebrated Bull Ring at Harfleur, not far, as the gull flies, from the scene of his triumphs in the Armentières sector but far enough to deprive him of prey whilst improving his stalking techniques. At Harfleur they taught him new but less precise methods of adjusting the imbalance between the Kaiser's hordes and the British Army, showing him, for instance, how to use a Mills bomb and a light machine-gun. He was an apt and attentive pupil, for although neither weapon demanded the degree of skill that had won him a reputation as a rifleman, he was the first to concede that they were likely to prove more lethal when he returned to the line. He was probably the happiest man in all the huge, dismal camp for, unlike most of his comrades, the ties that had bound him to his native heath had all but broken. The only thing awaiting Smut across the Channel was a couple of greenhouses and it seemed to him unlikely that people would worry overmuch about a shortage of petunias, lobelia and fuchsia so long as this gigantic spree endured. Meanwhile, for the new Smut, or rather the old one reborn, there were many compensations. The area was rich in merchandise of a kind that did not have to be watered or kept at an even temperature, all manner of things that careless people left lying around to be carted away and used, given away, or disposed of at a modest profit, loot as varied as sides of bacon, cases of spirits and French wines, items of harness, automatic pistols taken from dead German officers, high-grade German binoculars, boots, tins of jam, periscopes, torches, blankets and sometimes even a mule that had stayed within earshot of someone who knew how to persuade it to follow him without recourse to oaths and blows. To Smut Potter the untidy landscape about Harfleur was a kind of university wherein he was fed, clothed, housed, and even paid to perfect new skills and enlarge his mental horizon. For now he spoke a fluent patois that could engage and sometimes captivate the most grasping estaminet patronne. He could drive a Leyland lorry over bad roads at night without headlights or pilot a motor-cycle combination across a turnip field without clinking bottles stowed in the sidecar. He could strike an advantageous bargain with a Scotsman or a Yorkshireman who, in their home towns, had been the despair of professional salesmen and he could exact by way of toll almost any privilege from admiring company officers who often benefited directly from his highly developed sense of local loyalty. There was talk, now that spring had arrived, of an advance that would harry Fritz back over the Rhine in a matter of weeks but Smut hoped that the enemy would not be in too much of a hurry to depart. The prospect of resuming life as a reformed character had no attractions for him. He did not see how he could avoid becoming a poacher again once the Kaiser was accounted for and thought it likely that he would sign on for as long as they would have him and stalk other of the King's enemies, Arabs perhaps, or cannibals of the kind who had once engaged the attention of some of the time-serving men now instructing him. He liked everything about his present life, its constant movement, its boon comradeship, its glorious uncertainties and in this strange contentment he was not alone among enlisted Valley men.

Fifty miles south of the camp where Smut was perfecting new killing techniques the Bideford Goliath, sometime Lord of the Dell, had also had the seal of official approval placed upon dormant skills. As a private in a pioneer company Jem's weight-lifting techniques were invaluable. They had first advertised themselves when an ammunition limber slipped off the greasy pavé into a shell-hole and might have passed beyond recovery had not Jem, standing close by, grabbed a trailing rope, anchored it round a stump and held it there as nonchalantly as another man checks the flight of a frisky terrier. Others hurried to his assistance and the limber was hauled out but the story of his feat passed from mouth to mouth throughout the sector and soon assumed Homeric proportions, bringing to Jem the kind of notoriety that Samson must have enjoyed among the Israelites. After that he was watched every time he shouldered a load of iron staples to carry up to the line and it was remarked that, not only was he capable of shifting roughly twice as many as the strongest of his comrades could bear along a slippery communication trench, but also that he was, or seemed to be impervious to shell-fire. When a whizz-bang or a five-nine came crashing out of the sky, and others flung down their loads and flattened themselves in the mud, Jem seemed only to contract a little, carefully shifting his load to interpose between flying shrapnel and the upper part of his hulking body. He never winced. He never cowered. And he never got hit. Soon he became a kind of talisman so that men were comforted by his presence and under their admiration his personality began to flower. Once again he could take pleasure in the popularity he had enjoyed as a youngster in the booths of the travelling fair and had savoured, briefly, as Master of the Dell. He had never demanded much of life, no more than a full belly, a little affection and public acknowledgement that he was the strongest man in the world. Here, in a Pioneer battalion a mile or so east of Béthune, these simple requirements were

his and like Smut he thought it improbable that he would
willingly return to the Dell and readdress himself to the
hopeless task of guarding the virtue of his two wives. This
was not to say that he had resolved, like Smut, to prolong
his service with the colours. There were things he missed,
among them the evening Peace of the Valley, and the tang
of the sea meeting and mingling with the scent of freshly
turned soil, but he did not miss Ciss or Vi as much as he
had anticipated. The spasmodic chatter of machine-gun fire
in and about the cluttered pitheads was a fair substitute
for their clacking tongues and the occasional whoosh of a
five-nine, a split second before impact, sometimes recalled
their fierce, raucous laughter. On the whole, and on thinking
it over carefully, he preferred the overtones of war, so long
as projectiles fell on the extreme front line, or the back areas,
whence came all these miles and miles of wire and all these
millions of pit-props and iron pickets.

II

Smut was enjoying the war and Jem could bear it but less than
two days' march to the south-west was the very first of the
Valley volunteers, Will Codsall of Periwinkle, and Will shared
neither Smut's enthusiasm nor Jem's tolerance for the situation
in which he found himself alongside the Albert Canal, whence
he and the few survivors of the dismounted Yeomanry had
been sent after a hectic four months in sectors further north.
The appalling reality of modern war had been brought home
to Will before any of his neighbours had crossed the Channel.
In October, 1914, the Paxtonbury bunch had been fed into the
line to plug gaps torn in professional ranks by the First Battle
of Ypres and were at once engaged in a string of ding-dong
battles in shallow, flooded ditches running on and on through
unpronounceable towns and villages. In those touch-and-go
days Will had seen the Paxtonbury group shrink from three
score to about a dozen exhausted, lice-infected scarecrows,
who regarded themselves as a squad doomed to spend the

fag-end of their lives performing the horrid cycle of five
days in the line, five in support and five 'resting' in areas
that came in for nearly as much round-the-clock shelling as
those within pistol range of the Germans.

For a man who had never been able to bring himself to
drown a litter of kittens Will had acquitted himself well,
performing, in those first mad weeks, miracles of enterprise,
hardihood and even ferocity. He had seen at least a dozen
men fall to his rifle and had used the bayonet, cosh, and
crude bomb on many occasions but that was before the day
during a trench raid near Rue de Bois when he stopped in the
business of tidying up to look closely at a German Corporal he
had killed with a spade about an hour earlier. The sight of the
faceless thing lying on its back in six inches of churned-up clay
opened the door of an attic in Will's mind that had been kept
locked and chained for more than twelve years and soon after
that he began to see himself not as Will Codsall, the soldier
husband of the brisk and business-like Elinor but as Will
Codsall, son of Martin Codsall, whose craving for blood had
directed him to cut off his wife's head with a hay-knife. The
dissolution of his self-control was not instantaneous. Even in
his present pitiable condition, with nerves raw and brain and
body numb after terrible physical exertions and lack of sleep
Will was still game enough to coax the spectre back to the
attic and slam the door but the odds against keeping him
there were great. Soon the whole orchestra and landscape of
the battlefield enlisted with Martin and Martin's obsession, so
that Will began to see the churned-up fields not as violated
French farmland but as the margin of Four Winds' duck-pond
on a wet November afternoon, and hear the rumble of the guns
as an echo of Arabella's assaults on his privacy as she flushed
him out of hiding places during the struggle that had ended
in his flight and marriage. It was as though everything about
him conspired to re-create and widen the tragedy of long ago
and the sense of doom emerging from this vastly amplified
projection of destruction caused him to ponder aspects of the
murder and suicide that had not occurred to him during the
twelve-year lull. He came to believe, for instance, that his

father had not been mad at all, or not in the clinical sense but a man who had yielded to intolerable pressures upon his self-control, pressures supplied by the steady lash of Arabella's tongue, and it was during a pitiless bombardment a day or so after contemplating the man he had killed with a spade that Will understood precisely how his father had felt when he reached breaking-strain. From here it was only a step to personal identification with Martin at that point in his life where he had fired his gun at the Squire's boy, murdered Arabella in the bedroom and hanged himself in the barn.

No one around Will suspected that he had passed the extreme limit of endurance for as yet there was no such thing as 'shell shock' in the RAMC handbook. There were heroes and there were cowards and in between a majority who could endure a spell in the line and slough off the fear of death the moment they passed out of range of all but the heaviest artillery. It was this majority that Will Codsall envied but they were now cut off from him by the ghost of Martin, who seemed never to leave Will after they moved into a comparatively quiet sector, in April. Will came upon him in all kinds of improbable places, masquerading as the platoon sergeant in the bath-house, or sitting beside him on the companionable four-seater latrine, behind the billet, but it was not until Martin's ghost began to speak that the confusion became intolerable for then, largely out of cussedness, Will began to defy the old fool and curse him as he sat beside him at battalion sing-songs, and advised him to draw his bayonet and prod the belly of the corpulent reserve officer, who had replaced Captain Bagshaw, blown to bits at Rue du Bois.

Leave saved his sanity for a time. Once he was tidied up and embarked on the long, cross-country journey back to Base, Martin's ghost began to recede and by the time Will had reached Sorrel Halt, after a two-day journey of almost uninterrupted sleep in jolting trains, he felt reasonably assured that the old devil had been unable to escape from the lunar landscape about the Albert Canal and would stay there to be sniped, shelled, or bayoneted to death in the next local foray. And there, for all Will cared, Martin could suffer with all the other ghosts; he had never had much affection for his father when Martin was living and the recent persecution had put him on a par with Arabella.

III

Lieutenant Palfrey, the only man in the Valley to fight as a regular, spent the month of April, 1915, in the area of the dreaded Cuinchy brickstacks, where the Germans held one half of the rubble and the British held on to the lower, disadvantageous half. As a gunner and an officer he was spared a good deal of the terror, misery and discomfort that had driven Will Codsall to the edge of a mental breakdown but he saw more of front-line conditions than most heavy gunners for he was employed, sometimes for days at a stretch, as an artillery spotter and was either aloft in a captive balloon or, more often, checking map references with division infantry officers in and about the grotesque ruin where the two lines of trenches ran as close as fifty yards.

Ikey had now been in France for five months and the fact that he was a professional conditioned his outlook and moderated his prejudices. He was unable to view the sprawling, bloody muddle of Armageddon with the enthusiasm of Smut, the phlegm of Jem, or the frantic dismay of Will, for to most professionals the war was looked upon as a tiresome interruption in the fashionable art of soldiering mitigated, to some extent, by the chance of rapid promotion. Regimental protocol was still enforced and time-honoured mess customs were still sacrosanct, a frigid welcome being extended to youngsters drafted in to replace casualties. Ikey, who had always been inclined to look upon regimental ritual with tolerant contempt, was grateful for his keen vision and highly developed sense of observation, that offered an excuse to absent himself from the battery and regimental HQ. He cheerfully accepted the risk of being shot down from his balloon or sniped on his way to and from the front-line if he could spend whole days out of reach of the sahibs further back. By the time spring had come round he had developed a theory about the war that, to a degree, blunted its impact upon his sensibilities. All his life, or so it seemed to him, he had stood exactly half-way between the possessors and the possessed, between people who jingled the bell when the fire burned low and those who came trotting up to replenish it. He had been acutely conscious of this personal neutrality during his schooldays and whilst engaging in his clandestine association with Hazel, and although it would seem that, by marrying Hazel Potter, he had crossed from one social sphere to the other this was not really so. As long as the war continued or as long as he was actively engaged in it he still retained a foot in each camp. It was this time-truce that helped to clarify and then buttress his sense of detachment so that he came to see the war as a kind of surgical operation that civilisation was performing upon itself, an agonising but extremely interesting attempt to demolish class-barriers that had been building in Western Europe since the early days of feudalism. Possibly at that particular time, he was the only man in France who saw the war as the last eruption of feudalism, a gigantic and masochistic combined assault by masters and men upon the bonds they had forged for each other over twelve centuries of pride, bigotry and licensed greed. Unlike the majority of his comrades-in-arms he could not view it as an exercise in national rivalry or even, as the more sophisticated were beginning to regard it, as a cynical struggle for world markets that would last, perhaps another few months, or at worst another year. He saw it for what it was, the explosion of a magazine of myths and the trappings of myths such as flags and tribal cultures and although its barbarity horrified him, and he could pity the little people trapped in the cogs, he could also accept the slaughter as inevitable during a vast shift in the pattern of life on the planet. It was his sincere belief in this that enabled him to shorten the recoil of his emotional reaction to scenes that he would have thought himself incapable of witnessing without disgust and perhaps a protest that would have led, sooner or later, to direct conflict with brother officers.

His letters to Hazel encouraged the growth of his detach-ment. He enclosed one, at least once a week, in his cheerful,

factual letters to Paul, who now paid Hazel a weekly visit
for the express purpose of reading Ikey's letters to her. To
Hazel herself Ikey said little about the war but confined
himself to irrelevant minutiae, a patch of clover growing
beside a trench; the fatness and multiplicity of rats and their
dexterity in dodging revolver shots; the wandering flight of a
chalkhill blue butterfly braving shellfire over the brickstacks;
and sometimes even a comic quote from the gunners' letters he
censored. He did not know whether Paul, in reading his letters
aloud, ever attempted to convert his words into the brogue
that he himself had always used when talking to her but he
deeply appreciated Paul's kindness in fulfilling his promise to
keep an eye on wife and child and was touched when Paul
enclosed a letter allegedly dictated by Hazel, describing his
small son's attempt to wade the Sorrel that had ended in a
drenching. He had no means of knowing that it was Paul's
regular visits to Mill Cottage that precipitated a second crisis
at the Big House, or how near Claire came on his account to
allowing the wound inflicted by his marriage to fester.

IV

Claire had done her share of flirting. In the days before Paul
came to Shallowford when she was belle of the Valley she
had enjoyed the stir created by her arrival at a Hunt Ball
or at one of the charity dances in the Paxtonbury Assembly
Rooms and because he was proud of her good looks and fine
figure, Edward Derwent had given her far more freedom than
her competitors received. Then, after her humiliation at the
Coronation soirée, she had taken it out on the Tunbridge Wells
beaux but without a serious thought for any one of them. Since
her return to the Valley, however, and certainly since her marriage, she had never given anyone the slightest encouragement
to flirt with her although a good many tried, particularly
after the establishment of the camp on the heath where the
permanent staff included a dozen regular officers in their early
thirties, including one or two accomplished mashers.

She would certainly not have involved herself with Aubrey Lane-Phelps, the twenty-five-year-old musketry instructor, had her relationship with Paul resumed its tranquil pre-war course after the Hazel Potter incident but Lane-Phelps was not a man to wait upon encouragement. He possessed, besides hard and rather flashy good looks, an easy way with men and women, a small but adequate private income and, above all, a colossal but carefully camouflaged vanity. He met and marked down the Squire's wife on his first visit to Shallowford House and the suspicion that, in due course, he would be drafted to France applied a spur to his determination to make one more conquest before he was sucked into the Flanders mincing-machine, where the life of a junior officer was estimated at six to eight weeks.

He had sampled Claire, so to speak, at a Christmas party given by Paul for the permanent staff and had kissed her, very expertly, under the mistletoe in the hall, accomplishing this when everyone else's attention was engaged elsewhere. It was getting on for eight years since Claire had been kissed by any man other than her husband and she decided that it was a wholly pleasureable experience, particularly the way Aubrey Lane-Phelps went about it. All the same she broke from him rather indignantly and went out of her way to avoid him for the remainder of the evening. For several days afterwards her thoughts returned to him at odd moments when she was pondering how she could capitulate to Paul without losing too much face or when she was sitting in front of her mirror combing her long golden hair and wondering if, after all, she wasn't beginning to spread a little in certain directions.

Then he took to riding over to the house on one of the dejected screws they kept at the camp and usually appeared towards the end of the short winter afternoon, when Paul was out on his rounds, seeking the means of putting more acres under the plough or selecting timber to meet the demands of the Government's Forestry Commission.

At first she was rather distant with him but then, under the accurately sustained bombardment of his lively conversation, she began to thaw and at length made no secret of welcoming his company. The day he bent low over her hand and told her that he was in love with her she was far more flattered than outraged but after a moment of confusion, decided to treat his declaration as a joke, returning his heart with the sweet firmness of a broad-minded matron redirecting an infatuated youth. She misjudged him hopelessly. His experience was far wider than hers, so that he moved in smartly to pick up the next trick, projecting himself as a young man marked down for death, whose emotions had been cruelly mocked. Had she been less kindhearted, or better grounded in the business, she would have told him to mend his manners and not come again until he could resist the temptation to play the fool but it so happened that he caught her at a special disadvantage. Claire, at this time, was going through a very disturbing phase in her relationship with Paul. The quarrel concerning Ikey's marriage had died down but it had left a sensitive spot and whereas Claire had emerged from her long sulk, Paul unwittingly kept the issue alive by avoiding mention of Ikey or Hazel and keeping Ikey's letters to himself, so that a sense of strain crept into their relationship, showing itself in artifical silences and a marked slowing down of the physical rhythm of their marriage. It was not that he ever rejected her or she him but something of the gaiety and excitement of pre-war exchanges was missing and when they did make love it seemed to her that he roused himself with an effort, as though performing a duty expected of him. She had no way of knowing that this apathy on his part was due far more to his brooding preoccupation with the war, and his own uncertainties regarding it, than to their quarrel over Ikey's marriage but she had too much of her father's pride and obstinacy to broach the subject. It was because of this, and really for no other reason, that Lane-Phelps' interest in her as a woman and not merely as a convenient hostess excited and flattered her and when he threw in his reserves of pathos she faltered so that he was able to gauge her state of mind with considerable accuracy. He said, humbly, 'I know I haven't the slightest right to expect love in return, Claire. In any case, apart from you being married, I'm due to go overseas any day and my chances of coming back to you are not more than fifty to one. I've said what I feel for you because I had to but I can bow myself out with dignity I hope.'

It was a virtuoso performance, particularly as he knew well enough that there was not the slightest chance of him going to France until the new Kitchener armies were fully trained and that he meant to do his damnedest to land a staff appointment, for which he was fortunately placed. She said miserably, 'Don't say that, Aubrey! Let's hope to God it'll be over before any of you men up there are killed!' but as he turned away she caught his hand and the kiss that followed was somewhat more adventurous than that exchanged under the mistletoe, for in the course of the embrace his hands performed a light but very expert reconnaissance over two areas of his field of operations. Then, her Derwent commonsense catching up with her, she broke from him violently but experience told him that it was from motives of panic rather than repugnance and he decided not to press his luck but await a more opportune occasion. He picked up his hat, cane and gloves saying, 'If I should be posted suddenly, as usually happens, you'll see me again?' and she said she would, although he was not to call when Paul was out and she promised nothing.

She was in a very confused mood for the next day or so, a curious but not altogether unpleasant compound of guilt, fear, recklessness and elation. Paul seemed not to notice as much, being excessively engaged just then persuading the Government commissioners that, whilst they were welcome to all the soft timber on the estate, the war could be won without sacrificing Shallowford timber that had been maturing over two centuries. Suspense, and guilt also, made her amorous and at ordinary times he could not have failed to notice this, for she came very close to parading herself before him in the intervals between the time he came stumping up to bed and the turning down of the bedside lamps but although he was talkative it was not of love that he spoke but of Valley men overseas and the maddening perversity of officials pestering him for timber and agricultural returns, so that she was thrown back on her own thoughts and they were thoughts that might have dismayed him. She began to reflect that they must have reached a stage in their marriage where a spur was needed to remind him that she was something more than an audience for his rumbling complaints.

It was after the signal failure of her most brazen attempt to stimulate him that she made up her mind to adventure one step further with Aubrey. In the early days of her marriage Paul had always taken pleasure in brushing her hair and when they retired about eleven o'clock one night she made sure there was a bright fire in the grate, undressed, put on a beribboned summer nightgown, loosened her hair and invited him to brush it. His response would have made her laugh at any other time. He took the brush, performed a dozen, absentminded strokes and said, vaguely, 'Won't you be cold in this? Shouldn't you wear something thicker?', so that she snatched the brush away and climbed sulkily into bed, thinking, 'If Aubrey does call I'll receive him whether Paul is here or not! At least he'll pay me a few compliments instead of deluging me with estate problems and other people's troubles!'

He did call and with regularity, seeming to have accurate information on Paul's movements, for he never once appeared when she was not alone and able to be coaxed out of the orbit of the servants. They walked in the rose-garden and they sat in the little conservatory, talking gaily of this and that and sometimes skirmishing a little. By this time her feelings of guilt had almost disappeared and she flattered herself that she could handle him as surely as her sister Rose handled a young horse. There were half-a-dozen light kisses and one or two pats on the bottom, or make-believe accidental contacts between his hand and her breasts, but his progress was disappointingly slow until the afternoon when, in teeming rain, he came to tell her that he was expecting to join a draft in less than a week. They took tea in the conservatory where he kissed her rather more ardently than usual and she discovered, to her surprise and dismay, that his good looks, expertise and quietly aggressive masculinity roused her more than she wanted to be roused. It was only when his hand slipped from her shoulder, passing casually over her buttocks and then, swiftly and accurately, moved lightly between her thighs that she recollected herself and fended him off with genuine indignation. He said, sulkily, 'You can't blame me wanting all of you, Claire, not in the circumstances!' a protest that fell short of his usual high standard in the give and take of mashing. She replied as she turned for the door, 'It's a good deal more than you'll get, Aubrey, circumstances notwithstanding!' which at least showed him that she was learning. He followed her abjectly, mumbling apologies and blaming her magnetism for his unforgivable lapse, and although she parted from him coldly she remembered all he had said when she sat musing before the library fire that evening, waiting for Paul to come home from an overlong session of the local agricultural war committee in Paxtonbury.

Paul telephoned about nine saying he would not be in until midnight so she went yawning to bed, still unable to make up her mind whether or not she should forgive Aubrey's insolence sufficiently to say good-bye to him before he left for France. She decided, on drifting off to sleep, that she would; any man going out into that deserved the benefit of the doubt.

She was not much surprised when, soon after breakfast the next morning, a lance-corporal arrived with a message couched in impeccably polite terms. It told her that Lieutenant Lane-Phelps was due to leave camp within forty-eight hours and would appreciate an opportunity to thank her for her hospitality since he had been in the district. He added that he would telephone if she would tell the lance-corporal 'when she was likely to be on hand' and she did not miss this hint, telling the messenger Lieutenant Lane-Phelps might telephone mid-morning, a time when Paul was certain to be out. Sharp at eleven a.m. on the following day he 'phoned, first asking if she was alone. She said, hesitantly, that she was, astonished that the note of pleading in his voice brought colour to her cheeks.

'I'm due out of camp late tonight,' he told her, 'but I'm free all this afternoon. Will you ride out and meet me at the battery on the Bluff?'

She hadn't bargained for this; a sad, semi-platonic farewell in the security of her own drawing-room with delicately balanced cups of tea and Mrs Handcock within earshot was one thing. A meeting in the wooded country on the western slope of the Bluff involved risks she was reluctant to take but then she reminded herself that he was manageable and could hardly get out of hand if they were both on horseback – so she said she would do her best to meet him between three and four o'clock, providing he promised 'not to be silly'.

She was beginning to suspect that she had no talent for the role of erring wife and blew hot and cold all the morning, changing her mind half-a-dozen times. When, at lunch, Paul said he intended taking the trap to Whinmouth that afternoon – 'to have another go at knocking sense into those damned timber pirates' – she had difficulty in not exclaiming with relief, for somehow his absence from the Valley converted an act of gross disloyalty into a kind of schoolgirl romp and she thought, as he gave her a casual kiss and marched off, 'It isn't as if I was the least bit in love with the boy! I'm damned sorry for him – sorry for anyone going to France but even that isn't the real reason I'll go and say good-bye! I'm really going because all the sparkle has gone out of my life since last summer and this is the only bit likely to come my way until it's all over!', and she went into the yard and saddled Snowdrop, telling Chivers that she was riding over to High Coombe to see her brother Hugh.

It was a dull, windless afternoon when she emerged on to open ground from the high-banked lane that ran down to the woods. There was rain about but it fell on the Valley as mist, filling the hollows and blurring the landscape on the far side of the river. She rode at a slow walk, as though, by dallying, she still had leisure to change her mind but when the belt of mist had crossed the stream to idle at the base of the Bluff she was conscious of mounting excitement and almost admitted to herself that it was the prospect of being grossly flattered by a good-looking young man that made her feel so reckless. When she reached the outskirts of the Dell Wood, that clothed the western shoulder of the Bluff, she had renewed qualms of being spotted by one or other of the Potter tribe whose farm lay less than two hundred yards beyond the first trees, so she

made a wide circuit to within fifty yards of the river road
intending to skirt the garden of Mill Cottage and use a track
that ran across the steepest part of the Bluff before trailing off
into a gorse-grown section of the cliff, overlooking the battery.
From here, she thought, she could look down into the copse
without being seen and perhaps, even then, change her mind
and ride on to High Coombe, as advertised.

She had reached a point where the cottage came within
twenty yards of the road when she pulled hard on the bridle,
seeing a figure suddenly emerge from the river mist and turn
in at the wicket gate of the cottage. He was on foot and because
the stiff latch of the gate engaged his attention he did not look
over his shoulder and see her reined in between the high banks.
There was no mistaking the long stride and short-peaked cap.
The man entering Mill Cottage was her husband, who should,
by now, have been more than half-way to Whinmouth to
confront his enemies the timber pirates.

Her first reaction was extreme astonishment at seeing him
there and she only just checked herself calling out. Then,
like the crackle of Chinese rip-raps, came other responses,
all painful and most of them outrageous, for the sight of
him turning casually into the gate of Mill Cottage, as though
he visited there alone and on foot every day of the week,
set off a chain reaction in Claire's already over-stimulated
imagination, exhuming factors that her memory had recorded
subconsciously over the last three months. There was his
recent habit of walking rather than riding about the estate;
his extreme reluctance to mention Ikey, or the trollop Ikey
had married; his obstinate championship of the girl at the
time of the wedding and his evasiveness to engage in any
kind of truce-talk after the initial flare-up between them on
the subject. All this, she reasoned, as her brain skipped from
signpost to signpost, might or might not have significance but
there was something else that presented itself as a particularly
glaring piece of circumstantial evidence. There never had been
a time since their marriage when he had failed to enjoy her as
his bedfellow, not, that is, until recent weeks. In other spheres
she had, at one time or another, had self-doubts but never

in this respect for here was the thread they used to spin the pattern of their marriage, a mutual and deeply-rooted satisfaction in access to one another of the kind that Grace, as he had once told her, had proclaimed the true basis of marriage but had, for so many other reasons, been unable to achieve with him. Time and again over the last eight years she had exulted in her power to engage him at the level of an accomplished mistress rather than that of a workaday wife and while she had no yardstick but him to assess the vigour of men it had always seemed to her that his was exceptional. What pleased her even more was his boyish frankness regarding her power to stimulate him. She could look back on a girlhood and early womanhood when the topic of sexual adjustment between man and wife was taboo, not even discussed between mother and daughter. To her his approach had seemed not only healthy but immensely flattering. He had never used her without complimenting her, often in such wildly extravagant terms that she blushed in the secrecy of his embrace and as a lover he contrived to combine enormous gusto with a gentle reverence of her body. Sometimes she had not hesitated to exploit this when eager to win him over to her point of view yet, even here, he had knowingly submitted to exploitation, so that they had achieved a harmony she believed to be rare between two people. She was so conscious of this, and of her power to rouse him at will, that she often smiled at her own smugness but she had never ceased to value his need of her, hugging it to herself as the most precious acquisition of her life. It was because of this that the mere suspicion that her ascendancy was threatened frightened her as never before. To see him walking through that cottage gate, across the little garden and in at the back door without even knocking made her almost sick with rage and the alarm bell that buzzed most persistently in her head was not that he was clearly a regular visitor here but that he was prepared to lie about his visits.

She sat the horse without moving for five minutes or more while Snowdrop munched over the long grass growing out of the bank. She went over the evidence piece by piece,

balancing one fact against another without troubling herself
to seek alternative explanations. There could not, she decided,
be any other explanation, for everybody in the Valley knew
what the Potter girls had for sale. Their availability to any
man with a shilling or two in his pocket was a byword for
miles around and had been, ever since she had been a girl
growing up a mile or so above the Dell. It followed that this
girl, the half-witted Hazel, who was by far the prettiest was
also, on account of her lack of wits, the most accessible for she
would be unlikely to blab of her conquests. It was all, Claire
decided, very much of a piece – his moodiness, his deliberate
attempts to turn the conversation whenever Ikey's name was
mentioned, his obstinate advocacy of the idiotic alliance, and,
above all, his currently tepid approach to her own person,
for surely only a man who spent himself frequently with a
strumpet could fail to respond to her invitations during the
last week or so when she had, as she now realised, been
seeking reassurance from him.

It was the thought of Lane-Phelps, waiting for her at this
very moment in the copse under the Bluff, that changed her
dismay to humiliation. The base inequality of the sexes stuck
in her throat like a plum-stone, for here she was, feeling guilty
and troubled about a mere kiss or two, while her husband
was paying regular visits to a harlot whom he had married
off to his own ward! The reflection braced her to gather
up Snowdrop's reins and half-wheel in the lane with the
object of riding openly to her rendezvous with Aubrey and
avenging herself on the spot but she did not proceed with
this intention. Deep down, under the welter of indignation
that boiled in her, was a pinpoint of Derwent commonsense
and it told her that there was a chance, just a chance, that
she might be wrong, or half-wrong, or misled in some way,
so that she knew she would have to make certain before
committing herself finally and absolutely.

She judged that almost ten minutes must have passed
since she saw him enter the back door and he was not, as
she knew better than anyone, a man likely to make a ritual
of the business. By this time, no doubt, they were already

upstairs and in bed. The prospect of actually confronting them was dramatic, providing she could go through with it, which she doubted, but perhaps this would not be necessary. All she had to do was to creep into the house and listen and after that events could take their course. She swung herself out of the saddle, knotted the bridle round a young ash, and taking advantage of the overgrown bank moved down the lane to the gate which, most fortunately, he had left ajar.

The mist proved a valuable ally. It had been thickening minute by minute and now the hollow in which the cottage stood was half-filled with the seeping cloud drifting in from the south-west. Looking over her shoulder she could no longer see Snowdrop, so, moving with great caution, she approached the door and laid a hand on the latch. As she did this she glanced through the tiny rear window of the building, her eye attracted by the flicker of the fire within and here she stopped, hearing the murmur of Paul's voice rising and falling in a continuous rumble, as though he was reciting. He sounded so unlike a man passing a casual half-hour with a harlot that she hesitated and then, hardly knowing what she did, edged back from the porch, flattening herself against the cob wall and inching forward until she could look directly into the big room, with its window facing the river and its hearth on her immediate right. What she saw made her gasp. All three of them were there, Paul, Hazel and the child, the latter on his mother's lap with his fat legs dangling like great, pink sausages as Hazel listened attentively to Paul reading aloud from a letter. Claire watched in amazement. It was like looking in upon an animated scrapbook illustration, the tall, broad-shouldered man, still wearing his cap, his shoulder resting lightly on the mantelshelf and holding the letter in his hand, the young woman sitting in an old basket chair, an expression of rapt attention on her face, the child, disinterested but relaxed in the grip of his mother's forearm, his legs clear of the floor. Claire could even hear a snatch or two of the letter . . . *'thought of you when I saw the wind catch the poplar leaves and throw a handful of silver into the air'* . . . *'hoping to come on leave'* . . . *'heard your brother Smut had been promoted to corporal!'* . . . odd, inconsequential snippets that nonetheless made everything perfectly clear, so clear indeed that she could have smiled had she felt less ashamed at being here at all. She had been right about one thing, however. He obviously did come here regularly but for the purpose of reading Ikey's letters that were obviously enclosed in his own and Claire suddenly remembered that Hazel Potter had never learned to read or write, despite all Mary Willoughby's efforts to teach her the alphabet.

The long trailers of mist seemed to bore their way into Claire's bones and she shivered so convulsively that she could remain still no longer and began to retreat along the wall towards the door, and into the weed-filled garden, moving backward step by step, as though from something terrifying. On reaching the open gate, she turned and ran through the mist to the spot where the grey was tethered; seconds later she was in the saddle and using her heels vigorously so that the horse broke into a trot and then a slow canter, swinging left into the sloping field at the head of the path and finally, still at a canter, down the broad sweep of meadow to where the Shallowford track ran down to the orchard.

It was not until Snowdrop had been stabled and Claire was sitting hunched over a smouldering library fire that she spared a thought for Aubrey Lane-Phelps, still waiting for her in the mist below the battery but it was no more than a fleeting thought. 'Damn Lane-Phelps!' she said, aloud, 'he can go to France, Egypt or Timbuctoo for all I care! I shall squirm every time I think of him and maybe weep as well but not for the reasons he thinks!' and she snatched up the poker and attacked the fire as though the smoldering logs had been responsible for bringing her within a hairsbreadth of reducing her well-ordered life to chaos.

V

He did not come in to tea and when she nerved herself to make an inquiry from Chivers she learned that he had returned home about three-thirty, collected the trap and gone to Whinmouth as scheduled. She knew then that he would not be home again until supper and deciding that she could not face him across the table went up to the bedroom telling Mrs Handcock that she had a headache and was retiring early. She did not attempt to undress but sat in her favourite chair over the coal fire, curtains drawn against the world.

She tried to read and failed and tried to think and failed. In the end she just sat and looked at the shifting coals, awaiting his step in the library below.

About nine Mrs Handcock tapped on the door and said a Mr Lane-Phelps was asking for her on that there telephone. Claire said, shortly, 'Tell him I'm not available! Tell him that if he wants he can ring later, after Squire returns!' and her contemplation of Aubrey's reaction to this message was the one cheerful spot in an interminable evening. Soon after Mrs Handcock had gone she heard Paul come in and after a brief pause the chink of china, as his cold supper was set before him; she thought, 'Do I go down or do I wait for him to come to bed? If Mrs Handcock has told him I've got a headache he'll creep about for fear of disturbing me. Well, I could hardly be less disturbed and am likely to remain so unless I tell him everything now, before I weaken! I daresay it's inviting disaster but I'm sick to death of watching us drift the way we've been drifting since Ikey came home! He'll surely fly into a fearful rage and assume I'm going the same way as Grace but I can't help it if he does for anything's better than this. We had a good marriage, a wonderful marriage, and if we can't mend it and put it back on the rails it won't be for want of trying on my part!' She decided to wait for him to come up and undressed, putting on a winter nightgown, for this was no time for ribbons. It was whilst rummaging in the cupboard for her nightgown that she saw some of Simon's discarded riding kit, jodhpurs and jacket that he had outgrown put aside for the next jumble sale. There was a riding switch, a short brown cane that she picked up, recalling the story she had heard of the Bideford Goliath's use of a stick on the Potter girls every time they tried to make a fool of him. She thought: 'I wouldn't blame him if he treated me like Cis and Vi Potter for I'm really no better for all my airs and graces!' and the reflection made her more depressed than ever, for all her life she had regarded the Potter girls with a contempt not far removed from disgust.

He did not keep her waiting long. Soon she heard him call good night to Mrs Handcock, who usually drowsed by the kitchen fire until nearly midnight and then he came in, looking mildly surprised to find her sitting there and the lamps still burning.

'I haven't got a headache, Paul,' she said at once, 'but I came up early. I've got something important to say.'

He did not seem particularly surprised by this unusual greeting but for a moment looked almost amused and then straightened his face, kissed her lightly on the forehead, and said, 'Well, you do look a bit off colour. Anything unpleasant happened?'

She said, with a deliberation that surprised her, 'Yes, Paul, a great deal has happened and it is unpleasant but not nearly so bad as it might have been, or would still be if I made light of it.'

He sat down on the hard chair across the fireplace and shot out his long legs. He was still wearing his tall boots and breeches and he looked, she thought, a good deal more cheerful and relaxed than he had looked for some time.

'All right,' he said, 'if it's that important my news can wait,' and she experienced a wild flutter of alarm and cried out, 'You haven't enlisted!' at which he laughed louder than she had heard him laugh since before the war.

'No,' he said, 'I haven't enlisted, I doubt if they'd have me! It's just that I've saved out timber, at least for the time being.'

'I'm glad,' she said, slowly, 'and I expect you are!' and then, as though restarting a race after a false start, 'I've let you down rather badly, Paul! In two ways, different ways! I've been very unhappy about what's been happening to us lately and I suppose that's my only excuse, although it's a very poor one.'

He still did not seem much concerned although his expression hardened a little. He said, 'What the devil are you driving at? Come right out with it, it's easier that way and I'm damned sure it isn't half as bad as you think it is! *How* have you let me down?'

She said, flushing, 'I've been having a very heavy flirtation with Aubrey Lane-Phelps, up at the camp. *Only* a flirtation on my honour, but . . . well, it might easily have led to something more serious if I hadn't suddenly come to my senses this afternoon!'

'Why especially this afternoon?' he asked, so mildly that she was thrown off balance again and began to stammer, her cheeks flushing as bright as the core of the fire.

'I . . . well . . . I followed you to Hazel Potter's – Hazel Palfrey's cottage! I saw you go in. I was coming down the lane on the grey.'

'Yes, I know,' he said, grinning, 'I saw you and I wondered what you had in mind. Why didn't you call?'

For a moment she was speechless and then, her colour receding somewhat, 'You . . . you *saw* me?? You *knew* I was there while you were reading Ikey's letter to her?'

'Well no,' he admitted, looking surprised in his turn, 'I didn't know that. I had it in mind you rode off in a huff as soon as you saw me. As a matter of fact that's why I've never told you I always call there and read his letters. She wouldn't make much of them herself. What induced you to peep in and then creep away?'

She had to plunge now for what had seemed too certain this afternoon now seemed not only grotesquely ridiculous but downright insulting. She went on: 'Sitting here this evening I made up my mind to admit everything and here it is! I was certain you were calling there for . . . well, for the reason most men call on the Potter girls!'

If she wanted to astonish him she had succeeded at last. His jaw dropped and his heavy brows shot up more than an inch. Then, mercifully for both of them, his unpredictable

sense of humour came storming up and he let out a bellow
that might have been heard in the stable-yard on the far side
of the house. 'Great God!' he said, once he had composed
himself, 'you thought *that*! But you dear silly idiot, how often
have I got to tell you that Hazel hasn't a thing in common
with her sisters? Ikey's wife? And him in the trenches? Why,
Great Scott, even if I was so inclined she'd kill anybody
who tried to make a fool of Ikey!' Then, quite suddenly, he
became serious again and went on, 'What the devil is the
matter with you, Claire? It can't be just this nonsense with a
cocky young masher like Lane-Phelps. I knew all about that,
knew you were very flattered by his attentions anyway, but
it didn't worry me or not seriously! I suppose I was irritated
to watch him buzzing round like a wasp over a jam-jar but
since everybody is a little crazy these days I didn't grudge
you a bit of fun, so long as it remained fun!'

'It did, Paul,' she said, urgently and he ripped out, showing
his first flash of impatience, 'Good God, woman, I *know* it
did! Do you imagine I wouldn't have known after all this
time?'

Suddenly she felt both relieved and deflated, as though
she was a child with long plaits confessing a fault to an
indulgent parent, expecting a slap and getting nothing but
amused tolerance. The transition from one extreme to the other
was so painful that tears welled in her eyes and she made a
helpless gesture with her hands. He must have realised how
she felt for amusement and impatience left him at once and
he said, quietly, 'All *right*, Claire. I'll listen, if you really want
to unburden yourself and I don't mean that cynically! What
exactly did happen between you and that ass? He kissed
you once or twice, I suppose?'

'Yes he did, half-a-dozen times.'

He still looked indulgent, even when he said, 'And let
his hands stray a little, I wouldn't wonder? Well, I hope
his private technique is better than his public display for
his tactics went out with the crinoline! Dammit woman,
chaps like him are ten a penny in every mess or were
until we got caught up in a real war! I suppose he told

you he was being drafted to France and hadn't long to live?'

'Yes,' she admitted, 'he did, only this morning and I . . . I . . . was on my way to say good-bye when I saw you! He's going overseas tomorrow.'

'He's going tomorrow but not overseas,' Paul told her, shortly. 'When I saw him preening himself on his progress I asked the adjutant about him. He's going on a course to Aldershot, then straight back here and after that he'll land a staff appointment that'll keep him out of the firing line! He'll work it all right, the Lane-Phelps of this world generally do but what was it that made you "come to your senses" as you say?'

'When I looked in the window and realised why you were there.'

He pondered a moment. 'And suppose I had been upstairs with the girl? Would that have resulted in Lane-Phelps getting another scalp?'

'Yes, I think it would.'

'Well, I dare say you would have been justified, for I suppose it did seem I was lying about going to Whinmouth. I met the postman in the drive and thought I'd pop over and read her letter before I crossed the river. It's all rather silly, isn't it? I mean, not just this but the situation we've allowed to develop between us, and I daresay it's partly my fault; I couldn't have been easy to live with during the last few months.'

She was by no means disposed to grant him his share of the blame. 'That's rubbish!' she said, 'you've been grossly over-worked and because you identify yourself with the Valley you suffer for everybody in it! You always did but now it's a hundred times more strain and I should have tried to help instead of fooling around with a man like Lane-Phelps. Most men in the Valley would have given their wives a damned good hiding for far less!'

'Well,' he said, cheerfully, 'I haven't the slightest desire to knock you down and black your eyes but I'll turn you over and smack your handsome bottom if you insist!'

His facetiousness confused her, so much so that, in a perverse way, she felt cheated.

'I'm sorry, I can't laugh it off, Paul. The truth is I've never felt so small and mean and wretched in my life!'

'I'm sorry too,' he said, more seriously, 'but I find it difficult to go berserk over a show-off like Lane-Phelps!'

'But it isn't Lane-Phelps,' she argued, 'I see now that he was just a kind of game I was playing with myself. This afternoon was different. How could I have been so wrong and stupid? And suppose I hadn't waited and had ridden off to the Battery?'

'Well you didn't!' he said and she replied, biting her lip, 'I came within an inch of doing so and that makes me unfit to share a bed with a man as honest as you!'

Her contrition, carried to these extravagant lengths, exasperated him. He said, impatiently, 'Oh, for God's sake! Let's forget the whole bloody thing!' expecting her to shrug and climb resignedly into bed. In all their previous clashes she had remained open to reason and tact on his part, had even managed to half-heal the one serious rupture in their relationship. Tonight, however, it was as if she enjoyed wallowing in guilt and she stood staring at him with a curiously wooden expression that he had never seen on her face all the years he had known her. She said, at length, 'I don't seem to be able to convince you do I?' and he snapped, 'No, you don't! I think you're just being stupid and enlarging a peccadillo into a crisis!' but because she still regarded him with that odd, woebegone expression he suddenly relented and made one more attempt to laugh her out of it, saying, 'Look here, if it will soothe your conscience at the expense of your rump wait while I slip down and fetch my riding-crop!' and he reached out, intending to gather her up and throw her on the bed. To his dismay she stepped back sharply and backed against the cupboard. 'Whatever happens this is going to take me a very long time to live down,' she said. 'Your come-come-now-now approach isn't likely to help, Paul!' She turned then, flung open the cupboard and picked up the brown switch, thrusting it at him and throwing up her head with what struck him as a gesture of almost hysterical defiance. Then his astonishment was doused by laughter and he said, taking the cane, 'Very pretty, but if I took you at your word I daresay I'd never hear the last of it!'

Her head came down again and now, as defiance ebbed, she looked spent and defeated. She said, very quietly, 'It wasn't such an empty gesture, Paul. What you can't understand is that a woman who has behaved as I have would prefer a week with a sore backside to a lifetime with a sick conscience. Very well, leave it at that, but for God's sake don't stand there making excuses for me!'

It was only then, as she made a step towards the bed, that he realised she was in earnest, that she was in desperate need of some kind of penance and would have been grateful for a blow across the face the moment she had confessed to Lane-Phelps' fumblings and her suspicions regarding Hazel. He understood too that her emotions were essentially primitive, far more so than his, a newcomer to an area where the emotional relationship between man and wife had nothing to do with statutes and codes of behaviour written into books. He felt pity for her and compassion made him wiser yet without altogether banishing humour from such a grotesque situation. He said, thoughtfully, 'Has anyone ever beaten you?'

'My mother, when I deserved it.'

'Never your father?'

'He left that kind of thing to her. Perhaps it's a pity.'

'It's not too late. Bend over that chair and stay there until I tell you to get up!'

Even then she had power to shock him. Without a word or a change of expression she did as he bid, hoisting her nightgown and bending low so that her hair brushed the carpet. She was trembling but not from fear and no longer for shame. The very humiliation of her posture brought a sense of release as though, by calling his bluff, she was already atoning in some degree for the self-abasement of the day. She might have felt differently about this had she seen his expression as he stood contemplating her defenceless buttocks. It held no trace of irritation or astonishment now. He was grinning, broadly, and as the cane dropped to the floor, she felt in place of its bite, a tremendous slap that would have precipitated her over the back of the chair had he not saved her by grabbing the folds of her nightgown and robe. Then, before she had half-recovered her balance, he had spun her round and was holding her in a grip that drove the breath from her body.

'Don't be such a damned fool!' he shouted through his laughter. 'I'm no wife-beater and you're no Potter girl! Take those damned things off before I tear them off and get into bed and turn out the light! I know a way to teach you who is boss around here!' and he kissed her, swung her off her feet and tossed her bodily on the bed.

It was his tone more than the gesture that sobered her, that and his abrupt stalk round the end of the bed and into the dressing-room where he kept his riding clothes.

She got up and stood in the centre of the room massaging her tingling behind and then, catching sight of her reflection in the tall mirror, was amazed to discover herself smiling. They were over it, through it, and had the rhythm of their lives by the tail again and she could have shouted her relief and thankfulness at the top of her voice. She heard him grunting as he tugged at his long boots and called, after a moment, 'Do you want a hand with those?' and he shouted back, 'No! Get into bed for God's sake woman!' and a few moments later he was beside her handling her as impatiently as she ever recalled.

Yet it was she, exhausted by the emotional demands of the day, who slept first while he lay awake awhile, going about his familiar business of sorting out and docketing his impressions, his thoughts returning to her accurate diagnosis of his ill-humour over the last few months – his personal identification with the turmoil that had reigned in the Valley since Franz had 'phoned that August night telling him that war was inevitable and would be anything but the field-day-jubilee that everyone expected. She was right of course; she knew him better than anyone, better even than John Rudd who had shared the adventure from the very beginning. He saw the Valley people as a family, as dear to him as Grace's boy Simon and the twins, and his daughters Mary and Whiz, all sound asleep in their quarters along the corridor. He shared the mounting desperation of wives like Elinor Codsall and the misery of mothers like Marian Eveleigh, at war not only with the Germans but with her own husband. He worried, with Old Honeyman, over the shrinking manpower of the farms and dreaded the impossible tasks that would face them all at harvest time. He brooded, with Rose Derwent, on the probable fate of her horses, bought up and driven away by Government scavengers to drag great hunks of metal along foreign roads. He had saved the old timber of the estate for the time being, but how long would it be before they presented him with fresh ultimatums? And if the deadlock in France showed no signs of breaking how would it be possible, in two years or three, to reharness the Valley to his dreams? It was a depressing role, this witnessing of twelve years' thought and toil being swept away like bubbles of silt on a Sorrel freshet but tonight, for the first time in months, he felt comparatively optimistic and this was not on account of his victory over the timber pirates. His cheerful mood stemmed directly from the woman asleep in his arms, a wife of eight years' standing and the mother of four of his children but also, at this moment, a living symbol of the Valley, of its fruitfulness and beauty season by season. Her breasts were its contours and in her thighs lived its abundancy. 'And not so damned fanciful either!' he thought, 'for there were Derwents hereabouts when the first Tudor arrived and probably before that if they could be traced! I didn't get my hands on this land simply by paying the Lovell family a cheque but by taking her into partnership and giving her children in this house. All I've done since I got here is to play stud-horse and caretaker, and I daresay I'll go on doing just that as long as I live for it won't become Craddock land in the real sense until her children, and her children's children, take on where I leave off!' The conclusion and the glow of possession engendered by it, was a balm and warmed his belly like a glass of Bergundy. He pulled her closer, his lips brushing her hair and as he drifted off to sleep the knowledge that whole armies were locked in conflict across the Channel seemed a trivial thing compared to the eternity of red soil and the race who cared for it.

Chapter Five

I

John Rudd, Eveleigh, Sam Potter, indeed anyone who claimed to know Paul Craddock at all well would have argued that he was anything but an impulsive man. He had a reputation for slow, cud-chewing thought, and carefully weighed decisions, for assembling every scrap of available evidence and carrying it away to study in privacy before taking action on any matter involving the administration or development of the estate. And yet, viewed in retrospect, all of the important decisions of his life had been arrived at impulsively, almost recklessly – the purchase of thirteen hundred acres after a twenty-four hour survey; his marriage to Grace Lovell and later to Claire Derwent; his adoption of Ikey Palfrey and, finally, in the summer of 1915, his final conclusions on the war which led, more or less directly, to his personal participation in it.

Until then he had qualified as a guarded neutral, an object of distrust by the Kaiser-hating fire-eaters, men like Horace Handcock who saw in the conflict vindication of the prophecies of a decade. Almost alone among the menfolk of the Valley Paul was not visited by the virus of war-fever, devoting his energies exclusively to buttressing the Valley against the pressures exerted upon it from the hour Paxtonbury's newsagents' boys had run shrieking along the down platform proclaiming Armageddon and summoning the more impressionable to the Bosphorus and the Sweetwater Canal. On that momentous occasion Paul did not even get his feet wet. He looked upon the involvement of Britain in the Franco-German quarrel as a grave misjudgment on the part of the Government, whom he had always regarded as pacific and conciliatory. When it was clear that there could be no withdrawal and that, for good or evil, there would be a few months' carnage, he moderated his attitude, saying that he supposed they would all come to their senses sooner or later and he made no secret of the fact that he intended to continue minding his own business, taking full advantage of the Government's reawakening interest in the land. Fortunately for him (for patriotism could be menacing) he was qualified to stand aside. He was thirty-five when the war began and still suffered from the leg wound gained in the last epidemic of patriotic hysteria. He also had considerable responsibilities, including a wife, a young family, a seat on the local Bench and suzerainty over six prosperous farms each expected to do its share in stocking the national larder. At that stage, indeed, at any foreseeable stage in the war, he could have been said to be serving national interests more usefully at home than overseas and he continued to tell himself this until the war was about a year old. Then, brick by brick, the protective barricade he had raised against the outside world began to crumble so that he was obliged to take stock of it and ponder how long it could sustain mounting pressures from all sides and how much longer he could justify his neutrality. For thirteen years now his life had been the Valley, the people who lived there, the crops they raised and the cattle they reared, and for him no other obligations existed. Under the tremendous stresses of a war however, with half the world already involved and every participant bent on total victory, the entire social structure of the Valley began to change at a velocity that made his head spin. The slatternly camp arose on the moor and raucous north-countrymen flocked in like so many Viking invaders. Machines proliferated and their stench poisoned the air of the countryside but, what was worse, his own men drifted away in twos and threes leaving every farm short of labour and at a time when official demands on the yield of the land were assuming fantastic proportions. In one way he welcomed those demands. They gave him plenty to do and justified his faith in the land and in the improvements he had made over the years. With the expert knowledge of John Rudd, and his own not inconsiderable experience to help him,

he grappled with manpower and equipment problems, solving
them all one way or another but hard work and improvisation
could not rescue him from personal involvement in domestic
problems, or as time passed, from involvement in the tragedies
of the Valley. It was here that his detachment foundered.

In the last ten years Paul Craddock had developed a
knack found in the best type of regimental officer. He had
a remarkable memory for the kind of personal trivia that
convinced tenants and estate workers that their interests
were his and this was neither a pose nor an oblique way
of keeping the estate machinery oiled. He really did think
of the Eveleighs and the Codsalls as his friends and the
Derwents and Rudds not as relatives or deputies but as
allies and he went far beyond that, reaching right down
to the level of the two- or three-score hired men and maids
employed on the farms and in the workshops of the Valley,
craftsmen who were all, in some degree, dependent upon the
estate. He knew everybody in the vale by Christian name. He
knew whether they were married or single, how much they
earned and how many children they supported. He knew the
age of most of them and, in some cases, how long they had
occupied their cottages and what kind of home-makers they
were. Thus, when the men began to drift away to face death
or disablement he was concerned for every one of them and
for their families. Each brick knocked from his wall had a name
upon it and when a sufficient number had been removed, or
knocked askew, he was as deeply committed to the war as
the least of them and they all knew it and looked to him to
solve some of their immediate problems.

The first of these to confront him was the loss of Will
Codsall's labour at Periwinkle, smallest of the Valley farms
and as time went on, he and John Rudd formed a pool of
part-time, migratory labour to fill this and other vacancies so
that soon Valley farming became almost a communal venture.
This system broke down, however, after a mere eight months
and with far more land under the plough than in peacetime,
adjustments had to be made in the way of concentrating stock
and merging machinery and even borders. Some local trades

withered altogether. Thatching was the first of them and Nick Salter and his boys went to work at High Coombe and Four Winds. The fishing industry at Coombe Bay died after the recall to the Navy of Tom Williams and two of his crewmen and the local building industry was soon at a standstill, for Ephraim Morgan lost Walt Pascoe and three other specialists and although, in a sense, the failure of subsidiary trades was no immediate concern of the estate, Paul felt it incumbent upon him to do all he could to keep them alive against the return of the volunteers. Apart from using all available manpower on the denuded farms he also reduced nearly a score of his cottage rents and provided cart-horse transport for the pupils of Mary Willoughby's little school. He maintained good relations with the camp and indulgent officers sometimes turned a blind eye to his temporary enlistment of a craftsman or agriculturist from among the swarm of recruits.

Then the casualties began to occur, the first of them, Roddy, John Rudd's boy, who had written home in September, *'We are looking for Von Spee: when we find him we shall go to the bottom!'* thus fulfilling John's prophecy regarding the emptiness of boasts regarding the Navy's invincibility. After that came news of Walt Pascoe's death in Gallipoli but although Paul regretted Walt, whom he had liked, he did not waste much time on his widow, one of the few local women who seemed to be enjoying the war. After that, in May, 1915, came news that Tom Williams and his nephew had been torpedoed and of the near-riot that occurred in the churchyard when Tom was seen to put flowers on the grave of the German seamen buried there. Then a letter came from the old German Professor, who wrote from America to say that his only son, whisked into the Kaiser's Army whilst on holiday, had been killed in Champagne. It was foolish, perhaps, to mourn the death of an enemy yet Paul did regret a boy whom he had always regarded as a charming, friendly lad with a splendid physique and courtly manners. He did not and could not see Gottfried Scholtzer as a ravisher of Belgian women and bayoneter of infants notwithstanding the report that the Germans had just used poison gas at Ypres. For all that reports of the use of poison gas as a weapon of war between civilised nations helped to set Paul thinking along new lines, for it began to seem to him that unless the war was won, and that within a reasonable period, civilisation would go to the devil and, what was more to the point, all prospects of the Valley resuming its pre-war rhythm would disappear for his lifetime. In this context he said to Rudd, 'You can count me in from now, John! It might be the craziest thing that's ever been allowed to happen but it has happened and as I see it we've no choice but to win,' and old John, sucking his pipe, had replied, 'The longer it goes on the less chance there is of a negotiated peace. For my part I don't think it's possible; everybody's blood is up and it won't cool until all European males between eighteen and forty are dead, or home with a limb missing! There's another thing, too. Win or lose don't deceive yourself into thinking it can ever be the same again, here or anywhere else! All the wrong people are getting killed and all the flag-flappers are making money. Thank God I've had most of my life. Chaps your age will have to adjust themselves to something very different when the bloody thing does run itself into the ground!' In a year or so there were many who subscribed to this theory but in the early summer of 1915 John Rudd's views were regarded as eccentric and even his wife Maureen derided them.

And so the barricade began to tumble but there was no major collapse of Paul's defences until the Will Codsall episode. Once again it was a Codsall who supplied an unpleasant jolt to the Valley.

Will came home on leave in April and everyone was shocked at his appearance. He had left the previous August a thick-set, bumbling, broad-shouldered man, with a mild, friendly and slightly bucolic approach to all. He returned a shambling scarecrow, with a vague, shifty expression behind his eyes and a jumpiness that made his callers nervous when he handled his rifle and shot rats in the yard. Few could forget that Will's father had died raving mad and to those who remembered Martin there seemed a disturbing resemblance between Will and the man who had taken to staring out to

sea and had one day gone home to murder his wife. Will
mooched about, answering questions of 'What was it like?'
vaguely and unsatisfactorily, beginning sentences and leaving
them unfinished but everybody made allowances for the fact
that he had gone through a bad time after being rushed into the
line in October and seeing most of his Paxtonbury cronies
blown to pieces. They cheered up when Will, fortified by a few
pints of ale, worked himself up into a ferocious mood at The
Raven and described in detail, and with seeming relish, how he
had brained Germans with spades and shot them down at close
range when they advanced in close formation outside Ypres.
Then, on the night before he was due to return, Paul was summoned from his office to find a tense Elinor Codsall awaiting
him in the hall and Elinor, who seldom wasted words, went
straight to the point regarding her fears for Will's sanity.

"Er's goin' just like 'is old man!' she declared, 'and I've 'ad a
rare old do with him, I c'n tell 'ee, Squire! Tiz no good carrying
on about 'ow 'ee got 'isself into this ole pickle be joinin' they
Territorials backalong. The fact is he'll do someone a mischief
if us don't tell they Army people there's alwus bin daftness
in the Codsall family! He's talking about staying on yer and
hiding hisself, same as Smut Potter did time he crowned
Gilroy's keeper! Says he's done his bit 'an won't taake no
more part in it and if I hadn't got un half-slewed with cider
he'd ha' been gone by now an' us would have had the police
over yer to march un off to prison!'

Paul accompanied her back to Periwinkle where he found a
half-stupefied Will in the kitchen. Will had drained a gallon jar
of home-brewed cider but he was not uplifted by it. Although
he could hardly stand he was sour and intractable, declaring
with idiotic persistence that he had no intention of returning
to the colours but would 'lie up somewheres 'till tiz all over!'
Paul tried to reason with him but in the end he had to fetch
Doctor Maureen, who suggested getting Will's leave extended.
She made out a certificate to the effect that he was suffering
from chest trouble and got it countersigned by the camp
doctor, who was under an obligation to her for helping him
free of charge during an epidemic during the winter. The

Army doctor then examined Will and contacted his base at
Paxtonbury with the result that Will was put to bed and
remained there for a fortnight, after which he was, so the
camp doctor assured them, regraded for duty at the base and
was unlikely to be sent back to France for some months. The
night before Will left home for the second time he called on
Paul and at first seemed almost himself again but Paul was
disturbed by his declaration, made on leaving, that he had
seen his father on the battlefield. Under careful questioning
he admitted that it was only Martin's ghost he had seen and
Paul put this down to some form of hallucination brought on
by shock and exhaustion and was relieved to learn that Will
could now anticipate a few weeks' rest at base. Neither he,
nor Will, nor the camp doctor were aware at that time of the
tenuousness of the Ypres defences, after the counter-attack
that had followed the German use of gas. Will reported to
base on Saturday night; thirty-six hours later he was back
at Le Havre and a month later the second of the dreaded buff
telegrams arrived in the Valley. Will Codsall, the first man in
the Valley to go to war, had been killed in action.

The Valley mourned him as a hero and Elinor mourned
him as a grotesque sacrifice to local big-mouths like Horace
Handcock, the Valley's unofficial recruiting agent; they were
all wrong, for Will was neither Hero nor Sacrifice. He had
been executed as an Example!

The trial occupied far less time than the Whinmouth inquest
on Will's father and mother all those years ago. A row
of granite-faced senior officers heard another officer and
several witnesses describe how, during a local attack ten
days previously, one of a party of bombers who captured
a section of German trench threw aside his rifle, ran back
across no-man's-land, scrambled into and out of the British
trench and went on running until he was arrested by a
couple of Red Caps well beyond the supports. On the way
he felled two men who tried to stop him and one was
now a casualty with a broken jaw.

The sentence was death. It could hardly be anything else
for a man who had thrown away his arms in action, and Will,

asked if he had any comment, uttered four short words. To his judges they amounted to a confession for he said, in a low voice, 'They was right there!' The President of the Court, who had won a VC on the North-West Frontier, winced at hearing such a craven admission, particularly as there had been no Germans in the trenches when Will fled except, of course, any number of dead ones. How was Will to explain that it was the dead who had caused him to fly; not the German dead but two dead civilians, sitting side by side on the firestep of the captured trench and both shouting at him, which was very odd for Martin, his father, had a rope round his neck and Arabella, his mother, was headless.

It is doubtful whether Will understood his sentence or the plea of mitigation made by his defending officer. He felt more secure inside the buttery, which did service as a condemned cell, than he had felt for a long time. The door was barred and there was a sentry outside so that neither Martin nor Arabella could approach him. When they marched him out, blindfolded him and stood him against the wall he may have thought they were playing some kind of game for in the few moments before the volley he discovered that he could see through the bandage and was not much surprised to see Elinor climb the broken farmhouse wall, swinging a pail full of eggs and calling in her shrill voice to laggard hens. It was early but the sun was warm and beat on his face and neck and he wondered, although not urgently, what she could be doing there in a foreign farmyard, and how she came to look so slim and young, not the least as she had looked when he parted from her a month or so ago, with a tense, pinched face and a thickening figure but as she had looked when he used to slip across the Deepdene to do his courting. Then the sun must have burst for pieces of it exploded all around him and he knew he was in the line again and under bombardment and called to Elinor to look what she was about for shells could kill civilians as well as soldiers.

The provost, biting hard his stringy moustache, looked down at the body and said, under his breath, 'Poor sod! Any road you're out of it, chum!' and then barked at the firing-party who filed away, one of them reeling like a drunkard.

That same day in the House of Commons the Foreign
Secretary was asked how many executions for cowardice
there had been in France during the last ten months. He
replied that, according to his information, none at all. His
information must have been out-of-date. There had been four
that month in Will's division alone and there were many
divisions within a hundred miles of the place where Will was
shot. Perhaps it was to keep the record straight that they sent
a telegram saying Private Codsall had been killed in action.

A month or so later the Valley learned that Jem Pollock was
dead but this time the telegram was followed by a letter giving
circumstantial detail. The letter, written by Jem's company
commander, was addressed to 'next-of-kin' but as nobody in
the Valley knew Jem's next-of-kin it found its way to Paul.

It told a graphic story. Apparently Jem had been attached
to the Engineers for the purpose of tunnelling under the
German lines near Cuinchy, where the two systems of front-
line trenches sometimes came within forty yards of one
another. Rumours of his enormous strength had reached
REs responsible for the shaft and for more than a month
Jem shovelled away in safety while, overhead, men were killed
at the rate of about one every five minutes, for the Germans
had gauged the mortar range to the nearest yard. Then it was
discovered that the Germans were tunelling directly opposite.
When Jem laid aside his spade he could distinctly hear the
chink of tools and sometimes a man coughing. The officer
came along and listened with him and then left to telephone
HQ for instructions but while he was gone the sounds from
the German tunnel ceased and the sergeant left in charge
ordered work to recommence. It was an unwise decision,
for the German shaft must have progressed far beyond the
British and they exploded their mine soon after dawn, a day
before the British were scheduled to explode theirs and Jem,
just going on shift, was about twenty yards down the tunnel
when it went up. All the men in front of him were buried
alive but the entrance of the British tunnel had been riveted
with steel rails and held for a matter of about fifty seconds,
before slowly subsiding like a gently squashed matchbox.

It would not have remained open that long had not Jem instinctively reached up and braced himself against a key crossbar, an act that enabled the five men behind him to run back into the trench and crouch under the crumbling firestep. One of them reported what had happened and Jem's name was sent in for the Military Medal which he did not get because none of the witnesses had been officers. He was, however, toasted that night by the survivors, who thought of his death as almost biblical so that, in a sense, the Goliath of Bideford was transposed into Samson of Cuinchy who died supporting the pillars of a crumbling temple. The men who drank to him that night knew little or nothing of Jem's past so that they could not be expected to appreciate the roundness of Jem's end. All his life he had both paraded and used his strength for the benefit of others. In the jobs he held before joining the travelling fair his muscles had been at the disposal of North Devon craftsmen and in the fair ground he had drawn crowds and more than paid his way. Later, when he forsook the gypsy life and settled in the Dell, his strength had been at the disposal of the Potter girls and he had spent it freely, in the fields by day and in their beds at night, so that the Dell was rescued not only from weeds but from the threat of dwindling population. Then, when he went to France, he used his strength unsparingly on behalf of the Pioneers and there was still enough left over to save the lives of five of his comrades.

Paul, musing over the officer's letter, hoped Jem would get the medal and rode over to the Dell to pass the story on to Cissie and Violet whom he found pregnant and rather depressed. As Violet put it, 'He were a gurt handful was Jem, and us'll never see the like of him again, Squire!' He took the letter away with him and it was pasted into the back of the estate diary by Claire. She must, Paul thought as he watched her, have travelled a long road since the day she had railed against Ikey's marriage to a Potter, for when he told her that Violet had borne Jem a strapping boy, now aged six, she said, 'I'll fix the letter by the corners so that when he's old enough I'll be able to take it out and give it to him.'

He was touched by the thought and kissed her neck as she busied herself pasting the letter into the record. 'Claire Derwent,' he said (for he could rarely think of her by any other name), 'that flare-up we had over Ikey and Lane-Phelps did us a power of good! It cleared the air, like a heavy thunderstorm. I love you, woman, more than I ever did!'

'Prove it,' she said without turning aside from her task but he laughed and said, 'Not me, I've got to ride over to Hermitage. There's a problem blowing up over there, a very tiresome one!'

'Oh?' she said, 'and what's that?'

'I'll tell you about it in bed tonight,' he said and when she replied, laughing, that knowing him and seeing that spring was in the air she doubted this very much it struck him that since the crisis they had become lovers again and that she could cheer him up with a glance. He rode off reflecting, 'I'll soon settle this nonsense of Henry Pitts! He must be older than me and Hermitage can't manage without him! Damn it, if it comes to the worst, I'll write to the Agricultural Committee and get him starred for the duration!'

II

Paul's attempts to nail Henry Pitts to his farm for the duration proved unavailing. By early September, when everyone in the Valley was working sixteen hours a day getting in the harvest, Henry was plodding up and down a dusty parade ground near Oswestry, with a dummy rifle over his shoulder. By the time the British Army in the field had made good its losses at Loos he was in France.

Henry's urge to enlist was the outcome of his mid-morning visits to his piggeries, on the north-east corner of his holding. From here, high up on the shoulder of Hermitage Wood, he could look directly down into the basin of the camp parade ground where columns marched and wheeled all day and the hoarse shouts of NCOs reached him like the distant wail of gulls. Henry was fascinated by the patterned precision of their movements, which seemed to be animated by clockwork. He liked best to see a company respond to the command, 'At the halt, by the left, form close company of pla-*toon*!' and see the long, snaking column waver, break up, unfold like a spreading fan, reform and come to a tidy halt in front of the saluting base. As a child he had always liked playing with lead soldiers, forming them into assault columns and giving the closest attention to their dressing but here, before his eyes, was a game of soldiers come to life and played on a huge scale. The crispness and precision of their movements was a kind of poetry to him and he revelled in it, day after day, week after week, until it seemed to him that he could never be happy until he identified himself with those khaki-clad automatons, responding smoothly and ecstatically to the bark of their drill-masters. The precise beauty of drill banished all other aspects of soldiering from his simple mind. He did not ponder the possibility of wounds, or death, or discomfort in the trenches, or even prolonged separation from his land and his great tawny wife and plump, tawny children. All he could think of was the synchronisation of arms and legs *en masse* and at last he knew that, no matter what it might cost him, he must absorb himself in it at once.

He expected opposition from his wife, Gloria, and from his father, Arthur, but although there was an awed hush when he announced his intention to join up no one attempted to dissuade him except Squire Craddock, who was furious. His wife Gloria, the red-haired grenadier of a woman who had forsaken the Heronslea estate to marry him, openly applauded his decision. After Horace Handcock, Gloria Pitts was the most indefatigable patriot in the Valley and thought of any male out of uniform, if he was neither child nor dotard, as a poltroon. Gloria was the first woman in the Valley to engage in the popular pastime of distributing white feathers to civilians and actually slashed one of Martha Pitts' best down cushions for ammunition. She said, delightedly, 'Youm reely *goin'* Henry? Youm actually takin' a *smack* at that bliddy Kaiser? Well then, good luck to 'ee boy! And when you comes back on leave in kharki I'll show 'ee off all round the neighbourhood, you zee if I don't!'

Martha's reactions were more restrained. She pointed out that Henry was thirty-six and that they would probably keep him at home, guarding bridges and viaducts, but old Grandpa Pitts, who could recall watching redcoats embark at Plymouth for the Crimea, chose to regard this as an insult on the family and said that Henry would almost certainly return with a Victoria Cross pinned to his breast and a personal letter of thanks from Lord Roberts. They had told him several times that Bobs was dead but he chose not to believe it. Without both Bobs and Kitchener he could not believe in the inevitability of victory.

Paul argued that food-growing was just as important as killing Germans and that Henry, as a professional farmer, would almost certainly be rejected by the authorities. Henry countered by saying that his eldest boy was already big enough to take his place and Gloria, outraged by the Squire's attempt to snatch the halo of patriotism from the Hermitage, said she would never hold up her head if theirs was the only farm in the Valley that failed to contribute a man to the forces of the Crown. Seeing how determined they all were Paul withdrew his opposition and because of his personal regard for Henry did not write the threatened letter to the local committee with the result that Henry, fearing rejection in Paxtonbury, travelled to Bristol and enlisted in the Gloucestershire Regiment. Within a matter of hours, he was being taught the simplest of those great sweeping movements he had witnessed from his vantage point beside the piggeries.

His only grouse during his training period was that it was a long time before they issued him with a real rifle and until they did, until he could smack his huge, horny hand against a real gunstock, it seemed to him that he was only playing at soldiers. In due course, however, he got his arms and equipment and came home on embarkation leave about Christmas-time, when the Valley was under a light mantle of snow and everything looked lifeless and forlorn.

Everything, that is, except his wife, Gloria, who shrieked
with excitement when he marched into the yard, the living
justification for an entire handful of white feathers for now
she could say, as she distributed them, 'Get on an' join, boy!
My Henry's rising forty and he's out there, so what be you
doin' in corduroys?' Her delight in him was such that, had
Henry been given more than a short leave it is doubtful
whether he would have had the stamina to hump his fifty-
six-pound pack into Paxtonbury on the morning of departure.
Their relationship up to then had been cordial but humdrum,
for man and wife habitually worked a thirteen-hour day and
Gloria, with three children, had more than once declared
that she had no intention of cluttering herself with more.
Now, however, she had the immense privilege of actually
sharing a bed with a real live soldier, a man trained and
eager to slaughter Huns and she was determined to do her
part by sending him off to war fortified against a period
of celibacy. She had never heard of the Roman custom of
introducing harlots into gladiators' quarters on the night
before the Games in order to give them memories worth
fighting for but it was in precisely this spirit that she refused
to let Henry rise at the customary hour of six-thirty and
perform his usual duties about the farm. She clasped him
to her capacious bosom and enfolded him with her great,
muscled limbs, so that it was sometimes past nine o'clock
when they came down to breakfast and Henry began to
wonder if life in the trenches could demand more of a man.
He went off on Boxing Day with something like relief but
all the way to Paxtonbury he chuckled reminiscently over
his experiences of the last few days. 'Gordamme,' he said
to himself, shifting the weight of his pack as he braced
himself for the stiff climb to the crest of Blackberry Moor,
'I never knowed 'er had it in 'er, for 'er was always inclined
to ration a man after our first tacker showed up!' Then, as
he swung into the rhythm of a step that was brisk and
satisfying after the countryman's peace-time plod, he began
to whistle, 'Plum and Apple' and 'Do Like a Nice Mince
Pie', alien songs to a Valley man and learned during his

training period. Probably no man ever went to war in better
heart.

III

Pansy Pascoe, widowed nine months ago, expected Dandy
Timberlake to pay a courtesy call when he was invalided
home from Egypt that Christmas, but was surprised to see
him climbing up the steep, stony track to the Dell within an
hour of his return to the Valley.

Pansy was as good-natured and affectionate as any other
Potter but, like her sisters Cissie and Violet, she had always
found difficulty in throwing down roots strong enough to
bind her to any one male and although she was saddened
by Walt's death she did not mourn him long. As the months
passed she was able to bracket him in her mind with all the
other men of the Valley, including Dandy and his brothers,
and was therefore delighted to see the tall, stooping figure
amble into the yard pause, regarding the scene with distaste,
for it was washing-day and the Potter farmyard looked more
like a nomadic encampment than ever, an untidy crisscross
of lines supporting innumerable flapping garments and an
air of jerky, unplanned industry pervading the outbuildings
and washtubs.

Pansy abandoned her tub and ran to greet him, a big, beaming, blowzy woman, radiating a vitality that, for a moment,
affronted a man who had spent six months in a hospital
cot. She said: 'Why, Dandy, youm fair blown be the climb!
Come inside an' us'll brew some tay!' but Dandy refused the
invitation with a gesture, saying he preferred to sit in the open
where they could talk privately, and then, glancing round the
Dell once again, realised that he had forgotten the fecundity
of the Potters and exclaimed, 'Tiz like a bliddy fairground
yer! How many tackers be there for God's sake?'

'Oh, I dunno,' she said carelessly, 'getting on fer a dozen I
suppose but dornee mind 'em boy, nor the soldiers neither!
I'll get my li'l Liz to carry on with the wash,' and raising

her voice she bellowed to her eldest daughter, a dark girl of about eleven, telling her to attend to the tub while her mother took a breather.

The girl detached herself from a swarm of children round the waisthigh nettles and Dandy, watching them, said tolerantly, 'How many o' that lot be your, midear?'

She told him four and pointed them out, a boy favouring his father, two girls favouring her, and a toddler with straw-coloured hair who was staggering up and down with a huge marmalade cat that seemed not to mind being hooked under its belly and dragged about with its paws clear of the ground. It was the toddler who interested Dandy and he scrutinised the child carefully, noting his slightly buck teeth and narrow head topping a thick neck and solid little body. 'That little 'un,' he said, thoughtfully, 'what's un called, Panse?'

She knew, or thought she knew, why he asked and her generous mouth split in a grin, 'Albert,' she said, 'but I alwus thinks of 'un as "Dandy"! What's eatin' 'ee? Be 'ee thinking I was comin' down on 'ee for a maintenance order?' and when he was silent she pressed him, adding, 'Well? Do 'ee own to the boy? Do 'ee mind the night I come by him, you ole rascal?'

Her sophistry shocked him and he blushed under his tan. 'Did Walt ever guess?'

'Giddon no!' she said impatiently, 'for Albert were only a tot when you went off and bevore that, down at that cottage, us was treading on one another, so I don't reckon he ever got a close look at him! You baint *worryin'* about it, be you? Not after all this time?'

Dandy cleared his throat. It was embarrassing to confess to worrying over such a triviality to a Potter girl but he went on, desperately, 'Yes I be! I got to thinkin' on it many a time when Walt and me was out there together and that's why I made up my mind to speak, zoon as I set foot in the Valley! Fact is, me and the Army have parted company, Panse, and I'll be back at me old trade soon as I'm fit to do a day's work. There's no help for that anyways, for Pa and Ma are moving out come New Year, on account o' Pa's arthritis and theym goin' to live in one o' they new jerry-builts, at Nun's Bay.

With them gone, and the other boys away, Sawmill Cottage'll be empty and if I quit Squire will have to move a new sawyer in seein' house-room's mighty short about here.' He paused and cleared his throat again, irritated by the bewilderment on her broad, freckled face. 'Fact is,' he went on, with a rush, 'I got to thinkin' maybe you'd turn your back o' this knacker's yard and live decent again! There's room enough for all of us at Sawpits. The boys and the maids can share the two back bedrooms and we'll have the front! What do 'ee say, Panse? Dornee reckon Walt would sonner you took up with me than one o' those bliddy forriners? And baint there a good enough reason for it, seein' us've already made a start with a family of our own?'

She had been amazed and then amused by his stumbling earnestness when he began, astounded by his apparent willingness to accept responsibility for four children when only one of them was his but then, as he ploughed on, she was touched very deeply, not so much by his troubled conscience but by his eagerness to salvage something out of their past. It was as though he was offering her not marriage exactly, and certainly not what passed for respectability in the Valley, but something much more than that and of infinitely greater value, for here was a fruity slice of her half-forgotten youth being restored to her by someone who had once contributed to its gaiety. Then she reminded herself of the more practical issues, a father for her children and regular money coming in from his work and part disability pension but these things did not seem important. What impressed her was the tremendous compliment he was paying her and for the first time since she was a twelve-year-old, smarting under one of Ole Tamer's casual clouts, her eyes filled with tears and she was so disconcerted by them that for several moments she was incapable of speech.

He waited, having the kindness to avoid looking at her and presently, collecting herself, she gave expression to the warmth she felt for him by reaching out and letting her plump hand slide from his shoulder to his knee. It was the gesture that had won her Walt Pascoe all those years ago, when they stood together watching Coronation fireworks, and it

must have communicated itself just as surely to Dandy for
he suddenly grabbed her and kissed her so enthusiastically
that she was transported back to the time when she was a
neat-waisted girl of seventeen skylarking in the hayfields.
She said, with a slight quaver, 'You . . . you baint makin'
game o' me, Dandy? You baint, be you?' and he denied
hotly that he was, declaring that he would prove as much
by making arrangements with the rector this very day but
that in the meantime she was to restore Walt's wedding ring
to her finger – 'So as none o' they bliddy forriners get to
trespassing zoon as me back's turned!'

He left her then and she watched, with compassion, his
halting progress down the track before running to give Cissie
and Violet the news. She was not much given to vanity but
she could not help feeling elated by the thought that, whereas
the three of them had shared many men, she alone had received
not one proposal but two. It seemed to her, thirty-three and
with four children, confirmation that she was the flower of
the flock.

The big hearth at Sawpits Cottage had no time to cool. The
older Timberlakes moved out on New Year's Day and Dandy
and his bride, trailing their ready-made family, moved in that
same afternoon so that for the first time in close on twenty
years the whine of the Home Farm saw was challenged by
the tumult of children. Pansy, reconciled by the solid comfort
of the place to the loss of her regained independence, was in
high spirits, having drunk a pint of her mother's hedgerow
wine at the impromptu wedding breakfast in the Dell but
Dandy, exhausted by the excitements of the day, admitted
frankly that he felt unequal to the statutory exertions of a
bridegroom. 'Well,' she said, genially, 'we'm neither of us
chickens be us and there baint no particular hurry, seein'
youm back for good midear! Why dornee go up along an' rest
while I put the tackers to baid and make supper? I'll call 'ee
when I'm ready and tidden as if you dorn know what youm
be gettin' be it?' He took her advice and climbed the stairs,
thinking wryly on the days when he had bounded up them
three at a time and was soon so heavily asleep that when

she called there was no response so she went up to find him,
sprawled fully-clothed on the bed in his new blue serge suit,
its crumpled flower still pinned in the buttonhole. She thought,
smiling, 'He's aged, the poor toad! They must serve 'em cruel
in that bliddy war! I'll let un bide and take supper alone!' and
then she giggled, reflecting on the unlikeliness of her wedding
night, with four of her children under the same roof and the
groom sound asleep and still dressed in his Sunday suit. She
went out quietly and ate her supper in front of the fire, thinking
not only of Dandy, whose snores she could hear through the
oak floor, but also of Walt and Smut, and Henry Pitts and
poor old Will Codsall and young Gilbert Eveleigh, and all the
other Valley boys dead or scattered or just tired out like Dandy
upstairs and for the first time, not excluding the moment when
the buff telegram had been delivered to her, she thought of the
disruption of their lives as something sad and disturbing.

IV

Nun's Bay village was a small island of freehold land sandwiched between the coastal borders of the Heronslea and
Shallowford estates, a tiny community that had been no
more than a hamlet up to the time old Farmer Blair had
died childless, a year or so before the war. The Blairs had
freedholded here for generations but when the last of them
died the farm went up for sale. Local landowners had made
a bid for it but it eluded both Gilroy and Paul, passing into
the hands of a local firm that practised under the enigmatic
title of *The Whinmouth Development Company (Bricks and
Tiles) Ltd* whose boards had been mushrooming in the district
ever since Coronation year. The chairman of this shadowy
company was supposed to be old Widgery of Whinmouth,
but nobody believed this for Widgery was in his eighties
and his neighbours thought it unlikely that he would launch
out into land development after a lifetime as a dairyman.
Whinmouth folk said that Widgery, who owned a few houses
in the Whinmouth harbour area, was the front for a group of

men that included two or three Urban District Councillors who
did not want their association with local building publicised
but although these pundits were groping in the right direction they were wide of the mark. The secretary, and major
shareholder in the Whinmouth Development Company, was
a young man who was too knowing to waste time and
money fighting local elections or concerning himself with
other people's drains and water supply.

Sydney Codsall, as a qualified solicitor, had left Whinmouth
two years before the war and was now junior partner in an
older firm of country solicitors, with offices in Cathedral Yard,
Paxtonbury. Sydney had enlarged himself a great deal since
the days when he had courted Rachel Eveleigh in the hope
of getting a slice of freehold land for a wedding present. At
twenty-one he had come into the money left by his father and
mother. Ordinarily he would have only inherited half but in
the event every penny of it came his way, partly because
of Will's careless nature but more on account of Elinor's
independent spirit. Having abominated Arabella when she
was living she had no wish to profit by her death. Sydney
had an eye for a bargain and used the money wisely, chiefly
in the purchase of odd parcels of land. His years at a solicitor's
desk had taught him, among other things, that the only really
permanent form of wealth was land, and after land, bricks
and mortar, preferably unmellowed bricks and mortar. Having
ready access to advance information, and also the cash to
tempt impatient beneficiaries, he soon acquired an oddly
assorted patchwork of strips and corners in and around
Whinmouth and formed a loose kind of partnership with a
local builder called Tapscott, whom he tamed by taking out
mortgages when the builder's going was rough during spells
of bad weather. By the spring of 1914 he was in a fair way of
business and having temporarily exhausted the Whinmouth
vein, where Tapscott had a bad reputation, the partners ranged
further along the coast in search of promising sites. At Coombe
Bay they were blocked by the Shallowford estate, whereas
inland most of the property was in Gilroy's hands but the
death of old Blair, who owned over a hundred acres at the

mouth of Nun's Bay goyle, proved a godsend, for Blair's heir
was farming in South Africa and wanted a quick sale. The
farm was purchased and building began almost at once.

The war, however, caught Sydney off balance and after the
completion of a mere half-dozen of the twenty-four bungalows
planned, the scheme looked like petering out and might
have done if Sydney had not taken out insurance by cultivating the Paxtonbury Borough Surveyor who put him
in touch with the Government department responsible for
siting training camps in the west. The temporary camp on
the moor had never been very satisfactory. It was badly
exposed, south-westerly gales made havoc of tents and its
water supply was poor, so that Sydney was able to lease
his Nun's Bay site for the duration and secure Tapscott a
meaty contract for erecting a permanent hutted camp on
farmland overlooking the sea. There were several rewarding
by-products to this development, the most important being
the securing of Sydney's enrolment as a permanent member
of the Camp Siting Commission, and its off-shoot, a committee
concerned with the acquisition of local timber for Government
needs. Sydney could scent an Act of Parliament as a fox scents
the taint of man. He reasoned that, if the Army was so short
of manpower as to rush a clodhopper like his brother Will
into the front line, it would not be long before the supply of
patriots was exhausted and Lord Kitchener began prodding
the hesitant. Friends told him that England would never stand
for conscription but he did not believe them and was soon
proved right. Within weeks of his attachment to the camp-
siting and timber commissions the newspaper announced the
Derby Act, under which all single men below the age limit
were ordered to attest pending enrolment in the forces and
Sydney hastened to take out further insurance by getting
himself a wife. He also bought the services of a co-operative
doctor, who addressed himself to the task of discovering
minor ailments afflicting Sydney's person, ailments that had
been quiescent since childhood.

By this time Sydney had come to terms with the war.
The establisment of Nun's Bay camp enabled him to exploit

his somewhat panicky marriage to the only daughter of a Paxtonbury provision merchant and he persuaded his father-in-law to adventure into the field of confectionery and toys on premises adjoining the camp, where five thousand potential customers were wired in and ten miles from the nearest competitor. The village shop prospered under the personal supervision of Sydney's wife Dora, who was not as winsome as some girls Sydney had contemplated marrying during his apprenticeship days but had the advantage of a good head for business and a father with a cellar full of sugar bought at pre-war rates.

So much progress in such a short time would have turned the heads of some young men and would have mellowed others. Sydney not only kept his head but remained loyal to his original dream, a resolve to establish a new balance of power in the area surrounding the twin valleys of Teazel and Sorrel. He could have told you most things about his ambitions as a whole but would have found it difficult to describe this secret driving force, which was really no more than a resolve to arrive at level pegs with Paul Craddock, of Shallowford House. He could not have said why he resented the man, or why everything he did in the way of increasing his substance was an attempt to wriggle beyond the reach of Squire Craddock's patronage. It might have had something to do with Paul's championship of his brother Will's marriage to an ignorant farm girl, or the fact that Paul had been the first to look upon his butchered mother the night of the double tragedy, or something much more complex, a deeply buried resentment linking Paul in some way with all that had occurred at Four Winds that night, or a combination of all these factors that had made him a pensioner in the home of his father's foreman, Eveleigh, to suffer years of drenching pity from the uncouth children of Eveleigh and his wife. He had never explored his motives in depth, preferring to lump them together under the general title of *Getting On* or *Getting Ahead*, or *Being Someone*! And now, as the war entered it second year, he was someone, as was evident when he paid a call on the Squire in his capacity as a

Government forestry official and was sufficiently sure of himself to attempt reversing their roles.

Paul had already had one brush with the Commission when they had tried to make him include hard timber in the existing contract to supply pine-lengths for pitprops, so that it came as a wild surprise to him when he opened a letter bearing the official note-heading, informing him that a Mr Sydney Codsall would be calling on him by appointment on behalf of the department. Paul had always felt rather sorry for Sydney, whose spirit, he felt, must have been scarred his his terrible experience in 1904, when he had so narrowly escaped sharing his mother's fate. He had seen him often enough while he was growing up in the Eveleigh household but had lost track of him until their encounter on the land adjoining the Coombe Bay brickfield but Paul had almost forgotten that by now and decided that it was rather fortunate that the new local agent was under some kind of obligation to him, and not a foreigner eager to despoil the countryside of trees that had been growing before the German Kaiser's grandfather had pulled on his first jackboot. He was slightly amused by Sydney's pomposity when the young man was shown into the office but remembered that young Codsall had always been a pompous boy, utterly unlike his amiable brother, Will. He shook hands, offered Sydney a whisky and remarked jocularly that he had put on weight and seemed to be having a tolerable war. Sydney was disconcerted by this breezy reception and a little irritated by Paul's inclination to treat him as though he was wearing his first pair of long trousers. He said, in the slightly lisping accent he had cultivated since taking his articles, 'Time rattles on, Mr Craddock! Perhaps you have forgotten that I'm older than you were when you bought Shallowford from the Lovells!'

He hoped that this would put Squire in his place but all it did was to make Paul chuckle. 'By God, you're right, Sydney!' he exclaimed and then, looking at him carefully, 'You seem to have made good use of the time. Is this Government job full-time or a voluntary effort?'

Sydney considered this question so naïve that he disdained

to answer. He said, removing his rimless glasses with a deliberate air, 'I think I can put you in the way of doing yourself a bit of good, Craddock.'

Paul did not miss Sydney's self-conscious dropping of the word 'Mr'. He said, sharply, 'How do you mean, "good"? In respect of what?'

'Timbah,' Sydney said, smirking openly now, 'Timbah and Pocket!'

Paul suddenly decided that he not only disliked but distrusted Sydney Codsall, that he had always disliked and distrusted him, from the day he had paid his first call at Four Winds and seen the boy standing beside his insufferable mother. His first instinct was to pull him up short, re-establishing the relationship that had existed between them since Ikey brought him back to the big house but his curiosity was aroused by the young man's fatuity. He said, 'Why don't you say exactly what you have in mind?'

Sydney must have been completely deceived for he at once became conspiratorial, 'You're selling you pitprops well below par,' he said, 'I could get you another fifty shillings a load! Providing, of course, we came to an arrangement.'

'You mean other local suppliers are getting more?'

'There's no standard price, the Government have to have pitprops by the million so long as trench fighting lasts and a smart supplier can get what he asks, providing he stands firm and . . . er . . . providing he has contacts our side of the fence! It's the same with everything isn't it and after all, the Government don't have to make another profit do they?'

'No,' Paul said slowly, 'I suppose not but this . . . er . . ."arrangement" you mention; do I assume it would be between you and I?'

'Naturally,' Sydney said, not surprised by the Squire's ingenuousness. 'I should be satisfied with twenty-five per cent of the increase. It would be worth that much to you, wouldn't it?'

Something in Paul's expression must have warned him, for suddenly he faltered and made a play of replacing his glasses. Paul stood up, looking directly down at him, and finding it very

difficult indeed to check an impulse to knock him backwards
over the chair. The desire to do just this sprang not so much
from the amateurishness of Sydney's technique as from the
recollection of Will Codsall's tormented eyes shortly before
he returned to the Front to be killed and with this recollection
came others, equally unpleasant, as though, instead of looking
down on Sydney Codsall's neatly-parted hair he was staring
into a pool where scum gathered in poisonous-looking bubbles
which were bursting softly in his face. All kinds of bubbles
– the brutishness of the Coombe Bay mob howling under the
Professor's window, the stricken look on Marian Eveleigh's
face when he had called to console her on the death of her
boy Gilbert and the satisfied smirk, not unlike Sydney's, on
the face of Lieutenant Lane-Phelps who had done his best to
seduce Claire. He said, breathing heavily, 'There's only one
thing that stops me telephoning Paxtonbury Town Hall and
reporting every word of this conversation, Sydney! Do you
know what this is?' but Sydney, flushing now, jumped up so
quickly that he smashed his glass, making a gobbling sound as
Paul went on, 'The thing that holds me back is that everybody
associates you with poor old Will and Elinor, so for Christ's
sake get out of here before I kick you out and don't ever come
back on any pretext whatever!' and he passed behind Sydney,
flinging open the terrace door and glancing towards the porch
where a sallow man sat waiting in a trap outside the main door.
His movement gave Sydney a moment to recover a little of his
bluster. He said, shrilly, 'Look here, you can't play the God
Almighty Squire with me any longer! Things have changed
and they'll change a lot more before it's over! I could have
been a good friend . . .' but Paul made a vicious sweep with
his hand and Sydney dodged round him and leaped on to the
terrace as Paul shouted, 'If that's your trap get into it! I can't
think why you didn't arrive on a snake!' and then, as the last
of his self-control left him, 'Get out, blast you! Get out before
I kick your arse all the way back to Paxtonbury!' and at this
Sydney ran along the terrace, shouted something to the driver
and scrambled on to the box. A moment later the vehicle had
passed behind the screen of chestnuts, leaving Paul standing

with fists clenched and head thrust forward and that was how Claire found him when she came on to the terrace saying, 'I heard shouting! Who was it, Paul?'

He swung round aggressively, almost as though he expected to find Sydney had eluded him and returned to the attack and she saw at once that he was in one of his rare, white-hot tempers. 'Who *was* it, Paul? Who were those men?'

'I don't know who one of them was,' he growled, 'but the one I was talking to was a bloody sewer rat, the kind that seem to be proliferating about here!' and he stalked past her into the bedroom, pouring himself a whisky and tossing it back in a gulp.

She followed him not asking other questions but not leaving the room for she sensed that he would need her in a moment or two. When the spirit had steadied him somewhat he told her what had happened, cursing the social infection that was poisoning the Valley and declaring that the only place for an honest man now was alongside chaps like Henry Pitts and Smut Potter. She heard him out. She was growing accustomed to these outbursts, although they were seldom so violent and usually tailed off into a rumbling monologue that had as its theme the avalanche of change that had swept over the Valley in a little over a year.

'There are more Henrys and Smuts than there are Sydneys,' she reminded him. 'It's important not to lose one's perspective.'

'You're about the only one who hasn't, Claire,' he said but smiled grudgingly, adding. 'I was a damned fool to myself anyway! I don't want his filthy bribe but if I'd handled him more tactfully he might have saved our timber! Now he'll go out of his way to hit back any way he can.'

'I doubt it,' said Claire, 'he'll be far too scared you'll inform on him.'

'Not him! There weren't any witnesses. He'd deny it and say I was slandering him out of pique!'

'Oh, I wouldn't be too sure of that,' she said lightly. 'I was a witness, wasn't I? And in a cause like that I'd swear to it in Court if necessary! So would Horace Handcock because his patriotic principles would be outraged. One way and another we could sew Sydney into a sack and drop him in the river!'

Suddenly and irrationally he felt immensely grateful for her, for her balance and strength and her great granary of commonsense that made his own impulsive protests sound like the bleat of a child. He crossed to where she stood by the terrace door, pulled her towards him and kissed her on the mouth.

'Damn it, I don't believe you'd have the slightest compunction in perjuring yourself if the Valley was involved! I believe you would do it without a blush if you had to!'

'Certainly I would,' she told him cheerfully, 'and I should do it a great deal more convincingly than you! That's why I'm glad the children favour you more than me for there isn't an unblushing liar among them! Well, have you got Sydney's taste out of your mouth or shall I pour you another small one before lunch?'

'Go away,' he told her, good-humouredly, 'and attend to your business so that I can attend to mine! Whenever that perfume wafts about the room in the morning I get a dozen different answers to the same column of figures!' and he speeded her on her way with a slap on the bottom.

Her perfume remained, however, and it was not Sydney who hindered his concentration, so that presently he threw aside his work and began to browse through the pages of the estate diary, noting recent entries written in her neat, rounded hand. It was only then that he realised that he had not made an entry since the note recording the declaration of war but she had, more than four pages of them and he marvelled at her detachment for nobody could have guessed from the factual statements on subjects as commonplace as repairs to the tithe barn after a gale, that their lives had been mercilessly disrupted. Then he noticed, starred with an asterisk, an entry reading *'For enlistments, casualties, etc. see last page'*, and turned to the end of the book where, in fact, there were two pages devoted to war-time entries, one headed *'Shallowford Estate Enlistments'*, the other *'Casualties, Decorations, etc.'*. It surprised him very much that she had kept such a meticulous record, one that included the antecedents,

regiment and even dates of departure of recruits. He read the
long list of names under the Enlistment column, then turned
to the shorter list on the page opposite. Roddy Rudd's name
led it with the information *Falkland Islands, November 1914*
alongside and below were the names of Walt Pascoe, Jem
Pollock, Will Codsall and Gilbert Eveleigh and he thought
grimly, 'and I wonder how any more names will be there
before it's over?', resisting a strong impulse to score the page
through and reflecting that, despite an occasional flippant note
in some of the day-to-day entries, Claire took the job of local
Recording Angel very seriously.

Contemplation of the book led him to ponder the future of
the Valley as a whole and the ultimate effect the war would
have upon it. Right up to the last minute on August 4th, 1914,
everything had been reasonably predictable but what could
anyone be certain of now, save shrinking manpower, shortages
of things one once took for granted, and the brooding fear of
news that another familiar face had been blotted out? His
own detachment, maintained into the New Year, now failed
him altogether and he was fully committed, if only because
the Valley itself was committed, but involvement had not
yet convinced him of the justness of the war or enlisted him
among the patriots who seemed able to regard it as a latter day
crusade. And he was beginning to sense that he was not alone
in his reservations, that the Horace Handcocks and the Gloria
Pitts of the Valley were already outnumbered by the doubters.
Will Codsall's terrible apathy had sobered some of the men
in the bar of The Raven and the news that, notwithstanding
his shattered nervous system, he had been thrown back into
the whirlpool to vanish for good had shocked women whose
sons and husbands were in training camps up and down the
country. Only a few months ago people still hoped it would
end any day with a glorious victory in the style of Waterloo
or Agincourt, orchestrated by high-sounding sentiments of the
kind written by the poet Brooke that had found their way into
the *County Press* in 1914. Now the temperature had dropped,
not alarmingly but noticeably, so that the odd cynic raised
his voice, questioning the infallibility of news bulletins and

even the qualifications of generals like the pot-bellied Joffre, who had once been everybody's favourite uncle. Perhaps, after all, the smell of Sydney Codsall's hair-oil had not been entirely vanquished by Claire's whiff of Parma violets, for suddenly Paul felt restless and uprooted and, despite access to Claire's granary of commonsense, lonely and desolate.

Chapter Six

I

Winter in the Valley had been mild but generally wet, cheerless and without much promise. There had been no heavy snowfalls but ever since November the sun had been hiding behind seeping skies and by January the flurries of hail that came in horizontally, like a shower of assegais, had given way to a steady downpour that beat the dead bracken flat and changed the meandering Sorrel into a brown, froth-flecked torrent twenty yards wide carrying floating islands of driftwood imprisoned in briars that snagged in the shallows, causing floodwater to lap half-a-mile across the flat fields of the west bank. The woods, were thinned, strewn with the victims of the autumn gales blocking the rides or leaning drunkenly against hard-pressed neighbours and the river road below Hermitage Farm, robbed by Lord Kitchener of Henry Pitts' watchful eye, soon became pitted with potholes and obstructed by bank-slides. As winter groped its way towards spring the landscape withered under ceaseless rain and its inhabitants withdrew into themselves, almost forgetting to keep Christmas and New Year. The only really cheerful face to be met within the Valley that season was that of Horace Handcock, for he alone, it seemed, held the secret of the year's promise in his heart and was willing enough to share it with anyone with patience to listen.

For Horace this was the year of decision; the year when Kitchener's trained hosts, instead of being fed piecemeal into the line, would charge forward *en masse*, an irresistible force that would scatter the cowardly German hordes like stubble wisps and surge over the Rhine to Potsdam, carrying ropes for the Kaiser, Little Willie and the Junkers who had planned

to enslave the world but had forgotten that the British Lion
had strong teeth. They would be dealt with, Horace assured
everyone, as the Lion had dealt with everyone in the past who
made the fatal error of twisting the tail of the passive but
indomitable islanders and disposed of, once and for all, as had
Napoleon, the Mahdi, and Kruger but with a slight difference.
This time there would be no honourable banishment for the
defeated but an eighty-foot gallows for the leaders and years of
hard labour for the misled. Neither were Horace's hopes pinned
entirely upon the British field army. Poised to issue from Scapa
and Rosyth were the ironclads that would steam down the
east coast, corner the craven German Navy in or around the
Heligoland Bight and blow it out of the water so that never
again would the Hohenzollerns, or anyone else, presume to
seek parity with the super-national dispenser of justice which
was how Horace regarded the British Grand Fleet.

There were men of the Valley, however, who did not
share Horace's optimism in the early spring of 1916, men
who would have liked very much to look forward to a
midsummer victory-march down the Unter den Linden to the
music of 'The British Grenadiers' but who were prevented, by
evidence that they found difficult to discount, from believing
in the likelihood of gaps being torn in the German line for
the exploitation of Haig's cavalry.

Several of these dismal Jimmies lived within rifle range of
Horace's cowardly grey hordes whom they sometimes met face
to face in trench raids or on patrol in no-man's-land and who
saw no shame in flattening themselves in deep slush when
they heard the oncoming shriek of a five-nine, or watched the
deceivingly slow roll of the dreaded Minnenwerfer coming out
of the sky like a great wounded bird. Henry Pitts could be
numbered among the doubters for in one way active service
had disappointed him. He had arrived in France shortly after
the lost Battle of Loos but so far no one had ever asked
him to perform any of the evolutions he had perfected on
the home drill-grounds during the previous summer. Instead
they shuttled him to and fro along the greasy pavé, humping
a Christmas tree of equipment that taxed even his patience

and stamina when they left the road and entered narrow communication trenches where, every few yards, there was a shell-hole, a hangman's noose of barbed wire, telephone cables, a cave-in or a stretcher-party battling along from the opposite direction. He remained cheerful because, in place of precise, heel-clicking drill movements, they offered him comradeship. He had always preferred the company of men and here was good company in abundance, its society and steadfastness releasing the full force of his jovial, tolerant disposition, so that like Smut Potter and Jem Pollock before him, he soon became a great favourite in his company and could be relied upon to squeeze laughter from the most melancholy incidents, like the upsetting of the rum ration jar or a mortar explosion that smeared the section's breakfast rashers against the parapet. He had never had an eye for natural beauty so that the hideous disfigurement of the landscape did not distress him in the least and there was another aspect of active service that commended itself to him. When in the line nobody nagged him about his personal appearance, which was almost worth the sacrifice of home and family, for first Martha, his mother, and then Gloria, his wife, had never ceased to berate him for failing to care for his clothes or scrape the stubble from his chin. Over here, as long as he was out of range of the martinets, he could go days without removing mud that adhered to him and as to shaving regularly he often grew a tramp's stubble half-an-inch long. There was, in fact, a freedom that a man could not fail to appreciate after years of nagging at the Hermitage. For all this, however, he had no great hopes of seeing Germany's defeat by midsummer for what had impressed him most out here had been the apparent permanence of the war, with its miles and miles of deep ditches, its unending forests of wire, its deep, roomy dugouts (especially in captured sections of the German line) and the multiplicity of expensive-looking mechanical transport that swarmed everywhere between support lines and rest billets. To Henry's simple mind it seemed ridiculous to suppose that so much effort, and so much money, should have been poured into an enterprise due to end in a month or so. Frugal use of stock and plant had been practised by generations of Pitts at Hermitage, where a five-barred gate was expected to do service for twenty-five years, and sometimes the evidence of waste that he witnessed in France depressed him. He could not help thinking how useful some of these things would prove if he could have transported them to the farm.

A dozen or so sectors north of Henry's was another Valley man who would have challenged Horace had he heard him prophesying victory by June. This was Smut Potter, whose estimate of the duration of the war was based upon the strength of German counter-attacks during the Loos fighting last September. Smut had never shone at arithmetic. One of his drawbacks throughout life had been his inability to count beyond ten. At Mary Willoughby's little school he had used his fingers for counting but a fog descended on his brain when he had used up all his fingers and thumbs and was obliged to start again. Yet numbers impressed him and he made a point of counting the German dead when the company occupied one of the enemy's trenches. Until Loos this had been an easy thing to accomplish, for he was engaged in nothing but local sorties where the dead and prisoners seldom exceeded a dozen, but in the big push that autumn Smut's counting system broke down the first day, for he was in the second wave to cross no-man's-land and jump into a deep trench previously held by the Brandenburgers and here he found acres of Germans killed in the preliminary bombardment. It had seemed to him then, that the German Army must have been eliminated, that only a few dazed survivors would be left to scramble out of range of the British guns but he very soon discovered that this was not so for, by midday, he and his friends were counter-attacked, bundled out of the captured trench and were soon back at starting-point, where they were pinned down by fresh hordes appearing as from nowhere.

The seesaw went on for four days. Every time a few yards of rubble was won it was carpeted with German dead but the enemy soon reappeared with any number of fresh men until the offensive ground to a halt and the survivors of Smuts company were withdrawn for rest and refit.

During a spell in billets behind the line he pondered his experiences so deeply that he missed several chances of relieving his quartermaster's worries in respect of various shortages. At last, finding no answer to the mystery, he turned for enlightenment to his particular chum, a Stepney coster, called Harry. ''Arry boy,' he said, 'where do 'ee reckon they all come from?' and Harryboy, whose familiarity for humanity *en masse* was the natural product of an East End upbringing, replied, unhelpfully, 'All them mucking Fritzes? Blimey, doncher know? They collects all the dead uns after every show an' puts 'em through a bloody mincer in the Kaiser's palace! Then they cart all the sausage meat to a bloody great bakery where they bake it, an' out they come good as noo ready for the next show!' Smut, of course, did not accept this as a satisfactory explanation of the inexhaustibility of the Kaiser's manpower but secretly he felt that the real explanation came as close to necromancy.

Young Harold Eveleigh, seventeen-year-old brother of Gilbert, who had profited by Gilbert's false start and enlisted in a town a hundred miles from the Valley, would have taken issue with Horace on yet another account – that of the popular belief that all Germans were cowards, who ran away once they were bombed out of their deep shelters and called upon to 'face cold steel'. Harold had been in France since early September, despite his mother's frantic efforts to trace him and haul him out of the Army as she had once succeeded in doing as regards Gilbert. Harold looked at least twenty, having inherited his father's height and had joined up for devilment but whilst he was still in training, and serving under a false name, he learned that his elder brother had been killed in a bombing accident at a neighbouring camp. He and Gilbert, as the two elder boys in a long family of girls, had been very close and Harold had to take it out on somebody, so he managed to wangle his way into a draft on the point of leaving for France and soon became as enthusiastic a slayer of Germans as Smut

Potter, although he never approached the latter's efficiency. There was already a belief among veterans that a newcomer was at his best during his first few weeks in the line and that thereafter he deteriorated as a fighting machine. Harold Eveleigh's recklessness during the Loos push justified this theory. He arrived in France only a fortnight before the battle opened and when his shattered unit was withdrawn he had accounted for at least five Germans and probably one or two more. He came through unwounded, one of four in his platoon, and the experience taught him, among other things, that war correspondents who described the Germans as a nation of cowards were either deliberate liars or very badly informed for he witnessed acts of heroism on the part of enemy personnel that would have surprised him had they been performed by some of the élite British regiments, like the Coldstreamers, or the Royal Welch. He saw three Germans killed in quick succession trying to rescue a wounded comrade from the wire and the next day came across a dead machine-gunner, lying beside his weapon with seventeen wounds in his body and a deep trench down which he could have withdrawn within yards of his emplacement. He saw German stretcher-parties walk through a box barrage carrying British wounded and he studied the impassive faces of some of the dead Saxons who had refused to surrender a surrounded sap when their nearest reinforcements were pinned down by an incessant rain of shells. After Loos, Harold was in and out of the line for another six months and was sent back with a slight wound, in February 1916. During this period he learned many basic facts about the war but perhaps the most important of them was that a man's courage under fire did not depend upon his nationality but upon such factors as how much sleep he had had in the last seventy-two hours, what kind of training he had received, how much rum had been available before an attack and even on the arrival or non-arrival of his mail. It also depended, just as the veterans argued, upon how long a man had been out and what kind of sectors he had served in, so that when, to his amazement, he was included in a group of survivors and sent home to train for a commission he would have admitted to anyone, Horace Handcock included, that the respite he had gained represented the difference between Harold Eveleigh the Hero, and Harold Eveleigh the Coward.

It is doubtful whether Ikey Palfrey, still serving with the artillery in or around the Cuinchy brickstacks, would have bothered to argue with Horace Handcock upon the subject of how long the war would last but if, for some reason, he had been drawn into a discussion at The Raven his rebuttal of Horace's prophecies might have led to him being branded as a defeatist. After nearly eighteen months at the front, broken by a single spell of leave in June, 1915, Ikey had formed certain theories about modern warfare and they were not of the kind likely to win preferment for a professional. He had artillery-spotted for several small-scale offensives and two major pushes, including the Loos débâcle and had come to the conclusion that at least two drastic changes would have to be made on the Western Front before the Allies could advance as far as Roulers and Lille, much less Cologne and Berlin. In the first place all British ex-cavalry generals bent over maps at HQ would have to be put out of harm's way, preferably by a bullet through the head, although, in this case, shots would have to be fired point-blank for it was a well-known fact that all cavalry generals had bullet-proof skulls. This having been done, and a new General Staff having been recruited from men who had ceased to think of war in terms of Balaclava, some new tactical method would have to be devised as a means of penetrating the German trench system and covering the advance of infantrymen across open ground traversed by enemy machine-guns. Ikey had watched, through powerful binoculars, the advance of successive waves at Loos and for four days had seen the clusters climb out of their assembly points, plod a few yards over churned-up ground and wither away before they had travelled half the distance to their first objective. They looked, he thought, like a swarm of clockwork dolls moving across a brown tablecloth and when, during the first two days, attack after attack failed, he was at first surprised, then furiously angry and finally filled

with hatred for men who ordered their advance without regard
for the vulnerability of flesh and bone to bullets and shrapnel.
Then, as his duties required him to keep the surging attacks
and counter-attacks under constant observation, he was able
to eliminate the human element altogether and study the battle
in a tactical sense, reasoning that before the fortified ground
on either side could be taken and held something far more
imaginative than a preliminary bombardment was needed to
fortify the attacker during the initial stage of a breakthrough.
His mind began to toy with smokescreens, low-level aerial
machine-gunning and even bullet-proof vests but he rejected
all three as too clumsy, too revolutionary and too ineffectual.
Then, on the third day, he had the germ of an idea and it
excited him; what was surely needed out here, what would
have to be found before substantial progress could be made,
was some kind of war chariot mounted with quick-firing guns,
something impervious to all but a direct hit from a mortar
or long-range shell, a machine, moreover, that could crush
wire and circumnavigate all but the smallest shell-holes, a
moving fort behind which the hardy infantry could advance
without being scythed down by traversing machine-guns and
rifle fire. That night, back in his dug-out, he took pencil and
paper and began to sketch but he was less than half-satisfied
with the drawing he produced, thinking that it resembled a
memory copy of one of the sketches of military engines
made by Leonardo da Vinci that he remembered seeing in
a magazine in the mess at Quetta. He persisted, however
and at last evolved something that seemed to him to be at
least partially practical, a kind of squat armoured car, with
broad, steel-plated wheels looking a little like an armadillo.
He was so absorbed that he got behind with his real work
and it was not until the candle burned low that he put the
sketch-pad in his valise, marked his maps and finally rolled
on to his wire-netting bed to sleep. Outside the guns went on
grumbling, not violently but persistently, somewhere to the
south and before he slept Ikey thought the distant cannonade
sounded exactly like autumn thunder in the Sorrel Valley.

*   *   *

There was a woman, formerly of the Valley, abroad that same night not forty miles from the sector where Ikey sat sketching war-chariots and although she had always prided herself on being a realist, she would have done her utmost to extract a crumb of comfort from Horace Handcock's optimistic prophecies. Having come to regard the war as the most hideous tragedy that had ever beset the world she would have welcomed any terms, including unconditional surrender, that brought the suffering she witnessed each night to an abrupt end.

As an ambulance driver shunting regularly between casualty-clearing station and hospital, Grace Lovell was more familiar with the extremes of pain and human desolation than even a front-line infantry man. A fighting man was primarily concerned with his own plight, and either stuck it out, like a terrified mole, or was caught up in a struggle for survival demanding a quality of exclusive concentration. Grace Lovell did most of her work outside the range of all but the howitzers and therefore found it very difficult to isolate herself from the load of misery in her vehicle and devote her entire attention to the task of driving over shell-pocked roads with quarter-power headlamps.

She had been in France for close on a year now, having volunteered for ambulance driving after a brief, unhappy spell in a London hospital when the 1914 amnesty freed all imprisoned suffragettes. She emerged from Holloway half-way through her sixth sentence and her experiences during the previous decade had not been such as to encourage her to embrace a patriotic crusade. Ever since 1904 she had been hounded, hunted, man-handled, forcibly fed, and hectored by men and to the hard core of the Movement, some of whom, like Grace, were reduced to skin and bone by hunger-strikes and nervous strain, the war was regarded as a fitting punishment for a world of men who had been callous, sadistic and mulish in responding to a demand for basic human rights.

This savage mood endured through the autumn and into the spring of 1915, while she was recuperating at a holiday home in Scotland run by a wealthy sympathiser but she began to relent a little as the casualties of the first winter's fighting appeared on public platforms at meetings loosely associated with women's suffrage, men who, for the most part, were no longer men at all but patched-up parodies of men lacking arms, legs or even half a face. As news of the death or mutilation of some of her personal friends reached her, the shift of sympathies kept pace with her improvement in health and although she still regarded the war as the climax of years of blundering inefficiency on the part of the male cabals of Europe, she could find it in her heart to feel desperately sorry for the millions of young men urged to lay down their lives at the toot of a bugle and the flutter of a Union Jack. Veterans of the movement, women like Annie Kenney and Christobel Pankhurst, assured her that this was the opportunity for which they had been working since 1904 and that after the war every woman in Britain would have the franchise. She did not know whether she believed them but after a spell as a VAD in a London hospital it did not seem to matter much for the keen edge of her fanaticism was blunted by a factor removed from the purely physical suffering she witnessed in the wards. This was a creeping doubt as to whether women in authority were any more reasonable, or even as efficient as men. She had the bad luck to come within the orbit of a fat-rumped martinet whose only qualification for her position as Commandant was newly-acquired wealth and Grace soon had good reason to despise this type of woman as wholeheartedly as she despised Cabinet Ministers. The titled Commandant administered the hospital like an eighteenth-century school, treating her volunteer nurses much as the more ignorant of the wardresses had treated prisoners in Holloway. Grace came to suspect that, again like some of the wardresses, the Commandant was not only a bully and a snob but also a Lesbian for she made favourites of all the doll-faced little nurses from aristocratic houses and was hostile to any member of her staff who had been a suffragette. After two or three months of back-breaking toil and humiliation Grace knew that she would have to choose between resigning or changing her hospital, and since almost every reception-centre for the

wounded was in charge of middled-aged women enjoying the
exercise of despotism she managed, by pulling various strings,
to transfer to the transport section of the Department and was
sent to France in time to evacuate some of the casualties of
the battle of Veuve Chapelle, in April.

It was here, driving between clearing-station and base, that
her re-orientation really began, for during her ten years in
and out of gaol she had forgotten that men also possess
the capacity to suffer. Back in the hospital wards at home,
freshly washed, rid of their filthy uniforms and with their
wounds covered by clean bandages, wounded men could be
regarded with a certain amount of detachment but out here,
where they were lifted into ambulances much as they had
quitted the battlefield, compassion came near to prostrating
her until she was able to convince herself that every stretcher
case needed instant, practical help far more than tears. By the
time the Loos fighting began she had become an extremely
efficient driver and assistant orderly so that she was put on
a regular run through devastated territory wrecked during
the previous autumn's fighting.

Although the oldest woman in her section she withstood the
demands of active service better than most. Her experiences
had bred in her an iron self-discipline and once she was rested,
and had recovered from successive hunger-strikes, she put on
weight and regained her taut, resilient physique. She had need
of strength. In addition to the strain of night-driving over bad
roads, where every jolt produced screams of agony, and the
sickening morning routine of scrubbing out the ambulance,
her seniority made her a target for all the younger women
seeking a confidante. There were those whose health proved
unequal to the demands of the work but who wanted most
desperately to acquit themselves well, and there were those
who had rushed starry-eyed into the Service at the beginning
of the war and were now driven to distraction by nagging
superiors. There were others, perhaps the most pitiable, whose
greatest fear was to succumb to fear, and there was, of course,
a steady stream of pregnancies among girls from good-class
homes in city suburbs, girls whose staggering ignorance of

the basic facts of hygiene caused Grace to rage against the social taboos of the last few generations.

Some of the girls who came to her for help and advice were only half aware of how they had become pregnant and there were even more hopeless examples of girls who had been virgins when they stepped ashore at Le Havre and had contracted venereal disease in a matter of weeks. Grace did what she could, exploiting her many personal contacts at home, delivering impromptu lectures on sexual hygiene and contraception, using her campaigning and even her prison experiences to alleviate distress wherever possible, but sometimes it seemed to her she was distributing a handful of oats in a meadow full of donkeys. Whenever possible she conserved her nervous energies, making few close friends and spending her meagre spare time sitting alone in the sun and letting her mind go blank, a substitute for sleep that she had learned in the cells. But this was not always easy, particularly after an offensive, when, night after night, she had to handle men with wounds in the lungs, wounds in the stomach, wounds in the groin, legless and armless men, men with hideously disfigured faces and, worst of all, gas cases, so that she sometimes thought what a blessed relief it would be to look upon a young man who was whole and unblemished.

Perhaps it was this subconscious longing that urged her, in the early spring of 1916, to make a deliberate sacrifice of her privacy and involve herself, physically and emotionally, in what proved to be the most bizarre yet in some ways the most rewarding of her campaigns.

He returned to her for the third time in April, a gangling boy of no more than twenty who had been wounded in the shoulder at Neuve Chapelle and again, this time in the forearm, at Loos. She remembered him because of the terrible distress he showed after vomiting over her as they were helping him to board the ambulance and when they sent him back into the fight a third time in anticipation of the summer offensive on the Somme, he went to a great deal of trouble to seek her out explaining, naïvely, that he had never ceased to think of her all the time he was home and had written several times although his letters seemed to have gone astray.

She was oddly flattered by his attentions for it had seemed to her that never again would she earn the sidelong glance and smile of a young man. At thirty-four she still had an excellent figure but her dark curls were showing streaks of grey and her eyes seemed too big for her small, rather pinched face; in any case years had now passed since she had given more than a passing thought to a man who was not, automatically, a persecutor. Because of his insistence she let him take her out to dinner once or twice at a hotel that could still provide an excellent meal for officers attached to the transport centre, and she was touched when, on escorting her back to her quarters, he asked shyly if he might kiss her. For all his battle experience he was still no more than a timid boy and was also good-looking, she supposed, in the conventional English way, with his wavy, light-brown hair, a straight, short nose, clear eyes and fresh complexion. She let him kiss her, more as a joke against herself than from any desire to be kissed but the gentle pressure of his lips, and his reverential approach to her, renewed in her the yearning for a fresh, clean man, someone who was whole and whose clothes were not infested with lice and about whom there was no stale smell of sweat, blood and Flanders mud.

She must have responded to his kiss more eagerly than she intended for he began to pour out protestations of love, saying that the younger women at home meant nothing to him and that he had been unable to get her out of his mind during his convalescence after Loos. She tried teasing him, pointing out that, as an enterprising girl of fourteen, she could have been his mother but when he raised his hand and stroked her hair she succumbed to the crazy pressures of war and after one or two furtive embraces in the limited privacy of the base she promised to spend three days' leave with him after he had completed his gas course, at Montreuil.

She regretted it the moment he had gone, realising that she did not regard him as a person at all but as a symbol of all the millions of young men marched into this inferno by paunched, be-whiskered generals and ageing politicians on both sides of the line, boys who, like this one, would die virgins if they were too fastidious to visit the Blue or Red Lamp establishments during rest and training periods behind the front.

She kept her promise, however, and far from regretting it found his clumsy embraces a measure of solace for her years of deprivation and dedication before and during the war. They did not go to Paris, as he had urged, but to the village high up the Seine where, as a girl, she had boarded out for a time after her father had brought her back from India and where, among the friendly peasants, she might have found peace had she remained there to grow up as an exile instead of being fetched home after her father's remarriage.

They stayed at a little inn near the bridge. Before their window was the broad sweep of the river and its tidy fringe of poplars, limes and chestnuts and above them towered the walls of the castle, squatting like a white hen on a clutch of half-timbered, many-gabled houses. For Grace it was a recuperative interval, for here the war seemed to belong to another century. For David, 'The Boy David' as she called him, it was an idyll. He could hardly have been as deeply in love with her as he professed himself to be, yet she represented for him a romanticised ideal of womanhood who somehow struck a precise balance between a mother and a mistress, offering comfort in the one role and the grossest flattery in the other. He asked her many questions about her past but she parried most of them, telling him good-humouredly to mind his own business and although he talked eagerly about marrying her during his next leave, he did not press for details of her first marriage or her involvement in politics. On the final morning, just after dawn, she left him to sit by the tall window looking down on the sliding river and when she returned to the bed the terrible poignancy of his sleeping face brought tears to her eyes. To her he was as dead as though he was lying out on the battlefield and the knowledge that she had been the means of bringing him a little ecstasy seemed to her the most positive achievement of her life.

David was the first and perhaps the most innocent of them, for as the war dragged on she took other lovers, all of them young and resigned to death in the immediate future. She derived small physical satisfaction from these encounters for some of the boys were greedy while others were excusably clumsy yet she derived satisfaction of another kind that had nothing to do with their bearlike embraces and fearful impatience. She saw herself, as the Somme petered out and the even more costly assaults of 1917 began, as a healer and again as a kind of janitor, opening the door to give these condemned men a glimpse of a world they would never inherit. It was an extravagant thought and perhaps a vain one but it seemed to her a more rewarding endeavour than any she had attempted in all the years of platform storming and window smashing, or, for that matter, anything achieved during her short reign at Shallowford.

II

One morning in April, 1916, the Reverend Hubert Horsey, Rector of Shallowford, was shown into Paul's office in what Mrs Handcock might have described as 'zummat of a tizzy'. Like his son Keith he was afflicted by a slight stutter and Paul, aware of this, gave him a moment or two to collect himself before offering him a sherry which he politely refused.

'It's about my boy, Keith,' the rector said. 'I'm here to ask you a favour, Mr Craddock, or maybe find someone else on the estate who would do me a favour.' He went on to say that his son had recently been summoned before a Leeds tribunal to explain why he had not enlisted under the Derby Act of the previous December, Keith having declared himself a conscientious objector. Paul was not surprised. Both father and son had always been regarded as eccentric among the Valley folk and the rector was as unlike his predecessor, the Reverend Bull, as it was possible to be for he neither hunted, hectored his flock, nor challenged members of his congregation to explain why they had missed matins. He

had also succeeded in establishing cordial relationships with
the Nonconformists in Coombe Bay and for this reason alone
Paul had always liked the little man but Horsey had not been
a success in the Valley. Having been bullied by Bull for a
generation the local Anglicans regarded clerical tolerance as
weakness and church attendances had fallen sharply until
the war encouraged parishioners to seek Divine protection for
absent menfolk. Paul said, 'How convinced is he, Rector? What
I mean is, there seem to be many varieties of conscientious
objectors. Is Keith a religious boy?'

'I never thought of him as such,' Horsey admitted. 'We've
had a good deal of argument on religious dogma since he went
up to Oxford but he seems to have made a stand on this issue.
I have a newspaper report here; perhaps you should read it.'

It did not take Paul long to discover that Keith Horsey's
objections were political rather than religious. He had recently
resigned from the Paxtonbury tribunal himself and was
familiar with all the stock questions and most of the stock
answer. To the old chestnut, 'What would you do if you
saw a German soldier raping your mother or sister?' Keith
had replied, rather fatuously Paul considered, 'I have no
mother or sister,' and when pressed said he supposed he
would attack the rapist with his bare hands. There was
nothing dramatic about the examination. It had the same
tiresome note as the Paxtonbury hearings and the same
futility that had prompted Paul to resign.

'Will he do farm work?' Paul asked and Horsey said that
he probably would but that he, as Rector, had already made
the rounds of the Valley farms and had been unable to place
his son. At Hermitage Farm Gloria Pitts had abused him and
at Four Winds Farmer Eveleigh had refused to discuss the
proposition. There was no demand for unskilled labour at the
Dell or High Coombe and neither Willoughby at Deepdene,
nor Elinor Codsall at Periwinkle, could afford extra help.

Paul considered. He was aware that both the Pitts and the
Eveleighs could use extra help; indeed, Four Winds, with the
biggest acreage and a herd of seventy Friesians, was desperate
for a cowman and Keith could surely be taught to milk in a

week or so. He said, 'Leave it to me, Rector. I'll get him taken on at Four Winds. Get the boy down here and as soon as he's fixed I'll write to the Leeds tribunal.'

'It's very kind of you,' Horsey said. 'I couldn't bear to think of him going to prison, they say they treat them so badly, but I should be less than honest if I didn't say I understood how people feel who have a son or a husband out there.' Then, pausing for a second, he said glumly, 'This business makes me feel useless, Mr Craddock. I'm not one of those parsons who can unblushingly bless a cannon, or claim that the Almighty is fighting for us! Sometimes I wish I were; it would make things a lot easier and I daresay I should make more impact here.'

Paul, deciding that he had never liked the man so much as at this moment, said, 'I'm not all that enthusiastic myself, Rector! However, there's little you or I can do about it.'

The man's head came up and Paul noticed the baffled look in his brown eyes. 'Is there no prospect at all of a compromised peace this year?' he asked, and Paul told him that he had asked the same question of their MP, Grenfell, only a few days ago and had received a negative answer. 'Grenfell says the Government mean to fight to a finish,' he added. 'There are reasons for supposing the Germans have already approached both the Allies and the Americans and been turned down,' and then, when he saw Horsey was prepared to unburden himself further, he made the excuse that he would try and catch Eveleigh before the farmer went off to weekly market. He was not in the mood to share the rector's troubles, having more than enough of his own just then. As he was leaving however, Horsey said, 'This war and everyone's approach to it – it makes absolute nonsense of my work, Squire.'

'Mine too,' Paul said grimly, 'I put fourteen years into building this estate into a useful community and I thought I was progressing but here I am going cap in hand to one of my own tenants, to ask him to help prevent a brilliant brain like Keith's being scattered about France, or dulled by prison!' and he took his cap and went out, not in the best of tempers.

Eveleigh proved exceptionally stubborn. 'Look here, Squire,' he argued, 'I've had one boy killed and I've another in uniform! Why the devil should I help a damned shirker?'

'Maybe because he's your son-in-law!' Paul reminded him, 'and I'm sure your wife would be relieved.'

'I daresay she would!' growled Eveleigh, 'but the truth is I've never liked the boy! Rachel ought to have found herself a man, not a walking encyclopaedia who hasn't the guts to fight for his own kin! Besides, I've made arrangements to get a land-girl here.'

'You could do with two extra hands and I'm asking this as a favour,' Paul said.

Eveleigh hesitated. The war had changed him, more than any of them, Paul thought. He had always been dour and uncommunicative but in spite of this Four Winds had been a happy, prosperous farm since they had moved in, man, wife and children working in close accord and seeming to possess mutual respect for one another. Now the atmosphere of the farm was uncomfortably like Four Winds in Arabella's time, with Eveleigh snarling at his wife and younger daughters and the kitchen charged with explosive bad temper and suppressed resentment.

'Well,' he said at length, 'I'll do it on your account, Squire, for I don't need reminding it was you gave me my chance, backalong. If you hadn't I'd still be a hired hand living in the cottage, so get the boy here and Rachel too, and we'll see how they shape. If they pull their weight they can abide but I'll tell you straight, I won't have aught to say to 'em.'

That was the best Paul could do and a week later Keith and Rachel arrived from the North and took up residence in the cottage the Eveleighs had occupied during the Codsall régime. The rector called in to thank Paul but Keith himself did not seem particularly grateful for the reprieve and Paul guessed that he regarded farm work as an uneasy compromise. Rachel also was estranged from her sisters, who were inclined to share their father's view that Keith was a coward, a pitiful creature compared to their splendid brothers Gilbert and Harold but the arrangement served as a temporary measure and at least kept Keith out of gaol. Paul heard, however, that a month or two after their arrival, Eveleigh went ahead with his intention of employing a land-girl and soon after her arrival he saw her, a buxom, auburn-haired young hoyden, who looked as though she would be more at home in a munitions factory than a field of cows. Paul happened to pass her by Codsall bridge whilst she was driving the herd home from the river pastures and saw her take out a pocket mirror to apply a powder puff to her broad, freckled nose. He thought, 'Well, I don't know what Eveleigh's thinking of but Keith can't be much more of an amateur than her and at least Rachel can make butter and care for hens!' but he did not think any more about it until a week or so later when, on returning late from a meeting of an agricultural committee at Paxtonbury, Claire met him on the doorstep and he saw at once that she was worried.

'Rachel Horsey is in the library,' she told him, 'but don't go in until I've told you what it's about. There's been more trouble over at Four Winds.'

She took him into the little-used drawing room and shut the door.

'What do you know about that land-girl Eveleigh has over there?' Claire asked, and Paul told her nothing at all except that she did not look like a girl who could earn her wages on a farm.

'I daresay you're right at that,' Claire said, 'for it seems that Eveleigh isn't interested in her vertical activities!'

'Now what the devil do you mean by that?' Paul demanded, 'Eveleigh's not that kind of chap. You've been listening to gossip started by the fact that she's the first land-girl who has shown up here!'

'Not in this case,' Claire said, 'she was Eveleigh's fancy piece when she worked behind the counter at Foster's, the drapers, and has been for a year or more. He got her drafted to him by delivering cream and butter on councillors' doorsteps. Ben Godbeer, the seedsman, is on the County Council and allocates land labour, doesn't he? And Ben is an old crony of Eveleigh's. It looks to me as if Rachel has hit the nail on the head.'

'And what does she think I can do about it?' Paul demanded. 'Eveleigh's a paid-up tenant running the best farm on the estate and I'm already under an obligation to him on account of placing Keith.'

'Well,' Claire said, hands on her hips, 'you can't ask him to get rid of the girl just like that but Rachel thinks you might make some kind of indirect approach. Since this afternoon everyone at Four Winds knows about it.'

'What happened this afternoon?'

'A French farce,' Claire told him, 'Old Ned Fosdyke, the pigman, went into the loft over the barn to get meal and trod on the pair of them. Eveleigh had his breeches down and the girl was stark naked in the hay!'

'It's nothing to grin about, woman!' Paul growled, but Claire, still chuckling, said, 'I'm sorry, Paul, but I can't help it. If it were anyone else but Eveleigh it wouldn't be funny but he's such a sententious, self-righteous kind of chap and so strict with his children! The idea of him taking both time and breeches off for an ex-shop girl is enough to make a cat laugh!'

'Damn it, he might have been more discreet at all events,' Paul grumbled. 'How did Rachel come to hear about it?'

'How could she help hearing? Eveleigh was so mad he knocked poor old Ned Fosdyke down the ladder and everyone came running, including Marian! The point is he's absolutely unrepentant and won't even hear of getting rid of the girl!'

'He damned well will if I've anything to say in the matter,' grunted Paul and after a talk with Rachel, who was crying in the library, he would have accompanied her straight back to Four Winds had she not begged him to wait and hear something of her personal problems. 'It was good of you to get Keith fixed up,' she said, 'but it isn't going to work, quite apart from this development! Father's so changed you wouldn't know him. I don't know whether it was the boys going, or the war, or what, but life is impossible for Keith and I over there and Keith is thinking of walking out and taking the consequences. He thinks the war is a crime against humanity and that the only way it can be stopped is for people

like us to make a stand but what good will it do him going to
prison? Besides, I'm expecting a baby in the autumn!'

He looked more closely at her and realised that this was
a fact. Claire said, 'Then his first duty is to you, Rachel,
and not to a theory!' and once again Paul felt grateful for
his wife's grasp of essentials. He said, 'Leave me to deal
with Keith and when Ikey comes home on leave I'll get
him to talk to him. He's due in a day or so unless leave
is stopped. Meantime Keith can work on the Home Farm.
Can Rachel move in with us, Claire?'

'Certainly,' Claire replied, 'and the sooner the better. It'll
suit a plan I've had in mind for some time now.'

She did not tell them what her plan was and it was months
before they found out but Rachel, very relieved, accompanied
Paul to the Home Farm where he told Honeyman to make room
on the staff for Keith. They moved in bag and baggage within
twenty-four hours, making a home out of a ruinous cottage
adjoining the tack-room where Lovell's coachman had once
lived.

Feeling that the reins of the place were slipping out of his
hands, and that the spirit of the Valley was being poisoned
by the stresses of war, Paul rode over to Four Winds and
had a frank talk with Eveleigh on the subject of the buxom
land-girl. He found him truculent and unresponsive.

'You baint heard my side o' the business,' the farmer
growled. 'Marian's not been a wife to me for close on a year
now and I'll be honest, Squire! I'm a man as works hard, eats
hearty and damn' well needs a woman night-times! Alwus 'ave
and please God alwus will! I wouldn't have thought to get Jill
yer if things had been as they were between me an' the missis
but they baint an' won't be again. She holds me responsible
for Gilbert being blown to tatters and Harold runnin' off an'
enlisting, although you know same as I do that they'd ha' gone
be now in any case! As for Rachel, and that four-eyed scholar
she wed, I don't give a damn what happens to 'em, so long as
they get from under me feet! Jill stays here as long as I've a
mind to keep her and that's all I'm disposed to say about it!'
and he stumped off to his work leaving Paul to find his own

way out of the house. He saw one of the dairymaids in the hall and asked her if her mistress was available.

'No,' said the girl, carelessly, ''Er's table-rapping in Gil's room.'

'She's *what?*'

'Table-rapping! 'Er's at it all the time now. 'Er says if 'er keeps at it long enough 'er'll get through to Gil and vind how he's going on beyond the veil! It's a real carry-on I can tell 'ee, Squire.'

Paul began to understand why Eveleigh had sought solace in the barn and on the way out he passed the land-girl Jill forking hay in the yard. She gave him a smirk and the time of day but he did not acknowledge her greeting. It might have been fancy but, as he climbed on to Snowdrop and clattered out of the yard, the atmosphere of the place seemed so stale and sinister that he pushed the grey into a trot and had just reached the bridge when he saw a motor turn off the moorland road and accelerate along the flat beside the river. As it drew level he saw that the driver was Ikey and without knowing why his heart gave a tremendous bound and he shouted as the car slowed and stopped.

'We weren't expecting you yet, Ikey,' he said. 'Claire will be delighted! You look very fit, far more yourself than most of the youngsters who come home from time to time.'

Ikey grinned and Paul thought how much of the impudent gamin had survived the successive strait-jackets of public school, hill-station, and Armageddon.

'It's having had the sense to join the artillery, Gov,' he joked, 'the PBI do all the slogging and we chaps just sit around and make things tough for 'em by tickling up Fritz every now and again. I'm back in Blighty for several weeks, special course at Aldershot. Very nice and very secret!' and he winked.

Paul laughed, feeling cheered already and cutting through the paddock cantered ahead to give Claire the good news. That night, however, after everyone had gone to bed and they were sitting over their brandy, Ikey was not so flippant, warning Paul that within a month or two there was going to be a push to end all pushes on the Western Front and that, in his opinion, it was likely to be far more costly than Neuve Chapelle and Loos.

'The point is, will it be successful?' Paul demanded, 'will it break the deadlock and hasten things to a finish?'

'"Ah, that I cannot say",' quoted Ikey, '"but 'twas a famous victory"!' and then, seriously, 'Let's say it stands a better chance than anything we've tried so far. We've got some surprises and we shall certainly rattle old Fritz, the poor old sod but I can't say more than that, not even to you, Gov. Now, to hell with the war. What's happening on the home front?'

Paul did not think he could be seriously interested but Ikey listened attentively when Paul recounted the Valley news and seemed particularly struck by the information concerning Keith Horsey.

'I ought to have written to him,' he said. 'He wrote several times to me. I wouldn't like Old Beanpole to imagine I thought less of him for telling those bloody hearthrug patriots to look elsewhere for cannon-fodder! I'll go over and see him first thing in the morning.'

'What strikes me as odd,' Paul said, 'is that you chaps aren't anything like so emphatic about the war as the people at home. You don't foam at the mouth about the Germans and I get the impression you half admire people like Keith Horsey. Is that cussedness on your part or is it general among men on active service?'

'General I'd say, at least below the rank of colonel but I don't see why it should surprise you. Fritz lives under the same hellish conditions as we do and you can't help admiring his guts. Most of the chaps feel more akin to him than to the people at home and I daresay he feels the same way. You can't live a week out there and go on believing all the bloody nonsense people write and talk back here, not unless you happen to be on the staff that is!'

'But if things are as bad as that,' Paul said, 'isn't there a chance of it petering out of its own accord?'

'Not a snowball in hell's chance, Gov,' Ikey told him cheerfully, 'but if you ask me why I couldn't give you a short answer. It has to do with self-respect, regimental pride, the habit of discipline and even the warrior cult thousands of years old but more than any of those things it's probably reluctance to let other chaps down. I suppose that sounds facetious but it isn't, it's just that we're all so closely involved with each other and, in a way, with Fritz. I don't think things are like that on the other fronts, or at sea, but out there, in that great sprawling mud-bath where, to show the top of your head is certain death, a man ceases to have anything in common with ordinary civilised people. They've stopped believing in the war, or in the way it is regarded in London or Berlin, but they'll go on sticking it until one side breaks. Do you find that impossible to understand?'

'Not entirely,' Paul said thoughtfully and he did understand in a way, in fact he went to bed thinking he had learned more about the war from Ikey than from any other source over the last eighteen months.

Ikey crossed to the Home Farm the next morning and he and Keith went off together, high up to the source of the Sorrel, which had always been Ikey's favourite place on the estate. Here, where the river was no more than a shallow stream winding through thickets of brambles and shoulder-high ferns, he identified the locality with the first poem he had ever read, 'A Boy's Song' in Mary Willoughby's *Poetical Reader*. Paul never heard what they talked about that day but whatever it was it had an immediate effect upon Keith's thinking, for on his return he announced that he intended to volunteer for a stretcher-bearing unit, formed from conscientious objectors who had refused to carry arms and soon after Ikey left to begin his course he said good-bye to a tearful Rachel, and to Paul and Claire, and returned to the North. A month later Rachel received a letter from him from France. Two months after that she gave birth to a stillborn child and left the Valley for good.

III

The Somme offensive, following swiftly upon Jutland, fulfilled. Paul's gloomiest forebodings regarding the blank page at the back of the estate diary. In a single week, the first of July, a string of family names were entered under 'Casualties' by the dogged Claire, who had made a vow to keep the record up-to-date even though the task depressed her almost as much as it would have depressed Paul.

The first two names written in were Jutland casualties, Tom Williams and his nephew Dan, both lost aboard the battle cruiser *Queen Mary*. Within a fortnight Smut Potter was posted as missing, believed killed, and after Smut came the death of Evan Morgan, son of Eph Morgan, the Coombe Bay builder, and then Tremlett, the hunt servant, both killed on July 1st. Later the same week Nick, second of the Timberlake boys, Jeff Marlowe, son of the sexton, Will Salter the thatcher's son, Jim Willis, the wheelwright's younger son and two others, were killed, bringing Valley casualties up to fourteen. Despite these appalling losses the general news was encouraging. London papers, arriving a day late, told of spectacular advances, enormous German casualties and the capture of innumerable prisoners but long before the first of these prisoners appeared in a small POW camp, sited a mile or so north of Shallowford Woods the note of triumph had gone from the leading articles and Paul began to suspect that, as Ikey had prophesied, Fritz had been badly rattled but far from defeated. By harvest-time the familiar deadlock seemed to have been resumed, with no hope whatever of the war ending with a flourish of cavalry trumpets.

It was the establishment of a prisoner-of-war camp beyond the northern rim of the woods that led, indirectly, to the next outburst of Valley hysteria, an incident that pushed Paul that much nearer despair.

The camp was not a large one. It held no more than two hundred carefully-seeded Germans, mostly Saxons, selected from larger camps for timber-felling in the area. They worked in conditions amounting to freedom for none showed the slightest inclination to escape and Paul gathered, during a conversation with one of their reservist guards, that they considered themselves fortunate to be out of it and still sound in wind and limb.

They worked in gangs of six under the supervision of Sam Potter, the woodsman, and Sam, having free access to such splendid muscles, was not above allocating one or two of his charges to do urgent work on the estate, besides the felling and shaping of pitprops in the plantations between the border of Periwinkle in the west, and the boundary of High Coombe in the east. When Elinor Codsall complained to him that her patch of pasture under Hermitage Wood was reverting to moor and stood waist-high in brambles and nettles, he readily agreed to lend her a prisoner for a week or two to get it cleared. Soon the man arrived, a tall, broad-shouldered Württemberger, with a great moon face not unlike Will Codsall's and hands like raw hams that assaulted the briars and docks as if they had been collectively responsible for uprooting him from his farm near Ludwigsburg and setting him down on alien soil.

Nobody seemed to think it ironic that he should be clearing the land of a man at whom he might well have shot a year or so ago and that under the eye of his widow, who trudged to and fro among her shanty-town of hen houses on the opposite slope of the hill; nobody, that is, except Elinor herself, who was morbidly fascinated by the spectacle of the German's great broad back and the swift gleam of his scythe blade as it caught the sun in one of its wide, expert sweeps. Soon she found herself looking for him and sometimes wondered what Will would have said at having a German soldier working his way across the tussocks over which he had walked so often on his way to the fringe of the wood. His lumbering movements, Elinor thought, were strongly reminiscent of Will's, particularly when he stooped and gathered great armfuls of weeds to carry to the fire, and one day, impelled by nothing more than curiosity, she took him a stone jar of cider to refresh him at noon and thought, as he clicked his heels and bowed from the waist, that this was something Will would never have done, not even to a Lovell. He could speak a little English and she asked him his name. When he told her it was Willi, Willi Meyer, she walked swiftly away but after that, during the hot spell, she took him his cider each day and sometimes a hard-boiled egg and a crust of home-baked bread spread with butter from her churn. He seemed pathetically grateful for these modest gifts but whenever she approached he always dropped his scythe or billhook and stood stiffly to attention as though she had been an inspecting officer. Each time she saw him he seemed to have grown more like poor old Will and even the children must have thought so, for they often crossed the dip and climbed the hillside to talk with him and play about him as he worked and he was always careful to warn them to stand well clear of his scythe, although he beamed at them and sometimes made faces that produced squeals of laughter and excited jumpings up and down. There were four children, the elder, a boy, Mark, two girls, Queenie and Floss and the baby Richard. Elinor was glad to let Mark take them all out of her way as soon as he had finished his morning chores. He was a slim, serious-minded boy, with his mother's neat build and Grandfather Willoughby's beaky nose and grey eyes. When dinner was ready Elinor usually called to them from the farm wall on the opposite slope and she had summoned them one hot morning and seen them run down to the rivulet, when she heard a sudden outcry and saw the Württemberger throw down his scythe and dash down the hillside, moving at considerable speed for so clumsy a man. She ran down the slope to join them and was horrified to learn that Mark, in jumping the brook, had landed almost on top of a sleeping adder, curled on a slab of sandstone and had been bitten in the ball of the thumb. There had been one or two cases of snakebite in the Valley in the past year and one child, over at Coombe Bay, had died before she could be treated but it looked as though Willi Meyer had some experience in this field for he acted with commendable speed, sucking the puncture for a full minute, then whipping out his pen-knife, sterilising the blade in a match flame and scoring a deep double cut before sucking again. Then, still moving so quickly that he appeared almost to be turning somersaults, he threw the boy on his back, knelt on his forearm and made a tourniquet with his bootlace, twisting it until the leather bit into the flesh. Doctor Maureen said later that the German's first-aid had undoubtedly saved the boy's life for it was nearly an hour before she was located and could use the serum she had sent for after the fatal Coombe Bay case. Mark was out and about again in a week and boasting of his experience but Willi's skill and initiative made a deep impression on Elinor, who could not help thinking it strange that her son's life had been saved by one of the men who had helped to make her life and work meaningless. After this incident she made a habit of giving Willi a hot meal at the farm and gradually an undemonstrative friendship developed between them. He learned English rapidly, and seemed deeply interested in everything about the farm, particularly her methods of cross-breeding fowls to produce a good laying strain and soon they were on mildly convivial terms, discussing farm and family problems. He told her a good deal about his own farm in Württemberg, and how the South Germans always resented the domination of the Prussians and had only supported the war because Germany, as a nation, felt herself encircled by enemies. It was a point of view Elinor had never heard expressed and she thought, privately, that if most Germans were anything like the amiable Willi Meyer then the war was even more stupid and wasteful than she had supposed, and her husband's enlistment had been his first act of insanity.

The association never progressed beyond a neighbourly stage but it did not go unnoticed. Vicky Tarnshaw, a sullen, middle-aged woman who worked part-time for the Pitts family, at Hermitage close by, marked it and discussed it darkly with Martha Pitts and Gloria, the Valley Amazon. The good-natured Martha made allowances both for Elinor's loneliness and Vicky's addiction to gossip but Gloria was outraged. It seemed to her an act of the basest treachery to introduce a German, any German, into one's house at a time when half the Valley men were engaged in a life-and-death struggle with the baby-crucifiers and rapists overseas and having gone one noontime to the edge of Hermitage Wood, and watched Willi respond to Elinor's shrill call for dinner from the far hillside, Gloria convinced herself that there could be but one explanation to this act on the part of her neighbour,

telling Vicky, in Martha's presence, that Elinor Codsall's lust
for a man had driven her to form an association that shamed
the Valley. Martha, a kindly soul, pooh-poohed the notion
but Gloria argued, 'For what other reason would 'er ask un
inside? *Inside*, mind you! Gordamme mother, dornee lean
over backwards maaking excuses for everyone! Us 'ave 'ad
conshies an' our spies too 'till us bundled that Hun professor
out o' the Valley. So why shoulden us 'ave a woman who
dorn mind beddin' down with a Hun when there's nought
but children about the plaace?'

Thereafter Gloria and Vicky, taking turn and turn about,
kept a close watch on Periwinkle Farm but they did not, by
common consent, broadcast the story in the Valley. They
had a plan of their own and were reluctant to share the
pleasure of its execution with anyone.

One October evening, soon after supper, Gloria left the
house on the excuse of collecting mail from the box at the
end of the long track that led down to Hermitage Farm
from the river road but instead of going its full length
she climbed through a gap in the hedge and crossed the
shoulder of the hill to the wood. As she went she heard the
clink of hobnailed boots approaching higher up the lane and
wondered who might be calling on the farm at this hour but
she did not wait to find out for she had a rendezvous with
Vicky and soon located her, standing on the fringe of the
wood looking across at the single yellow blur that marked
the kitchen window of Periwinkle. 'Us'd better go about it
straight away,' Vicky said, 'bevore 'er locks up for the night!
Did 'ee think to bring the big scissors?'

'Arr, I did that,' Gloria said briefly. 'Come on then and us'll
make a quick job of it!' and they went down the slope and
up the opposite hillside to the farm where a peep through
the uncurtained window showed them that Elinor was inside
alone, bottling plums at the long table. They lifted the latch
and rushed in, startling Elinor so much that she jumped back,
smashing a large glass jar of fruit on the slate hearth. It
must have seemed to Elinor that her neighbour, together
with the hired woman who accompanied her, were victims

of the same homicidal urge that had destroyed Martin and
Arabella, for they rushed at her shouting curses and before
she knew what was happening they had her pinioned in the
high-backed chair, her feet in a mush of spilled plums and
broken glass that littered the hearth. Then she saw the big
scissors and let out a wild shriek and young Mark upstairs
tumbled out of bed and came pattering down the wooden
stair but by then Vicky, who was a powerful woman, had
the prisoner fast with her arms twisted behind the chair and
Gloria, hearing Mark approach, wedged an oak form under
the knob of the stairway door. After that the kitchen was in
an uproar with all three women shouting and screaming and
Elinor's wild struggles upsetting the table lined with bottling
jars that crashed and rolled in every direction. It was not until
Gloria had torn Elinor's hair loose and sliced more than half
of it away that the victim had an inkling of what lay behind
this assault, for Gloria screamed, 'There now! No one'll look
at 'ee twice now, not even that bloody Hun!' and went on
snipping away until all Elinor's honey-coloured hair lay in
the great pools of plum juice on the floor. It was the presence
of so much sticky liquid underfoot that gave Vicky Tarnshaw
another idea. She shouted, gibbering with glee, 'Now us'll strip
her naked an' roll her in it, Mrs Pitts!' and without waiting for
affirmation she ripped Elinor's cotton dress down the back and
did the same with her petticoat, while Gloria wrestled with her
drawers and stockings. It was this final indignity that gave
Elinor a brief access of strength. She kicked Gloria in the
stomach and lurched sideways so that the chair, entangling
itself in Vicky's legs, brought the pair of them crashing to
the floor within a foot or two of the fire. The struggle then
became general, with the winded Gloria joining in and getting
half her own clothes ripped off and they were all threshing
about in a whirl of garments and plum-syrup when the outer
door crashed open and Henry Pitts rushed in to stand with
mouth agape looking down at the extraordinary scene.

It had been his footfall, home on unexpected leave, that
Gloria had heard in the lane and when Martha Pitts seemed
evasive about his wife's whereabouts he lost no time in getting

her to voice her suspicions and had at once hurried in pursuit. Now he stood stock still on the threshold hardly able to believe his eyes. He was still wearing his uniform and patches of dried Flanders mud still adhered to his breeches and puttees. For a terrible moment he mistook the pools of plum juice for blood and assumed that the women were in the process of attacking one another with knives. Then he saw the shorn tresses lying behind the chair and it must have given him a clue for he started forward, seized his wife by the hair and hauled her clear, after which he planted a hefty kick on Vicky's behind that caused her to roll sideways and expose the crushed, hysterical Elinor whose cropped head was only an inch or so from a smouldering log that had fallen on to the hearth. He lifted her to her feet and saw that she was almost naked and plastered from head to foot in bottling syrup, as indeed, were all three of them. He said, with a trench oath, 'What in God's name be thinking of, all of 'ee?' and when Elinor, feeling her head, burst into hysterical weeping he turned to his wife whose dress hung down as far as the waist exposing her bare breasts and whose head and shoulders were dripping with plum juice so that she stared at him through a great mat of clotted red hair.

Vicky Tarnshaw was the first to recover. She scrambled to her feet and said, backing away, 'Us was marking her, Mr Pitts! 'Er's been lying wi' one o' they Hun prisoners up at the camp!' whereupon Elinor suddenly ceased her outcry, snatched up the scissors and would have plunged them into Vicky's face if Henry had not caught her by the shoulders and held her. Then Henry became conscious of a heavy thumping and wild cries from behind the stair door and asked Gloria who was there. She told him sulkily that it was the children trying to get in and the information seemed to steady him for he released Elinor, pocketed the scissors and went across to the door, opening it but blocking the boy's entry and saying, 'Tiz all right, Markboy. Us 'ave had a bit of an accident wi' the bottling and us was quarrelling who was to blame! Go back upstairs and quiet your sisters!' and then, very deliberately, he closed the door and addressing Elinor said, 'Now give over

snivelling, Elinor, an' tell us the facts. Is it true you been larkin'
wi' one o' they Fritzes? Not that I give a damn if you 'ave but
to satisfy these varmints, be it true?'

'No, it baint,' screamed Elinor, 'it baint true! Willi Meyer
saved my boy's life when he was bit by an adder an' ever zince
I give 'un a bite to eat mealtimes! You c'n ask the children, any
of 'em! Theym always yer when he comes inside the 'ouse!'

'Right,' said Henry, 'then go along upstairs and don't upset
the tackers telling 'em what really happened!' and as she
moved across the littered floor he picked up a besom from the
corner so that Vicky, mistaking his intention, made a sudden
rush to the door. He caught her a buffet on the ear that sent
her sprawling, shut the door and threw the broom at his wife.
'Clean this bliddy mess up,' he said briefly, 'every particle of it,
do 'ee hear?' and when Vicky, dazed from the blow, struggled
up on her hands and knees, he added, 'You too! Get to work
the pair of 'ee! Or I'll beat the daylights out of 'ee!'

He was very calm now, more deliberate and serious-looking
than Gloria had ever seen him. He took a seat astride a chair
near the door and watched their every movement and when
the litter of squashed plums and broken glass was shovelled
up he said, 'There's a bucket yonder, under the sink. Fill it
from the kettle and give the floor a swab over!'

'I'm not gonner scrub for the likes o' . . .' shouted Vicky
but she changed her mind when he got up and moved
towards her and scuttled into the scullery for bucket and
floorcloths. He reseated himself, placidly smoking his pipe
as they moved about straightening furniture and washing
the stone floor. When it was done, and the litter had been
thrown out, he said, 'Right! Get on home now, Vic Tarnshaw,
an' if you so much as shows your face at Hermitage again
I'll drown 'ee in the bliddy duckpond, you zee if I dorn't! As
for you,' he continued, addressing his wife, 'I reckon I'll serve
you zame as you served Elinor!'

'Don't you lay a hand on me!' shouted Gloria, jumping back
towards the fireplace but he turned his back on her and flung
open the door just as Vicky made a rush to pass him and
escape into the yard. She arrived there even quicker than she

had intended for, as she flitted by, he kicked her so accurately that she flew across the cobbles and landed face-down in the midden heap. He did not even wait to watch her scramble up and run shrieking into the darkness but shut the door, bolted it and crossed to the hearth, extracting Gloria's scissors from his pocket on his way. When she realised that he meant to put his threat into execution she let out a wild squark and tried to run round him and escape by the window, but he caught her easily enough, throwing his arm under her chin, dragging her across the window seat and making five quick snips with the blades. In a matter of seconds one side of her head was shorn even closer than Elinor's. Then she began to beg and plead – 'Dornee boy! *Dornee do it, Henry!*' and half-escaping his grip clasped him round the knees but he snipped and snipped until all her sticky auburn locks lay in a heap on the floor and the despairing face that looked up at him was the face of a stranger and not Gloria's at all.

He released her then, kicking the shorn tresses into the hearth, after which, still quite impassive, he took a ten-shilling note from his breeches pocket and laid it on the table, calling, 'Us iz goin' now Elinor! I've left 'ee zummat to pay for the damage and I'll be over to zee 'ee in the mornin'!'

There was no answer, no sound in the big kitchen but the loud ticking of the clock and the whimpering of the woman huddled under the window. He said, briefly, 'Be these our scissors?' and when she nodded he flung them in the fire saying, 'I woulden care to own 'em after this! Come on 'ome you gurt stoopid bitch, an' thank your stars I don't take a harness strap to your fat backside zoon as us gets there!'

She got up, still gulping and sniffing and went out into the yard. After a last look round he followed her, walking close behind as they crossed the shoulder of the hill, skirted the wood and went on down the far slope to the Hermitage track. It was a strange home-coming for a man who had been in and out of the trenches for the best part of a year.

The story of the assault on Elinor Codsall was common knowledge in a day or so. The Pitts did not broadcast it, and Vicky Tarnshaw left the Valley to work in a munitions factory in the North, but two closely-cropped heads on adjoining farms could not be concealed and Paul heard about it from the postman and made direct enquiries from Henry. Henry said, grimly, 'Ar, tiz true enough, Squire, I come 'ome after nigh on a year overseas lookin' for peace an' quiet an' what do I find? A bliddy war on me own doorstep, started be me own missis! Still, 'er won't start another I reckon, and I've squared the damage they did upalong. What the hell have got into the folk back here? Be they all clean off their bliddy heads?'

Paul said he thought most civilians were and after paying a call on Elinor arranged, through Sam Potter, to get the Württemberger sent away from the camp in case he was victimised. The sight of Elinor's unevenly shorn head distressed him more than anything he had witnessed in the Valley lately and leaving her he rode on up to the highest point of the estate, on the edge of Hermitage Wood, looking down across the autumn landscape and trying to understand the hysteria and savage intolerance that changed simple, workaday folk like Gloria Pitts and Norman Eveleigh into the kind of bigots one might expect to find in the fifteenth-century lynch mob whipped up by fanatical priests. Was it fear, he wondered, sponsored by the shattering of their settled way of life, or had a vein of tribal brutality always existed below the surface to be laid bare by the shock of war? It was hard to determine, particularly as the fighting men, like Henry, Ikey and Dandy Timberlake, seemed to have become almost gentle and were certainly more tolerant for their terrible experiences whereas cruelty only showed in the people at home. He sat his horse up there a long time deciding that he no longer belonged to any of them in the way he had belonged before the war. There were the fanatics, like Gloria Eveleigh and Horace Handcock, the Smart Allicks, like Sydney Codsall, and the passives, like Elinor Codsall and Claire; there were those in the thick of it all, like Ikey and Henry and the odd ones who saw the war as the negation of human dignity, people like Keith Horsey and poor, half-crazed Marian Eveleigh. He himself was a category of his own. By now he had learned to accept it as a kind of visitation, a plague that would one day die out and perhaps leave the land purified but today he felt utterly isolated, belonging neither to those under fire, to the patriots, or even to the honest doubters. He thought, grimly, 'Damn it, I'll have to find my way back again somehow and surely the only way to do that is to come down on one side or the other. I couldn't honestly proclaim myself a CO but I'm damned if I'll let my judgement be warped about the Keith Horseys and the Elinor Codsalls! I suppose the only thing left is to jump in head-first, alongside Ikey, Henry and all the others around here who have been sucked in!' and at once he felt more clear-headed but because he was doubtful whether they could use a man of thirty-six with the scars of the last war on his body he said nothing of his decision to anybody, not even Claire, until he had written to his old Yeomanry Colonel who had a staff job in Whitehall and asked for advice on the quickest way of getting to France.

He had made insufficient allowance for the terrible attrition of the Somme battles. A reply came by return of post and he was offered, subject to a routine medical check, a temporary commission in the Royal Army Service Corps, Transport Section. He sat staring at the letter hardly knowing whether to be astonished, elated or dismayed and then, remembering Will and Smut and Jem and all the others, and weighing their worth against that of Sydney Codsall and Gloria Pitts, he made his decision. Fearing that Claire would try and talk him out of it he filled in the application and posted it, asking for an interview at the earliest possible date.

IV

He confessed that same night, when he and Claire were sitting late in front of the library fire. Her temperate reception of the news confounded him, so obviously so that she laughed, telling him, in Mrs Handcock's phrase, that 'she could read 'un like an ha'penny book!' She could have said a great deal more on this subject, how she had watched him, anxiously and sympathetically, for months past as news reached the Valley

in dribs and drabs of casualties, as fissures opened between
combatant families and those who, by luck or design, had made
money and managed to remain uncommitted. It was this, she
felt, that was wearing him down for she had long ago accepted
the fact that the social health of the estate concerned him very
deeply, perhaps even more deeply than their domestic accord.
This was the yardstick he used to measure his worth as a
human being. She had watched him wince at the emergence
of the Sydney Codsalls and their ilk, at rifts between men like
Eph Morgan, whose only son had been killed, and men like
Abe Tozer, the smith, whose son-in-law was said to be coining
money in a Birmingham foundry. She too had been dismayed
by the attack upon Elinor Codsall and by the traces of slime
that survived Henry's earnest attempts to make amends and
yet, in the main, she had been unable to help him much for
although she was Valley born she still looked at the Valley
through clear glass and not, as he so obstinately did, through
a stained-glass window. It was because she knew him so well
that she had known it would end like this, in him going off in
the wake of the others and she said, in reply to his question as
to how she could know something he had not finally decided
himself, 'Oh, I knew you would go, sooner or later, and if I
were in your shoes I suppose I should do the same. I don't
say I'd do it in the spirit of the slop one reads in the papers
but, from a man's viewpoint, it must seem that all the best
are being sucked in and the discards spewed out! If you
were ten years older you'd have to grin and bear it; as it
is, thank God, you aren't likely to be sent into the line; if
they accept you at all, that is!'

'They'll accept me,' he said, so huffily that she laughed
again.

'Yes, I suppose they will, for you're a good deal lustier than
some of the men they've taken. However, don't run away with
the idea that leg of yours will stand up to unlimited demands.
What kind of jobs do they do in the Service Corps?'

He was so relieved that she accepted his enlistment as
inevitable and was not disposed to make a song and dance
over it that he became expansive. 'The RASC take all the

ammunition, stores and rations up the line. I shall try and wangle my way into a horse or mule section!' but she reminded him that Ikey had told them mechanical transport had now all but superseded the horse in France, and that if he was judged on his handling of the old Belsize he would prove an expensive addition to the forces of the Crown. He was not entirely fooled by her gaiety but caught himself admiring her performance.

'I don't know why you should be so ready to consign me to the awkward squad,' he grumbled, 'I was in uniform the first day you saw me and you fell over yourself to catch my eye if I remember rightly!'

'Yes I did,' she agreed, 'but you were young bones then! Besides you were the best catch in the county!'

'I've still got a shot or two in my locker,' he told her. 'Come over here and I'll prove it,' but she declined the invitation and instead sat on the hearthrug looking into the coals as Paul watched the effect of firelight on her hair. As he mused he thought of something he had always been meaning to tell her but had somehow forgotten, not once but a dozen times, since their encounter with Grace at the time of the Coronation visit to London.

He reached out, heaved one of the heavy books from the shelf at his elbow and thumbed through the pages until he found the colour reproduction of Rubens' young wife, Hélène Fourment, as Bathsheba, receiving King David's letter.

'I don't know whether you'll be flattered or otherwise,' he said, 'but this was something I always meant to show you. The first time you and Grace met, that afternoon you came here with Rose soon after we were married, she produced this as soon as you had gone, and said you were Hélène Fourment reincarnated. It wasn't wholly a joke either, I think she half believed it.'

She showed interest at once, taking the book and studying it carefully. 'Grace said that? All those years ago? But I was slim then and this girl would turn the scale to eleven stone! It was probably an attempt to put you off, I expect she saw you looking me over too attentively!'

He laughed, saying that even then he was inclined to think that Grace had been considering abdication. He could say that now and half-believe it for somehow, in the last year or so, he had begun to share a little of Grace's impatience with parochialism. 'You were never slim,' he said, prodding her. 'You had a neat waist and still have but you were always what the Edwardians called "a fine woman", meaning that you had plenty to catch hold of! However, Hélène was reckoned a great beauty, so I always regarded the comparison as a compliment, tho', if I remember rightly, she did use the adjective "ripe".'

'It's one that certainly suits me now,' Claire said. 'Are there any more of Hélène? Did he paint her often?'

'He was always painting her. Damn it, the man was over fifty and she was sixteen when they married so can you blame him? If I could paint I'd have you sitting for me nude, half-dressed or over-dressed, eight hours a day!' He took the book from her and looked closely at it again. 'That's an idea, Claire,' he said triumphantly. 'Would you like to sit for someone really good? After all, we look like being here permanently, so it's time we laid down an ancestor or two!'

She was secretly delighted at the suggestion but made a protest nevertheless, saying that it would have been a pleasant notion ten years ago but today, at thirty-three, it was too late for that kind of nonsense.

'Rubbish,' he said, 'look at some of these old hags of the Lovell family! I'd a damned sight sooner sit looking at you and pack this lot off to a sale. If we could get a London artist down he could do the children as well. I'll write off to Uncle Franz, for I wager the old codger would know someone and keep his price down.'

She said slowly, 'All right then but don't be so eager to throw your money away. As a matter of fact I've a confession myself. I didn't mean to tell until the plan was a lot further advanced but if you really are likely to go soon you ought to know at once. Had it ever occurred to you that *I* might want to play a more positive part in the war?'

'No,' he said, 'frankly it hadn't! You always seemed far better at carrying-on-as-usual than me.' And then he remembered that long ago she had an ambition to nurse and had taken a course at St Thomas's Hospital during her exile in London. He said bluntly, 'Look here, I'm damned if I'll stand for you working yourself to death as a VAD! I want you here when I come home and you have the children to think of.'

'Oh, it wouldn't involve leaving here,' she said, airily, 'but if you do go I don't think I could hang around here passing the time, living for leave periods or the end of the war. I should have to have something to keep me occupied and as long as John Rudd is active he can care for the estate far better than I. I had . . . well, it occurred to me that we could turn this barn of a place into a hospital!'

'A hospital! For stretcher-cases?'

'No, that isn't practical, something more modest like a convalescent home for about fifty to sixty wounded men who wouldn't arrive until they were on the road to recovery. As a matter of fact I've already discussed it with Doctor Maureen.'

'The devil you have!'

'She thinks it's a first-class idea. We've got at least ten rooms we now use for lumber. I could shift the children out of the east wing and clear the furniture from the big drawing-room that we hardly ever use. Then we could have a main ward on ground level and patients that could move about could sleep three to a room upstairs. If we needed more space we could get a couple of Nissen huts put up in the paddock. I got the idea watching Dandy Timberlake after he came home from Gallipoli. Men get patched up in big hospitals and then they go home on leave, most of them to industrial cities and some, I suppose, to near-slums. Then, as soon as their scars heal, they get reboarded but they aren't really well at all, they're still suffering from shock and nervous exhaustion like Dandy and some of the others about here who have been out a long time. A month or so in a place like this, with organised exercises, fresh air and sea-bathing from May to October would work wonders. I should like to do it, providing you agree.'

'Well,' he said, greatly impressed in spite of himself, 'I suppose it's possible but who would you get to run it?'

'I'd run it,' she said. 'I've kept up-to-date reading Maureen's journals and if we gave the house the Government couldn't very well turn us down, could they? As to staff, there are more than a dozen wives in the Valley who would be glad to do something useful. We could even organise a local crêche, with a roster of nannies and older children taking their meals at Mary Willoughby's so that their mothers could work part-time over here. They only drawback I can see is whether you really want the place knocked about by strangers and turned into a kind of barracks. After all, this is what you'll be fighting for, and in spite of anything you might think at the moment your dream isn't dead, Paul, only hibernating. Do you think I don't know why you divert every penny you receive from the scrapyard into a special account, earmarked for post-war development!'

'This is ridiculous!' he exclaimed, laughing. 'I don't have a shred of privacy! How the devil did you know I had made up my mind not to make a personal profit out of munitions or other fiddles?'

'Oh, I keep an eye on your papers when you're on your rounds,' she said carelessly, 'and for all you know I go through your pockets from time to time. You ought to know that, seeing you're likely to be turned loose in France among the mesdemoiselles and the WAACs! But don't sidetrack me, I've got to know exactly how you feel about this plan. It's got to have your blessing before I go ahead with it.'

He said, pulling her down on his knees, 'I think it's a damned good idea and with Maureen to keep an eye on the venture you'll make a sensational success of it! Yes, it has my blessing, Claire. You're nearer the truth than you know about the home background of those poor devils. There isn't one in fifty who owns a square inch of the land he's fighting for and Grenfell says their physique compares very poorly with the men they're up against! Take a look at some of those strapping Fritzes in the camp and see for yourself, it's a point worth taking!' Then, teasing her, 'I suppose when I do get leave and come back here pawing the ground I'll be met by a starchy matron who regards me as

a patient rather than a warrior in search of solace?' and he
ran his hands over her thinking what a fool he must be to
sacrifice her society for the desolation Ikey had described to
him in Flanders or even the cheerlessness of a base camp
populated exclusively by men. She said, after a moment
of this, 'I'm always telling you we're too old to do our
courting in an armchair! Let's go to bed,' but the prospect
of forsaking the warm fire and putting a term to one of the
rare moments of intimacy was uninviting, so she remained
where she was holding the future at bay and presently she
provoked him into enacting one of those boisterous scenes
that always made her chuckle in retrospect, as though they
were not man and wife, with a growing family and a longish
partnership behind them but a couple of youngsters making
the most of a lucky opportunity in the front parlour, when
everybody was out of the way.

V

Paul's summons to report for initial training at a nearby
Officers' Training Camp came in late November, 1916, but
before he left Grenfell travelled down from London and spent
a night or two at Shallowford. He was a very different
James, Claire decided, from the buoyant, quietly confident
professional they had often entertained in the days following
his return to Parliament. The strain of long-night sittings and
a share in decisions involving the slaughter of thousands of
men showed in the lined face and patches of white hair
above his ears. He had lost most of his jauntiness and
now walked with a slight stoop. He was not, he told her,
in the best of health, being sadly troubled with chronic
indigestion and periods of sleeplessness, aggravated by his
growing disgust for the jealousies and scramble for power
among some of his senior colleagues and opposition members
of the wartime Coalition. It was like, he told them, being
aboard a crippled vessel among a lot of elderly passengers
who had dismissed the crew and taken upon themselves

the job of charting the ship's course. Paul soon realised
that he was not only losing faith in his revered leader,
Asquith, whom Grenfell said was too much of a gentlemen
to survive in such a scrimmage but had also come to dislike
and distrust the firebrand, Lloyd George, who was openly
flirting with Unionists, men like Bonar Law and the newspaper
magnate, Alfred Harmsworth, in the hope of replacing Asquith
as Premier. 'I'm not so prejudiced as to think The Welsh
Wizard wouldn't make a good pilot,' Grenfell admitted, 'but
the way he's going about it could split the party down the
middle and we are going to need men of Asquith's integrity
when this business is over. Sometimes I find myself more
in sympathy with the men who had the guts to stand up
in August, 1914, and condemn the whole business as an
international crime! I wasn't one of them but I supported
the idea of a negotiated peace months ago and I've suffered
for it since! Maybe Old Keir Hardie was right when he
said, "If I had my time over again I should steer clear of
politics and preach the gospel!"'

He and Paul sat late over the study fire and Grenfell told
him something of the overall strategic position of the Allies
and spoke of hidden factors that influenced decisions and
could not be made public in the newspapers. The Dardanelles
campaign, James said, had almost succeeded, and might have
done had it not been bedevilled by inter-Service rivalry.
Now, in his opinion there was no real chance of either side
achieving a breakthrough in the West. James admitted to
being an 'Easterner', believing that a final decision could
only be reached on some other front but the High Command,
of whom he had an even poorer opinion than Ikey, were
now committed to a war of attrition in which the victory
was based on the Allies' superior manpower. 'Almost as
if they were playing with counters rather than people of
flesh and blood!' he declared bitterly. He deprecated Paul's
decision to join up, saying that he would contribute more
doing his part in making good the terrible losses caused
by the U-boat campaign. 'Damn it man,' he protested, when
Paul told him he was due to leave in a few days, 'hasn't

the Valley contributed its quota already! What sense is there in you rushing out in search of a medal and a lump of shrapnel to balance the Boer bullet that's still travelling round inside you? I should have thought Claire would have had the sense to talk you out of it!'

Paul realised that it was useless to try and explain how he felt about staying home while men like Smut Potter and Henry Pitts wallowed in the mud. By now Grenfell was incapable of regarding the war in a personal light but was compelled, by reason of his familiarity with the overall picture, to look at it as a complicated exercise in checks and counter-balances involving not merely men but entire races and imponderable economic factors. One other thing he said did impress Paul and made him increasingly anxious for the future and that was his contemptuous dismissal of the Russian 'steamroller' myth. He gave it as his opinion that Russia would be out of the war in a matter of months. 'And can you wonder,' he grumbled, 'when the Tsarist system if rotten right through! Peasants are going into action unarmed while scoundrels in Petrograd are making fortunes, and all the time that ass of a Tsar and his neurotic wife behave as though they are playing chess instead of a game that will sweep them all under the carpet, along with all that's left of human values!' He went off to bed in a despondent mood and presumably found it difficult to rest for in the small hours Paul awoke to find Claire getting him a bismuth mixture. She told him she had heard James pacing his room, assailed by one of his stomach cramps and said, on climbing back into bed, 'He's going to pieces, Paul! I don't think it's indigestion but something more serious, probably ulcers. I've insisted the Maureen gives him a good going-over in the morning and if necessary you'll have to persuade him to stay here and rest for a month or so.'

'I'll try but I don't think I'll succeed,' Paul said and he was right, for when, in the morning, Maureen diagnosed irritation of the duodenal cap he shrugged, pocketed her prescription, and said that while men who had voted for him were having their heads blown off in France, and dying of dysentery in

the Balkans, he could hardly take a month's holiday on
account of a bellyache. 'And in the circumstances,' he said
to Paul, 'who are you to argue with me? They'll probably
invalid you out halfway through your initial training, and
I hope to God they do! At least there will be one person
hereabouts to preserve a small corner of England that I
like to regard as a counterweight to all their damned factory
chimneys and red-brick jungles!' Paul saw him as far as
Sorrel Halt and as the train pulled out James leaned from
the window and waved his billycock hat, revealing, for a
brief instant, a flash of the jaunty campaigner who had
once shocked the Valley by barnstorming his way into the
heart of a Tory citadel. Paul was to remember his swift
smile, and the wave of the billycock hat. It was a long
time before he saw him again.

Two days later he stood on the same platform but this
time it was he who was quitting the Valley and Claire,
dressed in her fashionable best, who was putting a tolerable
brave face on their first separation since she had come home
in the spring of 1906. He said, jokingly, 'Well, cheer up,
I'm not off to France yet, just to camp over the county
border!' but there was finality in the occasion and they
both sensed it, possibly because, further along the train,
khaki-clad figures leaned from the windows watching them.
Paul said, as they awaited the guard's whistle, 'Listen, Claire,
get moving with that convalescent home the minute you
get back, it'll give you something to think about! As for
me, I daresay I'll put things in my letters aimed at taking
some of the starch out of the matron's linen!' She smiled
at that and said, 'It'll be odd getting a letter from you.
You haven't written me one for more than ten years. I
daresay, when you get down to it, you'll find it downright
embarrassing!'

'Not a chance,' he said, 'I could compose one between here
and the junction and maybe I will!' and with that the train
started and her hand flew to her mouth, and looking back
he saw her standing against the open skyline of the grey

landscape. It was confirmation, he thought, of the belief that had been gaining strength in him through all the years of their marriage. She and the Valley were one and could never be separated in his consciousness. There was comfort and a certain reassurance in the knowledge.

Chapter Seven

I

The first of them began to arrive early in the New Year, men wounded in the later stages of the Somme offensive, some having already spent up to four months in hospital and were now on the road to recovery, although about a third were permanently maimed in one way or another. These were the most cheerful. They had survived and could never be sent out again, whereas the more able-bodied lived in permanent fear of being reboarded fit for active service and were inclined to retard their own recovery, sometimes with Maureen's connivance.

At first there were only about a score of them but within weeks the Government sanctioned the erection of three Nissen wards in the small paddock on the right of the drive and thereafter the odd chronic case began to appear, including gas casualties, one or two who had lost limbs, and a few cases of shell-shock, men who sweated and trembled and dribbled and were sometimes sent off again to mental hospitals. By then a permanent Medical Officer had been allocated to Shallowford, together with three downgraded medical orderlies, themselves former casualties of 1914 fighting.

The weather that winter was cruel, with months of severe frost and several heavy falls of snow, so that, for the most part, the men remained indoors, some of them permanently in bed and it was this that compelled Claire to reorganise the staff almost as soon as it had been enrolled. She had not bargained for so many immobile casualties and the MO and his orderlies were fully occupied in the wards and could give no help in cooking, cleaning and organising recreational facilities. Doctor Maureen was equally busy, sometimes working an

eighteen-hour day but she seemed to thrive on it and soon
gained ascendancy over Captain Gleeson, the MO, who had
served with the Oxford and Bucks Light Infantry from Mons
to the battle of Loos, and been invalided home with bronchitis
in the autumn of 1915. Gleeson was a cheerful but irascible
man who looked a little like a grizzled Father Christmas and
could swear fluently in Hindustani. He was inclined, however,
to take things easily, reckoning that at fifty-eight he had done
his bit. He told Claire that only compassion kept him at his
post he had been on reserve when recalled in 1914. His three
orderlies worked extremely hard for they were anxious to
remain on home service but when, in early March, the number
of patients rose to eight-five the demands upon Claire, Mrs
Handcock, Thirza and the scratch team of dailies she had
enlisted in the village became intolerable and she began a
local recruiting drive that was met with immediate success.

Her first triumph was the enrolment of Marian Eveleigh,
whom she managed to coax from communion with the spirits
when everyone else, including Marian's exasperated husband,
had given her up for lost.

The death of her eldest son and the fear of losing Harold,
his brother, now commissioned and serving in the Near East,
had brought Marian to the edge of a nervous breakdown and
Eveleigh's uncharacteristic involvement with the land-girl Jill
had coincided with her change in life so that the wretched
woman's world had crumbled to pieces. She shut herself up for
days on end in the boy's old bedroom where she was alleged to
have established contact with a Red Indian spirit, who acted as
intermediary between mother and son. Her daughters and the
hired hands at Four Winds took it for granted that she was
going the way of old Marian Codsall but Claire had known
Marian all her life and remembered that she came from good,
yeoman stock and was therefore not prepared to accept this
verdict. In her initial approach she worked on the lines that,
by taking service at the hospital, Marian could do something
practical on behalf of her surviving son. She won her victory
on the afternoon she persuaded Marian to call at Shallowford
and meet some of the patients. One of them had served in

Harold's battalion in France and from that day on the cloud that had been setling on Marian Eveleigh's mind began to disperse and she agreed to go to work in the kitchen. Doctor Maureen described her as a classic example of the value of occupational therapy, declaring that Claire had a natural gift for healing. She then urged her to try her luck on Elinor Codsall who, since the night of Gloria Pitts' assault, had stayed within the confines of Periwinkle and was said to be developing into a recluse. Elinor proved more stubborn. To Claire's first appeal to hand over the outdoor work to Old Matt, one of the biblical shepherds (who was the Valley stopgap these days) she advanced a flat refusal.

'They took my man Will an' then spread bliddy lies about me so they can vinish their war without my help!' she said. Claire was puzzled by her truculence, remembering her not so much as the wife of Will Codsall but as the shy daughter of old preacher Willoughby tending chickens at Deepdene and Elinor's casual use of the favourite male adjective in the Valley was an indication of the changes that had engulfed the Valley in the last two years. She persisted, however, pointing out that the wounded men at Shallowford were ex-comrades of Will and therefore entitled to her concern and when Elinor protested that she had young children to care for in addition to thirteen-year-old Mark, Claire said that she might bring the toddlers to work with her each day and leave them in charge of Thirza, who had charge of the nursery for encumbered helpers. Elinor said she would think about it but when Claire artfully remarked that she looked years younger with her short hair, and reminded her of when they were girls on neighbouring farms, the widow's surliness disappeared and she even shed a few reminiscent tears, brushing them away with the query, 'What's to become of us all, Mrs Craddock? That's what I'd like to know, what with the Squire gone too at his time o' life!' and Claire hiding a smile, made a mental note to write and tell Paul that at least one of his tenants had ceased to think of him as 'Young Squire' and had already advanced him to his dotage.

Claire then enlisted the two Potter girls who grasped the opportunity to move within the orbit of eighty convalescent males, despite the fact that most of them were free with snapshots of wives and children. Time was pressing on the unmarried Potter sisters these days, for Cissie was thirty-three and Violet not much younger and although each could boast of a small spread of handsome, healthy children, neither could lay claim to a separation allowance or even a shared pension in respect of Jem, who had gone to his death unable to make up his mind which of them he would wed. As Violet put it to her sister, the night after Claire had offered them a pound a week each for a daily five-hour spell at the Big House, 'Us'd better taake 'er up on it, Cis! Tiz reg'lar money and us dorn zeem to be gettin' far with the boys zince they shifted that dratted camp the t'other side o' the Valley!' to which Cissie replied, thoughtfully, 'Aye, and us baint gettin' no younger neither, be us? They zay half the men downalong are short of a limb but they can't all be married, can 'em? Maybe tiz time us thought o' zettling down like Panse; after all, if theym took us'll get the pension, providin' us can get a pair of 'em to church, that is!'

And so they went and were soon in their element among the more cheerful and active of the patients and as more and more men arrived, and nearly half the women of the Valley were absorbed in shift work about the wards, kitchens and washhouse, they suggested to Claire that she signed on their sister Hazel, whose second child had been stillborn early in the New Year and whom they now described as 'Uncommon low in spirit on that account'. It was a sharp reminder to Claire that she had not called on Hazel since she had lost her baby but before going along to Mill Cottage she consulted Maureen on the possible usefulness of Hazel on the staff. Maureen's response surprised her. She said, shortly, 'Leave her be, she's not fit for any kind of work, although I daresay pottering about helping the sexton doesn't overtax her.'

'Do you mean she's ill, that she hasn't recovered from losing her baby?' Claire asked but Maureen only sucked her lips, looked irritated and said grumpily, 'Oh, she's well enough physically, and if I was asked for a professional opinion I should say her wits were sharper than they had ever been but having Ikey home for a long spell and then losing him again had a bad effect on the poor little wretch.'

'Well, since you've told me that much you might as well tell me the rest,' Claire said. 'I should have thought working here might cheer her up. She'll be with other people all day.'

'Not the kind of people we have here,' Maureen said, 'men lacking an arm or a leg and shell-shock cases! Hazel isn't a child any more. She was never really half-witted you know, just retarded and always, I thought, in a rather privileged way. For one thing time meant nothing to her. The months separating That Boy's visits were only days, perhaps even hours. She was never a prey to doubt, jealousy, or even fear of death in the way ordinary folk are bothered about these things. The fact is she's now beginning to grow up and could prove as much a shell-shock case as some of the lads yonder! Leave her be, Claire, I'll be responsible for her!' and with that Maureen rushed off on her rounds leaving Claire regretting that she had not found time to call at Mill Cottage the day Meg brought news that Ikey's daughter had been born dead shortly after his return to France. She resolved to go at the first opportunity but that night one batch of men left and another came in so that she was occupied every waking minute of the next two days. On the third day, as she was setting out, she met John Rudd trudging up the drive with news that put Hazel Palfrey out of mind. He reported, gloomily, that there had been a second rick fire during the night, this time at Deepdene, and that, following upon the first fire at High Coombe earlier in the week, it seemed probable that a pyromaniac was at large in the Valley.

II

John had had his suspicions after seeing the burned out ricks at High Coombe. He had a long experience of rick fires and this one, breaking out in the middle of the night after a week of drizzle, baffled him. Spontaneous combustion would have been preceded by smouldering and Hugh Derwent told him that he had passed the ricks only an hour before and would have certainly smelled smoke on such a windless evening. There were so many ways a stack could catch fire that John assumed that the outbreak was due to carelessness with cigarettes on the part of the soldiers taking shelter there earlier in the day. When news came of a second fire, however, this time at Deepdene, he realised that it must be deliberate and made a report to the police, circulating all the farms in the Valley to keep a sharp lookout and report the presence of any stranger in the lanes and tracks after dark. No information came in but within forty-eight hours there had been two more outbreaks, one on the extreme boundary of Four Winds and another on the eastern edge of Hermitage. John recruited a patrol from the officer at the Nun's Bay camp and for a week or more no new outbreaks occurred. Then, in the first week of April, smoke was seen coming from a large stack of pit-props in the plantation beyond the badger slope north of the woods and this time evidence of kindling was discovered and there was a whiff of lamp oil about some of the half-burned billets. John was in the act of telephoning the police when Claire told him that Meg Potter was asking for him and had expressed a wish to say something of importance to 'Squire's agent and the Lady Doctor'.

'What the devil does she want with Maureen?' John demanded and then, a thought striking him, added, 'I'll get her in any case, she's down at the lodge now.'

They assembled, all four of them in the library, the old gypsy standing with her back to the door, arms folded, face impassive, like a queen receiving an embassy. She said, without preamble, 'I can tell 'ee where to look for the rick-burner!' and when they exclaimed, went on, 'I dorn say I *will* but I could! Providing us keep it clear o' police an' foreigners!'

John said, sharply, 'Look here, we can't promise anything of that kind! The matter has already been reported to police and the military. The whole damned place is in uproar!' Then, when her expression did not change, 'Is it one of the patients here? A shell-shock case?'

'No it baint!' Meg replied stubbornly, planting her sandalled feet widely apart as though to resist a combined onrush. 'It's along o' my girl, Hazel!'

'Great God!' John exclaimed and Claire rose from her seat but Maureen sat still looking at the floor. 'Are you certain of that? You've seen her at it?'

'Nay, I've not seen her,' Meg said, 'but tiz Hazel right enough. The point is, what'll become of her if the police learn of it? Will 'er be shut up, same as my boy Smut backalong?'

Maureen said: 'Not in a prison, Meg, I could make certain of that!'

The gypsy turned, ignoring the others and said, '*Where* then? In one o' the asylums for mazed folk?'

'She'd have to be,' John said, 'you couldn't expect us to leave her free to do worse. Suppose she started setting fire to cottages with people asleep in them?'

'She'll not do that!' Meg replied grimly, 'tiz just the ricks and handy kindling, like the props up yonder.'

'How can you know that?' Claire asked and Meg said bluntly that she knew it well enough, implying that she had no intention of saying more than she could help.

'Listen Meg,' Maureen said urgently, 'suppose I could promise Hazel a course of expert treatment? I've got a friend in Bristol who runs a clinic. It isn't an asylum, or anything like an asylum. It's a place where they treat all kinds of people who have cracked under war-strain. I don't think this is a permanent derangement, it's linked to the girl's post-natal physical condition and maybe a sudden awareness of what's going on in the world. We'd get her well, given time.'

'Damn it,' protested John, 'what proof have we anyway? To put the girl away we should have to catch her in the act, wouldn't we?'

'Has she admitted the facts to you, Meg?' Claire asked.

'No,' said Meg, shrugging, 'I've not spoken a word to her on the matter and neither will I, except maybe to warn her should you and Mr Rudd set the police on her. I baint forgot what the police did to my boy backalong or the kind of place they kep' him shut up in for taking a deer and fightin' free o' Gilroy's men! Tiz like Mr Rudd says, you've no proof and us'll zee you don't come by none!'

'Then why are you telling us?'

The gypsy shrugged. 'Because you an' Squire always played straight with me an' mine!' she said and left it at that.

There was silence for a while. In a way, Claire thought, it was almost as if she was gloating over their impotence, yet if this had been so she would hardly have come here with information that her own daughter was a pyromaniac. She said at length, 'The Doctor could go and talk to Hazel, then report back to the four of us. Would you do that, Maureen?'

'It if served any purpose,' Maureen said, 'but it wouldn't, I can tell you that.'

'Why not?'

'Because, since her baby died, she doesn't trust me. I've tried talking to her, I've tried explaining about the war but it was easy enough to see she thought I was romancing. The only German she ever knew was the old Professor over at Coombe Bay. When I said Ikey was away fighting Germans she laughed in my face. She thinks of the Germans as a race of fat, wheezing professors, so it isn't surprising she finds it hard to believe Ikey and everyone else is fighting them. No, I could do something for her with Ikey's consent but she wouldn't admit anything to me.'

'She might tell her mother,' Claire said but the gypsy shook her head. 'I've generally known what the girl is about but there's no bond between us,' she said. 'In the old days I had to stand with Tamer, him being my man, and as for the others, they stood together. But Hazel, she's different, she stood alone 'till The Boy took up with her and now tiz his concern I reckon.'

'Could Ikey get special leave under these circumstances?' Claire asked John and John said he might, providing the facts were laid before the military authorities. Claire caught Meg's eye and said, 'We won't break faith with you, Meg, not unless we have no alternative,' and to Maureen: 'Would it do any good if I tried to talk to her?'

'It might,' Maureen said, 'she's always trusted the Squire, and you're Squire's deputy. Maybe, if you let her know that you know, fear of the consequences might stop the next rick going up. What do you say to that, John?'

John said, gloomily, 'I'm hanged if I know. It would depend on whether Meg was prepared to back us, providing, that is, Claire extracted some kind of confession from the girl. If I'd known when I came in here that it wasn't a shell-shock patient I'm damned if I would have given half a promise to keep the police in ignorance for at least they could have kept a watch on the cottage. My duty has always been to the estate and it still is. I don't clutter myself with personal responsibility for everyone who lives on it!'

'No,' Claire reminded him, 'but Paul does so it seems to me I ought to try and put myself in his place. Would you agree as regards that?'

John blew out his cheeks and groped for his pipe. 'Yes,' he said reluctantly, 'I suppose I'd have to agree to that. I've worked alongside the man fifteen years and flatter myself I know him that well. Go and see what you can do but if you run into trouble don't stay and handle it yourself, come straight back here for help!' He got up and went out, saying he would tell Chivers to bring the trap round to the front and Claire thought she had never seen him look so old and tired.

They had forgotten in was a Thursday, the day for the weekly war game over at the camp. Troops swarmed on the rising ground beyond the Four Winds' border, and the peace of the river road was shattered every now and again by a convoy of lorries, the ear-splitting rush of a despatch-rider's motor-cycle, or the passage of the big Crossley staff car that advertised its approach by a series of imperious honks. Claire cursed them one and all as she jogged along towards the cottage, for the noise and bustle put an additional strain on her nerves and the presence of transport here, where it had always been so quiet and changeless, underlined the fearful urgency of the war, as though a great bird of prey was beating its way up and down the Valley in search of fresh victims. She reined in beyond

the ford to let the staff car rush by and did not answer the
cheery wave of the officers in the back. The car disappeared
in a cloud of exhaust towards Coombe Bay and she went on
to the point where the lateral track joined the road beside the
cottage, tethering the pony to the gatepost. In the garden she
saw the child Patrick absorbed in the task of nailing pieces
of wood together with a hammer that seemed almost as
large as himself. She was struck not only by his neatness
and cleanliness but also by his likeness to Ikey. There was
little of the Potter stamp about his face or build for he was
very slender, with a dark, slightly sallow complexion and
sharp, intelligent eyes. He stood up when Claire asked him
if his mother was in the cottage.

'Arr,' he said, in the broad Valley burr, ''Er's upstairs,
ma'am. Leastways, 'er was!' and then, with an unexpectedly
engaging smile, 'I'm making a nairyplane! I'm gonner fly in
un when 'er's done!'

She had come without the least idea of how to approach
the matter but now she saw that, with a little luck, she might
use the child to win Hazel's confidence. She said, 'If I sent my
Simon over for you would you like to come up to the Big House
and play with the twins? They're making aeroplanes too.'

Patrick considered. He had, Claire thought, his father's
charm as well as his polite but definite sense of privacy. 'Arr,'
he said finally, 'I'd like that! When will 'er come, then?'

'I don't know, I'll go and ask Mummy,' Claire said and went
into the cottage.

It was, she thought, very neat and clean. It seemed a lifetime
since she had spied in at the window watching Paul read
Ikey's letter aloud, her heart torn with jealousy, but today
a different kind of confusion assailed her and she stood just
inside the door, wondering where to begin. Everything in
the room shone and twinkled in the afternoon sun and the
hearth had been newly swept. It did not look like the home
of a crazy woman who ran about the estate at night setting
fire to ricks and the responsibility of her mission dragged at
her so that, not for the first time since Paul had left, she was
conscious of her own inadequacy to deal with problems of

this kind, her uncertainty reminding her of his strange talent
for administration. Every man, woman and child living in the
Valley trusted him implicitly and he would have had such a
headstart on an occasion like this.

She went up the short stair and found Hazel sitting beside
the window looking out across the stubble fields beyond the
river. There was something birdlike about the way she sat
perched on a milking stool, her knees and hands pressed
tightly together, her expression not exactly tense but very
alert. She said, as Claire entered, 'Be'm still searching, then?
I zee the soldiers go by just now,' and Claire wondered if
this remark was a defensive diversion, as though Hazel
understood very well why she was here and was hoping
to forestall interrogation. She said, gently, 'I should like your
boy to come over and play with my twins. If I send Simon
over will you let him come? Tomorrow afternoon, say?'

'Arr,' Hazel said, readily, 'you could have un over to stay
for a bit if youm minded, for I fret sometimes on account o'
leaving 'un alone o' nights. 'Er sleeps like a winter squirrel
mind but if 'er did awake, to vind the plaace empty, I daresay
he'd be lonesome!'

'You have to go out? Of a night?' Claire asked, and was
dismayed to find herself trembling.

'Oh arr, sometimes,' Hazel said cheerfully, 'on account o'
lighting they beacons. Tiz a praper ole nuisance but seein'
theym all lost it has to be done, dorn it now?'

'Yes,' Claire said, feeling her way step by step as one might
descend an unfamiliar staircase in the dark, 'I suppose it does,
but does nobody ever help you light those beacons, Hazel?'

The girl looked sharply at her but then suspicion left her
eyes and she smiled.

'Giddon no,' she said, impatiently, 'for there's no one can
vind their way about in the dark like me! I'm accustomed to
it, you zee. There baint no plaace yerabouts where you could
lose *me*!'

It was her emphasis on the word 'me' that gave Claire
her first real clue and for a moment compassion choked
her. She reached out and took the girl's hand. It was very

soft, she thought, for a woman who had lived rough all her days and spent every morning in the churchyard helping the sexton dig graves and cut grass.

'How . . . how *long* have they been lost, Hazel?'

'Time enough,' said Hazel briefly. 'First one and then the other, and tiz puzzling, somehow. The Boy was lost first time I ever zeed him but he was a proper ole townee then, so there baint nothing surprising about *that*! Tiz the others losing theirselves that's queer – Henry Pitts, Will Codsall and young Gil Eveleigh, all reared in the Valley; and then Smut, that's queerest of all! Smut knew the place better'n any on account of the poaching he did from the time he was a tacker in the Dell! I should ha' thought Smut could have showed 'em the way home easy enough but 'er hasn't, zo it crossed my mind to zet light to they beacons. Tiz a rare pity there baint more ricks near the shore. If theym all across the water, like The Boy says, they won't zee the blaze unless theym looking for it!'

Suddenly it was very simple to understand, like a jigsaw puzzle when the centre pieces were assembled making a picture of what had been a jumble of torsos and severed heads. All the men of the Valley were lost and unable to find their way home again and the beacons were to guide them home. Claire said, releasing Hazel's hand, 'Suppose I took the boy back to the Big House now? The twins would like someone to play with and my trap is just down the road. The lady doctor is coming too and I think she wants to talk to you. Could I take Patrick, if I promise I'll bring him back as soon as his Dad gets back?'

'Arr, you taake un,' Hazel said, carelessly, and losing interest in the conversation resumed her scrutiny of the fields across the river.

Claire went downstairs, impatient with the tears blurring her vision and pausing for a moment in the living-room to absorb the terrible poignancy of the situation. Then, with relief, she was able to concentrate on the most urgent measure to be taken – the whisking away of the child outside, to a refuge where he would be secure in the company of her own children. She thought of other things too, what she would write to Ikey

and Paul and how Maureen would find the words to persuade
Hazel to abandon her vigil and quit the Valley for the first
time in her life but she pushed these misgivings into the back
of her mind and went swiftly out into the garden, telling the
child that his mother wanted him to go to the Big House
at once. He agreed eagerly enough and they went down the
winding path to the river road hand in hand. As she closed
the gate Claire looked up and saw the girl still sitting in the
same crouched posture, looking out across the slope of the
watershed between Sorrel and Teazel.

She was back within the hour with John and Maureen. The
agent was more relieved than dismayed at her report and
Maureen, having telephoned the Bristol hospital, suggested
they should persuade Hazel to join her child in the Big House
until arrangements could be made for her to be taken away.
Neither seemed to think it would be difficult to coax the girl
out of the Valley and, looking back on what happened with
such appalling unpredictability Claire sometimes wondered if
she exaggerated her own misgivings in this respect.

   She went on alone, leaving John and Maureen in the lane
but her return after such a short interval must have alerted
Hazel, for when she suggested she should move out and join
Patrick at the Big House the girl looked at her suspiciously
and said, flatly, 'For why? What would I do there, along o'
they voreigners?'

   'You could help me and your sisters,' Claire reasoned, 'we're
nursing wounded soldiers now and some of them are friends
of The Boy.'

   Hazel showed a flicker of interest. 'Do they know where he
be tu then?'

   'We could ask them?'

   Hazel considered a moment before rejecting the proposal.
'If theym voreigners they'll be worser lost than the Valley
men! I'll bide yer and look to the beacons!'

   Claire hesitated whether to accept this for the time being
and consult Maureen and then made what she later realised
to be her fatal mistake. She said, trying to sound casual, 'You

mustn't light any more beacons, Hazel. It's better that you should stay up to the house, really it is!' and laid a hand on her shoulder. It might have been the touch, the strained expression in the eyes of the Squire's wife, or the sixth sense that had served Hazel throughout her wild life in the woods; whatever the cause she leaped back, throwing up her head like an animal scenting danger and gathering herself for flight. Before Claire could utter a word of reassurance she had dodged round her and dashed down the stairs and within seconds she reappeared on the flood barrier that served for a front garden on the river frontage. Claire's shout brought John Rudd running but Hazel spotted him before he had moved two strides and changing direction without checking her pace crossed the patch and leaped down on to the road, turning south for the edge of Dell Wood a hundred yards distant.

It had all happened so quickly and so inexplicably that Claire, although leaning far out of the bedroom window, did not even see the big Crossley staff car until it came swinging round the bend at full throttle. There was no time for the driver to brake or even to honk and car and running figure met head-on thirty yards from the gate. Claire saw the car swing right and then left in a long, twisting skid as Hazel, mounting the bonnet, was flung upwards and outwards, to pitch like a bundle of rags in the iris clump at the stream's edge.

Maureen and the driver were bending over her when she ran from the cottage and like the sound of a far-off bell submerged in the thunder of shock she heard herself crying, 'Thank God the child wasn't here – thank God, thank God!', and after that images fused so that she had no more than a glimpse of men spilling out of the car and John Rudd, white and shaking, grasping her arm and saying, with a kind of pitiful emphasis, 'You couldn't help it! It had to happen – something like this! Maybe it's better!', and although Claire understood quite well that he was only trying to mitigate her grief and horror she remembered his words in the days ahead and derived comfort from them.

There was nothing Maureen or anyone else could do beyond lifting the broken body into the car to be driven to the potting-shed behind the Nissen huts, a place that had already done duty as a temporary mortuary that year. Hazel must have been dead when she struck the ground for her neck was broken, as well as her right arm and several ribs, but miraculously her face was almost unmarked and Maureen, sponging it clean and awaiting the arrival of the Camp Commandant and police, wondered at the curious serenity of expression reposing in the features of one who had died so suddenly and violently. She wept a little as she worked at straightening the clothes and tidying the hair, recalling her old affiliation with That Boy, who would have to be told by someone – not her, please God – that violent death was not the prerogative of young men in khaki. Perhaps Paul would come home and afterwards write, explaining as best he could that even this was preferable to shutting a wild creature like Hazel Potter behind walls and subjecting her, possibly for years, to the nameless indignities of the mentally deranged. There was the child to be thought of and mercifully he was young enough to be lied to until the memory of his mother grew dim. She supposed Claire would concern herself with Rumble Patrick and as she thought this she felt a terrible, choking pity for all of them – for Ikey, for Claire, for Paul, for the Valley wives and even for the miserable little Cockney driver of the car, who had whined in his thin nasal voice, 'She come straight at me! Never giv' me a chance, not a chance!' Well, that was true enough and luckily for him there were witnesses to back him up, so that he, at any rate, was out of it. She would have trouble, she suspected, with John, who was sure to hold himself equally responsible with Claire but was any one of them to blame in the smallest degree? It was, at bedrock, simply a case of the world's present madness catching up with one of the few who had managed to keep ahead of it for so long. Looking down at the calm, blank face of the girl Maureen found her crumb of comfort in the reflection that, when all was said and done, Hazel Potter's life had been more fruitful, tranquil and rewarding than most.

III

It was ironic that, within days of Hazel Palfrey lighting her last beacon to bring the Valley wanderers home, two of the strays should make such dramatic reappearances, the one on Valley soil, the other two hundred miles to the east where the youth of Europe was entering upon its third successive summer in the trenches.

The camp despatch-rider carrying the findings of the court of inquiry and coroner's report on the accident actually crossed beneath the route of the first of these returning warriors, who came sailing in at a height of about eight hundred feet, pushing his SE5 biplane up to its maximum of 120 m.p.h. as he swung into a following wind between the hills enclosing the two rivers. Then, to the delight and astonishment of every man, woman and child within running distance, the aircraft swooped down over the avenue chestnuts and went bump-bump-bump along the turf of the big paddock to stop barely a hundred yards from the house.

They came scrambling from every direction, spilling out of the barns of the Home Farm, crowding from the stable-yard and tearing new gaps in half the hedges along Hermitage and Four Winds boundaries, all converging on the dapper, leather-jacketed young man who half-rolled from the cockpit and pushed up his goggles to shake hands with the first arrival. This happened to be old Horace Handcock who nearly choked with excitement when the SE5 (a machine that he alone in the Valley could identify) dipped over the rose garden and, according to his account told later in The Raven, 'Dam' nearly knocked me bliddy 'at off!'

Few of those who crowded round the little machine, or reached to touch the smooth blades of its propeller, recognised the aviator. His snug helmet, heavy jacket and goggles gave him a Martian look and the nature of his arrival reinforced this notion. But Claire recognised him at once and told Thirza to take charge of the twins, who would have persuaded Simon to hoist them into the cockpit if they had not been held back.

Claire remembered the young man's half-apologetic grin, and
also a familiar smear of oil on his forehead, for Tod Glover,
the Valley's first motor mechanic, had always worn a smear
of grease on his face, carrying it like a trademark. When she
pushed forward to greet him Claire recalled the occasion,
years before, when Tod had rescued the family from the
ignominy of being towed home in the Belsize. He was a
fully-fledged pilot now, he told her, having completed his
course at Montrose, in Scotland, and been transferred to a
flying camp near Bristol. He had been there, he told his
astonished audience, only an hour or so ago and would have
to return at once but he decided to try a practice landing on
home ground, having remembered that the paddock was the
most level stretch this side of the river.

He stayed about half-an-hour, drinking tea (he refused
alcohol) and munching a huge slice of Mrs Handcock's plum
cake and still they surrounded him like the figures in the
engraving that hung in the bar of The Raven, entitled *News
of Waterloo*. He had retained his Devon burr but few among
them could recognise his slang and concluded that, on taking
to the air, these young men had been taught a new language.
He apologised for his short stay but on taking off promised to
loop-the-loop and the younger ones understood this well enough
and hopped about with excitement, clutching one another and
saying that Tod was going to perform the legendary feat right
over big paddock and that if the war lasted long enough not
one of them would enlist as a soldier but in the Royal Flying
Corps, like Old Tod, where they could kill more Germans in
two minutes than an infantryman killed in six months. As Tod
shook them off, warning them to stand clear whilst he swung
the propeller, Horace Handcock began a patriotic speech that
might have lasted some time had it not been obliterated by
the roar of the engine and a wind that carried his words
away like dry beech leaves. Then, after a short, uncertain
lurch across the turf, the SE5 was airborne and everybody
stared at the sky as it gained speed and height, sweeping in
a wide graceful circle round the fringe of Shallowford Woods
and then shooting downwind as far as Codsall bridge. Tod kept

his promise. Before heading off up the Valley he actually did
loop-the-loop, not once but three times. The ecstatic sigh that
arose from his audience was more prolonged than anything the
Squire's rockets and set-pieces had produced at either of his
Coronation displays. Then Tod and his trim little steed were a
disappearing speck over Blackberry Moor and all that was left
to remind the earthbound of his miraculous visitation were two
streaks and a brown skid-mark on the turf. The twins looked at
the scars reverently every day until they were obliterated by the
boots of hospital patients passing to and from the Nissen huts.
The patients, as a whole, did not share the Valley's enthusiasm
for fliers. One private almost caused a riot in the bar of The
Raven that same night by remarking, sourly, that 'The bloody
airmen had it cushy! They didn't have to face barrages and
they slept under a roof every night!'

The return of the second Valley wanderer did not create
such a sensation as the appearance of Tod Glover, for he
was unable to make a personal appearance but news of his
miraculous reappearance this side of Jordan was a nine-day
wonder. Smut Potter – poacher, gaol-bird, horticulturist, and
slayer of innumerable Germans, missing and believed killed
during the early days of the Somme offensive, returned from
the dead, seemingly none the worse for dying.

Smut had been given up for lost by everybody in the
Valley except, possibly, by Meg who consulted the cards on
the subject any number of times but had not turned up the
ace or jack of spades, signifying death or mutilation. She was
not much surprised, therefore, when an official letter arrived
informing her that Smut had rejoined his unit and would be
home on furlough in due course. This was followed, within
a day or so, by a single sheet written in Smut's laborious
scrawl, explaining that he had been taken prisoner in July
last year but had escaped and holed up until he could rejoin
the British field forces. Meg showed his letter to Horace and
Horace showed it to John Rudd but neither of them could
make very much of it for it sounded a very tame account for
someone who had returned from the dead. It was, however,

the simple truth and Smut himself was puzzled by the furore his reappearance caused in what remained of his battalion. He was interviewed by at least four intelligence officers, one of them a taciturn Red Cap whom Smut hated on sight. It was only when his own colonel interviewed him that the full story of Smut's survival emerged, and was copied into the regimental record, forming the basis of several newspaper articles, one of which Smut read but understandably failed to recognise himself as the hero.

His odyssey began ordinarily enough. On July 2nd, 1916, together with a wounded lieutenant and about a dozen other men, he was overrun in a shell-hole during a counter-attack. Smut, whose blood was up, was for fighting it out but luckily for the other men in the pocket the lieutenant decided to surrender when ammunition ran low. They were not murdered out of hand, as Smut rather thought they might be but were employed as stretcher-bearers until there was a lull and afterwards marched to a ruined farm behind Péronne. They were lightly guarded and Smut could have left the column without difficulty but he was tired, hungry and in no physical shape to attempt the feat of threading his way through the fluid German positions. An opportunity occurred, however, later in the day, when a large number of prisoners were packed into a large farmyard and dusk came down before they were recounted. On one side of the yard was a vast midden heap and near it Smut found a length of lead piping from a shattered pump. The pipe reminded him of an occasion, long ago, when he had given Gilroy's gamekeepers the slip by taking to a pond and breathing through a long reed while his pursuers beat a patch of marsh without flushing him out. His chum, 'Dinty' Moore, to whom he confided his plan, was sceptical of burrowing into the midden and using the pipe in the way Smut had once used the reed.

'I'd as lief spend the rest o' me bloody life behind wire as lay up in that stinking mush!' Dinty said but Smut, who had spent three and a half years behind bars, valued freedom more highly and was soon deep in the midden, his pipe projecting a few inches above the wall.

He lay there until he was half suffocated but the plan worked. As soon as the men were marched away he had no difficulty in emerging and walking unchallenged into the eastern outskirts of Péronne. By the time he got there, however, he was near the end of his tether. Forty-eight hours had passed since he had eaten his iron rations in the shell-hole and although by no means a fastidious man the stench he carried with him was enough to overpower a man travelling on an empty stomach. There was a shaded light at the back of the first house he reached, a tumble-down building with a large, stone-built barn abutting on to the street. Smut hesitated outside the half-open door wondering whether he could risk foraging for something to eat and perhaps lie up during daylight hours after making shift to remove traces of his sojourn in the manure heap. He was incredibly lucky. As he stood there, trying to make up his mind, he was assailed by a delicious smell of freshly-baked bread so that he pushed open the door and walked in, coming face to face with the baker, a handsome, statuesque woman of about forty, who might have weighed around eighteen stone. She came out of the inner bakery, stared at him in the dim light issuing from the open door, gave one or two long sniffs and then recoiled, as from a fiend of the pit but the smell of baking bread had now overcome the last of Smut's reservations and he followed her up, closing the door and announcing himself as a British soldier on the run. Thus began an association that was to last a lifetime and form the starting point of his miraculous return from the dead.

The woman was a Fleming called Marie Viriot and had been widowed twice, once by a sack of flour that fell on her first husband and broke his neck, and later by the Germans, when Monsieur Viriot was killed in the Ardennes offensive. She was now struggling to run her business in territory that had been occupied by the enemy since the first weeks of the war and her unremitting hatred of the Boche stemmed more from the innumerable petty restrictions than from the fact that they had killed Sergeant Viriot in 1914. She was a vigorous, affable woman, with a loud, neighing laugh and her sense of humour, dormant for so long, was revived by the appearance of Smut standing in her bakery steaming in the heat of the oven and giving off the acrid stench of a neglected farmyard. In her youth she had been a waitress in an Ostend teashop that catered for tourists and her quick mind had picked up a working knowledge of English. Smut's estaminet French was better than average so that they were able to converse freely almost from the start. They took to one another at once. Both Madame's husbands had been short, stocky men of Smut's build and after he had stripped and washed in her presence, and she had fed him on hot bread and thin vegetable soup she made her decision.

'You stay vile I brebare the bapers of my sister's husband, Jules!' she announced, in her thick Flemish accent. 'Then you vill work until the poilus return to cut the Boche into bieces!'

It was not until several days later, when she dragged him from hiding in the flour store and brandished a set of papers half-covered with official stamps that he understood his refuge was to be permanent. Madame Viriot's brother-in-law, it seemed, had decamped shortly after the Germans arrived in the district and had left his identity papers behind, together with wife and family, who afterwards obtained permission to go south to other relatives. In a strictly rationed area like Péronne Madame Viriot exercised considerable influence in official circles and it had been a simple matter to bribe civil authorities into converting Smut into the absent Jules Barnard. When Smut protested that his French was unequal to so great a strain Madame Viriot said, disdainfully, 'Poof! Jules was half the idiot! I shall give out that he has returned from the war all the idiot!', and thereafter she coached her protégé to such good effect that Smut was able to move about quite freely, indulging a hopeless stammer, a distressing twitch and a mild, cherubic grin. He rather enjoyed the charade and in any case was glad of a rest after more than twenty months in and out of the line. His obligations in the bakery by day were not as exacting as those by night, in Madame's vast, canopied bed, for Marie Viriot, husbandless for two years, was a virile woman and

used her stray Tommy with an energy and dexterity that
Smut found astonishing in one so ponderously built. He did
not mind, however. He was well-fed and well-housed and
when he was not at work derived a good deal of pleasure from
watching the enemy's second-line troops sweat and bustle in
their efforts to withstand the interminable British pressure on
the Somme. By the time the attacks had petered out he was
accepted everywhere as a bonafide French idiot and could
walk about the town without much risk, under cover of his
distressing stammer and carefully cultivated twitch. He soon
reverted to his war-time trade and brought home a variety
of carelessly guarded rifles. He collected information too of
a sort, the names and numerals of German drafts passing
through to the front, the type of transport used to shift stores
and ammunition and the approximate location of ammunition
dumps and long-range howitzer batteries, more than enough
to have got him shot had he shown more diligence as secret
agent. He was happy enough, save for occasional bouts of
homesickness. The monotonous, featureless landscape around
Péronne, he decided, must have been depressing in peace-time
but war had converted it into a half-rural, half-industrial slum,
housing a sullen population harassed by German regulations
and fear of death from air-raids and the long-range shelling.
Once, early in the new year, he gave expression to his
disgust for the French provinces, telling Marie that, après
la guerre, she would do well to sell up and take refuge across
the Channel where trees sometimes grew and occasionally
the sun shone for a week at a time. He was startled by
her reaction to this innocent remark. She bounced at him,
held him firmly by the ears, planted kisses on both cheeks
and exclaimed, rapturously, 'It iss the brobosal of marriage
you make! I accept! We will go to your native place and
establish ourselves as pastry cooks! Did not the fortune-teller
in Bruges tell me I should haf the three husbands but no
little ones? Come now! Embrace Marie, Tommy!', and she
crushed him to her buttressed bosom while outside the thin,
slanted rain fell and fell, and limbers moving up to the
front passed in endless procession.

Early in March rumours began to circulate of an imminent German withdrawal to a new line many miles to the east and soon afterwards all able-bodied civilians within the requisite age limit were faced with a choice of going into hiding or being forcibly evacuated. It was time, Marie announced, for Jules Barnard to disappear again so Smut was salted away in the flour store once more, remaining there while the town emptied. He had, by now, a very high opinion of Marie's ingenuity and naturally expected her to evade the evacuation order. But at the last minute something must have gone wrong for she suddenly appeared in his hideout with news that she was being moved to Lille and that a demolition squad would blow up the bakery at six o'clock the following morning. She did not seem to resent the wanton destruction of her property so much as her enforced separation from Smut, declaring that the French Government would be obliged to pay her compensation after the war and that she had already made out the bill. She made him memorise her new address and gave him back his uniform, which had been boiled, mended, and pressed against the day of liberation. She then issued final instructions, telling him to convert the flour store into a bomb-proof dugout, strong enough to resist the blowing up of the adjacent bakery and to be sure to write to her through the Red Cross as soon as he was free. If he failed in this respect, she said, she would hunt him down wherever he was, commencing the day the war ended.

The big bang came precisely at six a.m. and for a few minutes it seemed to Smut that Marie Viriot would be widowed a third time. The plaster ceiling of the store descended in an almost solid mass and only five layers of flour-sacks, reinforced by a girder, saved him from being buried alive. He poked a small hole through the debris but remained hidden all that day and the following night. Early on the second day he heard what he recognised as the sound of cheering and donning his uniform made his way across the ruins of the bakery to the street. By that time it took a great deal to excite Smut but he was more stirred by what he saw in Péronne that morning than by any experience that had come his way in the past. The advancing allied troops were Highlanders and they came swinging into the town to the bagpipe strains of 'Scotland the Brave'. Smut was still capering with excitement and cheering himself hoarse when he was arrested by two Red Caps as a deserter and clapped in the lock-up to await interrogation. After that it seemed to him that he told his story approximately five hundred times but in due course he was welcomed back to the rump of his unit. It was, he noted sadly, full of strangers. Only the adjutant, one former lieutenant now a captain and five men of his original company recognised him. All the others had been killed or wounded in the last ten months. The adjutant, however, was delighted to see him and promised to recommend him for a Military Medal on the strength of his experiences. He also re-enlisted Smut as his personal servant. He had had a string of servants since the previous July and had mourned Smut every time one of them returned from Battalion HQ with nothing but demands for returns on how many tins of plum jam had been consumed during the last ten days or what instructions were being given the men on keeping their feet dry. Smut had never bothered with this kind of thing but he had seldom returned without a bottle of whisky or a pound of candles.

IV

The day he received Franz's letter, telling him that he was now a sleeping partner in a firm producing grenades, pistol ammunition and other familiar articles, Paul had just returned from a night haul up to the support lines, behind Messines. He read the letter carefully, partly because its unconscious irony fascinated him but also to make quite sure that Franz had no commercial links with heavy pumping equipment, for that, Paul decided, would have been too grotesque. He had now been hauling pumping equipment up to Messines on thirty-five consecutive nights and had been strafed every night but two, when they had to turn back owing to traffic jams.

Paul's section had been assigned to the group of Engineers responsible for the fabulous mine-galleries running directly

under the ridge, mines that promised to provide the loudest
bang since the beginning of time and blast away a whole
section of the high ground from which the Germans dominated
the area, pin-pointing every cross-road and trench junction,
every artillery position and, or so it seemed to the Transport
men, every yard of pavé over which they moved. He had been
in this sector ever since he had arrived in France in January
and he already knew it as well, or better, than he knew
the Sorrel Valley. It was a landscape that fascinated him,
perhaps because, for so long now, he had been preoccupied
with landscapes. The starkness and emptiness of this one
was so awful that it sometimes took on a kind of beauty,
like engravings of Blake that he remembered having seen
in one of the books left behind by the unknown Lovell who
had a taste for art. It was not a merely tortured landscape
where nothing grew and not a single building of any kind
remained whole; neither was it a lifeless landscape for over
it, at widely-spaced intervals, little figures crawled and motor
and horse transport moved at funeral pace. But for all the
unlikely symmetry of some of the ruins and the presence
of half-a-million human beings, it had a kind of bloated
emptiness, like the mottled remains of a half-eaten crab
stranded above the Coombe Bay tide-line and everything
that crossed it was contaminated by its foulness, its utter
and stupid uselessness. At all events this seemed to be so,
until one stumbled across groups of men in dugouts or billets.
Then, hearing them laugh or cough, or noting their watchful
eyes and cumbersome moments, Paul discovered by degrees
that many of them seemed to have found fulfilment in their
troglodyte lives here and in the terrible intensity of their
personal experiences during their spells up the line or in
one or other of the offensives. They had acquired, almost
incidentally, the maturity he had been seeking so long in the
Valley and their communal life presented the kind of perfection
he had been striving to create in the community of the estate
but without getting anywhere near the ideal of comradeship
and interdependence of this array of clerks, labourers, factory
workers and schoolboy officers, in their faded, mud-stained

tunics and clay-caked boots and puttees. It was this sense of
discovery and his absorption into the fellowship that converted
Paul's initial pessimism into a secret optimism, an optimism
that grew a little every day as he moved to and fro across the
lunar landscape for it seemed to him that, if this almost holy
relationship between Englishman and Englishman survived
the war, no obstacle likely to be met with in peace could
defeat or discourage him. Had it not been for this Franz's
letter would have made him sick with shame.

The old man had not intended to sound so cynical. His
letter, in essence, was no more than a business bulletin
informing a shareholder that the firm was doing well under
the current demand for scrap and the end products of scrap.
Paul remembered that even in a sideshow like the Boer War,
Franz and his father had made modest fortunes so that it was
surely inevitable that ten such fortunes could be wrung from
Armageddon. He was also sufficiently balanced to appreciate
that his instinctive disgust on hearing that he personally
was profiting from the war was frivolous and emotional.
A British shell shortage would spell defeat and defeat in
the field would almost certainly entail the loss of another
half-million lives, even if its ultimate consequences were not
as terrifying as prophesied in Fleet Street. He looked at the
final page of the letter again and re-read the old rascal's
tailpiece, this time with a sour smile, Franz ended— 'So
keep your head low, my dear boy, and every time one comes
over inviting a Teutonic response remember it means another
threehalfpence, to your credit, another droplet to pour into that
bottomless pit of yours in the West!'

By the same mail there was a letter from James Grenfell
explaining at some length why he had sided with Asquith
in the recent Lloyd George coup that had ousted the great
patrician and split the Liberal Party from top to bottom. The
seizure of power by the Welsh Wizard had occurred when Paul
was still in England and had seemed an event of enormous
significance but out here it was very small beer, and although
he sympathised with James, who was appalled by the ruin of
his beloved party, Paul found it difficult to concentrate on

the closely written pages of his old friend. James rambled on about loyalty and integrity, of the importance of holding the Asquith group together against the days of reconstruction and then covered a page railing against the intrigues of public figures like Northcliffe. Over here, where men were being killed at the rate of about twelve thousand a day, the quarrels of politicians crossed the Channel as the echoes of kindergarten squabbles and if soldiers heard them at all they dismissed them as the prerogative of 'The Frocks'!

He put James's letter aside half-read and opened Claire's, the one he had been saving, as he might have saved the icing on a rather soggy cake. It was, he soon saw, one of her cheerful, gossipy letters which disappointed him but he paid it the compliment of close attention and although its content was even more trivial than Grenfell's it held his interest. She pattered on for several pages; there were now one hundred and four patients at Shallowford; a new attempt on the part of the forestry pirates to throw Shallowford beeches had been frustrated; there had been an outbreak of fire at the camp at Nun's Bay; the twins, little traitors, had succumbed to German measles but so far Mary, Whiz and Ikey's boy had escaped; and so on, down to the bottom of the page, where, in a postscript dated the following day, lay the promise of a real letter in the near future, for Claire had written: *'This is only a hotpotch dearest – jottings I might forget if I didn't set them down between times and even this has been two days in writing! I do miss you so. I'll explain how and why as soon as I get an hour alone late at night, when I can re-read your last letter in the library before going to bed. And talking of bed let's hope only the enclosed kind of letter is read by censors (are you quite sure you are right about officers' mail arriving uncensored?) because, although I can write shamelessly once I've locked the door I must admit to a blush or two when I get the kind of reply sparked off by the one I wrote last week! Good-bye for a little while, Paul darling, your ever loving, ever yearning Claire.'*

The postscripts pleased him and he sat thinking awhile on her strange and, to him, unexpected skill as a writer of love-letters. They came, perhaps, once a fortnight, spaced

by two or three gossipy bulletins such as the one he had
just received and each time he received one he marvelled at
the range and freedom of her self-expression, reflecting how
much their relationship had matured in the last few years,
particularly since their quarrel over that idiot at the camp and
her crazy suspicions regarding Hazel Palfrey. He remembered
the Claire Derwent he had met and flirted with when he first
arrived in the Valley, a pert and rather vain nineteen-year-old,
without a thought in her head beyond hunting and dancing
and catching a husband who would spoil her on account
of her red mouth and corn-coloured hair. How much of the
present Claire had existed when they met and how much
was the fruit of the fulfilment she had found in children
and her leading social position in the Valley? He took out
her last, intimate letter and read it for the twentieth time,
astonished to find that it produced the same excitement it
had stirred in him when he first received it before going up
the line on the night his friend Guy Manners had been blown
to bits at Vesuvius Cutting. It was fortunate that he had had
her letter to take his mind off death during the twenty-four
hours that followed, for out here the memory of friends' voices
and faces was short and Guy was almost forgotten in a matter
of days. He now re-read the letter as if it proclaimed some
extraordinary dazzling feat on his part, something that was
still able to inspire him with almost unlimited confidence in
himself and this was understandable, for his pride had never
completely recovered from the wound inflicted by Grace's
rejection of him. *'Oh my darling,'* she wrote, in that clear,
rounded fist of hers that recalled the pages of the estate
diary, *'I feel so desolate when I am alone at night in here
and when, after torturing myself with longing, I go upstairs
to invite an even more intense yearning by seeing your things
about the room. Then I tell myself I ought not to be miserable,
not really, when I remember the wonderful years we've had,
and the years that I know with absolute certainty we shall have
again! And the odd thing is this reassurance does seem to
work, perhaps because I have such sharp and sweet memories
of your love in this room right back to the day you brought*

*me here. So, when I've locked the door, I am yours again, as
completely as if you were sitting on the side of the bed tugging
off those long boots (which I keep oiled because Chivers thinks
of them as just boots) watching me undress and sometimes
being tiresome about letting my hair down, so that it wastes
a half-hour in the morning getting it presentable again! Dear
God, Paul how I enjoy being a wife to you and basking in
your admiration at times like that. I swear to myself that I
shall more than make up for every minute we're missing!
I like to think we have enjoyed each other far more than
most married couples but I think I can still surprise you
a little! I mean to try anyhow! I won't ever hold anything
back when you take me in your arms again. What I mean
is, I'll do and say everything that comes into my head no
matter how abandoned it is! I shall say how I revel in your
male gentleness and even more in your male roughness and
occasional impatience, which you might be surprised to learn
I find rather flattering after sharing a bed with you for –
wait, I'm counting! – twenty-one days short of ten years!
Good night my darling; I feel so much better for writing
this and if you don't mind having such frightfully immodest
letters from a woman old enough to know better I'll write
another every time I feel desperate!'*

It seemed to him a wonderful thing that he should have
been capable of inspiring a letter like that and it crossed
his mind, musing on it once again, that he might have
Grace Lovell to thank for it. Looking back he realised now
how raw and ingenuous he had been as a lover when he
and Grace had honeymooned in Paris at the beginning of
the Edwardian era, a time when only a street-walker dared
admit to a knowledge of the art of love, when complete
ignorance of all physical aspects of marriage was a bride's
(and often a groom's) title to respectability. It had been
Grace and no one else who had taught him what little he
knew of women. Because of her Claire had been spared
the painful, clumsy initiation reserved for the majority of
young wives. Yes, she could surely take some credit to
herself for the success of their marriage, for all she had

needed from the outset was his frank admiration of her body and she had brought to their relationship a prevailing sense of humour that was strange in a daughter of a glum old stick like Edward Derwent.

It was because his thoughts turned to Grace more than once that day that the encounter on the road up to Messines thirty-six hours later made such a profound impression upon him. Pot-bellied old General Plumer, probably the only high-ranking officer in the Salient who enjoyed the respect of his troops, blew his famous mines early that morning and their effect was as devastating as his chief-of-staff, Harington, had promised. The roar that accompanied the detonation of the nineteen undiscovered galleries under Messines sounded like the crack of doom and news filtered back that the attack had been a triumph, the first wave of troops walking over with virtually no opposition, for the German trenches opposite were a shambles. Paul realised this when he saw some of the gibbering survivors that afternoon, and although he pitied them he felt more optimistic about the war than he had felt for years. If it was ever to end, he told himself, then this was surely the way to wage it and the mere trickle of British wounded, compared to the flood that had accompanied every other push, was corroboration.

He went up the line that night with a convoy of corrugated iron for revetting the captured trenches. The outward journey was less eventful than any he had made since his arrival in the sector, and it was a quiet, windless dawn when he started back and became snarled up in a traffic jam two miles short of the dump. An ambulance, heading in the opposite direction, had swerved off the road and become bogged down on the edge of a flooded shell-hole and he sat watching as a party of pioneers attached a cable to the ditched vehicle in an attempt to drag it back on the road. Then, as he half dozed, he seemed to have had a particularly vivid dream for there was something familiar about the slim, uniformed WAAC, obviously the ambulance driver, who stood nonchalantly by the running board of the pioneers' lorry smoking a cigarette.

She looked, he thought, more like a boy than a woman in her laced-up boots and loose-fitting trench coat. She did not appear much concerned over the fate of her vehicle but rested her weight on the spare tyre of the lorry, inhaling deeply and letting the smoke trickle from her nose. Then he shook himself awake with a shout of amazement; the WAAC was Grace whom he had last seen after her hectic involvement in the House of Commons riot six years ago and although he knew this with complete certainty he was so amazed by her presence there that, for almost a minute, he stood half in half out of his lorry before shaking himself, jumping down and squelching across the slimed pavé to greet her in a voice hoarse and cracked with emotion. '*Grace!* It *is* you! It's you, by God!', and for some reason that he found difficult to explain to himself, he felt a tremendous surge of exhilaration as he seized both her hands and pumped them up and down so energetically that the cigarette fell from her lips and some of the pioneers, hearing him shout, looked up from their work to stare at them.

She did not seem so surprised as he but her eyes lit up and she smiled, slowly, almost sleepily, so that he noticed she was not only dog tired but also that she must have lost two stone since their last meeting. Her dark hair, crammed under the ungainly cap, had been cut short and there were flecks of grey over the temples. He had always thought of her as rather stocky and well-made, particularly about the shoulders but now she seemed so slim and fragile that, despite the few grey hairs and the circles under her eyes, she looked younger and infinitely more vulnerable than he recalled. He groped for his cigarettes and offered her one, noting that her hand shook a little as she put it to her lips. She said, in the low, controlled voice that was the only thing about her unchanged, 'I heard you were out, Paul. Uncle Franz wrote and told me about a month ago but it's a bore that you've caught me at such a disadvantage! I'm not usually this inefficient, it was a bloody staff car hogging the centre of the road. It would have been all the same if I'd been loaded with abdominals, blast them! However, what can you expect from red-tabs? Everyone is expected to make way for them, even the poor devils they've fed into the Mincing Machine!'

He was struck by the bitterness of her voice and also by the terrible exhaustion it expressed, as though the effort of greeting him made substantial demands on her vitality.

'Franz never told me you were out here!' Paul said, indignantly, 'I thought you were nursing in London.'

'I was,' she told him, 'but when I discovered women handle authority even more despotically than men I got a transfer! It was either that or braining the matron with a bed-pan! How long have you been out?'

Only three months, he told her, so apologetically that she laughed and said, 'Well, don't sound so bloody humble about it! After all, you're rising forty now and I daresay you could have dodged the column easily enough!' Then she looked at him rather pensively, adding, 'You wouldn't tho', would you? You were always a glutton for punishment!'

'Damn it, so were you!' he laughed. 'At least I enjoyed creature comforts when they were available! Look here, let me get some of my chaps to work on that crate of yours, those bloody pioneers will be fiddling about until Jerry drops something heavy on us!' and he shouted to his sergeant and walked over to supervise the salvage operations while she continued to watch, standing with her legs squarely apart, still dribbling smoke through her nose.

The ambulance was hauled clear at last, not before time for a range-finder crumped down in a field about three hundred yards to the west. Drivers in both halted columns began to hoot and shout ribald advice, and in the resultant flurry he almost lost her, for she scrambled into the driving seat and addressed herself to the controls while Paul's sergeant swung the starting handle, beaming with relief when the engine coughed and ticked over. Paul ran round to the offside just as the column began to move.

'Where can I get in touch with you? Let's have dinner somewhere?'

She called over her shoulder, 'Base hospital, I'm free tonight, six until midnight! Ask for Driver Lovell!'

She reversed expertly across the road and then edged away leaving him to scramble back into his lorry and move off in the opposite direction. He was heady with excitement, reflecting, as they nosed down the road to the dump, 'By God, but she's a remarkable woman! I don't think I ever realised how remarkable!' And then he pondered the startling changes in her looks and manner, neither of which, he felt, could be wholly explained by her occupation and drab uniform, for notwithstanding her almost insane embroilment in The Cause, he had always thought of her as all woman and now she was four-fifth male and as tough and embittered as the hardiest trench veteran. She was also, he thought soberly, near the end of her tether, used up, physically and spiritually but sticking it out in the way most of the men were sticking it, fortified to some extent by the mystic comradeship of the Western Front.

V

She succeeded in surprising him again that night after he had picked her up at the hospital transport depot and driven her into Béthune in the Douglas motor-cycle combination he had scrounged. She had changed her uniform and used a little lipstick and powder and the grey hair above her ears must have been camouflaged in some way for the tendrils that strayed below the rim of her cap were now as dark and curling as he remembered. She seemed also to have performed the miracle of developing a small bust during the day and was at least half a woman again but she did not seem to mind when he referred jokingly to this startling recapture, saying, carelessly, 'Well, it isn't every night one is taken out to dinner by an ex-husband! Other men will be there and I wouldn't like them to think you were that hard up for a girl!'

He found her surprisingly relaxed and easy to talk with, as though they were not an estranged husband and wife, who had been parted for twelve years, but a couple of old friends who occasionally spent an evening together. While they were waiting to give their order she said, looking round at tables occupied exclusively by officers and nurses from Advanced Base Hospital, 'It's almost a club, isn't it? Entrance fee a hole in you somewhere, or the permanent shakes!'

'You used to be just as hard on politicians,' he reminded her, laughing. 'Have you shifted your sights to the General Staff?'

'Oh no,' she said, 'I'm not murderous about anyone any more; I was, when I first came out and drove wounded back after the Loos fiasco but not now. It's got 'way beyond anyone's control! The politicians lost their grip years ago and even at HQ the old ex-cavalry Has-beens are the prisoners of their own inadequacies. You might say I've succeeded in reversing the Bourbon outlook – I've forgotten everything and am learning all the time.'

Paul realised that he was enjoying her society for the first time since their relationship had fallen foul of Roddy Rudd's motor-car, just before she ran away. 'I can understand what you've forgotten,' he said, recalling the free-for-all in Westminster Yard in Coronation week, 'but what exactly have you learned?'

'Compassion,' she said simply, 'and enormous admiration for the guts and patience of the underprivileged. Many other things of course but those in particular.' She spoke now, he thought, more as a Socialist than as a suffragette, and he asked her what she thought about the revolution in Russia. Did it mean there was a possibility of world revolution before all the licensed killing was done?

'That's difficult to prophesy,' she said, 'it depends on the breaking strain of us, the French, and even poor old Fritz over there. Big changes are already occurring in the European social structures but if we can adapt ourselves to this we can probably evolve some kind of compromise when it's over – providing the peace is reasonably merciful whichever side imposes it!'

She talked easily of all kind of things arising out of political, social, industrial and even strategic problems and he was impressed not only by her width of vision and lucidity, but also by her tolerance that seemed to enfold men who had flung her into gaol and forcibly fed her not once but many times. He was shocked by his own political ignorance and by the relative fatuity of the theorists, professionals like poor old Grenfell struggling with his conscience at home.

'You've changed tremendously, Grace,' he told her, 'I don't think I'd ever have the impudence to quarrel with you again,' and she laughed, her old, musical laugh and replied, 'You aren't obliged to, you've got a new wife to dominate!'

'I never came anywhere near dominating you,' he protested, 'and I can't ever recall trying!'

'No,' she said, seriously, 'I only meant that as a joke. The one real regret I've had about it is that I hurt you so badly at the time but even that regret is qualified.'

'How do you mean, "qualified"?'

'Well,' she said, 'I imagine you got a much better wife out of it all and certainly more lasting happiness. One only has to look at you to discover that! You are very happy with Claire, aren't you? All my informants tell me so.'

When she moved from politics and world affairs to human relationships her certainty abandoned her, exposing a slightly naïve facet of her compact personality, and through this chink in her assurance he realised that she had deliberately understated her feelings of guilt about him and was trying to convince herself that subsequent events exonerated her. It moved him a little that she should find this necessary after so many years and after witnessing so much real suffering at uncomfortably close range. He said, quickly, 'What happened was best for both of us, Grace, I don't bear any malice and never have, at least, not since I remarried. Yes, I am happy with Claire, happier than I deserve in the circumstances but if it's any comfort to you I can remind you of two things. One – it was you who virtually threw her at me and two – well, I don't imagine I could have succeeded anything like so well in a second marriage if you hadn't taught me how to treat a woman in and out of bed!'

'Did I do that?' she said, genuinely flattered all the same.

'You certainly did!' and acting on a sudden impulse he did a strange thing, tugging out his wallet, extracting the most thumbed of Claire's letters and pushing it across the table. 'You'll probably think I'm only being amiable by admitting that,' he went on, hurriedly, 'so there's proof of it! Go ahead, read that last page!'

'But it's a letter from her?'

'Yes but read it, or skim it if you like. I want you to!'

'Are you sure?'

'Quite sure. I owe you that!'

She took the folded sheets from the envelope and smoothed them out on the table, turning over the first three pages and glancing at the final page with unconcealed curiosity. The girl came with coffee and cognac but she did not look up although she was careful to shade the letter with her hand. Watching her he saw colour flood her cheeks and only then realised how parchment pale they were, not with the attractively smooth waxiness of the old days but a dry tautness that puckered the skin under the eyes and somehow deprived the face of width. Seeing her flush like that he felt a sudden tenderness for her. She seemed so small, lonely and desperate, so hopelessly inadequate to the fearful demands made upon her strength. She said, returning the letter, 'Don't ever be such an idiot as to tell Claire you showed me this, Paul! Ordinarily it would have been unforgivable but I can understand what made you do it and it was very generous on your part! She's lucky and you're lucky! I do remember telling you that what she quotes here is the basis of every successful marriage and it was obviously one of the less fanciful theories I had and still have! You've found something rare and precious, so hang on to it all your life! But I don't have to tell you that, do I?'

'No,' he said, 'I value it and so does Claire although I could never be absolutely sure of that until I came out here. We never put it to the test, I suppose.'

'Oh,' she said, smiling as the colour in her cheeks faded, 'that's rubbish! She's woman enough to have valued it from the beginning for I do remember that much about her! "Ripe" was the adjective I used, I believe, and you plucked her at the right time judging by that letter! I suppose you carry a photograph?'

He showed her snapshots taken with Simon's box camera, pictures of Claire alone and members of the family individually and as a group. He noticed that she studied the one of Simon intently but unemotionally.

'Is he troublesome, like his mother?' she wanted to know and Paul said no, not troublesome but far more introspective than the twins and even more sensitive to reproof than the six-year-old Mary.

'He'll be thirteen now. Have you any plans for him?'

'No,' Paul told her, 'except that he's bright enough to go on to 'Varsity if he wants to. He has your passion for facts and your wonderful memory. He's very good at history and writes a good essay, I'm told.' Then, seeing that she was interested, 'Look here, Grace, Claire isn't the least bit inclined to jealousy. When you get leave why don't you run down and see him? Or, if that would embarrass you, why don't you have him to stay? He knows all the essentials about what happened.'

'Not quite all,' she said, 'and neither, for that matter, do you. Anyway, I don't take my leaves at home, I use them to practise my other occupation.'

'What on earth is that?'

She looked at him steadily. 'Saluting men who are about to die,' she said. 'Youngsters mostly, some of them young enough to shock you but all young enough to need a little mothering.'

He was not shocked or even embarrassed. Somehow it was precisely what he would have expected of her essentially generous nature. 'I don't write them Claire's kind of letter afterwards,' she went on, smiling, 'but if I'm honest I get as much out of giving as they do taking and sometimes more! It keeps me sane, anyway.'

'Damn it,' he burst out, 'you've been out here far too long! Why the hell don't you apply for a rest? They can't keep you the way they can us.'

'I'll rest when it's all over,' she said, 'or maybe before, if I'm unlucky. In the meantime I get satisfaction from the thought

that at last I'm of real use to someone,' and as though she did
not wish to prolong the discussion she stood up and crammed
on her ugly cap. 'Come on,' she said, 'if I don't show up one
of the kids will be hauled out of bed to drive my ambulance,'
and marched out, leaving him to pay the bill.

When he regained the street she was sitting in the sidecar
and the engine was warming up. He said, stuffing the change
into his pocket, 'How are you off for money, Grace? If you
wanted any I hope you'd have the sense to ask for it.'

'Now what,' she said, 'can a woman buy out here? There's
nothing worth having in the few shops that are open and no
shortage of escorts with money to burn! Even at Advanced
Base we're outnumbered twenty to one. Get moving, Paul,
but in case I forget when you drop me off thank you for
everything.'

'Will you meet me again, same time same place next
week?'

'Certainly I will, that's the best meal I've had in months
and the best wine too! They probably know you tip well.'

'Then next Thursday,' he said, revving up and they bumped
off over the pavé in the direction of the hospital.

She rushed away as soon as they drove into the compound
although it still wanted twenty minutes to midnight. He
saw her flit like a shadow between two Nissen huts and
disappear with a casual lift of the hand.

He got a message to her six days later and arranged to call
at dusk and take her into Béthune again. He was surprised
to realise how keenly he looked forward to meeting her and
on the way to the hospital amused himself going over all the
things he had forgotten to ask her. When he inquired for her
at the transport section, however, a little Cockney driver, her
voice muffled by adenoids, told him that Driver Lovell, ''Er
Ladyship,' as she called her, was on duty having volunteered
for an extra run to the Field Dressing Station because she,
the informant, had a heavy cold. 'I woulden've let 'er go,' the
Cockney girl said, 'but I was asleep, see? We was busy las'
night and I slep' on. She did her trip earlier today an' scrubbed

out an' all but she's like that! Proper sport 'Er Ladyship is!'

'When is she likely to get back?' Paul inquired.

'Oh, any minnit now,' the girl replied, 'she's bin gone since dinner-time. I come out to scrub the crate for 'er. Least I c'n do, ain't it?'

Half-an-hour passed but the ambulance did not show up and Paul occupied the time amusingly enough pumping the Cockney driver about Grace. He soon realised that she was the acknowledged leader of the section, not only on account of her long service overseas (she was the only original member of the section still serving) but because she made everyone's problems her own, writing letters to parents, interceding with the MO on defaulters' behalf and generally mothering the group, especially new arrivals. 'Mindjew,' the girl said, with a wink, 'she's a rare one for the boys! Never withaht one and we younguns don't stand a look-in! Goes all the way too or so they say, 'though she's old enough to be mother to some of 'em who come sniffin' round! But what I say is, who cares? I mean, it ain't as if she's got anyone waitin' back in Blighty, is it? And you don't get no 'elpin' 'and from the 'oly sort, do yer? Catch one o' the Sacred Virgins standin' in for someone else's run to Casualty Clearing!'

The Sacred Virgins, he learned, were WAACs who, according to the Cockney, had reputations for 'leading men up the garden path an' slamming the summer-'ouse door in their dials!' Paul was still chuckling at this when a despatch-rider roared into the compound reporting a shambles a mile or so up the Messines road. A lone-flying Gotha, he said, had taken a crack at a convoy and there had been a few casualties. The road was temporarily blocked and two ambulances were required at once.

The Cockney girl had a vehicle ticking over in a matter of minutes and there was a good deal of scurrying to and fro. Paul, who was off duty until midnight, abandoned his Douglas and jumped up beside the girl shouting to the convoy leader that he was a transport officer and would help clear the road. Twenty minutes later, just as dusk was falling, they came to the scene of the incident. Two Leyland lorries, full

of captured material from the Ridge, had been blown off the
road, their crews killed outright by an aerial bomb that had
cratered the pavé midway between them. Close behind the
wreck of the second lorry an ambulance lay on its side
and orderlies were trying to extricate a screaming patient
from inside. Two other patients, deaf or unconscious, lay
on stretchers close by. The ambulance driving cabin was
empty. Suddenly the Cockney girl became frantic. 'Where's
'Er Ladyship?' she kept asking hurrying men, who brushed
her aside as they lifted the stretchers into the first ambulance,
and then he found her, about twenty yards back along the road,
a small, huddled form under a muddy blanket, guarded by her
orderly nursing a broken collar bone.

Paul lifted the blanket and looked down at the calm, waxen
face for a moment. It was dirty but not disfigured in any way
and the orderly, another Cockney, told him he had already
examined the body but could find no wound to account for
death.

'Muster bin blast, sir,' he told Paul, despondently, 'seen it
happen offen enough. Do fer anyone with a bad ticker, an' I
always reckoned she weren't strong enough fer the job. Game
tho', by Christ! Bin on the run four months with her an' never
see a woman with 'er nerve!' He was sorry, Paul noted, but not
overwhelmed and why should he have been? If he had been
helping her to shuttle wounded to and fro for four months
he must have seen scores of men die on this stretch of road.
Paul replaced the blanket and the Cockney driver, who came
running as soon as she was told, burst into tears, rocking to
and fro like a child with a grazed knee. Then, quite abruptly,
she pulled herself together and got Grace and the orderly into
the second ambulance as an RAMC sergeant arrived to take
charge. Paul, feeling numb, went back to help the pioneers'
trouble squad fill in the crater and make the road usable.
While he was directing the work the sergeant rejoined him.

'That driver, sir,' he said casually, 'a WAAC over there
says you knew her?'

'Yes, I knew her,' Paul said, 'she was a very old friend
of mine. I was to have taken her out to dinner in Béthune

tonight. We would have been there now if she hadn't volunteered for someone else's run.'

'That's the way it goes,' the sergeant said, philosophically,
'it don't never do to volunteer, sir!' and Paul said bitterly,
'A stray bloody Gotha! What the hell is a Gotha doing over
here in daylight, for God's sake? I'll never stop hating those
bastards!'

The sergeant looked at him quizzically for a moment, as
though trying to assess his grief and then said, gently, 'It's
not *them* so much, sir. Save your hate for the bloody fools
up yonder who sandwiched the Red Cross between lorries
carrying captured machine-guns and ammo!' and he moved
off, shouting to the pioneers to get a bloody move on if they
didn't want to cause a pile-up a mile long.

They buried her in a temporary war cemetery near the
advanced base hospital and Paul got permission to attend.
It was a brief, simple ceremony but they gave her all the
honours, including the 'Last Post'. Apart from the MO and
the pioneer diggers he was the only man present. The rest
were girls of the transport section and two or three nurses.

He stood watching them shovel the clay into the grave
and tried to come to terms with the crazy improbability
of the scene; Grace Lovell, once his wife and mistress of
Shallowford, neatly tucked away out of sight under a French
plain after being killed by the blast of a German Aeroplane
bomb. It was closer to fantasy than reality, the kind of twist
that tangled the skein of a bad dream, like foliage growing out
of a carpet or a coach lurching along on elliptical wheels being
driven by a two-headed dog; it was madly and hopelessly
illogical and past thinking about.

Before they were done it began to rain, the thin, slanting
rain that seemed always to be falling on this plain. He thought,
'God in Heaven, who could have believed it would end this
way when I first saw her standing in the nursery the night
I arrived in the Valley?' and then, as the notes of the bugle
opened a sluice on his emotions, he had difficulty in holding
himself rigid for he recalled her reply to his advice to apply
for a rest – 'I'll rest when it's all over, or maybe before, if I'm

unlucky!' Well, she had been unlucky. She had been unlucky
the whole of her life, with a father who goaded her mother
into drowning herself, a wretched and rootless adolescence, a
failed marriage, years of prison and persecution for a principle,
and finally a foreign bomb out of the sky. And yet, as he made
his way back to his lorry, he remembered to be glad they had
met again and, to a great extent, buried the past, and also that
he was here to salute her as a great war comrade rather than
a woman whom he had held in his arms.

The rain began to fall faster, driving in from the north-west
and the group around the grave dispersed. Only the pioneer
corporal remained to bank the earth round the wooden cross,
inscribed, *'Driver G. Lovell, WAAC Transport Section. Killed
in action, 14.4.17'.*

Chapter Eight

I

Henry Pitts, known in 'B' Company as 'Smiler', had never quarrelled with mud. It had always puzzled him why people got excited about it when it transferred itself to their boots and clothes, or why so many should go out of their way to avoid contact with it. His mother, Martha, was such a person, and so was his wife, Gloria. As soon as he presented himself at the kitchen door on a wet day they would rush out like a couple of furies, screaming, 'Dornee bring that mud in, boy!' or 'Keep that bliddy mud where it b'longs!' It astonished him, this almost universal hatred of mud which was, after all, only earth in a glutinous form and as the years passed he developed what amounted to a mild affection for it, partly because it seemed to him a warm, friendly element, lacking the malevolence of rain, hail, snow and the east wind but also because it was his silent ally against the assault of women's tongues.

Out here, in the autumn of 1917, mud enfolded him on every side and Henry's comrades had come to regard it as an enemy second only to German trench mortars. When, in the winter of 1916–17, a hard frost set in, and it was possible to walk the length of a communication trench without soiling one's boots, the men rejoiced in the weather, as though it was an advantage to have to stamp one's feet for half-an-hour to restore circulation, or wear so many garments that even a waddle round a traverse was an effort. He took issue with them on this, pointing out that, under these conditions, shells were far more lethal than when they pitched into soft, friendly mud but they dismissed him as a lunatic, a man who had been out so long that he had grown to tolerate mud and the curious thing was they were half right about this for when he was alone on watch Henry would sometimes mould handfuls of the thick, yellow stuff into elephants, or snub-nosed howitzers, or cottages, or, if it was not solid enough for use as plasticine, trace patterns on its shining surfaces with a cartridge tip.

It might have been his alliance with mud, or his natural amiability, or his slow, plodding, thoughtful way of making war that enabled him to survive the Passchendaele battle that summer and autumn and not merely survive it but emerge from it as an infantryman whom the Germans could neither kill, wound nor discourage. Men were swallowed up in their thousands during the successive stages of the offensive, falling in groups under murderously accurate machine-gun fire, disappearing in the brimming craters that pocked the landscape, going sick by the hundred or, in some instances, choosing suicide to a prolongation of their misery but Henry survived without so much as catching a cold in the head. When it was over, and the shattered remains of the army was pulled back after penetrating a mile or two at a cost of about 300,000 casualties, he had not only preserved his bland imperturbability intact but had also won the Military Medal, just like Smut Potter, downalong.

His acquisition of glory was due less to his invulnerability that had become a legend in the unit than a desire to prove a point involving mud, or mud as related to the new-fangled weapon now appearing on the Front and known, for some unexplained reason, as The Tank.

Henry had a profound distrust of all mechanical contrivances on wheels dating from his first glimpse of Roddy Rudd's motor on its initial trip down the Valley and when he saw his first tank he was derisive, sharing the prejudice of his commander-in-chief, Sir Douglas Haig, and expecting even less of tanks than the most prejudiced cavalryman waiting to advance against an entrenched enemy over ground marked on pre-war maps as 'Marsh, sometimes passable in summer'.

'They contrapshuns!' he declared, 'why, dam' me, I could bellycrawl faster'n a bliddy great snail like that! Theym not only useless theym a bliddy menace to everyone walking in front of 'em! Even the cripples yerabout could cross ahead of 'em, you zee if I baint right when us goes over!'

He was about as right as he could be. On the first day of the assault the tanks got bogged down far short of their first objectives and Henry, passing one stranded in no-man's land, shouted, 'Why dornee get out an' push, maister?' to an infuriated sergeant who found himself the target for half the artillery behind Château Wood. The attacks continued, more or less abortively, throughout July, August and September, and it was during a despairing attempt to push down the Menin Road in the final phase of the offensive that Henry had the satisfaction of passing the famous tank graveyard, where a dozen or more of the helpless monsters lay like a swarm of dying beetles trapped in a pool of syrup. It was this day that he proved his theory, won his medal and was promoted to sergeant.

About half-a-mile east of the tank graveyard the battalion was pinned down by a single, expertly sited machine-gun. The survivors of the first wave had been there all morning and despite urgent appeals to the artillery to silence it the gun was still traversing and keeping everybody immobile in a line of water-logged shell-holes. It was only a matter of time, Henry's sergeant said, before the German guns located and exterminated them but the machine-gun had already accounted for a score of men who had tried to get within bombing-range and the only thing to do was to stay under cover until one of the tanks could deal with it or cause it to withdraw. This was heresy to Henry who said, emphatically, 'No bliddy tank'll get this far, Sarge, and I'll bet 'ee a tin o' Goldflake on that! Us'll have to come at it on the flank or not at all, and it baint very healthy here, be it? You wait on the tank and I'll zee what us c'n do in the meantime.'

He took a haversack of bombs and set out on a wide detour, moving from hole to hole across the tormented landscape and at length arriving within extreme throwing distance of the gun that was still firing in an arc of about a hundred and eighty degrees; then, suddenly, it stopped firing.

Two years on the Western Front had taught Henry Pitts how to gauge the exact point where risk coincides with what the training manuals called 'the inherent military probability' but what Henry would have called 'plain, bliddy gappy'. His 'gappy' told him that the machine-gun, having been firing for over an hour, must be running short of belts and as he saw no signs of reinforcements arriving with replenishments a long silence implied that the gunners, if not helpless, were at least conserving every bullet to stop a concerted rush. He sat there weighing his chances very carefully; then he half-rose and gently lobbed a bomb over the lip of his crater. On the heels of its explosion he heard a short, hoarse cry that did not sound like the bellow of a victim but more like a despairing shout of 'Kamerad' and this, in fact, was what he had expected. He waited another moment before extricating himself from the embrace of the mud and plodding across the lips of several keyholed craters in the direction of the gun. No sound came from the emplacement and neither burst nor bullet was aimed at him from the summit of the ridge. For a few seconds he appeared as the only man alive in all that vast, glutinous landscape, a sole survivor of a race swallowed in miles and miles of soft, putrefying mud. At last, as he negotiated a spread of half-immersed corpses, to look down into the shell-hole, he knew triumph. There was the machine-gun team, their hands raised and there, huddled close by, were about a dozen other mud-caked figures too dazed and despairing to surrender, who looked up at him apathetically, hardly recognisable as human beings in their sodden, shapeless clothes and abject postures. The Devil's immunity must have been working overtime that day. It even succeeded in diverting the artillery and machine-gunners higher up the ridge for not a burst was directed at the group when Henry, a bomb in either hand, shepherded his fifteen prisoners out of the emplacement and back towards the halted British line of advance by the overland route. They got there almost intact. The last of the Germans, a whimpering boy who looked about sixteen, got hung for a moment on wire and yelped like a terrier when a stray bullet struck his hand. The sergeant looked at Henry with awe, too astonished to congratulate him but later, when they were back at the starting-point and digging in against the inevitable counter-attack, he listened with great respect to Henry's simple explanation of his coup and how it demonstrated the superiority of legs over tanks. 'Now take what happened outalong, Sarge,' he said, pausing in his revetting to scrape a pound of mud from his puttees. 'There I was 'avin' to maake up me own mind whether or not they was out of ammo and ready to give up. And so I did, an' you zeed the result. But suppose – just suppose – I'd been one o' they bliddy contrapshuns, all racket an' no bliddy brains? Could I have sat quiet an' worked it out for meself? And suppose I had? Ah, now, there's the real rub! could I ha' clawed me way along them ridges without bringing down a box barrage as would ha' blown us all to tatters? Would 'ee tell me that, Sarge?'

The sergeant, himself a Devonian, shook his head and admitted that Henry was probably right but he did not yield the argument unconditionally, saying, thoughtfully, "Tiz all a matter o' the ground, Smiler. On terra-firma tanks could make a clean breakthrough, providing there's enough of them mind you, but in a bloody mudbath like this they can't get started, can 'em? Youm right but it baint a fair test, boy! No, it baint a fair test!', and he went away down the trench to despatch Henry's fifteen prisoners to Battalion HQ for interrogation. He sent a note along with them, explaining how and by whom they had been acquired, but Henry did not hear about this until much later when, with the exhausted remnant of his unit, he was informed of official recognition whilst delousing his shirt over a candle-flame in a cellar behind Ypres.

II

The sergeant's claim that tanks had not had a fair trial at Passchendaele was advanced by an embittered tank officer in Gough's Fifth Army that same month. Among the most insistent that tanks should not be judged on their third Ypres performance was Captain Palfrey, now the commander of a squadron of Mark IV tanks, two male and two female, affectionately christened Alfie, Bertha, Charlie and Daisy.

It was given to very few during the twenty-four months intervening between Loos and Passchendaele to see their dreams come true but Ikey was of that minority for the vision he had had whilst artillery-spotting during the 1915 battle had materialised in the later stages of the Somme offensive when, as one of the first tankmen to pilot a Mark I machine into battle, he had cursed the idiotic use of the weapon by High Command. Tanks were dribbled into the line in ones and twos and although their initial impact upon the enemy was sensational, and those reaching the German line swept everything before them, the determination of the strategists to precede every big attack with a barrage that churned up the ground and advertised their objectives, effectually prevented exploitation of the arm. The tankmen were withdrawn as failures when the offensive petered out but instead of despairing they returned to their maps, probing and probing for a sector where they could prove their claim that tanks were the only answer to the Western Front stalemate.

By this time Ikey had been in and out of the line for three years but he was a bad example of the theory that a man's usefulness declined in direct relation to his length of service in the field. He had ridden out the shock of Hazel's strange death, had not become an alcoholic or been seriously wounded and after two years' active service his nervous system was more or less intact although some of his closest associates were beginning to think that he had deluded himself into thinking he was no longer engaged in a war against the Central Powers but against the cavalry-generals in their châteaux fifty miles behind the lines. Before the war Ikey's attitude to senior officers had been one of ironic and affectionate contempt. His mimicry of those above field rank had been a star-turn wherever subalterns assembled out of earshot of their superiors. With a little make-up he could even look like one as he delivered imaginary lectures by members of the staff, interspersing every sentence with the obligatory 'Haw-Haw'!

and ad libbing long and rambling reminiscences of campaigns fought in Upper Burma and the Sudan.

Long before the end of the Somme offensive, however, he had decided that senior officers were now beyond a joke, especially the over-sixties and their gilded protégés who infested Supreme Headquarters. They had enlarged themselves, he declared, from mere buffoons into homicidal maniacs and should be locked out of harm's way until the war was over, when they could be trotted out and driven through the streets of London, preceded by a banner with the legend: 'Victory in Spite of US'. In the meantime he placed his reliance in the improved Mark IV tank and when news came that at long last the tankmen were to be allowed a chance to show what they could do in a sector of their own choosing he was so elated that he told his crews they now had a chance of ending the war single-handed.

They were denied this distinction. The chosen sector was opposite Cambrai and at the insistence of the tankmen the attack was preceded by the briefest of bombardments. At first it looked as if Ikey's reckless prophecy would be fulfilled. In a matter of hours the tanks, with cheering infantry in close support, had advanced a distance of four miles, tearing just such a gap in the German lines as Douglas Haig (and before him Sir John French) had been promising since the spring of 1915. The tank experts had reckoned, however, without the price of Passchendaele. There were no fresh divisions left to exploit this astounding advance and when the Germans counter-attacked there was nothing for it but to withdraw and yield up two-thirds of the territory won. At the close of the battle all that remained on HQ maps to demonstrate the usefulness of tanks on the Western Front was a blunted salient a mile or two wide that ultimately became as big an embarrassment to troops in the line as the famous 'prestige' salient at Ypres.

Yet Ikey enjoyed his private victory. Inside the inferno of the leading tank he sweated and stewed as they rumbled forward over first, second and third lines of defence, barriers that would have cost the lives of a hundred thousand men on Somme and

Passchendaele estimates. He came through it all unwounded and sent in a detailed report on the engagement but with the advance of winter, activities in the new Flesquiéres salient came to a standstill and he was sent back to Étaples for a three months' technical course and here, to his mild astonishment, he learned that he had been promoted major.

His elevation, following closely upon the strain of the autumn battles, completed the profound psychological change in Ikey that had begun with the news that his wife's reason had succumbed to the shock of what most people would have called her awakening. Paul had told him the truth in a long, tactfully-worded letter but even Paul was largely unaware of the forces and stresses that had persuaded Hazel to appoint herself beacon-lighter to the doomed men of the Valley and, as Ikey saw it, every other Valley in Europe. Ikey, who understood her processes of thought better than anyone, not excluding Meg Potter, saw Hazel's act of madness as a protest, an instinctive protest against the more cynical and infinitely more lethal madness of civilisation and although, all things considered, he joined Maureen in regarding her death as an unlooked-for mercy, the events that had led up to it confirmed him in his steadfast belief that Hazel had been more sane than most people were nowadays; among this majority he numbered the patriots on both sides of the lines and, more particularly, the politicians and generals directing the Allied war effort.

For a long time now, ever since his first term at High Wood and up to, say, the beginning of the Somme offensive, Ikey had been armoured against fate by his ironic sense of humour and, even more effectively, by his social neutrality for it was this that set him apart from even the most detached of his fellows. He had never wholly rejected his childhood in a Thames-side slum but neither had he wholly accepted his status as the adopted son of a country squire and an officer in the forces of the Crown. He continued to maintain a foot in each camp for while his natural adaptability enabled him to survive the narrow atmosphere of the mess and polo ground, Hazel Potter had safely anchored him to his original habitat. He enjoyed, as it were, a unique look-out post in a private no-man's land. He found the position amusing and sometimes absorbing from an intellectual standpoint and it had special advantages in his dealings with the men who came under his command. He could communicate without patronage and they were not slow to recognise as much, so that among the other ranks he was always the most popular officer in every unit in which he served. He was also, because of his lifelong habit of taking a situation apart and studying the pieces individually before putting them together again, an accomplished professional and his seniors soon came to rely on him to a degree than encouraged their built-in contempt for technicalities that was a feature of the pre-war army. Ikey was not slow to exploit this trust and when he found himself in France, where professional ability often meant economy in lives, there was considerable competition for his services. His transfer from the artillery to the Tank Corps had cost him the goodwill of his superiors but because he was convinced that tanks, and tanks alone, could break the deadlock in the West, he had persisted and ultimately been successful. He never regretted the transfer. The officers of the Tank Corps were mostly ex-civilians, unhampered by the prejudices of gunners who had soldiered in India, and here Ikey found his creativeness given free rein. He also discovered that at last he could communicate without having to keep tongue in cheek.

As a major, a professional, and a man who had been out more than two years he could have adopted a superior attitude towards his fellow-officers without incurring their resentment but he now reserved the professional touch for comic turns in the mess. Yet, deep in his heart, Ikey no longer searched for humour in the present situation. As the months went by, as more and more conscripts were fed into the Mincing Machine, he grew bitter and desperate, not so much against the war itself but against the manner in which it was being waged. There were times when, like Siegfried Sassoon, he was tempted to voice his protest openly in the newspapers or through one or other of the left-wing organisations at home but the habit of discipline was strong in him and he reasoned that the only result of a one-man revolt would be his transfer to a mental ward. This, in fact, had already happened in one or two cases when Authority, unwilling to brand a man with a good war-record coward or traitor, found it convenient to downgrade him as shell-shocked and put him out of harm's way for the duration.

He was actually discussing one of these cases with fellow-officers in a bar in Étaples towards the end of his course, when his cast of thought was broken and remoulded by a chance meeting with a wounded French officer, employed about the camp as an interpreter.

He had noticed the Frenchman standing apart from the group, a man so hideously disfigured that it was difficult not to look at him with embarrassing directness. He was a tall, slim officer, lacking a right arm, and from his temples to the right side of his chin was what appeared at first glance to be a wide smear of plum jam but was, in fact, a terrible scar partially disguised by skin-grafting. When Ikey's companions left to go on duty the Frenchman came forward and said, in faultless English, 'You won't remember me, Major Palfrey?' and when Ikey admitted this but invited him to have a drink in any case, went on, 'I recall you very well! We met in India when I was French attaché, at Cawnpore, in 1912. We had a long discussion one night, on Napoleon's Russian Campaign. I believe I convinced you that it was not the blunder claimed in the history books!'

Ikey recalled him then and clearly, a handsome, intelligent, friendly individual called Bouvet, an expert on the new French '75', still regarded as the best field-gun in existence. Bouvet said, 'It is natural you should not recall my face. I was left for dead in the first Ardennes battle and was in hospital until February this year.'

Ikey murmured an expression of formal sympathy and they chatted on their Indian service but he soon realised that the man was impatient to be done with small-talk and express his opinion on Allied prospects and the general conduct of the war. No sooner had he broached the topic, however, than the Frenchman said, 'Not in here, my friend! We will talk elsewhere I think!', and led the way to his billet, a small cottage hemmed in by three-storey warehouses. They went in and Bouvet lit the lamp, revealing a room containing very little furniture but a great many books, papers and files.

'You must not think you British have the prerogative of stupidity,' he said. 'I could not help hearing your conversation in the bistro but it is even worse with us. There can be no hope of victory until we have a unified command and younger men at the top.'

'Well, that's on its way,' Ikey said. 'We already have a Joint Planning Commission and a central reserve and I imagine, as time goes on, it will take over from men like Haig.'

'As time goes on,' Bouvet sneered, 'that is very British of you, my friend!' and then, pulling his mouth into a hard line that tautened the ravaged flesh of his cheek, 'But we have no time! The Germans will attack in strength as soon as they can transfer their freed divisions from the Russian front and the result of that attack will be the finish!'

Ikey was familiar with this theory, an access of German strength in the spring after an armistice with Russia, but in spite of himself, he began to defend a more optimistic view, pointing out that the superiority of defence over offence had been proved over and over again in the last three years and that the war would probably end in a stalemate. The Frenchman listened politely but when he had finished he said, quietly, 'The enemy have their quota of idiots, my friend, but unfortunately their system of command is such that Junkers are ciphers, like Hindenburg, real power resting with the climbers, like Ludendorff. Ludendorff is no fool! Do you imagine he has not profited by the lessons of Verdun, the Somme and Passchendaele? I tell you, he will break through and dictate peace by midsummer! Everything points to that, including our mutinies!'

It was the first direct reference Ikey had heard from a Frenchman of mutinies that had resulted from the total failure of the Nivelle offensive and he was curious to learn more.

'You know about the mutinies?' he asked. 'They were more than a few isolated incidents?'

'I know enough about them to get me court-martialled if I so much as mentioned them to an Englishman!' Bouvet said, 'Yet I think it is my duty to mention them to you, if only to convince you that you have no one but yourselves to rely on once the German offensive is launched! The French south of the Somme cannot help you. They will hold the line, perhaps, but it is accepted that they will do no more than that until the Americans arrive in force. By then it will be too late.'

Bouvet then disclosed all he knew of the French mutinies and Ikey was shocked by his account. He learned that whole divisions of French infantry had walked away from the front, heading for Paris, and that the situation had only been saved by the prompt dismissal of General Nivelle, his successor's decision not to sacrifice another drop of French blood in an offensive, and by mass arrests and an unspecified number of executions. It was one of the methods employed to restore order that appalled Ikey. A small number of men, so Bouvet told him, had been shot but others, ostensibly pardoned, had been sent to a quiet sector of the line and there exterminated by their own artillery, supposedly firing at enemy defences. Bouvet could not say how many had died this way but he thought it was over a thousand and Ikey left his billet that night with his education on modern war complete. He no longer despised the Allied High Command buffoons but thought of them as a group of men from whom nothing could be expected but an eternity of blood-letting. It was this conversation, more than anything of his personal experiences in the last three years, that blasted him from his seat on the fence. The war had to be fought out, he supposed, but afterwards, immediately afterwards there must be a reckoning. The entire social structure of the old world would have to be changed, either by revolution on the Russian pattern, or by some less drastic process but changed anyway if human dignity was to survive. From then on he was committed and took little care to conceal as much notwithstanding the bright new crown over his shoulder.

III

The day she received Paul's letter saying that he had been promised nine days' leave in October Claire turned her back on patients, children, staff and all other time-robbers, saddled old Snowdrop and crossed the dunes to the gully to satisfy herself that Eph Morgan had kept his word about making the shanty habitable by the end of the month.

All good Shallowfordians had their inner tabernacle on or about the estate and Claire's preference was for the steep, narrow goyle that gave on to the beach within a couple of hundred yards of the rock-pool where her mother had taught her to swim and where Paul had proposed. She did not go there often but when she did she preferred to go alone.

In the mouth of the gully was a single dwelling, a tumbledown shanty once occupied by a local character known in the Valley as Crabpot Willie. Crabpot had been a very old man when Claire was a child but she recalled him as a shaggy-whiskered old rascal, who lived by catching and selling shellfish, who walked rather like a crab and who was said, on slender authority, to have rounded the Horn on a windjammer. Here he had lived until his death in the early 'nineties after which his cabin had fallen into decay for nobody cared to live this far from the village or so near high-water mark where spring tides would sometimes lap Willie's doorstep.

Claire first revisited the area whilst prospecting for a shorter cut to the beach for hospital bathing parties and recalling that the old man had been favourite of her mother's she turned aside to inspect his former home. She was surprised to find that the main roof timbers and pine floor were more or less intact, and that the shingle roof had been partially saved by overhanging firs marking the edge of the wood on the shoulder of the landslip. It was a secluded, pleasant spot in the summer. Sand had blown in from the beach, half-filling the little cleft and was held there by marram grass and sea holly. Higher up, beyond the pine-needles, grew campion, bugloss, trefoil and wood anemone in a grove of dwarf oaks and the place was

sheltered from easterly and south-westerly winds. Claire's first
thought was to convert the shanty into a beach chalet for the
convalescents but then she knew that she would resent sharing
it with anyone save Paul and another plan began to form in her
mind, resulting in her approach to Eph Morgan (then building
Nissen huts under Government contract in the paddock) and
an appeal to make it habitable as her retreat. Eph carried out
an inspection and said the shanty could be weather-proofed
easily enough but warned her that the only way she could
get the necessary materials was by compounding a felony
and signing a form to the effect that the work was a hospital
extension. She signed without a qualm and he went to work
on the promise of cash payment, hauling materials along the
beach at low tide and later helping her transport furniture,
bedding and kitchen utensils across the dunes.

When the job was finished, and the shanty looked snug
and inviting, she locked the door and kept the key on her
personal ring, against the time that she should have news of
Paul's homecoming, for the shanty was to be a place where
they could enjoy a few hours' blessed privacy away from the
racket of wards and nursery and safe from those who might
use his precious leave to importune for one thing or another.
There was also, she admitted to herself, a selfish element in
the scheme. She had long since made up her mind that she
needed him far more desperately than did anyone else in the
Valley and was prepared to maintain her claim at the expense
of tenants, employees and even the children.

In early October he wired asking if she would care to
meet the leave train at Charing Cross and spend a day or
two in town doing the popular shows but she wrote at once
declining the offer, saying that she would meet him at Sorrel
Halt in the trap. She knew that he would prefer this and her
plans were now well advanced.

On the morning of the day he was due to arrive she drove
the trap over the dunes for a last-minute inspection and
unloaded enough stores at the shanty to withstand a short
siege. The cabin looked spic and span under its new coat of
tar and creosote, crouching under the the cluster of firs like a

weatherbeaten toadstool. Inside it smelled fresh and clean and Claire spent an hour there, lighting a fire and banking it high with green wood, airing the bed with stone hot-water bottles, off-loading eggs, bacon, flour, and some bottles of wine laid down for Simon's twenty-first birthday and adding a touch of colour with some bronze and yellow chrysanthemums.

She sat for a moment watching the fire burn up feeling more like a young bride than a woman approaching middle age with a growing family and over a hundred convalescent soldiers on her conscience, but the latter could not have troubled her much for, as she laid her best silk nightdress across the pillow, she thought, gaily, 'I daresay he'll remind me it's autumn and hustle me back to the house in search of comfort after nine months at the Front but I'm damned if I don't do my best to maroon him here for twenty-four hours!' Then she locked the door and led the pony up the incline to the dunes, noting with satisfaction that the weather, although crisp, looked settled over Nun's Bay, the source of all the gales at this time of year.

She was astonished to note how fit and young he looked when he swung his valise from the train and came striding down the platform towards her. For so long, it seemed, she had, been shut up with sick, shambling men, short of a limb, jumpy and indecisive in their movements. She knew, of course, that he had been spared the worst of it and had at least slept under a roof since the spring offensive but she had not expected him to come to her looking braced, healthier and obviously more tranquil in mind than when he had been grappling with multiple problems during the first half of the war. She experienced a moment of embarrassment when he embraced her, recalling all those things she had poured into her letters during the last few months but the moment passed after they climbed into the trap and he took the reins with an air of having been met after one of his rare trips to London.

He told her a little of what had been happening over there, of the failure of the latest Ypres battle on account of the mud and how lucky he had been then to be in the relatively quiet sector far to the south and she began to feel slightly deflated, as though her role now was no more than that of dutiful audience to the returning warrior. Then, just as they were dipping down from the crest near the place where he had stopped to reassure himself after the suffragette scrimmage, he surprised her by pulling off the road, dropping the reins and kissing her with such zest that she exclaimed, laughing, 'I expected something like that on the platform but all I got was a peck and a war bulletin!'

'You can forget the damned war from now on,' he said, seriously, 'I only used it as a smokescreen while I got my bearings! If it was dark I'd let the pony nibble on that gorse for a spell and whisk you off into the heather before we got buried alive by well-meaning old busybodies like Mrs Handcock and the local Home Fronters! I was glad when you said you preferred not to meet me in London but we ought to have had the sense to find a place temporarily removed from everyone!'

He could hardly have given her a more welcome opening. She said, eagerly, 'Listen, Paul, do you remember that tumbledown old shack in the gully near the rock-pool where you proposed? I had an idea a month or so ago and I talked Eph Morgan into restoring it and when it was done I fixed it up. We can go there now. I took food over this morning and lit a fire. We can stay there for a day or so if we like because I took Maureen into my confidence and she said she'll think of something to spare our blushes! You don't *have* to go, of course, we could ride over tomorrow but . . . well, it's the only way I could think of to make sure the tenants don't descend on us in a body!'

She broke off, embarrassed to discover that she was blushing furiously under his amused stare and said, lifting up the reins, 'Well, there it is! Suit yourself! I don't mind either way!'

'By God I will!' he said, snatching the reins and flicking them across the pony's back. 'How the devil do you get there from here? There's no road, is there?' and as she directed him to cross Codsall Bridge and cut across the stubble fields to the dunes, 'And you don't have to apologise, either! I half thought that you . . . all right, let it pass!'

'What were you going to say?'

He looked at her with a grin. 'Only that I had a rather depressing thought at the back of my head – that those letters you wrote were prompted by loneliness more than anything else and that when we came face to face you'd feel shamefaced about putting your name to them!'

'And what makes you think I'm not?'

'Like hell you are, you little liar!' he said, chuckling, 'you've been plotting for months and why not? By God, Claire, I don't regret getting into the war when I might have stayed here but I don't think I realised how vital you were to my peace of mind, or how desperately I would miss you! I used to think it had to do with your identification with this place and so it had, in the beginning, but not any longer! It's you Claire Derwent and not the Valley! I could live anywhere if I had to, so long as I could be sure of waking up nights and finding you within reach!', and he threw his arm round her as they bumped off the Four Winds track and headed across the stubble for the coast. She said, choosing her words carefully: 'I've always pretended to be the Spirit-of-the-Valley, Paul, for I knew that was the kind of wife you wanted and played up to it! Even in the very beginning I admired your nerve taking on a job this size, and being a rather sensual little beast there never was a time when I didn't enjoy you as a man. Deep, spiritual need, however – real love, that's something one has to learn and I didn't begin learning until we had that stupid quarrel over poor Hazel and its sequel. Since then, and since your being away put responsibility on me, I understand your purpose better than anyone – except maybe John Rudd. I know somehow you'll come back for good, if only because you were meant to make this out-of-the-way corner live and flower. That's why, although I'm desolate without you, I don't worry myself sick like all the other women.'

He nodded, understanding and valuing every word she uttered. Then, as they reached the grove of dwarf oaks, he climbed down and led the pony along the ruts made by her hauls earlier in the year. When they reached the bottom it was dusk and the orange sun was playing a losing game with the silhouettes of the firs behind the cabin. He said, with the deepest satisfaction, 'This was an inspiration, Claire, and we'll keep this place for ourselves! We won't even have the children here,' and turned aside to unharness the pony and bed her down in the lean-to stable while she went inside to stir up the fire and prepare a meal. She had, he noticed, overlooked nothing. There was even a truss of hay and bucket of oats for the animal.

IV

Of the eight days he remained in the Valley they spent four in seclusion and the rest up at the house. The ninth he devoted to Simon who had gone to High Wood the previous month.

For Claire the time they spent alone was the highwater mark of her marriage, a lamp that was to shine down the years to the end of her life, lighting up periods of doubt and frustration, a fixed point to which she could always look for reassurance when her hair ceased to crackle under the comb and she began to thicken and lose some of her suppleness. Their hunger for one another denied them the leisurely love-making of pre-war days but instead followed a kind of graph, with a dozen rapturously high peaks and any number of swift dips into laughter. But midway between these two extremes were long, placid intervals when she would bring him up-to-date on Valley affairs and gossip so that when it was time for him to go a clear, balanced picture of Valley trends and Valley economics was etched upon his memory. The picture was to console him in the calamitous period ahead but he remembered more vividly the gaiety of their conversations and the blessed silence of the gully, disturbed only by the whisper of the firs and the measured suck of the tide, advancing and retreating up and down the deserted beach. The children brought him joy too, each in their several ways. Simon's adolescent earnestness, the twins' boisterous enthusiasm for all things military, the independence of little Whiz and six-year-old Mary's solemnity when she sat on his knee, begging him to make the other available to her protégé,

Rumble Patrick, whom he noticed she mothered like a little spaniel bitch foster-rearing a fox-cub.

But for Claire there was no such overall domestic pattern as this; for her the interval was at once more intense and far more personal, a time when she had reason to bless her forethought in providing a retreat where she was under no obligation to share him and where no exchanges between them were too unlikely and extravagant for a man and woman denied one another for so long.

After the initial transport, when they let the meal she had prepared go cold upon the table, she made up her mind to prolong the ecstasy of reunion by the exercise of some restraint but her resolutions came to nothing. As soon as he touched her her yearning became a frenzy so that she would not wait for him to take the initiative, as in the past, but would translate her written promises into action demanding of him as much as he could give and exalting in his greed for her. Yet always, as in the earliest days of their marriage, there was a residual of humour, for when they were still again she would say, teasing him, 'You don't act like a man home from a place where they work you hard! I believe you must have landed the cushiest job in France with nothing better to do but loiter about storing up energy on a honeymoon diet of oysters and champagne!' And he would respond with some rejoinder as, 'It was generated by your shameless letters – refined cruelty to a much-married man away from home and living in the open on a diet of bully beef!' Or, if she teased him about his techniques, saying he must have acquired them from the mademoiselles, he would heave her across his knee and spank her broad bottom for disobeying his orders to keep the war out of their conversation. As a honeymoon it was far more enriching than its predecessor ten years before and it was this she had in mind when she denigrated honeymoon couples as a whole, declaring that it was too much to expect young couples to adjust themselves so soon after the fuss of a tribal ceremony with the din of wedding bells in their ears. 'Why can't honeymoons be postponed for as long as this?' she demanded, and he had laughed, saying, 'Because, you idiot, they are designed for the prompt procreation of children! Suppose we'd waited ten years? We should have been a tetchy old couple of nearly sixty while the twins and Mary were still at school!'

'Well,' she said, with a conceit that made him chuckle, 'if you haven't procreated a second clutch in the last forty-eight hours I must be past bearing! If the estate falls into disarray because I'm busy nursing all next summer you'll have no one but yourself to blame, Squire!'

This was the way they talked and this was the rhythm of the days and nights they spent together, wild, ungovernable moments, spaced with intervals of laughter, speculation and reminiscence, but there were some inexpressibly tender moments too, as when they were undressing before the fire late one night after stealing back to the cabin like a pair of clandestine lovers.

She was in the act of slipping on her nightgown when he took it from her, bidding her to stand before the green and violet sputter of blazing apple logs, and when she did as he asked he sat absorbing the strength and symmetry of her body, as a painter might ponder the complexities of transferring physical perfection to canvas. She had already loosed her hair, and its lights danced the measure of the flames. She stood quite still, receiving and relishing his homage as he appraised every part of her, her long, slender feet and dimpled knees, the glowing health of her skin, the smooth sweep of her hips where they ended in a still-neat waist – every aspect of her that he had worshipped over the years. There was not a part of her, he thought, that was less than perfect in his eyes; the sturdy columns of her thighs balanced by wide buttocks and a long, straight back, her full, firm breasts, her strong neck and powerful shoulders offsetting the curious smallness and neatness of her head and, above all, those features of her that were so eager to demonstrate subjection to him, her generous pouting mouth, her lips, and eyes that seemed to him at this moment never to have held in their depths anything but promise. He said, soberly, 'You're not just Rubens' model, Claire, you're Velasquez's and every

other perfectionist who ever tried to express a feminine ideal!
You're quite beautiful and far nearer physical perfection than
you were in your early twenties! I swear to you that isn't
flattery and it isn't because I've been starved of you either! A
man could go on looking at you for ever and find something
new and exciting every second! How could any man in his
senses help desiring you, even if he did no more than keep
you to look at at moments like this?'

She emerged from the sensual reverie praise of this kind
induced and forked a shaft of mischief at him, the instinctive
provocation of a woman secure in the tenure of her lover.

'No one else ever has looked at me like this. If they ever do
I'll get the verdict endorsed! After all, one as flattering as that
deserves corroboration!', and then the mischief died and moved
by an impulse his commendation stirred in her she pressed his
face to her breasts, saying, 'I'm only beautiful as long as you
remember me like this, Paul! As long as the memory of our
time alone here is vivid and close to you! For as long as that
nothing can change for us dearest, not even if everything and
everybody around us changes!'

He was to remember that cry of hers at a moment when
the world around him was not merely changing but disinte-
grating in an everlasting series of thunder flashes and the
reek of cordite filled his lungs.

V

Although it was not for want of trying on Paul's part he had
never succeeded in establishing a relationship with Simon that
he had achieved with the other children, or, for that matter,
with some of his numerous godchildren in the Valley. The
boy hedged himself about with a special kind of privacy that
rebuffed most people and only Ikey, and, to some extent Claire,
could overcome. He was on friendly terms with most of the
tenantry, and some of the craftsmen and hired labourers, so
that it had sometimes irritated Paul to admit to himself that
Simon would talk more freely to Sam Potter, the woodsman,

or the hare-lipped dairymaid at the Home Farm than he would talk to his father. In Paul's presence Simon was respectful and noncommittal.

One of the by-products of Paul's 1917 leave was a partial bridging of this gap, for Paul was lucky to catch Simon with some of his defences down, moping through his first term at a sadly disorganised High Wood, staffed by an asthmatic temporary headmaster, invalided trench veterans and Grade III civilians.

Paul was depressed by the boy's dispirited manner when summoned to the Headmaster's study to meet his father and at once his heart went out to him, for he was reminded very sharply of Grace as Paul had last seen her in Béthune. He knew Claire had told Simon of her death and wondered if the boy was grieving, notwithstanding the fact that he could have no memory of her. There was no transport available so at the Head's suggestion the two of them set out across the moor to an isolated inn near Five Barrows, an ancient Celtic monument four miles from the school.

At first Paul thought it was going to be a miserably embarrassing expedition, for Simon answered his questions regarding school life with mumbled monosyllables. As they were threading their way through a beech grove, however, heading for the open moor, Paul succeeded in breaking the ice by chance when he said, 'I've really come to tell you what a brave woman your mother was, son!', and the boy stopped, looking up at him with a trembling lip and saying, in a cracked voice that Paul recognised as half-broken, 'Mrs Handcock said you were there when she was killed, sir, but I didn't believe it. I didn't see how you could be but that was what she said. I – I'd like to know if that was true, sir.'

Paul found to his embarrassment that his own voice was unsteady. They stood together on the edge of the wood, overlooking a tumbling moorland stream and then, by common consent, sat down side by side on a broken piece of fencing, Paul began, 'I didn't know how much you'd been told—' and then, impatiently, 'Look here, you don't

have to call me "sir"! Ikey always called me "Gov'nor". You
can call me Gov'nor if you like.'

The boy grinned and Paul realised what perfect teeth
he had and how, just like Grace, he was able to dissipate
any impression of surliness or distrust by a smile. He put
his hand on Simon's shoulder and when the boy did not
withdraw, as he half-expected he might, said, 'Well, it so
happens that old chatterbox had it right for once! I *was*
there when your mother was killed. She was driving badly
wounded men from Advanced Dressing Station to hospital,
and I came on the scene a few minutes after it happened
but before that we'd met by chance and had dinner together
and we talked about you. She was coming to see you when
she came on leave.' The lie, he thought, could be classified
as snow-white, for somehow it seemed important he should
draw them together in this roundabout way. Simon said, 'Do
you mind telling me about her . . . Gov'nor?'

'Not in the least. I always had a great respect for her
courage but after meeting her again in France, and talking
to some of the girls she was working with, I came away with
a tremendous admiration for her! She was as much a heroine
as any chap with the VC and don't ever forget it! That was her
second trip under fire that day and she volunteered for it.'

He told as much of the circumstances as he thought the
boy could absorb without feeding him material for mor-
bid reflections but Simon surprised him none the less, for
after Paul had told him Grace had been given a military
funeral, the boy said, 'Why did she leave us in the first
place? Did you quarrel over me?'

'Good God, no! Why should we do that? You were only a
few months old at the time.' He sat thinking hard, wondering
how to explain such an unlikely set of circumstances to a
thirteen-year-old child and finally compromised, saying, 'It's
difficult to put into words, old chap, but I suppose the truth
is your mother was never in love with me, not in the way your
stepmother is. It had to do with our aims in life. You see, she
wasn't a "country" person, so we ought never to have married.
If we hadn't we should have stayed good friends, the way we

ended up in France. Then she got a bee in her bonnet about votes for women and in the end this became more important to her than – well – me or the estate.'

'Were you against votes for women?'

'No, I wasn't, and neither was our MP, Jimmy Grenfell, who also admired her but the odd thing is I've come to believe your mother left because, in a funny sort of way, she thought it was unfair to me to stay.' He looked sideways at the boy. 'Do you find that hopeless to understand?'

'No,' said Simon, 'I believe I can see what you mean, Gov'nor.'

'Then try and tell me,' Paul said, gratefully, and Simon went on, 'She must have thought you ought to be married to someone keen on the Valley.'

'That's exactly it!' said Paul, excited by the boy's perception, 'she told me I ought to have married a farmer's daughter in the first place but what I'd really like to get home to you is that just because we got divorced she wasn't a mother to be ashamed of but rather the opposite. She didn't run off with anyone else, she just had to give herself to politics and she was prepared to go to prison for her beliefs which is a damned sight more than most politicians are!'

'Some of those Labour chaps have,' Simon said, unexpectedly, and Paul wondered how, in a conservative school like High Wood Simon could have known this and commented on it without labelling Socialist MPs 'dirty conchies'.

'Yes, that's so,' he replied. 'Some people feel about the war that way and most of the fighting men respect them for it.'

'They do?' He saw that he had astounded the boy at last and went on, 'Yes, they do, because people at home haven't any real idea what it's like, so they can't help talking nonsense about it like the newspapers and politicians. Did Ikey tell you about his friend Keith Horsey, the parson's son? He was a CO but he's out there in the thick of it stretcher-bearing.'

'Yes,' said Simon thoughtfully, 'I know about Horsey. Fellows here are ashamed he was a Highwodian you know, so I wrote to Ikey and told him and he wrote back saying they must be chumps because Horsey was braver than anyone if the truth was known!'

'Did you pass that on?' asked Paul, curiously.

'No,' Simon said, 'because I'd get hell for sticking up for a CO. You don't go around looking for trouble as a first-termer!'

Paul laughed and felt a rush of affection for the boy, thinking how badly he had misjudged him in the past.

'I see your point,' he said, 'it must be damned difficult to hold an unpatriotic point of view in a place like this!'

'What do *you* think about the war, Gov'nor?'

This was almost as difficult as explaining why Grace had exchanged home and husband for Holloway, for Paul feared to express himself too freely on the subject in case Simon quoted him in an unguarded moment.

'I *don't* think about it any more than I can help, son,' he said, realising he was evading the question, 'I just get on with it, like most of the chaps out there,' but the boy was not to be fobbed off with this and again reminded Paul of Grace when one of her principles was challenged.

'But you must know whether you think it right or wrong.'

'Well then, it's wrong,' Paul said, reluctantly, 'it's the biggest crime against humanity that's ever happened but I daresay some good will come out of it, at least, that's what most of us out there like to think, the Germans as well as the English.'

'If everybody fighting thinks that why isn't it stopped?' Simon persisted, with his mother's maddening logic.

'Because, for the moment, neither side is ready to give in. The men in the trenches would be very happy to call it a day but the war isn't directed by them. They just do what they're told and all the orders come from older men, most of them warming their backsides beside a comfortable fire. That's why it has to be fought to a finish.'

'It seems a stupid way to carry on,' the boy said and Paul agreed that it was indeed but that when the men came back they intended to make certain nothing like it would happen again so perhaps it would benefit their children and grandchildren.

After that they spent a rewarding day, talking easily of all kinds of things but when they parted in the quad as the bell rang for tea he realised Simon had absorbed every word he had been told about Grace for he said, shaking hands and pocketing Paul's tip, 'If they give my mother a medal could I have it? To keep?'

Paul had difficulty concealing the extent to which the request moved him but promised he certainly could keep the medal if there was one and the boy went off then, cheerfully enough Paul thought, envying the ability of the young to discard emotional problems in the struggle to adapt themselves to their immediate surroundings. The tedious journey home, however, was not wholly depressing, for at least he could congratulate himself on having got nearer to Simon than ever before and as he crossed the moor in the ramshackle motor-cab he had engaged at Paxtonbury he thought how small a part environment played in promoting character and how manifestly clear it was that Simon's personality was the legacy of the sallow, exhausted woman he had last seen lying under a groundsheet on the road to Messines Ridge. 'They can talk as much as they like about influences of social backgrounds,' he told himself, 'but what's in the blood stays there! Look at Ikey and that crazy marriage of his? And look at the way Eveleigh is making a fool of himself over that damned shop-girl! Come to that look at Simon – his stream of political thought already veering left at thirteen!' The rain slashed against the canvas hood of the cab and the darkness deprived him of his favourite view of the Valley.

Chapter Nine

I

January, 1918; snow blanketed the entire Valley, from the farthest fold of Blackberry Moor to the bleak, crusted dunes, from the blur of Shallowford Woods down through eight-foot drifts to the frozen Sorrel where the ice was said to be six inches thick. The frost had held fast since Boxing Day and even those with menfolk in the ice-bound ditches of Flanders were too cold, too tired and too discouraged to spare them much sympathy. For this was the fourth winter of the war that would never end and external pressures had shrivelled souls to the size and toughness of dried peas, sometimes putting an impossible price on neighbourliness.

Claire, depressed by this collective withdrawal, fought it wherever she could, for it seemed to her a loss more painful and damaging than the drain on Valley manpower. From time to time she went out of her way to marshal the survivors, reviving their flagging spirits with reminders of the approach of spring and the promise of a record yield from meadows now gripped fast by the frost and scoured by an east wind that searched through the heaviest garments a person could wear and still waddle up and down the lifeless lanes. The Valley, she would remind herself, was not only more populous but more productive than it had ever been. There were never less than two thousand men in the hutted camp at Nun's Bay, and often a hundred convalescents at Shallowford House. All seven farms had a record number of acres under the plough and were supporting twice as much livestock as in pre-war years and although so many familiar faces had disappeared, some of them for ever, their places had been taken by others not all of whom came into the category of foreigners, like the soldiers in camp or the German prisoners in the depot north of the woods. Men and girls had drifted in from the neighbouring estate of Heronslea which had lost impetus since Lord Gilroy had been killed on the Italian Front leaving no heir and two Whinmouth conscientious objectors were now employed by her brother Hugh at High Coombe, Hugh having neither the patriotic scruples of Eveleigh nor his preference for buxom land-girls. Yet the shifts and changes in the tempo of life were so various and manifold that Claire had great difficulty in keeping track of them all when she sat in the library late at night writing to Paul, or keeping the estate diary up-to-date. She applied herself to these tasks religiously, for the one was her sole emotional outlet and the other seemed to her a bridge to post-war continuity. The list of Valley soldiers and Valley casualties had now entered upon a second page. Dick Marlowe, the sexton's younger son, had gone down somewhere off the west coast of Africa bringing home a cargo of maize from Capetown, and news crossed the Teazel of the death in action of Dave Buller, Gilroy's keeper, who had carried the scars of Smut Potter's gunstock to his grave in a shell-hole on the slopes of Vimy Ridge. Then, as January passed, and the hard frost held on into February, news came of Parson Horsey's loss. His son Keith had been blown to pieces when a Minnenwerfer scored a direct hit on a stretcher party passing down a communication trench in front of St Quentin, and this time Claire had to do more than record the casualty, feeling under an obligation to call on the little rector.

She always hated these duty visits to the bereaved for whatever could one say to a broken old widower, whose hopes for years had been centred on an only son who had taken a double-first at Oxford and whose brains were now at the bottom of a French ditch? Expressions of sympathy had been all very well in 1914 and even in 1915 but they were fatuous after years of slaughter and the actual presence in the Valley of so many maimed men. She made the effort, however, borrowing Maureen's battered Ford, for she was now close on five months' pregnant just as she had predicted, although it no longer seemed a subject to joke about. A baby on the way was just one more responsibility at a time when she needed the maximum freedom of movement.

She found the rector at work in his glacial, book-filled study and although he looked tired and ill he seemed to her to have derived some kind of fortitude from his faith which was more than could be said of most of his flock in identical circumstances. He seemed also to have acquired a kind of pride in his son's share in the war, for he said, after showing her Keith's last letter praising the courage of some of the wounded he had tended, 'I was against him going to begin with, you know, but I realise now that he was right and I was wrong! I've since wondered if the early martyrs wouldn't have made their point just as forcibly by electing to serve in the arena, perhaps attending to wounded gladiators and animals. I always knew Keith would justify me but I never imagined it would occur in this roundabout way!' Claire, somewhat puzzled, asked him to explain and he went on, earnestly, 'Oh come, Mrs Craddock, you and your husband have never had any illusions about me being a failure here, just as I was in my last parish and the one before that! I was never unaware of it but I could at least say to myself, "I fathered a first-class scholar, whose personal impact may be as feeble as mine but whose brains will win him a real place in the world!" And they would have done that, you know. Now, I suppose, I must find consolation in the thought that his presence out there must have been instrumental in bringing a hundred or so back from the dead and I could hardly think that if Keith had been just one more man with a gun.' He smiled, politely and nervously, just as he did every Sunday on ascending the pulpit to begin sermons that were barely tolerated by his war-time congregations, and then he pointed at a large framed photograph of Parson Bull, his predecessor, still hanging over the fireplace. Bull had had himself photographed in hunting rig and contemplating the former rector's Hogarthian build, and insolent, bulging eye, it occurred to Claire that one could spend a lifetime looking for two more dissimilar priests. Horsey said, 'I keep it there to remind me there are various ways of preaching the gospel, Mrs Craddock. Bull's way was a century or more out-of-date but it worked far more effectively than mine. You have to admit that!'

'No,' said Claire, beginning to assess the parson's true stature for the first time. 'I don't admit it! Bull's way wouldn't work any longer and I think people about here are going to need your methods in the very near future. My husband never has thought of you as a failure, for at least you achieved something he always wanted by reconciling the Anglicans and the Nonconformists in the Valley. All Bull ever did was to hold them apart by brute strength!' Horsey accepted the compliment with a slight inclination of the head and thanked her for calling. At the door she said, suddenly, 'Look here, Rector, why don't you come up to the house and hold a non-denominational service for the convalescents? I daresay most of them are beyond any parson's reach but you might catch the odd lost sheep. Anyway, even the scoffers would like a change. The camp padre doesn't impress them very much.'

'Then I'm sure I should impress them less, Mrs Craddock. After all, can you wonder they've lost their faith? I don't think we parsons have come very well out of this war. Keith wrote saying every German has the words *"Gott Mit Uns"* emblazoned on his belt. Besides, what would I talk to them about?'

She had a sudden inspiration. 'Your son!' and he looked at her sharply, saying, 'Wouldn't that be parading a personal grief, Mrs Craddock?'

'No, I don't think it would. Many of them wouldn't be alive now if they hadn't been brought in by stretcher-bearers.'

He seemed vaguely impressed by this and stood holding the door, his eyes on the yellow slush that had accumulated on the step.

'Well, I'll think it over,' he said at length. 'Anyway, it was kind of you to ask and kinder still to call.' She went down the path to the car and heaved herself in, relieved to be done with the visit. 'Poor little beggar,' she thought as Marlowe, the sexton, who had lost two sons swung the engine, 'he's putting a brave face on it but I think this has about finished him.' But the Reverend Horsey was far from finished. Within the week he not only surprised Claire but several hundred others, including himself.

When the sound of the car had died away Parson Horsey went back into his study and sat down at his desk, poking about among the mass of papers until he found a closely-written sheaf of manuscript left by Keith after his last leave, in December. Horsey studied each page carefully, sitting there until the light faded. Then, lighting the lamp, he put the manuscripts away and began to re-read his son's letters, more than a score of them, written from France. When the housekeeper came in with his cocoa he was writing to Claire and his letter, delivered by hand the following morning, puzzled her. He said he would accept her offer to conduct a non-denominational service in the big ward next Sunday, subject to two conditions; attendance was to be optional and she must on no account circulate news of Keith's death among the patients. She sent a message to Nun's Bay camp informing the resident padre that the local rector would conduct a service on the following Sunday but was already half-regretting have invited Horsey to preach. The men, as she well knew, had shed what religious beliefs they held in France, and their approach to parsons was at best negative and sometimes hostile. 'We on'y saw a few o' the RCs up the line,' one of the men told her. 'Them others, they'd slip across during a quiet spell, dish out a few Woodbines an' nip orf ruddy quick! It's nice to 'ave one 'andy when you're buried they say but me, I don't go much on 'em! Sooner put me money on Jumbo I would,' and he showed her a small ivory elephant attached to his identity discs. Because Horsey was coming at her own invitation, however, she felt responsible for his reception and knowing that most of the more mobile patients would make themselves scarce before the service began she filled a couple of benches in the ward with household staff and a few of the VADs who had been allocated to her before Christmas. She was not really Commandant now, although she kept the title by courtesy. Her pregnancy had curtailed her nursing activities and a professional matron was due to arrive any day to cope with an influx of more seriously wounded men.

Horsey arrived about ten-thirty and the tepid service began, attended by no more than half-a-dozen of the active convalescents and, perforce, by those confined to bed. After the second hymn Horsey walked briskly behind the table they used as an altar and stood midway between the two nearest beds, blinking and fumbling with some notes he held in his hand. One of the men at the far end of the ward began to cough and deliberately prolonged the spasm but the rector waited quietly and when there was silence began, in an unexpectedly firm voice, 'I daresay most of you chaps are familiar with stretcher-bearers! I'm not going to bore you with a sermon and I haven't even thought of a text. All I want is to read you a piece of writing sent to me by a young man who spent a year in France and has since died. He calls this piece "*Truce, 1917*" and it tells of an incident that happened on the edge of a place called Pilckem Wood, near Ypres.'

There were several men present who had unpleasant memories of Pilckem Wood and one of them, who had lain under it a day and a night with a broken thigh, involuntarily advertised as much by exclaiming, 'Christ!', and left it at that. His exclamation had an unlooked-for effect on some of the others, who scowled and hissed, 'Shh!' whereas the man who had shown Claire his elephant charm, sat up and said, very sternly, 'Stow it, mate!' Claire, sitting on the end of the form under the window, glanced at Horsey and noticed that he seemed unruffled by the stir. He cleared his throat and at once began to read.

It was a straightforward piece of prose telling a simple, factual story of a fifty-minute cessation of hostilities towards the end of the Passchendaele battle, when men of both sides came out into the open to collect the wounded. There was nothing remarkable about this, Claire decided. Paul had told her that it often happened but it occurred to her that the writing was remarkable for its restraint. It made no attempt whatever to imitate the purple passages of a magazine story and, what was even more unusual, it contained no irony so that it was neither a conventional 'call-to-arms' nor an indictment of war but simply an account of what actually occurred during the lull, as seen from the point of view of someone grubbing about in the shell-holes in search of men with a chance of recovery. The dying, it said, were given morphine and the dead were left lying where they had fallen in the morass. Time was an essential factor in the operation. Every man in the open knew that the firing would begin again at any moment and soon enough it did when the infantrymen on both sides fired shots over the stretcher-parties' heads, warning them to return to their own lines.

When the rector had finished there was a silence such as Claire had never heard in the ward. At first she thought it was due to embarrassment but then, looking at the man she thought of as 'Jumbo', she realised that this was not so, for he was looking at Parson Horsey with a respect that she had never seen him bestow on any visitor, commissioned, civilian or clerical. It was as though, at any moment, he would embarrass them all by applauding but to Claire's relief he continued to stare straight at the little man standing between the two beds. Horsey used the pause to grope under his surplice and his hand re-emerged holding a small packet of letters tied with tape. He shuffled them carefully, selecting one with the air of a man who considers himself unobserved and then, clearing his throat once more, he said, 'The chap who wrote that was killed at the beginning of this month. The night before he was killed, however, he wrote two letters and one of them was passed on to me by his wife. I hope you will forgive me if I read this letter to end this little service. It isn't very long but I think it helps to clarify the motives of many of the conscientious objectors. You see, this chap was classified as a CO who felt strongly enough about his beliefs to go to face gaol for them. At the last minute, however, a friend home from France persuaded him to enlist as a stretcher-bearer. Now I don't know what you think of conscientious objectors; not much I imagine and therefore I would be less than honest if I failed to tell you this man once came to me and asked my advice and I told him he ought not to compromise in any way. I told him that partly because he was a brilliant scholar, the kind of man who might have something useful to contribute to the world after the war, but on reading this final letter of his I see very clearly that I was wrong. Perhaps you will agree, perhaps not, I don't know. I'm not nearly as sure of anything as I was a year or so ago.'

He laid the packet of letters on the makeshift altar and took the one he had selected from its field service envelope. While he was doing this Claire looked round the hut expecting some kind of reaction to an introduction that she found utterly uncharacteristic of the Horsey she had watched begin so many half-apologetic sermons in the parish church on pre-war Sundays. There was no reaction and Horsey began reading:

'This is the first anniversary of my arrival in France and it seems a good time to jot down a thought or two that I should have put on paper months ago but somehow never seemed to find time, either before or since the Ypres fighting. First, please don't bother to send the books you promised. I shouldn't have a chance to read them and in any case it seems a shame to subject a book to the kind of treatment it gets out here. It was thinking of books, however, that led me to think of the places they belong – libraries, schools and universities where, on looking back, it seems to me I spent so much time and largely wasted time at that because, in making out what you might call my first annual report, I see that a man would have to be a fool not to learn more in one week out here than he could cram into a lifetime in a university – that is, regarding essentials! Do you remember that old poem, the one in which Abou Ben Adam tells the recording angel to write him down as a chap who loved his fellow-men? Old Ben Adam could survive out here and might even enlarge himself but I doubt if poor old Shelley and Keats would last a week without going crazy!

'Well now, from annual reports to balance sheets. I've done some balancing up since we came out of the Passchendaele show and it's a pretty rum set of figures. On the debit side – carried forward from last year and the year before that – is death, blood, mud, lice, fear and boredom and on the other side? – call them hidden credits, sheer wonder at what a terrific pounding the

average chap can take without breaking; the strength of the bond between men who survive the same near-miss three days in a row and, above all, the comforting thought that Hell can't be so bad after all for this is Hell right enough but men can still laugh in it – laugh and sing and are doing both right now in this half a cellar, the one group over a game of pontoon, the other accompanied by a concertina. End of annual report and presentation of balance sheet – with time to say, in the light of the last half-inch of candle, that I'm glad I'm here, even though I don't retract a word of anything I ever said about the stupidity and brutality of war for if I hadn't come here I should have gone on cuddling my resentment behind prison bars and thinking myself no end of a martyr whereas here every poor devil is a martyr and there aren't enough stakes to go round! Some will survive, perhaps enough to draw up a fresh set of rules for the nations that used to call themselves civilised. Candle's going out. Good night. God bless.'

Horsey repeated his shuffling act with the flimsy sheets and then, retrieving the letters on the table, returned the one he had read to its sheaf. Nobody spoke and nobody moved. Not a cough or a shuffle broke the silence, until Claire heard a dry, indeterminable sound on her left and turning saw Mrs Handcock's handkerchief go to her nose as she blew and then blushed because everybody turned to look at her as though, by looking, they diverted attention from any emotional display on their part. Mrs Handcock, Claire recalled, would be one of those present who remembered Keith Horsey as a shambling adolescent drifting about the Valley with his long nose stuck in a book, a boy who had later married (or been married by) pretty Rachel Eveleigh of Four Winds, in defiance of her presently whoring father, but Keith's anonymity did not diminish the impact of Parson Horsey's sermon. Looking at him, and again at his congregration, Claire realised that here was a man who would never fear or falter again. She knew this, and the men knew it, but neither she nor they could have expressed in words precisely what he had told them that was new and therefore absent in any other sermon they had ever heard, or any sermon Horsey had preached in the past. She was aware of something else too – the enormous margin of error present in the snap judgments one sometimes made of other human beings.

II

Corporal 'Jumbo' Bellchamber, one of the few enlisted men present when Parson Horsey preached on conscientious objectors, came face to face with the rector a month later at a double wedding in the parish church. On that occasion Jumbo was a groom, together with his inseparable companion, Lance-Corporal Georges Brissot. The occasion was the only cheerful one in the Valley that season, a time when General Ludendorff and his highly-trained infiltration squads demonstrated that there was, after all, one way of breaking the deadlock in the West.

The Bellchamber–Brissot alliance was one of those improbable partnerships that sometimes emerge from service in the field. For a long time now they had never operated apart and it was therefore entirely fitting that they should take, as brides, two other inseparables, Cissie and Violet Potter, who had privately agreed that it was time they looked to the future and made a grab while there were still eligible men alive in the Valley.

They might have done worse. Jumbo, although wan and short of breath after three years in France ending with double pneumonia and pleurisy, was still more or less whole, whereas his big, swarthy, mild-mannered friend had a cork foot but, to offset this disadvantage, practical experience in farming dating from pre-war days in the province of Quebec. Brissot's injury had left him with an ungainly, bobbing limp, that gave people the impression he was forever on the point of tumbling head over heels but otherwise he was quite a catch, being strong, genial and capable of running a small farm. It was after Jumbo had discovered that the two Potter girls were in a position (once respectably wed) to obtain the lease of the Dell from the Squiress that a casual association developed into courtship and sundry slaps, chuckles and squeals were replaced with long, sighing glances and heavy breathing on the few occasions when Cissie and Vi could retreat to their familiar refuge in the laurels at the top of the drive.

Although Jumbo was barely half the size of his companion he was senior partner in the alliance, his ascendancy over the French Canadian dating from very early in the war, when the two had met by chance in the yard of an abandoned French farmhouse, near Château Thierry. Georges was a civilian then, who had been visiting French cousins when Von Kluck's hordes swept across north-eastern France and the visitor had been overlooked when his relatives decamped ahead of the British rearguard. Jumbo was a stray too, having been sent with a message to a British corps on the right, where he lost himself in a maze of unsignposted roads. He took refuge in the barn of the farm where Georges was stranded and they did not meet until a patrol of four Uhlans rode into the farmyard in search of forage. From an attic window the French Canadian watched all four German cavalrymen fall to the rifle of a single British straggler who had installed himself in a loft.

Georges was dumbfounded by the speed at which it happened. Down they went – one, two, three, four, just like wooden ducks at a shooting booth, the saddles emptying so quickly that Georges was persuaded the entire British Army had returned to rescue him. When he realised that his saviour was a single, bow-legged little soldier he was so impressed that he never recovered from the shock. From then on he was Jumbo's man and after helping him recover the Uhlan's horses on which they caught up with Smith-Dorrien's footsore column, he joined the Cockney's unit as interpreter, later enlisting and sharing his friend's varying fortunes through Neuve Chapelle, Loos and the Somme. They emerged from these disasters unscathed but the weather at Passchendaele was too much for Jumbo, despite a remarkable toughness, resilience and unfailing optimism. Then a carelessly-handled dud shell gave Georges the privilege of prolonging the alliance indefinitely, so that they found themselves wintering at Shallowford, where Jumbo's high spirits made him a great favourite with the Potter girls, who had always preferred the noisy, boisterous lovers.

The double proposal was put to the girls the day that Jumbo received his discharge, Georges having been invalided out a month or so before. Until then, Georges had never thought of marriage or settling in England for good but he accepted all his friend's decisions and reposed complete and utter trust in his judgments, despite the fact that Jumbo's speech was still largely incomprehensible to him. Georges spoke and understood English well but the Cockney idiom defeated him. He could never learn, for instance, that a 'butcher's' meant a 'look' or that when Jumbo announced he was ready to climb stairs and retire to bed he did not say so in as many words but said he was 'hitting the apples-an'-pears fer a kip'. Thus his announcement that marriage to the Potter girls would be an investment in the future bewildered him. Jumbo said, after studying his discharge papers. 'This is it, cock! We're both aht on our ear and we gotter get weavin' bloody quick, mate! I did think o' going fer moonishuns where they say you c'n earn a fortune but seein' as ol' Jerry 'as nearly shot 'is bolt, I don't reckon we'd 'ave time ter dig ourselves in before we start scrambling fer jobs with all the other bleeders in Civvy Street! Do yer fancy a nice bit o' country, like this here?'

Georges, understanding nothing but the final sentence, said that he found the locality very much to his taste, for it reminded him somewhat of wooded areas on the shores of the St Lawrence. Jumbo took this for unqualified assent, saying, 'Right! Then, Bob's your uncle! Them two bints 'ave got a farm, an' since they're only working 'ere while they look for a couple o' mugs to run it we'd better get stuck in before some other greedy baskit catches on! Since there ain't a pin to choose between 'em ser far as looks goes we'll toss for 'em an' after that you leave me to do the torkin'!'

They tossed, Jumbo winning Cissie and Georges Violet. When a local busybody pointed out that, although well over thirty and unwed, the girls had already raised a small family between them Jumbo was indignant, not with the brides-to-be but with the informant. 'What of it?' he demanded, unconsciously reiterating the claim of Edward of York, 'I'm a bachelor and I reckon I've got 'arf a dozen running around somewhere! Besides, they're bringing us house, farm an' furniture as a bleedin' dowry, ain't they? Gor blimey, who's askin' for jam on it?'

It was Parson Horsey's impressive performance in the ward that inclined Jumbo in favour of a church wedding and the ceremony was probably the best attended in the history of the church. Everyone was there, including Claire, all her family, and a motley guard of honour representing half-a-dozen regiments from the convalescents. Later the happy foursome repaired to the Dell to fortify themselves with a quart or two of Meg's hedgerow wine before beginning the task of spring-cleaning the decrepit farmhouse.

Claire wrote an amusing account of the ceremony to Paul that same night but it was a long time before the Squire of Shallowford was aware that the Dell, always the odd man out among his farms, had entered upon a new era under Anglo-French management. He never, in fact, received her letter, for the Potter girls were married on Saturday, the sixteenth of March and five days later the entire British line opposite St Quentin had collapsed, Ludendorff's stormtroops gaining as much ground in twelve hours as combined French and British offensives of the war had won in three and a half years.

There was another matter that would have interested him in the letter Claire posted the day after the Dell wedding; this concerned her personal handling of yet another Four Winds' crisis, events having reached a point where intervention on her part seemed essential.

Everybody in the Valley knew that Farmer Eveleigh kept a mistress but the scandal had died down after Marian Eveleigh had pulled herself together, turned her back on the spirits and spent all her working days at the big house where she was regarded as the most reliable local hand on the staff. One day in early March, however, Claire had found her weeping and distraught and persistent questioning uncovered the cause. Eveleigh, Marian said, had now taken his land-girl mistress into the house, offering his wife a choice between the room formerly occupied by the boys and the

cottage lodging vacated by the land-girl. The affront to a
woman who had borne Eveleigh six children and lost looks
and figure in the process, so outraged Claire that without
even consulting John Rudd, she checked the terms of the
Four Winds' lease, borrowed Maureen's Ford and drove to
the farm at such speed that Old Honeyman, herding sheep
along the river road, had to scramble up the bank to avoid
her onrush. She went in by the back door without stopping
to knock and finding no one in the kitchen stormed upstairs
shouting Eveleigh's name. He came out of the bedroom,
his face covered with lather and razor in hand, standing
gaping at her and looking, she thought, very seedy in his
long-sleeved woollen vest and dangling braces. It was some
time since she had seen him for he had kept clear of the
big house since Paul's last visit and Claire, who admired
his pluck and capacity for work without being able to like
him, was surprised at the change in his appearance. He
looked like an ageing man who was over-eating, drinking
too much and possibly over-worrying. She went straight
to the point, making no apology for her presence on his
landing at eight-thirty in the morning.

'You and I are going to have words, Eveleigh!' she snapped,
and when his hand went to his chin added, 'Never mind
shaving, come down just as you are!'

He followed her downstairs to the big, stone-floored kitchen,
looking bewildered and alarmed.

'Has anything happened up at the house, Mrs Craddock?
Is aught amiss wi' Marian?'

'You may well ask that!' Claire snapped at him. 'I've just
learned from her what's been happening here and I came at
once. It's got to stop, do you hear?'

His expression hardened and she realised that his initial
anxiety had stemmed from a guess that his wife had had
some kind of accident. As soon as he understood that his
own behaviour was in question he began to bluster but not,
Claire thought, with much conviction.

'I don' see what the 'ell it's got to do with you,' he mumbled,
'I'm not behind wi' me rent, am I?'

'I don't know,' Claire said, impatiently, 'I didn't stop to consult Rudd but I do know that if the Squire was here he wouldn't stand for what's going on at Four Winds!'

'But he knew about Jill,' protested Eveleigh, 'it's no dam' secret in the Valley!'

'He doesn't know that the girl has been installed in one of his farms and your wife turned out!'

'If she said that she's a liar!' said Eveleigh, flushing and wiping lather from his blue chin. 'We haven't been man and wife for nigh on two years but I never turned her out! You c'n ask Jill or any one about here!'

'I'm not going to ask that girl anything,' Claire said, 'except to pack her stuff and move out before I leave! I can't stop you making a damned fool of yourself, or making your wife miserable, but I won't stand for a chit like that being mistress of a Shallowford farm! I'll give her ten minutes and no longer; I'm busy!'

He looked at her open-mouthed and it struck her then that the change in him since the war had invaded his home and deprived him of his boys was almost as great as that wrought in Will Codsall by his spell in the trenches. She remembered that Paul had always spoken of Four Winds as the most prosperous but the unluckiest farm in the Valley, and had sometimes half-jested about it being hag-ridden by Arabella's ghost. She could understand what he meant now, less on account of this hesitant, truculent man, standing with his back to the door and trying, almost pitifully, to strike a balance between the respect he owed her as his landlord's wife and his rights as an individual than on account of the cheerlessness of the kitchen which had no feeling of home. In pre-war days this had been a cheerful room with its brasses gleaming, its hearth swept, its oak furniture highly polished. Now it smelled of dry rot and looked drab and tarnished, as though nobody used it except as a place to eat and loaf about. One or two grubby garments lay on the settle, and dirty dishes, coated with grease, were piled on the centre board of the great oak dresser. The fire was smoking and the curtains were stained and wrinkled. She said, with deliberate contempt, 'Jill seems to me a pretty poor exchange for a wife like Marian who gave you good service and loyalty! If this kitchen is anything to go by you made a damned bad bargain, Eveleigh!'

At the mention of the girl he scowled, drawing his heavy brows together. 'Leave Jill out o' this, Mrs Craddock,' he growled, 'you got no call to insult her and none to order her out neither! I'm master o' this place so long as I pay up quarterdays, and you show me another farm in the Valley that has my yield, year in year out!'

'I'm not discussing your yield,' Claire said, half-wishing she had brought John along to bully the fool, 'but I stand by what I said. Out she goes or you'll live to regret it!'

The door behind him opened so suddenly that it struck him and he lurched forward a pace to reveal Jill Chilcott. Claire remembered her now as a sullen, generously-built girl, who had once served behind the counter at a Paxtonbury draper's. She was dark and coarse-featured but possessed a heavy sensuality that would appeal to a man of Eveleigh's taciturn temperament. She was also every bit as sluttish as the kitchen suggested, her uncombed hair hanging in great hanks either side of a petulant face. She had obviously just risen from bed and had not bothered to dress. All she had on was a dirty whalebone corset that nipped her waist and forced her breasts so high that she looked as grotesque as one of the dummies in the window of the draper's where she had worked before the war. Her skin was very white but an unhealthy white, as though she ate too much starch and avoided exercise.

Eveleigh said, roughly, 'For Chris' sake get something on, girl! This is Mrs Craddock from the Big House,' and he threw her a flannel dressing gown that had been hanging on the back of the settle. She caught the gown but did not put it on, staring at Claire with far less embarrassment than her lover. Her wide, moist mouth was clamped in a little girl's sulk and she looked, Claire thought, rather too sure of herself in the circumstances.

'I bin listening,' she announced, 'I heard everythin' she said, an' you don't need to take no notice of 'er! None at all, see? Fact is, she's got no right 'ere an' you can order 'er out if you please!' She turned back to Claire who was shaking with rage. 'You wouldn't have no court order, would you? You know, one o' them notice-to-quit papers, signed by a Magistrate?'

The girl's insolence was so insufferable that Claire regained the initiative, ignoring her and concentrating on Eveleigh, who was now losing his truculence and was very embarrassed by the scene.

'I took the trouble to study your lease before I came,' she said, 'and I could have you out of here in three months! The Squire let you take over the Codsall lease on a triennial basis but it was never transferred to you. I'm sure Sydney, Martin's heir, would be very glad to let it revert to the Codsalls. He's already bought a farm in Nun's Bay and if he knew the circumstances of your tenure he'd probably apply to me for a re-transfer at once! Now get this slut out of here and reinstate your wife. If you do I'll ask Rudd to make out a new seven-year lease in your name but if you don't I'll write to Sydney Codsall this very day!'

It was a shot in the dark, or at least in the twilight, for Claire's study of the Four Winds' lease had been cursory but its effect upon Eveleigh was deadly and she saw this at once. Resentment and obstinacy ebbed from him and for a moment he almost cringed. She saw too that her threat had cut the ground from under the girl, who obviously knew Eveleigh as Paul and Rudd knew him, a man dedicated to these acres, someone whose entire life was bound up in stock and pasture between Sorrel and Teazel. She knew then that she had him, that nothing would be allowed to threaten his hold of the farm and that, in his heart and belly, he valued the least of his Friesian cows above the woman who had found a means of making a bad joke of his years of toil since Codsall's death.

The girl was a fighter, however, and made a final, desperate appeal, catching Eveleigh by the forearm and hanging there in what struck Claire as a kind of parody of an imploring wife in a Temperance magic-lantern show.

'Don' lissen Norman, she can't touch yer! She *can't*, I tell yer! She's bin put up to this by the old cow, Norman . . . !' but that was as far as she got for suddenly Eveleigh ceased to look either surly or hesitant but shook himself, like a man coming out of a daze and thrust her aside so violently that she was sent spinning across the room.

'Don't you call my missis names you bliddy whore!' he shouted, 'I told you before 'bout that and I'll not tell you again! Do like Mrs Craddock says! Pack yer things and go back to the cottage! Go on, damn you!' and swinging open the door he spun her round, planted a stockinged foot in her behind and projected her right across the hall to the foot of the stairs.

She fell on her hands and knees and remained crouching there but the terrible indignity of rejection must have sparked off her pride for, after a moment, she rose slowly and not ungracefully and said, in a little above a whisper, 'You won't get rid o' me as easily as this, Norman! I'll make you pay one way an' another, you see if I don't!', and as Eveleigh took a couple of strides in her direction she ran up the stairs and he came back into the kitchen, closing the door and crossing to the fireplace where he stood with head bowed and hands resting on the mantel as though the effort had exhausted him. It was so quiet that Claire could hear a hen clucking in the yard. She said: 'You didn't have to do that, Eveleigh. She didn't move in without your invitation.'

'Sometimes I could ha' killed her,' he said, '*lots* o' times I could ha' killed her and I daresay I would in the end if you hadn't come!'

He shivered and glanced round the room, so fearfully that Claire's flesh crept. It was as though she was listening to an echo of a scene enacted in the room during Arabella's time and described to her by Paul, years after the tragedy and this fancy was underlined by his next words. He said, bitterly: 'This is an unlucky house, Mrs Craddock. Sometimes I get the notion they'm still yer, the pair of 'em! I never thought o' that until my boy Gilbert got blown to tatters an' then my woman turned queer and didn't seem to take no pleasure in me but I've thought of it a lot since and maybe that's why I took up wi' that little bitch! She took me mind off me troubles I reckon,' and he spat in the fire, shaking himself like a big dog scrambling from water.

Suddenly she felt a terrible compassion for him, a far deeper and more urgent pity than she felt for his wife, or his dead son Gilbert, or his daughter Rachel now mourning Keith and involved in pity for him was a little for the girl upstairs, who had tasted power for the first time in her wretched life only to be thrown out in the end like a pan of washing-up water. But he had suffered and was suffering far more than any of them, a man whose lifetime of hard, disciplined toil had led him to this – his wife a neurotic, his children dead or scattered and his self-respect in ruins. She said, gently, 'Take a drink, Eveleigh. Is there whisky or brandy in the cupboard?'

Without shifting his position in front of the fireplace, he said, quietly, 'There's gin and bitters. That was her tipple!' and Claire crossed to the dresser finding there a bottle of gin and a jug of apple juice. She fetched glasses, washed them, and poured him a stiff measure and a smaller one for herself, carrying it across to him and bending to give the sullen fire a poke.

'I'll get Mr Rudd to make out a proper lease,' she said. 'You don't have to worry any more but you'll be far happier with Marian back to look after you. It's done her a lot of good working up there with the convalescents. She's almost over losing Gilbert now and I hear that Harold, your other boy, is doing splendidly in Palestine. He's commissioned, isn't he?' and when he nodded, 'We're all going through a bad time but it'll end, sooner or later. Would you like me to send Marian over to clean this place as soon as the girl moves out?'

She did not know whether her words brought him any comfort. He heaved himself away from the mantel, swallowed his gin and sat heavily in the inglenook, his big, brown hands clasped between his knees.

'I daresay it's hard for a lady like you to understand,' he said at length, 'but she helped get me through that time I heard about Gil and all that bliddy table-rapping Marian took to. That, and all the work an' worry and conniving, with everyone on at me to squeeze quarts into pint pots, an' dam' near every man and girl in the Valley going off to war or munitions! She was outside it all somehow. Never seemed to touch her, one way or the other. All she wanted was a strong man two–three times a night. It's hard to explain but . . .' Suddenly he got up and walked over to the window, as though confession was embarrassing him more than he could bear. Claire said, 'You don't have to apologise to me. I understand better than you think. And I'm not really a lady you know, just a farmer's daughter, who was lucky to get a good man and stay in love with him. That's why I'm here, I suppose. The Squire isn't just a landlord. He thinks of people like you as his friends, not his tenants, and he feels about this place just the way you do. You can say anything to me. It won't go further than this room!'

He looked at her gratefully and she saw that he was master of himself again and was glad for it excused the impulsive way she had challenged his privacy. He said, slowly, 'What I was going to say was, her being a young woman made me think a bit of myself, I reckon, took me back to the old days, when I first come here to work for Old Maister an' Arabella. I'm turned fifty now and it comes hard on a man that age to see most o' what he's worked for shredding away, a bit here, a bit there. The boys went off, then two o' the girls but me an' Marian never fell out over aught 'till Rachel took up with that parson's son, poor little sod an' then Gil joined an' got hisself killed. I was wrong both times and I'll own to that now but I didden know it at the time. You don't, do you? You just say an' do first thing as comes into your head and then the damage is done! I'd have come through it all right if Marian had turned to me fer comfort instead o' they bliddy spirits and suchlike! Then Jill see how things were between us an' tried her luck so to speak. She come to me in the barn one day after I'd had no sense nor comfort out o' Marian for three months or more. I was about desperate I suppose, an' one thing soon led to another. So long as she was there, ready to parade all she got any time I was minded I could muddle along wi' the work but youm right o' course, there's no future to it!' He stopped suddenly and looked at her under his heavy brows. 'Do you think Marian'd cry quits an' come back, same as we used to be?'

'Yes,' Claire said, 'I'm sure she'd be glad to do just that.'

'Right!' he said, 'then I'll pay that bliddy volcano off an' have done with her and we'll pick up where we left off!'

Claire heard the girl bumping a case down the stairs and Eveleigh went out to her. There was a low rumble of voices, then a pause and finally the front door banged. He came back rather jauntily with a reluctant grin on his face and the tread of a man who has just settled a matter of business to his own satisfaction.

'I give her fifty pounds,' he said, 'that stopped her snivelling! A pair o' trousers an' a bit to spend on herself is all she needs to keep her contented. We won't hear no more of Jill,' and then, resignedly, 'it'll mean tellin' the Squire, won't it? If you're thinking of getting the lease straightened out, I mean?'

'Only the essentials,' Claire told him, 'although I daresay it would cheer him up to learn we had our own kind of troubles over here.'

'Well, you tell him all you've a mind to, Mrs Craddock and send Marian over soon as you like.' He looked round the disordered kitchen with impatience. 'This place needs a doin' over, don't it? I reckon Marian'll make the dust fly! Funny thing about most women – present company excepted o' course – either they can't have enough of a man one way, or they can't do enough for him another! Now Marian, backalong, she was different. She kept the place fresh but didden seem to mind how many kids come along!' He smiled to himself and Claire thought his ability to do that again was the most encouraging thing to emerge from the interview.

III

On the night of March 20th, 1918, Paul took a convoy of lorries carrying ammunition up to a battery about two miles behind the Green Defence Zone, in front of St Quentin. The night was dry, muggy and unusually quiet. Not a single shell whined overhead and only very occasionally did a flare of one sort or another light up the blackness for a few moments. It was difficult to believe that somewhere up ahead were hundreds of thousands of men slopping about in trenches that were only just beginning to dry out after the thaw.

After arranging for the shells to be off-loaded, the major commanding the battery invited Paul into his spacious dug-out for a drink.

He was hardly more than a boy, with a boy's exuberance and lack of ceremony, and speculated gaily on the date of the long-awaited German offensive, saying that Jerry would probably wait for things to dry out a little more before trying his luck in the quagmire over which the British had tried to advance in the autumn, and when Paul asked if he thought the initial attack would be successful, he said, off-handedly, 'Oh, they expect Old Fritz to gain some ground but our defences are fluid enough to cope with it. We shall just bring up reserves and counter-attack and in the end everything will be as-you-were I imagine. Well, here's to a safe trip back and I wish to God I was going with you! Things are devilish dull here lately and I'm overdue for leave.'

Things remained dull until Paul's lorries were about half-way back to the dump. Then, about 3 a.m., all hell broke loose, first in the areas nearer the base, then in the artillery zone behind him and finally right where the convoy was travelling, a mixture of high-velocity and gas shells straddling the road with terrifying accuracy. It was suicide to push on so Paul ordered the men out of the vehicles and let them disperse in the fields and they were pinned here for more than half-an-hour as the shifting barrage grew more and more intense and the landscape erupted under a continuous rain of shells. Paul was not long in doubt that this was it, the big push they had been promised as soon as Jerry had transferred a sufficient number of troops from the Russian front but what appalled him was the terrible intensity and accuracy of the barrage, as though thousands of guns of all calibres were concentrating on a relatively small area, switching back and forth with a horrid rhythm that prevented anyone making a dash for it. With the first lightening in the eastern sky came fog and Paul spared a thought for the poor devils trapped in the underground front line, saturated with gas, crouching in crumbling trenches and awaiting the first waves of the German infantry to appear through the mist that now lay heavily over the countryside.

About six o'clock, when the barrage seemed to be re-concentrating on the forward areas, he started the convoy moving again but before they had gone far a howitzer shell landed smack on the head of the column and the road was impassable. The pattern of the drumfire now resolved itself into a steady pounding of extreme back and front areas and only occasional shells, mostly gas, fell in the intermediate zone so that there was no alternative but to return to the battery site and await the arrival of trouble-spot engineers to clear the road. The men in the leading lorries had been killed outright so, unencumbered with wounded, they were able to turn and head back the way they had come, driving directly into the sheet of flame on the horizon.

Moving fast they covered the distance in just over twenty minutes but there was no sanctuary at the battery, nor was there much shelter in the gunners' dug-outs. A direct hit, possibly two or three, had registered on the site and the place was a shambles. Every gun but one had been destroyed and the only living member of the crews seemed to be a bombardier nursing an injured hand. He was able to tell him that, apart from a team over on the right, he was the sole survivor.

'We'd only fired a few rounds,' he said, 'they had us taped to an inch! I was over by the dump which didn't go up, thank Christ. I bin out two years but never seen anything like this, not even on the Somme. It's a different *kind* of straffing, sir, a proper your-turn-next carpet pattern. Jerry 'as all the bloody luck, don't 'ee? Look at the fog out there!'

Paul's sergeant put a field-dressing on the man and sent him over to the remains of the officers' dug-out. It was useless to send him back to the dressing station for the fog belt in the west was masking a leaping sheet of orange indicating the barrage had switched yet again and was now firing at extreme range.

The gun on the right was still in action but its detonations sounded like apologetic coughs against the roar of the overall barrage. The ground quivered and heaved and the din penetrated the deepest recesses of the brain, slamming the door on every impulse not directly concerned with self-preservation. Paul staggered across to the battery HQ post and on his way recognised the remains of the boyish major who had entertained him three hours before, identifying him from among several blood-stained bundles by his military moustache and the crown on the lapel of his tunic. There was nothing he could do but get his surviving fourteen men under what cover was still available and there they remained until, through the tormented fog-belt, came the first of the beaten infantry.

They arrived in twos and threes, stumbling, blear-eyed men, some without rifles and about half of them walking wounded trying forlornly to find their way to a dressing station. Only one, a hard-bitten sergeant of a Midland regiment, was coherent and told Paul of chaos and carnage up the line where break-throughs had occurred right and left of the sectors his company had been holding.

'Couldn't do a damned thing to stop 'em!' the man said, with a curse. 'The saturation strafe they sent over at first light wiped out two-thirds of us. All the trenches up there are shallow and under-manned and then down comes this bloody fog to cap all! We held 'em off for a time with two machine-guns but they by-passed us and went round the flanks. It's a real bloody cave-in if you ask me and it'll take days to harden up, even if we've got plenty o' reserves back there!' He glanced bitterly at the fog which lay low on the ground all about them. 'By God!' he muttered, 'if we'd had fog like this at Third Wipers we could have gone all the way to Berlin!'

Then a wounded captain arrived and with him an astonishingly composed Engineer, a tall, angular Scotsman with iron-grey hair who had been in the support line all night installing a pump. Paul never forgot him, a polite, methodical man of well over forty who took command of the half-demoralised mob of wounded and stragglers now milling about the littered gun-site. The Scotsman said they would have to organise a road-block and rallying point until reserves came up and a counter-attack could be mounted and his quiet confidence

spread to Paul and some of the unwounded NCOs, who at
once set to work, driving the three remaining lorries broadside
on across the road, digging in each side and hauling timber
and wire from the shattered gunpits and dug-outs to make
some kind of entanglement to protect front and flanks. Men
and more men trickled in until there were about two or
three hundred to man the strongpoint, and as soon as the
barrage lifted Paul sent off two despatch-riders to the rear
with scribbled messages reporting their strength and position.
The Scotsman told him that they were on the furthest edge of
the Green Zone that had been designed for defence in depth
but that the German attack had been launched before the new
trenches were much more than surface scratches. There were
plenty of tools available, and the men dug furiously after they
realised they were out of range of all but long-range artillery
and that the very speed of the German advance would mean a
long interval must elapse before field batteries could be moved
forward to give their infantry support. The bombardment had
slackened appreciably and what there was of it seemed to be
concentrated on areas further back, probably in the hope of
checking the flow of reserves in the Green Zone. They had
dug and wired a semi-circular strongpoint by nine o'clock
and sited their three light machine-guns and two Lewis-guns
by the time the first parties of German infantry appeared
through the thinning fog at a range of perhaps four hundred
yards. By then the gun on the right, that had been firing
over open sites, was silent, having run out of ammunition
and the Scotsman, walking along the curving trench, did
not give the order to fire until the scattered groups on
the edge of the mist were within close range. They went
to ground at once and during the lull that followed some
of Paul's men brought up rations and a small jar of rum
salvaged from the battery command post. Paul tried to contact
the rear by telephone but the wire must have been cut to
pieces by the bombardment, so the Scotsman despatched
several of the walking wounded with orders to fan out both
sides of the road and take their chance getting through with
first-hand reports on the situation.

About midday the Germans attacked again, this time in greater strength and with at least two heavy machine-guns, but they were again beaten off and the Midland sergeant, who seemed to Paul the kind of man badly needed at Supreme Headquarters, forty miles back, said that in his view the enemy was employing completely revolutionary tactics in this offensive, pushing on wherever the resistance was weak and leaving the strongpoints to be mopped up by reserve divisions armed with mortars and supported by light artillery.

They were there in the improvised defence-hedgehog until dusk but had nothing worse than light machine-gun fire and sniping to contend with. The Germans out ahead had a flame-thrower but were never able to get close enough to use it. About six, to everyone's relief, a despatch-rider arrived on a Douglas motor-cycle, with orders to retreat to a map reference three miles in the rear and they pulled out, taking the less badly wounded along with them and probed their way over the shattered plain for hours, occasionally being fired on by other groups of stragglers from sectors south and north of the St Quentin trenches. In one of these blind encounters the Scots captain was shot through the head; Paul never knew his name.

In the early hours of the morning they came unexpectedly upon a new line of strongpoints where reserves, rushed up earlier in the day, were furiously digging in. Paul and the survivors of his group were sorted out and directed to a scratch MT centre, established in front of Rouy le Grand. It was, they told him, thirteen miles from the previous front line. At Third Ypres, Paul reflected, it had taken the British four months and something like half-a-million casualties to capture a couple of miles of liquid mud.

IV

He remembered that first day clearly enough. The intensity of the switched barrages, the bloody shambles of the battery site, the cool, angular Engineer who had organised the defence, and even irrelevant details, like the dead gunner's pathetic moustache and the bombardier's shattered hand, but he could never recall the day-to-day life of the next few weeks, remembering the period only as a grey, misted-over interval, shot through with stress, fear and constant movement that resulted in a terrible physical exhaustion. More often than not throughout April and early May he seemed to be asleep on his feet or driving a Leyland lorry over the remains of roads and tracks, weaving between an eternal patchwork of shell-holes and breathing stale air through his respirator. His senses were numbed by shock, noise and lack of sleep so that there was no rhythm to his existence, as during his previous fifteen months in the field. His unit, merged into other decimated units, was flung here and there, north, south and back again, wherever it was needed to bring up rations and wire and ammunition and sometimes the lorries seemed to be moving to no purpose for days on end. All the men whose names he remembered disappeared into the chaos of the shifting front but others replaced them, half-trained boys of eighteen and wary, workshy men of nearly fifty, who waddled about much like Old Honeyman tending sheep in the big paddock at home. No mail came through, or if it did he was never there to receive it and everywhere the front seemed to be crumbling and the war as good as lost. As soon as the St Quentin break-through was plugged outside Albert went north into the dismal basin of the Lys, again fighting as an infantryman during the break-through at Bailleul. Then, when the northern offensive was held, he was sent south again to lovely, unspoiled country around Vailly, north of the River Vesle, where the exhausted survivors of St Quentin and the Lys were just in time for the May offensive on Chemin des Dames, and Ludendorff's stormtroops smashed through on a broad front, penetrating to the Marne.

It was here, just before the supreme German effort, that he had a few days' respite, drifting up and down quiet country roads through villages still inhabited by civilians and during this blessed period he sometimes let his mind drift back to the Valley, to the view of the meandering Sorrel seen from the south-west corner of Hermitage Wood but before he had made contact with home, or even caught up on his arrears of sleep, the third hammer blow fell on the exhausted divisions manning the Vauxaillon-Craonne Line and suddenly he was a rifleman again, holding out in forlorn little centres of resistance and washed back by the indefatigable grey tide from the east, escaping death sometimes by inches and going back and back with the wreck of British and French units blasted from their positions by mathematically plotted barrages, like the one that had shattered the old front line opposite St Quentin. On the morning of the 29th of May the tide finally engulfed him, blotting out past and present for a period of fifty-nine days.

It came without pain, without even realisation. Just a sound-less explosion like the red-gold wink of distant shell fire at night and then an eternity of dreams, some troubled, like the recurring dream of his fever in hospital sixteen years before, some tranquil, like the memory of long summer afternoons in the Valley, with Claire coming down the goyle to Crabpot Willie's shack wearing an old-fashioned sun bonnet and waving as she approached yet never seeming to reach his side.

They had just made one more lurch south-westwards to-wards Soissons, no longer really an army after days of marching, counter-marching, of losing touch with their flanks, and being pounded by artillery and whipped by machine-gun fire that seemed sometimes to come from the rear. They retired, still struggling, a rabble of British, French poilus, and French civilians caught up in the backward heaves of the shattered divisions and it was Paul's quixotic concern for a wounded poilu that brought him down.

He had never shared the British contempt for their allies, seeing the French not as ragamuffins, whose trenches were filthy and uninhabitable, nor yet, romantically, as the inheri-tors of the Austerlitz tradition but as a nation of peasants and small craftsmen, like the people of the Valley who had been cruelly used by their militarists and politicians. Their countryside, parts of which reminded him vividly of the Valley, had been fouled by the passage of armies and their dwellings reduced to rubble by the cannon of both sides. And all this time their blood had been poured out like dish-water in the Ardennes, in Champagne, and in witless offensives like that of General Nivelle, the previous summer. Yet somehow they fought on, doggedly and savagely, little swarthy men, for the most part, with blue-black whiskers and dark, burning eyes and lately, or so it had seemed to Paul, they fought without hope.

Some such thought must have crossed his mind when he saw the poilu making a feeble attempt to apply a field-dressing as he lay on the blind side of a grassy hummock. They were retiring over fields not yet reduced to the grey morasses of the north, a rolling countryside where hawthorn blossomed and wild flowers grew. Two Northumbrian privates were humping the company's surviving Lewis-gun and clumsy ammunition buckets, so Paul was comparatively unencumbered. The Frenchman rolled his eyes upward as Paul knelt beside him. His shoulder had been laid open by shrapnel that was still scything down from a battery behind the hill and as Paul raised him, grunting under his weight, another splinter whanged through the poilu's helmet, scattering his brains and ricocheting into Paul's temple. They fell together, locked in a grotesque embrace and the Northumbrians, leaving their stray MT officer for dead, ran down the slope to find cover in a farmhouse, promising each other that they would go back for his papers and identity discs as soon as it was dark.

They never did of course, for dusk found them caught up in the mass exodus from Soissons and it was a German stretcher-party that found Paul still breathing at dawn the next day and conveyed him, with some of their own stretcher cases, to the Soissons infirmary.

He owed his life to the presence there of a Leipzig brain specialist called Quirnheim. Bored with abdominals and fractured limbs the man took a mild interest in the case, extracting the splinter but telling his orderly that the English lieutenant would almost certainly die during the next twenty-four hours. When, on his rounds the following day, Paul was seen to be alive the specialist's interest in the patient revived. He took a closer look, skilfully removed another half-ounce splinter from a shallow wound forward of the left ear and told the grinning orderlies that the Englishman evidently possessed an even thicker skull than his commander-in-chief, Sir Douglas Haig, and thus stood a chance of recovery. Quirnheim had no opportunity of following the case through for the tide of war swept back through Soissons and all the seriously wounded were left behind when the Germans abandoned the railhead to counter-attacking French and Americans. He lay in a ward alongside twenty to thirty other critical cases and in late July the Americans moved in, so that there was nobody who could identify him, his discs having been mislaid, his uniform burned and his few personal belongings looted.

The war rolled away to the north-east and days passed before a few muttered words, overheard by an American nurse, identified him as an Englishman, after which he was moved to a private ward and given individual attention. His ultimate emergence from the coma astonished and delighted the American surgeon, who, in the period ahead, was prone to take as much credit for Paul's recovery as his countrymen took for the overthrow of the German Empire. It was not until he was being invalided via Paris to England that a British doctor told him he probably owed his life to two factors, one French and one German. The shell-splinters, it seemed, had spent most of their force on the poilu's head but without Quirnheim's skill in replacing a section of bone with a silver plate the largest of them would have caused death. The information made Paul thoughtful. In later life he always felt diffident about the Croix de Guerre the French Government ultimately awarded him for his puny share in the Chemin des Dames battle; neither could he bring much enthusiasm to the post-war Hang-the-Kaiser campaign.

V

Claire's fifth child, another girl born early in the morning of July 1st, gave her as little trouble as her sisters, Mary and

Whiz. Maureen said, when she returned to the Big House after her morning rounds, that Claire was an example of the law of compensation, 'carrying with difficulty but bringing forth with despatch'. It was not until the baby was safely delivered, and Maureen, paying her return visit, was enjoying a quiet cigarette before beginning her evening rounds, that the doctor began to understand Claire's obstinate and utterly irrational optimism concerning Paul. It was not, she decided, simply a pregnant woman's talisman, for although both she and John considered Paul dead, along with all the others except those three indestructibles, Ikey, Smut and Henry Pitts, Claire's faith had never faltered. Maureen said, admiring her patient's composure, 'You're an unlikely cuss, Claire! You really have made up your mind that he'll soon be lounging in here on those long legs of his, haven't you?' and Claire said, 'Yes, I have. He'll be along soon enough and not all that much the worse for it – but this isn't just a lifebuoy, Maureen, of the kind all women grab at when they get a "missing" telegram – there's a link between people who have spent years building up a deep, personal relationship like mine and Paul's, and yours and John's. Separation and distance can't sever it and if death did then one would know. I'm not sure of much any longer but I'm confident of that! Now let me have another look at my baby.'

She struggled into a sitting position as Maureen lifted the child out of the cot and placed her in her arms. '"Now baint her a pretty li'l maid"?' Claire demanded, '"*baint* her, now"?' and Maureen, whose familiarity with babies had warped her judgment on these matters, agreed that she was indeed, with features of almost classic regularity, great tufts of hair a shade more blonde than her mother's and perfectly formed hands and feet. 'I'm so proud of her I could ask Parson Horsey to ring a peal of bells!' Claire said and Maureen added glumly that they could reserve that for news of Paul and an end to this idiotic slaughter, for although relieved for Claire, for whom she had always had a deep affection, she was miserably depressed by the hopelessness of life, what with poor old John laid up with the Spanish influenza scourge, half the Valley down with the same epidemic, and twice as much work as she could handle at her time of life. She came home, tired out, at eight o'clock and poured herself a stiff double whisky, carrying it up to sit with John for a spell. She tried to inject him with some of Claire's irrational cheerfulness, telling him what a handsome daughter the Squiress had just produced but John Rudd was gloomier than ever these days. He had never believed 'missing' was more than an indirect way of saying 'dead' and she knew that his friendship with Paul Craddock had always meant a great deal to him, as much and perhaps more than their marriage, or their seven-year-old boy, now boarding with Mary Willoughby at Deepdene in the hope that he would elude the 'flu virus.

'Well, I daresay it'll sustain her a bit,' he grumbled, 'but you know and I know that it's damned nonsense!'

'This morning I wasn't convinced it was,' she admitted, 'Claire talked about a thread between two people who grew fond of one another over the years and somehow it seemed to make sense, as though one spins a kind of strand from the heart and a final break registers itself physically.'

'By God we shall have you table-rapping before long!' he exclaimed and then, 'No! It's better to face facts and make one's dispositions accordingly!' For a moment he was racked with a violent fit of coughing and Maureen noticed, with renewed concern, how old and tired he looked.

'What *kind* of dispositions?' she asked, after he had taken a sip of his blackcurrant syrup.

'Oh, don't ask me now,' he said irritably, 'let's wait until the war's over! I don't see how she can run a place this size as a widow even though she won't be short of cash. Besides, all the heart will go out of her the moment she gets confirmation of his death and she'll sell up. Before we know where we are we'll have a damned profiteer moving in and when that happens I'm off, I can tell you! I shall put my feet up and spend the time left to me fishing and reading!'

She said, doubtfully, 'Suppose she never gets confirmation?' and he growled, as he pulled the bedclothes up to his chin, 'So much the worse for everybody, especially her! She'll turn into one of those damned neurotic women like Victoria, sniffing

about the place and complaining that someone has moved
his toothbrush out of line! I know Claire Derwent, my dear.
Without that lanky great dreamer she'd be lost and the
children wouldn't mean a damn thing to her,' and although
Maureen did not relish the thought she believed him for she
knew Claire and it had always intrigued her how far Claire's
children had lagged behind in her affections. She recalled how
eagerly she had turned her back on the family when Paul had
been last on leave and how jealously she had kept him closeted
in that love-nest of theirs, down in the goyle. 'I suppose the
truth is she's got an excessive amount of animal vitality,' she
mused aloud, 'and he's the only man with the key to release it.
I've noticed it often and, to tell the truth, it sometimes amused
me. The poor gel almost has an orgasm every time he slips
his arm around her waist!' She sat beside him for a few
moments before saying, 'It isn't just Paul, John! Everywhere
I call nowadays the sparkle and zest has gone, and most of the
hope too. How can any of us start fresh again, at our age?'

'We can't,' he said, 'but that isn't important. The new
arrivals, like that youngster born today will and I daresay
they'll make something better of it! A third of Europe's
population died in the Black Death and ten years later this
country alone was exporting enough wool to mine gold for a
thousand families like the Gilroys and the Lovells. You, me,
Paul, Claire, Will Codsall and the rest, we're just the latter-day
Black Death generation, the unlucky bunch caught at the
bottom of the dip. I daresay the replacements will learn from
it and if they don't they deserve all they get! Turn the light
down, old girl, I'm going to try and sleep before this blasted
cough gets a hold!' but Maureen's Celtic curiosity had been
awakened, not only by what he had said but by the memory
of Claire's steadfast faith in the face of near certainty regarding
Paul's fate. She said, 'Wait John – I'll give you a tablet and
some hot milk to quieten the cough and make you sleep – but
you've said that much, tell me a little more. Where does Paul
Craddock's archaic dream fit into this switchboard pattern?
Is there any justification for his stick-in-the-muddery, in an
age dominated by machines when the best brains in Europe

seem to have lost their way? What I mean is, what made him succeed here? Was it simple obstinacy, vanity?'

He thought a while before answering. It was a question that had occurred to him often over the years for, in its answer he imagined, lay the core of his deep attachment to the man.

'It isn't either,' he said, at length, 'but something a good deal more uncommon. Fundamental too. Nothing like it has been seen around here in a very long time!'

'What makes you say that?'

'I've spent most of my life among people with their noses in dirt,' he went on, thoughtfully, 'and he was the only one who neither looked on land as property or as a way of life that carried an insurance against hunger. To him it was the flesh and bones of humanity, the only true essential and whatever success he had here was the result of that plus a natural talent for administration inherited from money-grubbing ancestors on some other side of his family! And that isn't the whole of it either! There was something else that held him in – two things, and kept him from overreaching himself and forfeiting the backing of men he couldn't afford to lose.'

'Men like you, John?'

'Not just me, all the farmers and the craftsmen about here.'

'Well?'

'He never once put money before human dignity. All the time I knew him he only made one serious mistake.'

'Grace Lovell?'

'No, by God! That wasn't a mistake! He learned from Grace in all kinds of ways. The mistake was that a person with as much to give as Paul Craddock should go and get killed in a battle that was a damned shoddy affair compared with the one he was fighting. That wasn't simply his tragedy either, it was a tragedy for everyone in the Valley!'

She saw that he was hot and flushed and at once felt contrite. 'All right, John, I'm sorry I had to get you worked up at a time like this. I'll get your tablet and drink now,' and she hurried downstairs shocked and confused by his bitterness and by his acceptance of Paul's death as a fact.

And yet, as she pottered about in the kitchen waiting for the milk to warm, she was conscious of a sudden and inexplicable lift in spirits, so that she said to herself aloud, 'I wonder? I wonder if there could be anything in that thread-theory of Claire's?' She turned off the gas-ring and threw open the window, looking up at the stars in the clear, summer night and as she leaned there anticipation warmed her as it might a child counting the hours to Christmas Eve. 'Would *I* know?' she thought, 'if John had got himself blown to bits in China or Timbuctoo? Would *I* feel a sudden smart, like a half-healed scab coming off? Maybe I would, for who the devil am I to throw everything out the window that hasn't been laboratory tested? I learn something new about my job every day!' She poured the milk, dissolved the tablet and went up the narrow stairs a good deal more cheerfully than she had descended them ten minutes before.

Chapter Ten

I

The influenza epidemic ran its course from Whin to Sorrel and across the Valley to the county border, striking down about one in four and killing some of the very young and the elderly. Arthur Pitts of Hermitage died that autumn and so did Marlowe, the sexton, whose two boys had been killed, one in France and one at sea. Sam and Joannie Potter lost their youngest, a baby of eighteen months, and Cissie Potter, now Cissie Bellchamber, lost the child sired by Jem, the Bideford Goliath. Before that, however, there was a brief season of hope, when the country rang with news of the collapse of the famous Hindenburg Line and it really did begin to look as if the end might be round the corner. Then, just as the harvest was being gathered in, the Valley folk noticed a stricken look on the face of the Squiress and could only suppose that she had received confirmation of Squire's death and, for some reason, was loath to broadcast the news. They were not long in discovering the truth. The latest telegram to reach the Valley concerned not the Squire but his protégé, the boy whom they remembered him treating as a son from the days of his first coming among them, and although most of them were fond of Ikey they were none the less slightly relieved, for there was still hope that Squire would turn up, just as old Smut had returned from the dead a year or so ago.

Claire tore open the telegram with fumbling, sweating fingers. It told her that Major Palfrey, MC, of the Tank Corps, had died of wounds in a base hospital early in August and the heavy blow made her reel for somehow she had almost as much faith in Ikey's survival as she had in Paul's. A day or so later a letter arrived from Ikey's Commanding Officer.

Ikey, he said, had named her next-of-kin and it might comfort
her a little to know that he had received his wounds actually
in the Hindenburg Line, a few days after playing an important
part in the decisive victory over the Hun. It did not comfort her
at all. Apart from her own grief she realised how deeply Paul
would mourn the boy and how much a part of the family he
had become since that far-off day when he had unexpectedly
sided with her in the matter of young Simon's renunciation of
fox-hunting. She might have derived a little comfort, however,
could she have known that Ikey Palfrey was one of the very
few serving soldiers on the Western Front who had at least
seen his theories of the war completely vindicated before
his death and also, in the few moments of consciousness
vouchsafed to him after his transfer from Field Dressing
Station to hospital, had been able to direct a nurse to mail
a letter that had been several days in the writing.

On August 1st his had been one of the reserve squadrons
of a massed tank attack on what looked like an impregnable
section of the line, protected by formidable wire-belts and, as
far as the attackers were aware, manned by resolute troops
armed with the new anti-tank guns and well supported by
artillery. Yet it cracked like a stick when the tanks waddled
over it and Ikey's squadron, brought up for a heave against
the support line, was equally successful for the ground was
dry and the heart had gone out of many of the defenders.
The advance went on all that week until the tanks were
probing Proyart and Le Fisque, and the entire German defence line seemed to be crumbling.

A day or so later, feeling rather like the junior partner
of a huge, floundering enterprise saved from bankruptcy
by policies devised and initiated by him, Ikey went off to
explore part of the famous line and descended into a deep,
concrete-faced dugout, drawn there by curiosity and the lure
of souvenirs. That evening he could view the war as something virtually over and done with and he felt himself on
the threshold of a new era in which the long roll of dead
would have to be justified by the living and a new social
structure more flexible than its predecessor. The sense of

achievement made him pleasantly relaxed and reflective. It also made him criminally careless.

He directed his electric torch into the bunk recesses of the vast shelter, seeing a litter of abandoned blankets and items of kit and then, hanging on a bulkhead near the door, he saw the pickelhaube, the famous dress-helmet of the German Army symbolic of the very early days of the war, its patent leather and metal-tipped spike gleaming in the rays of his torch. Pickelhaubes were greatly prized as souvenirs and as he looked at it he suddenly thought of old Horace Handcock, the Valley patriot, who had been breathing fire and slaughter at the Germans ever since the dreadnought race of 1908 and the thought of old Horace made him smile for it occurred to him that Horace, crowned by this helmet, would caricature a fat German feldwebel. He had the same self-important gait, the same prominent blue eyes and thick, brick-red neck and Ikey made up his mind on the spot to present Horace with the pickelhaube as soon as he got home.

He stood up and unhooked the helmet from the nail on which it hung and there was a blinding flash, a roaring in his ears and then an advancing wall of blackness that lifted him and blasted him clear across the dugout. The pickelhaube was a very obvious booby-trap and as a man who, off and on, had served on the Western Front since November, 1914, he should have known better. Much, much better.

II

Another and equally freakish stroke of bad luck came close to depriving the Valley of one of its most celebrated soldiers in the last few hours of the war.

Smut Potter, who had sniped at Germans in the flooded trenches east of Armentières as long ago as autumn, 1914, had then spent almost a year masquerading as a French idiot in German-occupied Péronne and had since survived Passchendaele and battles in open country that followed the break-throughs, was shot and crippled by a machine-gun bullet on the morning of November 11th, only three hours before the cease-fire.

There was a kind of justice surrounding the circumstances in which Smut got his Blighty and got it far too late to show a profit except in the way of a small disability pension. In the four years he had been in action he had killed, or had a hand in killing, over a hundred Germans some of whom were notched on his rifle stock although he stopped keeping score after they had trained him to use the Mills bomb. He had collected a wound or two here and there but never one serious enough to keep him out of the line for more than a month or so and this he had in no way resented. He liked Army life, balancing the bad items against the good, the loss of sleep, danger and discomfort against the acquisition of an enormous variety of goods all of which he redistributed to his friends and favourite officers. He had lost his stripes three times for drunkenness but had always regained them in the next push and like most front-line soldiers, fought without rancour, looking on the war as a kind of gigantic poaching expedition and the men in the trenches opposite as homicidal but impersonal gamekeepers.

There had been rumours of an armistice for a week or more as he entered upon his fifth winter of active service but Smut did not take them very seriously. From what he had seen of Fritz lately there was still a good deal of fight left in him and, as it turned out, he was right about that. On the final day of the war his battalion was advancing on a village east of Valenciennes, where a wounded German officer told them the enemy rearguard had gone back before dawn. So they went in, some hundreds of them and were milling about the Square when two well-sited machine-guns opened up and Smut went down with a bullet in his hip. He would have been hit again, probably fatally, had not his poacher's sixth sense somersaulted him into a doorway where he was protected by the bodies of less experienced men while the last-ditch Germans, including the wounded officer, were rooted out and despatched with bayonet and bomb. The orderly who dressed Smut's wound commiserated with him, pointing out that hostilities were due to cease that very day but Smut, lying on a stretcher awaiting transportation down the line, was philosophical, deciding that he had had more luck than any one man deserved and that luck did not use a calendar. While the wounded were awaiting ambulances to take them back to the advanced Field Hospital an airman on the stretcher beside him died. With a good deal of wriggling, and a certain amount of agony, Smut managed to acquire the airman's fur-lined boots, reasoning that they would almost certainly be looted by the RAMC orderly who removed the body and that boots such as these would come in handy on the soggy fields above the Dell.

During his long spell in hospital at St Omer Smut's thoughts returned to Madame Viriot, the baker's widow who had sheltered him during his spell behind enemy lines. In retrospect she seemed a homely, friendly and industrious body. He remembered then that she had talked about setting up a bakery in the Valley after the war and ordered him to get in touch with her at Lille as soon as the opportunity presented itself. He was not much of a hand at writing so he dictated a letter to a VAD and, in due course, Madame arrived in person, quite beside herself with delight at being so miraculously restored to her stray Tommy. As soon as Smut could hobble about on crutches they were married by the Mayor of St Omer, an occasion for much merry-making by the patients and hospital staff. Then, to Madame Potter's chagrin, the authorities began to make a ridiculous fuss about her accompanying her husband back to England before numerous formalities had been completed. The business proved so protracted that in the end she was left behind to cope with it, while Smut was shipped across the Channel to await discharge. He limped home to the Valley, a civilian once more, in the spring of 1919, and when he told his friends that he had married a Frenchwoman, and that she would soon be starting a bakery in Coombe Bay they thought it was just another of Smut's leg-pulls. They soon discovered that it was not for Madame arrived a fortnight later, with a mountain of baggage and commercial instincts that proved disastrous to George Endicott, whose bakery had run down during the war and was now offered for sale. Madame got it for two hundred pounds and within weeks of moving in was putting inches on the waistlines of Coombe Bay housewives. She did not expect Smut to contribute to the running of the business, except for driving the old delivery van that she herself had assembled from a number of derelict vehicles rusting on the dump behind Nun's Bay camp. She was inclined to think that Smut had done his bit by ridding France of a hundred or so of the hated Boche and was entitled to rest on his not inconsiderable laurels that included the Military Medal. Smut took his good fortune for granted at the time but came to appreciate it when he ran across war comrades who were having the greatest difficulty in getting jobs and settling back into civilian life.

'I got to admit,' he would tell his cronies in The Raven, 'that I struck it cushy the day I met my ole woman! Them Frogs are diff'rent in all kinds o' ways but 'specially so when it comes to marryin' an' settlin' down. Now take Marie! She's boss from first light 'till lights out but from then on its me who takes over and a Frenchwoman wouldn't 'ave it no other way! In public you minds your Ps and Qs with 'em but soon as the shutters is up it's three paces be'ind fer the wimmin, just like the Wogs! Seems to work, too, seems to keep 'em happy and hard at it, although I offen wonder how we'd 'ave managed if Marie hadn't bin well past puppin'!'

He was to find out; before 1919 was done Madame Potter was proudly announcing to all her customers that the Ostend fortuneteller had been wrong after all. She was, by her reckoning, forty-two and had enjoyed, just as prophesied, three husbands but now (the Virgin be praised) she was *enceinte*, which Smut sheepishly translated as 'in the family way'.

'He will be a boy!' Madame declared with a whirl of gesture, 'and he will grow up to kill hundreds of the Boche like his father!'

III

Henry Pitts, the Valley immortal, faced the end as he had faced the beginning, with mild surprise, with a touch of awe, with patience, amiability and the slow rubbery smile so seldom absent from his genial face.

Most of the men fighting on the Western Front were bewildered by the abrupt cessation of gunfire at 11 a.m. on the morning of November 11th, but they soon adapted themselves to it. It was otherwise with Henry Pitts; the occasion made a deep and lasting impression on him.

Sergeant Pitts, DCM, was sitting on the firestep of a hastily dug trench in a turnip field, north-east of Mons, when the guns stopped firing. He too had heard rumours of an armistice but like his neighbour Smut he refused to take them seriously for by now he was completely absorbed in the war and it was not often that he thought of the Valley, or his wife Gloria, or even of his beloved saddlebacks in their sties under Hermitage Wood.

At eleven o'clock when it sounded as though every gunner and every rifleman in the Western Front was competing for the honour of having fired the final shot of the war, Henry's mind was more humbly engaged. He was trying to open a tin of bully beef with a very blunt bayonet and concentration had temporarily erased the rubbery smile from his face. Watching him, one on either side, were his two special pals, Corporal Watts and L/Corporal Eley, the one a former Blackburn cotton operative, the other a Cockney, who was entered on the battalion strength as bookmaker's clerk. They missed Henry's smile. It was like the sun going out and its absence augured badly for the peace for each of them had come to regard it as a Company barometer, indicating fair weather or foul in terms of light, heavy or medium strafing. The magic hour, and its accompanying explosion of firearms, seemingly left Henry unmoved for he could usually only think of one thing at a time but it stirred the imagination of his two companions. About five minutes past eleven L/Corporal Eley

began to jump up and down like a child seeking permission
to visit the lavatory. It was only when the racket had died
away, and a rocket or two was soaring from the German
lines, that Eley's fidgetings distracted Henry to the extent
of causing him to rise, cock an ear in the manner of a man
who suspects himself the victim of a practical joke, and say,
'Be it true then? Do 'ee reckon there's aught in it, after all?',
and without waiting for an answer he unslung his rifle saying,
'Reckon I'll get up over an' take a look!'

At once they began to remonstrate with him. To a cautious
man like Watts, one of the very few survivors of Kitchener's
1915 drive for recruits, it seemed madness to make a target
of oneself on the strength of information supplied by officers
a few months out of school and he laid a restraining hand on
Henry's shoulder. 'Nay lad!' he pleaded, 'don't be so bloody
daaft! Give 'em an' hour or so to cool off!' but by now Henry's
rubbery smile was back again and he said, impatiently, 'Oh,
giddon with 'ee, Bert! Hark to the silence! Tiz all over, baint
it?', and clawed his way over the parapet rising to his full
height and standing there, the only living thing above ground
in all that vast, dreary landscape.

He remained there for almost a minute and they gazed up
at him unbelievingly, expecting, any second, to accord him
the honours due to the last man killed in the war. Nothing
happened, so presently Henry squelched purposefully out into
no-man's-land, walking with his familiar splay-footed gait that
anyone born in the Valley would have recognised a mile away.
What astonished him most was the absence of shell-holes in
his path until he remembered that Fritz had been leap-frogging
back so rapidly that the area had never been subjected to
heavy bombardment or cluttered with belts of wire. He was
half-way between the lines when he saw a large, grey blob
emerge from the earth and begin to plod directly towards
him and in the first wake of the blob came another, smaller
blob, looking like a trail of disconsolate snails evacuating a
cabbage patch. He stopped then and waited, aware that his
mouth was dry and his stomach mutinous, as though he had
swallowed a quart of canteen beer in a great hurry. The

leading blob was now only some thirty yards distant and
Henry identified it as a German sergeant approximately his
own build, a big-boned, broad-shouldered man, very plump
about the jowls so that his coal-scuttle helmet adorned his
head like a small extinguisher on a fat Christmas candle.

The German did not seem as unsure of himself as Henry
but advanced steadily and close behind him came half-a-dozen
other Germans, still in file and led by a very thin officer,
who seemed to walk very slowly, as though he found the
clay too heavy for his boots. Then Henry noticed that the
sergeant was smiling and pointing with his left hand to his
right palm which held something that glittered and then
raising his other hand to his mouth.

'Well Christ A'mighty!' Henry said to himself, 'I reckon he
wants to trade fags for them bliddy cap-badges he's holding!'
and he hurried forward, fumbling in his tunic pocket for his
Woodbines.

Then the Germans came forward at a run and suddenly he
was surrounded by infantrymen of a Saxon regiment and his
Woodbines disappeared in a flash as the Germans pressed
upon him a variety of badges and emblems, including a
matchbox holder emblazoned with a double-eagle and the
legend 'Gott Mit Uns' that Henry recognised as having begun
life as a belt buckle. The German officer now came up with
them and Henry saw that he was a very sick young man and
was breathing hard, as though he had run a mile. In contrast
to the plump sergeant the officer's helmet was too big for him,
making his face look cavernous and pinched. He could hardly
have been more than twenty and he looked, Henry thought,
as if he was consumptive. The sergeant said something in
German and the officer translated, flashing a pale smile at the
Englishman. He spoke in rather lisping accents that reminded
Henry of the occasional nob like Roddy Rudd and Bruce Lovell,
who had strayed into the Valley from time to time.

'The sergeant asks if you will shake the hand,' he said and
Henry, impressed but embarrassed, said that he would gladly
shake hands and did so. He had always respected the German
front-line troops and, like most of the infantry, dismissed

most of the atrocity stories as newspaper twaddle. Then the
sergeant said something else and the officer, after a spluttering
cough, again translated, telling Henry that the sergeant said he
looked as though he was a farmer. Henry was so delighted at
this that he seized the Saxon's hand again and shouted, 'Youm
right first time, Jerry! Now for Chrissake 'ow did 'ee work that
one out?' and after some difficulty, arising perhaps from the
officer's unfamiliarity with the Valley dialect, the officer said
Henry's hands had given him away whereupon Henry turned
enthusiastically to L/Corporal Eley, who had come up at a run
to harvest more cap-badges in exchange for the half-opened
tin of bully, exclaiming, 'Damme, Bert, theym smart as paint,
baint 'em? Smart as paint they be, the whole bliddy lot o'
them!', and Eley said he had never doubted it and searched
his pockets for more Woodbines.

They stood there for perhaps ten minutes before officers
came out from the British lines and ordered them back,
announcing that an edict from Divisional HQ had strictly
forbidden fraternisation. Henry was unfamiliar with the word
'fraternisation' and said so but when it was explained to him
by a lieutenant of 'B' Company he was indignant. 'Why
damme,' he said to Corporal Watts, in an uncharacteristically
heated voice, 'the bliddy thing's over an' done with, baint it?
That Fritz was a farmer like me, an' that poor toad of a lieutenant, the one who could speak our lingo, was half-dead a'ready!
Whyfore shoudden us pass the time o' day with 'em?'

He continued to brood on the fraternisation ban. It seemed
to distress him far more than all the straffing and discomfort
he had undergone in the past and his natural respect for
officers, particularly front-line officers, began to fade, together
with his enthusiasm for the war. He remained aloof from
the unofficial celebrations (including a spectacular firework
display of coloured flares from both sides of the line) and
his mind continued to dwell on the bovine, broad-shouldered
Saxon, who had instantly recognised him as a fellow farmer.
Somehow it never occurred to him that the men he had been
fighting all this time were identical, men who, in better times,
plodded about tending pigs, herding cows, ploughing up land

and banking swedes for winter cattle feed. He had thought of them, if at all, as a race of efficient robots whose trade – if they had one – was war, who had never lived anywhere but in holes in the ground and whose tools included mustard gas and shrapnel. The encounter in no-man's-land undermined his entire philosophy of war and now, looking back, it seemed to him a very stupid, profitless business and he wanted nothing so much as to be done with it and go home. His dourness puzzled his platoon commander and also his intimates, men like Watts and Eley. Throughout all the bad times they had been able to look to him for reassurance, waiting for his slow, rubbery smile to indicate that the barrage had shifted further back, or north and south along the line but now his essential cheerfulness had deserted him and in its place was impatient pessimism.

They never really got to the bottom of it, although, from time to time, he tried to explain what had wrought such a change in his outlook and when, in late November, they followed the Germans across the winter landscape and entered Cologne he could be seen almost any day distributing pieces of chocolate and tins of plum and apple to clusters of pale, listless children at the street corners, thus openly defying the fraternisation order that he would describe as 'a bliddy lot o' red tape that dorn maake no zense no'ow!'

In late January he was weeded out on account of his age group and sent home for demobilisation and about a month later, when there was a light flurry of snow over the Valley, he detrained at Sorrel Halt and came tramping over the moor to the river road. It felt strange to be swinging along without the usual Christmas tree of equipment hanging about him and until he got used to the feeling he did not know what to do with his left hand that had always gripped the sling of the rifle hooked to his shoulder. Then the sky cleared a little and a fitful winter sun gleamed over the Teazel watershed, pin-pointing a million beads of moisture on the broad blades of the river rushes and he stopped to contemplate the scene, comparing it with the porridge aspect of the Salient. 'By Jesus,' he said to himself, 'I'm bliddy glad to be back! I'd clean forgotten how diff'rent it was!' and he marched on, unconsciously adjusting his route march stride to the slow, splay-footed tread of a countryman crossing the ridges of a ploughed field.

IV

Paul had been home three months then, having been discharged from a convalescent centre in Wales a day or so after the armistice.

His comparatively rapid recovery surprised everybody, including Claire, who had rushed all the way to Rhyl to visit him the moment she had received a letter confirming the wonderful telegram telling her that he was alive and lying wounded at Soissons. Alone in the Valley she was not overwhelmed by this news for she had never, not for a moment thought of him as dead. She was relieved, however, when she found him unmaimed and more or less himself, although he complained of severe headaches that his doctors warned would persist for some months but would grow more and more infrequent as time passed. Although delighted to see her he was somewhat abstracted, as though he could not yet accept the fact that he was not only alive but whole. He remembered very little of the last few months and nothing at all between the moment of stooping to lift the wounded poilu and that of hearing the voice of an American nurse in the ward some ten weeks later. Between headaches he felt fairly fit but he tired very easily and sometimes slept dreamlessly, ten hours at a stretch.

Claire's two brief visits did a good deal to encourage a steady self-adjustment. He relished the soft, warm plumpness of her hand in his and was touched by her timid hospital smile, saying, 'Don't fret, old girl, I'll be all right when I get out of here,' and although the doctor warned her that he ought to remain under direct medical care at least until spring she had an uneasy certainty that she was more aware of what was good for him than someone who had never ridden down into the Valley and through the autumn woods about the mere, and that what he needed far more urgently than drugs was the balm of familiar surroundings.

When she returned home for the second time she brought these thoughts into the open during a discussion with Maureen and it was Maureen's letter to the MO that swung the balance in favour of an early discharge. Less than a month after her second visit news came that he would be arriving on the afternoon train into Paxtonbury and so he did, descending slowly from the carriage and looking about anxiously until he saw the family clustered outside the refreshment room, a rather nervous Claire with seven-year-old Mary holding her hand, five-year-old Whiz holding Mary's hand, and the twins dancing a jig among a stream of passengers. Mary reached him first and he was touched by the abandon with which she embraced him. He remarked also how pretty and cuddly she looked, with her dark clusters of sausage curls and soft brown eyes, 'brown an' mild as a heifer's' as Mrs Handcock had once described them. Then he was almost bowled over by the two-pronged assault of the twins, who came at him like a couple of bullet-headed fugitives from a barrage, squealing with excitement, and he thought, fleetingly, 'I've always considered all four of them babies and here they are half-grown children, and each so individual that it hardly seems possible they are all mine and Claire's!' Claire stood back, letting the children enjoy their moment and looking, he thought, as though she was going to disgrace them all by bursting into tears. The, pulling herself together, she shepherded them into Maureen's battered Ford and they bumped off across the moor and down between the banks of crisp, half-dead bracken to the river. All the time the twins chattered gaily while Mary nestled against his shoulder and he thought, as they swung left and along under the paddock wall, 'It's a miracle! An absolute bloody miracle to be here again, seeing it and smelling it, with Claire as calm and pretty as ever sitting at the wheel, the twins prattling on about horses and conkers and school, and Mary and Whiz preening themselves but saying little except to tell him that poor Rumble Patrick, Ikey's boy, had been prevented from joining the welcome home party by 'the 'flu that everybody caught!' And then he remembered that he had yet another child, a girl Claire had named Jill, whom he had never seen and his mind leapt back more than a year to the hour of his child's conception in old Crabpot Willie's shanty during their second honeymoon, when the war had looked as if it was going on for ever. He felt an immense rush of tenderness and thankfulness for all of them and for everything about him; for the gleaming Sorrel and its sorry-looking autumn rushes, the sprays of late meadowsweet in the hedge, the twenty shades of brown in the avenue chestnuts and the breath-taking peace of a scene unencumbered by rusting wire, unpocked by gaping shell-holes and with every building roofed with thatch and pantiles that still held something of the summer's warmth.

They made no great fuss of him at the house, having been warned against a demonstration in advance so that soon enough everyone had gone to bed or returned to their own pursuits and he and Claire were alone again in front of the study fire.

It seemed to him a smaller, cosier room than he remembered, with firelight reflecting on the coloured bindings of the books and the comforting smell of leather and odd, ineradicable dust that lay between the dark oak shelves. She sat with the hem of her skirt on her knees and her long, elegant legs stretched to the blaze. Seeing her like that, after so long a deprivation, he would have thought that she would have hurried him into beginning one of their study-fireside tumbles but for the moment he could only contemplate her, letting relief and gratitude warm him like the logs in the grate. She had lost a good deal of weight he would have said, was thinner about the face, and in her eyes was a maturity that was new to him. And yet, if anything, it heightened her allure and he said, involuntarily, 'I'd almost forgotten how beautiful you were, Claire, how much of a woman!' and when she smiled absently but made no reply, 'I suppose it will take me time to get adjusted. So far it's a little disturbing, no more than returning to a place one hasn't visited since childhood but remembers as a source of joy and laughter.'

She said, 'It won't take you long, Paul! It won't take you forty-eight hours if you can relax and let the Valley seep into your bones!' She looked at him speculatively then, wondering whether she should take the initiative to search out the boisterous male in him that had so often responded to isolation here late at night but he was looking into the fire with a quizzical expression and she knew that she must be patient and walk carefully. His silence disconcerted her somewhat, for such silences were uncommon between them and one would have thought they had so much to discuss.

'What did you think of the baby? You were up there a long time but when you came down you didn't say?'

He recollected himself but she saw that he did so with an effort. 'Jill? She's quite beautiful!' and then, with a welcome flicker of his old-time raillery, 'She'll have the edge on Claire Derwent at seventeen plus! She's got perfect features.'

'Do you like "Jill"? Do you want to change it for any other name?'

'Since you ask me, yes. I'd like to call her Claire.'

She felt tremendously encouraged without knowing why. 'For any special reason?'

'She's the most like you for one thing and for another . . .'

'Well?'

She knew precisely what he had in mind but she wanted very much to hear him say it. He looked across at her and grinned and her heart gave a leap. It was going to be all right. It was going to be the same, in spite of her intermittent misgivings ever since she had looked down on a stranger when they showed her into the ward at the hospital. He said, 'You know damned well why. Do I really have to tell you?'

'Yes, you do!'

'All right. She's far more of a love-child than any of them. She had to be when you look back on how you came by her. That's a fact, isn't it?'

'Yes, that's a fact,' she said. 'They say a woman always knows precisely when she comes by a child but I'm hanged if I could give you chapter and verse regarding the other two girls. Who could with a man like you about the place?'

'Right then,' he said, settling back and feeling the room and her presence grow on him like a skin, 'it's "Claire" from now on! What made you think of "Jill" anyway?'

'I daresay because she came tumbling after,' she said and he laughed. It was the first time she had heard him laugh for longer than she cared to remember.

They were finding their way again and the certainty of this excited her so much that she had to make an effort to sit still and appear to share his mood.

'She's going to be a handful, I can tell you that already. I daresay it's because I worried so much all the time I was carrying her but you can't expect everything. She'll probably grow up into a thoroughly spoiled little brat, with everyone billing and cooing round her and all the young men within miles making silly excuses to call on us.'

'Well, damned good luck to her,' said Paul, emphatically. 'After what we've had to put up with I'm all for the next generation grabbing all they can get!' And then, suddenly, he thought of poor old Ikey and Hazel and of their child now asleep upstairs in the room he shared with the twins. He said, bitterly, 'It's a bloody shame Ikey couldn't have made it! To cop it like that, three months before the end!' and he scrambled up and looked down on her anxiously. 'Look here, Claire, if I have occasional fits of depression don't run away with the idea that you or the children are involved. I shall be remembering chaps like Ikey and Tom Williams and Will Codsall and all the other poor devils who went west!'

She looked at him doubtfully for a moment, as though debating with herself whether or not to pursue the subject. Finally she said, 'Was it *worth* it, Paul? Was it really worth it, do you think? I mean, couldn't it have been avoided with a little commonsense and more tolerance all round?'

He did not have to reflect long on an answer. He had already give the question a great deal of thought. 'It will have been well worth it if everybody has grown up sufficiently to throw bombast and national prejudice on the ash heap! Anyway, for what it's worth, that's the general opinion among the troops and they ought to know! As to whether it could have been avoided that's a different question. I suppose not, really. It could have been put off for a few years but no more, I think, not when you had gilded idiots like the Kaiser and the Tsar, and so many of our own windbags directing things! Sooner or later somebody would have pooped off the first shot so I suppose one has to regard it as inevitable in terms of the pre-war way of running things. It'll be different now, though, if only because it has to be! Nobody would ever stand for it again in any case and that goes for Fritz as well as us, and certainly the poor devils of French, who bore the brunt of it, for all our share in winning.'

The fire rustled and a half-burned log slipped, ejecting a spark with a sharp crack that made him wince. She saw the instinctive movement and suddenly she was beside him, holding him tightly and covering his face with kisses.

'Let's put a ban on mentioning it,' she said, 'let's rake the fire out and go to bed. You must be tired out and I ought to have sent you to bed hours ago!' and she seized his hands but perhaps, in doing so, defeated her intentions for the movement brought them face to face on the hearthrug and he kissed her on the mouth, not hungrily but with a flourish that was at least a positive reassertion. 'I'm not as tired as all that,' he said and then it was she who laughed.

V

On June 1st, 1919, the day of his fortieth birthday, he went out into the yard and asked old Chivers if Snowdrop, twenty-one by his calculation, was still capable of an hour or two of walking exercise and Chivers asserted that he certainly was and was even good for a trot on level ground, so Paul watched the old man saddle the mild-eyed grey and then hoisted himself up and climbed the orchard path through a forest of bluebells to the gap near the stile that gave on to the high-banked lane connecting Hermitage with the western edge of the woods.

There seemed to him promise of a long, baking summer, with everything far forward after a warm and windless spring.

He skirted the fringe of Hermitage Wood and picked up the narrow, circular bridle path that led to the little plateau that was his favourite vantage point. As he jogged along he looked up into a cloudless sky, enjoying the sun on his face and thinking that the weather was doing its best to make up for early autumns and long winters that had depressed the troops more than the shelling in France but then, he reflected, Flanders always had had a reputation for all-the-year-round drizzle and no matter where you dug out there you were bound to strike water a couple of feet below the surface. Then, as he had learned to do in the last six months, he was able to put France and the war out of his mind. Profit, he reminded himself, lay in the future and it was no use regretting an era when every child returning home from Mary Willoughby's little school would automatically tug his cap, or drop a dutiful little curtsy whenever he or John Rudd rode by. Not all that had disappeared was bad and surely patronage of that kind was something country life could do without in the years ahead. There were, of course, uglier trends, like the steady infiltration of men of Sydney Codsall's type into the coastal area east of Nun's Bay, war profiteers who seemed determined to disfigure the entire countryside with gimcrack bungalows, most of them in cahoots with faceless allies on local and county councils. 'Development' they called it, pretending their object was that of providing homes for old people and ex-service men but having watched Sydney Codsall grow from a toothy child into a scheming young shyster Paul had no confidence in this theory. Sydney now owned almost a third of Coombe Bay, including the old inn, The Raven, which he had already 'developed' into a Tudor sham but Paul made up his mind that he would see murder done before Sydney's tide pushed inland beyond the old brickyard, reflecting that he was nicely placed to hold it at bay for he was a war profiteer himself and a far more successful one than Sydney Codsall or any of his partners, not excluding Codsall's father-in-law, reported to have made a fortune in sugar.

The comforting reflection slammed a door in his resentment so that he found he could indulge himself in the luxury of a chuckle. All the time he had been wrestling with estate problems, all the months he had spent in France and in hospital, money had been piling up in his bank, the harvest of other acres he owned within a penny tram-ride of Tower Bridge. Its total had staggered him when Franz had come down with his ledgers and balance sheets in the spring and for a week or more Paul had gone about with a Bunyan's pack of guilt on his shoulders. It was not a very pleasant thought to realise one might have enriched oneself at the expense of the blood and bones of men like Ikey Palfrey and Big Jem of the Dell and his first impulse had been to get rid of it in a single dramatic gesture, as the politician Stanley Baldwin had done when he returned a third of his war profits to its source. Then he had a better idea and nothing Franz could say could make him drop it. He made over his holdings in the firm of Zorndorff and Craddock to the National Fund for War Disabled and afterwards transferred two-thirds of his accumulated capital, something like a hundred and twenty-thousand pounds, to a special Trust Fund earmarked exclusively for estate development. Not Sydney Codsall's development but real development, the restocking and re-equipping of every farm in the Valley, the rebuilding of every cottage over fifty years old and the purchase of stocks of fertiliser and tractors for all who would use them and plough teams for diehards like Henry Pitts who would not. Not one penny of this money, Paul told Claire and a sceptical John Rudd, would ever be rechannelled to his personal account, or be included in legacies to his children or grandchildren. Capital and incidental interest would be used to rehearten and reclaim land and modernise each of the seven farms. In the meantime (and this was what sent Uncle Franz away tapping his forehead) the Craddocks, one and all, would live on rents frozen at pre-war level plus the yield of pre-war investments and whatever the Home Farm produced under the management of Honeyman's nephew.

He had expected opposition from Claire, if only in defence of her children but she made no protest. She understood, far better than he realised, the compulsions under which he acted and being Edward Derwent's daughter she had always accepted land as the only true wealth, notwithstanding all the fortunes made by speculators and Paxtonbury tradesmen in the last four years.

It was signed and settled now, less than six months after his discharge and today was the first morning in over a month that he had deserted the office. The doctors at Rhyl had not lied to him. His headaches were now spaced by weeks instead of days and the worst discomfort he suffered from wounds in two wars was the occasional nag of rheumatism in the small crater left by a Boer bullet at the turn of the century.

The magic of the morning began to work on him as his shoulder brushed the lower branches of the elms overlooking Hermitage and at last he reined in on the spur of turf at the extreme edge of the escarpment. It was all under his eyes, more than ten miles of it, with the silver sliver of the river curving south-east like a bent rapier aimed at the heart of the Bluff. To the left and behind stood the big timber of Shallowford Woods, trees he had nearly lost in 1916 but which had miraculously survived while every wood in north-eastern France had been shredded to bare poles. To the south he could just see a grey-blue strip of water where the Channel lapped the edge of the dunes; to the west was Four Winds, squatting snugly among green wheat and well-trimmed hedges, and beyond, three miles or more, the gentle slope to the Teazel watershed rising more steeply as it curved north to melt into the moor. This was the outlook, south-east, south and south-west but there was as much to savour within yards of where old Snowdrop stood like a pipe-clayed veteran, comfortably at ease. A towering elm marked the precise corner of the wood, its green buds clothing the hole as far as the lowest branches. Ferns had come creeping out of the wood to seed themselves on the extreme limit of the shade and among them was a riot of colour, jostling for space. Foxgloves stood there, some of them six feet high and already shaking out pink mittens a month earlier than usual; campion ran along the southern margin of the wood like a belt of crimson fire and lower down the bank grew clusters of dandelion, daisy, periwinkle, stitchwort, bugloss and buttercup. There was only a pretence of silence up here. If you listened and thought about listening, there was subdued uproar, an orchestra of buzzing and whizzing and whispering and a rich, heady scent, the overall smell of everything that grows in England in the months of May and June.

He sat there with slack reins until Snowdrop began to shuffle and arch his neck and then he went on slowly down the escarpment to the point where the footpath joined the approach lane of Hermitage Farms. Clouds of flies followed him, seeking Snowdrop's eyes and the heat haze lay on the Valley like a blue, trembling veil. Prudence Pitts, Henry's girl, saw him approach and shouted, 'Me Dad be upalong wi' the pigs, Mr Craddock!' but he only smiled and lifted his hand. Of all the people in the Valley, save only Claire and possibly John Rudd and his wife, he preferred Henry's company but today he wanted to make the circuit alone, without having to wrench his mind from contemplation of the Valley as a domain rather than a community.

He reached the river road and let the grey nose the shallows, waiting while he drank his fill. A kingfisher flashed by and he remembered seeing one on this same reach the very first evening he passed here in the company of old John Rudd. Deliberately he counted both years and phases; that first hectic season when everything was new and strange and the whole Valley burning a sackcloth-brown under what Mrs Handcock called 'a praper ol' scorcher'; the false dawn of his first marriage and all the grief and confusion that came of it; the long, rewarding period with Claire that endured until another and more catastrophic 'scorcher' was over, and finally the interminable war years, with everything falling to pieces and hardly any of his former allies surviving to pull them together again. Well, it had been a long haul, getting on for a fifth of a century of ups and downs, but he was still here, sitting the same horse in the same river bottom; there was time enough, at forty, for the fulfilment of lingering dreams.

Chapter Eleven

I

On the afternoon of September 1st, 1929, the eve of the twins' 21st birthday, Paul saddled the sedate skewbald (who had replaced Snowdrop as his estate transport) and rode up to French Wood, the young plantation now growing up on the extreme south-western corner of the Hermitage plateau. He told himself he was going there with the object of calling on Henry Pitts and making one more attempt to convert him to tractor ploughing, but this was no more than an excuse to escape from the frenzied upheaval accompanying preparations for the all-night dance The Pair had organised, with the active connivance of their mother and sisters.

The house was already full of young people, most of them strangers to Paul, who bustled round and about him carrying armfuls of decorations, chairs, trestle tables and weird-looking band instruments and maintained a ceaseless hammering that made work in the office an impossibility. He said to Claire, standing on a stepladder with her mouth full of tacks, 'I'm going over to Hermitage, I won't be long!' but she only nodded absentmindedly. Clearly she had no thoughts for him today and neither, it seemed, had anyone else, for even Mary, the quiet one, had been sucked into the whirlpool of the first big-scale social event at Shallowford since Simon's twenty-first, more than four years before.

Paul rode up the orchard to the sunken lane, noting that the apple crop promised well and that Young Honeyman and Henry Pitts had almost done with harvesting. He never rode to the new wood without a feeling that he was going to church, for French Wood, which had been his own way of commemorating the Valley dead, was a kind of church, much more of one

than the precincts of all the other war memorials in the district
– plain granite crosses and pseudo-heroic statues of glaring
infantrymen, without the vitality or validity of his private
memorial to the eighteen local men who had died between
August 1914 and November 1918.

He remembered as he rode across the plateau how the
eccentric notion had come to him the week of his fortieth
birthday in June, 1919, when he had sat Snowdrop on the
crest overlooking the Valley and thought of all the cheery
souls who had turned their faces to the sun at this spot and
now lay in tidy graves in Picardy and Gallipoli. He thought too
of the maimed, of poor devils like Reg Willis the wheelwright's
son, who had lost the sight of both eyes and Davy Tozer, the
smith's son, who had come home minus a leg. There had been
talk of memorial stones and statues in all the papers just then,
for the Armistice was only seven months behind them but
now, as he entered the little wood growing up around him, he
was very glad he had planted a tree for each man instead of
carving their names on a lump of granite in the churchyard.
A living tree was surely more pleasant to behold than most of
the conventional war memorials up and down the country and
here, in 'French Wood' as the Valley folk insisted on calling it,
every man had individual representation, so long as a comrade
lived to come here and remember them once in a while.

The plantation was fenced with a stout wooden paling to
keep out the wild deer and against all the predictions of
the local wiseacres it was prospering, as though the wood
spirits favoured the idea. Paul had chosen each young tree
with care – a mountain ash for Ikey; oaks for the older
men like Tremlett, the huntsman and Tom Williams, the
fishermen; an elm for Jem Pollock already as thick as the
Dell giant's thigh and a small cluster of silver birches for
the younger set, men like Tod Glover who had once flown
low over this spot showing off his wind-riding skill like a
buzzard. In the centre of the wood was a flowering cherry
for Grace, killed hauling wounded back from Vimy and as he
crossed the turf Paul was not much surprised to find his eldest
son Simon sitting there, with a cherrywood pipe in his mouth

contemplating the metal plaque which read: *'Grace Craddock, ambulance driver, killed April 1917,'* and underneath the only Scriptural quotation inscribed on a plaque – *'Greater love hath no man . . .'* Simon said, without looking round, 'You should have done your bit of Bible thumping under Tom Williams' tree, Gov'nor! He was a Methodist and would have thought it fitting.' Then, with laughter in his eyes, 'She never had much truck with organised religion, did she?'

'No,' Paul said, aware that the boy was teasing him but not resenting it in any way, 'she didn't! As a matter of fact she didn't have much truck with anything except Women's Rights and Compassion.'

The boy looked at him in a way that Paul had learned to associate with his questing, mildly cynical nature, akin to his mother's but more tolerant and far less likely to give offence.

'It was a sentimental idea, this wood of the dead,' he said, 'but taken all round it does you credit, Gov'nor.'

'Thank you,' said Paul with a grin, for he suddenly remembered after all these years when and where he had invited Simon to call him 'Gov'nor' – sitting on a fence near his school, during a hurried visit on Paul's leave from the Front in the autumn of 1917. He thought of reminding the boy and then decided not. Simon affected to despise the past and to regard everything that had happened up to the Labour Government's first term of office, in 1924, as a pitiable failure of all human achievement. He said, instead, 'What made you come here, today of all days?'

'For the same reason as you; to get away from the racket! Anyway, I had some thinking to do. I've had a letter from Ned Stokes. He wants to know if I'd care to take over the literary editorship of *The Forum*. It's a new magazine his uncle is backing. Might have a future now that Labour is back again.'

Paul was resigned to Simon's false starts and news that he was contemplating a journalistic career, after turning his back on teaching and forestry, had no power to irritate him. He said, tolerantly, 'You're old enough to dispense with my advice, Si. I daresay you'd find it amusing for a time but those magazines don't last long as a rule, do they?'

'No,' Si said seriously, 'but what does?'

'Land,' said Paul, not unexpectedly, and Simon smiled and shook his head as though he had long ago accepted the fact that, when it came to the estate, his father was slightly off his head and everybody in the Valley acknowledged as much.

'I suppose your mob will want to nationalise us,' Paul said and without waiting for an answer, 'Well, I daresay it'll come to that in the end but until it does I'm staying put! It will take more than your precious Ramsay Mac' to shift me.'

Simon took his pipe from his mouth and ran his hand through his dark hair. It was a gesture that always reminded Paul vividly of his first wife, one of the many quirks she had passed on to the child she had abandoned for the Women's Suffrage Campaign, when he was no more than a few months old. He said, resignedly, 'You might just as well go over to the Tories, Gov'nor. You're a Tory in everything but name you know.'

'Don't be so damned patronising!' Paul told him. 'Jimmy Grenfell and I were the two people who showed the Tories the door round here before you were born!'

'Oh, I know about the 1906 landslide and all that,' Simon said, 'but for all your sound and fury you Radicals are as deeply rooted in the past as eighteenth-century landlords. Even the Tories subscribe to something new if there's a quick profit in it but you and Jimmy Grenfell don't. Surely you can see we've taken your places as Progressives?'

'I can't see anything of the kind,' Paul said, but genially, for secretly he never cared to quarrel with Simon's championship of the underdog, not even when it was larded with left-wing jargon borrowed from dull-looking books translated from the Russian. 'The fact is we were content to nibble whereas you lot will overeat yourself and give the electorate chronic indigestion. As soon as you begin to burp all your reforms will emerge as hot air and the Tories will be more firmly entrenched than ever! You see if I'm not right! However, I don't propose to spend a pleasant afternoon discussing politics with you, I'm going over to Hermitage to see Henry Pitts. Do you want to come along?'

'No thanks,' Simon said. 'I'd better go back and give The Pair a hand. Do you know how many those idiots have invited to stay with us overnight? Seventy-four! Where the devil are they going to sleep?'

'I don't suppose they will until the sun gets up and then they can doss down in the barns for all I care,' Paul said. 'Your mother and I are going to the shanty after the midnight toasts. You'll be in charge from then on!'

'An honour,' said Si, grinning, 'but one I could easily duck! The twins' set are morons but come to that so are the twins themselves. Have you talked to them since they came back from town yesterday?'

'Good God, no!' Paul said, 'they never talk to me! Mary is the only one of you who regards me as anything more than an amiable old-stick-in-the-mud with a fortune in loose change!' and he sauntered out of the enclosure and swung himself in the saddle, setting the skewbald at the steep path down to the river road and turning right towards the Hermitage farm track. Simon moved clear of the trees and watched him until he passed out of sight behind the Hermitage elms. 'Well, Gov,' he said to himself, 'Steve and Andy will be "talking" tomorrow or the day after and I daresay they'll succeed in knocking you more than I ever have! I've always been odd-man-out here and had time to get used to it!' He lit his pipe again and stood puffing thoughtfully and then, as he turned away, he passed the young beech planted for Keith Horsey, the parson's son, whom he remembered as an old boy of High Wood and sometime school friend of his boyhood hero, Ikey. He stopped to read the words on the plaque: *'To Keith Horsey, R.A.M.C. Killed February 1917.'* He recalled that Horsey had once been the Valley's conscientious objector and also that Number Ten Downing Street was now occupied by another. He thought, 'You should have held on a bit. Who knows? A chap with a good degree might have had a place in the Cabinet and then every damned flag-flapper in the Valley would have licked your boots!'

He lunged off, hands in pockets, pipe in mouth. He knew his duty as the heir of Shallowford at the forthcoming celebrations

but he did not look forward to hours of junketing in the
company of hearty young men who drove high-powered sports
cars with overlong bonnets and leggy girls who pretended
they were hot stuff and shouted 'Stop!' as soon as they felt
a hand above their knee. At twenty-five, and with his future
still undecided, he considered himself too adult for this sort of
nonsense; too old and too disillusioned with the entire bloody
decade.

II

Claire had been so busy preparing for the dance that she had
neglected to enter the momentous date in the estate diary.
Keeping the diary up-to-date was still largely her prerogative,
although Paul sometimes wrote brief entries in it and she
knew that he always read every word she wrote between
the heavy leather Bible covers of what had once been old
Sir George Lovell's pornographic photograph album. It was
a task she always found congenial inasmuch as it made her
aware of continuity and now that her youngest child was
eleven, and she herself forty-five, continuity was important
to her. About four-thirty, when the decorations were complete
and the buffet tables laid and covered with tablecloths, she
made a last-minute check of the guest rooms, and the Nissen
hut fortuitously left behind by the R.A.M.C. ten years before
and then went into the library and shut the door against
intruders.

She had always liked this room and liked being alone in it.
Its smell of stale dust and old leather reminded her of the early
days of her marriage and it always seemed to her that when
she was here at night, with Paul reading or dozing in the big
armchair on the other side of the hearth they recaptured the
intimacy that eluded them in a house full of strident young
things and servants who lacked the permanence of dear old
bodies like Mrs Handcock, long since retired to a cottage, or
Thirza Tremlett, who had been nursemaid until John Rudd's
boy had been born and she had moved down to the Lodge.

She fetched the diary and carried it back to the library table but as she set it down she caught a swift and not altogether pleasing glimpse of her reflection in the mirror over the sideboard. In the old days she had worried about putting on weight despite Paul's constant assurance that he liked rounded women but now she wondered if current fashions had not encouraged her to proceed too boldly in the reverse direction for her breasts seemed to have disappeared altogether and her behind, viewed sideways, looked nearly as flat as a board. Her hair had been bobbed as long ago as 1926 and the shearing of her long, golden tresses, for thirty years her pet vanity, had been an occasion almost as catastrophic as the declaration of war. Paul had stormed and she had wept, and the fact that the entire family had taken up her cause had not helped to convince either of them that her smooth, oval face was suited to the fashion. Since then she had compromised, unknowingly anticipating the long-bob of the immediate future, and now her hair reached her shoulders and curled under, masking what she called her 'rats-tails' on the nape of her neck. Her skin was still very clear and her eyes retained their blue depths but as she turned her back on the mirror she could not help regretting that the craze for boyish figures was taking such a long time to die, or consoling herself that the one aspect of current fashions to her advantage was that of short skirts, for her legs were still shapely and her ankles slim, whereas some poor wretches were condemned to expose calves as thick as banister rails and knees as knobbly as applewood faggots.

She opened the book and wrote: *'Today the Twins celebrated their 21st birthday with an all-night ball . . .'* and then stopped, thinking how Stephen and Andy would hoot with laughter if they ever saw tonight's event described as a 'ball', as though there would be sets of lancers and the mazurka, and all the gentlemen would wear gloves and the girls wait hopefully for their programmes to be filled. The thought took her back, however, to the first celebration she had ever attended in this house – the Coronation soirée in October, 1902, when she had driven here with her father, stepmother,

brother Hugh and sister Rose, one and all convinced that new
Squire would round off the occasion by announcing that he
intended marrying Claire Derwent of High Coombe in the
New Year. They had all taken a terrible tumble that night
and she could smile at it now but it had taken her close on
five years to ride out and perhaps she would be nursing
a grievance yet if Paul's first wife had not been such a
goose as to run off to London to smash windows and get
herself locked up in Holloway prison.

It was a day for musing. She wrote: '. . . *about two hundred
guests attended and toasts were proposed by the Squire at
midnight,*' but then she did what she usually did when making
a special entry of this kind and began browsing her way back
through the pages, noting entries relating to early triumphs of
her second daughter Karen (universally known as 'Whiz') in the
County show-ring, Simon's decorous 21st birthday celebrations,
in January, 1925, John Rudd's retirement in the following year,
and so on to the outbreak of foot and mouth disease at Four
Winds in the summer of the General Strike, the crash of a
Handley Page aircraft on the dunes, Jimmy Grenfell's narrow
electoral victories in 1924 and again last May and all kinds
of relevant and irrelevant happenings since Paul's miraculous
return from the dead in the last weeks of the war. It was all
here in her own or his handwriting and browsing over his
entries she found a theme that was absent from her own
recordings, a pattern of subdued anxiety running from page
to page, an undertone to the orchestra of Valley events. There
were terse entries like one in May, 1924, that read, *'Codsall is
developing east of Nun's Bay, blast him . . .'* and enigmatic ones
such as *'Quarry project through County Council; will block it
one way or another.'* It was the first time she had noticed
that he was using the diary as a safety valve or, indeed,
that Sydney Codsall's activities around the periphery of the
estate were so important to him and it worried her a little,
the more so because she could not remember him having
confided in her beyond making a glum comment or two on
local jerry building and the sins of war profiteers. She went
into the office and rummaged among the estate maps. John

Rudd had always praised Paul's administrative capacity and although he was proverbially untidy everywhere else he was never slipshod in here, the plainly furnished room that was the hub of the estate and had been since he had converted old Sir George's dark-room into an office. Everything was docketed and filed; every map, every lease and catalogue indexed with neatly printed cards. It was, she reflected, a side of him she hardly knew, even after twenty-two years of marriage, and today it intrigued her. She found a map dated 1929 and unrolled it, holding the ends down with ledgers and a glance at it confirmed her suspicion regarding his fear of encirclement, for whilst Shallowford land was shaded light pink and the sea pale blue, there were three areas shaded black and when she looked at the key she was not surprised to see them identified as *'Threatened Development'*. The extent of the areas surprised her. She knew that ever since the war had ended Sydney Codsall's Whinmouth Development Company (Bricks and Tiles), Ltd had been building bungalows on what had once been Blair's Farm, in Nun's Bay, a coastal island of freehold dividing the southern boundaries of the Shallowford and Heronslea Estates but she was largely unaware of Sydney's steady infiltration into Coombe Bay, two miles or more to the east, where, from time immemorial, most of the property had been owned by the Squire of Shallowford. There was a tracing pinned to the map which showed details of this infiltration. The old Manson brickyard was shaded in and so was The Raven, once owned by a local brewery and run by Minnie Flowers and her husband but now a Tudor sham renamed 'The Lovell Arms'. Now that she thought about it the deliberate reintroduction of the word 'Lovell' into the district smacked of an insult aimed at Paul and she wondered if there existed some quarrel between Paul and the toothy child he had tried to befriend when Sydney's father went raving mad all those years ago and killed Arabella Codsall with a hay-knife. There was a patch of black away up in the north-easterly corner of the map in the area where, during the war, there had been a prisoner-of-war camp. She had always thought of this parcel as land owned and administered by the Forestry Commission but it was clear that this too had now passed into the hands of the Whinmouth Development Company, for it was ringed in pencil and across it Paul had written 'Quarry Site?'

She was still bent over the map, the twins' celebration forgotten, when she heard his step beyond the office door and at once felt guilty, as though she had been prying like Bluebeard's wife. He came in with a tired smile, however, that at once reassured her so that her protective instinct drove her anxieties into the open and she said, 'I've been reading the diary and I came in here to check up. Why didn't you tell me you've been brooding about Sydney Codsall's antics?' He looked hard at her then, trying to make up his mind whether she was genuinely interested and that she understood his caution. He had never quite forgotten his first wife's contempt for his obsession with Shallowford and it had always seemed to her that this was the one wound of the many he had received at the hands of Grace Lovell that had been beyond her power to heal.

'It's a fair question,' he said at length, 'but right now we have to change for the big do tonight. I'll explain when the tumult has died down.'

'No, Paul,' she said obstinately, 'there's no hurry to change. Tell me now or I shall worry about it when I should have my mind on my job tonight.'

'Very well,' he said, 'although there can't be much you haven't heard. That little bastard won't be happy until he's boxed us in. His shantytown already extends as far as the dunes. He has about a third of the property in Coombe Bay under his hand and he's just bought the quarry behind the woods.'

'It looks frightening on paper,' Claire said, 'but hasn't he gone as far as he can? With farm prices as their present level you don't want any more land, do you?'

'No,' he said, 'I don't want more land. As a matter of fact I wouldn't mind unloading some, providing it went to a farmer and not to rascals who haven't the slightest interest in it beyond the quick profits they make exploiting it and fouling the countryside into the bargain!'

It was common knowledge that the shantytown on the old Blair farmland was the Squire's *bête noire* and privately she considered his attitude unreasonable. The bungalows there were almost all occupied by elderly retired couples from Whinmouth and Paxtonbury and, much as she shared his love of the Valley, she was not prepared to claim a monopoly of the coastline. She said, carefully, 'He's already built on every square inch of the Blair holding. There isn't room over there to put a shed up and all the land east is included in the country coastal preservation strip. Rudd told me that years ago, no one can build on it.'

'No one can build houses!'

'What else could be built?'

'A road,' he said, 'a glorified promenade right across the dunes as far as Coombe Bay and once that was approved we should soon have a little Blackpool on our doorstep!'

'This is possible? A motor road, between Nun's Bay and Coombe Bay?'

'Sydney and his Council stooges have been agitating for it for years. Why do you suppose he's bought up so many Coombe Bay freeholds?'

She understood and shared his concern because her resentment had deeper roots than his. A road along the coast would cut and probably choke the series of goyles that led down to the beach and one of the first to go would surely be Crabpot Willie's goyle, where lay the shanty that had a significance for her that she could never have explained to anyone, not even him.

'They've been trying, you say. What stopped them succeeding?'

He grinned and rolled up the plan. 'I've got my stooges as well,' he said. 'Fortunately it's a pretty expensive project and nobody likes to pay more county rates than they can help.'

'What about the land he's got behind the woods? Can he build another shantytown there?'

'It wouldn't pay him to,' Paul said, suddenly quite cheerful again, 'even if the coastal development matures, as I daresay it will in the end. His holdings in Coombe Bay and north of the wood will always be blocked by High Coombe, so he'll have to confine his activities in that area to quarrying. I daresay he'd give his eye-teeth to get hold of some of your brother's pasture and have direct access to the sea from that side.'

'What is he *really* after?' she asked. 'I mean, apart from money.'

'Me!'

'But why? You were almost a father to him when he was a boy. Ikey saved him from his crazy father, didn't he?'

'Yes he did,' Paul said. 'He fetched him down from the bedroom by ladder but Ikey would have saved everybody a lot of trouble if he'd left him there! Sydney hates me – I can't tell why exactly – it's probably because he knew I disliked his mother and because I showed him the door that time he came here during the war with his plan to cut me in on a side profit he was making out of pitprops. However, don't run away with the idea that I hate him back. I don't, you know, just what he stands for, what all Sydney Codsalls stand for. There are one or two operating in every area of the country. They stand up in public spouting about development and progress but what they really mean is exploitation and rural rape! They are the new *condottiere*, marching through England as the medieval mercenaries marched across France, taking everything out and putting nothing back! Some of them are old men who helped to push us into the war and drank blood for four years but there are plenty of others younger than me, men who made damned sure they stayed home and staked their claim while the going was good! Somebody has to stand up to the bastards or the country won't be worth living in in a generation from now.'

She had heard it all before, when some of the ex-servicemen called on him for advice or a loan, but never so exactly stated. She said, 'If you feel as strongly as that about Sydney Codsall why don't you run for the County Council yourself, Paul?'

'Not me!' he said fervently. 'I'll fight them where I find them, in my own fields and woods, thank you! Councils? They're for two varieties, well-meaning windbags and backscratchers, like Sydney's mob! I know better than to fight them in the open.

How long would it take them to tack a war-profiteer's label on me?'

'That's nonsense! There isn't a soul about here that doesn't know you've ploughed everything back into the estate. Suppose you had behaved like half the other landlords and unloaded the farms on the tenants as soon as taxes went up and prices kept going down? You've nothing to be ashamed of and a good deal to be proud of, Paul.'

He said nothing to this but dropped his glance to the diary, thumbing idly through the stiff, scrawl-covered pages. She did not have to be told where he had been all afternoon. Whenever he was in this mood she knew he had been to French Wood, as though a visit there established contact with men who had shared his love of the Valley and were able to renew his faith in the future. She was aware also that his return to the wood had some link with the day itself, the coming-of-age of the two handsome young extroverts she had borne him, and as she thought this she remembered something else that would have made her chuckle had she thought of it earlier. They had been conceived here, in this very room and not in a bed either, bless you, but on that old bearskin rug in front of the fire, one gusty night after they had come home cider-merry from one of old Arthur Pitts' Hallowe'en parties! She knew, after twenty-two years, how to coax him out of this things-aren't-what-they-were mood and surely tonight was an occasion he should enjoy as much if not more than the twins and a lot of boisterous strangers. She said: 'Right! We'll all battle along with you, Paul, but was there a special reason why you kept this to yourself so long? Kept it from me, I mean?'

'Yes,' he said, 'I suppose there was. You've always been so damned expert at keeping pace with change, Claire. Look at yourself! You don't appear more than a year or two older than some of those cropped-eared, flat-chested girls the twins bring into the place but my clock stopped after the war and I sometimes think of myself as constitutionally incapable of keeping abreast of the times. It worries me sometimes and that's the truth! I hate change but one day I'll catch myself resisting changes for the better. Simon as good as told me that today.'

'Well,' she said, smiling at his earnestness, 'you weren't always so desperately traditionist. Can you seen any direct link between that moth-eaten old rug we ought to have thrown out long ago and those lumping great boys, whose health you'll be proposing tonight?'

'No,' he said, looking very puzzled. 'I'm jiggered if I can! Is there one?'

'Certainly there is!' she said and reminded him, laughing at his slightly startled expression and the way he stared down at the rug as though he half expected it to turn back into a bear. He said, his features relaxing slowly, 'I might have known you would remember a thing like that! Will they be serving cider tonight, do you think?'

'We're not staying here tonight.'

'That's so,' he said. 'We're off to the shanty, aren't we? Well, you don't have to remind me of what happened there a long time ago. Come to think of it, it's a wonder we haven't a baker's dozen coming-of-age parties ahead of us!' and he kissed her on the mouth in a manner that implied Sydney Codsall and all his works would be out of mind for at least twenty-four hours.

III

It was not often that John Rudd came to the big house these days. At seventy-seven, and with a heart condition that had given him one or two frights over the last few days, he found the long drive too steep and the effort of climbing in and out of his wife's fussy little cars more exhausting than the ascent on foot. He was here tonight, however, and enjoying himself in an unexpected way, for this was the first big event at Shallowford in the past forty years when nothing was expected of him but to sit still, sip well-watered toddy and look amiable.

Maureen was off helping Claire and the staff with the buffet and Paul was consorting with some of his more active cronies – Henry Pitts, Smut Potter and the like, so that John, comfortably seated in what Claire was pleased to call the Minstrel Gallery (actually a kind of landing built on when the room was

enlarged after the war) could look down on the swirling
mob and make cynically good-humoured comparisons with
other special occasions that had occurred here since the days
of 'that old goat George Lovell and his rackety sons, Hubert
and Ralph'. The new dances puzzled him somewhat, prancing
embraces of the kind that were always popular among young
people but were confined, as far as he could recall, to the
bushes and would never have been allowed on a dance floor,
not even George Lovell's dance floor. The tunes puzzled him
even more, the old stamping music having been replaced by
a variety of near-dirges, almost all concerned with moons
waxing and waning over definite portions of the United States,
with here and there a snatch or two reminiscent of the songs
coons used to sing at concerts. Even the band instruments
in use were nothing like he recalled, not even in the early
days of the Craddock régime. The basic melody, it seemed,
no longer emanated from the piano or the violins but from
a kind of trombone called, he understood, 'a sax', the notes
of which were augmented and often drowned by the rattle
of kettledrum and clash of cymbals. The youngsters seemed
to enjoy it all and take the cacophony for granted but then,
in the decade that was just about to end, youngsters took
everything for granted – noise, speed, half-nakedness and
what was perhaps the most surprising, the virtual elimination
of class-distinctions. If he needed proof of this he had only to
lean forward an inch or so and look over the balustrade to see
Stephen Craddock, the stockier of the twins, whirling round
with Prudence Pitts, the red-headed daughter of Henry and
Gloria of Hermitage, a girl who was almost exactly Stephen's
age. Now that, he thought, would have been enough to bring
the ceiling down thirty years ago whereas, in the more free and
easy Edwardian decade, the glimpse of the girl's underclothes
as she was swung round in a final flourish would have almost
certainly led to her being ordered home by her blushing mama
and clouted on the way out by her father.

They were at it again, with hardly a pause for breath, one
of the swoonier tunes now – pretty enough in an unremarkable
way but tinged, as were nearly all their songs, with melancholy

and defeatism. He tried to catch the words of the lyric bawled
into a mechanical amplifier by the hired girl vocalist (another
undreamed-of innovation) but could make no sense of it, for
she seemed to be pleading for kisses from somebody called
'Babette' and Babette, unless he was far in his dotage, had
always been a woman's name and a rather tarty one at that. His
observations and the reflections they provoked switched from
the general to the particular. He spotted and contemplated
each of Paul's brood in order of precedence, beginning with
Simon, the Lovell girl's boy, and ending with the Craddock
postscript, the beautiful eleven-year-old, who had been given
special permission to stay up until 1 a.m. for the occasion.
They were a handsome bunch but also, as he knew from
their parents and from Maureen's fireside gossip, a highly
unpredictable spread of children. Simon, already twenty-five,
was said to be as mulish as his mother and likely to go
her way if Paul failed to pull him up short whereas the
twins, Stephen and Andrew, were as happy-go-lucky a pair
as one would be likely to encounter anywhere but had not,
so far as he was aware, done a day's work in their lives,
if one excepted the repeated stripping and reassembling of
motor-bikes and their redesigning of old Hocking's motor-
launch into a speed boat that had capsized at high speed
in the bay a month ago and came close to drowning them.
There was Simon, serious but tricky, and The Pair, feather-
witted but likeable, and then came the three girls, with more
permutations – Mary, the eldest and her father's favourite,
Whiz, the long-faced sixteen-year-old who rode superbly, won
bushels of awards and reminded everybody of her Aunt Rose
away in Gloucestershire, and finally the family Aphrodite,
Claire, whose classic profile, natural poise and astounding
precocity marked her down as a future Emma Hamilton or
Du Barry. Well, thank God, he only had one child to worry
about since poor old Roddy had drowned under the guns of
Von Spee and his Paul seemed normal enough, with plenty
of his mother's sense of humour but none of her pseudo-Irish
feyness, praise be to God! He sipped his whisky, pondering the
not inconsiderable compensations of old age as he saw Paul

come through from the hall, mount the rostrum and motion the perspiring drummer to give a long roll on the drums as a preface to the midnight toasts.

They swarmed into the already overcrowded room from all parts of the house and garden, some of the latecomers looking a little dishevelled and removing wisps of grass from their dinner jackets and dresses. In the old days, John thought, only the Potter girls slipped out into the shrubbery between dances but now almost everybody made these stealthy exits and re-entrances. There was a general laugh when Stephen made a breathless reappearance with the daughter of the Paxtonbury Archdeacon in tow, and then Paul gestured for silence and made a pleasant little speech, not too long and not too flippant but spiced with a little salty humour about his sons' shortcomings which was offset by the geniality Paul Craddock could always summon for a gathering such as this. There was not a man or a woman over forty present, John thought, who would not bear witness to the staying-power of the young greenhorn whom he had met off the London train more than twenty-seven years ago, and who had since rooted himself in the Valley as no Lovell had ever done.

John stood up to drink the twins' health but it was not of them he thought as he downed his final whisky that night. His congratulations – if he offered any – were reserved for the tall, slightly stooping man of fifty, raising his glass and looking down on the slightly tipsy company, and on the blonde woman who stood smiling at his side and whose attention, he suspected, was also directed at Paul rather than her sons, for no one who knew Claire Derwent (as he still thought of her) doubted that any one of her children came better than a poor second to the man she had come home to nurse and marry at the time of the German wreck in Tamer Potter's Cove. 'Dear God it seems a dozen lifetimes away!' muttered John aloud, as the music began to bray again and the couples swung off into the one recognisable dance of the evening, the Gay Gordons, and Maureen Rudd, appearing suddenly at his side, said, 'What's that you're saying?' But John was not prepared to admit to sentimentality, not even with only his wife as an audience, and replied, 'Nothing, old girl, only that it's time I toddled off. Stay on if you like, I'm for bed!'

'I'll tell Paul and Claire and get our coats,' Maureen said and disappeared again while John took a final glance at the kaleidoscopic scene below, thinking, 'Who'll be next? Mary, the quiet one? She's eighteen and has three years to go but maybe she'll marry and won't have a big house celebration. I doubt if I'll be around to see it anyway but good luck to them all, damned good luck, if only for his sake!'

Soon after two a.m., when most of the older guests had left, the blaring of a hunting horn expertly blown by Robbie Eveleigh, youngest of the Eveleigh boys (he had taken Tremlett's place as huntsman when the Sorrel Vale Farmers' Hunt was revived in the early 'twenties) summoned the younger generation of the Valley to join the traditional Tally-Ho crocodile, without which no Westcountry celebration could be said to be complete. Simon, as MC, thanked God that Paul and Claire had departed for the shanty, for already several of The Pair's inner circle were a little the worse for wear and the passage of the Tally-Ho crocodile through the house seemed to him a direct threat to furniture and fabric. There was no help for it, however, and the best he could do was to insist on a single crocodile weaving in one direction instead of two working towards one another with the object of head-on collisions. They set off to the scream of three horns, Robbie's and two others blown by Stevie and Andrew, and the uproar of their ascent of the stairs and progress along the main corridor from the old nursery to the west wing, shook the house in its foundations. The orchestra did not take part but added to the general din by playing hunting music at full blast so that elderly folk abed as far away as Coombe Bay stirred in their sleep as the waves of sound that launched Squire's twins into their twenty-second year crossed the stubble fields and lapped the inshore sandbanks of the bay. Paul and Claire, climbing into bed in the shanty heard the distant uproar and exchanged wry smiles; Marian Eveleigh heard in in the big bedroom at Four Winds, tut-tutting lest it should wake Norman who had been sleeping badly since his heart attack in the spring and had been persuaded to take a sleeping-draught against the noisy homecoming of his children; old Martha Pitts heard it over at Hermitage and wondered if Henry was home and whether Gloria, her daughter-in-law, had managed to keep him sober. Francis Willoughby at Deepdene, who had politely declined an invitation heard it, for it set his Welsh collie barking and the yaps were answered by the deep-throated bay of Jumbo Bellchamber's mastiff lower down the Bluff slopes at the Potters' old farm. Nobody minded much, however, least of all Simon who was bored by his six-hour stint as Master of Ceremonies. Alone among the family (young Claire had flagrantly disobeyed her mother's instructions and stayed up for the fun) he did not hitch himself on to the braying procession but wandered out on the terrace and down the broad, flagstoned path to the sunken rose garden, inhaling the night air with pleasure after the fug of the ballroom and watching the harvest moon ride over the avenue chestnuts down by the ford.

He had descended the steps that led to the lily pond before he saw a shadow and the glow of a cigarette over by the sundial. The lights from the terrace did not reach this far and the area round the column was cut off from moonlight by a tall copperbeech marking the southern limit of Grace Lovell's single contribution to Shallowford. He saw, however, that a woman stood there and that she was not a guest, for she had a coat thrown loosely over her shoulders and beneath it wore a high-necked sweater and tweed skirt. There was also something about her posture that suggested here was someone else impatient with noise and buffoonery, so he called:

'Hello there? It's only me, Simon Craddock. Can I find someone for you?'

The figure straightened itself and tossed the cigarette in a wide arc across the pond.

'No, thank you. I'm only waiting for my sister, Esther. Robbie, my brother, is staying on to help clear up so I brought the trap over for her; I'll give her another ten minutes.'

He realised then that he was talking to Rachel Eveleigh, one of the two elder of the Four Winds' girls and remembered

in time that she wasn't Rachel Eveleigh now but Rachel
Horsey, having married Keith Horsey, the parson's son, whose
memorial plaque he had read that same afternoon. He remembered her clearly as a pretty, fresh-faced girl, with light
brown hair, who used to help her mother make cream in the
Four Winds' buttery but had forgotten until now that Keith
Horsey, the CO, had had a wife, much less a local one. Her
presence here as an outsider puzzled him, especially as her
brother Robbie, the huntsman, and at least one of her sisters,
were among the more boisterous of the younger set in the
house. He said, diffidently, 'How is it you weren't invited?
I helped make out the list. You must have been overlooked.
I'm most terribly sorry,' and suddenly she laughed so that he
felt embarrassed for there was nothing diffident about her
laughter. Then she must have realised she had disconcerted
him for she said, earnestly, 'I'm sorry! I wasn't laughing at
you, Mr Craddock, just at the idea that anyone should be
expected to remember me when making out invitation lists
for a Shallowford beano! I've been away from here since before
my husband was killed. You may remember him better than
me, he went to your school, I believe.'

'I remember you both,' Simon said, still a little ruffled. 'As
a matter of fact I was thinking of Keith only this afternoon.'

'You were?' She sounded not merely surprised but defensive. 'Why should anyone around here ever think of Keith?'

'For the same reason as they think occasionally of all the
other poor chaps who went west. Oh, I'm not referring to
that mob' – he jerked his head towards the house – 'they're
incapable of thinking about anything of the smallest importance but local ex-service chaps must think of people like Keith
Horsey a good deal. My father does for one!'

She moved aside so that the moonlight fell on his face and
he had a curious certainty that she was weighing him up
and trying to make up her mind whether to continue the
conversation or break it off abruptly by walking away.

'You're different, aren't you?' she said, finally. 'They never
told me about you but – wait a minute, something gells – I
remember! You were madly anti-blood sports, weren't you?'

This time he could laugh for her directness, once you got used to it, was refreshing.

'I still am,' he said, 'it's a kink they never managed to straighten out but now they just pull my leg about it.'

'Ikey told us,' she said. 'I remember there was a family row over it at the time.' As she said this she recalled also that the Squire's eldest son, his child by the suffragette, had always worshipped Ikey Palfrey, and the memory of this bridged the gap between them so that her prickliness changed to a kind of relief. She said, before he could reply, 'Would you have a cigarette about you? That was my last and I'm an addict.'

He took out his case, a twenty-first birthday gift from his sister Mary and they lit up, moving by common consent across to the low wall that surrounded the lily pond; they were reconciled by each other's company to the uproar still issuing from the house. He said, rather glumly, 'Ah now, Ikey was one up on both of us! He would have *thought* the same as we do of that kind of horse play but it wouldn't have prevented him from joining in and outdoing the wildest of them! Then he would have gone to bed stone sober and laughed himself to sleep!'

'How do you know so much about him? You were still a child when he was killed.'

'I was fourteen-and-a-half and I should remember. The day they told me he was dead was the last time I shed tears. That was when Claire sent his last letter on.'

'A letter to you?'

'He wrote me many letters, fifty-three actually.'

'Describing what it was like out there?'

'About pretty well everything. I once thought of publishing them but then I thought better of it. It was the only legacy Ikey left to anyone, so why the hell should I share it with boneheads like The Pair, and the other idiots up there?'

'You don't share things at all, do you? Don't get me wrong, I'm not implying that you're mean but that you hate sharing yourself and anything important to you, anything you believe in or regard as fundamental?'

Her prodding among the private storehouse of his thoughts made him feel sufficiently resentful to stand up in protest but when she reached out quickly, and caught him by the hand, he suddenly felt more cheerful and expectant than for a very long time. He hardly knew why this should be so; he could not even see the girl's face clearly where she sat with her face turned away from the moonlight and he reminded himself that she was not a girl but a woman in her early thirties, widowed more than ten years ago. And yet there was an assurance in her voice and touch and as her hand tugged at him he sat down again saying, 'What the hell is wrong with us? What's eating the bloody heart out of us? Why is it we can't *be* young and *act* young, like all the others up there?'

'Well, I'm not young any more,' she said equably, 'but in your case I imagine it's part heredity and part on account of those letters Ikey Palfrey wrote you.'

'Do you remember my mother?'

'No, not really, but everybody in the Valley knew of her. I was about seven when she was headline news about here. She has significance for me because you might say that in a way she broke the ice for Keith.'

'How did she do that?'

'They were the only two rebels the Valley produced in a generation so it's fitting they should both leave their bones on the same battlefield, particularly as most of those who threw the brickbats are home and dry!'

She had given him the clue he had been fumbling for ever since her harsh laugh at his apology about the invitations. She had been embittered not so much by Keith's early death as by the patriotic persecution that had hounded him within range of the guns. His curiosity concerning her increased, perhaps nudged by the 'Oxford' accent she used, something utterly foreign to anyone growing up in the kitchen of Four Winds but something like the half-way voice of someone who had worked hard to shed the Valley burr.

'Keith was killed twelve years ago,' he said, 'what have you done with yourself all that time?'

'All kinds of things except marry again.'

'You don't sound like a Valley girl any more.'

She laughed, pleasantly this time. 'Should I? I left here for the North in 1914.'

'It always shows up in the vowels.'

She was silent for a moment. The racket in the house had died down and dancing had evidently been resumed for the sound of a waltz drifted across to them, a thin, warbling tune, pleasant to hear after the frenzied scream of the hunting-horns.

'What's that they're playing?' she asked suddenly.

'It's one of the talking-picture tunes called "I met her in Monterey".'

'Ah,' she said, 'one of their "if-only" tunes! You might think they were all in their 'fifties if you judged them on their dance music.'

'You haven't told me what happened to you.'

She said with what seemed to him something of an effort, 'The real waste of the war wasn't the blood, you know, it was the brains! That's the currency your generation will have to pay in. Keith had brains, not just exam-passing brains but the ability to select and interpret what he learned. After he was killed it seemed to me I should at least make some effort to compensate for the waste. I took a degree in Economics at Leeds University.'

It did not surprise him overmuch. There was something about her that suggested not only stamina but initiative.

'You went back to school?'

'Night school up to Matric standard; then I got a county grant. They go out of their way to cater for the morally earnest in the North, you know.'

'And then?'

'I ran headlong into the sex-barriers your mother spent her life storming. They are still there, you know, bristling with patronage, complacency and fly-buttons! I tried accountancy, then teaching, then actuarial work and flopped in all three! They say the professions are open to women now but it isn't true of course, not unless a woman is prepared to wear a tight skirt and leave all the decisions to the men, even the one about what time she likes to go to bed.'

He ignored all her jibes. 'What do you do now?'

'I supervise a chain of working men's clubs and do part-time secretarial work for a Member of Parliament. The clubs interest me. The MP doesn't, I'm afraid.'

'A Socialist MP?'

'A very temporary one; he'll be looking for a job himself before he's acquired a taste for House of Commons sherry.'

There were so many things he wanted to ask her – how secure was the recent Labour victory at the polls, how sincere was her avowed contempt for men of whatever political persuasion, and above all what remedies, if any, she prescribed for the anaemia of Western civilisation but at that moment the music stopped and he heard Stephen bawling for him from the terrace.

'I'll have to go,' he said. 'Won't you at least come up and have a drink of some sorts?'

'No thanks,' she said, 'I'll bring our trap round to the front if you tell my sister I'm waiting. I promised Mother I'd get her back at a reasonable hour and I suppose three o'clock is reasonable by Esther's standards.'

He offered his hand and she took it absentmindedly.

'Couldn't we meet again before I go back to town?' he suggested. 'I'm thinking of going on the staff of a new magazine but nothing's settled yet.'

'What kind of magazine?'

'A long-hair; it's to be called *The Forum*. Have you heard about it?'

'Yes,' she said, 'I've heard about it,' and then, with another crackle of candour, 'You could do a lot better than that, Simon!'

'Then let's meet and discuss it. Tomorrow evening? I can pick you up and we could have a bite to eat at The Mitre, in Paxtonbury.'

'Very well.' She sounded unenthusiastic but he was still young enough and vain enough not to care. He went off along the flagged wall calling to Stephen but as he went he wished he could have seen her in the light, especially when she was talking about Beanpole Horsey.

IV

The twins 'did their talking' that same week, before all traces of the celebrations had been removed and it was as well for them perhaps that Simon was still at home to act as a buffer, and also that they had had the foresight to summon reserve artillery in the person of Uncle Franz Zorndorff who had been talked into paying one of his rare visits to the Westcountry.

The old man, whom Paul declared was going to live for ever, appeared the Monday after the party, spruce and chipper as ever, although, by Paul's reckoning, he was now only a year short of ninety. He bowled up the drive soon after lunch in his huge, black Daimler, driven by a chauffeur wearing chocolate livery and Paul thought, as he watched the flunkey double round and give Franz an unnecessary arm as far as the porch, 'The old rascal loves ostentation everywhere but in his counting-house. In there he'd too damned careful to spend sixpence on a new blotter!' But he was pleased to see his father's old partner nonetheless and made a mental note to seek his advice about farm prices and land values. The wily old Croat might spend his entire life between his luxury flat in the West End and his disputable Thames-side scrapyard, but his advice on any subject remotely connected with money was worth having and usually worth following. He called from the garden door as Claire ran out on to the porch, 'Now what the devil brings you down here? Is the plague raging in town?'

The aged dandy waved his silver-topped cane and submitted gracefully to Claire's embrace, and then Simon and Mary ran out, and after them the twins whooping with glee, so that Paul began to suspect there was more in this than met the eye and went back into the study to rake among memories of recent hints on Claire's part connected in some way with the twins' harebrained schemes for making money – for 'getting aboard the jolly old bandwaggon' as they would have put it. Their bandwaggons, Paul reflected, were gaudier than Simon's but just as flimsily constructed and somehow far more calculated to irritate him. Simon's false starts had about them a few rags of dignity whereas the twins' were balloons full of blather that soared and were forgotten in a matter of days. The presence of Franz, however, made him more than usually curious to know what was brewing and he would have gone through into the hall had not Stephen appeared suddenly in the doorway and said, 'Uncle Franz is swilling tea, Gov! He says to leave him with Mother for a jiffy. Andy and I want to jaw first, is that okay with you?'

'You don't have to tell me something's afoot,' Paul said and grinned in spite of himself for it was impossible to resist the impact of The Pair. 'Come on in, both of you, and out with it! Your brother told me you had another rod in pickle for me.'

'Won't cost you a sou, Gov, and that's a fact,' said Stephen, sidling in and shutting the door after his twin. 'Isn't it a fact, Andy?'

'Fact,' said Andy, who habitually used fewer words than his brother.

'Well, what is it? Not another madcap scheme like that marine engineering lark, I hope.'

'Nothing like it,' said Stephen, sitting and throwing his long legs over the arm of the chair, 'this is a corker and Uncle Franz is right behind us, isn't that so, Andy?'

'Money in it,' Andy said, 'real money! No outlay either.'

'At least not from your standpoint, Gov,' Stevie added promptly.

'Well that's a change anyway,' Paul said watching their exchange of glances with sardonic amusement. 'I suppose it's too much to hope that you've decided to take my advice and pick up where you both left off at Agricultural College?'

'Look, Gov, farming's a dead duck. Honestly it is!'

'Dead and buried,' confirmed Andy. 'Ask any of your tenants, they'll soon get you up-to-date!'

He knew it was useless to argue with them. They had been over the ground so often since both had left school without matriculating; they had been over it, through it and round it, with and without benefit of supplementary arguments and suggestions contributed by Claire, John Rudd and the Principal of the County Agricultural College they had attended for a couple of terms. 'Well,' he said, resignedly, 'get to the point, I'm listening.'

'Uncle Franz has asked us to take over his Birmingham Branch,' said Andy, rather too bluntly it would seem for his brother's liking for Stevie swung round in protest but was checked by a gesture on the part of Andy, confirming Paul's theory that although Stephen was the more dominant of the two Andy was the brains of the alliance. He said, trying to keep his voice level, 'What the devil do you mean? *What* Birmingham branch? And branch of what, for God's sake?'

Stevie, already out of his depth, was content to leave the matter with his twin but Andy went on, deliberately, 'Uncle Franz has a yard up there. It's been open a year but it's being run by a crook and isn't paying off! It could tho', particularly with another slump around the corner. Uncle Franz thinks we'd make a go of it.'

'A "yard"?' Paul queried, repressing an impulse to shout. 'You mean – a *scrapyard*?'

'What else? Franz is the king of scrap, isn't he?'

'Yes,' Paul said, 'he is, and when I was a year or two older than you he did his best to make me the Crown Prince! I declined the honour and looking back on my life I count myself very fortunate!'

'But that's just it,' Andy said, leaning forward and speaking with great emphasis, 'looking back on *your* life, Gov! We're concerned with *our* lives and neither of us have the slightest inclination to vegetate down here!'

Out of the corner of his eye Paul saw Stephen wince but Andy, unrepentant, went on before either of them could comment. 'I don't mean that you've vegetated, Gov! Nobody around here could accuse you of that, but what you've done you wanted to do and were good at whereas Stevie and I, we're neither of us particularly bright and have to grab at what chances present themselves! I reckon we could tackle this lark and might even make a go of it! Anyway, we've talked it over and we'd like to try.'

It was a longish speech for Andy and left him a little breathless and red in the face. Paul said, as his mind still boggled at the project, 'You say you've talked it over? Do you mean with your mother, as well as with Uncle Franz and Simon?'

'No,' admitted Stephen, 'we thought of doing so but didn't. It didn't seem fair to involve her in case you blew your top!'

Strange that, Paul reflected, calming somewhat. Strange and a little touching that they should have reservations in that respect. It did them credit he supposed, but it also showed how accurately they had measured Claire's loyalty. Then, as he got his second wind, he had leisure to ponder the irony of the situation. From scrap to scrap in one generation! How Franz must relish the proposal after all he had heard from Paul on the subject of scrapyards over the last twenty-seven year! He said, very curtly, 'Very well, you've had your say. Run along and let me talk this over with that old rascal.'

'Don't you want to hear details?' Stevie asked and Paul said no but if he had to listen to them he preferred hearing them from Franz.

They got up gratefully enough but as they reached the door he relented slightly and said, 'Well, at least you didn't taunt me for using scrap money to keep the Valley alive since the war!'

'We thought of it, Gov, but decided it was below the belt!' Stevie said and they both vanished under cover of his grunt of laughter.

Paul went over to the window and looked down the curving line of the avenue of chestnuts. He still felt winded and was glad of a moment to compose himself before Franz appeared. From the angle of the window he could see the glint of afternoon sun on the ford and the shadow-play on the long swell of the Codsall stubble fields where they climbed to the watershed on the edge of the moor. He remembered the first time he had stood here and looked westward to the boundary, the day before the Lovell sale, in the long, dry summer of 1902, just before he had made up his mind to buy the place and years before those two young idiots had been thought of; well, it was pretty well full circle now, with all three of his sons opting out of the estate and the demands it made on a man. They would find their way, he supposed, but it would be their way not his or Claire's and there was, after all, some justice in their argument. He had a right to want at least one of them to follow on here but he had no right to insist on it and he knew before he heard Franz's step what the outcome would be. If he had a successor here it would have to be a grandson and even that, he felt, was unlikely.

The old man advertised himself with a cough, then shuffled in and stood with his back to the door. Paul thought he had seldom seen Franz so unsure of himself and it cheered him. It was not often he had the old man at a disadvantage.

'Well, Franz,' he said. 'I suppose they told you I took it on the chin, although I must say it makes nonsense of everything I had in mind for them. Was it their idea or yours?'

'Mine, Paul,' Franz said, 'and common decency demands I make some effort to hammer the motive into your thick skull.' He lowered himself gently into Claire's armchair and lit one of his long Dutch cheroots. He looked, Paul thought, like a centenarian gnome got up for a wedding – trim Van Dyke beard and sidewhiskers, razor-sharp creases in his striped trousers, puffed grey stock fixed with a diamond pin, gnarled fingers crowded with gold rings. He said, puffing a thin stream of bluish smoke, 'I *have* a motive and it's a disinterested one, I assure you.'

'You imply you agree with Andy when he says British agriculture is dead and buried?'

'No,' Franz said, 'but it soon would be if their sort had a hand in it! The fact is, Paul, my boy, you haven't made allowances for the gap between their generation and yours. It's a great deal wider than the usual gulf between father and son.'

'The thing that defeats me,' Paul said suddenly, 'is that those boys are good farming stock on their mother's side. Simon I could understand – any child of Grace would have to behave eccentrically but Claire's boys – old Derwent's grandchildren . . . !'

'It isn't eccentric to want to clear a fresh circle for yourself at twenty-one, Paul! After all, you did and were damned obstinate about it if I remember rightly! In any case, those boys are as far away from us as we were from men born during the French Revolution. You can blame the war for that but don't blame them.'

'But what the hell could they do in a Birmingham scrapyard? They'll only lose money and you'll ship them back to me the moment they do. I know you that well, Franz!'

'My boy,' said Franz, with the air of taut patience that always irritated Paul when they disagreed, as they did over almost everything they discussed. 'Why will you persist in looking on the scrap-metal industry as the prerogative of a man in a leather apron, driving a donkey-cart? Did you ever see me touch a piece of salvage? What will they do up there? They'll do what I tell them to do, make friends and contacts, hob-nob with steel-masters, used-car dealers, machinists, boiler-makers, wholesale meat-purveyors and wiremen! They'll join clubs, buy drinks, dress well, drive fast cars, back steeplechasers and flirt with women, I hope; anything calculated to broaden their outlook and nail down new sources. I've done precisely that for the past fifty years and you can't tell me that it hasn't paid dividends!'

'It sounds the kind of occupation well suited to them,' Paul said, 'but I hope you realise they can't add a column of figures three times without getting three different totals, and that their scrawl is usually illegible.'

'We maintain clerks and book-keepers,' said Franz, acidly. 'It wasn't to learn how to run my business that I made the effort to come here, Paul.'

'Neither was it to win my approval for my sons leaving me in the lurch,' said Paul cheerfully, 'for you've always been too damned arrogant to seek a blessing from anyone!'

Franz smiled, accepting the thrust as a compliment. 'I won't quarrel with you there, my boy, but the fact is I was wrong about you and admit it! The only real success is living one's life the way one wants to live it and, taken all around, you've been successful. Damn it, how many men have survived two wars and two marriages and stayed sane and solvent?'

'It wasn't just luck, Franz, it was often more a matter of holding on.'

'Whatever it was timing had something to do with it, which brings me to the only real point I want to make.'

'Well?'

'You had a twelve-year apprenticeship before the rot set in. You settled in here smug and cosy when the pound stood for something abroad, when everybody knew their place and you and all your bucolic friends could take tea on the lawn without the tablecloth blowing away and wasps crawling up your corduroys! You ought to remember that when you expect those boys to use your set of values! I'm nearly twice your age and I don't expect them to use mine! They have to make a new mould and they can't do it here growing prize artichokes and playing cricket on the green! Make 'em and they'll go sour on you, sour and rotten, I promise you! I've seen too many rich men's sons warped by Papa's conceits not to know what I'm talking about. I've given you good advice in the past – it was me who put you on to this place at the start of it all – and I'm giving you more now! Let 'em go, and Simon as well if he wants to, and do it with good grace! Let 'em find out for themselves what it's really like out there in among the grime and brickstacks. Either they'll adjust and do you credit or they'll come home with their tails between their legs, in which case you might found your neo-yeoman family after all!'

By the time Franz had finished and thrown his cheroot butt into the grate as a kind of full-stop Paul was chuckling, not so much because, in his heart, he agreed with the old man, but because his explosive vitality had the effect of cutting everything down to size and making Paul's initial distaste for the project seem as prejudiced as Henry Pitts' stonewall opposition to selling his plough horses and accepting the gift of a tractor. He said, pacifically, 'All right, Franz, you don't have to break a blood-vessel on their behalf! They're all three of age, anyway, and I couldn't stop them doing what they wanted. Good luck to them and to you and you're the one who is going to need it most! However, since you seem to be in such a pontifical mood, and since I rarely see you where we're not interrupted by the telephone, will you give *me* some advice? There are pretty clear signs of another slump setting in. Is it likely to be easier or more difficult to ride out than the last one, from my viewpoint I mean?'

'Now why the devil should you ask me that?' Franz said, playing at being ruffled. 'What do I know of livestock and land values this far from civilisation?'

'About a hundred times more than the best-informed local Agricultural Adviser who ever quoted an out-of-date white paper to me,' Paul told him, remembering that all the success the old man had achieved since landing in England as a political refugee had not made him immune to flattery.

'You're genuinely asking my advice? About selling or buying land?'

'About selling it; I've come out of things better than most farmers since the war but it's time I retrenched if I want to keep money in hand against emergencies. One of my tenants has been pestering me to sell for some time.'

'You trust him?'

'Good God, yes, he's my brother-in-law. It's Claire's brother, Hugh.'

'Then sell! Sell tomorrow! And retrench too if you have time!'

'It's as bad as that?'

'We're heading directly into the worst economic blizzard of our lifetime.'

'Oh come, Franz, you aren't that scared of another Socialist Government?'

'The Socialists have nothing to do with it this time. The Tories ought to be damned glad they're not holding the baby. As a matter of fact some that I know are!'

Paul was more interested than alarmed. He knew that the sensitive fingers of this dry old stick never left the economic pulse and recalled how, on the night of August 1st, 1914, he had been hauled out of bed to answer Franz's laconic telephone call urging him to insure against a long war; only Kitchener and Uncle Franz had been right about that! He said, 'If it isn't all this talk about the investors going abroad and taking their money out of reach of our tame Bolshies what's causing the anxiety?'

'The American Stock-market. You don't still cherish the fiction we're still the financial hub of the world, do you? We're in for a bad time, the whole lot of us!'

'Well,' said Paul resignedly, 'the first to feel it will be the farmers.'

'Oh don't try that one on me,' Franz said testily. 'I've never seen a poor one yet and at least they can always eat! By this time next year that'll be a privilege among the unemployed.'

'Then why are you branching out in Birmingham? Wouldn't you do well to retrench?'

The old man smiled and stood up, brushing the ash from his faultlessly cut jacket.

'I always maintained, Paul, that you were not a man of business and certainly not of the scrap business! In a month those boys of yours will make rings round you. The scrap market is the vulture in the flock. That's why I can smell carrion long before anyone else's nostrils twitch. Sell to your brother-in-law and count yourself fortunate. I would advise you to pretend to sell reluctantly and keep the price up but I know your Nonconformist conscience would torment you if you didn't tell the buyer everything I've said to you today! Besides, you have a duty to your wife's family, I suppose, you owe her something for putting up with you all these years! What time do you dine in this wilderness?'

'We don't,' Paul told him, 'we have high tea at six-thirty and don't expect any frills.'

The Croat took out a large gold watch and studied it. 'Time for a nap,' he said, affably. 'Half-an-hour with you, my friend, is as good as a day's grind.'

He went out with his curious shuffling step and Paul, still grinning, escorted him as far as the landing, pointing the way to the guest room. As he descended the stairs his grin broadened. Simon, Andrew, Stephen, and behind them, Claire, were all gazing up at him from the threshold of the hall. They looked like a group of anxious children whose ball has just sailed over an alien fence and were calculating the risks of retrieving it.

Chapter Twelve

I

Paul remembered, looking back on that time, that Franz had used the word 'blizzard' and had seemed to mean it but the depression that resulted in three million unemployed in Britain, and had most of its cities and great areas of the countryside sick and gasping by 1931, did not visit the Valley as a blizzard, or anything like a blizzard. Instead it crept in from the north and east like a malign, leisurely blight, touching first one family then another, plucking at a farm here, a man there, leaving any number of small, scabrous wounds that were slow to heal and seemed at first unrelated to one another or to hurts such as those caused, say, by the war. Yet, in some instances, the wounds were just as lethal. At Periwinkle, for example, which decayed structurally, and in the relationship between the Big House and High Coombe, where the period of stress left a scar that never did heal while there was a breath in the body of Paul Craddock and his wife, formerly Claire Derwent.

Echoes of the Wall Street crash reached the Valley by courtesy of Fleet Street. During the autumn Stevie and Andrew left for what Paul thought of as its storm-centre, the industrial Midlands, but when they reappeared on Christmas Eve that same year they did not look like the survivors of the economic disaster. They roared up in a red MG sports car, with long silk scarves round their necks and golf clubs protruding from an overloaded boot. They rampaged about the Valley for a spell shouting at everyone they encountered, coming home at four in the morning and spending freely in the Paxtonbury pubs. Then they disappeared again without anyone having the least idea what they did in Birmingham or how they acquired sports car, golf clubs or the skill to use them.

It was a hard winter. Snow fell early and Valley noises were muted for a period of weeks; then, with the arrival of a cheerless, seeping spring, came news that foxes were active west of Hermitage Wood and that luckless Elinor Codsall had lost thirty-seven point-of-lay birds in a single night.

Paul went over to pay her hunt compensation, knowing that she was having a struggle with the price of eggs at an all-time low and her son Mark laid up with a broken leg caused by a motor-cycle skid during the cold snap. He was accustomed, by now, to Elinor's pessimism but was puzzled by the way she took her loss of hens to heart, as though the dog-fox who got into the run had singled her out for special persecution.

"Er made straight for me, zame as all bad luck do!' she said and when Paul tried to laugh her out of her grievance she said, challengingly, 'Well, baint it zo? Baint I alwus zo? My man was the first to get called up an' be blown to tatters! Then us struggles on 'till that red-headed bitch Gloria Pitts comes yer raisin' creation about me an' that German! Then us loses the pigs in the first voot an' mouth outbrek an' when us is making headway again Mark has to break his bliddy leg. Now, to top all, nigh on forty point-o'-lay crossbreds, the best I ever reared, makes one meal for bliddy Reynard!'

There was no comforting her and she continued to grumble through the summer when Mark was back at work but likely to be slightly lame for the rest of his life for the accident left him with one leg an inch shorter than the other.

The Codsalls perked up for a time after Paul found them a hired hand called Rutter but after a few months at Periwinkle the new man had an invitation from his brother-in-law in Tasmania and announced that farming here was a mug's game and he was getting out while the going was good. After that Paul noticed that land Will Codsall had patiently reclaimed from the moor began to go back, so that before the year was out Periwinkle was reduced to its original holding, a mere sixty acres and although Elinor was only paying a pre-war rent she fell behind in that and Paul, only too aware of the narrow profit margin of more prosperous farms, could not be persuaded by John Rudd to find a billet for Mark Codsall somewhere' else and cut his losses by letting Elinor live on in the old Hardcastle farmhouse while her land was divided between Four Winds and Hermitage.

It was the final piece of advice John was to give him. In the event the Periwinkle problem was solved by a near miracle but before Paul could justify his extreme reluctance to do as the agent suggested John was dead.

If a man can be said to have died thoroughly at peace with his world this was achieved by John Rudd. He died in the cramped bedroom of the lodge that he had occupied ever since the Lovells had left and in the presence of the only three people in his life who mattered to him, his wife Maureen, the slim, fair-haired boy, whom she had astonished everyone by producing soon after her late marriage, and Paul Craddock, whom John always claimed to have restored to him a purpose in life.

He caught a severe chill in early autumn and coughing aggravated his heart condition. On the third day after he had taken to his bed it was arranged that he should be admitted to Whinmouth Hospital and Maureen sent for Paul asking him to come before the ambulance was due. Paul was shocked at John's appearance. He lay propped up by pillows looking more than his age and his gruff voice was reduced to a dry whisper. Yet he seemed philosophic about his chances of survival. 'Tried to tell Maureen to leave me be,' he said, 'but she fussed, so I couldn't be bothered arguing. Prefer to die here if I've got to go. Been my life best part of fifty years.'

Paul reminded him that Maureen's purpose in transferring him to hospital was his need of an oxygen tent but he made no attempt to indulge in conventional sick-bed denials. He knew Rudd better than that and recognised an old, tired and moderately satisfied man when he saw one. John went on, after some coughing, 'Should like to have left you on a crest instead of deep in a damned trough. Think you'll struggle out of it?'

'We've always bobbed up before, John,' Paul told him, 'and there's no sense in you worrying about it at your time of life.'

The agent's old-fashioned moustache twitched. 'You're a damned sight tougher than you look, Paul,' he said grudgingly. 'A Boer bullet in your knee, lump of shrapnel in your head, your ribs bashed in that time of the wreck, and this white elephant on your back! But you wouldn't have it otherwise, would you?'

'I could have done without the bullet and the shrapnel,' Paul said, 'but I'm not nearly as bothered as you seem to be by current land values and farm prices. These things come and go like women's fashions.'

'Talking of fashions . . .' whispered John and stopped as his son came in with a draught of medicine, put it down on the bedside table and said, in a sickroom voice, 'Mother has just heard on the 'phone that the ambulance will be a bit late, Father. It seems they're clearing up after a road smash on the main road, a bad one.'

'Good,' John croaked, 'hope it keeps 'em busy all night!' and as the boy tiptoed out and he reached out to pick up his medicine, 'I wish to God he and his mother would be as realistic as you, Paul. She's tough enough with her patients but she clucks all day long over me! Like a schoolmaster spoiling his own children!' and he chuckled at his own modest joke.

Paul said, for something to say, 'You were making some comment on fashions.'

'Ah yes,' John muttered, his medicine glass clutched in a hand that shook so much that Paul reached across to steady it, 'it made me think of bosoms!'

'Whose bosom in particular?'

'Everybody's! Time was when every woman about the Valley tortured herself to look like an hour-glass. Now every damned one of them, your wife included, delights in making herself look like a tube!'

It struck Paul as so grotesque that bluff old John Rudd should beguile the time awaiting his ambulance by jesting about bosoms that he laughed outright and the patient, catching the infection of laughter, joined in so that for a moment they were both comparatively young again, riding together through Shallowford on their way home from a day's hunting before the war. Then, with tragic suddenness, John's laugh changed to a rasping cough and the draught of medicine shot over the coverlet as he bent forward spluttering and groping with outflung arms. Maureen rushed into the room and after her the boy but it was over before they could hoist him back into his former position.

It was sobering, Paul thought, to witness the extremity of their distress, for although death was a new experience to the boy his mother must have seen a thousand die in almost identical circumstances. She looked across at Paul with her face ravaged and Paul, taking control, motioned to the boy to leave which he did at once, trying in vain to stem an unmanly flow of tears. Paul said, 'He loathed the prospect of dying outside the Valley, Maureen! He told me so the minute I came in here. Surely you must have known what his chances were!'

She made a gesture of hopelessness and turned her back on the disordered bed, crossing to the window and opening it a notch so that a swishing wind threading the chestnuts banished the stuffiness of the little room. Paul took advantage of the moment to lay the body straight and arrange the sheet, after which, thinking to give her son something to occupy his mind, he called down and gave instructions to cancel the ambulance and notify the hospital. He turned back to Maureen, still standing by the window. 'Can I get you a drink, Maureen?' and when she shook her head, 'He had a good life once the Lovells went out of it and especially good after you came to share it.'

'He told you that?'

'He implied it often enough. It was a tremendous piece of luck for him to find you about half-way through.'

'For me too, Paul,' she said, and he saw that she had herself in hand again.

There seemed nothing more to say, or not at this stage, and when Maureen indicated she would like to stay a while and compose herself before she went back to the boy, he left without saying anything to his godson who was talking hoarsely into the telephone. He went out into the drive and found the night warmish but gusty, with only a sliver of moon over the Bluff and a hurrying breathlessness in the south-westerly wind that promised more rain, possibly an autumn gale. He went through the open iron gates to the ford which was high and noisy and stood there a moment gulping down mouthfuls of the moist air, quickly coming to terms with the sharp break in a line of continuity that led right back to the blazing afternoon thirty years ago, when he had first trotted along this road with John. That was all that John had cared about – continuity, pattern, ordered progress and it was that, he supposed, that had linked them from the beginning, building a relationship that had resulted in each of them having complete confidence in the other and in Shallowford as an institution. Yet he remembered John telling him before the war that he no longer needed an agent, that he was perfectly capable of running this place alone. It wasn't true of course, no single man's care and capital could nourish the Valley, no matter how single-minded and dedicated that man might be. It needed a dozen or more and they were getting fewer as time went on. Some were not being replaced as surely as Arthur Pitts at Hermitage had been and Edward Derwent, his father-in-law at High Coombe but he had been lucky so far. Of the seven farms only Periwinkle and Four Winds were in rough water, the one because it had always been too small and inadequately staffed, and the other because Eveleigh's eldest son had been killed in the war and none of the others seemed interested in carrying on. He stood there in the wet wind making a sort of accounting to the dead man in the lodge. Prices were atrocious, more and more skilled men were drifting into the towns, hedging and ditching was in arrears because of labour shortage, reliefs and government subsidies were unrealistic, and old men like Henry Pitts and the failing Eveleigh were slow to take to new methods and develop new markets like those of sugar-beet, cereal wheat and peas for local canning. If it were not for Paul's policy of keeping rents at a minimum figure, and feeding fresh capital into the estate by way of pedigree livestock, farm machines hired out at nominal rates and free gifts of chemical manure to those who would use it, the estate would have contracted long ago and land would have been sold off to keep what remained in good heart. As it was only Hugh Derwent's High Coombe had broken away and even that was still in the family and might return some time seeing that Hugh was a bachelor and likely to remain one. John had seemed worried in his last moments regarding his ability to hold on to the place and now Paul wondered if he had convinced him of his determination and wished that he had emphasised it more. 'Well,' he muttered to himself, as he turned for home, 'he ought to know me after all this time! I'll see it through one way or another until one of the boys comes to his senses, or one of the girls marries a sensible chap and has children to pass it to!' and feeling renewed rather than depressed he repassed the lodge and lifted his hand in salute to the man who lay behind the little latticed window. It was very difficult to think of old John as dead.

II

John Rudd was buried on one of those left-over days from late summer when the broad, steep street leading down to the church glowed in pale sunlight that suggested rather than provided warmth for the mourners. After the committal, when he was heading for the lych-gate to rejoin Claire (no women had attended at the graveside although many had been present in the church), Paul found himself noting any number of odd, inconsequential things that John might have remarked upon had he been in a tranquil mood – a squadron of rooks circling the church elms, the drunkard's flight of a bumble bee who had evidently lost his calendar, the curious, crab-like progress of old Aaron Stokes, the reed-gatherer, who must, by Paul's reckoning, have attended two hundred funerals during his eighty-odd years in the village but his reflections were cut short by confrontation with young Mark Codsall, yet another godchild, at the fork in the church path and Mark's apologetic – 'Could I have a word with 'ee, Squire? Worn taake but a moment; tiz about Mother!'

He turned aside, wondering if this meant fresh trouble but Mark seemed no more than bashful and said, as they drew aside from the stream of mourners, 'She's thinkin' on gettin' married again, Squire! Tiz true! I baint jokin'! But it'll mean her leaving Periwinkle an' she abben the nerve to tell 'ee! Anyway, tiz all happened zo zudden I'm praper mazed meself, that I be!'

Paul said, 'I'm absolutely delighted to hear it, Mark, and so, I'm sure, would your father have been. She needs to make a new life for herself and that's been her main trouble but I hadn't the faintest notion she . . .' and he stopped, noticing that Mark was now flushed with embarrassment.

'Nor had I, nor our Floss, nor any of us,' Mark added, 'but on'y me's in favour of it! Them others, they don't understand, havin' gone off an' lived away so long, but I remember the bloke well enough. Reckon I ought to – he saved my life when I was a tacker.'

'Who did?' asked Paul, more mystified than ever and the young man blurted out that the German prisoner who had been loaned to the farmer twelve years before had reappeared on the doorstep a fortnight ago and informed his mother that he was not only a widower but a prosperous one, having inherited an extensive market-garden from an uncle in some unpronounceable German province like 'Shinivwig'.

'Schleswig? Schleswig-Holstein?' suggested Paul and Mark said yes, that was it, and Elinor had asked him in for a meal and afterwards they had driven off to Paxtonbury in his hired Essex saloon and that his mother had 'shown up that night in a praper old tizzy, laughin' an' cryin',' and that since then the German, who was called Willi Meyer, had called every day and had finally taken Mark aside and asked him his views on the prospect of having a German stepfather.

'Good God!' said Paul laughing and then, recalling where he was, straightened his face. 'What did you say to that?'

'I told un 'twas no biziness o' mine,' Mark said, 'seein' 'er was old enough to marry whom 'er plaised! Point is, I got no hankering to stay on there meself. I bin courtin' Liz Pascoe and Liz has zet her heart on one o' they new houses in Nun's Bay and woulden give us a thank-you for our ratty old plaace.

Besides,' he looked a little ashamed, 'I baint zet on varmin'
like Mother and Dad were, I'd as zoon try something wi'
steady money, zo long as it had to do wi' driving and mebbe
a chance to ride once in a while.'

Paul knew very well what Mark was hinting at. Chivers,
the Shallowford groom, had died a year ago and had never
been replaced and Mark Codsall was a judicious compromise
between the post-war motor-clad youngsters and the older
men who still liked a day's hunting. He said, on impulse,
'How would it suit you to move into Chivers' old quarters
at Shallowford and be our chauffeur, groom and odd-job man
in the garden? The stable flat has mod cons, tell Liz, and it's a
damned sight more comfortable than any of those jerry-built
bungalows at Nun's Bay. You won't make a fortune but I
daresay you'd earn more than you've been getting lately.'

'It'd suit me fine,' Mark said, his eyes shining, 'Liz an' me
could get married zoon as mother but . . . well . . . dornee
mind about her marryin' a Jerry, Squire?'

'Not in the least,' said Paul, 'a Jerry saved my life soon
after that prisoner-of-war tackled your snakebite. Would she
be embarrassed if I rode over and wished her luck?'

'Well, I daresay 'er'd blush an' carry on a bit,' Mark admitted, grinning, 'but if I was you I'd call unexpected an'
catch 'em at it! He's always around dinner-times but you
worn have no trouble with 'ee, 'ee's a nice enough chap,
even if he does click his heels and bob about all the time.
He's got our lingo off too! Damned if he don't sound like he'd
swallowed a bliddy dictionary sometimes!'

Paul rode over to Periwinkle about noon the next day and
it cheered him to see the astonishing change in Elinor Codsall,
who flitted out to the gate in a way that reminded him of the
Elinor Willoughby wooed by Will Codsall over at Deepdene all
those years ago. Her greying hair was neatly dressed and her
apron (a piece of sacking when he had last called) was clean,
frilled and gaily patterned. She was so shy and excited that
she whisked him into the presence of the tall, sombre Willi
Meyer, a man about her own age and then disappeared into the
scullery like a rabbit into a hedge burrow. Fortunately, at this

point, Mark stumped into the kitchen and dispensed tankards
of home-brewed cider, so that Paul and the German soon
found common ground in battlefield reminiscences which led,
naturally enough, to an expression of Meyer's doubts about
the local reaction to the marriage between a German and the
widow of a man killed by Germans fourteen years before,
explaining earnestly that Elinor herself seemed entirely free
of prejudice and regarded the entire conflict as an act of folly
on the part of their respective rulers. As for him, he did not
blame the luckless Kaiser (as most English people did) so
much as the Junkers, who had always been a thorn in the
side of the South Germans. He himself, he hastened to add,
had nothing but admiration for the British, who had treated
him with far more lenience than he had been led to expect
after his capture near St Quentin. All the time he talked he
stood stiffly to attention, making his points with a series of
stiff half-bows from the waist and every time he bowed Mark
Codsall choked into his cider. Paul could not help comparing
Meyer's elaborate courtesy with the bucolic manners of poor
old Will, his predecessor, and it crossed his mind, whilst listening patiently to the German's preamble, that it was not every
woman who could achieve such a range in husbands. This led
him to reflect upon what this punctilious Saxon could find to
admire in the tubby, middle-aged widow, still holding out in
the scullery, or, for that matter, how Elinor herself could have
taken his proposal seriously. The German answered one of
these questions almost at once, declaring that he had forgotten
neither Elinor's kindness when he was a prisoner nor her skill
in raising poultry and it seemed to Paul that his determination
to take her back to Schleswig with him was prompted largely
by her promise of extreme usefulness when he got her there.
In Germany, as in England, he pointed out, poultry was the
prerogative of the farmer's wife. He had no children and
after eight years as a widower looked upon marriage as an
insurance against lonely old age. What did the Graf think?
Was it not a very sensible arrangement for both parties?

Paul explained, as well as he could, that he had no juris-
diction whatever over Elinor, that she was his tenant and had

been for nearly thirty years but that his interest in her was limited to that of an old friend. If she was anxious to become Frau Meyer he could give assurance that nobody in the Valley, much less himself, would think any the less of her and that the majority, he felt, would wish them luck. The people round here, he told the German, now resented the French more than the Germans, particularly since it had been made public that the French Government charged rent for the use of track and rolling stock employed to repatriate British wounded, whereas in recent years, especially since the publication of Remarque's *All Quiet*, anti-German hysteria had spent itself.

'Ach, so!' said Meyer, thoughtfully, 'that is good to hear from the lips of an English Graf! It has never been otherwise in my country. Tommy fed our children in the Ruhr and in defiance of orders, yes?'

He seemed to regard this as a suitable point to terminate the interview, clicking his heels and conjuring a blushing Elinor from the scullery with a despotic clap of his hands. Elinor's prompt response to the summons released another spring of conjecture in Paul's mind, for he reflected how, when Will Codsall was nominated master here, it was common knowledge in the Valley that Elinor wore the trousers. Elinor said Willi was anxious to get married before his return early in the New Year and this meant that everybody concerned would have to hustle. Mark could take what he liked of the furniture and the remainder would be put up to auction for she was taking nothing but her linen.

'John Rudd's notion was to split Periwinkle acres between Hermitage and Four Winds,' Paul told her, wondering if Elinor would resent seeing half her acreage pass to the Pitts' family, for she had never forgiven Gloria for her unique expression of patriotism during the war.

'Tiz your land, Squire,' Elinor said carelessly, 'and tiz for you to parcel it out but I'd be plaised if you could see your way to givin' me away when the time comes! Would 'ee now? Would Mrs Craddock think it zeemly?'

'I'm sure she would,' Paul said, 'but wouldn't your brother Francis like to do it?'

'Giddon no,' said Elinor, impatiently. 'Francis baint had collar an' tie on zince Father died and he give up attending chapel! Us'd zooner it was you, woulden us, Willi?'

'Please?' said Willi, never having mastered the Devon dialect, whereupon Paul translated and the German said it would be an honour, none of his family having had a Graf present at their weddings.

'For God's sake what *is* a "Graf"?' demanded the indulgent Mark but Paul said he would explain later and they parted on a cordial note, Elinor accompanying Paul to the post where he had tethered his skewbald.

'What do 'ee really think, Squire?' she asked as he put his foot in the stirrup, 'do 'ee think I'm mazed to go marryin' a forriner at my time o' life? I dorn mind if you says zo tho' my mind's zet on it, whether or no!'

'I think it's a splendid arrangement,' Paul said, laughing, 'so long as you're sure you'll be happy in a strange land, away from all the folk you've grown up with. He's a thorough decent chap but I suppose you've considered the obvious difficulties, language and so on?'

'Arr,' she said thoughtfully, 'I have that and I daresay I'll be terrible homesick come springtime an' autumn but a woman's plaace is where her man has his work. If old Will had up an' trotted off to Australia that time his folks tried to come between us I would ha' followed to whistle an' neither Arabella nor my folks could have stopped me! Zeems away off, that ole fuss dorn it, like another lifetime? To tell 'ee the real truth, Squire, Willi Meyer showin' up like he did saved me from actin' about as stupid as Will's father! Things was closin' in like they do sometimes an' you can't fight free of 'em like you can when youm young an' spry!'

'You're as young and spry as the best of us,' Paul told her and then, looking down at her earnest face, his curiosity broke the bounds of propriety and he said, 'Was there ever anything between you and Willi Meyer when he was working here during the war? I don't give a damn one way or the other, but *was* there?' and was not the least surprised when a sly grin lit up her face and she said, cheerfully, 'Arr, naught but slap an' tickle in the barn a time or two, Squire, but dornee let Gloria Pitts know, will 'ee now?'

'What kind of a fool do you take me for?' Paul said, chuckling, and before he swung himself into the saddle he turned and kissed her weather-roughened cheek, not waiting to witness her surprise but riding down over the weed-grown western slope to the track that led to the river road. 'By George!' he said to himself, as he broke into a trot, 'what the devil do any of us know about the people we live among? I don't think I ever thought of that story Henry told me about the fight in the Periwinkle kitchen without choking with indignation but it seems Gloria had been right after all! Maybe everyone was a little mad those days, even Claire with that ass at the camp, the one who came close to prompting me to tan the hide off her!' He went on down to the river, riding into a flurry of rain and feeling a good deal more cheerful than he had for a long time.

III

There were three Valley weddings that winter but only those of Elinor Codsall and her unlikely German, and Mark Codsall and his Liz Pascoe, were on home ground. The third, a ceremony entirely without trimmings, took place in a Manchester Registry Office on the same day as Elinor's wedding.

Valley gossips were wrong when they told each other Squire Craddock had refused to attend the wedding of his eldest son, Simon, to Rachel, the widowed daughter of his tenant, Norman Eveleigh, and they were equally wrong surmising that neither Squire nor Squiress had been aware of the match until it was accomplished. Their failure to attend was due to the clash of dates and no other reason. Paul had been given a bare twenty-four hours' notice of the wedding by telephone but would have hurried north, grumpily enough no doubt, had he not felt that Elinor Codsall had prior claim on him.

Simon telephoned his father and stepmother with reluctance. Only the prospect of an eve-of-wedding quarrel with his fiancée got him into the 'phone booth for her insistence seemed to him maddeningly illogical having regard to her refusal to notify her own parents. She could not make him understand that their cases differed or that she had never found grace to forgive her father for his bitter opposition to her marriage to Keith Horsey during the war. She and Norman Eveleigh had never exchanged a word since that day and she still held him partly responsible for Keith's death, which was even more illogical. It was not Eveleigh's bellicose patriotism that had made Keith Horsey a conscientious objector, nor his sour nagging that had encouraged Keith to enlist as a stretcher-bearer instead of sweating it out in gaol. The rift remained however, and when Simon tried to strike a bargain with her, offering to delay the wedding a week and invite all four parents, she refused point blank but still held to her view that Paul should be notified and given the chance to attend.

'It's a damned lopsided arrangement,' Simon grumbled, 'but I'll do it if you insist. I've got nothing against the Gov'nor or your father and I don't see much sense in asking either of them to make a five-hundred-mile round trip in mid-winter to attend a five-minute civil ceremony! However, if we ask one we should ask the other. What on earth has our difference in age to do with it?'

Rachel who, since his proposal, had not drawn attention to the fact that she was eight years his senior flashed out at this.

'It hasn't really any bearing at all except, possibly, that you were a child of ten when my father made everybody at home wretched about my marrying Keith! Can't you get it into your thick Craddock-Lovell skull that I still find his attitude unforgivable?'

'There's your mother,' he argued, 'you've nothing against her, have you?'

'Marian's very loyal,' she told him, 'and she'd stick by Father no matter what but that's as it should be, particularly since the bite has gone out of him! Do as I say! Go into the kiosk and tell your father when and where, for if you don't I'm hanged if I won't change my mind after all!'

He capitulated at that. He knew her by now, a woman of strange inflexibility in whom infinite prejudice was mixed with infinite compassion in about equal proportions. He had seen her in draughty church institutes and parish halls, raging against social injustices to an apathetic audience of a dozen people, and he had watched her help an incompetent midwife deliver a child in a bug-infested tenement where whole families lived in single rooms on diets of fish, chips, and bread and margarine when they were lucky. He had admired her, worshipped her, and sometimes feared her, knowing that dedication to a cause to the degree that Rachel Horsey was dedicated could make sentimental mush of his own dilettante socialism. He went into the booth and dialled trunks, watching her through the streaked panes as she stood with her coat collar turned up against the wind and her brooding eyes fixed on some point beyond the spot where the railway bridge laid a shadow across glistening setts. He felt desperately sorry for her, standing there in the cold and drizzle, sorry and half-choked with a range of emotions in which awe and a deep yearning to share her life were the two extremes. The operator told him he was through and he heard Paul's voice on the line.

'Hullo? Craddock here! Who is it?'

'Simon.'

'*Simon!*' The voice sounded agreeably surprised. 'Are you coming home?'

'Soon, Gov'nor, but I've got news. It'll rock you but it's nothing unpleasant.'

'Are you all right?' The voice was urgent now.

'Sure I'm all right. I rang to say I was getting married to Rachel Horsey.'

'Married?' The voice sounded incredulous. 'For God's sake – *When?*'

'The day after tomorrow.'

'Day after *tomorrow*! Great God! Wait a minute, I'll fetch Claire . . .'

'No don't, Gov! No, I don't mind her knowing – of course I don't – but, well . . . I haven't any more change and Rachel is standing in the rain. Can you come up? It's only a Register

Office "do" but Rachel seems to think you and Claire should be invited. Otherwise I'd have written and left it at that! Are you still there?'

Paul's voice broke the silence and sounded a little less cordial, Simon thought. 'Yes, I'm still here. Listen, I've got to give Elinor Codsall away the same day. Can't you postpone it?'

'No Gov, I'm afraid not. We had to fit it in with all kinds of things up here, including a bye-election. *Who* did you say you've got to give away?'

'Elinor Codsall of Periwinkle. The widow! She's marrying a Jerry she met during the war! I've promised and she's relying on me. I honestly don't see how I could let her down flat at the last moment.'

'Of course you couldn't!' Simon tried to keep the relief out of his voice. 'You go ahead and wish her the best from both of us.'

'It's damned sickening tho'. Claire will be very disappointed. You say Rachel Eveleigh is there?'

'Right here but she isn't Rachel Eveleigh, Gov. She's a widow too.'

'Of course, I'd forgotten.' He had forgotten, not only the fact that she had been a bride of one of those rushed war-time weddings but also that she must be years older than Simon, he could not say how many until he consulted Claire or the diary.

'Do her parents know?'

'Not yet,' said Simon, 'she's writing her mother.'

'I see!' He understood the girl's prejudice far better than his son. He had thought of that strange contretemps at Four Winds several times since Simon had written saying he was engaged in some kind of social work in association with the girl. Yet it had never occurred to him for a moment that one of Norman Eveleigh's daughters would end up as his daughter-in-law and bewilderment prevented him from getting a clear mental picture of the girl. There were so many Eveleighs. There had always been so many Eveleighs, ever since that awful night he had hammered on Norman's door in the teeth of a south-westerly gale and told him his employer was hanging from a beam of the barn. Then he remembered something relevant. That was the night Simon had been born, and one of the children who had peeped over the banisters and been shooed back to bed must have been the Rachel, now 'waiting in the rain'. He said, emphatically, 'Listen, Simon, if the operator cuts in tell her to reverse the charges. Get Rachel into the box, you idiot, boy!'

There was a long pause and he heard Claire calling from the library, 'Who is it, Paul?'

'Simon! He's 'phoning from Manchester,' and she came into the hall as Paul heard a crisp, unrecognisable voice on the line. 'Mr Craddock? You remember me?'

'Good Lord, of course I remember you, Rachel! Listen, before we're cut off. Would you like me to go over and tell Marian? I'm sure she'd appreciate it.'

There was a brief pause, during which Claire joggled his elbow and he shook her off, impatiently. 'Did you hear, Rachel?'

'Yes,' she said quietly, 'I'd like that, Mr Craddock, and tell her I'll write. I'm sorry you can't come but we both understand – and, Mr Craddock . . .'

'Yes?'

'I'll look after him well. You don't have to worry.'

'I hope he'll look after you, Rachel – but thank you, I . . . I'm happy about it, even if it is a bit sudden, and I'm sure Mrs Craddock will be. Can we ring you anywhere later?'

'Yes, you can. We're going to town just for the week-end to a conference actually,' and she gave him a number that he jotted down on the pad.

'There are the pips,' she said, 'don't reverse! Simon's getting wet now! Good-bye, Mr Craddock.'

'Good-bye, my dear. And good luck, both of you.'

The wire clicked and began to purr. Slowly he replaced the receiver and turned to meet Claire's bewildered gaze.

'Who on earth was it? You said "Simon", didn't you?'

'Yes,' he said, 'it was Simon who called but that was Rachel Horsey, née Eveleigh.'

'Eveleigh's second daughter? The one who married the parson's son and never came back?'

He nodded. 'What do you remember about her?'

'Only that she was a pretty girl with a generous share of Norman Eveleigh's pigheadedness. Why?'

'She'll need it, she's marrying Simon the day after tomorrow,' and as she gasped and her hand shot to her mouth as it always did when she was surprised, 'Come out of this damned draught and I'll tell you what little I know. Fix me a drink too. It's a wonder I'm not a dipsomaniac with my crazy family.'

Simon's letter duly arrived, a breezy statement of fact, 'Like an extract from one of his damned statistical reviews on malnutrition,' Paul muttered, but he made no such comment about a letter Marian Eveleigh handed to him a day or so later, after he had ridden over and told her the news. Marian was flushed and excited, although half-inclined to apologise for her daughter having married into the Squire's family but it seemed to Paul that Norman, her husband, had some difficulty taking it in. He kept shaking his head and fidgeting with his hands and his only remark when his wife repeated the news into his one sound ear was, 'Arr, Rachel's alwus gone her orn way! Nothin' new about that, be there?'

When Marian walked him to the yard he said, 'How is he these days, Marian? He doesn't seem too great,' and she said, defiantly, that he could still do a good day's work but that the deafness that had followed his partial stroke a year or so ago sometimes gave people the idea that he was wool-gathering. The Lady Doctor, she went on, using the term the Valley had applied to Maureen Rudd since 1906, had urged him to give up work altogether but she knew this would be fatal to him. 'He'd only moon about and die of boredom,' she said, 'so let un carry on, long as he can. As to our Rachel, she's a hard one and no mistake! She's never forgotten that war-time bust-up. Maybe this'll make a difference. I wouldn't like to think they kept it up until he was taaken.'

She seemed, Paul thought, resigned to him dying although he could hardly be more than seventy and looked strong enough physically. She was equally resigned to tending him and sticking by him, having found it easy to erase the memory of a war-time peccadillo with the land-girl who had once moved into her bedroom and been ejected by Claire. He said, briefly, 'Well, I don't know what you think about it, Marian, but I hope you'll believe me when I tell you I think Rachel is what Simon needs. She's had plenty of trouble of her own and I daresay she'll mother him and persuade him to settle down somewhere.'

'None of 'em will ever do that be our standards, Squire,' she replied, 'and I don't reckon it's their fault altogether. Nothing's ever been quite the same since, has it?'

'No,' said Paul, cheerfully, for he heard this kind of remark every day from one or other of the older generation, 'but there's a good deal I'm not sorry to see gone. Taken all round people are kinder and at least we're unlikely to see another war again, so we must have learned something from it.'

'Lord God, I do hope you're right,' said Marian fervently. 'Would you like to see the letter she writes me if 'er does?'

'Yes indeed,' Paul said, privately hoping it would be more explicit than Simon's telephone conversation.

It wasn't, or not much. Marian sent it over a day or so later and it looked fat enough to be informative until he realised that the envelope contained a sealed letter addressed to him as well as a brief letter to Mrs Eveleigh. He thought, as he took it out, 'Now why the devil didn't she write direct? She hasn't forgotten where we live has she?' but he ceased to wonder when he saw, written slantways across the inside envelope, *'For Mr Paul Craddock! Personal!'* and his jaw dropped at the first paragraph, which read: 'Dear Squire Craddock, – I'm sorry, I can't think of you as a plain "Mr" although, to be frank, I wouldn't like you to think I subscribe to patronage of any kind!' His curiosity overcame his surprise as he read on – 'I haven't told Simon I'm writing for obvious reasons and therefore enclose this with Mother's letter. I wouldn't have thought of writing if I hadn't got to know Simon well enough to understand *you* far more than I did in the old days, when I was a child growing up in the Valley. Ordinarily I set my face against landlords of all kinds but you are an exception apart from the fact (whether we like it or not) we're now related. Any prejudice I might have had in your respect has gone

long ago and not only because – as I say – I've learned about
you through Simon, but also because you've never shown my
family, particularly my mother, anything but consideration
and therefore you don't qualify as a landlord in my book!'

His unpredictable sense of humour was already at work
and he found himself grinning broadly. 'By God,' he muttered
aloud, 'young Simon's met his match here and no mistake!' and
because her uncompromising style reminded him so vividly
of Grace riding her sex-equality hobby-horse he readdressed
himself to the letter with enthusiasm.

'Well,' she went on blandly, 'that will do for a preamble; now
to the grist. Honestly, Mr Craddock, you've made a real mess of
Simon and sometimes I feel it's almost too late to unravel him!
I'm going to try, though, for Keith persevered with me and I
was even more hopeless material. I remember the fearful row
we had about the time we married when I curtsied to his father!
You see, Simon has terrific potential – a receptive mind, good
reasoning powers, good health, a first-class memory and so
on, but what are these worth without *drive* and *purpose* and
direction? When I met him he was ambling along like a sick
mule, feeling so sorry for himself that whatever capacity he
had to do something practical for anyone else was a spluttering
fuse that led nowhere and would have ended blowing himself
up with a faint pop! I imagine you were always handicapped
by the fact that his mother dodged the job of bringing him up
and that made you lean over backwards to make allowances
for him. That damned public school you sent him to didn't
help either but that's another story. The point is, he's my
responsibility now and I want you to know that I'm serious
to the point of priggery about any responsibilities I take on!
That's why I always take my time accepting a new one
as I did by marrying Si. After all, he's twenty-six and I'm
thirty-four, so there was plenty to worry about had he been
adult, which he certainly wasn't when I met him the night of
his brothers' twenty-first party.'

He knew it was important to digest this letter line by line
so he went back and started again. He knew, also, that she
was not merely forthright to the point of arrogance but that

her judgment was sound and that every shot fired scored a
bull's-eye. He had leaned over backwards to make allowances;
Simon had all those qualities she named and he did lack
purpose and direction; he was not fully adult and never
had been, as though some hidden streak of Lovell indolence
blunted his natural talents to a degree that made him seem
rootless and ineffectual and yet, somewhere inside him, was a
persistent flicker of Grace's fire. That a child of Norman and
Marian Eveleigh, whose education could not have exceeded
a rudimentary grounding at Mary Willoughby's little school,
should have perceived this astonished him. Could she have
learned so much in her brief marriage to Keith Horsey? Or
had it been dinned into her during the long struggle to make
ends meet and keep her head above water, without whining to
a father she despised? He realised that this was something he
would never know. Clearly she was not a person to proclaim
her own triumphs. He read on: 'I'm going to make something
of Si, Mr Craddock – *really* make something of him! What
emerges may not be the kind of person you admire but at
least that person will amount to something. I think it's right
that I should tell you this because, in a way, I need your help.
I want you to promise you'll never send him money. He has a
little (about three pounds a week) from his mother's estate and
that's more than enough to tide us over until he can stand on
his own feet. If he thinks he can always come back to you
I'm beaten from the start. Some of the people we work among
raise families on less than this and if there is one thing I can't
stand it's a theorist who preaches Socialism when his own
belt is let out to the last notch! Believe me, Mr Craddock,
we get plenty of those in the Movement and I wish to God
they would stop pretending and go over to the Opposition! I
haven't made up my mind yet exactly what Simon will go for
but meantime he's teaching in the WEA (Workers' Education
Association) and soon I'm hoping he'll take an external in
Economics. After that, if things work out as I hope, he'll
get electoral experience in a hopeless seat and finally, with
more luck, stand for somewhere with a chance of winning.
All this, of course, is dependent upon him and also on my

hunch about him. Meantime, if Mrs Craddock fusses (and I wouldn't blame her a bit if she did, for she obviously knows him better than you!), do try and convince her I'll make him as good a wife as he'll let me. He's a very lovable boy and although I'm sure I don't sound it I'm a naturally affectionate person. Yours very sincerely, Rachel Craddock.'

It took his breath away for a moment and then the chuckle that had been trying to escape for the last ten minutes emerged as a bellow and he stood by the window with the letter still in his hand and enjoyed the joke as he had not enjoyed one in a long time.

Slowly the more sober aspects of the situation filtered through to him and he thought, with some satisfaction, 'Dammit, it might be the best day's work he ever did in his life marrying that girl! She's got all his mother's idealism pickled in several generations of Eveleigh commonsense. Shall I show this letter to Claire or shall I let well alone? It's something I shall have to think about damned carefully!' and he folded the pages, put them back in the envelope and locked it in a drawer of his desk, along with his Will and insurance policies.

He was preoccupied for several days, so much so that Claire mistook his withdrawal for worry about the failure of the new Government to halt the decline in agriculture. As was her custom she challenged him when they were going to bed one night.

'There's no sense in worrying yourself silly, Paul,' she said, for perhaps the hundredth time in the last decade. 'Farming will bob up just as it always does. That's the one sure thing about the land. It's indestructible and indispensable.'

'Who the devil is worrying?' he demanded, off guard. 'Did I say I was particularly worried?'

'I can always tell, it's the Tudor look again!'

The 'Tudor look' was a family joke. Ikey, the family jester, had once produced a miniature, supposedly by Hillyard, of a long-faced Elizabethan worrier, and pointed out the close resemblance of the portrait to Paul in one of his baffled moods.

'Ah,' he said, beginning to brush his teeth vigorously, 'you're 'way off course this time, old girl! I wasn't worrying, just pondering. About the newly-weds!' He put down his tooth-brush and glanced at her humorously. 'Come to think of it you haven't had much to say on the subject. The last time one of the family married a tenant's daughter you sulked for weeks!'

She was long since proof against this kind of gibe and laughed over her shoulder as she climbed into bed. 'That's libel,' she said, 'and you know it! I began sulking about Ikey marrying Hazel Potter but there were other reasons for maintaining it and I don't have to remind you of those, do I?'

'No,' he said, 'you don't! It was a guilty conscience about that young squirt up at the camp . . . what was his name again?'

'You haven't forgotten his name, you fraud but why worry about newly-weds of their age? Were you thinking of mailing them one of those Marie Stopes books there's so much talk about?'

He said, slowly, 'I had a letter from her, Claire, and I've been wondering whether or not to pass it on to you. I've decided I will. I think you'll enjoy it as much as I did!'

She had been drowsy for the last hour but she was wide awake now. 'Give it to me at once! Go on, give it to me!' and when he protested that it was locked in his office she said, 'I don't give a damn where it is! Go and get it this instant, you traitor!'

He fetched it and sat on the edge of the bed watching her read it and any misgivings he might have had disappeared when he saw her stifle a giggle, then a series of giggles. 'Oh dear,' she said, laying it down, 'poor Simon! All those capitals and underlinings! The Movement! Opposition! The WEA! There wouldn't be any point in sending him Marie Stopes would there? He's gone and married one, the silly boy!'

'Now how can you justify that?' he demanded. 'I'm all for Simon having a sober wife as a sheet-anchor but don't tell me any fun and games will go along with it!'

'Rubbish!' she said, 'she gives herself away in the tailpiece. Don't take that crusading preamble of hers at face value, it's no more than a smokescreen!'

'Are you trying to tell me she isn't in earnest about her determination to make something of the boy?'

'Oh, I daresay she thinks she is,' Claire said, 'but she's covering up nevertheless and any woman could tell you as much. See here – she's healthy, Valley-bred and thirty-four. She's been without a man twelve years and if she's an Eveleigh she's no prude! Along comes Simon, young, good-looking but, what's more important, pliable! Why bless you, she needs him more than he needs her but because of the age gap she has to justify herself! So what does she do? Sets about convincing herself the marriage is near-platonic but you can take it from me that now she's got him she won't address herself exclusively to the task of healing sick society!'

She always amused him when she came out with one of these down-to-earth pronouncements and he chuckled as he switched off the light and climbed into bed, saying, 'The trouble with you is you've got a one-track mind and always have had!' whereupon, not altogether to his surprise she said, 'Thank God we're old enough to let the world get on with it and concentrate on essentials,' and enfolded him in a way that left him in no doubt at all about what she regarded as essential.

Chapter Thirteen

I

That was the season of Rumble Patrick's disgrace, the time when the long-suffering Headmaster of High Wood decided that a less conventional establishment was required to battle with the young man's restless sense of humour. Whilst it could not be said that Rumble Patrick made family history by being expelled from school it is certain that his career there ended prematurely, following a letter from the Headmaster suggesting that withdrawal would save everyone concerned a great deal of unpleasantness.

So Rumble came home at seventeen, puzzled but not deflated by the world's rejection of his efforts to cheer it up and Paul was not surprised by the turn of events. Indeed, the surprising factor was that High Wood had tolerated Rumble so long.

And yet was it all that surprising? From earliest childhood Rumble Patrick Palfrey had been able (and that simultaneously) to bewitch and exasperate his peers and nobody knew this better than Claire, who had been slightly awed by the child ever since the day she had brought him to Shallowford after Hazel Palfrey had been run down and killed by the Army staff car. There was something demoniac about Rumble who was, as Mary once declared, half-cherub, half-poltergeist. It was as though, shortly before his birth, he had been given the rare privilege of assembling his own psychological make-up from material available from both sides of his family and had rejected all but the risible and the bizarre. He had, for example, a broad streak of urchin impudence, the legacy of Ikey's Thames-side forebears and fused with this was the cheerful contempt for authority that had been a characteristic of the Potter clan for generations. This was by no means all. Woven into his character were the strands of Ikey's objectiveness, Mother Meg's pride, Old Tamer's cussedness and Uncle Smut's initiative, all subject, it would seem, to a belief that every day was April Fool's Day. It added up to a most engaging personality but one that offered certain problems to those charged with fitting him for a career in a competitive world.

Paul had sent him to High Wood out of habit. Neither Ikey nor Simon had taken kindly to the credo of the late Doctor Arnold of Rugby, and whereas The Pair had distinguished themselves at games, both had failed the Junior Cambridge examination three times in a row, having taken six years to grind from Second Form to Lower Fifth. With the arrival of Rumble Patrick in 1926, however, High Wood faced an altogether sterner challenge. By the time Rumble was fourteen his explosive energy had settled into a deadly rhythm that expressed itself in volleys of elaborate practical jokes, many of which would, no doubt, become hallowed by tradition but at the time of launching did nothing for the peace of mind of the staff.

It would be unprofitable to list the efforts of Rumble Patrick Palfrey to enliven the school's day-to-day life. They began, conventionally enough, with run-of-the-mill pranks – the sudden elevation of the chalk on a length of thread suspended across the blackboard, the insertion of a dead rat under the teacher's rostrum, the ghostly creakings of an isolated upright piano moved on to the edge of a warped floorboard shortly before Speech Day ritual began, the organic rumblings in blocked hot water pipes to illustrate a geography lesson about earthquakes and so on, but it was soon evident that Rumble was warming up for the big league, in Middle School. At fifteen he abandoned this kind of nonsense to the professional time-wasters, devoting himself to the planning and execution of more ambitious diversions and the inspiration of some of them must have derived from long-dead ancestors, jesters and tumblers in medieval Hungary perhaps, passed onto him by his emigrant grandmother. He was not only as good a mimic as his father had been but a better actor and was able, by the exercise of some strange Jekyll and Hyde alchemy, to assume all manner of personalities with the minimum of disguise. His voice had a wide range, his soft, cherubic features astonishing mobility and he was, above all, a persuasive salesman of comic ideas. There was never any malice in his jokes but his intense curiosity to witness what would occur if a certain number of actions were put into effect sometimes produced alarming results, as when he opened the sluice-gates of High Wood's millpond and flooded a road to the depth of two feet or when, in less desperate mood, he persuaded the village signwriter to paint and erect a large board advertising an isolated section of school property for sale by public auction. Sometimes he would operate as leader of a band of jokers but more often he would work alone, as when he disguised himself as a grizzled labourer and rode about the country all one Sunday on a Douglas motor-cycle owned by the school cricket coach. He took his inevitable punishments cheerfully enough, counting them mild in exchange for the entertainment they represented, and for all his crazy unpredictability and nuisance value he somehow contrived to remain popular with the staff, even the Headmaster, who sat down to write his ultimatum to Paul with reluctance, reasoning perhaps, that life at High Wood after Rumble Patrick's departure would be restful but dull. The letter was sent the day after Rumble, disguised as a deputy stationmaster, sent the school eleven on a cross-country trip to Cornwall when they should have been playing away to Somerset Stragglers. In writing to Paul the Head admitted that 'the boy could, if trained and tamed, prove a credit to himself and family' but honesty compelled him to qualify this by adding 'he might find it difficult to adjust in a society where the patterns of general behaviour were already established', which Paul took as a hint to despatch Rumble Patrick to an outpost of the Empire where his originality would have free play among the primitives.

The day Rumble and his school trunk returned to Shallowford Paul left word that the boy was to report at once to the library. He did not consult Claire on the matter, knowing that she had long since succumbed to Rumble's spell. In any case he always hated these occasions which embarrassed

him and left him with a feeling of inadequacy as a father.
When Rumble arrived, however, he saw at once that the
boy was determined to make things as easy as possible,
for he entered with Ikey's engaging grin and said, without
preamble and without hypocrisy, 'I'm sorry I let you down,
Gov'nor, but you don't have to involve yourself any more you
know. After all, I'm not a kid any more.'

Paul looked at him as he stood by the tall window and
found himself comparing the boy to Ikey in his scrapyard
days. He had Ikey's sense of detachment and Ikey's small,
neat head but his frame was all Potter, sturdy, thick-set,
suggestive of speed as well as power. He thought, sadly, 'I
wonder what the devil poor old Ikey would have made of
him? Or Old Tamer, his grandfather?' and his spirits lifted
somewhat when he recalled that on both sides of his family
Rumble had heroes of a kind and stamina that ought to be
good survival currency in a world drained of security by the
demands of the last sixteen years. He said, with more curiosity
than reproach:

'Why is it you prefer to live in hot water, Rumble, when
most chaps your age are content to take a dip in it now and
again?' and the boy answered, with unexpected promptness,
'The world is so lopsided, Gov'nor. Everyone is tearing themselves to pieces looking for answers and all they come up
with are more and more questions!' and he looked across at
Paul shrewdly, as though it occurred to him he would have
to elaborate a little if he was to make his point but Paul
understood, having not only known and reared Ikey, but also
observed Hazel when she was running wild in the woods. He
meant, of course, that most people were so reluctant to laugh
at themselves and that Rumble's pranks were no more than
an attempt to redress the balance.

'Everybody's finding life pretty tough these days, Rumble,
and they aren't all endowed with your kind of bounce. The
point is, what the devil am I to do with you now? You can't
earn a living pulling people's legs! Your father was a rare
handful but at least he compromised and made a success of
the Army. Suppose I passed you on to a crammer's? Would

you promise to stop acting the goat for once? It's high time you did, you know!'

The boy, serious for once, said, 'Simon and The Pair have gone off and only the girls are left. It must be a bit frustrating for you, Gov'nor – to have no one to carry on, I mean.'

'You think you could make a career of farming?'

'I wouldn't want to step in ahead of them, it wouldn't be fair, would it?'

'Then what?'

'I'd like to get out and about for a couple of years. Not like Simon – politics are a fearful bore – and not like Steve and Andy either, for I'd make a fearful hash of a commercial career. I mean *really* out and about; overseas.'

So here it was again; none of them had a particle of affection for the Valley. All they wanted was to escape as from a noose that threatened to throttle their initiative. They saw him, one and all, as an anachronism, clinging to a way of life that had begun to wither as long ago as the summer of 1914. The conviction that this was so made him feel defeated and old beyond his years.

'Have you anywhere particular in mind?'

'Yes,' said Rumble, unexpectedly, 'I'd go to Australia first There was a chap I was friendly with at school, a fellow called McPherson, whose pater had a sheep farm inland from Brisbane. He was always keen for me to visit and I've heard from him lately and the offer is still open. It's a big place, Queensland.'

Paul glanced down at the Headmaster's letter and remembered the hint, '. . . a place where the patterns of behaviour were not fully established . . .' Claire wouldn't like it, or Mary, who, of all his children, had been the closest to Rumble. Yet the idea had obvious advantages. Australia was probably populated with unconventional people and any one of the numerous Diggers he had met in France during the war would be more than capable of knocking commonsense into the boy with the flat of his hand. Maybe a year or two roughing it among strangers was what he needed and yet, with Simon and The Pair already gone, he was reluctant to help empty

the Valley of young men. He said, resignedly, 'Check on
that invitation, it might have gone cold; in the meantime I'll
think things over but while I'm doing it for God's sake try
and keep out of trouble, Rumble!'

Suddenly the boy was himself again, mischief sparkling in
his eyes, so that Paul, recalling Ikey's impudence, hardly knew
whether to laugh or clout him across the head as he rushed into
the hall calling to Mary. Paul heard his daughter's joyous shout
from the top of the stairs and then, as she relayed the news of
Rumble's home-coming to her sisters, a rush of feet across the
landing. He went out of the garden door and down the drive
to see Maureen, who had always shown a great interest in
Rumble Patrick, but she only gave the advice he expected.

'Damned good idea!' she said. 'Head him that way and don't
let Claire or the girls talk you out of it!' and when he protested
that all the young to whom one might look for succession
were leaving the Valley, she added, '*He'll* come back! That
one will always come back! Too much of his mother in him
to stay away long!' and went briskly about her business,
leaving him to reflect glumly that she herself had not been
much help since John had died and her own boy had gone
off to study medicine in Dublin.

These days he was beginning to feel more and more isolated,
more and more turned in upon himself. The decade that had
closed with the death of old John, his chief confidant, had not
only deprived him of all three of his sons but several of his
intimates, men like Arthur Pitts, of Hermitage, and his dour
father-in-law Edward Derwent, who, on his son buying the
freehold of High Coombe, had deliberately placed himself
beyond the sphere of interference by moving into a quayside
cottage overlooking Whinmouth harbour. Mary, the dreamer
of the family, kept to herself when she wasn't mooning after
Rumble Patrick and even Claire seemed to have withdrawn
from him a little as her two younger daughters claimed more
of her attention, Whiz with her eternal round of gymkhanas
and hunter trials, the youngest with the business of growing
into the most sought-after adolescent within riding distance.
Sometimes, as today, he was very sorry for himself, wishing

the whole boiling of them would give him leisure to concentrate on his own concerns while making themselves available to help form a decision once in a while. He went down the river road a mile or so and for once found a little comfort in the distant prospect of Henry Pitts hup-hupping his three-horse plough team across the red down-slope of Undercliff, the farm's southernmost field. He stood leaning on a rail watching Henry's broad back from a safe distance, reflecting how often and how fruitlessly he had tried to talk him into selling his horses and buying a tractor like Francis Willoughby, Eveleigh's foreman, and Brissot, the cork-footed co-tenant of the once sterile Potter holding. 'Well,' he told himself, as Henry dragged his team round and came back towards him, 'there's one thing that won't change – Henry's methods of husbandry and his hatred of "bliddy contrivances"!' and although he had no wish to talk to Henry today the sight encouraged him to make his way to French Wood, a direction he often took when he was in the dumps.

He approached it from the south, climbing the escarpment above the big bend in the Sorrel and pushing his way through the tall thistles and docks that crowned the little plateau in front of the plantation but here, on the very edge of trees, he stopped short seeing the hunched form of a girl sitting with her back to him on a log near Grace's flowering cherry. It was his daughter Mary and he did not have to see her face to realise that she was in tears.

She had not heard his approach so he stopped and drew back below the crest, his mind assembling the pieces of the puzzle with a speed and certainty that surprised him. Less than an hour ago he had heard her greet Rumble from the stairs and the note of pleasurable excitement in her voice told him that she must have been unaware until that moment of Rumble's return; now she was here alone, more than a mile from the house, and even a man to whom feminine changes of mood remained a mystery after two marriages did not need to be told why. Rumble must have blurted out his harebrained plan and, equally obviously, the prospect of Rumble removing himself half-way across the world had devastated her. Here

then, was something new, Mary and Rumble Patrick linked in a
way that he had never suspected and he wondered if Claire had
an inkling and if she had whether she was amused, displeased
or indifferent. The revelation, complicating an already teasing
problem, irritated him and he thought, impatiently, 'Damn it,
surely I must be imagining things! He's not eighteen yet and
she's less than two years older!' and he stole back to take
another look but found to his relief, that she had disappeared
and the distant crackle of dry bracken below the crest told
him that she must have ridden up here on one of the ponies.
He made up his mind then to watch her closely at supper and
if she gave herself away to consult Claire at once but then, as
though it had dropped through the trees and struck his head
like a pebble, he had another and even more extravagant idea.
What if it turned out that his eldest daughter and the son of
Ikey Palfrey and Hazel Potter were to succeed him, the Valley
passing not to his sons, as he had always assumed, but to
his grandsons? He sat down on the stump to think and it
astonished him that he could contemplate the irony of such
a twist without resentment, could even find in it a kind of
inevitability as he followed a loose end of the skein all the
way back to the scrapyard beside the Thames. 'I daresay it's
no more than wishful thinking on my part!' he grumbled to
himself. 'But then, do I really wish it? Would I prefer events
to have taken a more natural course and the valley pass to
Simon, or one of the twins?' He found himself unable to answer
the question but he could not put it out of mind; the memory of
his daughter's hunched figure was too poignant to support the
theory that he was deducing too much from too little. He sat
musing a long time and then, crossing the grove, he picked
up the pony's tracks in the dust that lay thickly on the path
around the northern bulge of Hermitage Wood. As he left the
trees and walked into bright sunlight a hen pheasant whirred
up less than a yard ahead and flew squawking across the dip.
'I daresay you're wiser than I am, old girl!' he said aloud.
'Kark-kark – Kark-kark! That's about all any of us can say
when it comes to explaining other people's motives, especially
when they are your own flesh and blood!'

II

It would have astonished him even more to have learned that he made his discovery, or half-discovery, only an hour or so before Mary herself gauged the strength of the bond that linked her to Rumble Patrick. Alone among the Craddock children she remembered his actual arrival at Shallowford, a small, plump, easily-delighted child of four, speaking an even broader Devon brogue than Mrs Handcock and Martha Pitts, and because she was the eldest girl, and no one in their senses vested responsibility in The Pair, her mother had taken her aside that same evening and told her frankly that Rumble's mother had been killed and that his father, Ikey, was away at the war and that she was to do all in her power to make Rumble feel at home in the Big House. It was not, she soon discovered, a particularly onerous charge. Rumble Patrick made himself at home anywhere and in a week or two seemed to have forgotten everything about his mother and the enclosed life he shared with her at Mill Cottage, becoming almost at once one of the Craddocks, sleeping in Mary's room until he was six, riding her ponies, sharing her toys and Claire's good-night kisses. Mary soon noticed that her mother showed him special tenderness and would have found it difficult to believe that Rumble's appearance in the world, and the war-time marriage that followed it, had sparked off the only important quarrel between her father and mother in the history of their marriage. When the child had been thoroughly absorbed, however, Mary did not relinquish her post as playmate extraordinary. Her maternal instinct, naturally strong (she was the only one of the Craddock girls who played with dolls), had been matured by Rumble's presence and as her sisters grew up to develop their own interests and needed her less and less, she became Rumble's sole companion in his eternal wanderings in the woods and valleys, where he constantly surprised her with his knowledge of fieldcraft, wild flowers and the habits of the thousand and one creatures who lived out their lives within a mile of the Sorrel springs on the moor. He never treated her as a girl, as did Simon and The Pair, but expected her to climb the same trees, wade the same streams, and disdain tears when brambles clawed at her bare legs and nettles left their smart on her wrists. Because he never seemed to want to ride but preferred to penetrate into places inaccessible to ponies, Mary soon ceased trying to compete with Whiz, the equestrienne of the family and thus lost favour with her Aunt Rose, who sometimes invited them all to stay at her sprawling Gloucestershire home that was a kind of horse-barracks. But there were compensations. By the time she was ten, and Rumble was eight-and-a-half, each of them knew the Valley better than Paul, or John Rudd, and among the tenants only Smut Potter, who drove the bakery van for his French wife's business in Coombe Bay, could challenge them on the termini of the rabbit-runs in Shallowford Woods or the exact location of the principal otter holts along the weaving courses of the Sorrel and Teazel. They liked Smut, who would often stop his van and pass a pleasant half-hour with them during his rounds, telling them where to find nests and sometimes recounting his poaching exploits of pre-war days, and they had their favourites among the tenants, farmworkers and Valley craftsmen. They liked old Martha Pitts up at Hermitage, who would sometimes bake them savoury pasties, telling them she had done as much for Rumble Patrick's mother when she had lived wild in the woods before her marriage. They liked and respected Grandmother Meg, whom they encountered in out-of-the-way places where she was gathering herbs or selling her rush mats and baskets and Meg, unsmilingly and with a deliberation that fascinated Mary, would sometimes tell their fortunes and prophesy that Mary would marry a gypsy and have blue-eyed children, a pledge that Mary secretly doubted for she could not imagine marrying anyone but Rumble, whose eyes were the colour of his mother's name. They were fond of Henry Pitts, with his great, rubbery smile and were well-received by the Timberlakes at the sawmill, and also by the cork-footed Frenchman, Brissot, who did most of the work in the Dell while his partner, Jumbo, stood around cracking jokes in his thin, Cockney voice. Mary found it difficult to believe that both Mrs Brissot and Jumbo's wife were Rumble's aunts. Each of them seemed so old and each treated him with the respect they showed the Squire's children but it was so, for Paul made no mystery of Rumble's background and once took them up to French wood, pointing out the two trees he had planted in memory of Rumble's parents, saying that Ikey, his father, had been a very brave soldier and his mother, Hazel, had known even more of what went on in the coverts and goyles of the estate than Smut Potter, a statement that helped Mary to understand Rumble's instinctive knowledge of woodcraft and fieldcraft. They had their dislikes too, usually avoiding High Coombe and thinking of Mary's uncle, Hugh Derwent, as an aloof, tetchy man plodding about his business without a smile, and although they got along well enough with Marian Eveleigh, at Four Winds, it was never a farm they frequented much for they were half-convinced that old Norman Eveleigh was a little soft in the head, partly because he looked at them as though they were not there but also because one side of his mouth dribbled a little, as though he had left his handkerchief at the farm. Rumble told Mary this was nothing to wonder at; Norman Eveleigh had evidently been touched by the Four Winds' curse and sooner or later every master of this particular farm went mad.

So they wandered about, looking for and finding small, everyday adventures, but the idyll came to a sudden end in 1922, when Rumble Patrick was sent away to prep school and Mary put up her hair and had to pay some heed to her clothes. Then Mary went as a weekly boarder to the Convent of the Holy Family, in Paxtonbury, and there were only the holidays when they tried but failed to pick up where they had left off. Something went missing and neither of them could discover what it was; then Whiz grew old enough to invite her pony-mad friends back to the house, and some of the twins' friends from Paxtonbury and Whinmouth began to notice Mary's dark, shy charm and employ all kinds of strategems to get her alone and kiss her behind the barns or in dark corners of the house. At first she was indignant at such tomfoolery, thinking them very soppy but later both her mother and Whiz urged her to be 'more sociable' and she did try very hard, and even fancied for a week or two that she was in love with a red-headed boy called Gussie whom Stephen brought home to stay for a fortnight one summer. Yet the secret bond between them was never completely severed; it only stretched as the years went by, and the house was full of strangers who kept passing between them with their crazy horse dance steps and ukeleles and horseplay, so it was not until the week Rumble disgraced himself at school and came home with wild, frightening talk of going to Australia to learn sheep-farming, that the memory of their childhood alliance became vivid to her. Before that, *just* before that, something happened that made her particularly sensitive to Rumble's callous declaration of independence.

A night or two before Rumble's return there had been a Junior Hunt Ball at Whinmouth and, as usual on these occasions Mary was told off to chaperon her younger sisters, Whiz and Claire, respectively seventeen and fourteen, after they had been driven to the dance in the family Austin by Mark Codsall. The role of chaperone was largely fictitious these days, especially in the Craddock household, but Mary got her routine instructions – 'Keep an eye on them and make sure you're all ready to leave by midnight.' Claire Craddock was very broadminded in the matter of her daughters' upbringing, not only because she trusted Mary implicitly and remembered her own youth had been singularly free of restrictions but also because, far more than Paul, she had come to terms with the new freedoms. It seemed to her both natural and healthy that young people should want to grow up fast and enjoy themselves out of range of adults, and whenever Paul challenged the wisdom of her tolerance she could be relied upon to dismiss his growls as evidence of a hang-over from an era dead and buried in the 1914–18 earthquake.

'No one quarrels with your preference for horse-transport and horn-lanterns, dear,' she told him on this occasion, 'but you really must try to see the world through their eyes! All I'm concerned with is getting them there safely and getting them back at a reasonable hour. I've enough faith in my daughters to know that they'll conduct themselves sensibly in company and this is a perfectly respectable company, composed of people we know. It might interest you to learn that it actually goes on until two a.m. but I've told Mary to have them back here by one!'

'I should damn well think so!' he replied but he did not make an issue of it. He would never have admitted as much but he had respect for her judgment in these matters and was obliged to admit that she had made a more successful job of raising the girls than he had of tailoring the boys.

Whiz was particularly excited, being currently involved in a double flirtation with two young thrusters from the Paxtonbury Farmers' Hunt and looked forward to the certainty of being sure of partners for every dance and perhaps the cause of a quarrel. Fourteen-year-old Claire (whom everybody mistook for sixteen) was eager to show off her new apple-green organdie, her first real dance frock bought on the occasion of her fourteenth birthday, in June. Mark got them there too early and the first hour or so was dull but the dance warmed up when all the young men came in from The Mitre and Mary soon lost track of Whiz, suspecting that she was spending more time in the parked cars than on the dance floor, whereas it intrigued her to see young Claire blush for the first time in her serene existence, when the Master's son, a willowy young man with a reputation for being Paxtonbury's most expert ballroom dancer, partnered her to win the fox-trot competition. She was watching her sister come down from the platform and marvelling, as she often did on these occasions, at Claire's breathtaking poise and composure, when Bob Halberton lounged across and asked her for the next dance. She was glad to see him, even though he did seem to have consumed rather more than a safe quota of beer, for up to then her dancing had been limited to potluck stumbles in the Paul Jones. She had known Bob all her life. His father was a doctor, practising in Whinmouth and he was a genial, heavy-featured boy, who was often out with the Sorrel Vale Hunt on Saturdays. He was engaged, he told her, in studying law and was finding it a terrible bore, so much so that he was thinking of throwing it up and trying for a short-service commission in the Air Force.

'That's the life!' he told her, clutching her tightly as they shuffled round the crowded floor. 'I've already joined a Flying Club at Reading, where I'm bogged down in an office so I get a flip most weekends. Who the devil wants to be chained to a stool grubbing among conveyances and affiliation orders? If it wasn't for the fact that the old man has sworn to cut me off I'd sign on without even asking him and to hell with the consequences!'

She had always rather liked Bob Halberton, who had the gaiety of the twins plus, she suspected, a good deal more intelligence and she thought of him as kind-hearted and masculine. She also liked him for not being sure of himself, or as good-looking as most of Whiz's friends and the amateur sheikhs the twins brought home but she had never suspected that he was interested in her so that when he said, on the long drum roll, 'Look here, Mary, it's stuffy in here. Let's go out for some air!' she was flattered but reminded him of her responsibilities as chaperone. He said, laughing, 'Oh, to the devil with that! They ought to be looking after you!' and then, as though she was feinting, 'Is there someone else? I always took you for the unsophisticated one!'

The gibe (for she accepted it as one) hurt a little and she replied, with a crackle of defiance, 'I'll get my wrap.' and on the way to the cloakroom told Whiz that 'she was going out with Bob Halberton for a cooler'. Whiz laughed and looked surprised. '*You.* And Bob Halberton? My word, Mar, you're coming on but watch out, they say he's hot stuff!'

'He won't be "hot stuff" with me,' Mary retorted, suddenly feeling annoyed with herself and everyone in the room, excluding Bob Halberton, to whom she felt she owed her escape from the company of wallflowers but as they made for his car, an Austin Seven painted to look like a racing car, she decided that he was not safe to drive and told him so and to her relief he said, 'I daresay you're right!' and motioned her into the back, climbing in after her and losing no time in clasping her in a bearlike embrace.

She did not mind being kissed by him, accepting the sad fact that almost every man who kissed you at a dance, or a celebration of any sort, was certain to smell of liquor but she had never been kissed so enthusiastically as Bob kissed her and wondered if it had anything to do with being in need of solace. People usually were when they sought her out and his grumblings about office life were still fresh in her mind. She drew back at last and said, 'Could I have a cigarette, Bob?'

He laughed rather unpleasantly at this, recognising it as a time-honoured manoeuvre in the art of self-defence but he gave her one, saying, 'I didn't know you smoked?'

'Well, I've started!' she said, so sharply that he laughed again, saying, 'Don't think I don't understand! All your life you've been stuck with the job of Little Mother. Well, it's time you started having fun, so why not let rip!' and he kissed her again, this time letting his hand slip over her shoulder and rest on her breast. She remembered then what Whiz had said about him being 'hot stuff' but in her new role as a rebel she did not see how she could protest without seeming a prude, so she puffed stolidly at the cigarette as he stealthily extended his hold but realised, rather forlornly, that she was deriving no pleasure at all from his mauling and wondered how all her contemporaries could welcome this kind of thing as they apparently did whenever they were alone in the dark with boys. He said, as though to relax her, 'You're very sweet, Mary! I've always thought of you as the flower of the flock!' but instead of pleasing her the comment touched her pride and she replied, 'If you're referring to my brothers and sisters I should like to know what's wrong with them!'

He took up her challenge more ruthlessly than she expected. 'Well, let's face it, Mary; your brother Simon is a bolshie, the twins are a pair of nitwits, and although both your sisters are damned pretty they know it, even that kid Claire! I'm not a fool, it must be sheer hell living with younger sisters who do everything so well that everyone looks over your head at them!'

His appalling honesty made her shudder but because she recognised a strong element of truth in what he said she kept her temper in check, thinking, 'At least he has the guts to say what everyone else thinks! That's more than anyone will, even Mother!' and she said miserably, 'I suppose that implies I'm the flop of the family? Well, I am! I'm not at ease with people like young Claire and I can't win prizes at every field event like Whiz. I'm not gay and dressy and gregarious like the twins, or even bolshie and clever like Simon! Would you mind telling me exactly why you asked me to come out here? Was it out of pity?'

It was his turn to recoil. He sat back, taking her by the shoulders and turning her face to him under the unflattering glow of the parking-ground lamp and for a moment seemed at a loss what to say. Then her instinctive sympathy for him gave him the wrong clue, as she said, hastily, 'I'm sorry, Bob! That was a beastly thing to say! Let's go back inside,' and she reached to open the door.

'Don't be such a damned fool, Mary!' he growled, throwing his arm around her. 'Have fun yourself for once!' and he began to kiss her with such determination that she was crushed against the hard leather cushions of the tiny car. Then he was almost on top of her, his hand slipping the shoulder strap of her dress over her arm in a clumsy attempt to fondle her small bosom. There was hardly enough space to resist but she did her best, pressing herself against the door and drawing up her knees so that her short dress wrinkled high on her thighs but even this he took as a gesture of encouragement, extricating his other hand and groping between her knees. Then fear and distaste gave way to fury and she dragged her nails down the side of his face and taking advantage of his wincing recoil rolled to the floor, grabbed the handle and fell out on to the tarmac. She heard him shout, 'Mary, I'm sorry . . . wait!' but she picked herself up and ran, not back to the hall but round the building into the shadow and across the little square to

the quay where she stopped, steadying herself against the
harbour guard-rail. She felt sick with misery and shame but
still consumed with a terrible anger, not for Bob, whom she
reasoned would be very sorry for himself when he sobered
up, but with the world as a whole and her allotted place
in it, the plainest, gawkiest and shyest of a family of six,
a girl who had no more finesse when faced with a routine
dance-hall hazard than to scratch a man's face raw and then
rush off into the dark like an outraged virgin pursued by
a satyr. Whiz was two years her junior but Whiz would
have extricated herself from such a situation with dignity
and hauteur and surely even Claire, at fourteen, would have
had enough sense not to climb into the back of a car with a
half-tipsy boy, imagining that all he wanted from her was a
dry peck or two and a sympathetic audience. Bob Halberton
was clearly right when he implied that she was the family
flop, the predestined maiden aunt, who would sit at home
knitting woollies for a chain of nieces and nephews until her
life grew dim and purposeless. Why was she so different from
all the others? Why did she find a tussle in the back of a car
degrading and humiliating, when most girls her age would
have shrugged it off as no more than tiresome and others, a
majority, perhaps, would have found it flattering, especially if
they had spent two hours watching others enjoy themselves.
She could find no answer to these questions that did not point
to personal inadequacy and suddenly, to her renewed shame,
tears began to flow and her whole world clouded over as she
went back over Bob Halberton's summary of the Craddocks
of Shallowford – a bolshie, a couple of empty-headed idiots,
two vain extroverts and a reject! Did everyone outside the
Valley – and perhaps those inside it – view the family in this
light? It was a chilling thought for, until that moment, she had
always tended to think of the Craddocks as the acknowledged
leaders of the community. Perhaps this was a fallacy? Perhaps
people in places like Whinmouth and Paxtonbury had always
regarded her father as a man who was playing Squire with
money earned in a scrapyard, and her mother as a lucky
farmer's daughter, shrewd enough to have grabbed him on

the rebound after a disastrous marriage to real gentry?

Bob found her there dabbing her eyes and trying, in the wan light of the harbour lamps, to repair her make-up. He seemed contrite and deflated, showing three curving lines of nail-furrows on each cheek and said, as soon as he saw her, 'I'm sorry, Mary! I didn't realise what an ass I was making of myself . . . I've always liked you a lot, honestly, and after all you did give a chap the impression . . .' and he tailed off, shuffling from one foot to the other and dabbing his scratches with a handkerchief. There was, she decided, small comfort to be derived from his abjectness, for even now he was careful to use the verb 'like' rather than risk a second misunderstanding. Then her fatal pity took a hand again and she said, quietly, 'You can't go back in the hall with your face in that state, you'd better go home and forget what happened. It was my fault really, I shouldn't have come out. At eighteen, it's time I learned what's expected of a girl who does,' and she walked back across the square with Bob trotting alongside like a terrier who has been whipped and is hoping to find a way of wriggling back into grace. He found none; she said, decisively, 'Good night, Bob,' and went straight into the hall, where everyone was bobbing round the floor to the rhythm of the latest bit of nonsense:

'There ain't no sense,
Sitting on the fence,
All by yourself in the moonlight . . .'

and although Mary found the theme appropriate to her mood its irony had no power to cheer her as she sat waiting for Mark Codsall to call and take them home. When he did appear, on the stroke of midnight, she summoned her sisters with such impatience that Whiz complained, 'You needn't be in such a panic just because your Bob has taken himself off!' and Mary felt she could have boxed her ears on the spot. To Whiz's subsequent demand for an account of what happened, she snapped, 'Nothing! Nothing but silliness!' and that was her sole contribution to the lively recapitulation of the evening's triumphs that beguiled her sisters all the way home.

And then, after a day and a night of brooding, Rumble was restored to her and she tore downstairs in response to his shout only to learn, to her bewilderment, that he had been politely expelled and had made up his mind, presumably with her father's blessing, to remove himself to Australia! What was more galling than this monstrous decision was the eagerness with which Rumble embraced it. All through the autumn, while letters and cables were passing to and fro between him and his future hosts, and his great black cabin trunk was being filled, he ranged about the house practising a ridiculous Australian accent and spicing his conversation with outlandish words like 'pommie', 'outback' and 'fair dinkum'. It was as though, like Simon and the twins before him, he could hardly wait to scrape Valley mud from his shoes and whilst she had understood the restlessness of her brothers, Rumble's rejection of the old life – a time that had once seemed eternal – mystified and depressed her.

It was not until his last afternoon that she had an inkling of what lay behind this renunciation of their past. It was almost Christmas then and a cheerless Christmas it promised to be, for there was little point in decorating the house for a family reunion that might last two or three days and would not, in any case, include the twins, who were in the Tyrol, and Rumble, who was due to sail on December 22nd. The weather, however, did its best to help the Valley show off its autumn clothes and when she accepted his invitation for a final ramble she found that October still lingered among the oaks and chestnuts of the southern rim of the woods, and that when they went down the long, tangled slope to the mere the water was slate-blue in pale sunshine and the evergreens on the islet were fortified against winter by a gloss that still held the ripeness of June. She noticed, a little maliciously, that he had lost some of his bounce and that his fresh, squarish face now had an almost stoical expression. He said nothing, however, until they moved along level with the ruinous old pagoda where he stopped, took her arm and said with rare earnestness, 'Will you promise something, Mar? Will you come here sometimes, to this spot, and – well, remember me once in a while?'

The finality as well as the strangeness of the request dried her mouth and her voice was as strange to him as his sudden seriousness was to her.

'Yes, of course – of course I will, Rumble, but, oh God, you make it sound as if I won't ever see you again! You make it so horribly final! Why do you *have* to go? You needn't! Even now you could cry off and we'd all understand! I think Daddy would be relieved really and I'm sure Mummy would!'

He seemed to consider a moment so that hope fluttered in her but then he said, slowly, 'I couldn't you know – cry off, I mean. I've let him down just like the others but at least I know it and can do something about it and I think he understands that or will do, some day!'

'But I don't understand! What has Daddy got to do with you going all that way off? He hasn't thrown you out, he wasn't even upset about you getting sacked from High Wood. Where does he enter into it?'

He looked at her solemnly for a moment and then, relaxing, gently pushed her down on a stump where the path crossed one of old Aaron Stokes' tracks to the reed beds.

'It's because of him I got into this, Mar,' he said, 'but I'll never forgive you if you pass that on, even to your mother or to Simon! Don't you realise what a sickener it was for him? The twins going off like that, and Simon never having the remotest wish to carry on? It was part of his dream that at least one of them would finish what he started. I imagine that's why he had a family in the first place!'

'Well, even if that were true,' she said, and privately thought he was taking far too much for granted, 'You could go to Agricultural College and take on the Home Farm in time.'

'It wouldn't be the same,' he said, shaking his head. 'I'm not his son you see, just the byblow of a kid he fished out of the slums and the scattiest of the Potters. We respect one another and he's been more than a father to me. It would be a poor sort of return if I paid him back by horning in ahead of his children! Surely you can understand that, Mar?'

'No I can't!' she said, stubbornly. 'For you've just said neither Simon, Steve nor Andy want to stay here and farm. The Valley has never meant a thing to any one of them!'

'They may come round to it, one or other of them, sooner or later,' he said, 'but they certainly wouldn't if I got my oar in first and staked a claim! Simon is too unselfish and the twins would just use me as an excuse. You must see that, Mar.'

She did see it and gave him credit for his sagacity. Until then her sense of deprivation had been so personal that it had never occurred to her that he might be making a deliberate or half-deliberate sacrifice, and the realisation enlarged him enormously. She said, with awe in her voice, 'Then you aren't really so . . . *keen* to go, Rumble?'

'*Keen?*' He sounded outraged. 'Leaving *here*? Why, turning my back on this place is the hardest thing I've ever done or ever will do! And there's more to it than that too! Leaving you makes it that much harder. The Valley is my home and you're the one person that makes it so, and it's never been any other way with me, although I don't think I understood that until a week or two ago, until . . . well . . . until I'd burned my boats!'

There was sweetness as well as pain in his declaration, a sweetness that seemed to rend her and gush into her breast so that she reached out and took both his hands and held them tremulously. In the pincer grip of fear and relief she was unable to utter a word of protest or pleasure and they sat there on the many-ringed stump, linked less by physical contact than by the intensity of their emotions, by a tangle of ties reaching back to their earliest childhood compounding all the days they had spent together soaking up sunshine and drinking wind and rain. It was a magic moment, less transitory for her than for him, for now, out of understanding, came reassurance of a kind and a conviction that, if a person as splendidly resourceful and enterprising as Rumble could travel to the ends of the earth, he might well find his way back again, so that this might not be the end of everything but a beginning. She said, in a steady voice, 'I love you, Rumble! I want you to know that I love you and could never love anyone else, could never want anyone else to touch me, you understand?' and as she said this she thought fleetingly of Bob Halberton's prying hands on the night of the dance and was conscious of a release from shame, as though Rumble's touch had exorcised an unwholesome memory and restored tranquillity to her being.

He looked at her in a way that he had never done in the past. There was joy in his glance but apprehension also, as though he welcomed her pledge but doubted her strength to make it good against the demands of time and distance. Then he raised his hand and touched her lightly on the cheek and in the shy gesture was all she needed to know, at all events for the present, until she had leisure to contemplate this moment of time in privacy. He kissed her mouth so gently that she was half afraid to return the kiss but did so with hardly less restraint and it was a bestowal that must have liberated him from the silence of wonder, for he said, stroking her hair, 'I've thought of this, Mar. Many times! I've imagined it but that's as far as it went. It's late enough in the day for us but it has happened, and I suppose that's the important thing!' And then, nerving himself, 'But it doesn't bind you, Mar! You must understand that! It mustn't spoil things for you after I've gone!'

'But I want it to bind me, Rumble,' she said, fervently. 'I wouldn't want to remember it any other way and I don't care for how long, you understand? I don't care any more!'

They sat through the last moments of the short winter's afternoon, saying little of any consequence, too shy now to do more than utter short, broken sentences about letters, pledges, promises and a raggle taggle of trivialities, but for Mary all the stresses of the last few weeks had been eased, like the slackening of a cable hitching her to a drag-load of despondency and deprivation. She wondered, as they went hand in hand up the escarpment to the slope above the house, whether anyone would notice and comment on the change in her when they assembled for high tea but decided that she did not care a rap if they did.

Nobody exclaimed. They were all too concerned with the ritual of his departure and in any case it would be days before the great change in her advertised itself in an added brightness of the eye, a lightness of step or a tendency to hum a tune instead of taking up a challenge thrown down by Whiz or young Claire. By that time he was gone and they had received his first card posted at Lisbon. Claire read it aloud and Paul, catching Mary's eye and seeking confirmation of his thoughts in French Wood back in the summer, was reassured by what he saw, or thought he saw, thinking, 'Well, she seems to have reconciled herself to his going after all! I daresay I was imagining something that wasn't there,' and he dismissed the subject, forgetting it in a welter of new troubles. It was some time before he realised that he had been right after all.

III

The seasons had their cycles and the years their rhythms, a small graph within a larger one that was then caught up in the rhythm of the world outside. There were good years and bad, years recalled with laughter and others with memories that the people of the Valley stowed away like limber to take out only in times of prosperity and good cheer. The war years fell into this grouping but even these had faces that reflected an odd note of laughter or excitement, like the arrival of the first aeroplane in the Valley, or the ripple that ran down the Sorrel when news came that Smut Potter had returned from the dead. Some of the slump years had this same, mitigating sparkle. The year 1926, when prices were down and foot and mouth rampant and the general gloom was relieved to some extent by the astounding news that Francis Willoughby had won a national cattle award and was taking one of his bulls all the way to the Argentine. Paul watched these rhythms closely and sometimes wrote of them in the estate diary, jotting down forecasts between solid wedges of Claire's trivia, and his extreme sensitivity regarding all things pertaining to the Valley regulated his alternating moods of optimism and pessimism, particularly round about January, the bleakest time of year. He would say, 'This year will be good in most

respects . . .' or, 'This year's damp is already in my bones . . . !'
pretending that his barometer was the wound in his knee, or
the small crater in his temple where the last piece of shrapnel
had been extracted in 1918, but this was only a family joke,
like his 'Tudor look'. His gift of local prophecy, if indeed he
possessed one, was geared to a far more complicated machine
assembled from the cogs and wheels plucked from the years,
from signs and portents passed to him by gypsy Meg, or by
weather sages like Arthur Pitts and old John Rudd, but even
Paul himself never mastered the art of starting or stopping
this machine at will. It seemed to generate itself and run on
through a given number of revolutions and when at length it
stopped of its own accord he knew they were all set for one
of their unmemorable spells, when things were neither good
nor bad and the seasons came and went unnoticed.

The machine began to roll in the first week of January,
1931, and its whirring was so urgent that he was worrying
hard before the year was forty-eight hours old, the nag setting
him reading through the pages of the diary as far back as 1904
when the new year had opened with the Codsall tragedy and
the tempo built to the whirlwind of Grenfell's first victory
and Grace's flight. Perhaps it was the vivid memory of this
time, and its link with the first event of 1931, that put him
on his guard, for just as the bumpy run of 1904 began at Four
Winds, so the 1931 run of bad luck began with an event that
left Four Winds masterless and laid open the flank to the west.
It was a vulnerable flank, particularly since Elinor Codsall had
given up and Periwinkle had gone derelict, for although in
the east High Coombe had been pinched out by the sale of
freehold Paul never considered this as a sign of impending
dissolution. Hugh Derwent was his own brother-in-law and
also a first-class farmer. It did not matter if his land had
been erased from the estate map for Hugh had told Claire
more than once that he was unlikely to marry now and
he had no kith or kin other than the Craddock children,
and his childless sister, Rose. To the west, however, it was
another matter. Not only was Four Winds the largest and
most prosperous farm of the original six, it was also the

closest to Nun's Bay shantytown and the proposed route
of the coastal road to Coombe Bay. Failure, or withdrawal
in this direction might mean all manner of things and could
not be shrugged off like the break-up of Periwinkle in the
north-west. Four Winds was a bastion in the economy of the
estate; it needed a strong man in possession.

It was with these thoughts that Paul, learning of Norman
Eveleigh's second stroke on January 3rd, threw a saddle
over the skewbald and took the shortest route to the gate
in the park wall. It was the route, he reminded himself, that
he and Ikey had taken the night he answered a previous
summons to Four Winds when Norman Eveleigh, tousled
but cool-headed at three in the morning, had recommended
himself as a likely successor to the man hanging in the barn.
Now, according to Marian, Eveleigh was done for, lying in the
kitchen where he had been carried by two of his men after
collapsing in the yard an hour or so before whilst clearing
a blocked drain. He did not recognise anyone, not even his
wife, but lay on a makeshift bed staring up at them with
uncomprehending eyes. The thick fingers of his left hand
twitched and his left leg kicked but these were the only
movements he made when Doctor Maureen peeled off his
long, woollen pants and probed the flesh. Marian stood beside
the log fire and old Ben, Eveleigh's aged pigman, remained
in the doorway, twisting the ends of his white moustaches
in embarrassment at witnessing the sudden helplessness of
a man he had feared and respected for more than thirty
years.

'Will us get un upstairs?' Marian asked, after Maureen had
finished her examination. 'Us coulden manage it at first but I
daresay us could now, tho' he's a turrible weight.'

'He'll do here for the time being,' Maureen said and then,
without lowering her voice, 'I'm afraid this is it, Marian!'
and when Eveleigh's wife shot her a look of reproach, added,
'He can't hear and he can't see much either. Maybe the
difference between light and dark with his left eye but no
more.'

Marian's face crumpled and she began to sniff so that

Maureen at once summoned Debbie, Eveleigh's unmarried daughter, telling her to look after her mother. Paul said nothing but remained after Debbie, Marian and Ben had left the room. The hulk on the makeshift couch was enough to depress anyone who had known Norman Eveleigh in his prime, a tireless machine that could harvest round the clock, and milk faster than anyone in the Valley, a man to whom hard and regular toil was the breath of life, so much so that he had somehow carried on after his first stroke years ago and still managed a better day's work than some of the younger hands who had come to the Valley since the war.

'I'd sooner see him dead!' he said suddenly. 'He'd have wished it, I can tell you that!'

'Most people wish it,' Maureen said, repacking her bag, 'but we have to take what comes our way. We were right about keeping him hard at work as long as possible. Any other finish would have been cruel.' Then, straightening herself, 'He was a damned hard man, Paul. Hard on himself and hard on everyone around him.'

'He was a good farmer,' Paul said, 'and taken all round a good family man. I never regretted putting him in here after Codsall. It was one of the few times I followed a hunch and wouldn't let John turn me aside.'

'How old would he be?'

'Sixty-seven,' Paul said and she smiled, recalling that Paul and her John had vied with one another on knowing the exact age of everyone in the Valley. It was one of the small vanities they shared.

'Well,' she said, 'I suppose you might say he worked himself into the ground but the older ones do, don't they? There aren't many of the originals left now, are there?'

'There are none,' he told her gravely, 'but the farms of four of the six I began with have passed from father to son. That's not a bad average and I'll warrant it can't be said of any other estate round here.' He lifted Eveleigh's hand, holding it for a moment and setting it down on the blanket when Eveleigh's stare did not waver. 'How long is he likely to last?'

'Hard to say,' Maureen replied, 'but not long. We could get him into Paxtonbury Hospital if Marian prefers that. It'll save her trouble for he'll have to be nursed day and night. What do you think?'

She had grown accustomed to deferring to him on matters like this. The Valley people trusted her by now but not in the way they trusted him.

'He ought to die here,' said Paul.

'But he won't be conscious of where he dies and he'll certainly survive longer in hospital if we can get him there.'

'There isn't any point in him surviving, Maureen, and no matter how stricken he is he'll know if you shift him!'

'How? He can't see or hear!'

'He can smell!' Paul said, 'and I don't want him to go with the stench of a hospital in his nostrils! He's one of us, Maureen, and he'd prefer to die on his own land.'

She did not argue with him; John had taught her that he knew all these people better than anyone alive and she was confident that he could handle Marian Eveleigh, a woman who had always accepted him as God's deputy.

'Very well, Paul, tell them to fix him up down here. It'll kill him to be dragged up that stairway. I'll look back tonight.' She went out and climbed into her ramshackle car, touched by his sadness and finding in it confirmation of an accelerated rate of change and the merciless shift of pattern in their lives lately. Who would he get in Eveleigh's place, she wondered? There was no son or son-in-law to follow on, for Gilbert, the only real farmer of the brood, had been blown to pieces practising with a short-fuse hand-grenade in 1916, and the eldest daughter, Debbie, was one of those Valley girls who preferred to go to their graves mourning a man killed in the war – who was it now? – one of the Marlowe boys, or Dave Williams, the fisherman? Well, that was Paul's problem, she had plenty of her own with a mild 'flu epidemic on her hands and she slammed the car in gear and drove off towards Codsall bridge, noting that the river was high and that another day's rain would flood the lower road as it usually did at this time of year.

Paul remained at Four Winds most of the morning, helping
Marian and Debbie convert the kitchen into a sickroom but he
was more concerned with the problem of succession. He said,
when Norman had been made as comfortable as possible, 'Do
you suppose your youngest boy, Robbie, would be interested?'
and Marian said Robbie wouldn't, he was far happier as a hunt
servant whereas Harold, the second boy, was doing too well
in the North to change his factory job for farming.

'You can't blame him for that,' Paul grunted but he could
see they were worried about their future and said, hoping to
reassure them, 'Don't think I'll ever send you packing, we'll
think of something. In the meantime you had better let Rachel
know and see if you can get her home to take her turn at
nursing. Someone will have to sit with him night and day
and there are only two of you.'

He went out and rode slowly down the track to the river
road, unable to shake off his gloom. Eveleigh's death had not
been entirely unexpected but it was a pity that it had to
happen now with skilled labour so scarce, all the younger
men drifting into the cities, and the Valley feeling the pinch
of war-time losses more sharply than at any time since the
Armistice. What a splendid thing it would have been if young
Gilbert had been there to step into his father's place or, failing
that, his own son Simon bring Eveleigh's daughter home and
work out an apprenticeship at Four Winds under Marian's
experienced eye? He thought, savagely, 'Damn the younger
ones! Where's the sense in them turning their backs on the
land and joining the bloody dole queues in the city?' and then
it occurred to him that this was unfair because the natural
successors were not children who had grown up in the last
decade but those who lay in graveyards all over France and
the Near East. Who could blame their younger brothers and
sisters for seeking a more rewarding life than that of the hulk
sprawled in the kitchen at Four Winds, used up at the age
of sixty-seven? One needed to have had a glimpse of what
the Valley could offer in pre-war days before one could be
reconciled to the sweat and grind of the job. Maybe, after
all, he had it wrong and his sons, and young sparks like

Rumble Patrick, had it right; maybe The Pair had talked sense when they described farming in England as a dead duck.

In the event Eveleigh lasted no more than a month and they buried him a pebble-toss from old Willoughby, Tamer Potter and Arthur Pitts. All the family were briefly united for the funeral and Paul had a word or two with Harold, the second boy, now in his early thirties and serving as Welfare Officer (whatever that was) at a jam-making factory in Manchester. He looked, Paul thought, an odd man out among Valley mourners, in his neat black overcoat, trilby hat and striped pants. Paul asked him how he was doing and he said, wryly, 'Oh, so-so, Mr Craddock! There's a hell of a lot of unemployment up there but I'm on the permanent staff, thank God! I cashed in on the welcome-home-the-heroes boom in 1919 and flashed my 'accustomed-to-handling-men' qualifications under their noses! I had damn all else to offer, except a good line in killing Turks!' Paul also had a chance to meet and reappraise Rachel, his daughter-in-law, but found to his dismay that both Simon and his wife bored him with their clichés and endless chatter about the dictatorship of the proletariat and the various manifestations of the class-struggle. 'Don't they ever come down off the bloody platform and become human beings?' he complained to Claire, after Simon and Rachel had rushed north again to take part in yet another bye-election but Claire only chuckled and said, 'They'll get over it, poor dears. They are talking about adopting a child so all we have to do is to wait until the proletariat has to be fed at four in the morning!' and privately he thanked God for her commonsense and was ashamed of his own intolerance. Then, as March came round, he was sucked into the political maelstrom himself, for Jimmy Grenfell, Liberal Member for the Paxtonbury Division since half-way through King Edward's reign, announced that he would not stand again when the present Parliament dissolved and intended to devote what remained of his life to writing a history of the Chartist Movement, a task that seemed to him more rewarding than shoring up a Labour Minority led by the

Duchess-kissing Ramsay MacDonald, now a prisoner of the
Tory Opposition. Paul, who hated abrupt changes of any
kind, was shocked by his decision.

'Who the devil can we find to take your place, Jimmy?' he
grumbled. 'I've looked to you as our spokesman up there ever
since I came here.'

'Why don't you stand yourself, Paul?' Jimmy said but
only in jest, for he knew that his backer would as soon
go and live in Hong Kong as spend most of his time in
London.

'We'll lose that seat if a Socialist makes a three-cornered
fight of it,' Paul warned him but Grenfell said, dryly, 'We'll
lose it anyway. The Tories are putting up a local man, a real
local, not a phoney like they have in the past.'

'Who?'

'You know him; a young speculator called Codsall, the son
of one of your former tenants, I believe.'

'*Sydney* Codsall? That young bastard? You must be joking!'

'I'm not joking, they've had their eye on him ever since he
got on the County Council a year or so back.'

'Then we have to find someone with an even chance of
beating that young scoundrel,' Paul declared and his emphasis
puzzled Grenfell for it had seemed to him that Paul had
been losing interest in politics of late. 'He's the man behind
everything shoddy round here and he doesn't know a damned
thing about representing an agricultural constituency! He's a
small-town shyster on the make and I've known him since he
was a child. Even then he was a slippery little swine!'

'They say he's made a pile,' Grenfell said. 'Is that true?'

'I daresay, he's dabbled in jerry-built property and runs a
quarry over beyond High Coombe. He had hopes of 'developing' Coombe Bay, God help us, but I've scotched that by
blocking his direct access to the sea.'

'Maybe that's what set him on his way to Westminster,'
said Grenfell, grinning. 'You'd be surprised what they get
up to there nowadays, It's one of my reasons for getting
out.'

'You're absolutely resolved on it, Jimmy?'

'Yes I am,' said Grenfell and gave Paul a narrow glance. 'You've taken a beating since the slump set in and your boys went off. Could you take another wallop?'

'You've decided there's no alternative to Tories and Socialism?'

'No,' said Grenfell, 'nothing so drastic. That last time I was in dock – just before the last General Election – I asked them to give it to me straight. They did! Cancer! I'd like to have a crack at something creative before I go.'

It should not have been much more of a shock than Eveleigh's stroke. For a long time now Claire had been worried about Jimmy Grenfell's health and his spells in hospital, but Paul, regarding him as a frail man but knowing him for a fighter had never shared her concern, certainly not to the degree it merited. Grenfell gave him a moment to ride out the punch and said, placidly, 'I told Claire months ago and advised her to keep it from you. I didn't really believe she would but I see I misjudged her. Come now, it's not all that much of a shock. You knew I'd never make old bones and I'm pretty well satisfied with the run I've had for my money.'

'How long did they give you?' Paul asked, feeling like a child in the presence of Jimmy's size and toughness.

'Oh, they blathered about another operation,' Grenfell said, 'but who the devil wants to die the death of a thousand cuts in a clinic noisy with lamentation? I'm like your old friend Eveleigh, I prefer to die on my feet. However, I might as well choose the locality and I'm damned if I want to spend my last few months listening to professional liars like Stan Baldwin and Ramsay. They're all pitiful when you measure 'em against real men, chaps like Asquith, Grey, Haldane and even poor old Bonar Law. Post-war change isn't limited to the Valley, Paul. You'd have to face it no matter where you went.'

'What are your plans, Jimmy? Will you wait for another election?'

'Oh yes, it'll be this autumn in my view and I need daily access to the Public Record Office and the library of the House while I finish my research. This book means a lot to me, Paul. I've been at it, off and on, for ten years. After that, I'll find somewhere down here and watch the sunset.'

'You'll watch it from Shallowford,' Paul said, 'and don't let's have any polite excuses! Claire would wish it, Maureen will be on tap, and the place has been half-empty since the boys left.'

Grenfell's face lit up with pleasure. 'You mean that? It isn't a sympathetic reflex?' and when Paul grunted impatiently, 'Then I'd like that, Paul. It has shape, for in a way it all began in your library – that time I called uninvited, remember? And I'm not such a fool as to imagine I should ever have won the seat if I hadn't had you behind me. I've never had more than a slim majority and it was made up of people who trusted me because they liked and trusted you. Will you write to me after you've talked to Claire? It's her decision, you know.'

He talked to Claire that same night, anticipating her approval and getting it. She had always understood the strength of the bond between the two men and, like most of the women in the Valley, had long since succumbed to Jimmy Grenfell's shy charm and integrity. She said, 'He can have Simon's old room. It faces south and is big enough to use as a study. He can do his writing there and come and go as he pleases by the garden stair. When will he move in?'

Paul said he thought after Parliament had dissolved for the summer recess but that between then and now they had to get busy looking for a challenger to Sydney Codsall's pretensions. She said, with a yawn, 'I wouldn't try too hard, Paul. If Jimmy says he'll get in he will. We only scraped home last time because of Jimmy's personal following.'

'But we can't just hand that little bastard the seat on a plate! I'd sooner stand myself than let that happen!'

'You won't do anything so silly!' she said emphatically and when, like a thwarted boy he challenged her, she got up and crossed to the rug, looking down at him with a mixture of sympathy and impatience.

'You ask why? For any number of reasons! In the first place an MP has to spend at least half his time in London; in the second you don't really give a damn about what happens outside this Valley and never have, but most of all because, as an MP, you'd lose the thing about you that's more important to me and everyone else about here, that makes you different and easy to love!'

'Now what the hell would that be?' he demanded, laughing at her but she did not smile.

'Your faith in people and your instinctive trust in them! You wouldn't keep that once you started bandying words with that glib bunch! No, Paul, you can put that out of your mind, and Jimmy, Henry Pitts or anyone else with your true interests at heart will tell you the same if they're honest!' and she went off to bed, leaving him to ponder her advice by the fire. She was right, of course, and in any case, when it came to the touch, he doubted if his pride was equal to a defeat at the hands of a man like Sydney Codsall. It occurred to him, however, that she might be out-of-date in her estimate of human beings and Valley folk in particular. He still liked and trusted the hard core, men like Henry, Francis Willoughby, Sam and Smut Potter, and women like Marian Eveleigh and Martha Pitts, and even some of the latecomers like the French Canadian, Brissot, and his sky-larking partner, Jumbo Bellchamber, but he was not nearly so sure of the youngsters, of his own sons, of second-generation Potters and the Valley flappers who plastered their faces with make-up and seemed to spend most of their time waiting for the 'bus to Paxtonbury and Whinmouth. Sydney himself was of this generation, too young to have suffered in the war but old enough to join in the scramble for the wreckage of a civilisation that had once offered security and serenity to anyone who did not complain of an aching back or expect too much in the way of bonuses.

'Well, I daresay she knows what she's talking about,' he thought, heaving himself up and shelving a final decision until he could assess the prospects of drumming up a candidate with a sporting chance. 'Maybe most people see Sydney as I've always seen him and won't take him too seriously.'

Some did, however, as he was obliged to admit before this year of setbacks had lurched into a crisis that rang alarm bells as far west as the Sorrel Valley.

Chapter Fourteen

I

Perhaps the first of the Valley uncommitted to take a markedly serious view of Sydney Codsall was Hugh Derwent, freeholder of High Coombe.

No one had ever seemed to get the true measure of Hugh. At the age of fifty he was unmarried, seldom moved more than twenty miles east or west of the Bluff and was, in a sense, the Valley sphinx, a man who kept very much to himself and had no real friends, apart from Francis Willoughby, his next-door neighbour at Deepdene. Often enough his dogged neutrality puzzled Francis, who nevertheless ambled to Hugh's defence when his name came up for periodical speculation in the bar of The Raven or the Paxtonbury cattle-market, those two changing-houses of Valley gossip.

Paul had confessed to Claire often enough that he had never been able to guess what her brother Hugh was thinking and Claire said this was not really surprising for Hugh had never had a thought at all but got by very well on instinct. He was a prudent if unenterprising farmer, without his father's prickly pride, his sister Rose's amiability, or his sister Claire's natural sparkle and quick temper. In a sense, but without setting out to deceive or conciliate, Hugh Derwent was all things to all men. Some said he was 'near', which, in the Valley idiom, meant careful with loose change. Others said he was not mean, silent and withdrawn by nature but was exceptionally shy and shyness made him difficult to know. The children thought of him as even crustier than old Edward Derwent and kept clear of his neat fields but Francis Willoughby held Hugh was not so much crusty as lonely, and missed the bustle that had prevailed at High Coombe when Rose's riding school had been

based there and the place was always full of laughing girls
and young men mooning after Claire before her elevation to
Squiress. His purchase of the freehold from his brother-in-law,
towards the end of 1929 surprised nobody, for it had long been
known that all the Derwents were land-hungry. On becoming a
freeholder, however, and taking over from his father, Hugh had
withdrawn even more from his neighbours and although he
gave them all the traditional Valley salute – a circular flourish
of the right hand and a sound midway between a grunt and a
cough – he rarely gave them anything else but went about his
business with ponderous tread and level gaze. Paul, who had
always been curious about him, occasionally plied Claire for
information about his youth. Had he ever been any different?
Had he ever shown an inclination to specialise, as had Francis
Willoughby with his beef cattle? Had he ever fallen in love?
To the last question Claire, taxing her memory, said there had
been a phase in Hugh's life when he was about nineteen when
he had begun to brush his clothes, wear a necktie instead
of a choker, and plaster his hair with grease and that these
actions were outward manifestations of his obsession with
Queenie Pitts, a cousin of Henry's, who had spent summer
holidays at Hermitage. But Queenie had married a sergeant
of the Royal Marines, after which Hugh had reverted to his
old morose habits and had seemed, she recalled, more relieved
than heart-sore. What was Queenie Pitts like, he asked, and
she said she was a plump, jolly girl, with Henry's smile, lots of
freckles and a propensity to say 'Ooo-ahhh!' in her earnestness
to agree with everybody and keep the atmosphere congenial.
  'She sounds as if she might have done him a lot of good,'
Paul said and Claire agreed, adding that the Derwents were a
warm-blooded lot and that Hugh's moroseness was probably
caused by his never having enjoyed a woman, for she was
ready to swear he was still a virgin.
  Virgin or not Hugh Derwent set Valley tongues wagging in
the summer of 1931.

  Francis Willoughby was the first to get an inkling of what was
happening. He was crossing his top field adjoining Derwent's

land one day when he noticed a smart new car parked in High
Coombe's approach lane but did not remark on it until, on the
third occasion it was there, he saw Hugh and Sydney Codsall
emerge from the yard, stand talking for a moment and shake
hands before parting. After Sydney had backed out he went
along the hedge and called, genially, 'What's young Bighead
after, Hugh?' using the name Sydney's detractors had coined for
a son of old Martin, who had taken to wearing town clothes. To
his surprise Hugh Derwent flushed, mumbled something noncommittal and at once withdrew, obviously disinclined to
discuss the visit, but a surprise of a more dramatic nature
was in store for Francis that week. A day or so later an earth-
moving machine arrived in charge of a squad of Whinmouth
navvies and began to bite into Derwent's northern boundary
hedge, clawing its way across two clover fields and swallowing
soil and hedgerows like a starving mastodon let loose on the
countryside. This was too much, even for an incurious man
like Francis. He crossed over to High Coombe, sought out
its master and said, with the resentment of a traditionist
witnessing a landscape change, 'What the hell be 'em about,
Hugh? Be 'em laying a culvert or zummat?'

Hugh looked, he recounted later, very shifty but said,
'They'm coming through, Francis! Tiz all zigned and zettled!'
and when pressed for more detailed information, admitted
that he had sold a freeway connecting Codsall's quarry
and the main road north of Shallowford, to the cliff-top
fields east of the Bluff. Francis was amazed and said so
but Hugh, with a flash of Derwent temper, replied, 'What
business is it of anyone else? Tiz my land now and I
paid for it!' after which he stumped off and Francis,
greatly troubled, pondered developments a day or two
before seeking out Claire and telling her what was happening on the eastern edge of the Valley. He was prepared
for indignation but not the dismay she displayed the moment
he explained what was occurring.

'You're sure of this? Codsall's men are actually working
there now?' and when he confirmed that this was the case
and it looked as though the new road would pass within fifty

yards of the farmhouse, she said, quietly, 'Thank you, Francis! Don't tell anyone else and be sure you keep it from Squire! I'm going over there right away.'

She was bumping down High Coombe approach track within the hour and found her brother drinking his morning cocoa at the kitchen table. He seemed displeased but not surprised when she burst into the room and sent his daily woman Flossie Waring packing, with a curt 'Leave us, Floss!'

'What the devil is going on here, Hugh?' she demanded. 'Have you leased Codsall a right-of-way, or have you been such a fool as to let him talk you into selling a strip?'

He said, with defiance that did not fool her, 'He's bought it! Paid a crazy price for it! It's like I told Francis, tiz all zigned and zettled, and nobody's business but mine!'

'*What* is signed and settled?'

'The sale! What else? I've done wi' farming, drat it! I got more sense than any of 'em, I reckon.'

Claire was so appalled that she could only echo his words, the full meaning of which took some time to register. '*Done* with farming? What on earth do you mean "done with farming"? How can you be done with farming? You're still here, aren't you?'

'Yes,' he said, 'but I won't be, come Quarter Day! I'll be long ways off and married too, mostlike.'

At any other time the mere possibility of her brother Hugh marrying, or even contemplating marriage, would have put every other thought out of her head but under the shock of his admission she let the incidental news pass as irrelevant and said, breathlessly, 'Look here, Hugh, who do you think you're fooling? Paul sold you the freehold because he knew you and Father always hankered after it! It was me who persuaded him and you can't sell it, not even if you wanted to!'

He put down his mug and stood up. She had never realised how much weight had been added to his lumbering frame since the war. Today he looked gross and out of condition, and his eyes, which had always held a puzzled, slightly worried expression, were as cold and blue as a March sky. She said, with sudden concern, 'What *is* it, Hugh? You aren't sick, are you? If you are . . .'

'Never felt better!' he said shortly, 'nor more pleased wi' meself! And tidden a particle o' use asking me to change my mind because it's like I said, all zigned and zettled!'

'I keep asking you *what* is signed and settled!' she almost screamed, and his rather pursey mouth twitched, almost as though he found her extreme exasperation amusing.

'You'd better get it straight and go back so as your man can swallow it in one piece,' he said. 'It'll be less sour than nibbling, piece at a time! Codsall been badgering me for more than a year to sell him Eight Acre and Top Warren. Offered me near as much for two meadows as I paid for the whole parcel. Well, I held him off until I run across Queenie – Queenie Pitts that was. She's been a widow twelve years or more, did you know that?'

'Never mind Queenie Pitts! Did you sell Sydney Eight Acre and Top Warren? Did you?'

'Aye, I did,' he said, watching her carefully, 'and more!'

'How much more?'

'The whole of it.'

'High Coombe? The *house*? *This* house?'

'He woulden have it no other way, so we settled on Saturday.'

Suddenly her knees began to buckle and she half turned from him to sit on the end of the long oak bench running the length of the big refectory table. There wasn't a thing about this kitchen that lacked association with her childhood, especially those years before the day they brought her mother into the yard and she saw her through the inglenook window, a bundle under a covering of coats. Sitting here, her head in a whirl and her body shaking, it was as though the most terrible moment of her life had returned to gloat and reduce her once again to a little ghost with two swinging plaits and pointed dancing shoes, worn for the first time that day in anticipation of Mary Willoughby's Christmas party. She said, in a whisper, 'Is it final, Hugh? There's no crying off?' and he answered gruffly that there was not, for he had made up his mind to change the entire pattern of his life and Codsall's price was 'the daftest ever paid for a Valley farm and likely to be 'till the crack of doom!' The mention of money seemed to relax him and iron away some of his truculence, for he stood over her grinning and said, 'Here, lass, what's there to fuss about? I only sold what was mine since Father took himself off. Dammit, your husband would have sold at that price if he'd known about it!'

His reference to Paul restored to her the power of protest. She shouted, 'That's a damned lie, Hugh! Paul wouldn't have, no matter what Sydney was offering!' but his grin broadened so that suddenly he was no longer a paunched, balding man of fifty but a teasing brother, enjoying the time-honoured High Coombe game of 'making Claire's eyes spark'. He said, genially, 'Now see here, Claire, what's wrong with me sitting in a dish o' cream for a change? You been squatting in one ever since you nabbed young Squire and Rose weren't long following suit! Why damme girl, you've got pretty nigh the whole Valley under your hand, an' Rose spends more on her hunters in one year that I earn in two! I'm gone fifty; I don't want to stay an' wear out, like old Norman Eveleigh yonder. Besides, like I said, I ran into Queenie, and she's that bonny you'd never believe and her not a year younger'n you!'

It was his seeming inability to understand the nature of his betrayal that baffled her for when she turned away he grabbed her arm and she saw that he was holding up a snapshot for her inspection, almost as though he felt confident that she had only to glance at it to approve his act. She saw that it was a picture of a blowzy, smirking woman in a bathing costume, and although just recognisable as Queenie Pitts, it had little relation to the bucolic girl she remembered in her teens. It was inconceivable, she thought, that a cautious, unimaginative man like Hugh should be eager to exchange land he had farmed all his life for a late-flowering courtship with a fat, rather coarse-looking woman, but perhaps he did not see her as she was but as she had seemed to him the better part of thirty years ago. It was this that prompted her to make a final attempt to shame him if he was capable of being shamed. Behind him, hanging where it had hung throughout much of her childhood, was a large, oval-framed portrait of their mother, a picture sadly dated and taken God knows how many years ago in a Whinmouth studio, of a handsome, smiling woman, under a broad picture hat and wearing a blouse with leg-o'-mutton sleeves that looked like a pair of waterwings. She pushed past him and unhooked the picture, tucking it under her arm and making for the door but the action increased his truculence and he moved to stop her, shouting, 'Now lissen here, Claire, tidden a particle o' use your man storming over here, and making a scene . . .' but when she evaded him he followed her out into the yard, trotting alongside as she climbed into the car, started the engine and began to reverse rapidly up the lane. Tears blurred her vision so that she struck the bank more than once but she outdistanced him easily enough and swung into the Dell road, leaving him behind in a cloud of exhaust. She thought, 'I've got to be the one to tell Paul! I won't be answerable for what he might do if it passed to him as Valley gossip!' and she calmed a little, pushing the car up the one-in-four gradient on the shoulder of the Bluff.

She found him in the Home Farm strawyard talking to young Honeyman and drew him aside, pouring out her tale and waiting for him to erupt. He did not; instead he heard her out, interposing one or two terse, factual questions about the farm's conveyance, the proposed route of the new road and other aspects of the sale, questions that she was unable to answer. His voice was steady but she noticed that his cheek twitched when she repeated what Hugh had said about herself and Rose. Then, quite suddenly, she realised that he was not angry at all but was regarding her with sympathy, and his arm went round her as he led her to the far side of the rick, out of earshot of Honeyman and his men. He said, briefly, 'You're taking this on yourself, aren't you? Well don't! It was my decision to sell to your father and how the hell were you to know he'd pass it to Hugh almost at once? For that matter, how could you or anyone else anticipate a thing like this? The real wrong Hugh has done is not giving me a chance to buy it back again; I don't care what that young bastard Codsall gave him, I would have covered it, even if I had had to mortgage the entire bloody Valley! However, it's done and I don't suppose it can be reversed at this stage – that depends on the conditions your father handed over to Hugh. I'll drive over and see him right away and I'd prefer you not to come. Will you walk across the fields, or shall I ask Honeyman to run you home in the trap?'

'I'll walk,' she said gratefully, 'and . . . thank you, Paul!' and she brushed his cheek. She wanted to say much more. She wanted to tell him he had never seemed so big or so dignified as at that moment, when it must have seemed that everything he had striven for over the years had been mocked and belittled but he turned and left her and a moment later was driving down the river road towards Whinmouth.

Edward Derwent was not at home when Paul knocked at the door of his quayside cottage but Liz told him that he had had a letter from the local solicitor that morning and it had seemed to upset him. He had gone out with his breakfast half eaten and that was unusual for he 'did zo take to his bacon an' eggs'. Paul said, 'Where's the nearest 'phone-box, Liz?' and she pointed to one outside the harbour-master's office no more than a step away, so he said good-bye and crossed the quay to telephone Snow and Pritchard, the firm the Derwents used on the few occasions they needed a lawyer. They told him that Mr Derwent had indeed called that morning but had gone again, they understood to visit his son. The information troubled Paul. He knew Edward Derwent for an impulsive man if his dander was up, so he jumped in the car and put his foot down all the way to the moor highway that linked up with the dust road running across the headwaters of the two rivers. It was the longest way round but the way the old man would have taken if he made the journey by trap, and he remembered that Edward Derwent neither hired cars nor drove them. He reached the junction of roads in half-an-hour and it was not until he was descending the hill that the sourness of Claire's news rose in his throat, tainting his palate like bile. He had a swift and agonising vision of what the estate map would look like when Codsall had finished with High Coombe, had cut his road and blocked the whole eastern boundary of the estate with bungalows, quarry shacks and God knew what else. Shallowford would be punched into an ungainly figure eight, with 'development' reaching as far as the edge of the Dell and then all the way to the coast. Coombe Bay would change overnight, becoming, no doubt, a snappy little resort, with a prim promenade, shelters and 'attractions' of one sort and another, and whom would they attract? Not men with a craft at their fingertips, like old Tom Williams and Abe Tozer the smith but carloads of week-enders, strewing paper bags and cigarette packets all over the gutters and townees to man shops displaying mass-produced goods behind chromium-plated windows! Well, no one alive could stop it altogether, he supposed, but where was the sense in accelerating the process and this, it would seem, was what Sydney and his kind had in mind, and for no better purpose than to line their own pockets. God damn the lot of them, he thought, and especially that bloody traitor Hugh Derwent, and he swung the car off the road into a passing bay to allow the passage of a two-horse farm wagon approaching at a walk.

It was not until the vehicle had drawn almost level that he noticed the waggoner was Hugh Derwent himself, hunched on the box with the reins slack in his hand. He shot out his hand to open the offside door and leap out and then he stopped halfway out, checked partly by his brother-in-law's dejected air but more so by a livid cut spotted with congealed blood on his cheekbone. He opened his mouth to say something but Hugh did not even glance at the car. In a moment the waggon had gone creaking on its way leaving a debris of twigs and leaves where it had brushed the nearside hedge. In another moment it had passed out of sight round the bend in the narrow track.

Edward Derwent was standing in the centre of the yard when he drove up, waiting beside the pump almost as though he expected him and Paul noticed that he looked very trim in his serviceable tweeds and the deerstalker he had affected since his retirement. 'More like a retired colonel than a farmer,' Paul thought, with a grin, and without knowing why suddenly felt a great deal more cheerful, although, from where they

stood, he could hear the chink of spades on flint as Codsall's
workmen dug their way across Eight Acre. Paul said, 'I saw
Hugh near the crossroads and he looked pretty sorry for
himself! You're not going to tell me you thrashed him?'

'I caught him one or two before he ran for it,' the old man
said but with no answering smile. 'It's damned lucky for him
I brought this instead of a double-barrel!' and he lifted a heavy
walking-stick tipped with a brass ferrule. 'I was coming over
if you hadn't shown up. Not that there's much to say, you
can't do a thing to stop it, lad.'

'I didn't imagine I could,' Paul told him. 'I just hoped, I
suppose. Claire was very upset. What happened exactly?'

'I threw him off,' the old man said, 'the same as I would a
poacher. Oh, he owns the place legally, at least until Codsall
moves in on Quarter Day, but I told him if I found him about
the place between then and now I'd shoot him, even if I had
to hang for it! Aye, and I would too, that's no boast!' Paul
said, quietly, 'Is there a drink in the house? We could both
do with one, Edward!' and led the way inside, noting that
the kitchen showed signs of a hasty evacuation, with dresser
drawers open and furniture pushed to one side. Old Derwent
went into the scullery and came back with a bottle of gin in
one hand and an orange in the other and Paul watched as
he poured two measures, sliced the orange with his penknife
and squeezed a half into each glass. 'That's so like him,' he
thought. 'The old boy has probably never heard of bottled
fruit-juice of the kind they'll soon be selling from kiosks in
Coombe-Bay-on-Sea!' and they sipped in silence. Paul said, at
length, 'Someone will have to tend the stock, Edward. Shall I
tell your man Gregory to carry on?'

'No,' Edward said, 'I'll have a word with Gregory before I
go to bed. I shall stay unto the last minute. I ought never to
have left here; never!' and his eyes ranged the room, stopping
at the patch of discoloured wallpaper between window and
fireplace.

'Claire took it,' Paul told him, 'it was a gesture, I suppose,
but I'll ask her to bring it back when she comes over.

'You never knew Claire's mother, did you?'

'No, she was killed a few years before I got here. She was very popular and very beautiful, I believe.'

The old man walked across to the slate hearth and stood with one arm on the mantel looking into the empty grate. Paul had always thought of him as a prematurely aged man; this afternoon he looked ninety, although Paul knew he was no more than seventy odd.

'She was the pride of the Valley,' Edward said. 'To see her in full-cry was to see wind crossing standing corn, boy! Claire favours her in looks, and Rose in style, but neither one could hold a candle to Molly in her prime! Damned if I ever could understand what she saw in me. Thought about that many a time and never found an answer.'

'I could give him one,' Paul thought, 'but it would only embarrass him. The readiness of a man ready to kill his only son for selling off land to a jobbing builder probably had something to do with it; that, plus his guts and integrity. With five men like him I could hold the Valley against all comers but there aren't five, only three now – him, me and Henry Pitts. The reinforcements haven't shown up so, from here on, it's digging in and that's an end to it!' Something still puzzled him, however, and he said, 'Didn't Hugh fight back? He could have held you off with one hand and laughed in your face, Edward!'

'He hasn't a ha'porth of real guts,' the old man said. 'I don't know how Molly and me came to spawn a boy like Hugh. Seems all our spunk went into the girls!' And then, cocking an eye, 'He'll not show his face in the Valley again until I'm six foot under! You'd better warn Claire of that.'

'She'll lose no sleep over it,' Paul said but the old man shook his head. 'A family ought to stick together to the end. I always tried to teach 'em that after their mother went but I must have taken a wrong turn somewhere.'

'You didn't,' Paul said, 'but I daresay Hugh did when that girl of his showed him her backside. There's a lot of us who would like a chance to catch time by the tail and I suppose he sees the chance of doing it, or thinking he can,' and as he said this he felt an alien current of sympathy for Hugh Derwent, remembering his own desperate loneliness after Grace had gone and before Claire took her place. He said, in an effort to cheer Edward, 'I suppose we've got a lot to be thankful for. I could never bear a brother of Claire permanent ill-will and I'll tell you something else too. Whatever I've managed to do here in the last quarter century I couldn't have done without Claire, so you still have a generous share in it, Edward.'

The old man pushed himself off the mantel, turned and retraced his steps to the table and as he reached for his glass his moustache twitched. In a man of Edward Derwent's temperament this was the equivalent of Henry Pitts' braying laugh. He said, 'I'll tell you one thing young-feller-me-lad! When you first settled here I wouldn't have wagered a flagon of cider on your chances! I was wrong about Hugh and wrong about you, so you can write me off as a dam' bad judge o' character! Nobody could have done more for this place and the way you've gone about it has been right – right all the way down the line, so don't let that Martin Codsall's boy or my boy, or any other Clever Dick tell you that isn't so, now or ever! I'll drink to you, lad, to get the taste of my own kin out of my mouth!' and he drained the glass and began moving round methodically shutting drawers and straightening furniture.

'Will you want your things sent over tonight?' Paul asked and Edward said he would. Claire could telephone the harbour-master and ask him to tell Liz to pack them up and get ready to move back.

'Will she want to do that just for a few weeks?'

'She'll do as I bliddy well tell her!' the old man retorted. 'I've yet to get a back-answer from my second wife, although I got plenty from the first!' He stopped what he was doing and looked at Paul. 'Tell me, lad,' he said, 'have you ever had any tussles with my girl? I always reckoned she'd take some managing. Did you ever have call to belt her?'

'Only once,' Paul said, smiling, 'and it was a long time ago. Maybe that once was enough.'

The old man looked at him with admiration. 'I always did tell Willoughby and old Arthur Pitts that there was a deal more to you than you could tell by looking,' he said, 'so at least I was right about one thing!'

Paul left him on that and went out into the yard. The hot sun sucked humid steam from a neatly-piled stack of manure and already the farm seemed half-deserted. A dog was sound asleep over by the pump and a blue-check pigeon was the only moving thing between byre and house. From over the hedge came the persistent chink of spade and the rumble of a wheelbarrow rolling along a plant track. He looked over the wall beside the building where Rose had had her stables and saw a seam of earth glowing red, like the wound on Hugh Derwent's cheek. A few workmen pottered to and fro and beyond was a man in town clothes setting up a surveyor's tripod. He went back to the car and eased it along the lane until he could turn and then drove home, thinking not of the eastern defences, which had crumbled, but those in the west, of the deserted Periwinkle and the masterless Four Winds. 'It's time,' he told himself, 'we had a little luck but I daresay it will all run Sydney's way until the election. After that who knows? Who knows anything at all?

II

By the time Quarter Day came round he had other things to think about and so, for that matter, had most people. The alarm bells of national bankruptcy were ringing in Fleet Street and urgency ruffled the bland voices of radio announcers so that even in the Valley, where people were very slow to panic, folk became aware of the crisis and the possibility of a general election, 'To Give the Government a Mandate For Economy'. That, thought Paul, was how it was always projected, in stunning capitals, with the emphasis on what was expected from the governed rather than what could be expected from the governors. Henry Pitts must have noticed as much for one morning, meeting Paul on the river road, he shouted, ''Ave 'ee 'eard the latest, Maister? We'm goin' broke, on account of all that bliddy cash you an' me 'ave been sploshing about zince us was demobbed, backalong!'

That was about it, thought Paul. The men in charge muddled along, bickering one with the other and trying this and that expedient until the machine slithered to a halt. Then, like the feckless head of an improvident household, they announced that there would have to be a cut in housekeeping, sacrifices all round and no more pocket money for anyone. His cynical attitude towards politics, fostered by a decade of agricultural depression, had been deepened by the arrival of Jimmy Grenfell, with the benefit of thirty years' close-range experience of professional politicians. Sentence of death had put a cutting edge on Grenfell's sense of humour and he beguiled some of his sleepless hours in front of the library fire after Claire had gone to bed sketching for Paul a gallery of lively portraits of the shady, the earnest and the pompous with whom he had hobnobbed since he first entered 'The Club', as he called it, about the time the Tsar's fleet fired on British fishing smacks in the belief that they were Japanese warships. Listening to him Paul began to doubt the practicability of democracy but when he admitted his doubts Jimmy only said, with a shrug, 'There are really only two choices, Democracy and Muddle, or Dictatorship and Tyranny. I admit I've sometimes wondered which is preferable but I've always come down in favour of muddle, if only because it can always be temporarily tidied without a blood bath. I daresay we shall stagger on for another decade or so, but as for finding the right answers, as we believed ourselves capable of doing in 1906, that's just a pipe-dream! The Holy Grail was lost long ago and it's not likely to turn up in Westminster.'

Paul went along, accompanied by Henry Pitts and Smut Potter, to Sydney Codsall's adoption meeting in the Paxtonbury Drill Hall and found it a less humiliating experience than he had anticipated, largely on account of his companions' lively commentary. The prospect of Sydney Codsall as a Member of Parliament struck Henry as so uproariously funny that all that shushing on the part of rosetted stewards could not prevent him from expressing opinions that would have led to him being thrown out in days when Paxtonbury folk took their politics seriously.

'Giddon, tiz a bliddy miracle!' he kept muttering. 'Marty Codsall's boy, zitting up there like a tailor's dummy, askin' us to zend un to Parlyment! Why damme, I never zeed ole Marty in collar an' tie in his life and all the politics he ever knowed was how much water to add to 'is milk!'

When Henry was only warned to keep quiet, and not expelled from the meeting, Smut joined in, saying that they ought to have had his mother, Arabella, up there on the platform. ''Er voice could carry furthest of anyone in the Valley,' he added, half-way through Sydney's personal promise to build the League of Nations into an effective instrument for peace. 'You could have heard Arabella from the far zide o' Cathedral Close and I can't catch no more'n the odd word o' the boy's, can you, Henry?'

'No,' said Henry, 'but I'm sure o' one thing, I baint missin' much!' and Smut's barking laugh made so many people turn that Paul hustled them out and they adjourned to the public bar of The Mitre where Henry, suddenly more serious, said, 'Lookit, Maister, is us goin' to let un get away with it? Tiz the daftest thing ever happened yerabouts, a toad like 'ee standin' for farmers! Baint there nothin' us can do about it?'

'Not much,' Paul told him, 'for we still haven't got a candidate. He won't be unopposed, however, a Labour chap is putting up, a University lad sent down to get experience.'

Smut said, with a picturesque oath, 'A bolshie is wastin' his time yerabouts. If you stood us'd 'ave a sportin' chance anyway. Dammit, we voted solid Liberal here nigh on thirty years, so why have us let this happen? Politics never bothered me much, apart from the larks us got up to in the old days, but to see Marty Codsall's boy standing gives me the gripes, I can tell 'ee!' to which Henry added, 'Why *dornee* 'ave a go, Squire? 'Twould liven things up any road.'

It was not the first pressures that had been applied to him as the weeks passed and still no acceptable successor to Grenfell presented himself. Liberal farmers from the villages north of Paxtonbury made approaches and some of the Old Guard, who had helped to send Jimmy back to Westminster several times in succession, seemed to resent his steadfast refusal to involve himself. He continued to stand aloof until mid-September, when the date of the election was announced and the Socialist party split down the middle with the Premier, Ramsay MacDonald, and others making common cause with the Opposition. Grenfell said, on hearing this news over Claire's new four-valve radio set, 'Well, there's an end to the Liberal Party. We've been slowly bleeding to death ever since Lloyd George knifed us, in December, 1916. Now we shall have to choose Right or Left, with no hedging of bets! Thank God Asquith didn't live to see it!'

It was Grenfell's comments on this occasion that reminded Paul of his own broadly-based faith in Democracy, a credo that, in his view, offered few fireworks but rather a steady promise of improvement for those dedicated to the ideal of personal liberty practised within a framework of disciplined free enterprise. It was very difficult for him to stand aside altogether and see a man who despised farmers as clod-hoppers seek to represent the Valley in national councils, yet nomination day would have come and gone without him taking positive action had not Claire done a sudden right-about-face and ranged herself on the side of Henry, Smut and all the others urging him to take up the challenge.

They were sitting before the library fire one night listening to the midnight news-bulletin when she said, without preamble, '*Do* it, Paul! I was wrong! You won't win but do it anyway, as a gesture!'

He was amused but also slightly alarmed at her insistence. It was not losing he feared but losing ignominiously. He said, 'You weren't wrong, you know; all the arguments you used against my standing were valid. Why this sudden change of heart?'

'I think Hugh has something to do with it, Hugh and the man who bought him. I went over there today to help Father and Liz pack up.'

'Well?'

'It was pitiful, not just the old couple having to leave but the place itself, so empty and lifeless, with the stock sold off and not even a hen scratching about in the nettles. It was a kind of death.'

'I don't see the connection between the write-off of Hugh Coombe and me standing for Parliament.'

'There is a connection,' she insisted, 'but I'm not clever enough to state it. It has to do with standing up for our way of life, a banner that has to be picked up and waved by someone, if only for a few moments!'

He pondered this and with it the issues, most of them unconnected with the everyday life of the few hundred people living between the main line and the sea – far wider issues, involving tariffs, overseas payments, war debts, the League of Nations, the guilt of Germany, the truculence of France, on which he would be asked to pronounce and in which he was not, and never had been, deeply interested. If he stood at all it would be as a candidate in the old-fashioned sense, a local man seeking to represent local causes which was a role not even Jimmy Grenfell had been able to play for much of his time in Westminster. And yet, she was right again, even if she did stand in flat contradiction to herself. 'A banner to be picked up and waved, if only for a few moments . . .'

'All right,' he said, finally, 'if you're behind me I'll have a go and to hell with it! Do we go up and tell Jimmy now? He's probably awake and reading.'

'No,' she said, 'it can keep for tonight!' and then she did something she had not done for a long time, kicking off her shoes, coiling herself on his knee and saying, 'I know I'm a good deal heavier but you'll have to put up with that! After all, it's an occasion!'

It was a brief, breathless campaign, waged, for the most part, in thin rain that seemed now to have been falling for months, ruining the harvest and converting the Sorrel streams into brown floods that burst their banks and spread far across the flats, greatly hindered movement from one point to another. Looking back on that autumn election Paul found his memories of it fragmentary and insubstantial, a succession of dashes to and from draughty village halls and littered committee rooms, of open-air meetings in a dripping raincoat, and intervals of talk and endless cups of tea in steamy kitchens. He remembered the smells after he had forgotten the occasions, a salad of drying laundry, wet macintoshes, stale dust rising from the cracks of Institute platforms, and the sharp, schoolroom smell of freshly-printed leaflets and election addresses. His speeches were short and factual, concerned almost exclusively with the heavy slack of farm economy since the all-too-brief boom of ten years ago. He warned listless audiences of the steady drift from the land, urging the necessity of a sound agricultural policy if the country was not to become completely dependent on imported food. It was, he supposed, a very parochial campaign, with little appeal to voters living in the suburbs of the cathedral city, or elderly couples who had retired on fixed incomes to bungalows in places like Nun's Bay but it won over a sizeable number of the farmers who had been Tories all their lives and it detached from Labour's interests some of the unemployed who, in better times, had been rooted in local crafts like coach-building, shoeing, fishing, thatching and brick-making. He had a very zealous committee headed by Henry Pitts, Sam and Smut Potter, Marian Eveleigh, Parson Horsey and a few of the faithful living north of Paxtonbury. He also had a number of unexpected allies whom he used as supplementary speakers, men like the humorist, Jumbo Bellchamber, and Rose's aged husband, Major Barclay-Jones, who came down from Gloucestershire and cantered about the Valley like a vintage Paul Revere, scorning the use of committee cars. Mary, his eldest daughter, was with him heart and soul, endlessly addressing envelopes and answering the telephone, or waiting for him with a Thermos flask of coffee in the brief intervals between one meeting and another, and Claire's enthusiasm touched him even more for she had always professed to regard politics as a bore, as though to emphasise the contrast between herself and Grace. The constant rushing to and fro, and the vast expenditure of nervous energy listening to constituents' grumbles and remembering so many names and faces, made him feel his age but with only a few days to go he began, almost subconsciously, to rate his chances far better than at the outset of the campaign. He met, and made friends with, the young Socialist candidate, a rather forlorn figure who reminded him a little of his son Simon, and he found it possible to admire the earnestness of a lad whose deprived youth in a north-eastern shipbuilding town had made him an apostle of militant socialism. The Socialist candidate was called Hardcastle and his appearance in the Valley was a forlorn hope on the part of Labour but he fought cleanly and doggedly, and Paul went so far as to put him in touch with Simon and Rachel, currently campaigning in a Welsh mining area. He did not come face to face with Sydney Codsall during the campaign. It was not until all the ballot boxes had been collected in Paxtonbury Town Hall that he saw him, outwardly smug but showing nervousness when the counting began, and wondered what attitude he would take if Sydney was disposed to be patronising. He was spared a decision; Sydney and his agent kept their distance while he stood waiting with young Hardcastle, watching the votes pile up on the long trestle tables, three creeping stacks, his own and Sydney's maintaining a level advance and Hardcastle's almost a non-starter. He was familiar with the tense atmosphere of a count, having attended any number in the past and was surprised at his own indifference. He had picked up the banner and waved it, and that was all that mattered. When Claire and Mary joined him, and Claire (far more concerned with the result than he was himself) sought his hand for comfort, he said, with a grin, 'You needn't worry, old girl! It isn't going to be a walkover!' and shuttled her on to Hardcastle, who looked as if he needed mothering.

The result was far closer than anyone had anticipated having regard to the landslide in favour of the National Government all over the country. They told him the totals but he was almost too astonished to take them in and at one p.m., with everyone congratulating both leading candidates, the Returning Officer went out on to the balcony where a crowd awaited the result in the eternal drizzle. Only at the very last moment did Paul feel a void in the pit of his stomach and a parched feeling in the back of his throat that reminded him of nights behind Vimy, when he had been on the point of moving up to support areas with a convoy of shells or wire. Then, as he pulled himself together, he heard the fruity voice of the Returning Officer challenging the steady hiss of the rain:

'. . . Codsall, Sydney Algernon; thirteen thousand, one hundred and forty nine . . . Craddock, Paul; thirteen thousand . . .' but the next words were drowned in the roar that ascended from a crowd raised to a pitch of enthusiasm by the obvious closeness of the contest.

'. . . Craddock, Paul; thirteen thousand, one hundred and one!' Sydney had won but by so small a margin that it was nothing to crow about and certainly not so when his massive organisation was taken into account. To Paul it was better than a victory, for it meant justification without the horrid necessity of turning his back on the Valley and his relief was so great that he felt almost sorry for his opponent faced with the prospect of making good his electoral promises and discovering, as Grenfell had prophesied, that attendance at Westminster called for a great deal more stamina than the old-pals atmosphere of County and Urban politics in the provinces. Perhaps Sydney already realised this; his formal speech of thanks was delivered in a high, piping voice and interrupted by a volley of catcalls, organised, Paul suspected, by stalwarts like Henry and Smut. He left them at it and went back into the hall where Claire, pink with excitement, said, 'You don't look like a defeated candidate!' and plucked his sleeve nervously when he said, with unabashed heartiness, 'I don't feel like one either, old girl! Don't you ever push me that near the cliff again!' He shook off a swarm of supporters, saying, 'For God's sake let's get on home and pick up where we left off! Codsall can keep the seat warm until we can find someone who means business!'

Claire remained in what old Mrs Handcock always described as 'a bit of a tizzy' for the rest of the day but when the house was quiet, unnaturally so after the turmoil of the last three weeks, he poured her a double brandy and stood watching her sip it. He said, thankfully, 'My God, it's like coming home from the war! Like being turned loose again from hospital or the trenches! Why did we ever take such a risk?'

'We neither of us realised it was a risk. Frankly I thought you'd poll about a third of his total. It only goes to show.'

'To show what?'

She turned her back on him to set down her glass, at the same time throwing a glance at him over her shoulder that somehow reminded him of the saucy, provocative girl who had once helped him decorate this room for King Edward's Coronation soirée. 'It's like Father always says! There's a lot more to you than meets the eye!'

'Well,' he said, crossing to her, slipping his hands behind her and genially pinching her bottom, 'you should know! I suppose you would call this another of your famous "occasions"?'

'Look here,' she protested, 'all our married life you've been hard at work convincing yourself that I was a wanton! I daresay it flatters you but it isn't true!'

'Oh yes it is,' he said, 'and you've got six children to prove it! Do you want another drink?'

'No,' she said, 'and neither do you it seems!' and disengaged herself to throw a log on the fire and switch off the light.

'You're a lusty fifty-two, Paul,' she told him, 'so maybe I'm lucky you didn't win and get yourself a London flat and an admiring secretary!' but as she said this her mood shifted again and holding his face between her hands she said, 'We've been wonderfully lucky in spite of everything and we ought never to forget that when we run into the occasional bad patch! I was beginning to and so, I think, were you,' but his relief was too deep to share her sudden earnestness and all he replied was, 'Stop preaching, woman, it doesn't become you!' and began to treat her as though they had just returned, laughing and half-tipsy, from one of old Arthur Pitts' Hallowe'en parties in days when fashions in clothes made this kind of frolic a far less casual enterprise than it was today.

III

The long run of back luck ended almost at once. Within days
of the landslide election, when supporters were still pointing
out that he, alone of Westcountry candidates, had increased
the Liberal vote notwithstanding a massive Coalition victory,
Claire came into the office and said that young Eveleigh
wanted to talk to him. Paul looked up, expecting to see
Robbie, the baby of the family, now huntsman to the Sorrel
Vale pack but it was Robbie's elder brother, Harold, whom he
had not seen since Norman Eveleigh's funeral. Harold, the war
hero who had been commissioned in the field and decorated
for gallantry, looked apologetic and declined a drink, saying,
'Perhaps later, Mr Craddock, I'd prefer to talk first. The fact
is, I'm in the fashion – on the dole and have come to you with
half an idea.'

News that Harold was unemployed surprised him for he
had got the impression from Marian, as well as Harold himself, that the temporary gentleman of the long family has
done very well for himself and had continued to earn good
money throughout the Depression.

'I thought you were dug in,' he said and Harold replied,
bitterly, 'So did I, but it seems I didn't dig deeply enough! The
boss had a son down from 'Varsity and didn't know where to
place him. Then he remembered me and reckoned the war was
so long ago that we were due for the next, so out I went on
my ear! They didn't put it that way, of course – just the usual
cock about hard times and unavoidable economies! Odd how
these chaps can make a virtue of necessity. This crisis has
been a Godsend to some of them I can tell you!'

Paul said, sympathetically, 'We all get a kick in the pants
now and again and ex-service chaps more than their ration.
What was the idea you had?'

'Mother wondered if you would consider me as tenant at
Four Winds.'

Paul made no attempt to conceal his astonishment. Like all
the Eveleighs Harold had grown up on a farm but he had

enlisted at eighteen, and after the war had gone straight into industry. To come home with the notion of running Four Winds implied that he was either supremely self-confident or desperate; it was important to discover which for Four Winds was no place for a desperate man, using it as a temporary haven and Marian would surely be aware of that.

'You say it was your mother's idea.'

'No, it was mine; Mother doesn't think I could make it and she only let me apply because she's sorry for Connie and the kids.'

'You've got kids?'

'A boy and a girl, seven and five.'

'You've been able to save a bit?'

'A bit, but not much, the pay wasn't all that good.' He hesitated, then went on, 'I pretended it was better than it was when I came home! I always was a bit of a show-off, remember? The pips went to my head, I suppose. I daresay you heard about the time the old man had to clear my mess debts?'

'No, I didn't and you don't have to tell me.'

'I'd prefer to!'

'Well?'

'I never really settled after demob. Everything seemed stale and flat. It was a come-down to have to take one's place in the queue and be grateful for the odd glass of beer after whisky! I soon got out of my depth and the old man paid up but only on condition I resigned my commission. That was back in 1922.'

It was, Paul reflected, a familiar story – a boy boosted by his own courage and initiative and being spoiled by older men, whose experiences on the Western Front bred in them a terrible pity for the very young. Then peace and reaction, with any number of sprees in the Mess, and maybe a love-affair or two with girls overseas, who would encourage him to show off and spend freely. Finally Father's ultimatum and the bump back to earth, the assumption of parental responsibilities and the need to hold down a job in a competitive world. It must have happened a million times since 1918. He looked sharply at the young man and thought he could detect fear behind the eyes. Harold Eveleigh must have faced death many times but it needed a different kind of courage to tackle the challenges of the last year or so. And yet, pitying him and understanding his situation so well, Paul resisted the impulse to welcome him with open arms. Four Winds needed a dedicated man unless it was to go the way of High Coombe and tear yet another gap in Valley defences. He said, aware that he was temporising, 'You're over thirty now, Harold, and I don't suppose you've milked a cow or ploughed a furrow since you were seventeen. So far as I'm aware you've never even wanted to! That's what's important and that's why your mother was reluctant to encourage you. It won't be news to you that agriculture is down and out, or that it's damned low on the priority list of politicians.'

Harold said nothing but Paul could see he was digesting every word. 'It isn't that I wouldn't like to see an Eveleigh back at Four Winds,' he went on, 'but there's more to it than sentiment. I've poured a small fortune into the estate since the war but I can't go on doing it. Unless things mend very soon I shall be obliged to contract or throw in my hand.'

Harold Eveleigh shifted his weight from one foot to the other trying, without much success, to conceal his growing desperation. 'I see your point, Mr Craddock. You need someone with experience, the kind of farmer my brother Gilbert would have been if he hadn't had the bad luck to meet a bloody fool of a bomb-instructor.'

'No,' Paul said, 'not necessarily but I need someone with Gilbert's love of the place. I daresay your mother could supply the experience but let me put it this way; what I *don't* want is a man using Four Winds as a bolt-hole, someone who will move on when something less mucky turns up! I daresay that sounds priggish but I don't care if it does. This place means everything to me and I'll fight for it the way you fought Johnny Turk, with every bloody weapon I can lay my hands on!'

He gave him a moment or so to ponder, crossing to the sideboard and pouring two drinks. When he turned the young man was hunched by the window, hands deep in pockets, chin lowered as he looked beyond the leafless chestnuts to the point where Four Winds' boundary met the skyline midway between the rivers.

'Here's to Gilbert and all the others anyway,' Paul said, nudging his elbow and Harold said, slowly, 'I daresay I should have been as good a farmer as Gil if I'd stayed behind like Francis Willoughby, over at Deepdene. Come to that, we can't swear to how Gil would have reacted if he had survived and had to pitch in with the rest of us and make the best of it. Sometimes I think they were the lucky ones, Mr Craddock; chaps like Ikey Palfrey, Big Jem and all the others who went West! At least they died still believing in one another!'

'I still believe in the Valley and Four Winds is a vital part of it,' Paul said but he was touched nonetheless. There had been times when identical thoughts had occurred to him, particularly during the last few months.

Eveleigh went on, 'What can I say that won't sound like a bleat? I can't tell you I'm longing to trudge behind a plough, or that I think raising a crop of mangolds is Mankind's noblest endeavour, but ten years in industry has at least taught me there are far dirtier ways of earning a living! If I had my time over again I'd settle for mangold-raising as the lesser of two evils. I've got farming in my blood, I imagine, the same as Gil and all of us and I've got a flair with some animals. Apart from that I've got a duty to Connie and the kids, and two other things in my favour are that I'm fit and still old-fashioned enough to keep my word if I give it. If you like to take a chance on those qualifications I'll do my best and at least I'd accept guidance. I was pigheaded once but not any longer!'

Paul found himself drawn to the man, liking both his honesty and his awkward humility. It must, he thought, cost a son of Norman Eveleigh a great effort to admit so many shortcomings. He said, on impulse, 'Would you bring your wife over to see me, Harold?' and Harold said, 'She's here now, I left her in the kitchen having a cup of tea with Miss Mary but she knows even less than I do about running a farm. She gets on with Mother, however. She's a Lancashire lass and worked in a chocolate factory up to the time we married. Shall I fetch her?'

He sounded eager and Paul wrote this down as a point in his favour. He remembered Arabella, and how essential it was for a farmer's wife to accept the limits of the life if her husband was to succeed. A Lancashire girl, who had worked in a chocolate factory and who got along with Marian Eveleigh, sounded promising material. 'By all means,' he said, 'and bring Mary with her in case she's shy.'

Harold shot off like a boy at the end of an unpleasant interview and was back almost at once with a pretty brunette in tow, a tall girl with a very clear skin, soft brown eyes and a child's mouth. Mary, always at her best with shy people, came to the rescue saying, 'Shake hands with him, Mrs Eveleigh! He always scowls like that when he's introduced to anyone!' and Harold laughed, adding, 'She's not such a mouse! She thinks we're a soft lot in the South but says the climate makes up for us!'

'She can make Lancashire cream cheese,' Mary said, 'and I think she'll like it here,' but Harold said quickly, 'She might not get the chance, Miss Craddock! Your father is chewing it over and I'm hanged if I blame him! We're both rank amateurs and it isn't as if Mother was still young.'

'She's young enough to teach you a thing or two,' Paul said, 'so I'll get the new lease drawn up this afternoon. You and Marian can be joint tenants for three years and we'll see how things shape. Will that satisfy you?'

He saw young Eveleigh and his wife exchange a quick glance and read their relief. The girl Connie said, in a strong Lancashire accent, 'We'll make a go of it, Mr Craddock, I'll see to that!' and suddenly Paul knew that they would, that Harold and this pretty young wife of his were much-needed reinforcements and that Four Winds would soon regain its place as the natural bastion in the West. After they had gone Mary confirmed this impression. 'I took to her at once,' she said, 'she's down-to-earth and doesn't say things she doesn't mean!'

'That's a Lancashire characteristic,' he told her, 'we had hundreds of them about here during the war. The thing that decided me was the fact that they're prepared to take advice from Marian!' and then he smiled and when Mary asked the reason, added, 'I was thinking of the buzz in Four Winds' kitchen that led up to this – Harold and his wife trying every trick in the pack to talk Marian into acting as their spokesman, knowing that she would be a damned sight more likely to win me over than he would!'

'Well, it so happens you're wrong, Daddy. Marian wanted to come but the girl wouldn't let her. She told me she didn't want his mother talking-up for Harold. If you had turned them down they were leaving in the morning to look for work in London!'

He was struck by this and it reinforced him in the rightness of his decision. They had their troubles, these youngsters, but were probably maturing under them and somehow the entire interview now presented itself as a hopeful signpost into the future. Then, following this chain of thought, he remembered Rumble Patrick's last letter in which he talked of quitting Queensland for Alberta.

'You hear from Rumble a good deal more frequently than we do,' he said. 'Does this Canadian venture mean he's tired of sheep-farming and must needs fly off at another tangent?'

He saw the colour rush to her cheeks and instantly regretted the question. Her head came up sharply and she said, defensively, 'He's having to feel his way, like anyone else far from home! You don't have to worry about Rumble. He'll surprise you one of these days!' and she left the room with an abruptness that left him in no doubt at all but that she preferred to keep Rumble and Rumble's letters to herself. He thought, with a smile, 'Well, she'd damned touchy about him! I wonder if Claire knows as much as I think I know, and whether we ought to pool the evidence?' but postponed a decision as something that could wait and went into the office to find the old Four Winds' lease, drawn up the day after the inquest on Martin Codsall and his wife. Searching for it he came across the estate diary and opened it to see what Claire had written about the election. The entry startled him. Under October 19th, 1931, she had written: *'General Election: a three-cornered fight here with Paul Craddock standing as successor to James Grenfell,*

*Liberal MP for Paxtonbury since 1904. He was defeated, but
only just. General opinion is he could have won if he had tried.'*
That was all, a reasonable if prejudiced statement of fact, for
he had to admit that he was more elated over the Eveleigh
succession than he was deflated by defeat at the polls and
this must surely mean that he would carry his parochialism
to the grave. He turned a page and wrote, *'Harold Eveleigh,
second son of the late Norman Eveleigh, tenant of Four Winds
for twenty-five years and foreman prior to succeeding Martin
Codsall, today applied for and was granted the lease which he
will hold jointly with his mother, Marian Eveleigh. He is aged
32, married and has two children.'* It seemed incredible that
the man who had just asked for the lease had been the smaller
of the two night-shirted boys peering down at him the night
he thundered on the Eveleigh front door to pass the news that
Martin Codsall had killed Arabella and hanged himself.

Chapter Fifteen

I

Traveller, the oldest and craftiest fox inhabiting the country of the two rivers, could usually be found in Folly Wood, north of Heronslea, when said to be at home but it was not by remaining for long in one covert that he had survived any number of cracking days on the part of the Sorrel Vale Hunt. Robbie Eveleigh, huntsman to the local pack, had ceased to regard Traveller as a legitimate quarry and had his hounds succeeded in running the old rake to earth (which was unlikely, for Traveller had come to doubt the security of earths before he was half-grown) he would have probably called them off and cast around for a fresh scent; Traveller, he might have reasoned, had provided everybody in the district with so much sport for so many years that he had earned the right to die of old age.

Traveller was readily identifiable by less experienced men than Robbie. All the Heronslea keepers knew him, recognising his drooping left ear and abbreviated brush when they caught a swift glimpse of him on routine patrols beside the pseudo-Gothic tower raised by the mad Gilroy nearly a century ago. They also recognised his curious lop-sided gait, caused by an old injury in a gin-trap when he was in his prime and now that he was very old his coat was so shot with grey as to pass for brindled. Yet age and infirmities had done little to restrict Traveller's movements about the country or impair in any way his prodigious memory for nooks, crannies, short-cuts or places where a decoy scent could be found, or a stream forded on dry pads. And within this web of knowledge was another, with threads feeding back to an instinct that taught him how to differentiate between danger areas and safe areas, dependent upon the people occupying them. He knew the Valley and Valley folk far better than Paul Craddock and Smut Potter, better than Smut's gypsy mother, or Marian Eveleigh, neither of whom had ventured far beyond the Whin or the county border. Indeed, the only two-legged creature who had known it as well had been Hazel Potter and she had died before Traveller was born.

He had not acquired this detailed knowledge without working hard for it and neither had it been dinned into him by being chased over it in peril of his life several times a season. He had built it up bit by bit during countless forays, east and south-east as far as the backyards of Coombe Bay cottages and the marram grass tunnels of the dunes, sometimes going there in search of food and sometimes to look for a mate, for there were always young vixens to be found in Shallowford Woods and a favourite of Traveller, who had already borne him several litters, still hunted the landslip terrace under the Bluff. His survival was therefore no miracle of hardihood or ingenuity but simply the result of keeping abreast of every change that took place in the country of the two rivers. As regards this, the constant revision of the map imprinted on his mind, he was a pedant among foxes, like an old man who has sworn on oath to achieve the age of a hundred and is prepared to regulate his life accordingly. At certain seasons of the year he would make one of his great, circular sweeps of the Valley, noting every minute change as it presented itself – a sagging gate here, a new plank footbridge there, a different pattern of lights at one farm, a variation in an occupier's step at the next. Methodically and painstakingly the new scents and sounds were absorbed and filed away for future use. Not one was overlooked or forgotten.

In the late spring of 1932 Traveller padded free of the trailing briars of Folly Wood and set out on one of his routine reconnaissances, moving swiftly over the mile or so of bracken as far as the barrows on Blackberry Moor, for there was no profit in lingering near home where nothing had changed for a long time. His goal lay further east, where things were constantly

changing, and he did not slacken his urgent pace until he
reached the old hunting ground above Periwinkle Farm. Here
he lingered a few moments, his pace slowed more by nostalgia
than curiosity. The farmhouse was empty. He knew that well
enough, having passed this way often since Elinor Codsall
had gone, taking her succulent hens with her. Periwinkle had
been a winter larder to Traveller in his heyday for all Elinor's
vigilance had never succeeded in denying him occasional
access to a hen or a duck. Tonight he did not have to descend
into the hollow to make certain that the yard was still derelict,
or the rotting hen-houses empty of anything larger than a
shrew. He climbed to the top of the hill, looking across the dip
at Hermitage Wood, then turned north heading for Hermitage
itself but tensed himself nevertheless for the Pitts family
was unpredictable and many a buckshot had come his way
in these fields and the rutted lane that bisected them. Old
Arthur had never fired at him (he had not seen the old man
about for some time) and Henry, the ponderous, splay-footed
master was content to bellow 'Be off, you bliddy varmint!' if
Traveller broke cover in his line of vision, but the younger
Pitts, David, did not hunt and regarded all foxes as vermin to
be exterminated by any means, fair or foul. Tonight, however,
none of the men-folk were astir although there was a car
parked at the head of the lane and as he slipped by he
heard a woman's soft laugh and a voice say, 'Dornee now!
Tiz late, boy . . .' but he paid little heed to sounds or taint.
Whenever he descended Hermitage lane between late spring
or early autumn there was a car of some sort in the passing
bay and Prudence Pitts was sitting in it, with one man or
another. Traveller knew it was here, identifying her by the
sickly scent that clung to her, a scent that suggested dog
violets but was not violets or any other flower of the woods
but a bastard alloy of some kind and usually competing with
whiffs of human scent and petrol exhaust. He went on down
to the yard, noting a fresh rat-hole that would give access
to the cattlecake store and the mice who lived there but he
did not explore, preferring to reconnoitre on an empty belly.
There was a square of orange light above the rain tub so he

scrambled up and looked into the kitchen. There was not much to be seen. Henry, and his son David and the old crone were there, all three crouched round the oblong box with a trumpet on the top, their attention devoted to the caterwauling issuing from it, a medley of sounds dominated by one not unlike the bray of a hunting-horn. He jumped down, skirted the yard where there was a chained and very observant collie and went past the sties, wrinkling his lip at the sour stench of pigs. Then he climbed the long, sloping field to the sunken lane that circled the escarpment and headed north-east for Shallowford Woods where, in his day, he must have given hounds the slip on a hundred occasions.

It was a mild, pleasant night and he was enjoying himself in his own quiet way. The woods were full of safe, springtime scents, so that his nose told him precisely what ride he was crossing at any one time. Down here by the mere anemones and irises grew and the sap in the split reeds gave off a scent that recalled long summer days in the holts under the bank, where he often met otters. Otters fished for a living and had no quarrel with him but he knew they were hunted like himself and sometimes envied their ability to take to the water. He passed the pagoda and circled Sam Potter's cottage, recalling the big man's joyous whoop whenever he saw him bound out of a bracken in the area further north, where Sam spent most of his time felling timber. Traveller liked Sam, who had no malice but he did not care for his younger boy, Ted, who was prodigiously fast on his feet and could leap across broken ground at the speed of a whippet. Once or twice, in this part of the woods, he had come close to running Traveller down but there was no risk tonight, for Ted was always early to bed like his father. Only Joannie Potter and her long-faced daughter, Pauline, sat up late and as Traveller paused outside the tightly wired hen enclosure Pauline came out of the back door calling the cats to their supper. She was, he recalled, crazy about cats, who were strangely pampered at this house and not left to fend for themselves as at all the other farms in the Valley. Coddling them had made them soft so that he did not fear them as he feared the half-wild cats at Deepdene or the Dell. He jumped the stream, threaded the rhododendron maze and climbed the hill where the Shallowford badgers lived. One or two of them were pottering about and bristled at his approach. They were excessively fastidious animals and only a dire emergency would drive him to use their holts as a refuge but he had refuged there from time to time until hounds were called off to another part of the woods. Every animal in the woods was leagued against Man and the badgers were no exception.

He padded through a forest of bluebells to the head of the slope and then, at a leap, dropped down into Derwent territory, or what had been Derwent but was now a wilderness, recalling in its sordid disarray, the old camp on Blackberry Moor before it was overgrown by creeping colour. Unlike the camp, however, there were few pickings to be had here now. He did not understand what had been happening in this part of the preserve but had remained curious ever since the downslope of the hill above the farm had been ripped open by great clanking machines, like those that rushed down the shining rails near Sorrel Halt and now, he noted, there were other changes, none of which fitted into the broader pattern of agricultural pursuits as he had observed them over the years. Some of the great engines stood about, protected by tarpaulins that lifted in the breeze and momentarily deceived him into thinking men were on hand although the wind carried no taint of men. Then he saw them for what they were, coverings of the kind used on haystacks and he snarled at them and crossed the red weals in Eight Acre to inspect a long row of squarish pits, cross-covered with beams and surfaced underneath with a hard, gritty substance that was neither earth, grass, rubble nor the familiar tar of made-up roads. The pits puzzled and disturbed him and he wondered if they were a row of gigantic traps of a new and hazardous design; then it occurred to him that they were not unlike dwellings, although it seemed improbable that a man like Derwent would have so many people cluttering his land. His reasoning powers were considerable but they were limited by his experience and he had no previous experience of building sites, Nun's Bay having been completed shortly before he was born. The changes here were immense since his last visit and instinct warned him against change of such catastrophic proportions so that he could not help but link the disarray at High Coombe with the dissolution at Periwinkle on the far side of the woods. Viewed separately they were singular; taken together they were alarming.

He padded down the long slope towards the sea and whilst crossing the approach lane of Deepdene he wondered what had become of the old woman who had so many children for whom she would sometimes ring a bell, the clang of which carried over the river on certain winds. Then he heard the heavy crunch of hobnail boots on gravel and at once took cover in a bed of docks as Dick Potter, Farmer Willoughby's cowman, checked his stride, sniffing the air before moving on with a grunt. Dick, as Traveller well knew, had affiliations with the cottage back in the woods and it struck him that the Potters, one and all, were a tribe to be watched. Each of them, it seemed, possessed some special skill; Sam, the woodsman, could throw a hatchet and kill a rabbit on the run and his son Ted, could outpace a whippet over a given distance; now here was Dick, Ted's brother, who could smell a fox on a windless night and Traveller was grateful that the moon had yet to rise. He waited until the sound of footsteps had died before taking the steep, winding path to the Dell. Here there was nothing to fear. The two farmers and their fat wives were an amiable lot and Traveller had a special interest in one of the men because he had a curious, lop-sided walk, not unlike Traveller's own. There had been a time when the Dell was sown with traps but that was before Traveller's time. Today neither Farmer Bellchamber, Farmer Brissot, nor anyone else about here bothered to keep down the conies which abounded in Low Coombe. Traveller killed one in passing and then wished he had not for the rabbit's shriek set the dogs barking and one of the women came out into the yard and shouted to them to be quiet. The dogs he knew were chained so he lingered in the area for a spell, remembering the times he had given hounds the slip in the fields of kale about here; then he trotted off and turned left-handed, emerging from the wood at the head of the Bluff where he was just in time to see the moon rise and tip twenty cartloads of silver into the bay. He paused, looking down, half inclined to descend the rock-ledges to the landslip terrace and visit the vixen who lived there but he thought better of it. He was already tired and it was a long way home and his need of vixens was less urgent than in the past.

It was in an enclosed garden above the forge that he was made aware of other changes since he had passed this way. The village seemed to be extending up the hill and, whereas evening loiterers had usually gathered under the one roof of The Raven, tonight a group of them, all men, were standing in the soft glow of the forge that spread beyond the open door. He went closer and looked directly down on them, their taint reaching him like an advancing wall, their cigarettes glowing like a scatter of watch fires. Some he recognised and some he did not, according to their occupations and habitat. Abe Tozer, the aged smith, was there, leaning on a long-shafted hammer, his white whiskers reaching the top of his leather apron and close by two or three of Abe's cronies – Morgan, the pot-bellied builder, Noah Williams, the sailor who never went to sea, and Thorn, the new sexton whom Traveller had often watched at work on the churchyard. With them was a sprinkling of younger men, like the hideously disfigured Gappy Saunders, and the blind man, Willis, who walked with a white stick. The rumble of their voices came up to the fox as he rested and again the pattern of change was revealed to him for not so long ago this street would have been empty under the stars at this time of night.

He circled the forge, crossed the street and climbed the hill to the dunes where the smell of the sea vanquished every other scent until he caught the reek of gorse growing among the marram grass. Then he turned inland along the river bank as far as Timberlake's sawmill, a place where he had often refuged from hounds and watched them overrun his scent among the newly-sawn logs before he doubled back to the nearest covert. The house behind the sawpit was silent and shuttered, as though its occupants had turned their backs on the Valley like Elinor Codsall and Farmer Derwent, and for the

third time that evening Traveller sensed change and a shifting
pattern, so that suddenly, from being merely curious he felt
uneasy, despite the reassuring scents of resin, dry sawdust
and woodsmoke and leaving the yard hurried on his way,
crossing the river at the ford and taking a short cut across
the stubble to Four Winds. Here, to his relief, nothing had
changed at all. The yards were still tidy and spotlessly clean,
the fences in repair, barns and byres bolted. There were no
rat-holes in the weather-boarding and lights burned behind the
neatly-curtained windows; all the same he went on through to
the watershed without pause. The fat Boxer kept by the new
landlord was a pet and was therefore almost certainly asleep
beside the fire in the kitchen but all his life Traveller had
feared the Four Winds cats of which there seemed to be a
baker's dozen, all as aggressive as stoats. By the time the moon
was high he was safe across the Teazel and heading through
Heronslea coverts and within minutes of reaching his culvert
beside the tower he was curled muzzle to brush, or what little
remained of his brush, but before he slept the changes he had
marked during his circuit had been filed away in his memory.
Hunting had finished until autumn but when it began again
every scrap of information acquired that night would multiply
his chances of outwitting hounds and the tyrant who fed them
as a reward for betraying every other beast of the field.

II

The changes Traveller had marked during his fact-finding
foray seemed abrupt to him for, alone in the Valley, he and
Squire Craddock were half-rebel, half-conservative. To most
people in the Valley post-war changes were accepted as the
wear and tear of years – incidents like the death of old
Arthur Pitts, or the decision of Mary Willoughby to close
her little school and spend the remainder of her days sharing
a bungalow with an elderly cousin, in Dawlish. Everyone had
noted, of course, the inroads of Codsall's shock troops at High
Coombe, and some of them smiled and shrugged when they

heard the story of the irascible old farmer's assault on his son
Hugh at the time of the sell-out, but for the most part they did
not share the resentment of father, sister and brother-in-law.
A man was entitled to do as he liked with land bought and
paid for and the bungalows Codsall's partner Tapscott built
in Top Warren were soon sold, the row of shops in Coombe
Bay High Street soon let. The proposal to build a permanent
camping site for tents and caravans, with its own row of
shops in Eight Acre, caused a somewhat wider ripple of
comment but once the site was cleared and the foundations
that had so mystified Traveller marked out, few were outraged by what was happening along the eastern border of
the estate. Farms were being sold off everywhere nowadays
and it was accepted that there was no future in agriculture.
Young men like Dick Potter, and Will Codsall's younger son
Mick, who clung to the industry were the exceptions. Maybe
they were too idle to leave the Valley and learn a trade in
Paxtonbury, maybe there were too stupid.

Most of the young ones had left by the end of 1932, some
to look for work in the cities, others to marry and one or two,
despairing of finding regular jobs, to join the Services or go
abroad like Rumble Patrick Palfrey. The Valley was not at
all surprised to learn that he had sailed away to Australia;
anything might be expected of a child born in a cave above
the Shallowford badger sets but as the Depression deepened,
and the national tally of unemployed topped the three million
mark, some of Rumble's contemporaries had second thoughts
about his hereditary daftness and themselves wrote away for
details of Government-sponsored emigrant schemes. Young
Sally Pascoe, for instance, the younger daughter of Walt
Pascoe and 'Pansy-Potter-that-was', left in 1931, writing within
six months to say that she had found herself a husky husband
in Ontario. Brother Albert (the hidden persuader of Pansy's
second marriage) soon followed her and after him went Esther
Eveleigh and her husband George, only son of the blind
wheelwright, Willis. Yet somehow the broad outlines of the
Valley did not change much, at least not along its northern
and western boundaries. Periwinkle remained derelict; nobody

would be fool enough to move into Elinor Codsall's farm, where the acres Will had reclaimed from the moor were already waist-high with dock and thistle and the farmhouse, never much shakes as a dwelling, was partially roofless and soggy with damp. In the south-east the Willoughby holding continued to prosper, Francis Willoughby having proved that it paid to specialise and his success with beef had attracted two local youngsters to sign on with him at the new agricultural rates. Deepdene was a very democratic farm these days, Francis and his two hired hands (one a Potter and the other a Timberlake), living a carefree life with a daily woman to cook and clean for them. Master and men made regular jaunts to Paxtonbury where, it was rumoured, Francis learned to lose his woman shyness in the roystering company of young Dick Potter, his foreman. Whether this was true or not Francis must have mellowed since his trip to the Argentine for when teased by Claire on the subject of his bachelor status he had shocked her by quoting the famous Churdles Ash quip – that the act of taking a wife at his age was akin to leaping into a river to quench thirst! Claire thought this evidence that Francis' success had done much to enlarge the son of Preacher Willoughby, the old prophet who had once stalked the Valley warning the unrepentant against an eternity of hell fire.

Lower down the long slope, where the unlikely partnership of the lame French Canadian Brissot and the Cockney Jumbo Bellchamber had now entered its second decade, there was hope that the Dell would continue to hold its own, for Brissot was a good farmer and his talkative friend a better salesman. The two Potter girls had sobered beyond local recognition and had even been known to express disapproval concerning the shameless behaviour of girls like Prudence Pitts, who, to some extent, had inherited the Potter reputation of tasting every dish in the Valley before making a final decision. Prudence's mother, the once tawny, now greying Gloria, was outraged when the comment reached her as it did within hours. Like everyone else among the older generation she had vivid memories of the Potter girls' reputations up to the moment they had married at the end of the war and it seemed to her grossly hypocritical on their part to quarrel with her daughter's efforts to make the most of the shrinking supply of men in the Valley. She carried her complaint to Henry, demanding that he confront the slanderers but Henry only laughed and said, 'Dornee talk so bliddy daaft, woman! Us dorn mind what the Potters zay an' never did! Besides, tiz true baint it? I baint zeed 'er with the zame chap three times in a row!' Gloria complained that he was deficient in family loyalty but she had regarded herself as the dominant partner but the shearing episode, in the disordered kitchen of Elinor Codsall in 1917, had taught her otherwise. Since then she had made one or two half-hearted attempts to regain the ascendancy but all they had earned her was the traditional penance of a valley shrew, a profound reluctance to sit upon anything unupholstered for a day or so. Apart from an occasional flare-up between man and wife, and a brief sulk on the part of Prudence when she was between boy friends, life pursued an uneventful course at Hermitage. Henry's son David, now twenty-six, had his father's and grandfather's reverence for large whites and saddlebacks and in the main he upheld Henry's refusal to abandon traditional tools for one or other of 'they bliddy machines'. Paul declared that Hermitage was the most old-fashioned farm in the county, a holding that had never heard the stutter of a tractor, or the clatter of the muck-spreader but deep in his heart he counted Henry Pitts his most reliable tenant. Their relationship, always cordial, had now ripened into friendship and they would sometimes ride the rounds together, talking of old friends and old adventures that led all the way back to the rescue of shipwrecked sailors in Tamer Potter's cove. Paul was not alone in his affection for Henry. Everyone in the valley welcomed his broad, rubbery smile and his high-pitched, ''Ow *be* 'ee then?' His aged mother, Martha, still treated him like a child but she respected his judgment as she had never minded that of her amiable husband, Arthur.

Over at Four Winds Harold Eveleigh had made good his pledge to regard farming as a way of life rather than a temporary alternative to the dole queue. The farm had almost regained its pre-war rhythm for Harold's wife, the pretty

Lancashire girl, was quick to learn from Marian and from Deborah, her sister-in-law, whereas Harold brought to his new occupation the serious application that had promoted him from private to captain in three years of active service in the East and afterwards in Ireland. It heartened Paul to see Four Winds surface again and shake off its gloomy reputation, and when Harold's son Norman was born he broke his resolution to cease adding to the long roll of his Valley godchildren. Mary, his daughter, and Harold's wife Connie, became close friends and Whiz, his second daughter, taught Connie to ride. Paul never had cause to regret his snap decision; from the time Harold took over his western flank was secure.

The fox's uneasiness when he paused outside the silent, shuttered sawmill was justified, for that very day Dandy Timberlake had died, indirectly as the result of the lung wound he had received in the Dardanelles seventeen years before. He and Pansy Potter had made a good marriage and Walt Pascoe's children found him a tolerant and conscientious stepfather. Walter's eldest son, Tim, stayed on at the mill as sawyer, assisted by Dandy's own child, who bore the name of Pascoe notwithstanding the fact that everyone in the valley was aware that he was the product of a walk home in a storm on the night of the Coronation fête, in 1911. The boys were both single and after Dandy's death their mother lived on at Mill Cottage, where Hazel had settled after bearing Ikey's child in the woods. In spite of having had a largish family and two husbands Pansy held middle-age at bay more successfully than either of her sisters. At forty-nine she was still a very handsome woman, with enormous reserves of Potter vitality, and although she regretted Dandy in the way she had regretted Walt, she made no secret of her intention to marry a third time as soon as opportunity presented itself.

'I made two of 'em comfortable and I baint ready for the rocking-chair yet!' she told Claire, the day after the funeral. 'Poor old Dandy was only half the man 'er was before 'er was shot about be they ole Turks but the poor ole toad did his best, bless 'un! Las' thing 'er zed to me bevore he give up was, "Panse midear, dornee wear no widdow's weeds for

me! You show a leg an' get yourself a bit o' winter comfort
zoon as may be! Youm too lusty o' woman to run to waste
and youm not fifty yet so get out an' about midear, and
dornee mind what the gossips zay!"'

Pansy took him strictly at his word. That summer, by means
of Dandy's insurance money, she transformed herself and then
took a job as barmaid in The Raven where, at first glance, even
her oldest associates had some difficulty in recognising her.
Her hair, that had been a dead-leaf brown flecked with grey
at the time of Dandy's death, now shone like sun-kissed brass
and her mouth was as red and welcoming as a coal fire on a
cold night. She disdained the slimming diets urged upon her by
her daughters but settled for the policy of making the utmost of
what she had, lacing herself into a pair of pre-war stays that
induced a pink and permanent flush on her cheeks without
recourse to rouge. Pansy's new self, indeed, was a study in
pink. She wore coral-pink earrings and tight pink blouses that
revealed a bewitching cleavage. Round her waist she wore a
patent leather belt of piratical design, relieved by a pink rose
the petals of which were proof against fading for they had
been made by Pansy herself from part of a window-blind, a
trick learned in one of the many women's magazines she read.
Her black shiny skirt was so tightly stretched across her hips
that it would never have remained there when she leaned over
to draw beer had she not equipped it with press-studs as large
as the bosses on a suit of mail. Her shapely legs were encased
in flesh-pink stockings and the heels of her patent leather shoes
obliged the new landlord to renew the bar linoleum every six
months. He did not complain, however, for the new barmaid
proved a transfusion to an establishment that had been going
downhill since it was rebuilt to look like a Tudor tithe barn.
Bar profits took a sudden upward leap and there was soon
civil war between the regular patrons of private and public
saloons, both of whom clamoured for Pansy's ministrations.
She was an enormous success from any point of view and,
next to her figure, the male clientele admired her endearing
trick of pretending to be shocked at the remarks tossed at her
when she was teetering across the floor with a tray of drinks

balanced on the tips of vermilion finger nails. Men began to drift back again from Abe Tozer's forge in ones and twos so that old Abe and Eph Morgan, who were both lifelong teetotallers, soon had it to themselves again and resumed their interminable games of draughts on the anvil. Among the reclaimed was Alf Willis, the wheelwright, who had been blinded by gas on the Somme and had recently become a widower. Alf (christened 'Reginald') was thankful that he had learned a trade before losing his sight and was still able to pursue it as well as draw a disability pension. His wife had been a rather anaemic woman and the strain of living with him during the difficult period of his readjustment had exhausted her, so that now he was looked after by his thirteen-year-old daughter Bessie and occupied one of the new bungalows at the top of the village. Willis could not see Pansy's late-flowering charms but he had not lost his sense of touch and because he was sightless, and everyone pitied him, she went out of her way to be especially kind to him, allocating him a reserved seat in a corner where she had to brush against him every time she served the tables under the window. Her sidelong passage past Alfie became a regular source of Raven ribaldry as the weeks went by for every time she lisped, ''Scuse me, Alfie!' and pressed herself against him, his broad face glowed with unabashed pleasure and Alfie's cronies would pretend to offer cash for his seat. Encouraged by this, or by Pansy's thoughtful offer to relieve his daughter Bessie of the nightly walk to The Raven to fetch Father home, Alfie soon proposed and Pansy promptly accepted, so that Smut, whose experience of his sister went back a very long way, declared, ''Er had it in mind from the day she took the job, the crafty bitch!' but at once qualified this implied criticism by adding, 'She'll play the game by 'un tho'! Panse usually does, pervidin' o' course, that Alfie's minded to keep 'er served!' Presumably Alfie was for, to the delight of The Raven's regulars, Pansy presented her astonished husband with a ten-pound boy thirty-seven weeks to the day he led her to the altar. It was her sixth child and she celebrated her fiftieth birthday two months before delivery. Although inclined to be a trifle vain of her record (three husbands and progeny by each) she worried over the possibility of being replaced at the pub but her employer hastened to reassure man and wife that Pansy was irreplaceable and promised to keep open her job if she liked to come in and serve five evenings a week. Her wages and tips, added to Alfie Willis's earnings and pension, were more than enough to offset the cost of a regular baby-sitter so she soon made a triumphant reappearance, still in pink and showing, if anything, rather more cleavage. Dandy would have been delighted and so, perhaps, would Walt, whose happiest hours had been spent in the court where Pansy now reigned.

That was the period Claire called 'The Marriage Year', the twelve months between the spring of 1932 and the early summer of 1933, and Pansy's marriage to Alfie Willis was only the final peal of wedding bells in the Valley. Mark Codsall led off by marrying Liz Pascoe, Pansy's eldest daughter and taking the cottage her mother had vacated on moving into the pub. Then, to the vast relief of Gloria Pitts, Prudence accepted Young Honeyman, manager of the Home Farm, and the least hopeful of her many suitors. Gloria Pitts suspected that it was panic rather than Honeyman's relatively good prospects that inclined her daughter to choose Honeyman instead of one of her flashier beaux, young men with oiled hair who had raced her about in the countryside in their second-hand cars and lingered so long in the passing bay of the lane. She was, in fact, on the point of demanding of her daughter specific information regarding matters that had come to her notice when Prudence announced the engagement. She went on to say – as if it was the most natural thing in the world – that they had 'decided not to wait and would be married almost at once' and that 'this was Nelson's idea because he was scared I might change my mind!' Young Honeyman's name 'Nelson', derived from his father's obsession with the Navy League in pre-war days and only a threat on his wife's part to shame him at the christening, had prevented the boy being named Horatio-Grenville-Hood, Nelson being a compromise. Gloria kept her suspicions to herself and Henry, who liked

Honeyman, swore that he would give his daughter a 'rare ole zend-off, like us had in the old days yerabouts'. He kept his promise. Over a hundred guests attended the wedding and Squire himself proposed the principal toast, for Prudence was one of his tribe of godchildren. Everyone declared that Prudence was the most radiant Valley bride of recent years and the junketings at the Hermitage that day were reminiscent of a less sophisticated era. There was an open-air breakfast and a procession down the track to the festooned honeymoon car, the couple riding the first stage on a farm-waggon drawn by drag-ropes. After that there was rice, old shoes, nosegays and silver horse-shoes all the way to Sorrel Halt, where Nelson and Prudence entrained for 'an unknown destination' that proved, disappointingly, to be Ilfracombe. Young Honeyman could hardly believe his luck when he found himself alone in the compartment with the most popular girl in the Valley but Prudence, carefully combing confetti from her red-gold hair, looked more relieved than ecstatic when he shyly showed her the marriage licence. It had been, she reflected, a very close call. Notwithstanding the falseness of the alarm that had precipitated the engagement, Henry would have had her marry Ronnie Stokes if she had not had the sense to keep her suspicions to herself and the odd thing was, now that she had Nelson, she actually preferred him to Ronnie. He was rather stolid she supposed, and his courting tactics were years behind the times, but he was healthy, high in the Squire's good graces, and had no eyes for anyone but her; as to the techniques, she could supply those as part of her dowry.

Within two months of Prudence Pitts' marriage Whiz, Paul's second daughter, announced that she was engaged to a Flight-Lieutenant Ian McClean, recently attached to the new RAF base, a mile or so east of Paxtonbury. She told her parents that they would probably be married before Ian left to complete a tour of duty in the Near East. Whiz had had almost as many local admirers as Prudence but the name of 'Ian' was new to Paul, although not to Claire who, although appearing to pursue a policy of extreme tolerance, nonetheless maintained a watchful eye on the least tractable of her three daughters.

Up to the moment Whiz announced her news Paul had always pretended to be piqued by his daughters' disinclination to 'look about with an idea of settling down' and had seemed, indeed, to take it as an affront that nobody had asked either one of them for her hand. Now, to Claire's amusement, he began to bluster, demanding to know if 'this Ian McShane was present to make a formal request'. Whiz laughed outright at this. 'Good heavens, of course he isn't!' she said, 'what year do you think this is? 1066? And anyway, you might as well get his name right. It's *"McClean!"* – a small "c" and then a big one!'

'I'm obliged to you for pointing that out,' Paul grumbled, disconcerted when he sensed that Claire shared her daughter's view in that he was behaving like a Victorian papa, 'but how the devil am I expected to approve of a prospective son-in-law I've never even met?'

'You have met him,' Whiz said coolly, 'he was one of a tennis party here at Whitsun but even if you hadn't it wouldn't make much difference, would it? After all, I'll be twenty in April.'

Claire stepped in quickly now. She had no illusions regarding the lack of communications between Paul and all his children, with the exception of Simon, whom he had come to understand of late, and Mary, whom he adored. Between him and Whiz there had always existed a zone of neutrality that extended, to some extent, to their youngest child, whom he accused her of spoiling on account of her striking good looks.

'Listen you two,' she said, briskly, 'what's the point of quarrelling over the poor boy? Ask him to lunch tomorrow and let him speak up for himself! I'm sure your father will like him, Whiz, he seemed a polite, level-headed sort of chap to me,' and with that Whiz drifted off to bed, reappearing at noon the following day with a uniformed Scot in tow, a cautious, thick-set young man, with sandy hair, good if rather distant manners, and a profound disinclination to engage in small talk. Paul spent an uncomfortable half-hour with him alone but neither of them mentioned Whiz and as the day wore on Paul realised that his daughter had been quite right – there was little expected from him one way or the other. Everyone of her generation was obviously equipped to make their own decisions, even at the age of nineteen. He noted with approval, however, that Ian McClean was neither fool nor weakling but a man who kept his emotions, if he had any, double-locked and chained and instinct told him that this kind of man might get the best out of a girl who had been inclined to put on side after so many successes in the show ring. Ian, it seemed, had a little money of his own, an income of about three hundred a year plus his pay and was due to fly off to the Suez Canal zone in September, returning the following spring. After that, he said, he would move about here, there and everywhere, sometimes in this country but more often in far off places like Hong Kong, Singapore, the Arabian Gulf and India. Whiz, once married, could accompany him to most of these places but not all, for there were certain areas closed to the wives of junior officers. When, at last, the subject of the actual wedding nosed itself into the conversation and Ian bucked at delay, Paul had a gleam of insight, reading into the young Scot's insistence on a short engagement determination to stake his claim before Whiz went out of circulation, and he felt a certain sympathy for the man. Although by no means as beautiful as young Claire, Whiz (Ian gravely referred to her by her given name, Karen) was pretty enough to prove a bad risk and, like her twin brothers, she had the knack of attracting about her a small court of admirers, some of whom Paul reminded himself, were far less eligible than this taciturn Celt. In the end he found himself wholeheartedly approving the match and it made him chuckle to see the subtle change that the prospect of marriage wrought in Whiz, for she became almost affectionate towards him as her moods ranged from one of brittle excitement to a kind of dithering uncertainty, not as regards Ian but the trivia inseparable from weddings. Claire, however, seemed to have an instinctive knowledge of how to cope, both with her daughter and with the mounting tensions in the house as the day approached. She was quite prepared, he noted, to organise the most spectacular wedding ever witnessed in the Valley but by mid-August Whiz had backed down, settling for a comparatively quiet affair, with a mere sixty guests, most of them family or local equestriennes. Mary and young Claire were bridesmaids (Paul thought he had never seen anyone look quiet so enchanting as Mary in her sprigged organdie and long, Victorian mittens) and in the absence of any close friend at Ian's temporary base, Stephen, the more talkative of the twins, stood as best man. To Paul's relief he was not called upon to entertain the groom's family. McClean's father had died with most of the Cameronians at Loos, and his mother a year or so later, in India. Aside from a few RAF acquaintances from the camp the groom was represented by a formidable aunt from Perth, whose speech was as broad in its way as old Mrs Handcock's, and who seemed to regard everyone living south of the Cheviots as something midway between a tyrant oppressor and a confidence trickster. Paul made the mistake of trying to draw her out on Scottish history but was soon sent packing with a flea in his ear, Aunt Elspeth being unaware that the last blood-letting between English and Scots had occurred at Culloden Moor, nearly two centuries ago. Picking up his dignity he wandered among the guests, feeling rather like a lucky amateur exhibitor at a professional flower show whose entry, the bride, had unexpectedly won first prize. He was consoled, however, by the presence of the wanderers among his brood, finding a sympathiser in Simon who dismissed all religious ceremonies as 'social opiates', a view that did not seem to be shared by his wife Rachel, who was clearly enjoying the occasion and looked, Paul thought, attractive in her simple blue dress, wide straw hat and elbow-length gloves. Simon told him a little of their life in the mining valleys and shipyard towns and it all sounded desperately dull and unrewarding but he noticed that the boy seemed to be maturing under the stresses of his nonstop guerrilla war against what he called The Establishment. He was, for instance, more restrained in his judgments and more disposed to make allowances for the terrible complexities of building a social system that guaranteed fair shares for all; he was also prepared to find room in his brave new world for a revitalised agriculture and for this small blob of jam Paul was duly grateful.

The Pair were as irrepressible as ever. They came skidding up the drive in a huge car of American make, scrambled out and at once proceeded to fill the house with noise and strangers, of the kind that attached themselves to the twins wherever they went. They must have introduced him to a baker's dozen of their friends but he forgot their names instantly and could only think of them as carbon copies of his own boys and of each other. The young men, he noticed, used a laconic argot of their own that was almost a foreign language and drank a great deal without becoming the worse for it; their womenfolk – who reminded him of a bevy of medieval pages in a Flemish picture – had nicely waved peroxided hair, doll-like faces and were not above letting themselves be pawed in public, although they received these attentions absentmindedly, as though they were thinking of more important matters like their next hairdressing appointment. He found himself wondering how many of them were virgins, or whether their silly talk was no more than the backlash of Victorian and Edwardian cant. It was Henry Pitts, another wanderer in this post-war wilderness, who put these thoughts into words when he said, watching the young people milling about at the reception, 'Us is vallin' behind, Maister, and there baint two ways o' lookin' at it! There's a bliddy great hairy fence betwext them an' us, an' whereas the wimmin zeem to be able to jump it when they've a mind to, I'm jiggered if I c'n nerve myself to take off! I can't never be zertain zure what's on t'other zide!' There really was such a fence, Paul thought, and the only gap in it accessible to him was Mary, who seemed to have a password enabling her to move to and fro between the generations but preferred, on the whole, to stay in the safe old world that she could not have recalled, having been no more than three when the gates slammed on it in 1914.

One big surprise did emerge from the wedding, the totally unpredictable recapture of Stephen by his old flame, Monica Dearden, the Archdeacon's daughter from Paxtonbury, whom Paul had almost forgotten. Claire met her in the Cathedral Close a week or two before the wedding and sent her an invitation, saying that it was at Stephen's request, which was not true although he had asked her in one of his infrequent letters. Paul could never imagine either of the twins married. They seemed so self-sufficient, so satisfied with their hectic round of golf, jaunts to the Continent and business luncheons with potential suppliers of scrap iron in the North and Midlands. He was wrong, however. Before the end of Claire's 'wedding year' both were brought into the fold, Stephen by the elegant Monica, who seemed to combine the unlikely roles of blue-stocking and playgirl, Andy by a little Welsh nurse whom he met during a spell in hospital after a road crash in one of his dashes down to South Wales in search of scrap. Paul like both his new daughters-in-law, although he was slightly intimidated by Monica Dearden and bored by the Archdeacon's wife. Stevie and Monica were married and off on their honeymoon to Venice before he had the slightest inkling that Claire had, in fact, manipulated the match and regarded it as a personal triumph. He learned of this the day of the wedding in Paxtonbury Cathedral, when Stevie and his bride had gone, and he and Claire were driving back over the moor after seeing the couple off.

'Well, I think I managed that very neatly indeed!' she crowed, 'and moreover my part in it will establish just the right relationship between mother-in-law and daughter-in-law!'

'I suppose you're boasting of your share in helping that dull, well-meaning old duck to cope with all those beaming clergymen?' he asked and she laughed and said, 'Oh dear, Paul, you really are dim about some things! Haven't you realised I arranged that wedding singlehanded?'

He stopped the car on the first stage of the descent, pulling off the road not fifty yards from the point where, more than twenty years before, she had helped him to adjust himself to all that had happened as a result of the suffragette riot in Westminster Yard.

'What the devil are you talking about, Claire? *How* did you arrange it? Stevie has been blowing hot and cold about that girl for years and it seems to me all that happened is that he got a fresh look at her when she turned up at Whiz's wedding, looking extremely fetching!'

'Well, to begin with it was *me* who invited her with that

end in view,' she said, 'and after that it was *me* who told
Monica where he was based and advised her to manufacture an excuse to bump into him!'

'Good God, you did that?' he exclaimed, genuinely amazed.
'But why? What made it so important to you to see Stevie
married?'

'I don't see why a mother shouldn't work as hard to get her
sons safely married as to find someone suitable for her daughters! As a matter of fact sons usually stand in greater need of
the push, especially ours! In this case, however, I had a special
incentive. I was determined to split the partnership and now
Andy will have to get married too, you see if I'm not right!'

'Have you anyone special in mind?' he asked but his sar-
casm was tinged with admiration.

'No,' she admitted, seriously, 'but he'll find someone and
soon for he won't enjoy himself nearly so much without Stevie
as an audience! Don't you realise that most of their trouble
stems from the fact that they have been playing "Betcher!"
ever since they were toddlers?'

He knew it of course but her talent for practical intrigue
startled him. He said, 'What exactly did you do? Apart from
the invitation and the tip-off?'

'Oh, I had a long and rather blushing talk with Monica when
she came home after "meeting" him in Birmingham. We met
by appointment at The Mitre and, as the saying goes, she
emptied her heart, poor dear! Well, it wasn't in vain, I told
her to leave it all to me and that I'd have Stevie roped and
delivered in less than a week!'

'Knowing The Pair that was a damned reckless offer but
I'll wager the cards fell your way. They usually do in the
matrimonial field.'

'No,' she said, unblushingly, 'as a matter of fact they didn't,
or not at first. Those two maniacs of ours got involved in the
crash the next day. You remember – the first we heard about it
was Stevie ringing up after being discharged from hospital.'

He chuckled, recalling the way she had exploited his own
helplessness shortly before he proposed but his only comment was, 'Well, go on, finish it.'

'In a way I *was* lucky. Andy was crocked but Stevie escaped with scratches, tho' I daresay I should have thought up something if it had been the other way round.'

'You bet your life you would! What precisely *did* you do, you scheming hussy?'

'I just mentioned, ever so casually, that there was talk of Monica Dearden marrying Alderman Gratwick's son – you know, the ironmonger one – and then I told Monica to get young Gratwick to take her to the Territorial Ball. I knew Stevie would rise to that bait and sure enough he did! He was in Paxtonbury Town Hall before the orchestra had tuned up and now – well, now they're on their way in a gondola!'

'Well, I'll be damned!' he said. 'Did it occur to you that if the marriage goes on the rocks you'll be directly responsible?'

'No, it didn't and doesn't! He's kept that poor girl on tenterhooks for years and with all the opportunities he must have had that must mean something! Monica played up much better than I expected, however, and in view of her ecclesiastical background that was rather surprising.'

'Just what do you mean by that?'

He saw that she was not only enjoying her triumph but also the prospect of shocking him. 'Well,' she said, 'knowing The Pair, and the fact that, behind their display of fireworks, they are basically decent human beings with tender consciences, I encouraged her to let Stevie go almost the entire length of the garden path providing she didn't let him into the summer-house! It seemed to work. She brought him to the boil in less than a month!'

She had often amused him with her half-baked schemes, and her transparently counterfeit logic, but never quite so much as on this occasion. He said, when he had done laughing, 'You're an absolute travesty of a wife and mother! I don't know where you get it from – certainly not from your father – and I can't bring myself to believe from your mother either. Now, I suppose, you'll go to work on Andy?'

'No,' she said, 'I don't have to. You see, Andy will go wife-hunting himself now that he's thrown on his own resources. Stevie was always the real leader.'

'And how about Mary?' he asked cautiously but there was no mischief in her eyes as she replied, very levelly, 'Mary? Oh, she's your problem, not mine! That's one for you to tackle without any help from me!'

He had no need to be reminded of that and thought briefly of Rumble Patrick, now in Alberta doing God alone knew what, but still, he was sure, holding Mary's heart to ransom. She had been very quiet of late, an island of serenity in a sea of to-ing and fro-ing, willing to smile at the antics of her brothers and sisters but not to contribute much to family high jinks. How far did one's parental responsibilities extend? His eldest, Simon, was now twenty-eight, and his youngest, Claire's favourite, was fifteen and quite the daintiest creature he had ever seen. Of the six of them three were now 'safely' married and two of the others likely to be in no time at all but of the six not one had inherited his obsession with the Valley, or was prepared to get behind it and help to push into the future. Simon, inheriting Grace's wider outlook, was already immersed in the troubles of the world at large and perhaps, like his mother before him, secretly despised the limits Paul had alway set· upon himself. The Pair made no secret at all of their impatience with his parochialism and had reverted to type, deriving more satisfaction from a discarded boiler than a good harvest. As to the girls, Mary loved beauty and seemed content to seek it at home but suppose Rumble Patrick turned up 'whispering of lands where blaze the unimaginable flowers'? Then, he supposed, she would turn her back on the Valley without another thought and he would never see her again, except for an occasional visit from somewhere thousands of miles away. As for the remaining two, Whiz and young Claire, he expected nothing at all from them. Whiz was married anyway and the Valley had never been more to her than a place to cross at breakneck speed on a mettlesome horse. Claire, the baby, whom his wife and almost everyone else spoiled outrageously, would find nothing more absorbing in a Sorrel pool than her own reflections, so that, taken all round, they were a disappointing bunch. Claire said, with a smile, 'I don't need a penny for them! I suppose you were wondering whether they've been much of an investment after all?' and he replied, without rancour, 'Something like that but a man is a fool who expects a dividend from flesh and blood. I look for my return in the by-products!'

'Such as?'

'I've still managed to hang on to most of my capital, haven't I?' and he made a wide sweep with his hand; she realised that he was not referring to money.

III

Claire made good her boast. Within three months of Stevie's marriage to Monica Dearden, and their settling in what Paul thought of as a rather vulgar Edwardian house in a suburb of Birmingham, Andy appeared and presented his intended with the flourish a magician uses when he whips the curtains aside to reveal the missing lady still in one piece. Claire did not say, 'I told you so!' but her glance implied it when Andy came bounding into the hall one crisp, February morning, having driven through the night from the Welsh valleys where, he crowed, he had gone to rescue his Margaret and whisk her over the border like a marauding moss-trooper in search of a bride.

His choice presented Paul with no puzzles. Contemplating Margaret he reflected that perhaps, after all, at least one of his sons had inherited something from him, for at Andy's age Margaret Highton's ripeness would have made instant appeal to him. The girl's qualifications for an extrovert's bride were all on show – a happy-go-lucky temperament, a trim little figure, Celtic sensuality and an obvious capacity for enjoying the bonuses of life, good food, pretty clothes, lots of laughter and a regular roll in the hay. She was small and neat, with exceptionally pretty legs and a fashionable pageboy bob framing a fresh, gently rounded face. Her brown hair reflected firelight in the way sunshine teases the polished husk of a chestnut and she had large brown eyes, a *retroussé* nose and a wide red mouth that turned up at the corners and would probably stay that way if kissed often enough. Paul took to her at once and Claire, watching him, understood why; Margaret had promise and to Paul a woman without it was not worth a moment's attention. Claire, for her part, was fascinated by the girl's Welsh lilt that suggested sad Celtic songs sung round the camp-fires of forgotten kings with long, unpronounceable names full of 'u's and double 'd's. She thought, the moment she saw her, 'Well, I'd say Andy was luckier than Stevie! She's got something, apart from pretty-prettiness and I daresay they'll have a string of handsome children and enjoy watching them grow up!' and she left Paul to show Margaret around while she listened to Andy's unlikely account of his courtship that began in the casualty ward of a cottage hospital in Glamorgan, and ended a few days ago with Andy storming the dispensary at three in the morning, being ejected by an indignant night sister, and returning at breakfast time to persuade Margaret that, until the British paid its nurses better wages, they didn't deserve to have any! Claire said, laughing, 'Did she take much persuading, Andy?' and he said not after she had seen the ring that he had purchased from one of his seedier contacts in Cardiff, getting a seventeen-and-a-half per cent reduction on condition he gave 'Solly' (who dealt in scrap metals as well as expensive jewellery) twenty-five shillings a ton 'over the odds' for the rusting remains of a coaling barge!

'I hope you didn't tell her as much as you're telling me!' Claire laughed, 'for the idea of a man bargaining for my engagement ring would have made me think twice at Margaret's age!' but as she said this she felt a wave of affection for him that embraced not only Andy, and his sexy little Welsh girl, but the whole of Andy's generation who seemed so miraculously liberated from the conventions of the preceding generations. The very notion of buying an engagement ring from a scrap dealer, rushing into a girl's place of work, and carrying her off like a freebooting soldier at the sack of a city, would have been preposterous in her day and she remembered the scandal that had led to her virtual exile from the Valley throughout the years of Paul's first marriage. She could never agree with Paul and other traditionists that all post-war changes were regrettable. A few were but the majority were long overdue and one was surely the disappearance of hypocrisy among the young, giving them the freedom to act on impulse and indulge their natural appetites without artlessness. Andy had simply looked at this plump little partridge and, after prodding her here and there, had decided that he liked what he saw and here they were, as good as in bed together, and enjoying every moment of it! 'Damned good luck to them!' she thought. 'I wish Paul and I had been able to use that kind of short-cut!' and she bustled off to order a special dinner but found time during the afternoon to enter Andy's engagement into the diary immediately under recent entries devoted to Whiz and Stevie.

The April wedding was a very simple affair, more intimate and relaxing than either of its forerunners. Margaret's father, a retired miner, made no excuses for his inability to do more than provide a modest reception in the institute adjoining the local chapel and Paul found both him and his wife refreshing contrasts to Ian McClean's formidable aunt, and the patrician dignity of the Archdeacon and his wife. Claire, watching them talking and laughing together, was amused and relieved, for although she freely admitted to being a bit of a snob she would have hated to witness her husband or children putting on side. These were his kind of people, she reflected, whose company he had sought ever since she had known him and they brought out the best in him, whereas the twins seemed equipped to move freely on all levels of society. She noticed, however, that Stevie's wife, Monica, tilted her nose an inch or so as she took her seat at the trestle table and toyed with lettuce salad, and thought, briefly, 'It's odd they should have been so close all their lives but split on their choice of wives! I still think Monica was absolutely right for Stevie and there's no doubt at all that the little Welsh girl is ideal for Andy, but will this prove the fork in the road that The Pair have travelled all these years?' Then she found herself looking directly into the eyes of Simon, saw that he was smiling and realised that they were sharing the same thought. He came over and said, in his diffident voice, 'It's all right, Claire, you don't have to worry! If Monica tries to snub her Stevie will sit on her, hard!'

'There's not even privacy in thought when you're around, Simon,' she said. 'Sometimes I think you must be Ikey, reincarnated.'

'Well, at least I was trained by Ikey,' he said. 'Thank your lucky stars he never taught Gov the noble art of thought-reading!'

She laughed, feeling, as always, relaxed in Simon's company. He was mellowing a good deal, she thought, since leaving home and marrying that earnest but tiresomely intense wife of his and she wondered if Paul was right when he said Simon was growing a shell. She held to her point, saying, 'How can you be so certain? Stevie might even agree with her!'

'No,' he said, seriously, 'the twins are vulgarians but just ones! They'll make money, pots of it I daresay, but they'll never let money makes fools of them. How could they? You and Gov had them until they were seven and you know what the Jesuits say!'

It struck her that he was paying her a rather gracious compliment, that he was saying, in effect, no one who had grown up at Shallowford would find it easy to lose the classlessness that had been such a feature of the Valley since Paul had reigned there but she was never less than honest with Simon and said, 'I can't take a ha'porth of credit for that, Simon! I was a terrible snob when I married your father.'

'Oh, I daresay,' he said, cheerfully, 'but you were humble enough to learn from him and loved him enough to want to. As a matter of fact, Claire, that's something I've always admired about you two, you borrowed tolerance from one another, whenever you needed it! I suppose that's what made the marriage so successful.'

'Stop it,' she said, 'you'll have me blushing in a minute!'

'So what? If you can't fly a happy marriage like an ensign on a wedding day when can you? You don't have to apologise for it, it's rare enough these days.'

'Yours seems to be working well enough.'

'Yes, but "well enough" doesn't win prizes, does it? You

have to remember Rachel took a beating over Keith. She'll never quite get it out of her system.'

She would have liked to have asked him to be more explicit but at that moment the bridal pair took their seat at the top table and Stevie, as toastmaster, called for order. She continued to ponder his rather enigmatic conversation and it bothered her so much that she missed half the fun of the send-off, when all Margaret's neighbours converged on the pavement shouting expressions of goodwill that sounded like Celtic battle-cries. It was during the inevitable anti-climax, when they were returning to the hotel to say their good-byes and disperse, that she was able to draw him aside again and say, 'I've been thinking . . . it was Paul's second go, you know, and that gave me a flying start . . .' and she stopped, remembering too late that she was addressing the son of Grace Lovell. He noticed her confusion and rescued her with a smile and a squeeze of the elbow.

'There was a big difference, Claire. Rachel was in love with poor old Beanpole Horsey but you and Paul . . . it was in the cards from the start! I was the product of a misdeal!'

'And a very lucky one for me,' she said quickly and kissed him, remembering how she had once felt impelled to kiss Ikey Palfrey for roughly the same reasons. It was strange, she thought, as she watched Simon and Rachel drive off in their battered Morris, with the tatters of the last election posters still adhering to the doors – strange and a little spooky how vividly that boy recalled Ikey Palfrey, whose understudy he had always been.

And yet, taken all round, she felt elated, reflecting that if the success of her marriage was so obvious to him, the son of the woman she had replaced, it must be doubly so to everyone and perhaps this was something to crow about after all. Her elation bubbled over when they were packing for the drive home and she said, suddenly, 'Look here, Paul, why do we have to go home? It's spring, and not all Wales is as down and out as this place! Why don't we take a few days off?'

He never like staying away from the Valley for more than a day or two but she saw by his smile that she had anticipated him and suddenly remembered why. Last year had been their Silver Wedding anniversary but there had been no celebration for it had clashed with Prudence Pitts' wedding, then the whirl of Whiz's engagement and marriage, and, within weeks, Stevie's marriage to Monica Dearden. He had always promised her some kind of celebration and now it was far too late to arrange one they could share with all their old friends in the Valley.

'I had it in mind to suggest we slipped off and did some overdue honeymooning ourselves,' he said. 'Maybe it's all this nuptial syrup we've been dosed with lately! Suppose we "go back", just for the weekend?'

She knew what he meant by 'go back'. Never, in the twenty-six years of their marriage, had they revisited Anglesey, where they had spent their first fortnight together in 1907, and now, Heaven help them both, it was 1933, and the same season of the year. She said, eagerly, 'I'd love that, Paul! And Mary and young Claire have never seen the mountains. Why not drop a line to Honeyman . . .' but he interrupted her, saying, impatiently, 'Don't be so damned silly, woman! Do you want to hawk proofs of fruitfulness all over the island? Mary and Claire can tour the mountains under their own steam if they want to and if not they can go home by train!' and he went downstairs to telephone the Home Farm and tell Honeyman that he would not be back until early the following week. In the meantime Claire had collected the two girls to tell them of the change of plan and was annoyed to find herself blushing when she said, in response to her youngest daughter's 'Why can't we come along?' 'I don't think your father wants that, my dear . . . it's . . . well . . . it's his idea of a Silver Wedding trip, and you know what a sentimentalist he is!' and she was vastly obliged to Mary when she helped her out by saying, 'I think it's wonderful for you both! Come on, Claire, we'll check the trains and if there's one tonight we'll take it, no matter what. I only hope North Wales is a bit less dingy than South, Mother!'

'Believe me, it is!' Claire told her. 'From what I recall of it it's not unlike home!' and she hurried away to redistribute the contents of the cases.

They set off that same evening, driving almost due north, putting up for the night at a little hotel among the low hills of Radnorshire and moving on after an early breakfast along the southern valleys of Snowdonia. She took her turn at driving the big Austin so that he could look around a bit and sometimes they travelled for miles without exchanging a word but both, in their own way, were enjoying the experience of being cut off from the Valley, with the family turmoil of the last hectic months behind them. As they crossed Menai Bridge, meeting a stream of returning Easter traffic, he said, 'I don't recall seeing anything but a horse and trap up here in those days. One might think it was a century ago judging by externals!' and she said, with a smile. 'How about internals? Do you feel your age? No hedging, tell the truth without bragging!'

'Mentally I do,' he admitted, 'but not physically. That's the result of making the effort to ride and walk as much as I could. The youngsters will have to pay for this tearing around in cars when they come up to the fifty mark. No, I don't feel more than forty. How about you?'

'Forty-one,' she said, 'and a year or so younger after dark!' and he gave one of his sudden schoolboy laughs and pinched her knee as they turned inland towards the north-west corner of the island, where they had stayed the second and more rewarding week of their honeymoon in a farmhouse, after making an excuse to vacate a hotel full of Methodist clergymen assembled for a conference. Over here there were changes to be noted but they were not remarkable, a limited amount of new buildings on what had been open country, a few caravans in fields on either side of the unsurfaced road leading to the bay where, twenty-six years before, they had bathed and picnicked all day, without seeing anyone but children with shrimping nets. The old Roman road beyond Tynygongl had not changed at all and wild flowers, rarely seen in the Sorrel area, still grew in profusion among the outcrops of rock about the Druids' Circle. Everyone about here spoke Welsh and used English with difficulty, and, to their delight, the old farmhouse was still there, overlooking the bay, a snug, Tudor homestead, squatting so close to the soil it looked as permanent as the rocks that broke the shallow soil and made ploughing here a tedious business. They knocked on the door with some trepidation and the old woman who answered them, and gave them a polite Welsh greeting, was the same who, as a woman in her early forties, had bustled about her unexpected guests seven years before the war. She did not recognise them, of course, but when Paul explained who they were she broke into a torrent of Welsh, rushed to the dresser and produced a photograph album containing a yellowing snapshot taken with Paul's box camera on the porch, a picture of himself and Claire taken at his direction and with, he recalled, a great deal of fussing on the landlady's part. They all peered at the blurred images and Claire said, 'My goodness! Look at my waist in those days! And I'd quite forgotten you had a moustache, Paul!'

The woman, Mrs Hughes, told them that her husband had died several years before and Paul said, 'You had a son. He was called . . . wait a minute . . . David, and couldn't speak a word of English! Does he still carry on farming?'

'No, David was took,' the farmer's wife replied, unsentimentally, 'he was took an' never come home, you see!' and she pointed to a photograph standing on the oak sideboard showing David in khaki presenting bayoneted rifle in the inevitable pose of Kitchener's volunteers, when they rushed into studios within hours of being kitted out. 'There's not so many of the younger ones left around here,' she went on. 'Those who come back look you had different ideas, and crossed over to the mainland. There's no money to be earned farming and Evan's land iss sold off, mostly. My daughter Dilys's man, Owen, he works what iss left, but there are no children whateffer! There's a pity it iss but things is that changed, don't you know?'

Paul consoled her by saying his part of the world had changed too and from similar causes and it consoled him to think that post-war problems were universal among the farming communities. The old woman asked if they had a family and when Claire told her two boys and three girls she exclaimed with delight and patted her, as though she had

been a prize-winning cow, so that Paul had to turn away
to hide his grin and leave them together, lifting the cases
out of the car without asking if the farm still accommodated
visitors.

It was soon arranged, however, and he was directed to the
same low-ceilinged bedroom with its enormous, locally-made
oak bedstead and view of the sea through the mullioned
window. He thought, as he began to unpack, 'I suppose,
taken all round, we've been a damned sight luckier than
most! Hardly more than one in three of the chaps who were
young then would be alive now, or, if they were, sound in
wind and limb,' and then Claire came in and said, practising
Simon's thought-reading trick, 'I felt desperately sorry for the
old dame, Paul. It's almost as though we were flaunting our
survival! That boy of hers married before he went off and
got killed but she hasn't any grandchildren and no prospect
of any.'

'She's still got the farm or what's left of it,' he said, 'and
that's more than some of them have. Do you really want to
stay?'

'Yes,' she said, 'but more for her sake than ours. It's all
rather chastening, don't you think?'

'It always is,' he replied, 'and I imagine that's what they
mean when they say one shouldn't look back.' Then, seeing her raise her arms to take off her little straw hat and
noting, notwithstanding her continual complaints regarding
her waistline, that her figure was very trim for a woman a
few months short of fifty, he was glad they had returned and
catching her round the waist, said, 'I don't give a damn if
I do feel smug about us! We've earned the right to preen
ourselves a bit, Claire!' and he spun her round and kissed
her mouth with an urgency that was communicated to him
not only by an awareness of where they stood but also
by the thought that there was a limit to the span when
a man could kiss his wife as though he was still courting
her.

It was this thought, and the deliberate nostalgia they were
invoking, that injected a special kind of gaiety and youthful

abandon into the brief period they remained in hiding at Tynygongl. Paul, for his part, found himself recalling some of the spring tides of the years. As he lay in bed watching her undress, for instance, he remembered with amusement his impatience with the fiendish complexities of her 1911 Coronation finery, in the hotel room overlooking Green Park and again, when she teased him by prolonging her going-to-bed ritual involving creams and lotions, he saw her as the laughing girl who had thrown her cap at him in the long, dry summer of 1902. He did not communicate these memories to her, preferring to enjoy them in private but deduced from her lightheartedness that she had equally stimulating memories of her own, for she came to him each night with an enthusiasm reminiscent of the time they had spent together in Crabpot Willie's cabin during his final leave from France, encouraging him to use her not gently and diffidently, as he had done when they first lay in this room together, but as though she too had heard a clock ticking in the bowels of the old house.

It was within these terms of reference, or something like them, that she communed with herself while he slept. Had their marriage never had much more than a strong, physical basis, and if so would the colours fade altogether when time finally caught up with them and remembered ecstasy was all they had? It was a sombre thought but the terminus still seemed immeasurably far off, for they derived more satisfaction from one another than when they were thirty and far more than when they had first come here, she as nervous and gawky as a Valley milkmaid, he curbed by the failure of his first marriage. How quickly and finally those initial handicaps had been overcome! And how smoothly had they arrived at a stage where intimacy was achieved on her part with the uninhibited enthusiasm of a Potter wench, and on his with the casual expectancy of an uncomplicated creature like Henry Pitts? Well, if that was all there was to it, a bed and the procreation of healthy children, she couldn't help it and, what was more to the point, she didn't care! Not a hoot! Not one of his hearty smacks on the bottom signifying his impatience to have her naked in his arms caressing every part of her body. It was not quite what she had expected of marriage in that beginning but it had worked and that was all that mattered.

She turned over, tucking his arm under her breasts and returned the wink of phosphorescent light in the bay.

Chapter Sixteen

I

The year of weddings ended with a funeral. Paul and Claire arrived back in the Valley on May Day, the first anniversary of the wedding of Prudence Pitts, to learn that Jimmy Grenfell had persuaded Mary to shift him to a Paxtonbury Nursing Home, declaring that there were limits to the hospitality one man could claim from another, and that it was bad taste to die in an old friend's bed. He must have know that Paul would never have agreed to him going, and would, indeed, have done all in his power to dissuade him from submitting to another operation, so he took advantage of his hosts' absence and convinced Mary that her parents would have fallen in with his plan. Paul hurried over to see him the day before his operation and found him very weak but as cheerful and resigned as ever. The history of the Chartist Movement was proofed, he said, and all that remained now was for Paul to send the MSS to the publishers and countersign a document he would find in the drawer of the desk on which it lay.

'What is it, Jimmy?' he demanded. 'I must know what I'm signing before I promise anything.'

'Only some mumbo-jumbo drawn up by the agent,' Grenfell told him, 'allocating the royalties, if any, to you.'

'Dammit, man,' Paul protested, 'I don't want to profit by your death! Haven't you any relatives you want to pass it to?' But Jimmy said all his relations were staunch Tories who would be embarrassed by a book on a revolutionary movement. 'In any case,' he added, 'the money isn't a straight bequest, it's an endowment. I'm told the book is expected to do well, both here and in America, and I had an idea that I could flatter you and, at the same time, make a post-mortem gesture!

It ought, over the years, to produce enough to give one boy, or girl for that matter, a decent education and send them on to university. It's laid down in the deed that if any such person is found, and named by you, that they read modern history and philosophy. You'll administrate, of course, so I leave it to you to see the clause is followed.'

'That alters things,' Paul said, 'and I think it's a splendid idea! What kind of geographical limits had you in mind?'

'Only that whoever takes advantage of this is the child of one of your tenants, or, if there are no local takers, the child of one of our old stalwarts in the constituency, someone who stood with us through the heat of the day.'

'Well,' Paul said, 'let's hope you can tackle the paper work yourself, Jimmy,' but Grenfell said, 'You don't believe that, Paul! I'm a gonner and you know it; I only agreed to this operation because I knew it would mean curtains. There's really no point in hanging around any longer and becoming a damned nuisance to everyone. I've already had a couple of years more than I expected and I owe that to you, to Claire, and that charming daughter of yours. I'm afraid this is good-bye, Paul.'

Paul said nothing. He was aware, more than anyone, of the pain Jimmy had endured over the last few years and could no more regret his release than he had regretted old John Rudd's more merciful death not so long ago. Both men, he reflected, had been bonny fighters and it was pitiful to see them grow entirely dependent on others. He said, finally, 'It's been fun, Jimmy, and an adventure in its way, ever since you bowled up the drive in that yellow trap, wearing that damned silly billycock hat and looking more like a squire than I ever did! I've learned a lot from you; it was you who kept me in touch with what was going on outside and stopped me from becoming dangerously parochial.'

'Taken all round you had the right idea from the beginning, Paul,' Grenfell said. 'I didn't always think so but I do now.'

'Well, I believe we're getting on top of things, Jimmy,' and as he said this it struck him that, in his final moments old John Rudd had also been concerned with the future of the Valley, as though each of these men had donated part of themselves to a task that had absorbed his own interests throughout the greater part of a lifetime. He left then, with the uncertainty that he would never see Jimmy Grenfell again and neither did he. Within twenty-four hours they rang through to say the patient had died under the anaesthetic.

Parson Horsey called as soon as the news got around and said Grenfell had asked him if he could be buried in the Valley and Paul was more impressed by this than by Grenfell's eccentric legacy.

'He wasn't a local man, he belonged up North,' he told Horsey. 'Jimmy didn't set foot in the Valley until he got himself adopted as Liberal candidate at the beginning of the century. What did you promise him?'

'I told him we would certainly find room for him when his time came,' Horsey said. 'He's one of the few politicians I ever met who based his election addresses on the Sermon on the Mount. There aren't so many of his kind left, Mr Craddock. Will Wednesday suit you? His grave will be the first in the new annexe, beyond the wall.'

Paul remembered then that Horsey had recently acquired a triangular plot east of Churchyard Lane, directly behind the church and its overcrowded graveyard. It brought home to him that the rate of wastage in the Valley was accelerating and, for the first time perhaps, he realised that the Craddocks, when their turn came round, would not lie in the same acre as old Tamer Potter, Edwin Willoughby, John Rudd, and Norman Eveleigh, of Four Winds.

He completed arrangements with the parson and went into the office to record Grenfell's death in the diary but when he turned the book to its first blank page he saw that Claire had anticipated him and had written, under Monday's date, *'Today James Grenfell, MP (with a single brief break) for Paxtonbury from 1904 until 1929, and who spent his last years in Shallowford writing his "The History of the English Chartists", died at the age of sixty-five years. He was a good man, genuinely regretted by everyone in the Valley, and particularly so by the Squire, whose close friend he was during the whole of*

that time.' The entry touched him. Claire had never been one
for politics and what she had written underlined the respect
and affection she felt for Grenfell as a man, rather than as a
politician. There was nothing he could add to the entry so he
went upstairs to the room Jimmy had occupied since retiring
to Shallowford. To his surprise he found Mary sitting at the
desk, so absorbed in the proofs of Jimmy's book that she
did not hear him come in. He knew his eldest daughter was
an enthusiastic devotee of lyrical poetry (she was the only
female member of the family, he would say, whose mind
strayed outside a woman's magazine) but he had never before
seen her reading a political book.

She said, noting his smile, 'All right, so it's a new field! But
it's one of the most absorbing books I've ever read. Have you
read it?'

'In manuscript. What makes it specially interesting to you?'

'The way people lived, the working people and the fight
they had. You don't hear about that kind of thing in school
history lessons, at least I never did – just kings, battles and
treaties.'

'You must have had a very old-fashioned history teacher!'

'No, seriously,' she went on, folding her hands and clasping
her wrists, a gesture he always thought of as Mary's equivalent
to putting her hands in pockets, 'what staggers me is that
it wasn't all that time ago, less than a century. Your father,
and Grandpa Derwent, must have been alive, and realising
that makes everything so much – well – relevant, even things
about here if you see what I mean?'

He did not but he was anxious to; he had never held a
conversation like this with any member of his family except
Simon and Simon always retreated into bluebooks and party
pamphlets.

'How do you mean, "even things around here"?'

She said cautiously, 'Well, you know how we've always
teased you about having a bee in your bonnet as regards the
Valley . . . ?'

'You don't have to apologise. As regards that my skin is
several inches thick! How does the Valley come into it?'

'This book, which I began dipping into simply because I liked Uncle Jimmy made it so clear that there have always been two kinds of people in charge, those out for all they could get and those – well, those like you!'

It was, he felt, one of the most roundabout but acceptable compliments he had ever received, certainly out of the mouth of one of his children, and it confirmed his prejudice in favour of this willowy, inarticulate, sensitive girl, whom he had always preferred (and been ashamed of preferring) above her brothers and sisters. He straddled Jimmy's chair and said, gravely, 'I see. It looks as if it has finally got through to you. It's about time I must say! Does this mean the rest of the family still regard me as half-dotty?'

'Oh no,' she said earnestly, 'not dotty, just . . . well . . . just the tiniest bit eccentric about the Good Earth, and The-Man-with-Mud-on-his-Boots! And in any case, you mustn't include Mummy in the family write-off. Your word has always been gospel to her.'

'For quite different reasons, I'm afraid. Well, you'd better finish it and if you want to talk about it after you can, any time. Incidentally, "The Good Earth" is an article of faith with me and always has been ever since the day I came here.'

'Why *did* you come here, Daddy?'

'Why?' He had to think hard. It was a question he had not asked himself for more than twenty years now. He said, at length, 'Because of a dream, I suppose, a dream I had when I was in hospital after the Boer War but it's far too complicated to recount and right now I have to arrange Uncle Jimmy's funeral.'

'*Will* you explain? Some other time?'

'Yes, if you like but it will only convince you the bees must have been in my bonnet when I was born. It's too late in the day to expect them to swarm!'

'I'll hold you to that,' she said and turned back to the proofs while he went out, quite forgetting what had brought him there but musing on the conversation for the rest of the day as he sat telephoning and writing to everybody who might want to attend Jimmy's funeral.

*   *   *

It happened that, about this time, there was a very active bee in Claire Craddock's bonnet but it was a recent lodger and she had yet to come to terms with it. Within a month of Jimmy Grenfell's death, however, it led her to pay one of her rare calls on Doctor Maureen.

She saw Maureen almost every day, for the Lady Doctor (as everyone still called her) lived on alone at the lodge that she used as a surgery, but it was a long time since Claire had had occasion to seek her professional advice. Unlike a majority of Maureen's patients Claire was deeply ashamed of ill-health and had, in fact, never sought a doctor in her life except during confinements. She went now much against her will, convinced that she was approaching, if not entering, the dreaded Change.

She had returned from the Welsh holiday in splendid health but ever since had lacked an appetite and had been subject to mild spells of dizziness when she got up in the morning. Nothing to worry about, she told herself, but enough to set her thinking. Her horror of The Change (she always saw it in capital letters) dated back to her childhood when she had overheard a doctor tell her father that this had been a contributory factor to her mother's death, inasmuch as it had probably warped her judgment at the fatal jump. Yet this half-recalled episode from a time of trouble was not the main cause of her anxiety. She was aware of others, with sources far closer the surface, and they were all rooted in a fixation about the milestone of fifty.

On her fiftieth birthday she took a good long look at herself in the dressing-table mirror and the scrutiny failed to reassure her, notwithstanding recent memories of the second honeymoon. She saw facial muscles that were undeniably sagging a little, wisps of hair over the ears that had outgrown their last rinse in a fortnight, eyes that, in her view, had lost a good deal of their sparkle, lips that seemed slightly less full and – this was certainly no fancy – an inclination to put on weight nothwithstanding years of dieting. She weighed herself on the bathroom scales and at once regretted it, for the needle proclaimed an impossible increase of two pounds in just over a week. She said, stepping down, 'It's wrong! The damned scales need seeing to!' but Paul and the children noticed that she did not open her birthday presents with much enthusiasm and when they teased her about it she had to make a genuine effort to pretend not to mind. A few days later, telling herself that she needed a tonic, or change of diet, she walked across the paddock to catch Maureen between morning surgery and her forenoon rounds, knowing that with no time to spare Maureen would probably confine herself to questions and a prescription. Maureen called from upstairs, 'Hullo there! Don't tell you're for surgery? I've just got rid of the last malingerer!'

'Come on down,' Claire said shortly, 'I'd like a word with you!' and Maureen said, '*Professionally?* You must be joking!' Then, judging Claire's tetchy mood from a distance, 'Go along in then, I won't be a moment,' and Claire went in, looking round distastefully at the cheerless little room with its dog-eared calendar, row of hard chairs and worn oilcloth. There were no magazines; Maureen did not encourage her patients to linger.

'You do look a bit off colour,' Maureen said as she bustled in. 'I noticed it as a matter of fact but knowing you I wasn't going to be the first to mention it!'

'You noticed it?'

'Oh, it's nothing, I can tell you that from here! I daresay you've been over-dieting. Overtiring yourself too – all those family upheavals on lettuce leaves and charcoal biscuits! Don't say I didn't warn you!'

'I think it's more than that,' Claire said, ignoring her banter. 'I think it's The Change and if it is you can give me a tonic and some advice!' but in Maureen's presence her confidence returned. They had been friends now for over a quarter of a century and if there was one thing Claire knew it was that she could count on directness and no 'Now-now-there-there' talk from Maureen Rudd. She spoke of her occasional dizziness, her increase in weight despite dieting, loss of appetite and, above all, recurring spells of depression. Maureen was as blunt as she had expected. 'Well, I daresay you're right, girl, but there's very little I can do about it! There are tablets, of course, but I never had much faith in 'em. It's more of a mental than physical readjustment and its effect on a woman is often regulated by willpower and plain commonsense. You've got more than most women around here and should get through it easily enough, providing, of course, that you don't mind me having a word with Paul on the subject. His attitude is important, or will be in your case. He mustn't mind you flying off the handle every now and again!' She looked at Claire with amused affection. 'Cheer up! Most women round here who reach the point of no return are delighted. I can tell you that for nothing!'

'I don't suppose you'll believe me,' Claire said, 'but Paul and I have never tried not to have children, not once!' and Maureen, with an appreciative chuckle, replied, 'I certainly do believe you! What kind of a family doctor do you think I am!' and then, because Claire's mood made her seem a great deal younger than fifty, she put her arm round her, saying, 'Getting old inside a family circle is nothing to be frightened of! It's getting old alone that's the real spectre!' and Claire suddenly felt ashamed of her neglect and made a promise to come up to supper, remembering that she must be very lonely in the evenings now that John was gone, and her son rarely returned to the Valley after qualifying and taking a practice in Scotland.

She remained cheerful for a spell but then the steady increase in her weight, and a tendency to tire very quickly, began to disturb her again. The tablets made her sleepy by day and restless at night, and she found she was morose on wakening, so that it was with less hesitation that she paid her second call on Maureen and submitted to a check-up despite a protest that all she really needed was sanction to throw 'the damned tablets in the dustbin'. Maureen said, sharply for her, 'If there's one type of patient who makes me swear it's the sort who come here with their own prescriptions and expect me to sign 'em! Get your clothes off, girl, and let's take a good look at you! There's not a thing wrong with you that isn't in your mind and I must say you surprise me! Next thing you'll be joining the procession of middle-aged women who come in here insisting they have cancer of the breast!'

Maureen's cavalier handling of her patients was notorious so she submitted with good grace as Maureen made her check, grunting a little, Claire noticed, when she stooped, so that the patient got one back, saying, 'You sound as if you could do with a diet yourself! You must turn the scale to something around twelve stone!'

'Twelve-three to be exact,' Maureen said, straightening, 'but I'm not pregnant and you most certainly are, my girl!'

The certainty that Maureen must be joking irritated Claire, who thought this was carrying a joke too far. She sat up, swung off the cold leather couch and said, 'For heaven's sake, Maureen, I'm not one of your silly hypochondriacs who has to be bullied into . . .' but then she stopped, for something in Maureen's expression as she stood with arms akimbo and back to the window, made her pause. Maureen said with a shrug, 'You can protest as much as you like but it's a fact, so don't let's have any more snivelling about grey hairs, and youth calling from the far side of the hill! You're three months pregnant and there's an end to it! I don't know whether I should congratulate you or ask Parson Horsey to ring the church bells!'

Then she waited. Half a minute elapsed before Claire could make any kind of reply, for her tongue was stilled by the confusion of mind resulting from such a preposterous explanation. Pregnant, at fifty-plus! Pregnant, after a gap of how many years since the birth of her youngest child? – 1918 – and it was 1933, and young Claire would be sixteen next birthday! She said, in a voice so strained and uncertain that it seemed not to belong to her, 'There can't be any mistake? It's a certainty, you say?' but she did not seriously challenge the fact, reasoning that Maureen would be very unlikely to fall into such an error after seeing her through all her previous pregnancies, including an unsuccessful one as long ago as December 1907. She said, hoarsely, 'What is it, Maureen, a . . . kind of . . . freak-miracle?' and Maureen, who seemed to be extracting a certain amount of sardonic amusement from the situation, retorted, 'Good God, woman, of course it isn't! I told you you were exceptionally healthy and it isn't all that uncommon when a woman has already had a string of children. Nature's last fling, I imagine, and it will be the last if that's any consolation!' but Claire continued to sit balanced on the edge of the couch,

gasping and blinking, as though she had just been dragged
from cold. Maureen said, curiously, 'Once you've got over the
shock will you be pleased? Will Paul, do you think?'

'How would I know that? It's all I can do to . . . to
absorb it! I feel as if – well, as if I'd been caught out doing
something shameful,' and then, correcting herself, 'no, not
shameful exactly, but something horribly embarrassing, a
practical joke in very bad taste that didn't amuse anybody!'

Maureen, who thought she knew her patient as well as
anybody, was not only baffled but a little worried. She said,
'Look here, Claire, I've always thought of you and that hulking
husband of yours as two people marvellously adjusted to one
another, a couple who had the sense to give their instincts
a chance, instead of relying on one or other of these damn
silly books on sex and psychology that people are churning
out nowadays! I haven't been wrong, have I?'

'No,' Claire said, slowly, 'you haven't been wrong, Maureen.
I've always found joy and fulfilment in the physical side of our
marriage and I think he has too, but – how can I explain? We
don't have to . . . to proclaim it from the housetops do we?'

'You were proud enough of the others,' Maureen said, not
liking this turn of talk at all, 'so why worry about a few sly
giggles at your age?'

'Age is the operative word,' Claire said, beginning to dress
at a speed that suggested she could not be out of the surgery
quickly enough. 'The "others" are all grown up, and going
their own way, so to the devil with starting all over again,
and having Paul's attention directed elsewhere! I've earned
the right to have him to myself, haven't I?'

She went out with a rush, not even pausing to say good-bye
and Maureen, who was rarely astonished, looked after her
with mouth wide open. 'Great God!' she said aloud, as she
watched Claire cross the stepping stones to the ford instead
of turning for home. 'I do believe the woman's jealous of
her own womb! Her appetite for that man has never had
anything to do with children at all – they were just by-
products!' and suddenly she felt angry with herself for her
total failure to plumb the emotional depths of a patient she

had always thought of as an open book and a well-thumbed book at that. She thought, 'Well, I don't know how Paul will react but he's going to hear about this from me and I hope I can find him before she does!'

She was lucky, meeting Paul in the drive before Claire returned from her breathless walk along the river road and, to Maureen's relief, he let his sense of humour take over, once he had ridden out the shock. But although glad enough to hear him laugh she deliberately sobered him, saying, 'Right, but see that you straighten your face before she comes to you with the news, and I don't have to tell you to pretend it's first-hand when you get it! You're going to need more tact over the next six months than I've ever seen you display!'

'Oh, stuff and nonsense!' he said. 'I daresay it's staggered her but once she's got used to the idea she'll be delighted. She isn't likely to have a bad time, is she?'

'Physically, no, she's always produced children with less difficulty than most women but what I'm trying to prepare you for is something quite different. I'm beginning to get an inkling of what's bothering her and I must be half-way to my dotage not to have spotted it before. How can I put it without seeming fanciful? Listen – in the old days she had youth, and vanity that goes along with youth. The children were close enough together to amuse one another, the house full of women to attend to them and you were out and about your business most of the day. It's very different now. The children are grown up or scattered and the staff, such as they are, won't do a stroke more than they have to! On top of that you're now of an age when you'll be more likely to spend your time at home but, above all, remember that when Claire looks in the glass she sees a middle-aged woman whose figure isn't going to be improved by another child! If you think I'm exaggerating ask yourself how she behaved towards the children when they were toddlers.'

'She was a damned good mother to them.'

'I'm not questioning that but what was her overall approach to them? Was it mother-hennish?'

'No it wasn't! Now that I come to think of it it was always pretty casual.'

'Right, well I'm asking you to think about that and for your sake as much as hers.'

He said, wrinkling his brow, 'You know it is odd, Maureen, I don't think I've ever remarked on it before but there was something undemonstrative about her approach to the kids, all except young Claire that is.'

'Don't be taken in by that,' Maureen said, 'I've noticed her approach to Claire myself and it's no more than an inclination to bask in the reflected glory of the child's looks and poise! No, Paul, we might as well face it. She fell head over heels in love with you the minute you rode into High Coombe yard when you were youngsters and all the years between have done nothing but pile coals on the fire! That's why you're in this pickle, isn't it?'

'You really think of it as "a pickle", Maureen?'

'Well, let's put it this way, it's six months' walk through a mine field and all I'm saying, as your doctor and friend, is watch where you put your feet, lad!'

It was as well that he had this warning for Claire's humour during that summer and autumn baffled him to such an extent that it was difficult to believe he was sharing bed and board with the same woman. It was not that she was quarrelsome or intractable – in some ways he would have described her as subdued and withdrawn – but that he, and everyone else about Shallowford, found her wildly unpredictable. Sometimes she would show a spurt of temper over a trivial omission on the part of one or other of them but at other times she seemed to have lost contact with the family. In between these two extremes she was unsure of herself to a degree that recalled the very earliest days of her marriage, when she found herself in authority over such well-established limpets as old Mrs Handcock and the unsmiling Thirza Tremlett. Towards early autumn, when her pregnancy had ceased to cause much comment in the Valley, she took to wandering off alone in the old yellow trap (Paul had forbidden Mark Codsall to let her saddle a horse) and the curious would watch her drive out

along the river road to the moor, or across the pasture track
to the head of the goyle that led down to Crabpot Willie's cabin
and the beach. Paul was nervous of these solitary excursions
but, after a word with Maureen, he made no protest and had
to admit that they had a calming effect on her nerves, for she
was often more herself when she returned to preside over
family high tea at six. Then, as the evenings drew in, she
took to retiring early and would be asleep when he came
upstairs but she rarely slept until dawn and sometimes she
would be up by the time he awoke, pottering about the house
before the earliest riser was astir. Not always, however. There
were occasions when he caught a swift and disturbing glimpse
of the pressures a fancied insecurity was exerting on her
mind, as when he awoke one night to find her out of bed
and crouched on the floor beside him, her head touching his
pillow. He reached out to turn on the bedside light, thinking
that she must be unwell and had blundered round to his side
in an effort not to disturb him but she dragged his hand from
the bulb and then began kissing him with a desperation that
stirred his pity. He said, gently, 'What *is* it, dear? Tell me
what's worrying you so badly? I'll help if I can, we'll all help . . .'
but he learned very little even then, for once she had climbed
back to bed he realised that it was not words of comfort she
wanted so much as reassurance that her swollen body was
not repugnant to him. He gathered this from her impatient
dismissal of his half-hearted protests and his silent possession
of her, without either the tenderness or the humour that had
attended their love-making in the past. After that he followed
Maureen's advice to drop the half-invalid approach and a
subdued Christmas came and went, the family assembling
and dispersing without anyone making more than an indirect
reference to her condition. She seemed to approve of this collective disregard of the embarrassingly obvious yet she remained
withdrawn, so that Paul found himself noting the passage of
days with the attentiveness of a castaway or a prisoner.

When at last it happened – on the 30th January, 1934 –
he was away from home, just as he had been in 1910 when
Thirza Tremlett met him at the gate with news of Mary's

arrival. Henry Pitts' wife, Gloria, had died whilst on a visit to her sister in Cornwall, the victim of her own obstinacy and a virulent influenza epidemic, for Henry said she had been severely troubled with her chest throughout the winter but had insisted, against his advice, on making the trip to the remote village where she had been born in order to attend her aged mother's funeral early in the New Year. She caught a severe chill at the graveside, developed pneumonia and had been too ill to recognise him when he responded to an urgent summons to the bedside. To his surprise and indignation he learned that Gloria had expressed a death-bed wish to be buried in the family grave near her original home and it required the united pressure of all Gloria's Cornish relatives to overcome his objections to such an act of disloyalty. Paul, who thought it his duty to attend Gloria's funeral, found Henry's grief somewhat mitigated by his wife's eccentric preference to lie in foreign soil, and on their way back from the funeral tea (it was, Henry grudgingly admitted, a very sumptuous one) he voiced his complaints with what seemed to Paul an exaggerated bitterness.

'Tidden right!' he kept saying, 'an' tidden zeemin' that 'er should lie down yer, half-way across the bliddy country! Never 'eard o' such a thing, not in all me born days! A Pitts, buried all the way down yer, among a horde o' flamin' Cornishmen! Tiz 'er own wish I know but 'er won't rest easy! There's been a Pitts in the Valley for I don't know how long and 'er's the first to be buried out of it! 'Er was alwus obstinit mind but I never dreamed 'er was so mazed about Cornishmen!'

Henry's rumbling complaints took some of the sting out of the occasion as they recrossed Bodmin Moor in driving January sleet and Paul, a tolerant listener, was tempted to confide some of his own troubles to his old friend, if only to distract him from his grievance but he thought better of it and held his peace until they drove into the frontier town of Launceston, where he left Henry to console himself with a tankard of beer and telephoned Shallowford to say he expected to be home in two or three hours.

Mary answered so quickly that she might have had the receiver to her ear. She said, quietly but incisively, 'Come straight away, Daddy! The baby's arrived! It's a boy and everything's fine but we need you!'

Paul said, with a gasp, 'Your mother is all right? You aren't keeping anything back?'

'No, honestly. Maureen says it was a very straightforward affair but . . .'

'To hell with what Maureen says! Maureen told me there was no possibility of the baby arriving until partway through February! When was he born?'

'It started soon after you left.'

'Why the devil didn't somebody get in touch?'

'We couldn't. I wasn't sure of the address and there wouldn't have been a 'phone, would there?'

'No, you're quite right. Give her my love and tell her I'll be with her in about three hours. And Mary . . .'

'Well?'

'How has she taken it?'

Mary said, carefully, 'It's a bit odd, Dad. You know how she's been but I thought – well, when the baby actually arrived I thought she'd change.'

'And she hasn't?'

'No, she doesn't seem interested. Just hurry along, she'll be all right when you show up!'

He replaced the receiver and stood looking across the hotel lobby at the sleet slashing down on the little square and leaping up from the cobbles. He felt tired and dispirited, finding no pleasure in the news although, secretly, he had been hoping for another boy. He thought, impatiently, 'Claire's right! We're both too old for this kind of nonsense and it's time we both had a little peace and quiet!' and then homesickness came down on him, as it always did when he was more than an hour's ride from the Valley, and he called to Henry to hurry along and went out into the rain to the car.

It was like playing an old, old scene over again, with words and actions clearly remembered but all the spring and gaiety gone from the step. She was in the same room and the same bed and the only difference, he was quick to notice, was that the baby's cot was not by the window as it had been on every previous occasion. She looked, he thought, extraordinarily fresh and young but there was still hostility in the eyes, or perhaps it was not hostility but simply an unconscious expression of the same, baffling impatience with life he himself was experiencing. He said, with an effort, 'I'm sorry I wasn't here, Claire, I could kick myself for not trying to find a public 'phone in that God-forsaken country. I ought not to have gone, I suppose, but Henry is our oldest friend left around here and he wanted me at a time like this. Mary said it was quick, like the others. Is that true?'

'Yes, it was very quick,' she said. 'I suppose you're pleased it's a boy?'

'Yes, I am but all I really wanted was to get it over and done with.'

He wanted badly to use this opportunity to talk frankly to her, to make some attempt to climb the fence that had grown up between them during the drift of the last few months, but she would not give him the necessary encouragement so he remained standing by the window, feeling more shy and gawky than when he came here to visit her after the birth of the twins. What they had lost, he decided, was the sense of humour that had always been able to bridge these embarrassing moments. When she asked if he had any name in mind he said, groping wildly for laughter, 'I don't know . . . something to single him out from all the others ten laps ahead; how about "Tail-piece"?' The small joke was a failure. After a wretched pause she said, settling herself, 'Yes . . . well you had better go and look at him. After all, he's all yours, Paul!'

He would have protested and perhaps, stung by injustice, hit back in some way but he remembered in time that she was at a disadvantage and that if this tension between them persisted it must be met and faced as soon as she came downstairs. He went along the corridor to the old nursery where, to his astonishment, he found Thirza Tremlett sitting beside the cot making the obligatory noises she had made

over the cots of all the children up to the time she left the
Big House and became nanny to John Rudd's boy. She was
wearing her faded nanny's 'uniform' and for some reason
her presence cheered him a little.

'Now what the devil prompted you to rejoin the column?'
he asked, remembering that Thirza had married after leaving
Maureen's service and had not been seen in the valley for some
time past. Thirza told him that she had heard through old Mrs
Handcock that Mrs Craddock was 'expecting again' and had
applied for reinstatement after she and her husband had 'gone
their seprit ways'. He recalled then that Thirza had ultimately
married a Whinmouth sailor who had, it was rumoured, been
courting her since the bustle was in vogue. He said, looking
down on the fat little bundle who was gesticulating with
a small, business-like fist, 'And what do you think of this
surprise packet, Thirza?' She replied that she supposed he
would do but pointed out that, with a gap of fifteen years
between him and his youngest sister, 'he was zertain zure
to be spoiled' and he might depend upon her to do her best
to see that he wasn't.

''Ave 'er got a given naame yet, Squire?' she asked and Paul
said no, it was something he would have to think about, and
because Thirza was more of an old friend than an employee,
added, 'Mrs Craddock doesn't seem particularly pleased with
him, Thirza? Have you any idea why?' She did not seem in
any way embarrassed by his mark of confidence, considering,
no doubt, that it was her prerogative to pronounce upon such
matters. 'Well,' she said, unsmilingly, 'I baint surprised to
learn that! Mebbe Mrs Craddock thinks tiz high time 'er was
done wi' such tiresomeness!' and the look she gave him as he
withdrew was loaded with reproach.

He drifted off to seek Mary, wondering whether 'tiresomeness' on the part of Thirza's sailor-husband had played its part
in the failure of the marriage but he was far too grateful to see
a fragment of the old pattern restored to resent the implied
rebuke. Mary was not to be found so he went up across the
long orchard, conjuring with names and recalling the fun he
and Claire had naming the other children, sometimes amusing

themselves for nearly a week before settling on Andrew, Stephen and Mary. 'Karen', the name Whiz never used, had been Claire's choice, he remembered, and she had hit on an equally fanciful name for young Claire which he had rejected on his return from France, in 1918. As he went down the lane towards the western tongue of the woods confidence began to return to him, a bonus, perhaps, of crossing a landscape where every tree and every contour was as familiar to him as his own features. 'I daresay it's something to do with the metabolism of the body' he told himself, still pondering the baffling changes in Claire, 'and as time goes on it will sort itself out, like everything always does in and about the Valley.' After all, there had been times when he had despaired of finding his own way, and plenty of occasions when whole families, like the Eveleighs at Four Winds, had been written off but something always turned up to adjust the balance in the way spring converted this belt of trees from a witches' back drop to a maze of green tunnels. He turned away from the woods and went down the long, sloping field to the house, just as a watery sun came out and the sky over the Sorrel cleared for a few moments. It looked quiet and workaday down there, with wavering columns of bluish smoke rising from the twisted chimneys and a line of limp washing on the cord that crossed the kitchen garden. Peace returned to him and with it the memory of the fat little bundle in the cot knuckling his fist and looking up at him through eyes slitted against the light. 'John!' he exclaimed suddenly. 'It will be good to have a John around the place again and if there is a more English name for a farmer I've yet to hear it!' He went on down the slope feeling almost cheerful again.

II

'Almost' was as far as he got that season. As spring came round Claire edged back into the family circle but far too guardedly for Paul's liking, so that imperceptibly their roles were now reversed, with his own edginess causing his daughters and the men about Home Farm to tread warily, whereas it was Claire who held the watching brief that had been his throughout autumn and winter. He was aware of the sources from which his surliness stemmed, not merely his semi-estrangement from Claire but a long, rumbling quarrel with circumstances that held any number of new problems in reserve, depriving him of the mental ease he had enjoyed in the pre-war days when the world was sane and the wary peace he had enjoyed in the years leading up to the slump, when his children were growing up around him and he was still young enough to respond to a challenge. Yet, even now, there existed no open quarrel between him and Claire. She had abandoned her solitary expeditions in the trap and was, in fact, less inclined to fly off the handle when something displeased her, but what exasperated him most was her neutral attitude to the baby and her tendency, at least in his view, to give free rein to young Claire who was now, as Mrs Handcock would have said, 'of an age', which meant she was too old to be smacked and too young to respond to reason. It was no consolation to reflect that Claire had never been over zealous in her duties as a mother, that she had left all the fussing to people like Thirza, Mrs Handcock and old Chivers, the groom, for he remembered also that the children, one and all, had always been able to make her laugh and arouse her interest, so that her relationship with them had been that of an elder sister rather than a mother and he had never quarrelled with this. As to the new baby, she breast-fed him, as she had all her other children but that was all. She took no pains to conceal that he was little more than a tiresome addition to household chores and Paul sometimes wondered if the baby's plainness had anything to do with her attitude. At this stage in their lives all her children had a pink and white prettiness whereas John, a sturdy child and one that gave little enough trouble, was surprisingly sallow and even Thirza had to admit that his wrinkles had something in common with those of old Aaron Stokes, the doyen of the Valley, still to be seen outside his cottage on fine mornings making bird-tables to supplement his pension.

When the baby was about six months old Paul stopped by the lodge one morning seeking further advice from Maureen but was not surprised by her impatience with his complaints.

'Women are often withdrawn after childbirth,' she reassured him, 'so in the name of God don't be cultivating another fancied grievance!'

'Now why the hell should I go looking for trouble?' he demanded but she said, with a laugh, 'Oh, I'm not saying it's deliberate on your part but she tried your patience pretty sorely all winter so this is your subconsious getting its own back!'

Neither he nor old John Rudd had ever had much patience with Maureen's pseudo-Freudian explanations for human oddities of one sort or another, so he protested that she was now talking nonsense, 'Damn it, you admitted yourself that she was jealous of the poor little beggar before he arrived. Now that I've come round to your point of view you back down on it and feed me a lot of psychological claptrap! It would have made John hoot with laughter and you know it!'

She said, regarding him with affectionate amusement, 'Oh, you and my John were two of a kind. Everything you came up against had to be black, white or khaki and stated in two-syllable words! Well, thank God, we've learned something about human beings since those days and the plain fact is life isn't that simple! A thing like this could have gone either way. A majority of women producing a healthy child at fifty would have whipped up their husbands' temper for quite another reason!'

'How?'

'They would have screamed with triumph, turned their backs on their man for good and gone to goo-gooing over the new arrival and if it had taken Claire that way we should have had you in here with an even bigger chip on your shoulder! Very well, you've asked for it. I'm going to give it you straight whether you like it or not! How often have you made love to the girl since the package was delivered?'

'Now you're just a nosy old woman dredging for prurient details but if you don't wheedle them out of me I daresay you'll get them from her so I'll tell you! We haven't been man and wife since John arrived, and as things are right now we look like heading for honourable retirement!'

'Then you're both bigger fools than I took you for!' Maureen replied. 'There's not the slightest chance of her conceiving again and setting up a new record in the Valley!'

'I don't think it's that, Maureen.'

'Then what is it? Are you both sulking, at your age?'

He said, trying to state his case as honestly as he could, 'We never have been lovers from habit and what's more I can't remember a time when an occasion wasn't mutually prompted and mutually enjoyed but the impetus has gone somehow. Maybe it's burned itself out and the very lack of it is poisoning our relationship.'

'But that just isn't true,' she said with an earnestness that half-convinced him in spite of himself. 'This is no more than a phase and both of you are prolonging it artificially. Listen here, Paul, I know an old stick-in-the-mud like you finds it difficult to take psychological factors into consideration but they do exist and very much so in a woman as sensual as Claire and a man as vigorous as you! The years ahead of you could be your happiest yet for I never saw a better-matched or a healthier pair, but you are letting your prejudices react against one another and if you don't do something about it you might have a real issue on your hands before you've realised it!'

'What do you suggest? That I don't wait for the propitious moment and demand my rights, as they say?'

'No, I don't,' she said emphatically, 'for that might easily result in your making an ass of yourself and coming back here waving your pride at me like a head on a pike! I know it's asking a lot of you to be subtle – neither you nor my John ever really understood the damned word – but subtlety is your cue now. Stop bellyaching and start courting and I promise you the propitious moment will appear without any prompting on your part, you great numbskull!'

'Well,' he said slowly, 'you're beginning to make sense but even if you're right I don't see how a thing like this can be resolved by a tumble or two on the bed,' and she sighed, so deeply that he had to smile.

'You can be so *thick* sometimes!' she said. 'Who am I, a woman who married an elderly man when I was over thirty, to be giving you and Claire lessons in this kind of thing? I'll spell it out for you. Claire Derwent, as I've told you before is crazy about you, not as Squire of Shallowford but as a man – M.A.N – and the only man she has ever enjoyed or ever wanted to and when I say enjoy I mean it! I remember telling John more than once that she goes limp at the knees every time you enter a room and women like her don't change, not even when they produce "proofs of affection" as they used to say, at the age of fifty! Well, here she is, back in the race again you might say, but how are you giving expression to the relief she must be feeling? By holding back out of mistaken consideration and by working off your bad temper looking for qualities in her that aren't there and never were, not even when she was a day-old bride! You remember what I told you in the beginning of all this? That the children are no more than by-products to her, this last one especially, but if she ever suspects that baby is causing a permanent rift between you you'll really have something to blow about! You haven't put this in words to her, I hope?'

'No, I haven't said anything but Mary and Thirza must have noticed her attitude to the kid.'

'Let them both mind their own damned business! One's made a mess of her own marriage and the other is still waiting on Mr Right! This concerns no one but you and Claire, and my advice is to stop expecting her to sit opposite you with a shawl on her shoulders and rock the cradle! Dammit, when I think of most of the middle-aged couples you don't deserve your luck, either of you! There won't be an old age for you or her unless you open the door to it!' She paused for breath and concluded, 'Have I made any impression on you at all?'

'Yes,' he said, 'I think maybe you have but I'm not one of your wide-eyed witch-doctor patients, who swallow everything you prescribe without question. I like to be told the ingredients and make up my own mind. Would you give me a hint how to start courting at fifty-four? You ought to

know something about it, John was about that age when he
married you. What was his line?'

'He pretended to anticipate my every wish. It was only later
I discovered that his technique was simplicity itself. He would
pay out three yards of slack and pull in two-and-a-half when
I wasn't looking and I loved him for it! You start with an
advantage no man deserves. Claire's already broken and the
jerks won't even surprise her!'

'Well,' he said, 'you won't find that in any of your
Psychology-for-the-Million textbooks but I suppose it's the
kind of advice I was looking for and I'll take it. There's a
big-supper-dance at the Paxtonbury Town Hall on Thursday,
the annual "do" of the county Dairymen's Association. The
girls wanted to make it a family excursion but I turned them
down. I've suddenly changed my mind.'

'Quite proper!' she said. 'Why the hell should the kids have
all the fun? Has she got a new frock to go in?'

'No, but she's got her eye on one!' and he walked out almost
jauntily so that she called after him, 'Don't waste my surgery
time coming back here with a progress report! I live on your
doorstep, remember?' and slammed the door feeling justifiable
pride in her achievement but regretting that old John wasn't on
hand to hear an account and share the joke. Time and again he
had prevailed upon her to break confidence with the patients
he liked as well as those he did not.

The dance was in full swing when they arrived about nine
o'clock and the two girls at once disappeared to find their
friends, leaving Paul and Claire to begin the evening with the
Military Two-Step, this kind of item predominating an event
organised by and for the middle-aged rather than youngsters.
By Paxtonbury standards it was an impressive gathering and
reckoned the event of the season, if Paxtonbury could be said
to enjoy a season. Most of the local landowners were present,
including the Somerset Gilroys, near relatives of the Heronslea
family, who had recently let their property and gone to live in
France. Humphrey Gilroy asked Claire to dance and Paul found
himself partnering Gilroy's wife, a statuesque woman who

seemed to tolerate him solely on account of his relationship
with Rose Barclay-Jones, organiser of the well-known two-day
event in Gloucestershire and described by Mrs Gilroy as 'a
dashing gel', which struck Paul as a curious description of his
gaunt, fifty-nine-year-old sister-in-law. After they had shed the
Gilroys, danced a waltz, and watched Mary win a spot-prize
(young Claire seemed to have adjourned to the carpark but
Paul, in tolerant mood, did not remark on it) they sat out
eating cold turkey and Claire, who had seemed nervously
elated ever since he had insisted on buying her a green velvet
dance frock she had admired in a Cathedral Close window,
said, 'I suppose you know all about the Dairy Queen Contest?
They have the preliminary canter tonight and we've never had
a finalist all the years it's been going.'

'Yes,' he told her, he knew all about the Dairy Queen
Contest. Old John Rudd had always referred to it as 'The
Heifer Parade', declaring that its popularity lay less in its
avowed purpose of advertising Britain's farm products than
in the opportunity it offered farmer-judges from all over the
provinces to enjoy a close-up of young women in bathing
costumes. 'I'd forgotten it was on the programme,' he admitted and she said, doubtfully, 'Honestly? You aren't holding
out on us?' and then laughed so that he at once linked her
expectant air with the mysterious flutter in the family when
he had announced that they would be attending the dance
after all.

'Look here,' he demanded, 'what *is* all this? What gave
you, young Claire and even Mary the jitters when I suddenly
changed my mind about coming tonight?'

'Oh, never mind,' she said, smiling, 'just sit back and wait!
Frankly I thought you were double-bluffing us but it seems
I was wrong!' and before he could dig deeper the drums
rolled, the floor cleared, and the Paxtonbury Town Clerk
stepped on stage to proclaim in a town-crier's voice that
there would now be an interval while Mr Humphrey Gilroy
CBE, and three other judges representing four Westcountry
counties, would select Devon's entry for the national final of
the British Dairy Queen of 1934.

It was then, as the curtains swung aside to reveal a dozen contestants grouped in a half-circle on the dais, that Paul experienced one of the sharpest jolts of his life. Fourth from the right, looking like a young Aphrodite in her scarlet swimsuit and ermine-trimmed cloak, was his youngest daughter, and Claire, watching him nervously, saw his body go taut as he exclaimed, 'Good God! It's young Claire! Whose idea was this? And why they devil wasn't I consulted?'

She said, rather desperately, 'Shhh, Paul, not here – please! I'll explain everything but don't make a scene, she'd never forgive you!' and she let him simmer as the audience cooed, the band struck up a Danubian waltz and the girls began to circle the dais, their high heels clattering as they passed to and fro in front of the judges in the orchestra pit.

She was, he had to admit, the most staggeringly attractive female he had ever seen but it was not the classic regularity of her features, or the singular maturity of figure in one so young that gave her such obvious advantages over the others. Her distinction was centred on her poise, a kind of relaxed sophistication that armoured her against the nervous embarrassment of the older girls. She was, he reflected grimly, a smooth professional among a crop of buxom amateurs; then his attention switched from the stage to his own predicament.

He knew that if he made no effort to hold himself in he would make a scene of their conspiracy of silence, if not here then the moment they returned home. Alternatively, if he once admitted to feeling slighted and belittled by their exclusion, such progress as he had made with Claire in the last day or so would be cancelled out. In the resultant flare up (for she would certainly side with her daughters) the chance to recapture the elusive rhythm of their lives would be lost, perhaps for good. He saw then, and clearly, that he must either capitulate or compromise but there was really no room to manoeuvre. He knew his youngest daughter sufficiently well to appreciate how much this occasion meant to her, particularly if – as was barely credible considering her age – she went forward to the national final. He was so absorbed in making private decisions that he paid little heed to the judges and it was the

familiar ring of his own name issuing from the mouth of the
Town Clerk that jolted him into awareness that the stage was
now empty of bathing beauties, and a decision was on hand.
He thought, as sweat struck cold under his armpits, 'Damn
it, why should I let a prejudice destroy the peace and quiet of
my own home? This is a time to borrow old John Rudd's trick
of paying out slack and not haul in again until my feet are
on surer ground than they have been during the last twelve
months!' and then the tension broke in the seats behind and
he felt Claire's hand grasp his wrist as a fanfare of uncertain
trumpets summoned his youngest daughter back on stage and
he watched her advance towards the Lady Mayoress who had
materialised from the wings carrying a garish-looking crown
on a red, velvet cushion. 'Good God!' he exclaimed, 'she's won!'
but because he saw in his wife's face a radiance that had not
been there for a very long time, he found it easy to counterfeit
a nonchalance he did not feel and even to add, 'There was
never a doubt about it, was there?'

He got his reward on the spot. Her relief seemed to burst
like a bubble and for the first time in almost a year she looked
at him in a way that he recognised and remembered.

'You rotten fraud!' she whispered, enlarging her grip on
his hand, 'you had me scared for a moment!' and then, to
his acute embarrassment, she and Mary began to applaud as
frenziedly as anyone in the hall.

III

'In for a penny, in for a pound,' Maureen told him when she
heard the news and again he took her advice so that the
Craddocks descended upon London in a body in September
to swell the gathering of provincials from all over England
and Wales who were involved in the Dairy Queen finals, held
in a Park Lane hotel.

The competitors, viewed as a contingent, taxed the ingen-
uities of all but the most ingenious of the Press corps, who
found most of the girls blushingly inarticulate when faced

with the stock questions. All but Claire that is, of whom
the journalists made a mascot, not only because she was
the youngest finalist by almost two years but because she
seemed to know exactly where she was going and why.
This was something that Fleet Street not only understood
but applauded.

Mary, who was present at most of her interviews, looked
on with awe as Claire fenced, joked and flirted with hardbitten
men more than twice her age and seemed, by exercising an
inborn skill, to know precisely what they required in the way
of copy, so that Claire's profile, Claire's expectations, and even
Claire's pronouncements on such diverse topics as clothes,
love, cows and cheese were featured in all the journals and
periodicals. She even made a fleeting appearance on Gaumont
British News, assisting at the opening of a hospital wing.

One way and another it was a sensational week and the
first occasion for Paul when London, as a city, touched him
with her magic for the weather was fine and warm, their
quarters comfortable and the general excitement contrived
to keep at bay that depressing anonymity he had always
felt when caught up in this whirl of traffic and stampede of
grey-faced millions who somehow reminded him of prisoners-
of-war milling about the compounds behind Compiègne.

Perhaps the sense of family unity had something to do
with it, for on the second day the twins and their wives
roared up in their big, shiny cars, Monica and the laughing
Welsh girl, Margaret, both dripping with furs and inclined,
he noticed, to convert their 'a's into 'e's and discard the 'g'
in words like 'ripping' and 'topping', which they used a great
deal. Like Claire, and a few of the Pressmen, the twins were
already assured of victory and Paul feared for them all when
finalists intermingled for the first time at a tea dance and he
realised that the competition here was far more formidable
than at Paxtonbury. She could, he thought, outclass some
of the chubbier girls from the remote counties, places like
Cardigan and Cumberland (although, if he were in search of
a living advertisement for cream and butter these were the
very girls he would choose) but it was obvious that city

sophistication had lapped over the farmlands within shouting distance of the big cities and Miss Suffolk, for instance, looked far more like a film star than a dairymaid. He enjoyed talking to Garstin Schroeder, the improbably-named Organising Secretary of the British Dairymen's Association, finding him extremely well-informed on the subject of farming prospects generally, and he found common ground talking to some of the fathers of competitors, whose dolorous experiences on the land during the nineteen-twenties were identical with his own. As a rule, however, he stood aside and let the women enjoy themselves, grateful for Mary's watchful chaperonage of Claire, even more grateful for his wife's sparkle which dated from the very moment he gave his reluctant blessing of the enterprise in the Paxtonbury Town Hall. He did not have to follow Maureen's advice literally; so far, he told himself, he had paid out a great deal of slack and gathered none in but it was a relief to hear her laugh again, to see her preen herself in her smart new clothes and watch her soar off on a series of shopping sprees with her elegant daughters-in-law, Monica and Margaret, neither of whom, he reflected, seemed eager to pause in their eternal gallivanting long enough to produce a grandchild for his delight. It was reflection on his lack of grandchildren, in fact, that had modified his pleasure in the reunion. The Pair had now been married more than two years and Simon, who showed up on the final day, for four years, but neither one had yielded a dividend, male or female. Whiz, they told him, was expecting a child but Whiz and her dour Scots husband were far away in Singapore and if things went on like this it might be years before he could hoist a toddler on to the crupper of his saddle and ride down across the Codsall stubble fields, as he had ridden with all his own children at one time or another. He mentioned this to Claire one night after they had returned from a noisy drinking session in the hotel lounge but she did not seem to share his regrets.

'Oh, there's time enough,' she said carelessly, 'they're all young and healthy and girls nowadays want a bit of fun before they settle down the way we did in our day. I can't say as I blame them, either. Everything has been so topsy-turvy

since the war that one can't see more than a few weeks
ahead.'

One could not indeed, as Simon was not slow to point out
when they had a quiet chat during the parade rehearsal on the
morning of the grand final. The boy, he thought, was a great
contrast to his splendid brothers, in his off-the-peg suit and
weather-beaten trilby. He had some kind of job, he said, editing
a left-wing paper in Manchester, and Rachel, his wife, who did
not accompany him, brought in extra money as a lecturer for
the Workers' Education Association. Between them they had
contested three by-elections and had emerged at the bottom
of the poll at each of them but repeated failure to penetrate
beyond the fringe of politics seemed neither to depress nor
surprise him.

'I'm living the kind of life I want to live, the only kind I could
live, Gov'nor,' he said, when Paul suggested he should swim
with the tide until a real opportunity presented itself. 'The
fact is the whole damned lot of us are living on borrowed time
but so few people seem to realise it. Take what's happening
in Germany. All pretence of freedom has disappeared over
there and anyone who opposes that little bastard Hitler has
his throat cut, or is slammed into one of his concentration
camps. Nobody seems to bother. All that really concerns most
people is how to make a fast buck, how to find the money for
the new Morris Eight, or the down payment on 'Mon Repos'
and 'Shangri-La'. They'll wake up eventually, however. They'll
have to or go under overnight!'

It was the first time Paul had considered Adolf Hitler as a
potential menace and he could not help feeling that Simon's
obsession with the underdog had led him to exaggerate. He
said, 'I'll go along with you, son, when you say things aren't all
they should be, and that the Government is the laziest, shiftiest
bunch we've had for a very long time, but surely nobody takes
tinpot ranters like Hitler and Mussolini seriously? From where
I stand it's ninety-five percent blather!'

'The Kaiser blathered,' Simon said, and not for the first time
of late Paul had the impression that, in his quiet way, his son
had the same political prescience as old Franz Zorndorff, who

boasted that he could smell burning powder half-way across the world.

'What are the chances of a general turnover at the next election?' he asked, remembering that since Jimmy Grenfell's death he had lost contact with the political scene, apart from a perusal of leading articles and Simon said, 'None! We'll dodder on and on, doped by our football, films, greyhounds and the distractions that even dairymen go for nowadays. Then, one bright morning, we shall wake up and find the Fascists not merely on our doorstep but in bed with us, and chaps like Mosley and his Blackshirts hanging a "To Let" notice on the Houses of Parliament. That is, of course, providing Hitler doesn't take a crack at Russia; if he does he'll get all the backing he needs in the West.'

Paul wondered, as Simon said this, precisely how far to the Left his son had travelled in the years since the Slump and asked, bluntly, 'Do you still look at Russia with starry eyes, Simon? Is it really any better than Fascism?'

'No, I don't go along with it,' Simon replied unexpectedly, 'it's not the answer and never can be – people handing down decisions from the top. We have the real answer here if the mass of people would use the machinery got together by the pioneers, like the Tolpuddle Martyrs and old Tom Paine!' He smiled, and added, 'You see? Basically I'm just as old-fashioned as you, Gov'nor! At least, Rachel says I am.'

'You and she seem to get along well enough,' Paul said, more as a feeler than a statement, and Simon replied, 'As people? Yes, we do; I respect her and she tolerates me, but she's a Marxist and the trouble with poor old Karl was he never learned how to laugh.'

Somewhere near at hand trumpets brayed and ushers appeared to shepherd everyone to their seats. Paul regretted the interruption, knowing that in the scurry that followed the verdict he would have no chance to continue the discussion and it was so rarely these days that he had a chance to talk to the only one of his children whose intelligence he respected. Soon, however, he forgot Simon, being drawn, willy-nilly, into the vortex as the twenty finalists were whittled down to twelve, then seven, and then four, with Claire still in the running and his wife, daughter and daughters-in-law gibbering with excitement, and triumph still hidden behind the red and gold curtains where the survivors had retired to await the ultimate choice. The Pair, Paul noticed, although jubilant, were far more realistic than their womenfolk, Andy declaring that young Claire would forfeit the title on account of her age, Stevie trying to console his mother by saying, 'Look here, she's got this far, and holds the Devon title for a year! That's something to be going on with, isn't it?'

'It's not enough,' Claire said, emphatically, 'she's got to win! She's just got to win!' and when Paul said, 'Why, Claire? What's so terribly important about it? And why is it so vital to you?' the cold glance she turned on him reminded him uncomfortably of her recent moods. 'It isn't important to me but it's terribly important to her! Why? Because it's all she's got, don't you see?' and to Paul's astonishment Monica came out in full support of this astonishing verdict, saying, 'I go along with that! I was a Claire, not as pretty maybe but with nothing to offer but a face and curves in the right places! I never had any real confidence in myself in a last year's dress; no brains, no special skills, nothing but myself.'

'And the pity of it is that it's expendable,' Claire added. 'One loses a little of it every day after one's twentieth birthday. Now a thing like this – public recognition I mean – is something one can look back on all one's life without having to console oneself with a photograph album!'

As she said this, almost as though addressing herself, the cancer of the last year was suddenly revealed to him for he remembered how vain she had always been of her body, and her ability to keep pace with changing fashions, all the way from leg-o'-mutton sleeves and picture hats to the bandeaux and short skirts of the 'twenties', and the more feminine styles of today. It occurred to him then that she must always have thought of their partnership as something that owed very little to the shared adventures of three decades but hung upon factors like the weight of flesh about her thighs, the size and sag of her breasts and the clarity of her skin. Comprehending this for the first time in nearly a year he had an inarticulate desire to comfort her but at that moment the curtains swung aside and the Master of Ceremonies emerged with a slip of paper in his hand and announced, 'The final decision of the judges, ladies and gentlemen . . . Miss Cheshire, fourth place, Miss Shropshire third place . . .' He saw Claire, then Mary and the others, rise in their seats and heard the Twin yelp with triumph. 'Miss Kent, runner up . . . Miss Devonshire, Dairy Queen of England and Wales for the year 1934–1935 . . .'

The orchestra crashed out and the applause stormed over their heads. He saw the other finalists file in, noting their glumness and pathetic attempts to smile as Claire was led to the central dais, moving with infinite grace, utterly composed as the silly little crown was placed on her head by last year's winner, and beside him his wife looked so pale that he thought for a moment she was going to faint and caught her arm as trumpets blared and everyone rose to their feet, clapping. He said, with relief, 'Well, there you are! She'll have something to look back on after all!' but the thought struck him that, at the age of sixteen, the salting away of memories was a macabre compulsion.

By the following day they had dispersed, the twins and their wives roaring away up the Great North Road, Simon, about some mysterious business in the East End and then to Euston for Manchester, Paul and Mary by taxi to Waterloo, with Claire left behind to stay with her daughter until Tuesday. At the last minute Schroeder, the Organising Secretary, came to them with a sudden change of plan. Arrangements had been made, he said, for the winner to fulfil her first public engagement at an Agricultural Fair, due to open in The Hague later that week but prior to that she had to be 'groomed', whatever that meant. Paul was anxious to get home. The harvest was late and in any case he and Mary had arranged to take part in a County Gymkhana but he would have waived Valley commitments if he had been persuaded that wife or daughter needed him. As it was, in the upheaval that followed the triumph, he was almost overlooked and when Claire said that she would like to stay on a day or two to help choose dresses, and that he would be bored by a two-day shopping expedition in the West End, he took the broad hint and said, 'You don't mind if I go back with Mary? I'm a droop when it comes to this kind of thing!' she regarded him with her head on one side and replied, 'You're dying to get out of here and I must say you've been far more patient than I expected! Go along home with Mary and meet me on the three o'clock from Waterloo, on Tuesday. I can't really leave her alone until she flies off and I have a feeling she'd sooner have me around than Mary!'

'I'm quite sure she would,' Paul said, 'and I believe you're getting an even bigger kick out of it than she is!'

'Yes, I am,' Claire admitted, 'for it's something I should have loved to have happened to me at her age, although I couldn't have carried it off with her aplomb!'

'I'm damned certain you could,' he said, 'but I don't think your father would have stood for it for one moment!'

'Neither would you! I can just see your face if I wiggled up and down in front of those latterday George Lovells in a tight bathing costume! Did you think of that old rascal when the judging was going on?'

'Why yes, I did as a matter of fact,' he admitted, surprised and pleased at this evidence of a return to their old-time jocular plane, 'but I would have said it was the last thought to occupy your mind.'

She said, frankly but without looking at him, 'It's been a difficult time for you, Paul, and don't imagine I don't realise as much! But we're over the hump now, I can tell you that! This has been a real tonic to me! Would you be interested in learning how, exactly?'

'Yes, I would. Very interested indeed!'

'Well, I suppose, up to the moment of young Claire winning the preliminary I was just plain envious – envious and resentful of their youth and high spirits, of the freedom they enjoy that we never had and of their good looks and expectation of life! I was even jealous of Mary's tranquillity but now, well – now I've got the whole thing into better focus, just a matter of counting blessings I imagine! After all, we're still solvent and in good health and Claire owes this triumph to the legacy of our health. But the really important thing is I'm still important to you! I'm convinced of that at any rate!'

'Did you ever doubt it?'

'Yes, both before and after John was born. Don't ask me why but I did!'

'I wonder what happened to all that famous Derwent commonsense?'

'It evaporated the minute I knew I was pregnant. Maureen tried to explain it but she didn't really get through to me.'

'Or to me either,' he admitted.

'It's partly a physical change, I suppose. I told her before I left that I'd try and put it on paper some time so that she could write an article for one of her medical journals.'

'Don't you do anything so damned silly,' he said, 'it's one thing having a daughter displaying all her equipment in public, but quite another having one's wife strip herself naked for the British Medical Journal! I'll say good-bye to Claire and wish her luck,' and he turned to go with a sense of enormous relief but as he reached the door he said, as an afterthought, 'From now on it's going to be us, Claire! They can bloody well fend for themselves, one and all! One thing Maureen said did get through to me – that the time we've got left could be the happiest years of our life. Did she say that to you?'

'Yes and I didn't believe her but I do now. That's all that counts, isn't it?'

'It's what counts with me,' he replied emphatically and crossed the corridor to the room shared by the two girls.

Mary was in the lobby arranging about luggage but his youngest daughter was there and he was at once struck by her remoteness of expression which was something new to him, although she had always been a very self-contained person, far more so than any of his other children. She was so still and rapt as she sat by the window that she did not turn her head as he entered and he felt the curious embarrassment that had always plagued their relationship. He said, with assumed heartiness, 'Well, Kiddo, you saw them all off and your mother's bursting with pride! She's staying until you take off at Croydon and I've come to wish you luck, I'm going home with Mary.'

The child looked at him as though he had said something she only half understood and again he caught the half-puzzled, half-anxious expression in her eyes, eyes a shade bluer than her mother's and half veiled by long, golden lashes. He thought, 'Well, here's an odd turn-up! She isn't as confident as all that now that she's launched!' and somehow felt closer to her than ever before, the shift prompting a protectiveness she had never seemed to demand of him.

'Are you scared after all, Claire? If you are it's nothing to be ashamed of, and if you want to talk about it I'll listen.'

'No,' she said, in hardly more than a whisper, 'I'm not scared, Daddy. I'm terribly excited but—' and suddenly, against all probability, she seemed on the verge of tears so that he went across and put his arm on her shoulder, saying, 'You can still back out if you want to! Nobody can make you go through with it. After all, it's only a kind of advertisement, and apart from expenses you aren't being paid for the job.'

'Oh, I wouldn't want that,' she said, 'I'd want to go through with it, no matter what happens.'

'But what could happen, Kiddo? Apart from pleasant things?'

'I don't know,' she said, uncertainly, 'nothing, I suppose, but it's queer – I had a feeling it was all – well – *bound* to happen, just the way it has! Just now, before you came in, it seemed – well rather *creepy* somehow. Does that sound stupid?'

'No, not a bit stupid. The fact is you've had a devil of a lot of excitement and no matter how much you pretend to be adult you're still only a kid. It's perfectly understandable you should feel nervous. It it was me, I'd be scared stiff.'

She made the only joke he ever recalled her making, saying, with a smile, 'You'd look like hell under a crown, Daddy!' and because it was the first time there had ever been real communication between them he threw his arm round her, saying, 'Neither you, nor Whiz, nor your brothers, ever had the slightest respect for me! However, if you'd like me to stay and see you off I can easily 'phone through and get Henry Pitts to do my judging at the Gymkhana. Would you like me to do that, Claire?'

'No,' she said, 'because I know you hate London and I think you've been pretty sporting over the whole business. You haven't even warned me not to talk to strange men in foreign cities! Go on back to your precious Valley and let me find one of my own, like Whiz and The Pair! All I'd like you to be sure of is that – well – that I don't *really* take everything for granted! It's just that I'm not very good at saying "thank you",' and she took both his hands, stood on tiptoe and kissed him very deliberately on both cheeks. The unexpectedness of words and gesture overwhelmed him so much that all he could say was, 'Do you need any money?' She shook her head, held him for a moment and then resumed her seat by the window. He may have fancied it but it seemed to him that she turned her head away deliberately and he went out hurriedly, never having suspected her of doing anything so human as to shed a tear at the prospect of leaving home and family.

IV

It was a rather sombre journey back to the Valley. He found it difficult to rid himself of a feeling of guilt, of having abandoned her at a time when, for the first time in her life, she seemed to need him but when he tried to describe what had passed between them, first to Claire and then to Mary, it sounded trivial and insubstantial so that he was not surprised when they told him that maybe young Claire had bitten off just a tiny bit more than she could chew and that a little humility, the product of nervousness, would do her far more good than harm. When he urged that he should stay after all, or even accompany her to Holland, they laughed at him for reverting to one of his 'duty-moods', another hoary source of merriment among the family, yet the feeling of unease persisted, clouding his pleasure at the sight of the Valley under warm September sunshine, with its fields dotted with golden stocks and its streams unseasonably high after a wet August.

All that day and all the next he had difficulty in picking up his routine, his mind constantly returning to the picture of young Claire sitting at the hotel window looking out on nothing or perhaps on something only she could see, and he thought too of her sudden spurt of affection, wondering what instinctive fears might have prompted it. The feeling was strong enough to drive him to the telephone on the second night, the last of her stay in London, only to learn from an impersonal receptionist that 'Mrs and Miss Craddock had gone to a theatre and were not expected back until after midnight.' He declined an invitation to leave a message and went to bed with his favourite copy of Jorrocks and when Jorrocks failed to entertain him he lay awake a long time listening to the screech of owls in the paddock, thinking it was the one night-sound of Shallowford he preferred not to hear on the rare occasions sleep evaded him.

If Shallowford House could have been said to possess a radio fan the title would have gone to Mary, the only member of the family whose musical tastes extended beyond Strauss waltzes and jazz. Mary's room, the first on the nursery corridor facing west, was the most feminine in the house. She had chosen her own carpet and curtains and converted two deep alcoves into arched bookshelves. Her furniture was small and neat, an assortment of birthday and Christmas presents over the years and she had accompanied Paul to local auction sales to buy little pieces of Coalport and Rockingham china, mostly vases and baskets which she kept filled with wild flowers from February until late autumn. These little posies, dotted about the room, were her calendars. In late winter there were usually snowdrops and celandines on the mantelshelf and the lower shelves of the alcoves. In March and April there were primroses and dog-violets, with arrangements of pigmy daffodils and narcissi as spring advanced and after that came the blue and yellow iris that everyone else in the Valley called 'flags'. Later still the room was gay with foxgloves and bluebells (cut short to spare the bulbs), honeysuckle, meadow-sweet, campion, bugloss and shyer flowers gathered in remote corners of the woods revealed to her by old Meg Potter, with whom Mary was on intimate terms. She spent a great deal of her free time in this room writing her diary, trying to compose rustic sonnets in the style of Wilfred Blunt (her favourite poet) and writing long, rambling letters to Rumble Patrick, with whom she had now maintained a regular correspondence for more than three years. Rumble's photograph stood in a silver frame on a papier-mâché bedside table, not the roundfaced Rumble Patrick who had decamped to Australia as long ago as December, 1930, and had since wandered half-way round the world, but a lean, cheerful-looking young man, in what she took to be a Canadian trapper's outfit of fur cap, fringed jacket and top boots. The photo was signed *'As always, Rumble'* which satisfied her but did not seem to impress anyone else.

On the afternoon Paul drove to Paxtonbury to meet the 3 p.m. out of Waterloo she declined his invitation to come along, saying that she had to write Rumble an account of the Dairy Queen final so that it was about half-past five, just after Paul had left, that she sat down at her little rosewood desk and began to marshal her facts, making no effort to restrain the pride she felt in the family triumph and pinning caption slips on each of the snipped-out photographs of Claire, on which she wrote such comments as *'This doesn't do our Claire justice, it was one of those awful flashlights and she looks startled!'* or *'The girl next to Claire is Miss Cheshire who was a very pretty brunette but a cat!'* About ten minutes to six she reached out and turned her wireless set on, continuing writing against a background of Jack Payne's light orchestral music, a Palm Court broadcast dribbling out tinkling tunes like 'Little Man you've had a busy day', or dreamier ones like 'A Night in Napoli' and 'Little Old Church in the Valley'. Mary paid no heed to them but unconsciously cocked an ear when the announcer began to read the news. Then she stopped writing, in the middle of the word 'gorgeous', used to describe the white satin ball-dress the Dairymen's Association had presented to Claire to wear at her maiden public appearance. Her hand clutched the pen so tightly that its nib spluttered and for a moment the little room, flooded with early evening sunshine, rocked and receded as the announcer said, in a voice nicely pitched for tragic announcements, '. . . there are believed to be no survivors in this afternoon's air disaster, involving the British Dairymen's contingent on their way to exhibit British products at The Hague. Among those aboard the aircraft, which is believed to have crashed about twelve miles north-west of the Hook of Holland, was the recently-chosen British Dairy Queen, Miss Claire Craddock aged only sixteen. Rescue craft went out on receipt of the first distress signals and, together with other aircraft, are still searching the area. A report has come in that one body, believed to be that of a crew member, has been recovered but apart from a small amount of wreckage no traces of the fuselage have been found. The total complement of the aircraft was sixteen. Further bulletins will be issued at nine o'clock and midnight . . .'

Mary waited, her hand on the knob, until the announcer went on to talk about something else. Then she switched off and stood up, steadying herself by the little brass rail that surmounted the desk and it was necessary to grip hard for the walls continued to expand and contract and all the time the sun poured into the window like a blinding light, causing her to raise a hand still holding the pen and press the palm to her eyes. The movement left a smear of ink on her cheek.

Claire dead! Drowned and probably mangled, somewhere off the coast of Holland! Claire, the spoiled beauty of the family, whose photographs lay strewn across the desk covering the pages of Rumble's letter. Claire! Who had somehow stood for success and glitter and adventure in the world outside the Valley, the beautiful little child whom she had accompanied to so many dances, gymkhanas and fêtes, noting how everyone turned their heads when they passed, the girl who had caused men of all ages to stand aside and pay silent homage to her radiance and grace, as though she was some classical statue transformed into flesh and blood and loaned for each occasion. It was incredible and yet, as Mary fought for her breath, she knew that it was true and that even at this stage to hope would be futile. There had been clinical finality in the announcement but away and beyond this there was also a terrible inevitability about it, as though young Claire had come to the end of the road the very moment the little crown had been settled on her head and that somehow, if only they had taken the trouble to find out, it could all have been found in Meg Potter's pack of cards.

And then, as tears began to flow, she forced herself to think of the effect of this appalling news on the others, on her mother, now more than half-way home and isolated from news in a speeding train, and of her father, half-way to Paxtonbury, likewise ignorant of what had happened and liable, she thought with a shudder, to read it in a newspaper whilst awaiting the arrival of the express.

She crossed over to the window groping for handholds on bedhead and table and her blundering hand brushed and tipped over a small vase of flowers spilling water and a shower of yellow blossoms across the table-top. At last she found the window seat, summoning every ounce of resolution to think, to hit on some way of softening the blow if God was merciful and Paul and Claire arrived home unaware of the disaster. For she would have to break it to them. Somehow they would have to be cushioned against the savagery of a flat, impersonal wireless announcement, or the professionally sympathetic voice of a policeman telling the story over the telephone. From far away downstairs she heard the telephone ringing insistently and levering herself up went out into the corridor to the stairhead. Thirza, crossing the hall, turned aside to lift the receiver but Mary called, with an urgency that made Thirza's head jerk upwards, 'Don't! It's for me!' and ran downstairs as Thirza, shrugging, marched through the swing door into the kitchen quarters.

A voice said, quietly but distinctly, 'Shallowford House? Is Mr Craddock available?' and Mary said, choking back her tears, 'Who is it? Who wants him? This is Mary Craddock, his daughter!' and when the voice said, 'Ah yes, is your father anywhere about, Miss Craddock?' she recognised it as that of Sergeant Beeworthy, the policeman stationed at Whinmouth and responsible for the Coombe Bay area. She said, with a tremendous effort, 'Is it . . . is it about the aircrash? About my sister Claire?'

'Yes, Miss Craddock, I'm afraid it is. You know about it?'

'I just heard it, on the six o'clock news.'

'I see.' The voice expressed relief and there was a pause before it went on: 'Have you told your father? Is he there?' and Mary said no, he had gone to Paxtonbury to meet her mother on a train due in about six o'clock. 'Listen, Sergeant,' she went on, as the power of coherent thought returned to her, 'I . . . I'd much sooner you left this to me! Unless he buys a paper at the station he won't know, he'll simply pick up Mother and come straight back here without stopping! I'd much sooner you left it to me and didn't try to contact him! Will you do that? *Will* you?'

'Certainly, Miss Craddock,' and Beeworthy sounded grateful. 'I think it would be best in the circumstances. I just had word from London and it would have been my job to make sure that he knew.'

'There's no further news?'

'Nothing good, I'm afraid. They've located the wreck, it seems, but there's very little hope. There were no survivors. It was some kind of engine-failure, they say. I'm . . . I'm terribly sorry for all of you, I knew her well of course.'

'Everybody did. Thank you, Sergeant. I'll tell Father you rang.'

'There's one thing more, Miss Craddock.'

'Well?'

'In the circumstances the Press will soon be on to you. I expect they'll jam your line.'

'What can I do . . . just for the time being?'

'You could leave the receiver off the hook but then nobody else could get you. I think it might be wiser to ring the Coombe Bay operator and ask her to put all incoming calls through to me. I could filter them for you, for a couple of hours or so, and I daresay I could head the Press off. I could say you were all in London.'

'That would be very kind, Sergeant.'

'Right, then ring the operator right away. Perhaps Mr Craddock or you would ring me later. I might have more news.'

She rang off, passed the message to the operator without comment and looked at her watch. It was six-twenty. Paul would be meeting the train in a few minutes and it would take him less than an hour to drive back. By eight o'clock they would be coming through the door and she would know by looking at them whether or not they had heard. She went upstairs to the bathroom. Any weeping that had to be done had better be done now.

She waited until they had had some tea, listening over the banisters to the rise and fall of their voices and hearing Claire's laugh. Then she went down to the library and Paul, jumping up, said, 'I thought you must have popped out somewhere, Mary . . .' but stopped, looking hard at her as she stood with her back pressed to the door, groping for the words but finding none.

'What is it, dear? You're upset? You've been crying!' and Claire put down her empty cup and turned towards her so that, fleetingly, Mary was grateful she had been betrayed by her eyes despite incessant bathing, for this surely meant that they would not be swung from a mood of relief at being home and together again, with all the excitement behind them, to one of utter despair. They had warning; some kind of warning.

She said, biting her lip, 'Something's happened. Something . . . bad! Don't let anyone in, I've got to tell you first!' and then stopped, her tongue filling her mouth.

All her life she had admired him at times of crisis. He had always seemed to her a big, dependable man, whose inclination to fuss was reserved for the smaller, unimportant irritants, a broken harness strap, a sudden quarrel resulting in unnecessary noise but in the wider sphere she had never once seen him rattled and it came to her now, faced with this hideous task, that this might be the secret of his reputation in the Valley. He came over to her and took her by the hand, leading her to a chair near the tall window, saying, 'Is it about Rumble, Mary?'

She shook her head and swallowed and they waited until her tongue became manageable.

'Claire, *our* Claire!'

Her mother's head came up sharply. 'She's ill? Someone's telephoned from London?'

She wished now that she had tackled Paul alone. It would have been much easier to have told him and let him pass it on, for her mother's favouritism of Claire had never been a secret in the house, just another family joke, and surely a shock like this would be too great for her to absorb without a collapse. The thought gave Mary a little strength. She said, choosing her words with the utmost care, 'There's been an accident. A bad accident!'

'Where?'

It was Paul who spoke and he sounded tired rather than frightened.

'Flying Holland – it was on the wireless – then the police rang. No one was saved!' and she bowed her head and was silent.

There was no sudden outcry, no movement of any kind. The library clock ticked on. The mellow light filtered by the avenue chestnuts flooded the room as each of them fought with the whole of their strength to ward off horror from each other and then Claire, twisting her handkerchief into a hard knot, stood up and she said, quietly:

'There's no hope? None at all?'

Mary shook her head and there was silence again. Claire crossed to the sideboard cupboard taking out a brandy glass and a decanter. She poured four fingers and carried it back across the room.

'Take a drink, Paul!'

'You—?'

'It doesn't help me but it will you.' He took and swallowed it like a child taking medicine and it was in the act of putting the decanter away that Claire, out of the corner of her eye, saw Mary sitting with her head bowed, her hands on her lap. The abject pose communicated the girl's misery to her as nothing else could have done. She moved to the window and touched her head lightly, the gesture releasing a spring of tenderness that had never flowed for a daughter who seemed to belong less to her than did Paul's son by Grace Lovell. 'I'll never forget you made yourself tell us, Mary! *Never*, you understand?' Then she went out, leaving them alone, understanding that, at a juncture such as this, she was the odd one out.

She paused in the hall undecided which way to go and what to do first, yet astonished at her own steadiness. Then she made her decision and climbed the stairs to Claire's room, one room along from Mary's. It was still strewn with the debris of Claire's departure and she wondered for a moment why nobody had tidied up after they had gone. Then she remembered that Claire had always been the litterbug of the family and that long ago instructions had been issued to Thirza and the others not to encourage her slatternly habits by following her round and picking up discarded garments.

Tears began to flow as she set about the job of clearing up and as the first of them fell she knew the source of her strange, numb calm. It was not, as she had thought on quitting the study, the almost instinctive lurch towards the routine obligations of telephoning and writing, or a summoning of willpower to withstand the flow of condolences or the clamour of the Press. This rally would occur in an hour or so but for the moment she found a reserve of strength in a deep conviction that what had occurred was not a terrible accident but a cycle of circumstances, all of which were inevitable and quite beyond anyone's power to alter or mitigate. She had always known that something like this would deprive her of Claire, suddenly and completely, and it was because of this that she had spoiled the child so shamelessly. She was very far from being a superstitious woman in the accepted sense of the word and yet, as regards Claire, a child conceived against a background of death and deprivation in the deepest trough of the war, she had always been half-aware of a kind of bargain made with death that involved not only the child but her father whom everyone in the Valley, herself excepted, believed dead at the time. All the time the child had lain in her womb death had squatted over the Valley, and his favourite roosting-spot had been the chimney-pots of this house. Yet, in the end, he had been vanquished, or perhaps not vanquished but bought off, and now, after a respite of more than sixteen years, he had returned to claim the talisman. She did not know why or how such a train of reasoning could cushion her against the terrible shock of Claire's death but it did, so that a kind of emotional petrification checked her tears and she braced herself against the demands that Paul and Mary and all the others would be certain to make on her in the weeks ahead, weeks of mourning that were denied even the focal point of a committal.

When the room was tidy she opened the window, took a last look round and went downstairs to the telephone, lifting the receiver and asking for the number of the Whinmouth police station. Her hand and her voice were steady as the bell tinkled, and when Thirza emerged from the kitchen to answer it, she turned aside and said, crisply, 'Go and fetch the Lady Doctor, Thirza. Tell her Mr Craddock wants her urgently and hurry!'

She turned her back on the woman's puzzled expression and re-addressed herself to the telephone but there was no more news, only confirmation of the disaster. She replaced the receiver and wondered whether to await Maureen in the hall but then she had another thought, retracing her steps upstairs, and going along to the nursery. The baby was awake, threshing away with his little fists, and as she stared down at him she found herself smiling. She thought, 'I wonder why he always struck me as a plain child? He isn't plain, just – comical!' She picked him up, carried him downstairs and out on to the terrace, holding him tightly and occasionally brushing his head with her lips. They were still standing so when Maureen and Thirza came hurrying up the drive.

Chapter Seventeen

I

No other bodies were recovered so it was as Claire had suspected, a mourning without a corpse, with a memorial service in Coombe Bay Church that Paul authorised only after strong pressure from The Pair and their wives, who were, it seemed, very conventional in some respects and thought it essential Claire should have her public tribute.

The weather broke the day following and autumn rain seeped down on the stubble and a countryside that had rallied during the sunny spell following a wet summer; by the end of the week it might have been late November. The Sorrel was in flood and all its culverts choked with sodden leaves.

It was strange that the elimination of Claire, who had never been noisy and energetic like her brothers, or even gregarious like her sister Whiz, should invest the house with such gloom and emptiness, but this was so and it was Mary, without an absorbing occupation, who noticed it more than the others. Sometimes, when it pressed too heavily upon her, she put on macintosh and gumboots and slogged up across the orchard to the lane and round the rim of the woods to the mere, or, turning left instead of right, climbed to French Wood and dropped down past Hermitage Farm to the stream that fed the Sorrel here, then up the long slope to the ruin of Periwinkle. She had always liked Elinor Codsall and it increased her depression to see the rain dripping through the thatch and thistles marching down the slope that Will, whom she dimly recalled, had reclaimed from the moor before he went off and got himself 'blowed to tatters', as Martha Pitts used to say.

She was here one October afternoon, about a fortnight after Claire's death, when she heard, or thought she heard, the sound

of footsteps in what had been Elinor's kitchen. She stood on
the bank and listened, half-deciding that she must have been
wrong but then she noticed a wisp of smoke rising from the
chimney and guessed who must be inside, almost certainly old
Meg Potter. Meg sometimes used the ruin for boiling herbs she
had gathered this side of the Valley and thus saved herself
the trouble of hauling them all the way to Low Coombe where
she lived if she could be said to live anywhere. It would be
comforting, Mary thought, to take a brew of tea with Meg
and tell her her troubles. Maybe she would tell her fortune
again, as she often did when they met by chance in isolated
places. Meg did not tell anybody's fortune but she was always
ready to tell Mary's and she would never accept silver for her
services. 'You'll never maake money, tho' you'll live a long
time in peace,' she would tell her gravely, 'and I donr't need
me palm crossed to tell that to man nor maid!'

She jumped down from the bank and crossed the muddy
farmyard, meaning to stand beside the rain-tub and peep in
the window, in case it wasn't Meg but one or other of the
wayfarers, who sometimes slept a night in there *en route*
for Paxtonbury's tramps' lodging house. Then she stopped,
convinced that she was the victim of a hallucination brought
on by delayed shock, for inside, engaged in measuring the
room with a long, notched yardstick, was Rumble Patrick!

At least, she thought it was Rumble Patrick, although the
young man absorbed in the task of estimating the floor-space
of the littered room was much taller, more broad-shouldered
and somehow more rawboned than the Rumble who had
kissed her beside the mere all those years ago, and to whom
she must have written at least two hundred and fifty letters
during the the last three and a half years. He was much
browner too and more weather-beaten about the face and
his dark hair, that had been thick and unruly, was now
close-cropped, so that his reddened ears, always inclined to
protrude, seemed set at an angle of about forty-five degrees.
His clothes were outlandish, serviceable breeches and a kind
of lumber-jacket with a fur-lined hood, and strong, laced-
up boots, like those her mother was seen to be wearing in

photographs taken before the war, only these had metal-tipped high heels that looked oddly effeminate on the long legs of a broad-shouldered young man.

She remained by the window oblivious of the dripping thatch as warmth stole into her, animating every nerve in her body and bringing the blood rushing to her cheeks already whipped by the wind. She tried to call out but her tongue was as unresponsive as it had been when she had brought the news of Claire's death to her father and mother and it was all she could do to lift her hand to the pane and drum with her fingers on the cracked glass. He turned then, as sharply as a hare surprised in long grass but when he saw her he did not seem surprised but grinned broadly and beckoned, so that she ran along the slippery cobbles and under the cascade of drips at the porch and the next moment she was in his arms, laughing and crying and still struggling with a sluggish tongue.

He said, holding her and running his big, rough hands over her damp hair, 'I suppose that rascal Smut Potter gave me away? He was the only one who saw me jump the train, at Sorrel Halt. I meant to tip him to keep his mouth shut but I had to run along the line for my rucksack and forgot!'

She told him at last that she had not had the least idea he was home and that he was a pig to have given her such a shock, and that he couldn't have come from Sorrel Halt that day because the first train that stopped there was the four-thirty and it was only three-forty-five now but he said, grinning, 'Who said it stopped? It slowed down and I couldn't see the sense of going on to Paxtonbury and hiring a taxi so I jumped for it! We're going to need all I've saved to put this joint in order! What's the matter with Gov'nor, to let one of his places run down to this extent? Another year and even I couldn't have fixed it!'

He spoke, she noticed, with a slight but unmistakable Colonial drawl, using words like 'fixed' and 'joint' without self-consciousness so that for a moment the implication of what he said did not strike her; when it did she could have cried out with relief and joy. Being Mary, however, she admonished herself for leaping to the most exciting conclusions and said, instead, 'You mean you intend to *farm* Periwinkle? To do it up yourself and . . . and *settle* in it?'

'You bet,' he said, casually, 'unless there's anything better going and I'm pretty sure from your letters there isn't! The others are all occupied, aren't they? Even if they are operating on a horse-and-buggy economy!'

Yes, she told him, almost gobbling with excitement, all the other farms in the Valley were tenanted and High Coombe had been sold off and was now a building estate and caravan camp. Her father had long since written-off Periwinkle and what remained free of weeds had been split between Hermitage and Four Winds, after Elinor Codsall had married her German prisoner-of-war. He looked thoughtful at this and she noticed that when he concentrated his expression reminded her sharply of his grandmother, Meg Potter; he had Meg's deep-set eyes and bushy brows and the same obstinate chin.

'That's bad,' he said, 'for I don't suppose either Pitts or Harold Codsall will take kindly to surrendering land. They could be compensated, I suppose. I've earmarked two thousand dollars for contingencies.'

'Good heavens!' she said. 'Daddy wouldn't let you pay money for that! He'd come to some kind of arrangement with Henry and Harold,' but he said, sharply, 'If they can be persuaded to let it revert I'll pay for it! I'm aiming to be a freeholder, not a tenant farmer. Come to think of it, it's probably a good idea the Gov let the place run to seed. He might even be glad to get it off his hands. Would he, do you think? After we're married, of course?'

The sheer casualness of the afterthought made her gasp and she said, drawing back a little, '*Married?* Good Lord, Rumble, you haven't even proposed to me yet! I was always hoping you would in your letters but for every paragraph in them that made me hope there were five hundred about sheep-dip!'

He said, with his slow grin, 'Ah, you'd be surprised how many trial proposals I used to light my pipe winter evenings!

Fact is, I'm too down-to-earth to put that kind of guff on paper but then, where's the point, seeing I never looked twice at any other Sheila?'

'Sheila?' she said, with a sharp stab of jealousy, 'who is Sheila?' and he threw back his head and laughed, telling her that 'Sheila' was nobody in particular, just Australian slang for 'girl-friend'.

'Well,' she said, much relieved, 'you haven't even told me how and why you're here. I suppose you decided to come as soon as you got my letter telling you the awful news about poor little Claire?'

'No,' he said, 'I didn't wait for a letter. I went East the day after I read about it in the papers. She was only about eleven when I left, poor kid, but she would have had my vote at a beauty contest even then. How has your mother taken it, Mary?'

'Oddly enough a good deal better than Father,' she told him. 'He's frightfully low but you being here will cheer him up. He was always asking about you and I had to read him all the farming bits from your letters. I think he approves of you very much, Rumble.'

'Well, I hope so,' he said, 'seeing that he's likely to be stuck with me for a son-in-law!' and suddenly he reached out and grabbed her again with a kind of proprietary flourish that made her giggle but his embrace was no laughing matter; his grip promised to crack her ribs.

'Oh, Rumble,' she cried, as he swung her off her feet and carried her triumphantly into the yard, 'you'll never know what a difference it made, looking into that filthy window and just seeing you there! I can't get Claire out of my mind and the others can't either. It seems almost wrong to feel happy after what happened to her but I do, I do, terribly happy, and . . . safe somehow! Can you understand that? No, I don't suppose you can, not having been here when it happened, and not having seen any of us in years!'

He said, cheerfully, 'Whether I can understand it or not it sounds very flattering!' and when he seemed disposed to march clear across the yard and into the lane with her, she said, 'For heaven's sake put me *down*, Rumble! Suppose Henry Pitts or anyone came down moor road?'

'Oh, they wouldn't begrudge me a celebration,' he said, 'not even in England, where they still go for the gooseberry-bush guff!' but he set her down, kissed her mouth with the air of a man sealing a bargain and set off down the eastern slope at such a pace that she had to trot to keep up with him. When they reached the wicket gate in the park wall, however, he suddenly became shy and said, 'Hadn't you better run on ahead and warm them up a little? After all, this isn't the Outback or the Rockies, where anyone passing by is expected to stay a fortnight!' but she seized him by the hand saying that Paul and Claire would be delighted to see him and that he was just what was needed up there, so they crossed the Big Paddock, skirted the Home Farm and came on the drive near the final curve, Mary running across the gravel forecourt shouting, 'Mummy! Daddy! Look who's here!' and thinking that even decorous Claire would have whooped for joy to see Rumble back in the Valley at last and at a time when they could all do with a little good news.

II

He had his father's flair for lighting up shadows, for coaxing laughter from such reluctant subjects as the poker-faced Thirza and the solemn Mark Codsall. From the moment he flung down his rucksack in the hall, and was dragged by Mary into the library, stillness left the house and voices were raised again. He was, Paul thought, like the sun and wind, radiating vitality just as Ikey had done whenever he chose and it was quite astonishing to see the effect he had upon Mary, who hardly ever took her eyes from him, although she had an irritating habit of interrupting and throwing him off on a fresh tack just when he was explaining something interesting, like the latest kind of reaper operating in the wheatlands of the North-West. The two men soon got down to business and, as Mary had predicted, Paul was very willing to have

Periwinkle reoccupied, promising to see what he could do to recover the hundred-odd acres leased to Hermitage and Four Winds. Harold Eveleigh, he said, would probably be glad of shrinkage, for Four Winds was about as much as he could handle with only one man and one boy but Henry's son, David, might protest at yielding up the Undercliffe pasture, for he had put a good deal of work into it since it was ceded. Supposing this could be achieved, however, Periwinkle would still be a farm of well under two hundred acres and not, he would have thought, an economical unit these days. Would not Rumble be better advised to cross the river and take one of Gilroy's run-down properties? He understood that the Heronslea estate was in very bad shape, with some of the smaller farmers being welded into larger units, and two or three ruinous and tenantless at the moment.

'I wouldn't care to go outside the Valley,' Rumble said. 'I've done all the travelling I intend to do. From now on, if you catch me north of the railway line, or east of the Coombe, you can take a shot at me with a twelve-bore!' and he obviously meant it, for he at once plunged into a detailed description of what he intended doing with Will Codsall's old place, and how he could make it as prosperous a farm as Four Winds in Norman Eveleigh's heyday. 'Two-thirds of it are southern slopes,' he said, 'and dear old Elinor, bless her, had her nose so deep in the hen-roosts that I don't think she ever realised it, or Will Codsall before her! Once I've reclaimed the moor strip there's not much I couldn't raise there and I've learned what can and can't be done in a climate like ours! Cereals can be produced here cheaper than in Canada, providing mechanisation is one hundred per cent and the biscuit factories prefer English wheat to any other kind.'

'Then why has three million acres passed out of cultivation since the war?' Paul asked, and Rumble said it was largely on account of the English farmer's resistance to new methods and reluctance to combine for the purposes of buying and marketing. Paul, who had been trying to build a co-operative system ever since 1911, had to admit that Rumble was right and asked if Periwinkle would specialise or follow a policy of mixed farming, like that practised by most of the Valley farmers for generations.

'That depends entirely on available markets and the growth of Government subsidies,' Rumble said. 'The canning industry is bound to go on expanding and when it does it might pay to try fruit on the western side. In the meantime I shan't bother with beef or pigs, and if I follow Elinor in the matter of hens you won't catch mine outside of a deep-litter! Free range is old-hat and damned wasteful on farms as small as they are in this country. What do you want for Periwinkle as it stands, Gov? I shall have to make a start right away if I'm to be ready for spring sowing, and there's not so much as a fence in repair over there!'

Paul said, smiling, 'What shall we say? Ninety acres at sixpence an acre . . . ?' but Rumble's jaw shot out and he said, briskly, 'I'm not joking, Gov'nor! If I can't buy it I won't have it!'

'Then have it as a wedding present,' Paul said, 'providing I got the message in Mary's eyes!' and he thought how times had changed, for here was everybody blandly assuming that Rumble and Mary would marry almost at once and so far no one had mentioned the matter either to him or to Claire, save by implication.

'No, I'll not have that,' Rumble said obstinately. 'I wouldn't feel I owned it and I always wanted to own a piece of the Valley, ever since I was a kid.'

'Did you now?' said Paul, much surprised, and reflecting how odd it was that such a thought had never entered the head of either one of his own sons. 'Well, I see your point, and I daresay I'd have felt the same at your age, but the farmhouse itself is derelict and it's my responsibility to get that right before I make the place over. I'll ask Eph Morgan to look at it. He'll give me good advice.'

'I've already looked at it,' Rumble said, 'and I don't want anyone else messing about over there! I can make that place shipshape in three months, providing I can hire one pair of unskilled hands. Where I've been we don't waste money on builders, plumbers and electricians, we do things ourselves. All I want out of you is your price. And your daughter!'

'Ah, I was wondering when you were coming round to that,' Paul said, 'but supposing you can make Periwinkle habitable, when do you intend getting married?'

'The day the last shingle goes on the roof,' Rumble told him, 'for I'm damned if I'm going to re-thatch! It looks pretty enough but a man's never done with it. Can you buy Canadian shingles around here?'

'I'm sure *you* can,' Paul said, responding to the boy's tremendous zest, and remembering precisely how he felt himself when he first vowed to put new life into the Valley, 'but if you won't let me set you up there I'll buy you a tractor for a wedding present and Claire will chip in with some furniture. By God, but it does me good to see somebody with a bit of real enthusiasm for land! I'd begun to think we'd seen the last of it in your generation and quite made up my mind that you would stay in the Dominions. Weren't you tempted to? Honestly?'

'No, never, although it was fun while it lasted and the best place to learn because class cuts no ice at all over there! A man's judged on the skill in his hands and the ideas in his head.'

'Then apart from Mary what made you return?'

Rumble said, wrinkling his brow and looking, for a moment, extraordinarily like his grandfather Tamer assessing the cash value of a piece of flotsam, 'It's home, I guess. I could have sent for Mary and I daresay she would have come but there wasn't a day out there when I didn't sniff the air and find something missing! Spring-time and Fall were the worst. You could never smell rain, or come to terms with the colours. All manner of things tug at a man but one can't put a name to 'em until one's back. In the train, on the way down, I got a clue – everything's real green – that is, neither parched up, as it almost always was in Queensland, or green-sombre, like the pine forests back of the Rockies. And the sky is different too, maybe because it doesn't stay the same two minutes together!'

'Well,' Paul said, laughing, 'Mary often told us you weren't any great shakes at writing a love-letter, Rumble, but you seem to me to have the instincts of a poet, of the old Walt Whitman variety! Did you ever read him?'

'Never,' Rumble admitted, 'but Mary's been threatening me with poetry ever since I got back! Maybe I should be grateful to all the guys she quotes. They seem to have kept her in cold storage while I was away.'

'I don't think it was the poets altogether,' Paul told him, remembering the glimpse he had of his daughter in French Wood, the day Rumble had made up his mind to go overseas. 'I think it was Valley magic. After all, your roots here are a lot deeper than mine!' and he got up as Mary came bouncing in, shouting that Henry Pitts and his son David had called, that she had shown them into the office, and that a message had come from Harold Eveleigh saying he would be over as soon as he could to see about the redivision of land and when Paul, astonished, said he had not even broached the matter to either of them, Mary said gaily, 'No, but I did and I think you ought to see to it at once, Daddy!'

He went along the corridor hiding his smile. It was extraordinary, he thought, how the certainty that she was coveted put sparkle into the girl. Maybe there was more of Claire in her than either of them had suspected.

Mary's was far more of a Valley wedding in the old-fashioned sense than that of any of his other children, all of whom had married what Mrs Handcock or old Tamer would have dismissed as 'forriners', notwithstanding the fact that Whiz's groom, Ian, and both the twins' wives, were a mixture of Saxon and Celt. Here, however, both bride and groom had been born within hailing distance of the Sorrel, and nobody (except possibly Claire) recalled that the latter had first seen the light of day in a cave over the badger slope in Shallowford Woods.

So many responded to the general invitation that Paul was reminded of the wedding of John Rudd and Maureen O'Keefe, getting on for thirty years ago, the last occasion he could recall when children presented horseshoes to the happy pair on their way down the drive.

He prayed for a fine day and his prayers were answered, April borrowing a few hours from June and the sun throwing down a cloth-of-gold cloak that spread from the summit of the Bluff to the crown of the Teazel watershed. It was the first family reunion since the day of the Dairy Queen final but, as though by common consent, nobody mentioned this and the occasion was further heightened for Claire by a sight of her first grandchild, the three months old daughter of Whiz, home on leave from Malaya. There were prospects of more to come, she noted, when the twins' wives appeared, putting all the women to shame with their smart London clothes but unable to disguise the fact that both were pregnant. Simon and Rachel turned up, both, she thought, looking rather tired and old, and Smut Potter, by virtue of the fact that he was uncle of the groom, hired himself a topper and striped pants from Whitby's, in Paxtonbury, and so astounded his brother Sam that he exclaimed to Henry Pitts, 'Would 'ee think, to look at 'un, that he ever did time for poachin'? Damme, you could almost mistake him for old Gilroy himself!' All the Valley originals attended the church and reception; Marian Eveleigh, Eph Morgan, now in his eighties, and Martha Pitts also in hers, Maureen and her son Paul, Abe Tozer, the smith (who now shoed no more than two horses a week), together with a score of second-generation couples, mostly Pascoes, Timberlakes or Codsalls. Old Edward Derwent was bedridden but he sent Liz and Rose came down from Gloucestershire. To Paul, looking out of the library window while the guests were assembling after the ceremony, it was proof that many of his fears regarding the Valley's vitality were groundless but perhaps this was less because so many familiar faces were to be seen than the reassurance that had been his watching Rumble rebuild Periwinkle almost single-handed, and also the light in his daughter's eyes, when she came downstairs to share a ten-minute vigil with him after Claire and all the others had left for the church.

'There's no hurry, sir,' the car-hire man had told him on the telephone, when he was dressed, fidgety and waiting for Claire to come down, 'it's customary for the bride to be five minutes late at the church. There's only the one car, I believe?'

'Yes,' Paul told him, 'just the bridal car, my wife and the others are finding their own transport but you will be here sharp at eleven, won't you?' Then, having survived the last-minute panic surrounding the departure of the family in what looked like a motorcade, he retired to the library for a double brandy and was enjoying it when the door opened and Mary came in, looking as serene and composed as young Claire would have looked in similar circumstances but, to his mind, the most ravishing bride of the century. The brandy had steadied his nerves and he said, gratefully, 'This is something very special for me, Mary. All the other weddings – well, perhaps I shouldn't say it – but they were just occasions! You and Rumble represent the continuity I always wanted and worked for and my only regret is that Ikey didn't live to see it! I think he would have derived as much satisfaction from it as I do. You don't remember him, I suppose?'

'No, and I've only the vaguest memory of Rumble's mother, but you loved the pair of them, didn't you?'

'Yes I did,' he admitted, 'as much as my own children, although they were probably the most unlikely pair who ever produced a child, even in a community like ours which has been throwing up eccentrics for generations! You don't look as if you need a drink but you can have a small one if you like.'

'No,' she said, arranging herself on the humpty as deftly as a swan on a nest, 'I'll wait, I think. I always thought I'd be sick with panic but I'm not and when you come to think of it why should I be? How old was Rumble when Mother brought him home that day?'

'Four; you're not telling me you remember his arrival here, are you?'

'That's the funny thing,' she said, 'I do, and quite distinctly! It was only an hour after his mother was killed, wasn't it? Mother told us he'd just been orphaned and we had to make it up to him but I think I was the only one impressed!'

He thought he knew what she was thinking – of the seeming inevitability of this marriage, something that had seeded itself and emerged from a shared childhood but he could remember the original link in the chain that connected her with Rumble Patrick Palfrey to the Valley – an impulsive act of his street-urchin father in the scrapyard during the long, hot summer of 1902, a tiny, insignificant incident that had prompted him to adopt Ikey, first as a stable-boy, later as a kind of son; he did not remember ever having told her how casually it had all begun.

There was no time now; the car advertised its arrival by a screech of tyres on the gravel and she stood up, unhurriedly rearranging the folds of her gown.

'Well,' he said, offering his arm, 'here goes the last of the Craddock girls!' and she replied, rising to the occasion, 'Well you needn't sound so beastly relieved about it! I may have been the retiring one of the family but I had my chances!'

'I'm damn glad you didn't take 'em!' he said, and they passed out on to the terrace and into the forecourt where the car stood flaunting its broad, white ribbons.

III

Edward Derwent died that spring and neither Paul, Claire, nor anyone else who was on intimate terms with the old man could regret his death. He had been bedridden for the better part of a year and had confessed, often enough, that confinement to a bedroom was purgatory. Liz told Paul he was a tetchy invalid and Paul could believe it. He had always been a very active man, even in his declining years, and when Paul called on him for the last time he admitted that he had made the biggest mistake of his life retiring at seventy and 'handing over to that damned son o' mine!'

'I should have carried on and died on my own acres, same as Norman Eveleigh!' he said, 'for that way High Coombe would ha' stayed inside the boundaries and I shouldn't have to lie here knowing there was a rash o' red-brick spreading across

Eight Acre and Cliff Warren! However, tiz too late to think o' that now!'

'I don't ever think of it,' Paul had comforted him, 'and neither does Claire! At the time it happened it stuck in my gullet but at least it was a means of keeping the coastline open. If Sydney hadn't got direct access to Coombe Bay through your land he would have hammered away at the County Council until he got a road over the dunes from the west. As it is we got off fairly cheaply. Young Harold Eveleigh's return to Four Winds shored up the landslide to some extent.'

'Ah!' Derwent said, with real regret in his voice, 'I should ha' had more sons and I would have had if I hadn't lost my first wife, backalong.'

'You've done all right by your daughters, Edward,' Paul reminded him, 'and you can't expect your bread buttered both sides. I daresay, if you had had a spread of sons, they would have been killed in the war!' and the old man must have pondered this for presently he said, 'Arrr, I daresay you're right at that, boy! It never struck me that way before and the girls did me credit, just as you say, tho' I should have liked our Rose to have married a bit earlier and had children!'

It occurred to Paul, looking down at the broad, red face, spiked with grey bristles, that Edward Derwent had always been a man who concerned himself exclusively with fundamentals. Land, stock, and children to follow him, were the only things that he had ever considered worthy of serious contemplation. Everything else could go hang. He wondered if this was one of the reasons why he had always got along with his gruff old father-in-law and said, hoping to comfort him a little. 'Well, Edward, you did me a damned good turn producing Claire. It's been a good marriage, right from the start.'

'Aye, you don't have to tell me that, son,' the old man replied, 'although I daresay she's been a bit of a handful now and again. You can lay that to my door for I spoiled her after her mother went and sometimes it looked to me as if you did the same. The times were against us, mind you! A man's position in the house baint what it was, I can tell you! Why, even Liz'll answer back when she's a mind to!' and as though making a final effort to assert the doctrine of male superiority he raised his voice and bellowed for his wife, who at once made nonsense of his complaints by popping into the room like a cuckoo on the hour, saying, 'What *is* it, dear? Do 'ee want for anything?' and Paul had to turn to the window to hide a smile.

Rose came down when the old man's condition grew worse and she and Claire were with him when he died. He was buried in the churchyard extension, within swearing distance – as Smut Potter irreverently observed, of his one-time neighbour Tamer, with whom he had once maintained a long-standing feud about water-rights and the depredations of the Potter clan on his well-kept acres. 'I sometimes wonder,' Smut told Paul at the funeral, 'what might have happened downalong if the Almighty, in his infinite wisdom, hadn't planted Preacher Willoughby between the two of 'em. I reckon you would have come looking for an estate and found a bliddy battlefield!'

Paul offered Liz a home at Shallowford but she declined. Edward she said, had left her sufficient to buttress her old age and she had made many friends in Whinmouth and preferred to live out her years in the quayside cottage. 'Us likes to watch the people go by,' she said unexpectedly, 'and I would miss my whist so! Tiz kind o' Claire to want me, tell her, but I'll stop where I be, thanking you!'

A more cheerful entry found its way into the estate record a week or so later, when preparations for celebrating the Silver Jubilee of George V and Queen Mary were in progress. Paul was leaving the rectory one morning in early May, having been discussing with Horsey the street-luncheon and the distribution of commemorative mugs to the schoolchildren, when he saw a blue Morris Cowley zig-zag down the village street, its horn blaring and its course so erratic that pedestrians instinctively withdrew into shop doorways until it came to an uncertain halt a few yards short of the church. Paul saw the driver waving but the sun was in his eyes and it was not until he crossed the street that he realised, to his amazement, the driver was Henry Pitts. Beside him, snuggled down like a sleek little dormouse, sat a pretty, very diminutive woman of about thirty-five, whom he recognised as one of the newcomers to the area who had recently bought one of Sydney Codsall's bungalows at the top of the village. Henry, who was in an ebullient mood, insisted they all adjourn to The Raven close by. Like everyone else in the Valley he deliberately avoided calling the pub by its new name, 'The Lovell Arms'. Paul was so astounded to see Henry driving a car that he followed them without a word and it was not until they were sipping their drinks that he found his tongue and asked Henry to introduce him to the lady and incidentally explain his inexplicable surrender to the twentieth century.

'Well, Maister,' Henry said, breezily, 'I had to come to it, zame as everybody else yerabouts, but 'twas a pistol held to me head and Ellie's finger on the trigger, baint that zo, midear?' and he slid his arm round the little woman's waist and drew her towards him with a familiarity that left Paul in no doubt at all but that Henry was planning to fill the gap left in his life by the death of his wife, Gloria. 'Do 'ee know Ellie? Do 'ee know the Squire, midear?' and when Paul said he had not had the pleasure, and Ellie giggled her denial, he continued expansively, ''Er's new yerabouts, you zee, and a widder, baint 'ee midear? Us on'y made up our minds this morning, zo fitting you should be the first to know. Truth is, I told Ellie you'd stand for me when us gets to bizness. Will 'ee, now?'

'Certainly I will and I'm delighted to hear it,' said Paul, reaching down to shake hands with Ellie, who seemed to stand no higher than Henry's massive chest, 'but I don't see the connection between finding a wife and buying a motor-car, Henry. Damn it, you've always set your silly face against everything that's appeared on the market since Edward the Seventh was crowned!'

Ellie seemed to regard this remark as a brilliant witticism on Paul's part, laughing so heartily that she spilled half her gin-and-orange down her chest and Henry brought her another and made a great show of removing the droplets from the front of her frock. When his ministrations were complete he said gravely that the car was not his but had belonged to Ellie's late husband, a commercial traveller for a well-known brand of pickles, who had died of thrombosis whilst opening up new territory in Hampshire, six months ago. '"Twas very suddenlike, wasn't it, midear?' he said gaily. 'Dropped stone dade, he did, in the act o' taking his boots off! And him all alone, poor toad, in one o' they dismal little places commercials stay in when they'm peddling!'

If it had not been for the fact that Henry was acknowledged to have the largest and softest heart in the Valley Paul might have found elements of near-relish in this recital, particularly as, all the time Henry talked of her husband's fatal collapse, little Ellie beamed at him and then added, by way of extenuation, 'Oswald was twenty years older than me, Mr Craddock, so it weren't that much of a shock, if you follow me!'

'I see,' said Paul, reflecting that, although only half her size, Henry's intended had the same philosophic approach to life and death as her predecessor, and at once bought another round, asking, 'What finally overcame that daft prejudice of yours towards all things mechanical, Henry?' and Henry explained that Ellie had the car but could not drive and that he, at fifty-eight, declined to walk the four miles between Hermitage and Coombe Bay every night to do a bit of courting, so he had hired a man from the Whinmouth Motor Company, taken a course of driving lessons and could now 'push her along middling-like!'

'Middling-like is about right,' Paul commented but comforted himself with the reflection that a man who had survived three years on the Western Front without a wound would almost certainly die in his bed, especially as his grandfather had come close to breaking the Valley record for longevity.

'Perhaps Ellie can talk you into getting a tractor after you're married,' he suggested, 'for it's something I've never been able to do! Here's to both of you, and jolly good luck! Will it be a church wedding or a quiet affair at the Registry Office?'

'Oh, not church, Mr Craddock,' said Ellie, in a shocked tone, very much at odds with the congeniality she had shown over the eclipse of the traveller in pickles, 'I mean, it wouldn't *look* right, would it? Not with the pair of us hardly out of mourning!'

'No, perhaps not,' conceded Paul and suddenly decided he liked her for her honesty and remarkable inconsistency, both of which promised to contribute something towards the happiness of his oldest friend in the Valley.

'Well, tiz a rare bit o' luck us running into you today,' Henry said, 'for us was racking our brains about how to break it to young David and Mother! Seeing you reminded me o' the part you played getting Elinor Codsall clear away, with that bliddy Squarehead she married! Do 'ee think you could bring yourself to sound the boy on how he'd feel about me bringing Ellie back to Hermitage? I dorn mind tellin' 'ee, Squire, tiz something I don't relish doin'.'

'Damn it, that's surely a job for you, isn't it?' Paul protested but Ellie said, earnestly, 'Oh, we've already given 'em the *hint*, Mr Craddock! What Henry means is – well – could you bring yourself to pop over today and sort of walk in on us, after we'd put it to 'em? Henry told me his Ma thinks a rare lot of you, and if we can bring her round to it I don't reckon we shall have trouble with Henry's boy. You see, I always get along with men!' and she winked so impudently that it was Henry's turn to soil his waistcoat with liquor.

It began to look like a conspiracy and must have been hatched, Paul decided, the moment they saw him in the street. He said, with a sigh, 'Your father warned me thirty years ago what I was taking on with this place, Henry! I'll come but only providing you take the plunge now. For all that I don't see how my presence will help much.'

'Giddon, doan you believe it,' said Henry, finishing his pint at a gulp. 'Mother alwus did think the sun shined from your backside, Squire! Hop in, Ellie, and us'll get it over an' done with, midear!' and he led the way out to the little car and after killing the engine five times managed to start and drive down to the river road, where he soon built up to thirty-five miles per hour. It was a breathless but triumphant journey. Along every yard of the route Henry kept his finger on the horn and when he had occasion to change gear the car proceeded in violent

leaps and bounds, so that Paul was relieved to be put at the
top of Hermitage Lane and watch them drive on to the farm,
'to warm things up a bit' as Henry put it.

He gave them fifteen minutes' grace and then ambled into
the yard advertising his approach by calling to the dogs, so
that Henry emerged on the porch and exclaimed, for the
benefit of his aged mother and son, David, 'Why damme if
it baint Squire himself! Come along in! Youm just in time for
the shock of a lifetime, Squire! I was just tellin' Mother I was
thinkin' o' bringing Ellie to care for her in her old age, wadden
I, Davey boy?' whereupon he solemnly reintroduced Paul to
Ellie and then treacherously withdrew, on the feeble excuse
of showing Ellie his saddlebacks.

It was obvious that the news had not come as a thunder-
bolt to the old lady and her grandson and equally clear
that they were not wholly in favour of the arrangement,
for Martha Pitts, invariably cheerful and welcoming, now
had her nutcracker jaws well clamped and Young David
was glowering at the stone flags, his enormous red hands
hanging loose, like a pair of hams in a butcher's window.
Paul realised that the initiative was his and took it, as much
out of his sympathy for them as Henry.

'You might have done a good deal worse, Martha!' he
said, bluntly. 'She's a cheerful little body and I think she'll
make Henry a good wife. These things are never easy for
the people concerned but when a man has been married as
long as Henry he's far easier to live with if he cuts his
losses and starts all over again.'

'She baint varmin' stock!' Martha grumbled, 'and you c'n
zee that be lookin' at her!'

'And suppose I had it in mind to marry an' zettle in
yer?' demanded David, and they both awaited his verdict,
not exactly resentful but with a certain shared glumness.

'She may not be farming stock but she's obviously used to
a hard day's work,' Paul said. 'Moreover, she's genuinely fond
of Henry and certainly isn't after what money he's got. In fact,
it seems to me she's doing precisely what he's doing – finding
a means to insure against a lonely old age!'

'He's got us!' said Martha, defensively.

'Both of you are different generations and that's important to a man his age. And talking of ages, he's not old enough to retire and hand over to you, David. If he did he'd soon run to seed if I know Henry. *Were* you thinking of getting married yourself?'

'Well, no, I got no one particular in mind,' the young man admitted, 'but I got a right to if I do want!'

It occurred to Paul now that here was a situation that often cropped up in local farming families, where life revolved around a single, indivisible unit of land but it was a problem he had never been called to solve. Sometimes the older generation lived on and the sons soldiered as junior partners until they wanted to marry, but so far none of the Shallowford farms had supported three working generations under a single roof. He said, on impulse, 'Suppose I agreed to build a house nearer the river if and when you think of marrying, Davey? Hermitage is large enough to support two families and I daresay Martha would get along with Ellie well enough, once she set her mind to it. If she didn't could she move in with you?' and he was relieved to see the old lady's face relax, for it was known that she had always worshipped Henry's son and that the boy's presence here had made it easy for her to get along with the sharp-tempered Gloria in the past.

'What do 'ee say to that, midear?' she asked, glancing at her grandson with the furtiveness of the very old and insecure, and Davey, wrinkling his brow, said, 'Well, I daresay 'twould be the best way out, Gran! I'd always be glad to 'ave 'ee, you knows that well enough!'

'Very well, you've got my word for it,' Paul said. 'There's an ideal site on that flat piece below Undercliff where the brook runs under the road. I'll get my son-in-law Rumble to survey it tomorrow, for he seems to have made a first-class job of tidying up Periwinkle. You're good neighbours, I hope?'

'Arr,' said David, with a flicker of enthusiasm, 'he's a dabster an' no mistake! Can do well-nigh anything with his own two hands an' most of it a bliddy sight better'n a tradesman! Coulden wish for a better chap upalong, I couldn't.'

'Then it's settled,' Paul said, 'and the pair of you do what you can to make Ellie feel she's wanted in the meantime!' and he withdrew to find Henry and Ellie hanging about the yard, having eavesdropped on most of the conversation at the scullery window. They were obviously relieved and Henry said, "Ow much will it cost to build that bungalow downalong, Squire?' and Paul said, shortly, 'A good deal less than it would to have a bad atmosphere up here, Henry! This has always been a happy farm and I want to keep it that way!'

'Arr,' Henry replied, thoughtfully, 'youm right about that, Maister! Gloria had her moods, mind you, but Martha could always manage her, 'cept that one time, when she left it to me and a pair o' scissors!'

'What was that?' piped Ellie but he replied, with one of his slow, rubbery smiles, 'Mind your own bliddy bizness, Ellie! Tiz between me an' Squire and I won't tell 'ee till I 'ave a mind to!' and he emphasised Valley dominance of male over female by the proprietary slap on the behind that made them seem man and wife already.

Paul declined an offer of Henry's to run him back to the house, walking over the shoulder of Undercliff pasture to the slope below French Wood and congratulating himself on a good morning's work, albeit one that would set him back by several hundred pounds. High Coombe was gone but Four Winds had been saved and Periwinkle was burgeoning under the hands of Rumble and Mary. Now Hermitage, always one of his favourites, had been insured against dissolution, so that, taken as a whole, the future was more promising than it had been for a long time. He stopped at the crest and looked down across the Valley. Next week, he remembered, there would be Silver Jubilee celebrations, and although it seemed probable they would lack the spontaneity (and certainly the imperial aggressiveness) of 1902 and 1911, official jollifications were at least evidence of continuity and that alone, in a rapidly changing world, brought him a measure of satisfaction. He felt the urge to hurry on home and write in the estate diary about proposed changes this side of the Valley and relief must have shown in his face when he appeared at lunch, for Claire greeted him with a cheerful, 'What's cooking? You look smug?' and he replied, 'I feel smug, and I've every right to! No one in this house ever has fully appreciated my stupendous talents as an arbitrator!'

IV

It was, one might have said, his Indian summer of smugness. With the Slump behind him and the family, apart from the baby, off his hands, even his feud with Sydney Codsall became almost extinct after the bricks of the bungalows on the eastern border had mellowed and the County Council (with whom Sydney seemed to have lost his grip) compelled him to shift the caravan park nearer the main road where it was screened, to some degree, by the tongue of the woods.

The Silver Jubilee celebrations were tepid judged by earlier and more robust jamborees, as though the British were honouring the royal family from habit. Public luncheons were eaten, races run, mugs distributed, loyal addresses delivered but purely local festivities had lost their appeal in an age when radios were switched on all day and there was a two-hourly 'bus service between Coombe Bay and Paxtonbury, and all the youngsters roared about the countryside on motor-cycles. People went further afield these days and looked for more sophistication in their leisure. There were two cinemas in Paxtonbury and one in Whinmouth, and their bills were displayed regularly in the window of Smut Potter's baker's shop, giving him and his French wife free access to Hollywood entertainment every day of the week had they cared to avail themselves of this tremendous privilege.

And yet the Valley remained a unit, buttressed in the east by dedicated, middle-aged men, like the cork-footed Brissot of Lower Coombe and Francis Willoughby of Deepdene, and in the west by the bastions of Four Winds, Hermitage and the resurrected Periwinkle. There was still no more than a wandering path along the dunes and over the goyles and liaison between the estate and the National Trust kept the great woods in being and the slopes of Blackberry Moor free of bricks and mortar.

On Midsummer's Day, 1935, when all the Jubilee litter had been gathered up and burned, a casual perusal of the estate diary sent Paul off on one of his great circular sweeps, his first in a long time. He had been entering up after breakfast when something prompted him to turn back the pages, a whole fistful of pages, to the same season of the year a quarter-century ago, when he had made the rounds to acquaint tenants of King Teddy's death, in 1910. The recollection of this set him musing on the great patterns of change that had overlapped one another in the last two-and-a-half decades. It struck him that the very act of conveying such news across county on horseback was something linking him to Tudor and Stuart eras, for today, supposing the ailing George V died, everyone in the Valley would be aware of the fact within minutes. There was hardly a cottage that did not possess its radio and London papers arrived in Coombe Bay at breakfast-time on the morning 'bus. The bright sun threw golden darts across the little room so that the prospect of paperwork depressed him and he pushed his tray aside, letting his mind rove back to the day, clearly recalled, when he had ridden old Snowdrop over the Sorrel and back across the edge of the moor to the mere and the farms in the east. It seemed more than twenty-five years ago. Four of his seven children had been unborn and young Ikey Palfrey had only just left school. Old Tamer and Willoughby were already dead but Arthur Pitts, John Rudd, Norman Eveleigh and most of the old brigade were thriving and so were the second generation, Will Codsall, Big Jem, and a score of others commemorated in French Wood. The sight of a motor-car in those days had set everyone running and no one in the Valley had ever seen an aeroplane, or heard of Hollywood. There had been but one telephone in the district, a thing that looked like an ear-trumpet in Coombe Bay Post Office and the main road running behind the woods had been white with dust all summertime. He said aloud, as he re-read his 1910 entry, 'God, it's another world!' and then, hearing Claire clearing the breakfast things, shouted, 'I'm going out for a spell! I'll be home to lunch!' and went along the terrace to the yard calling Mark Codsall to saddle the skewbald.

He took the same route, across Big Paddock to Home Farm, where he stopped for a brief chat with his goddaughter, formerly Prudence Pitts, now mistress of the place, and as he sat his horse talking to her he reflected how quickly these flighty girls let themselves go once they had settled for a man. Prudence had once been the belle of the Valley and the giddiest flirt for miles around; today she looked as though she had been married almost as long as her landlord. He gave her good-day and rode on, his mind occupied working out her age which he judged to be twenty-seven. She was not, he thought, wearing so well, despite her lavish use of cosmetics and fortnightly visits to the Paxtonbury hairdresser. Her figure had already begun to sag and rumour had reached him that she nagged her husband but the farm itself seemed in good order, with its outbuildings freshly whitewashed and its yard free of nettles. He emerged on to the river road and crossed the bridge, once a plank affair but now of metal plates bedded in concrete piers and rode on down the Four Winds' approach lane to the biggest but no longer the most prosperous farm on the estate. Harold Eveleigh and his eldest boy were there, tinkering with a tractor parked alongside the barn where Martin Codsall had hanged himself more than thirty years ago. He called, 'Lovely morning, Harold! Anything you can't fix yourself?' and Eveleigh straightened himself and grinned.

'If I can't, Bob can,' he said and the boy beside him grunted, 'Carburettor trouble! This fuel is second-rate and she clogs. Dad will start her on it, no matter how many times I tell him to switch over and start on pure gas!' He tinkered awhile and then, with a stuttering roar, the engine suddenly burst into life and the boy leaped up and tuned it to a smooth *bub-bub-bub*.

'Got to keep him handy all the time,' Harold said. 'I wish to God he didn't have to go to school! I could do with Bob around me all the week. I was going in for a mug of tea. Will you join me, Mr Craddock?'

'Thanks, no,' Paul told him, 'but give my regards to your wife. I'm just doing the rounds and I've promised to be home for lunch. Everything okay over here?'

'Ticking over,' Harold said. 'Milk yield is up but we're down on pigs. Poor old Ben is past it, I'm afraid. Time we pensioned him off!' and he nodded in the direction of an incredibly old man doddering across the yard carrying two buckets of swill, completely absorbed in the task of keeping his balance on the sun-slippery flags.

'He must be nearly ninety!' Paul said, recognising the labourer to whom he had once delivered the drunken Martin Codsall after taking him home from the bay one winter's afternoon, shortly before the Four Winds' tragedy, and he called, 'Hi there, Ben!' but the old man disappeared round the corner of the barn without looking up.

'Stone deaf!' Harold said, 'but a better worker than most of them for all that! I've tried to persuade him to pack it in but either he can't hear or deliberately misunderstands. He was here in Codsall's time, wasn't he?'

'Yes,' Paul said, 'and I daresay he's another who would prefer to die in his boots. If you retired him he'd fade out in a fortnight. It's routine that keeps that kind going.'

'My God, it won't keep me going at his age!' Harold said, 'I shall be damned glad to put my feet up and let the boys carry on.'

'Do they want to?'

'Bob does, he's got a mechanical flair. Must be from his mother's side, it certainly isn't from mine.'

'Well, there's hope for you yet,' Paul said. 'You heard Henry Pitts has acquired a tractor since he remarried?'

'I never believed it until I saw him cruising across Undercliffe the other day but if he drives it the way he drives his Morris we shan't have him around for long!'

'Don't bank on it,' Paul said, moving on. 'Henry came through Third Ypres. It'll take a damned sight more than a tractor spill to kill him!'

He rode down to the river, feeling, as he would have said, 'comfortable' about Four Winds. Harold Eveleigh would never be the kind of farmer his father was, or his brother Gilbert would have been, but he had more than enough staying power to see him through, and domestic peace anchored him to the place in a way that was rarer today than it had been a generation ago. He forded the river where it was no more than a fetlock deep and punched up the swell of Undercliffe and under the lee of French Wood to Hermitage, passing on his way the cleared site of Davey Pitts' new bungalow. Davey, it seemed, had been evasive when he had told him a month ago he had no plans to marry, or perhaps his father's second marriage had jogged his elbow. He had appeared at Shallowford within three days of the confrontation and taken Paul up on his offer to provide alternative accommodation for himself and the old lady. Later it had leaked out that he had become engaged to one of the Timberlake girls living in Whinmouth, so that the danger of relationships going sour at Hermitage had been sidestepped.

The old lady was sunning herself in the porch when Paul rode up and he was just in time to see Ellie emerge with her tea and biscuits. Old Martha, he noticed, received her ministrations as a right and he thought, 'The sooner the old girl goes and leaves Henry and his new wife to themselves the better!' and apparently Ellie thought so too, for she made a grimace of resignation with her mouth as if to say, 'It isn't for long, thank God! But I'm not giving her a stick to beat me with!'

He passed the time of day with them both and learned that Henry had taken his new tractor down in the hollow near the moor road fork. On the rim of the western boundary he saw him, trailing blue exhaust along the bowl of a field they called Barley Mow and it was obvious, even from this distance, that he was using his tractor as a plaything and not as an implement, for the trailer he was towing was empty and Paul watched as Henry, hunched like a chariot driver, charged a narrow gateway and roared up the incline towards the north-westerly tip of the wood. It was, he felt, a cheering sight, and evidence that none were proof against the lure of gadgets. Not a hundred yards from where Henry joyously tackled the gradient was the road junction where, in the early years of the century, he had stood on the bank and gaped at his first horseless carriage, the fidgety little contrivance driven into the Valley by Roddy Rudd. From that moment, it seemed, his mind had hardened against machines and his prejudices had been increased rather than diminished by his experiences in the glutinous mud of Passchendaele, yet here he was, wedded to the machine age by a widow and eight-horse power car. In a way, Paul thought, it was a comic miracle.

He left Henry to his play and rode across the shallow valley to the Periwinkle boundary where the skewbald, full of spring grass, and with the hunting season well behind her, threw up her heels and took the ascent at a gallop, Paul entering into the spirit of the frolic and hallooing Mary as she emerged from the wash-house with her mouth full of pegs – rubber pegs, he noticed. Rumble Patrick must have talked her into throwing her wooden pegs on to the ash-heap.

Every time he had come this way in the last few months there had been changes and all of them good. The new shingled roof of the farmhouse, the creosoted split-rail fences and the general air of sleekness that the ugly duckling of the Valley had acquired under Rumble Patrick's dynamic direction, made his heart swell with pride, not only because the marriage was so clearly a happy one but because he felt he could take credit himself for having produced a daughter with enough sense to sit waiting for the right husband when other girls would have compromised. And yet, although the wedding was only three months distant in time, he found it difficult to regard the new occupants of Periwinkle as newlyweds. To him they seemed always to have been man and wife elect and what had happened last April was no more than ratification of contract. As he reined in at the gate Rumble appeared from the kitchen wearing nothing but a pair of khaki shorts and, improbably, an apron. The boy's back and shoulders were burned a golden brown and Paul thought, 'Now dammit, why can't I tan like that? If I take my shirt off I go brick-red, endure two days' agony, peel and then go fish-belly white again!'

'What's the idea of the badge of servitude?' he asked. 'No other man in the Valley would be seen dead in an apron!' and Mary, spitting her pegs into a basket, called, 'Don't come between man and wife! Rumble does the cooking on washdays and he's a better hand at it than most of the women around here! Are you going to stay and sample one of his hashes?'

'Not likely,' he said, dismounting and leading the skewbald into the lean-to stable, 'but I'd like to see what kind of job you've made of it inside? You're about finished now, aren't you?'

Yes they were, she told him, and he smiled at the queenly way she marched ahead of him into the house leaving Rumble to off-saddle the mare and resume his weekly chore. He had seen the renovations in various stages but was unprepared for the pleasant impact of Elinor's old kitchen, always a tumbledown old place, with its crumbling beams and bulging cob. Today the place seemed not only solid and commodious but one of the most cheerful rooms he had ever entered, its great stone fireplace softened by large earthenware jars filled with lupins, delphiniums and gladioli, the slate floor laid with brightly patterned rugs and primrose curtains over the windows. There was a new stove in the enlarged scullery, a covered-way for boots, coals and logs, and what had once been a deeply recessed bacon cupboard had been converted into a backstair leading to the landing where the beams had been treated with a preservative that gave off a pleasing resinous smell. She obviously took immense pride in showing him all they had done and pouted when he said the place looked more like a pocket Manor House than a run-down farm.

'I don't see why all farmers should have to share a sty with their pigs,' she said, 'and most of them around here do! Rumble can solve any problem once he puts his mind to it but it was me who took charge up here,' and she led the way into the low-ceiling bedroom, where the walls were painted the colour of old parchment, every piece of cottage furniture gleamed and the double bed was covered with a lavender-blue bedspread. There were night tables either side of the bed and on them were gleaming silver candlesticks, complete with original snuffers. It all looked so trim, fresh and elegant that he thought, 'They aren't really farmers at all, they're more like a couple of kids playing house!' He said:

'I was only teasing. You've got a better home-making in-stinct than any of us, Mary, and this would have made old Elinor Codsall's eyes start from her head. As for poor old Will, he would have rolled himself in a blanket and slept on the floor!' Then, looking at her pink nightie and Rumble's striped pyjamas folded on the pillows like props in a magazine advertisement, 'You're obviously well-matched and I don't have to ask if you're happy.'

'No,' she said, without a trace of the shyness that had characterised her up to the very moment of Rumble Patrick's reappearance in the Valley, 'No, you don't, Daddy! He's wonderful but sometimes I find it very hard to believe he's only twenty-two. He seems so much more mature than any of the younger set round here and yet – well – it doesn't make him in the least stodgy, if you know what I mean.'

'I know exactly what you mean,' he said, 'for his father Ikey had the same quality. It was something I always envied him!' and he gave her a swift hug to express his extreme satisfaction and they went downstairs to the scullery where Rumble was stirring a savoury-smelling stew in a large, black saucepan which he lifted aside and said, as he slipped his arm round her waist, 'Did he think it was a bit fussy up there? Above stairs it was her doing, not mine, Gov'nor!'

Paul said, seriously, 'You've made a wonderful start here and it frightens me to think I thought of bulldozing the place after Elinor left, and letting it revert to rough pasture. What have you got in the way of stock?'

'Nothing to boast about as yet,' Rumble said, 'but I'm buying some Friesians from Eveleigh. The new generator's installed and the milking machine arrives on Friday. I shan't bother with pigs while the price is so low but I'm going ahead with the cereal wheat as I planned. That way I can manage with one extra hand. After we've reclaimed fifteen acres of moor we'll see about getting another on piecework basis. Would you and Claire like to come over to a meal on Saturday night? It's rather special, the official switch-on!' and he pointed to the empty light-socket over the stove.

'We should be delighted,' he said and Rumble told Mary to watch the stew while he showed Paul the electric plant housed in what had been Will Codsall's cowshed and then, as Rumble led the way out of the house, his face assumed a slightly wary expression as he said, 'Did she drop the dutiful hint about a little stranger, Gov?' and went on, before Paul could exclaim, 'Oh, I talked the usual guff about waiting until there was money in the bank but . . . well . . . you know these things have a way of making up their own minds! Maybe there's some sense in her view – that kids are the better for having young parents!'

'Well, you certainly haven't wasted much time, Rumble,' he said, smiling, 'but taken all around I think she's right and you're wrong!' He glanced down the slope to where the river gleamed between the willow clump on the wide river bend above Codsall bridge. 'It's a nice spot to be born in and grow up, so damned good luck to the three of you!'

He rode off along the crest towards the bulge of Hermitage Wood feeling more elated than ever. He already had three grandchildren, all girls, but Mary's he felt sure, would be a boy and perhaps take his place here in the 'fifties and 'sixties. Somehow he had always known that his successor would derive from Mary and also that, somewhere along the line, Ikey would have a stake in it, and it was to Ikey that his thoughts returned as he cut across the northern boundary of Hermitage to enter the woods by a little-used bridle path running round the shoulder of the badgers' slope. It was about here, so Maureen told him, that Hazel Potter had been delivered of Rumble Patrick in a cave, on a summer evening the year before hell broke loose and changes rushed down on them so rapidly that it seemed the pattern of life would be shattered for all time. It had not, thank God. Somehow they had been able to save the main fabric, sort out the pieces, and begin all over again and this, surely, was what Oliver Cromwell (himself a well-meaning vandal) would have called 'a crowning mercy'.

The woods were at their midsummer best, the bracken shoots mushrooming as high as the skewbald's ears, the flowering rhododendrons immediately below looking like a fleet of purple galleons anchored in an olive-green bay with their crews asleep or ashore. Beyond the stream, in the hollow east of the mere, Sam Potter's cottage reminded him of the cottage Tom had seen from Hearthover Fell, in his favourite childhood book, *The Water Babies*, and as he advanced down the steep slope he caught a glimpse of the ponderous figure of Joannie Potter, wearing red, just like the old lady who had befriended the fugitive sweep. The mere itself, on his right, was very still but as he reached its northernmost tip he could see the tiny V-ripples of voles swimming along the bank towards Smut Potter's old hideout, and, over by the islet, a moorhen and her chicks making the circuit and again suggesting a fleet, only this time one of rowboats led by a small, brown ketch. The orchestra began as the path flattened out, a low muted hum of innumerable rustlings and warblings and dronings, pitched in the identical key that he heard when he first rode here in the drought of 1902, and he thought, 'This will almost certainly be the last place to change! Even Sydney's bulldozers would be defeated by this tangle, thank God!' and he called to Joannie Potter, twice as heavy as when Sam first brought her here at his instance and she answered in her high-pitched, broad-vowelled voice, 'Zam's downalong! Word came Mother Meg wanted un. Do 'ee want un special, Squire?' and Paul said no, he was just taking the air, and asked after Pauline, his first Valley godchild, now married to a railwayman in Paxtonbury.

''Er's vine,' Joannie said, 'and expectin' another. That'll mak' zix grandchildren, what wi' Georgie's last one! Who'd ha' thought it now?'

'Who indeed?' said Paul, with a smile, for he had always had a warm corner in his heart for Sam and Joannie, the very first of the second generation round here to raise a family and name one of their children for him, although her sex called for a little cheating and one extra syllable.

'What's Sam doing downalong?' he asked and Joannie told him that word had come from the Dell that Meg had had 'one of her spells' a week since and Smut had had to take the van and fetch her back from the moor, leaving her horse to find its own way home.

''Er's over eighty now and 'er reely shoulden keep traapsing about, the way she does,' Joannie complained.

'You'll not stop Meg moving around,' said Paul, 'not unless you tie her down!' and he rode on beside the mere, passing the spot where, on the left, he had first romped in the grass with Claire, and on the right was the islet holding his happiest memory of Grace. At the sloping field he turned left, hugging the edge of the woods past the favourite haunt of the Shallowford butterflies for about here, years before he came to the Valley, someone had begun planting an ornamental shrubbery and a few of the imported shrubs had lingered on, notably a buddleia that seemed to hold a special delight for butterflies of all kinds. They were here now, wavering irresolutely over the flowers, a host of Red Admirals, Peacocks, Meadow Browns, Tortoiseshells and Cabbage Whites, two or three hundred of them going about their business whatever it was, and pausing to watch them Paul remembered the neighbours of the old German professor who had been driven from the Valley in 1914, for his hobby had been lepidoptery and he had had cases of butterflies in his study.

He gave Deepdene a miss and rode instead down the winding path to the Dell to inquire after Mother Meg but she was not there and neither was Sam, the French Canadian Brissot telling him that, against her daughter's advice, Meg had set out on one of her basket-selling trips early that morning.

The Dell looked far tidier than it had ever looked under the hands of Old Tamer, his wife, or even Big Jem. There was not a nettle or dock to be seen and green wheat stood shoulder high in what had once been a tangle of briars on the southern slope of the wood.

'You seem to be keeping hard at it about here,' he said to Brissot, a man he respected, although he could never understand why he had carried the Cockney Bellchamber on his back all these years. 'Do you ever feel homesick for Quebec?' and the Frenchman said politely that he had never regretted settling in England because the winters were so mild, particularly down here, and even as a child he had hated snow. Violet, Jumbo Bellchamber's wife, came out with her washing while they stood talking and smiled a welcome. Like Joannie Potter she had put on a great deal of weight and it was difficult to picture her as a slim, fleet-footed girl, who had once set Valley tongues clacking and driven the young sparks wild. 'They all seem to have settled for a quiet life at last,' he told himself, 'although I would never have bet a shilling on it happening!' and he took the track that led over the western shoulder of the Bluff and was soon clattering down Coombe Bay High Street.

Not much of the original village was left and what little there was seemed populated with strangers, loafing about the church green in holiday garb. Almost everyone about here, he reflected, catered for summer visitors and in a month or two, when the school holidays began, this street would teem with Cockneys and Midlanders in shorts and coloured shirts, with children scrambling about in the harbour with shrimping nets and toy boats. He was in such a relaxed mood, however, that the thought of Coombe Bay as a holiday resort did not bother him this morning. It was probably good for trade and who the devil was he to deny city families a fortnight by the sea, or begrudge people like Smut Potter and that French wife of his selling their confections? As he drew level with the Vicarage he saw Parson Horsey, a bent, shrunken old man now, with a halo of silvery hair circling his brown, polished skull. The old man was still very active, however, for here he was hoeing his flower-beds and stooping every now and again to pluck a weed and toss it in a seed-box close by.

'I had to get out in the sun this morning,' Horsey confessed, after Paul had hailed him and Paul said, 'Me too!' and reined in, asking after Abe Tozer, the smith, who had taken to his bed a week or so before.

'He'll not last the summer,' Horsey said, 'but he hasn't any regrets. After all, he was swinging a hammer up to last week and his wife tells me he's well over eighty. I suppose the forge will close when he dies. There's more call here for a good garage than a smithy. Your good lady is well, I trust?' and Paul said she was and told him the news from Periwinkle. Horsey said with a smile, 'Well, it doesn't surprise me, Squire. That girl of yours is a lovable lass and as for that lad of Hazel Potter's, one should never be surprised at how a Potter turns out! I've just seen Pansy taking her third husband for an airing. He's a powerful swimmer, you know, and she marches him down to the beach every morning of the week about this time between May and October. There's some very good stuff in that woman somewhere. They say she's made that poor chap a very happy man. It isn't everyone who would take him on.'

It was a judgment, Paul thought, that old Parson Bull would never have passed and not for the first time he congratulated himself in installing this little gnome of a man as rector all those years ago when Parson Bull, last of the sporting parsons, had ridden himself into the ground chasing foxes.

'Do you ever hear from Rachel these days?' he asked and Horsey said he did, now and again, and that the last time she wrote she said she had just been adopted as Socialist candidate for a Glasgow constituency and seemed to have a chance of being elected if Baldwin went to the country in the autumn. He waited to see if Paul would respond with news of a letter from Simon but when he did not, added, 'Your boy is her agent. I expect you'll be hearing!'

'I doubt it,' said Paul. 'They're generally too absorbed in politics to waste propaganda time writing to an old Diehard like me! What do you really make of them? Honestly now?'

Horsey said, with a smile, 'I think maybe they have the right idea – broadly speaking that is! Things are badly shared, no one can deny that, so perhaps it's right that the younger generation should chivvy those in authority. Frankly I find their outlook a bit cold-blooded and I daresay you do as well, but if they can goad the Establishment into knocking down a few slums, raising the general standard of living, and stopping another war, then all power to their elbow! Our lot were a bit too complacent, don't you think?'

'You weren't,' Paul said, remembering Claire's tale of the sermon he had preached to wounded soldiers, 'but probably I was and still am! I've always known my limitations and they don't extend beyond the Teazel and the Bluff, yonder!'

He said good-bye and walked the skewbald down to the harbour where he saw the blind Alf Willis, supple and well-muscled for a handicapped man of over forty, emerge from the

water and watched Pansy hand him his towel and help him on
with his sweater. It was just another facet of the morning's ride
that pleased him and he turned the horse into the sandhills,
meaning to follow the coastline as far as Crabpot Willie's goyle
before riding the last mile home in time for lunch.

It was much cooler here by the sea and the flies, which had
bothered the skewbald in the woods, dropped away so that he
put her into a steady trot. In five minutes he had reached the
gully and turned inland, heading through the scattered pines
above the shanty but halfway up the incline he reined in, his
eye catching a sparkle of metal on the summit of the opposite
hillock. There was a trap over there, stationary in a cleared
patch about a hundred yards west of the goyle, and when he
looked more closely he could see someone sitting motionless
on the box, slumped against the iron backrest. He rose in his
stirrups and called 'Hi, there!' but the figure did not move and
the pony, after raising its head, went on cropping the sparse
grass. He thought, 'That's odd, it looks like Old Meg's trap,'
and he crossed the goyle at its shallow head, circling round to
the clearing and coming alongside the shabby little equipage.
It was Meg's trap and Meg was in it. The reins had slipped
from her hands and she sat with her eyes wide open, looking
out over the tops of the lower pines to the bay. He did not
need to dismount to discover that she was dead.

The sight of her sitting here, staring out across the Channel,
was impressive and a little awesome. She looked rooted and
statuesque, her knees spread and her hands resting lightly
in her lap. She might have been part of the background,
something that belonged there, like one of the fully-grown
pines or the outcrop of sandstone against which the trap-wheel
had come to rest in the pony's search for grass. He dismounted,
hitched the mare's reins to the rear step and, after feeling her
pulse, knelt on the footboard and eased her into the trap-well,
which was half-full of rush mats and besom brooms. She was
very heavy and the effort required all his strength but he
managed it and gently, for he had a great affection for this
hulk of a woman, who had always gone her own way with
dignity, earning her own bread and keeping herself, and often

her indolent family, with coppers coaxed from the twin trades of hawking and fortune-telling. It was strange, he thought, that she should die the morning he had news for her of another grandchild, one among so many, yet he did not find her death shocking or startling. It must have come upon her very stealthily, while she was returning home across the dunes and perhaps, hearing its rustle, she had reined in to take a last look at the sun baking the sandbanks a mile or so out to sea. It was, after all, a pleasant way to die and one might 'envy her some day, death in the open and the fresh air, after a long lifetime of breathing fresh air; a good deal better than John Rudd's death in a stuffy little room and a far more natural one than poor Claire's. He thought of Old Tamer's death in the breakers off the Cove, hardly a mile east of this spot, and wondered if man and wife would now meet again after all this time and if so what would they have to say to one another. It seemed unlikely. If Heaven and Hell were Old Testament realities, then Tamer would still be working out his time in Purgatory, whereas Old Meg, who had never stolen so much as a clothes-peg, would surely get her reward if rewards were going.

He lifted the reins and clicked his tongue at the pony, turning the trap in a half-circle and setting off across the fields in the direction of the ford.

V

Uncle Franz Zorndorff paid his last visit to Shallowford that September, his last visit anywhere as it happened, for a few months later he died at the age of ninety-three. His final meeting with Paul was almost accidental.

He had written in May saying that he was going to Austria for a holiday and Paul was very surprised, not so much that a man of his advanced years should feel a sudden urge to travel, but because Franz's wish to see his homeland again after so many years indicated an unsuspected streak of sentiment in the old man. By Paul's calculations Franz had fled the Continent seventy years ago, when the Emperor Franz Joseph had ruled over his hotch-potch of a dozen quarrelsome races of which Franz's people, the Croats, were then a persecuted minority. Paul had never heard the Croat speak of Austria-Hungary with affection. It was the home, he would say of *Schlamperei* – which he translated as a policy of deliberate drift, a tolerance for romantic nonsense, and to a man with a lifelong dedication to money-making *Schlamperei* was an unforgiveable sin. It was therefore with some astonishment that Paul had read into the old man's letter a kind of confession, for Franz had written, '. . . I've had a very long run, my boy, and can't expect more than another year or so. Before I go I should dearly love to see what they have made of it over there, since the old Empire broke up and everybody chose their own road to perdition. You might find it difficult to believe but I have always had a filial affection for the Old Man' (he meant, presumably, Franz Joseph, who had ruled from 1848 until 1916) 'and before I die I have a ridiculous desire to ride in a carriage along the Prater, and take a final sniff of the air of Transylvania. I daresay the journey will kill me but if it does then I shall have no complaints. Whilst the City of London is undeniably the only place where a man can put on weight whilst making a fortune, it is not, I think, a place where one would wish to leave one's bones! Last week I made a shorter sentimental journey to your father's grave, in Nunhead Cemetery. It was, perhaps, the sight of those grey acres that suggested this grandiose display of sentiment!'

Franz did not leave his old bones in Transylvania. Judging by the series of luridly-coloured picture postcards received by the twins, by Claire and others, his return to Vienna, after a lapse of almost three-quarters of a century, invigorated him and in mid-September that year Paul was again surprised to hear Franz's precise voice on the telephone and to learn that he had that day landed in Plymouth.

'What the devil are you doing in Plymouth, you restless old rascal?' Paul demanded, and Franz said that he had made the outward journey by trans-Continental express but had returned home by sea from Trieste and would be passing through Paxtonbury in an hour or so. If Paul cared to meet

him there he was welcome; there was a later train on to town
and they could spend an afternoon together.

'I'll meet you, of course I'll meet you,' he said, beginning to
wonder if the old chap was senile, 'but why on earth don't
you stop off and stay with us for a week or two? There isn't
all that hurry to get back to London at your age, is there?'

'As a matter of fact there is,' Franz replied, unexpectedly.
'To my way of thinking even minutes count but don't expect
me to explain that from a public telephone-box! My train gets
in at one-fifteen and if you intend to meet me be there, because
I shan't get out unless you are, do you understand?'

'I'll be there,' Paul said, resignedly, and replaced the receiver
with a suspicion that Uncle Franz's apparent hurry might have
something to do with the twins who had been left in charge
of the patron's various enterprises during his absence. He
mentioned as much to Claire but all Claire said was, 'You're a
born worrier, Paul! Why on earth should you suppose anything
like that? Those boys are perfectly capable of looking after his
interests. They've been more or less running his business for
years!'

'Nobody runs Uncle Franz's business!' Paul said, 'and I shall
get to the bottom of this! It wouldn't surprise me in the least
if those two hadn't been monkeying on the Stock Exchange
while he was away!' and he drove off across the moor, his
disquiet causing him to arrive far too early and spend an
impatient three-quarters of an hour stamping up and down
the platform, awaiting the boat train.

He saw Franz leaning from the window before the train
came to a halt and was relieved by his obvious chirpiness. The
old fellow was as spruce as ever, his face sunburned the colour
of an old walnut and his Van Dyck beard curled Continental
fashion, so that he looked like the most elderly character in
Rembrandt's 'Night Watch', one of Paul's favourite pictures.

He went along to the compartment and supervised the
unloading of Franz's cases, more than enough to load a barrow,
and with the note of tolerant impatience he reserved for the
Croat, said, 'You don't have to bother with all this clutter. I'm
taking you along home whether you like it or not. Put all this

stuff in the left-luggage office and we'll have lunch at The Mitre and get back to Shallowford for tea. Claire's expecting you.'

'Then I shall have to disappoint her,' Franz said, flatly. 'I'm catching the late-afternoon train and only my duty to you disposed me to break my journey to this desert staging-post. If I survive I may well join you for Christmas but in the meantime there's salvaging to be done, I assure you.'

'So those boys of mine let you down after all?' Paul said and the old Croat's Father Christmas eyebrows shot up an inch as he looked at Paul with humorous concern.

'Good heavens, no!' he said. 'Whatever gave you that idea? I've been in constant touch with them and they've been splendid, quite splendid! I can't imagine how you produced a pair of smart operators like Steve and Andy. Are you quite sure Claire didn't cuckold you one day while you were out ploughing?'

'Then what the devil is your hurry?' Paul demanded. 'At ninety-three you can't be all that essential to the business!' and Franz said, with a twinkle, 'I don't suppose I am but I like to pretend to myself that it is so! After all, it's all I've got to hold me to life and I daresay, at my age, you'll feel precisely the same about your damned fields and dripping woods! The fact is, I've learned a good deal in the last few months, and perhaps it's lucky for all of us that I made that trip. I had my suspicions, mind you, but I have to admit that I was scared once I saw it at close quarters.'

'Suspicions about what? You've only been on holiday in Vienna, haven't you?'

'To get there I crossed Germany,' Franz said, 'and I was sufficiently misguided to stop overnight in Munich. A month or so later I stayed a few days in Nuremberg, and even in Austria I was able to confer with certain associates. The truth is, my dear fellow, the balloon is almost ready to ascend!'

'Damn it, *what* balloon?' said Paul, impatiently, and Franz replied, settling himself in the car and adjusting the impeccable creases in his trousers, 'Ah, I thought that would confound you! It's what follows from having your nose in the dirt all your life! I suppose you have heard of Hitler, have you not?'

'Well, of course I have,' Paul said, 'who hasn't? He makes more noise than the Kaiser used to but what of it?'

'What of it?' said Franz crisply. 'The Kaiser turned everything upside down, didn't he? And made you a small fortune into the bargain.'

'Are you trying to tell me you think there's danger of war?'

'Indeed I am,' Franz said, 'but a very different kind of war from anything in the past. There won't be anything gentlemanly about this one!'

'There wasn't anything gentlemanly about the last!' Paul retorted, 'ask anyone who was at Ypres or on the Somme!'

'Oh, I'm not talking about the actual waging of it, the mere fisticuffs part!' Franz said, with a blandness that Paul found irritating. 'I'm talking about the political aspects, the impact on Western civilisation as a whole! That maniac means business and unless we people wake up in time that disgusting swastika of his will fly in all manner of unlikely places; Buckingham Palace maybe! Oh, you can chortle, but I don't think you would if you've seen what I've seen this summer, or talked to people whose near relatives are actually populating his extermination centres!'

As usual Paul found himself impressed, in spite of private reservations that the old man was exaggerating. Franz was a Jew, of course, and he supposed that made a difference, for even Henry Pitts had expressed indignation of *pogroms* in Germany since the Nazi party had taken control, and yet, the prospect of actually being called upon to fight Germany again, had never cost Paul, or anyone else in the Valley, a moment's loss of sleep. He said, more soberly, 'Very well, Uncle Franz, what did you actually see? One of those idiotic rallies, with everyone goosestepping, wearing fancy shirts and shouting "Heil Hitler"?'

'Yes,' said Franz, without the customary spice of his professional cynicism, 'I saw that but I also saw elderly women and seven-year-olds scrubbing the streets and being kept at it by arrogant young thugs with dog whips! I saw whole Jewish shopping centres wrecked and looted and, in Vienna, I was infected by the panic of men I have known gamble twenty thousand pounds on a hunch and then spend the evening drinking schnapps and listening to folk music without so much as telephoning their broker! I have lived a very long time, my boy, and seen a very great deal. I have not lost my touch or my sense of smell and can still sniff powder a long way off. And even though I find it difficult to read small print without spectacles I can still recognise a vulture when I see one.'

He seemed abstracted during the meal they had at The Mitre in the Cathedral Close and reluctant to return to the subject but over their coffee, after Paul had given him the family news, he said, suddenly, 'There was a reason for my returning by sea! I couldn't bring myself to cross Germany again, not even to fly over it, you understand?'

'I can't help feeling you're exaggerating a little,' Paul said, 'for I can't imagine anyone, even the Germans, starting another war. Incidents and an occasional bickering, no doubt, with plenty of sabre-rattling and a financial crisis or two, but when it comes to the actual point anyone would think twice; three times! Anyone, that is, who was actually there and Hitler served on the Western Front.'

'Precisely the same might be said of 1914,' Franz said. 'I defer to you when it come to recalling actual conditions on the battlefield but someone like me, a man whose ear has been to the ground for nearly a century, doesn't have to read history books to know that in August 1914, no one, not even the Junkers, actually willed the war! It simply happened. All but the lunatic fringe were terrified of the actuality by the time the guns started firing themselves.'

'Aren't there enough of us to contain him?' Paul argued. 'What about Russia and France?'

'You can write off France! I've done business there lately and count myself fortunate I collected fifty per cent of my bad debts. As to Russia, there are plenty of wiseacres who think he'll turn East and if he did they would encourage him, finance him I don't doubt, but they would be doing themselves a very poor service. It's no more than a question of who is first. That man is after world domination.'

It was difficult not to be convinced by the old man, particularly when one looked back on his accurate prophecies of 1906, 1914 and 1929. He had forecast, among lesser catastrophes, the German Naval race, the World War and the Wall Street crash, when those in a position to know, people like James Grenfell for instance, had been hopelessly wrong. Paul said, 'Isn't there a way to head it off?'

'Yes,' Franz said, 'but I very much doubt if you English are realistic or ruthless enough to use the means at your disposal! You could blow Mussolini's transports out of the water when he gobbles up Abyssinia in a week or two. That might convince German financiers and chauvinists that they were playing with fire. The Abyssinians are barbarians, of course, but we might as well confine barbarism to Africa if we can.' His eyes, usually as bright as a ferret's, seemed to cloud and he looked across at a portly Dickensian waiter and a couple of clergymen toying with their fish course. 'You know, Paul,' he said, 'it's your world that's at stake, not mine! We people, the usurers of this world, learn to come to terms with these things but you never could. Win or lose you'll sacrifice all you managed to salvage from the last dog-fight – provincial peace and social patterns, a code of decent behaviour and places like this, that are the focal points of your out-dated civilisation. You'll be lucky if you don't lose your precious Valley.'

'How do you suggest I insure against it?' Paul asked grimly, for it began to dawn on him that Zorndorff's telephone call and his decision to break his journey, were no more than thinly-disguised manoeuvres to exercise the protectiveness shown towards the son of his old partner, a habit that had coloured their relationship for more than thirty years.

'I can tell you that, my boy,' Franz said, cheering up at once, 'you can act independently of that idiot Baldwin and any windbag who succeeds him, and set course between the present and Doomsday.'

'Well?'

'Buy!' Franz said, earnestly. 'Lay up the treasure of the fat years against the dearth of the lean! Buy all the pedigree stock you can afford and all the latest machinery. Build a reservoir at a safe distance from the house for reserve fuel, for fuel will be one of the first things to run short. Make yourself as tight and self-contained as Noah, who received his warning from a somewhat more infallible source, but above all, ignore anything you read in the newspapers about pacts and arms agreements and Germany being too poor to wage a war of aggression! Even over there plenty of people old enough to know better are depending on that and more still are falling into the error that they are still in the driver's seat. I daresay they were until a year or so ago but time doesn't stand still for people like Adolf Hitler. It's get on or get out, the same as it is in any competitive business, and nobody seems to have recognised him as that very rare phenomenon indeed!'

'Come again!'

Franz said, with his familiar, sneering smile, 'They do not recognise an Austrian who is uniquely free of the taint of *schlamperei*! I am such a one, and Hitler is another. Dangerous fellows both! Like an Englishman unhindered by tolerance, someone who would even cheat at cricket if there was a sizeable stake on the match! Well, it is time for my train, I think,' and he stood up, taking out his wallet and putting a five-pound note on top of the two-pound bill.

'I'll pay for this, Uncle Franz,' Paul said but the old man waved his hand.

'Certainly not,' he said. 'I doubt if I shall ever have the pleasure of lunching with you again,' and, to the hovering waiter, 'The meal was excellent! My compliments to the chef and share the change!' He swept out, past the two clergymen and the gratified waiter, and Paul reflected that for all his shrewdness he was still as vain as a mongrel who has confounded the judges by winning a first at Cruft's.

He drove home very slowly, pondering the old man's Jeremiad and wondering if, in the next year or so, he should plough his reserve (only just replenished after the drain of the slump) into building the fuel-tank and investing in stock and machinery at the County Show. 'Maybe I will,' he told himself, 'the old rascal was right about everything else but I'm not that much impressed, in spite of it all! At the age of fifty-six there's really no reason why I should be.' But then, as he looked up and saw the slender silhouette of French Wood on the skyline, he remembered that he had sons and sons-in-law, the eldest thirty-one, the youngest still a baby, and he hurried on, saying, 'Christ! Not again! Not after what we endured for four years at the hands of boneheads like Haig!' then, as the park wall began, and he caught the gleam of sun on the shallow river, he compromised, 'I'll buy, just as he advised,' he told himself, 'but as an investment in sanity not in suicide!'

He swung into the drive and blew his horn to give Claire warning of his approach.

Chapter Eighteen

I

Franz did not return to the West for Christmas. In mid-December Stephen wrote to say that the old man had gone into a nursing home and in late January, the week Valley radio sets broadcast news that King George lay dying, Zorndorff died in his sleep.

Paul thought it his duty to travel to London in thick, January murk to attend the cremation at Woking and when he returned to the old man's home in Sloane Street one of a small army of the solicitors Zorndorff had employed drew him on one side and gave him a letter Franz had dictated, with orders that it be handed to Paul Craddock after his death.

'He made a number of codicils to his will during the last few months,' the man said, rather resentfully. 'All in all it made matters very complicated! Up to that time his dealings with us had been very straightforward.'

'I daresay you were well paid for it,' Paul said, shortly, and the solicitor, regretting his unguarded remark, buttoned his lip and said, 'Oh, I certainly wouldn't like you to think we objected in any way, Mr Craddock. It was just that – well – we felt some of his last minute changes were rather impulsive!'

'Since you've told me this much you can tell me what they were,' Paul grunted, for he was always a little edgy in London, particularly when required to go there in winter.

'I . . . er . . . I think perhaps your sons are better qualified to explain that, sir,' the man said. 'After all, we handled his latest will but we were not his exclusive advisers. The Five-Year dispersal of the estate was executed by another firm. He only came to us when the partner of his regular solicitors died.'

Paul relented somewhat, reflecting that Uncle Franz must
have been a particularly troublesome client to men whose
minds ran along prescribed grooves and when he was alone
with Stevie and Andrew he reported his conversation with the
lawyer, asking them how much they expected to benefit from
the will. The boys were practically strangers to him now. It
was getting on for seven years since they had launched themselves into this bizarre world of scrap metal, golf tournaments,
mysterious trips up and down the country in bigger and better
cars, and hole-in-corner conferences with shady characters
who lived, Paul suspected, on their wits, and only just inside
the law. Neither Stephen nor Andrew had maintained any real
links with the Valley or, as far as he could judge, with any
aspect of country life that was not synthetic. They wore Savile
Row suits and smoked big cigars but there was still something
vaguely flashy about both them and their equally well dressed
wives, so that he thought with relief of Rumble Patrick and
Mary, in their snug farmhouse, overlooking the Sorrel.

'There's not all that much duty to pay,' Andy explained,
with a grin. 'Uncle Franz saw to that when he split everything
up a year or so after we horned in on the racket! It was lucky
for us he lived out the span. Stevie and I were made partners,
you know, but most of his capital was ploughed back in the
Birmingham and Liverpool branches and since then we've
opened yards in half-a-dozen other places. You might say
that what the Old Boy really left us was goodwill, bricks
and mortar. Plenty of it but not much cash. About five thou
apiece I'd say, wouldn't you, Stevie?'

'Plus legacies in trust for the kids,' Stevie said. 'They won't
have to bother, I can tell you that, Gov, so if you ever think
of making a will you can cut us out and no hard feelings.'

It was impossible not to respond towards the sheer impudence of The Pair, Paul thought, and he could readily
understand how the old buccaneer had taken them to his
heart.

'I'm not at the will-making stage yet,' he told them, 'but I
should be interested to know how the old fellow disposed of
his cash. He had hordes of Austrian relatives, most of whom

sponged on him for years, but somehow I don't think the hangers-on will benefit. The lawyer I spoke to seemed to imply he had had all manner of second thoughts after his trip abroad.'

'Yes he did,' Andy said, 'and he was damned cagey about them but from what I can gather he left a hell of a dollop to the Zionist Movement. He was very needled about what was happening to the Jews over there but, aside from that, I hope he didn't overlook you, Gov! You mightn't believe it, but he had a lot of time for you, even though, privately, he thought you were a bit . . . well . . . a bit set in your ways, if you follow me.'

'I follow you,' Paul said, 'and it's about the politest way either of you have ever put it! He left me a letter to be read after his death and I've got it here. I purposely didn't open it until I could share it with you,' and he thumbed open the stiff, parchment envelope, extracting a single, folded sheet, with an antedated cheque attached to it by a paper-clip. The cheque was for ten thousand pounds.

'Good God!' Paul exclaimed, 'this is absolute nonsense! I parted with what interests I retained in the firm during the slump!'

The letter was brief and very much to the point. 'My dear Paul,' it ran. 'I enclose this because, knowing lawyers, I realise that it might be a year before you get your hands on it. You can draw on this almost at once and, as I warned you, there isn't that much time! I don't suppose you followed my advice and stocked up but this may prompt you to begin. You ought to be a rich man in your own right but I know very well that you are not. You still might be, in spite of yourself, if you ever approach my age! It's my guess that in the years ahead land and property will skyrocket as never before and for all manner of reasons, among them over-population and slum-clearance by bombing squadrons. However, I found on getting back here, that I was in a very small minority. Few people take that little rascal any more seriously than you did. That's why I made some last-minute alterations in my will and left the bulk of my pile to those who are going to need a refuge few of them deserve! Despite your holier-than-thou judgment of me, my boy, I never really had much use for money *as* money. It was making it, beating them all at it, that was the breath of life to me, even in your father's time! One small thing; I had someone do a little digging in Somerset House after our last meeting and uncovered a little that explains your life-long obsession with mud, red necks, thatch, well-water and hairy forearms! Your mother's maiden name was 'Endicott' and she came from a Somerset village, either Curry Rivel or Chard, I was unable to determine which, although I daresay you could find out by checking parish records. She was born in 1848 but I couldn't get a copy of the birth certificate as there were hordes of Endicotts thereabouts. All I wanted to prove to myself was that you did, after all, revert to type! Good luck always, dear ploughboy – affectionately, Franz Zorndorff.'

He read the letter aloud and the twins listened respectfully. Andy said, finally, 'Well what do you know? He was an amazing old bird, wasn't he? But I can't help feeling that last trip of his threw him off balance a bit. After all, who cares about a bloody little whipper-snapper who used to hang wallpaper and bites carpets whenever he gets stoked up? Someone will bump him off sooner or later!'

'As a matter of fact the cheque isn't all that much of a surprise to me,' Stevie admitted. 'The last time I talked to the Old Boy he launched into a diatribe about the submarine fleet Hitler is building and how we should all be starved out in war. Damned funny the bats that start whizzing around in your belfry when you get to that age! There was that final instruction we found on his desk, the day the ambulance called for him.'

'What was that?' Paul asked sharply, not sure that he cared for their flippancy.

'He asked us to scatter his ashes in the boneyard,' Andy said. 'Can you beat that? Down among the scrap! Ashes to ashes you might say.'

'That's a revolting idea!' Paul protested, 'and if it was left to me I should ignore it.'

'Well, it was a special request,' Andy said, 'we've got it in black and white.'

'Have you told the solicitors?'

'No,' they said together, obviously awaiting a lead.

'Well don't!' Paul said. 'He was a wonderful friend to me, and although we seldom saw eye to eye, I had more respect for him that you seem to have! I'll take care of his ashes and I'll do what he advised about stocking up.'

'You mean you really fell for that stuff about war?' Steve asked and Paul said, no, he didn't, but he wasn't going to be caught off balance by another slump and it amounted to the same thing! Then they all took a drink, and felt better for it and the twins drove him to Waterloo in time for the five o'clock train. It was not until he had shaken them off that he could laugh at them, and as the train gathered speed, and the yellow-brick labyrinth was left behind, he re-read Franz's letter, finding that the old man's quixotic search for his mother's antecedents touched him more than the legacy. He thought, 'I'll drive over to Curry Rivel and Chard in the spring and take a look at those parish records. It's odd that I never thought of contacting Somerset House myself but had to leave it to him!' Then his mind conjured with expansion on the basis of the money. One could do a very great deal with ten thousand and it seemed disloyal to spend it in any other way, or simply invest it against a repetition of 1929–31. Two thousand would cover all the stock and machinery he could house at Home Farm and perhaps another thousand would provide a fuel-storage tank and pumping equipment, housed in the hollow on the western edge of Big Paddock. What could he do with the remaining seven? Some of it, he supposed, could be used to foster the co-operative that he had been nibbling at for years, a couple of heavy lorries, a combined harvester for the use of every farm on the estate, perhaps improved outbuildings, Dutch barns and modern byres at places like Deepdene, Low Coombe and Four Winds. That French Canadian, Brissot, and young Eveleigh could do with some help – he didn't know about Francis Willoughby and Henry Pitts, who had always preferred to solve their own problems but they were tenants and he was entitled to improve his own property if he wished. Periwinkle was the exception. It was being bought by Rumble Patrick over a period and already a third of the money had been paid over. Then, as the train glided into Salisbury, he had an idea, and as it took shape it appealed to his sense of humour. He explored it for flaws and could find none and by the time he had finished dinner, and the train was rattling into Paxtonbury, he was resolved on it and made up his mind that he would confide in no one but Claire.

He left the train and made his way in driving sleet to his car, setting the windscreen wipers threshing and settling himself for the sixteen-mile trip over the moor. It was fortunate, he reflected, that he knew every bend in the road for there were patches of fog wherever the trees fell away and his eyes were not as keen as they had been when he drove up to the artillery positions behind Vimy nearly twenty years ago. He was relieved when the gradient told him he was over the crest and dropping down to the river where the elms behind the park wall kept the mist high and comparatively thin. 'Tomorrow,' he told himself, shivering, 'providing Claire doesn't head me off, I'll ride to Hermitage with the news. Rain or no rain it's always a damned sight warmer with a horse between one's thighs!'

Claire did not head him off. All she did was laugh and say that she supposed he was interpreting the spirit of Uncle Franz's implied conditions. She did suggest, however, that Simon and Whiz should benefit to some extent, pooh-poohing his argument that he was pledged to Rachel never to give Simon money, even supposing he was willing to accept any.

'Nonsense,' she scoffed, 'Rachel has had time to outlive those high-minded notions! You offer her a little and see! As for Whiz and Ian, they don't really need any, but I won't have any of them saying we're showing favouritism. I know you always have done as regards Mary and that I did towards little Claire, but never as regards money. That's the one sure way to split a family.'

'You're right about that,' he said. 'Suppose we send them £500 apiece?'

'You'll have to do better than that,' she said. 'Rumble won't accept a penny if he thinks it's a gift. You'll have to make it appear a direct legacy from Uncle Franz to Mary. Get one of the twins to forge a letter of confirmation and produce it in a day or so.'

'I had something like that in mind myself,' he said, 'but not enough guile to put it into words!' and he kissed her, absurdly grateful to be home again and reflected that, when they were alone here, with all the older children grown and dispersed, and two-year-old John and the staff asleep upstairs, there was a tranquillity and timelessness about the old house that made him feel half his age.

He rode over to Periwinkle the next day, a mild, damp morning, with the mist lying in the bottoms and everything drooping and glistening in the hedges. Mary, busily baking her bread, looked ponderous but very fit and when he asked her if any precise date had been quoted she told him Maureen had 'pencilled in' St Valentine's Day.

'Don't let her take you in,' he said, 'she generally contrives to get things wrong. I was away from home when four out of my seven were born!' and he called through the covered-way to Rumble who could be heard swinging an axe in the strawyard.

'Come in for a minute, I've got news for you!'

Mary said, laughing, 'He won't like it, whatever it is. The one thing he really enjoys is chopping. Someone in Canada taught him to split sixpences edgeways and whenever he's out of sorts all I have to do is hand him the axe and lead him to the chopping block! In ten minutes we've not only got more than enough for the evening's burning but he's worked off all his bad temper on stumps.'

'I don't believe that boy ever shows bad temper,' Paul said, as they went back into the pleasant kitchen, where a great log fire burned and everything twinkled, and Mary told him he was happy enough most of the time but had been worrying over the struggle to maintain monthly payments on the farm, and also the fact that he couldn't expand as fast as he had planned without hiring another hand. 'He says farmers will never get a square deal in this country until they find a way to cut out the middleman,' she added.

'He sounds just like his grandfather,' said Paul. 'Every time I called on the Dell in the old days Tamer blathered about bankruptcy. When you're as old as me you'll realise this is no more than a built-in pessimism that the British farmer claims as a birthright! It comes from thousands of years' sparring with our weather!'

Rumble came in, his face streaked with sweat and said, nodding at Mary, 'She looks like a penguin, doesn't she?' and Mary countered with, 'Kick off those filthy boots! I don't want half the yard in here!' so that again Paul thought how easy was their relationship and how greatly it differed from the more guarded exchanges between Simon and Rachel, or between the twins and their sophisticated wives. He said,

'I've got a windfall for you; Uncle Franz Zorndorff left money to split between the family and Mary will get her share in a week or two.'

He saw them exchange glances and it seemed to him that Rumble's eyes sparkled.

'That's encouraging! How much?'

'Round about fifteen hundred,' Paul lied happily and Rumble's cheeks turned a deeper shade of pink as his arm slipped over Mary's shoulders and they stood with their backs to the fire looking, Paul thought, like a couple of children on Christmas morning.

'That was damned decent of the old boy!' Rumble said. 'I don't recall seeing him more than twice. Why didn't the twins get the lot? After all, they worked for him.'

'The twins have done very well,' Paul told him. 'They get the Empire and we get the leavings! He left us ten thousand on condition I spend half on the estate. I've earmarked five and the rest, less lawyer's fees, passes to Mary, Whiz and Simon. That was what he had in mind when I last talked to him and that's how it will be split!'

He wondered if Rumble suspected that this was largely a fiction and also how he would maintain it if Simon and Rachel declined to accept their share of the money. Rumble said, deliberately, 'That's terrific, Gov, but don't give us Mary's share, keep it towards the balance of the freehold and I'll make it up to her later. It will mean this place is really ours that much sooner!' He glanced at Mary; 'Do you go along with that, Mar?'

'Of course!' she said, 'it's by far the best way of using it. We don't want for anything right now and in a couple of years we shall be in the clear. Do what Rumble says, Daddy!'

They had, he reflected, outwitted him after all, and he thought how Claire would laugh when he got home and reported as much. 'There's at least one thing you can say about my brood,' he told himself, 'not one of them is greedy for money and that's something to crow about these days!'

'You're sure you wouldn't rather have it as a float?' he persisted. 'I'm in no hurry to be paid off and I never cared for the arrangement in the first place. I realise you want to be independent and I admire you for it, but you might just as well have stayed tenants until you got some capital together!'

'That's the way I want it,' Rumble said, looking very obstinate, 'for I don't care to be a tenant, not even with you as my landlord! If I farm land I've got to own it! Maybe it's something they dinned into me in the Dominions.'

'Very well,' Paul said, 'that's the way it will be. It will mean Periwinkle is two-thirds yours already and that's not bad going for twelve months.' He looked at Mary again. 'Are you determined to have the baby here? You wouldn't rather your mother made arrangements to go in St Theresa's, at Paxtonbury?'

'He'll be born right here!' she confirmed. 'Mother had all her children at home and Rumble was born in the Valley. It wouldn't be the same if he was born elsewhere, even tho' Paxtonbury is just over the hill, and now I must see to my bread!' and she went out leaving Rumble to walk him to the gate.

'I've had the telephone installed,' Rumble said, expressing an anxiety Paul had never felt for Claire, 'and Doctor Maureen looks in every day.' Then, with a diffidence that struck Paul as uncharacteristic, 'Do you happen to know Grandfather Potter's real name? I always meant to ask Mother Meg and never did!' and Paul, racking his brains, said this was a teaser, for he had never heard anyone in the Valley call the old man anything but 'Tamer'.

'Do you want to name your boy after him?' he asked and Rumble said, almost apologetically, 'Yes, I should like to but don't ask me why, something to do with your famous "continuity" I imagine. Do you think Uncle Sam or Uncle Smut would know?'

'If they don't we can easily look in the parish records,' Paul told him. 'I'll ride down there right away and ring through. What's your number?' and he jotted it down in the memoranda block he was never without when he rode about the Valley.

An hour later he was chuckling and when Parson Horsey asked him the joke he said, returning the register, 'I look like being saddled with a grandson called Jeremiah and I must say it's an apt name for anyone destined to farm hereabouts! Do you christen many babies with Biblical names these days?'

'Not one in fifty,' Horsey said, 'all the boys are named something fancy, like "Trevor" or "Bevis", and all the girls are named after film stars!'

Well, thank God we can shorten it to something manageable,' said Paul and rang through from Coombe Bay public 'phone booth to pass the information to Rumble.

He was there again in under a fortnight and for once Maureen had calculated the date accurately. The baby, christened Jerry ('Jeremiah is asking too much of family loyalty' Rumble declared) was born on February 14th. Mary was exhausted but delighted, and Claire said the baby had 'an Italianate look', having inherited Paul's narrow features and his parents' dark complexion. 'There's certainly not much Derwent about him,' she said ruefully, when she came downstairs, and Rumble had promised to add the name 'Edward' to keep the record straight. Then, Valley-fashion, they all wet the baby's head and Thirza was loaned as nurse for a fortnight, less because Mary needed her than for fear of giving offence, for Thirza regarded this function as an hereditary right and would have sulked for a week if she had been denied it.

'Well,' said Claire, as they drove down the track to the river road, 'I suppose you're satisfied now! You look almost as smug as Rumble I must say!'

'It's a matter of satisfaction to both of us,' he said, 'for it means that at least one of our children is anchored here. If young John stays put, and doesn't take it into his head to go rooting in scrapyards, or taking the world's troubles on his shoulders like Simon, then we're in business for another two generations!'

She glanced at him affectionately, wondering at the astounding durability of the roots he had thrown down since the day he had first ridden into High Coombe yard in his stained Yeomanry uniform, and she had handed him sherry and pikelets and held his hand a little longer than necessary. In some ways it seemed a thousand years ago and in others only a month, and as she thought this she experienced the familiar, comforting desire to be possessed by him as though it was twenty years ago. 'Maybe it's an instinctive awareness of the cycle caused by another birth,' she thought and wondered, even whilst laughing at herself, how she could get him to go to bed earlier than usual that night without making it obvious and pandering to his vanity, for even at fifty-six he was still inclined to parade his virility.

II

In the old days the ripples of the world beyond Paxtonbury seldom reached the lower reaches of the Sorrel. A few did, much trumpeted events, like the death of a monarch and the coronation of another but it was not often that Valley folk involved themselves, even objectively, in international topics. Before 1914 the latest titbit of scandal from the Dell could always be sure of winning more word-coverage in The Raven than, say, an Agadir crisis, or the latest Armenian massacre. The first international event that really captured the imagination in the Valley had been the war but even then not because Valley men were claimed and killed but on account of the invasion of the Valley by so many foreigners passing through the moor training camp and the convalescent home. After the war the Valley did its best to revive the policy of deliberate isolation, counting London, and the affairs of the Continent, well lost after so much cackling, scurrying and heartbreak. They were aware, of course, that all kinds of things did happen east of Sorrel Halt and west of the Whin, but no one, not even Horace Handcock (whose patriotism had managed to survive the General Strike and the Invergordon Mutiny) made more than a passing reference to events such as Lindbergh's flight of the Atlantic, the Saar dispute, or the airship disaster at Beauvais. Farm prices interested them, and so did sporadic outbreaks of foot and mouth disease, but events like the trials of Metro-Vickers men in Moscow, and the perennial squabbles of French politicians went unread. The Valley was like a tiny community in the hinterland of a remote island; everyone living in it was intelligently aware of what went on in the local capital but only vaguely conscious of events further afield, especially those enacted in places separated from them by stretches of salt water. Few people in the Valley took a newspaper other than the *Country Weekly* and not all that number listened, with much attention, to the news bulletins although there was a radio of sorts in most of the farms and cottages.

All this began to change rather abruptly between the autumn of 1935 and the summer of 1936 and Paul, whose finger and thumb never really left the Valley pulse, was the first to notice this and become aware of the end of a deliberate dissociation with the world outside. The realisation came to him quite suddenly one frosty morning in October, 1935, when he was hailed by Henry Pitts from the lower stretch of Undercliff.

Henry, riding his tractor like a Roman charioteer, saw him testing the ice in one of the oxbows of the river and called, cheerily, 'I zee that ole varmint be zettin' about 'em niggermen, Maister!' and somehow Paul at once knew that he was referring to Mussolini's attack upon Abyssinia.

He went across to him and they talked for a spell on world events and it was soon after that, in the public bar of The Raven, that he heard people like Smut Potter and the blind veteran, Willis, engaged in argument over the probable fate of the sad-eyed Negus, currently a fugitive on his way to Britain.

Paul's personal interest in world affairs had waned since Jimmy Grenfell's death. Jimmy had always kept him in touch with the broad outlines of what was happening outside but now that both Jimmy and Uncle Franz were dead he found himself less and less addicted to reading leading articles in *The Times* and the *Mail*, preferring late-night symphony concerts to the nine o'clock or midnight news-bulletins on the air. It was the voice of Adolf Hitler, that he heard by accident one night, that first made him conscious of his withdrawal and he said to Claire, absorbed in her favourite Priestley, 'Good God! Can you imagine a man who sounds like that running a country populated by chaps with as much sense as Old Scholtzer? It's fantastic! He sounds like a maniac in a fit!'

'What was that, dear?' Claire asked, mildly, dragged from the interminable odyssey of *The Good Companions*, and he said, smiling, 'I'm sorry, I was only thinking aloud!' but all the next day his mind returned to the phenomenon and although he spoke no word of German the speech had seemed to him to contain elements that a man could associate with the howl of the long-dead sheepdog of Preacher Willoughby, a dog that had caught rabies and had been shot by Smut Potter.

Then he noticed that others were equally concerned or, if not concerned, at least interested in the antics of the German Fuehrer and, to a somewhat lesser extent, in those of the Italian Duce and his eternal postures and extravagant claims to the Mediterranean, Corsica and Nice. Both of them became, in a sense, comedians, always good for a wry joke or a gibe, in a way that men like Stanley Baldwin and Ramsay MacDonald were not, for these men were at least recognisable whereas Hitler and Mussolini were not and seemed different even from such flamboyant characters as the ageing Kaiser, now reported to be chopping trees in Holland.

Then the Spanish Civil War began and circumstances combined to compel Paul to take a more than casual interest in world affairs, for one morning, when he was at work in his office, Claire came in carrying baby John and said, 'We've got a visitor, Paul. It's Rachel!' and when he said, with pleased surprise, 'Simon too?' Claire said Rachel was alone and wanted to see him at once. 'She's in the kitchen,' she told him, 'she was wet through, the silly girl! She walked up from the 'bus stop in Coombe Bay!'

'Why the devil didn't she ring and ask one of us to fetch her?' he demanded and then, because Claire looked worried, 'Is she all right? Is Simon all right?' and he got up to go into the hall but she stopped him, saying, 'I think she wants to talk to you alone. I'll take John down to Maureen for his inoculation and join you at lunch. She's agreed to stay on a day or so.' Rachel appeared, looking, he thought, not merely bedraggled after a two-mile walk in pelting rain but extremely unsure of herself.

Claire took her hat, coat and gloves, told her to stand against the fire and went out, carrying the protesting two-year-old with her. Paul said, 'I've forgotten, Rachel. Do you drink or don't you?' and Rachel said she would be glad of a whisky if there was one going and her clothes began to steam in the heat of the library fire.

'I ought to have had more sense, I suppose,' she said, 'but the fact is I just didn't think of telephoning. I've got too much on my mind and that's why I'm here!'

'Is Simon ill?'

'No, he's very well, or was the last time I saw him.'

'You . . . you've not parted?'

'No, at least, not in the conventional way. We've had a big row tho', the first in six years, and it doesn't make it any easier to reflect that basically he was right and I was wrong! But even if I climbed down it wouldn't stop him now. You might but I couldn't and that isn't surprising when you think of it. It was me who headed him that way in the beginning.'

He said, handing her a large whisky and soda, 'Sit down and take it easy. Where is Simon right now?'

'In Falmouth, unless he's already sailed.'

'Sailed where?'

'For Spain, as a volunteer.'

'Good God!' Paul exclaimed, deeply shocked. 'What the devil made him do a damned silly thing like that?'

She said, regarding him carefully over the rim of the glass, 'How much are you interested down here? I mean, it's common currency with us but I realise it mightn't be for you. He got it into his head that every able-bodied man who gives a damn about the future ought to stop talking and do something and, as I said, he's probably right! But after all, he's well over thirty and was almost certain to win a seat in Glasgow next election. I think he could do more good right here, fighting this non-intervention farce but maybe that's only my way of kidding myself. What really frightens me is the idea of him being killed or captured. It's a no-holds-barred war you know!'

'He must be off his head!' Paul said. 'What can he hope to do out there? One man, caught up in a war between two bunches of foreigners? What possible purpose does he think he'll achieve?'

'Solidarity of the Left I imagine,' Rachel said. 'That's what got him as far as Falmouth. There's an International Brigade forming, people like us, who think this is a dress-rehearsal for the Fascist take-over in Europe.'

'*You* think that, or only Simon does?'

'Oh, I think it, and surely it's evident, even to our home-grown Fascists, but that doesn't reconcile me to losing him. You remember what I wrote to you at the time we married? I said I'd do everything I could to make him a good wife and I seem to have succeeded too well. He's quite dedicated now, far more than I am or ever could be! I found that out when we argued about his going. I suppose you'd call me Frankenstein, of the rose-pink variety. In the last year or so I've paled but he's gone several shades deeper red!'

'How on earth do you think I can help?'

'I don't know really, I came here because I was . . . well . . . desperate I suppose. I thought you might hurry down to Falmouth before the boat sails for Bordeaux – that's where they're said to be congregating – and try and talk him out of it one way or another.'

'If you can't how can I? He thinks of me as an anachronism and always has!'

'He's got a very great affection for you nonetheless.'

Paul was surprised to hear it; mild respect, perhaps, in a slightly contemptuous way, but hardly affection. 'What makes you think that?'

'We were talking about it a night or two ago. What he admires about you is your consistency. That, and your genuine concern for the few people you think you can influence along broadly progressive lines.'

'The trouble with you and Simon and everyone else of your persuasion,' he complained, 'is that you slot every idea and abstract into a labelled bin and forget that politics consist of people with toothache, mother-in-law troubles and rate-summonses! I daresay I seem very old-fashioned to you but at least I've never overlooked that! And touching his mother I might as well tell you she's still very much alive in Simon and always has been. She seems to have passed on this . . . this mania for bannerwaving, like a congenital defect, like cross-eyes or a weak chest.'

He sounded so exasperated that she laughed and then he laughed too, adding, 'Listen to me! Preaching at you! I'll go to Falmouth right away if you can tell me where to locate him but only on condition you stop here and let Claire mother you for a week or two. Will you do that?'

'Yes,' she said earnestly, 'and I'll never cease to be grateful if you can talk sense into him.'

'I can't promise to do that,' he said, 'but I'll try. Of my seven children only Mary ever regarded me as anything more than an amiable fuddy-duddy. Maybe I should have been a bit more Victorian in my methods of bringing them up.'

'You did all right, Squire,' she said, 'ask my mother or anyone else about here!' and she walked across to the tall window and looked out across the dripping paddock at the distant outbuildings of Home Farm. 'It's odd,' she said, with an air of apology, 'a bit of me is beginning to think you might have been far closer to the truth than any of us – accidentally one might say, like a man who made up his mind to pursue a path even if it did appear to lead in the opposite direction! After all, the world's round isn't it? You might be the odd one who goes the whole way while all we short-cutters get lost in the woods!'

It seemed to him the most oblique endorsement of his policy that anyone ever stated to his face.

The directions she gave him were vague. Simon was supposed to be boarding a coaster in Falmouth and crossing to Brest where, if everything went according to plan, he would meet volunteers from countries as widely separated as Mexico and Bulgaria and travel overland to Bordeaux. Here a Republican coaster was scheduled to pick them up and take them on to San Sebastian. It was typical, Paul thought, of the sheer muddle-headedness of the Left, an itinerary based on hope, faith and slogans, rather than steamship tickets and a thick-soled pair of walking shoes. He found the coaster easily enough, a grubby little cockleshell called *Hans Voos*, out of Amsterdam, but the only man aboard her appeared to speak no English save the single word 'Okay', which he repeated, with varying degrees of emphasis, whenever Paul asked a question. He booked bed and breakfast at an hotel near the harbour, fortified himself with a couple of stiff whiskies and went looking for Simon but it was not until the following day that he located him through a wharf-loafer, who said the Dutch vessel was due to sail the following morning and that some young Englishmen had been recruited as crew. Paul never learned how the vessel had arrived there from Amsterdam with a crew of one, or what the ship was supposed to be transporting apart from British idealism.

Simon was in high spirits, looking and talking like a young missionary who, after innumerable setbacks, had just been given sailing instructions to New Guinea and promised the likelihood of being eaten by cannibals. He did not seem surprised to see his father, admitting that he had thought it probable Rachel would approach him in the hope of bringing about a last-minute cancellation of plans.

'I can tell you now, Gov'nor,' he said, 'that there won't be any change, although I appreciate your coming all this way for her sake. She ought to have known better than to involve you for, damn it, I'm thirty-two not seventeen! I know precisely what I'm doing and what's at stake.'

'It's my belief that you don't!' growled Paul, 'and frankly I think you're in for some nasty shocks once you embroil yourself in that free-for-all! Don't think I'm not on your side – in the general sense that is. I hope to God these chaps give Franco and his mercenaries a damned good thrashing and bundle them back to Africa but I think it's their concern, not ours, nor Russia's, Italy's or anyone else's! I've seen two wars and unless Britain was directly involved they could fight another in my stableyard before I'd join in!'

'But hang it, Gov'nor, this is a dress-rehearsal and how it goes will resolve the future for every one of us!' Simon argued although good-humouredly. 'We don't expect chaps your age to join in but how the devil can I preach solidarity against Fascism if I'm not prepared to peel off my own coat and take a crack at them? I tried to make Rachel see that, and she ought to see it, but all she could say was that I would do more good staying home and helping to organise public opinion against Non-intervention.'

'And I'm by no means persuaded she isn't right at that,' Paul said, wishing Jimmy Grenfell was alive to back him up. 'I'll grant you we've been drifting pretty hopelessly since the war, and that things are getting in a hopeless muddle one way and another, but if that's so isn't it the duty of chaps your age to become legislators rather than Robin Hoods? She says you would win your next fight at the hustings.'

'Suppose I did?' Simon said, bitterly, 'where would I go from there? I'm been stumping the country for six years and Capital is more firmly entrenched in Westminster than it was when you and old Jimmy Grenfell held the platform, in pre-world war days! We were getting somewhere then, if history books are to be believed, but we've been backsliding ever since and if you don't believe me look what's happening in Germany and Italy right now! Anyone with enough guts to oppose racialism and rule-by-rubber-truncheon is shot out of hand or sent to rot behind barbed wire! Have you really thought about the logical outcome of Fascism, as practised by bastards like Hitler and Mussolini?'

'I've thought about it a great deal,' Paul said, 'and all I'm saying is that insurance against that kind of thing happening here won't be bought by your death in a Spanish ditch!'

'Well, we must agree to differ I suppose,' Simon said, cheerfully. 'You'll wake up sooner or later and I hope to God it isn't too late!' Then, with a boyish grin, 'Would you like to meet the troops? Deckhands all, tho' I doubt if any one of them has ever sailed further than the Isle of Wight on Bank Holiday,' and without waiting for his father to accept this dubious honour he led the way to a ramshackle pub where Paul was introduced as 'the Gov'nor' to a group of piratical-looking young men drinking beer out of tankards and seemingly as full of missionary zeal as his son. There was a slim, pallid youth, whose clothes looked as if they had been borrowed from a younger brother's wardrobe, a squat, broad-shouldered Scot, who spoke with a thick Glasgow accent and was addressed as 'Tam' by the others, but the recruit who impressed Paul the most was a handsome young chap with a public-school accent, who said his name was Barnaby and had, Paul learned, interrupted his studies at Cambridge to sign on as a deckhand on the *Hans Voos*, which was the only legal way of leaving the country for the rendezvous in Bordeaux. The obvious sincerity of the group touched him in spite of himself and deep in his heart he envied their faith in their own convictions, their high spirits and derring-do. He thought, 'They're only a later edition of the young idiots who thronged into the Yeomanry after Black Week, 1899, and went off to fight Kruger, and I daresay they'll soon be as disenchanted with International Socialism as we were with Imperialism.' Then, glancing at Simon (deep in a dialectical discussion with the Glasgwegian and talking, as far as Paul could hear, straight from the textbook) 'I wish Grace could see him now! He's so very like her in her suffragette days, with the same passionate belief in theory and the same compulsion to put theory to the touch! Well, I only hope he's luckier than she was and neither rots in gaol or finishes six feet down on a Continental plain!'

Simon said, 'Will you stay and see us off, Gov?' and Paul said no, he wouldn't, because he had a strong suspicion that they wouldn't get further than the harbour entrance before a Government official came aboard with a court order and returned them to the shore. 'I'll bail the lot of you out if I have to,' he promised, 'but only on condition that you all go home and tackle whatever you're trying to do in a country where you can be understood from a platform.'

They seemed to think this was meant as a joke and certainly accepted it as one, thumping his shoulders and forcing him to drink another tankard of beer, as though he had been a parent conferring with daredevil prefects on Speech Day. Then he and Simon went outside and back along the quay to his hotel. 'It's coming in thick again,' Paul said, 'and it's a four hours' drive, so I'll say good-bye and good luck and try and think of something cheerful to tell Rachel when I get home.'

'Tell her to keep my candidature warm,' Simon said. 'I'll be back inside six months and you'll find out what it's like to have an MP in the family. You haven't said anything about Mother and the kids. Are they all well and happy?'

'Mary is,' he said, dolefully, 'but I wouldn't know about the others. Whiz seems settled enough with that airman of hers but they spend most of their time abroad. As for The Pair, they're still making money I suppose, spending most of it on their wives and the rest on the sort of rubbish everyone prefers to something worth having these days!'

'Well, cheer up, Gov!' he said. 'You look good for another thirty years as an eighteenth-century squire and by that time things will almost certainly have sorted themselves out a bit, even if all the surviving squires are in museums!' but suddenly his smile faded and he looked serious as he said, 'Listen Gov, I'll write . . . I'll write anything important direct to you, understand? I'm more glad than I can say I had this chance of seeing you and all I want you to understand is that I'm doing what I think to be right – what I think *has* to be done by some of us, some time, so why not now? Put like that I suppose it sounds like an attitude but even if it is it's my attitude and deeply felt! The minute I get an address I'll write and . . .' he stopped suddenly and came as near to blushing as anyone with his sallow complexion could.

'Well?'

'I daresay this sounds hopelessly sentimental but . . . would you have a photograph of my mother at home somewhere?'

The question startled him so much that, for a moment, he was too occupied controlling his emotions to reply. He had come down here prepared to be persuasive, angry, contemptuous even, but he had not expected to be ravaged. The boy might be thirty-two but when making that request he looked no older than on the day they sat side by side on a log near his school in 1917 and he told him of Grace's death in France. Simon was sensitive enough to give him a moment or two to recover and looked out across the harbour so that finally Paul managed to say, 'I've got several. Studio portraits and early snapshots. I'll pick the best of them and send them if you like.'

'Thanks!' Simon said and they shook hands, and after that Paul could not be gone quickly enough. He glanced in the mirror as he drove back along the littered quay and there was Simon, his raincoat fluttering in the stiff wind, his mop of dark hair, the same texture as his mother's, streaming out like a black pennant. Paul thought, 'God help us all, will I ever see the boy again? I very much doubt it, for it seems to me he's been heading for this all his life, before he was born even! In some ways I'm damned unlucky with my children!' and he drove into the rain, pressing up the central road of the peninsula at twice the speed he generally travelled. The open country on each side shared his deep depression, and he remembered the last time he had driven across Bodmin Moor, nearly three years ago, when little John was being born and he was half-way through that uncomfortable interlude with Claire. Well, that had turned out well enough, so perhaps this would in the long run. He badly needed a drink but decided not to stop and waste driving time for, as usual, he felt lost and lonely out of range of the Valley and almost envied Simon the companionable squalor of the forecastle of the *Hans Voos*. 'At least he has someone to share his convictions,' he thought, 'and that's more than I have, or have had since old John Rudd died! Claire and Mary are all very well but they're women and can't really understand, whereas Rumble Patrick, who comes closest to my way of thinking, is another generation and can't range back far enough.' The struggle, it seemed to him, was too long and too demanding. One ought, by now, to have entered upon an era of serenity, with little or no risk of switchbacks ahead, but the long hauls and the steep dips that succeeded them were becoming more frequent every year and used up far too much of a man's nervous energy. What was even more depressing was a conviction that, week by week almost, the struggle was enlarging itself, so that a man now had to worry about factors entirely outside his control, like this damned war in Spain, and the creeping tide of barbarism in Europe. He thought about the span of years before the world ran off its rails in 1914 – 'The Edwardian Afternoon' people were already calling it, as though it had been a marathon garden-party but had it? There had been the pleasure of working and planning within settled terms of reference but even then one needed the resilience of youth to absorb the shocks and disappointments of life. Grace had tinged his days with sadness and the element of strife within her seemed to have clung to Simon ever since. Then, when he had survived that breaker, the war had rushed down on them, and after that the stresses of the 'twenties culminating in the slump. One accepted personal tragedies, like the death of young Claire, and with them the ransoms of time, like the elimination of old friends and old partners, but lately – just when they seemed to be adjusting themselves to the post-war pattern – fresh shock waves came out of nowhere and a man was flat on his back again if he didn't keep looking over his shoulder! People like Henry Pitts and Smut Potter seemed to ride them without much trouble, and Claire had acquired the knack of bracing herself to meet every new cross-current but he couldn't, or not indefinitely; unlike them he was burdened with a sense of involvement that was at once a curse and an inspiration.

His sense of isolation joined forces with the wind-driven sleet that rushed at him across the open moor and he pressed on over the border like a tired fugitive on the run.

III

Simon wrote within the month, giving a Madrid address but no personal news beyond the fact that he was well. For progress of the war Paul had to turn to the newspapers and one needed a good deal of ingenuity to thread the maze of prejudice implicit in the reports. Even the names of the antagonists were interchangeable. To Right-Wing journalists Franco's Moors were 'Nationalists' and the elected government 'Reds'; to others, who shared Simon's dress-rehearsal theory Franco's side were 'The Fascists', or 'Insurgents', and their opponents 'The People's Army'. Paul hardly knew what to make of it and was still trying to puzzle it out when, in common with everyone else in the Valley who read newspapers or listened to radio bulletins, he was caught up in a different kind of civil war, one of words raging around the bachelor King whom everyone had assumed would replace his father in the days when there was still a real, personal relationship between Monarch and subjects. Here was an issue, he thought, that did not require Fleet Street guidance and Paul came down heavily in favour of the morganatic marriage to Mrs Simpson (whoever she was) and was mortified to find himself in the minority when the topic was discussed in the Valley. Only Henry Pitts and Smut Potter proclaimed their allegiance to 'The King's Party', whereas people like Marian Eveleigh, Thirza Tremlett, and even the former Potter girls (whom he would have thought could be relied upon to take a tolerant view) ranged themselves alongside Baldwin and the pharisaical Archbishop of Canterbury, Violet Bellchamber declaring, 'Us dorn want the likes of 'Er for Queen, do us? 'Er's been divorced twice and if he can't do no better'n that then he should bide single and vind his bit o' comfort where he can, zame as King Teddy did!'

At first Paul found this attitude amusing, especially when it was adopted by women who seemed to have forgotten their own carefree youth but as the crisis mounted, and the cleavage of opinion became sharper, their intolerance exasperated him and Claire, sensitive to his moods, called him to task when he admitted losing his temper with Harold Eveleigh's wife on the subject.

'You're getting everything out of proportion these days,' she told him bluntly, 'and if you don't watch yourself you'll develop into a real old griper in your old age! What on earth does it matter to you whether he marries Mrs Simpson or not? You never had much time for royalty in what you're now pleased to call the Good Old Days just because they're behind you!'

'I had a lot of time for him!' he countered, 'and it makes me vomit to hear people discard loyalties like sweaty socks! Damn it, there was a time when that chap was the most popular man in the world, and unlike most of his kind he bloody well earned it, trapesing all over the world advertising the damned country! I remember him in France too! He wasn't like all the other Brass Hats, warming their fat backsides at a fire at Supreme Headquarters. He did everything he could to get up to the front and the chaps loved him for it! Now, because he happens to fall for a mature, intelligent woman, everybody suddenly becomes a bloody Sunday School superintendent! I tell you, it turns my guts sour!', and he flung himself out of the house and took it out on the skewbald in a breakneck gallop across the dunes where, as luck would have it, he ran into Maureen driving her ancient Morris up from the red-tiled bungalows in Nun's Bay. Maureen had news that took his mind off the troubles of the King and Mrs Simpson. She braked and hooted the moment she saw him and shouted:

'Hi! Hold on there! I've just heard a rumour that will set tongues wagging! Sydney Codsall is flat broke and resigning his seat. Have you heard anything to confirm it?'

It was not quite true but had elements of truth, as everybody between Whin and Sorrel soon learned. Sydney's business associate, Tapscott, the builder, had gone bankrupt for what seemed to Valley folk the astronomical sum of £28,000, but it soon leaked out that Sydney, although partially involved, had saved his bacon by withdrawing capital before the crash. It was true that he was resigning the Parliamentary seat, won in 1931 but this, it seemed, was due to domestic rather than financial difficulties for his wife was suing for divorce on evidence gathered by a private detective, so that the Valley soon found itself in the Sunday newspapers for the first time since the wreck of the German ship off the Cove, in 1906. It made, as Vi Potter declared, 'tolerable gude readin'', particularly in one of the Sunday papers that featured a picture of Sydney's alleged mistress and horsefaced wife side by side, under the banner headline, *'MP flees Love-Nest by Fire Escape'* and below, *'Nude Woman hits Photographer with Table Lamp'*.

In the resultant scramble for details the King and Mrs Simpson departed for France almost unnoticed and Paul, never a malicious man, nonetheless commented to Claire that weekend, 'Well, he's been sailing close to the wind twenty years and was due to capsize! I wonder if Tapscott would be interested in an offer for what's left of High Coombe? It would be a feather in our cap to get it back, don't you think?'

She could not be sure whether or not he was joking so she temporised, 'What would you do with half a farm if you got it? They've already built all over Eight Acre and Cliff Warren. I don't suppose there's more than a hundred acres left of the original.'

'Periwinkle was smaller than that to begin with,' he said, rubbing his hands and looking so pleased with himself that she felt ashamed for him. 'There's no harm in getting Snow & Pritchard to put out a feeler!' and he left the table whistling between his teeth so that she thought, a little ruefully, 'He's hardening up! There's no doubt about that, and I'm not at all sure that I like it!'

Tapscott was only too eager to sell and before the New Year was a fortnight old the rump of the old Derwent Farm had been repurchased, a parcel consisting of the original farmhouse, some ruinous outbuildings and about ninety-five acres between the tail-end of Tapscott's bungalows and the

north-eastern tip of Shallowford Woods. Paul got it, he told
Claire, for a song – less than half the price paid to Hugh
Derwent by Sydney five years before, and not much more
than Paul had been paid by Hugh two years before that.
She drove out there with him one windless March day and
they poked about the farm and grass-grown yards, finding
that the old building was still in reasonable repair, Sydney's
agents having used it as an administration centre for the
caravan camp inland from Eight Acres. For all that the air
of neglect depressed Claire so much that she said, pointing at
the cracked and peeling paint on what had once been Rose's
stables, 'I wish I hadn't come. It's revived all my anger against
Hugh! I suppose we shall have to pull it down and include
what's left in Willoughby's farm.'

'Not a bit of it!' he assured her. 'I've got an idea
but it'll need time to work on. Anyway, I'm glad some
damned speculator didn't jump in ahead of us, for this
is like recapturing occupied territory. High Coombe was
always my private Alsace-Lorraine!'

He went to work at once, making an appointment with
Francis Willoughby that same evening and when Francis,
guessing why he had called, asked, 'It'll be about what's
left of High Coombe, won't it?' he said that unless Francis
was desperate for more pasture he had a plan that required
a sacrifice on the part of Deepdene and he would appreciate
Francis speaking his mind, notwithstanding the landlord-
tenant relationship between them.

They made an appointment and Francis was awaiting him
at the extreme southern end of his land when he rode up
from the Dell about ten o'clock the following morning. He
looked, Paul thought, about as unlike his father, Preacher
Willoughby, as was possible. The preacher had been tall and
spare, with a saint's halo of soft white hair, whereas Francis,
broad-shouldered and grizzled, looked precisley what he was,
a middle-aged man who had never had a thought unconnected
with cattle-rearing. He was short and square, his thick calves
encased in spotless leggings and a hard hat wedged firmly
on his round head, as though to advertise that inside there

was no room for frivolities of any kind. He was respectful, however, greeting Paul with the grave politeness that still lingered among the older tenants.

'I came downalong to saave 'ee the journey up to the house,' he said. 'My two varmints are upalong in the rickyard and they stop work if I bide talking to anyone!'

'It's about one of your varmints I've called,' Paul said, dismounting. 'How would you feel about young Dick Potter branching out on his own? I'm sure a chap with your reputation wouldn't have trouble replacing him.'

Francis looked blank and then thoughtful. Not given to making snap judgments he took his time answering.

'Dick's got the makings of a good farmer,' he said at length, 'which is surprising, considering the blood that runs in him but then, you can't judge by that, or not entirely. That Potter son-in-law of yours over at Periwinkle is a lively spark and may do well once he's outgrown his fancy notions! Where would you be thinking of zettling my cowman? On what's left of old Edward Derwent's plaace?'

'Why not? There's over a hundred acres if I threw in the sloping meadow that backs on the Big House. It's small I know but he'd be on his own, except for a boy if he could get one and I believe he's a good man with dairy cattle?'

'Arr!' said Francis, guardedly, 'he is that! Better than he be wi' the beef. If he hadn't been I wouldn't have kept him all this time!'

It occurred to Paul that this eastern side of the estate bred an altogether different kind of man than the west or south. Within living memory Edward Derwent, Tamer Potter, Willoughby Senior and now Willoughby Junior had all grown to maturity on the exposed side of the Bluff. Perhaps the eastwinds, sweeping across the Downs, had tempered them in a way that it had not tempered amiable families like the Pitts, the Honeymans and the younger Eveleighs.

'Dick Potter, by my reckoning, is twenty-six. If he stays on with you another year or so he won't want to shift and he'll be a hired man all his life. I've already had a word with Sam, his father, and he's desperately keen we give the lad a chance, Francis. I'd appreciate it if you'd part with him and forgo any hopes you had of enclosing High Coombe within your own borders. However, I'm not going to do more than put it to you. If you're opposed to the idea then we'll forget it and say nothing to him. You've been a first-class tenant ever since your father died and I wouldn't want to upset you. Take a day to think it over.'

'Nay,' Francis said, slowly, 'I don't need time to think on that. Tiz right to give the lad the chance, for I've not forgotten you gave me mine backalong. I can make do on the land I've got, I've managed well enough so far!' His last sentence was a challenge and Paul, recognising as much, said, 'You certainly have and there isn't a man in the Valley who isn't proud of you. Should I put it to Dick or would you like to sound him?'

'I'll do it,' Francis said and heaved himself off his five-barred gate, 'but I wouldn't bank on him accepting. There's a lazy streak in the Potters but us'll zee what us'll zee!'

Paul never learned what took place between Francis and Dick Potter, son of his woodsman, but the upshot of it was that Dick set about repairing the Derwent farmhouse and outbuildings and somehow contrived to find time to do some spring sowing on the neglected acres inland from the cliff fields. Paul and Claire went over in late April to see how he was getting along and found him with Smut Potter's lad, the impish, seventeen-year-old son of the ponderous Fleming, who had clasped Smut to her corseted bosom in 1917 and never let him go. Dick favoured his father, Sam, a tall, rangy young man, with the Potter trademarks of brown, impudent eyes, stiff unruly hair and bouncing, spring-heeled gait. Paul handed the new tenant of High Coombe his lease and learned that Dick proposed to specialise in dairy products.

'Not Friesians, Guernseys,' he told Paul. 'There's a big local demand for clotted cream in Coombe Bay and Whinmouth and it's growing all the time. 'Bonbon' is going to work for me, so he says, but I doan reckon he'll stay; he's always cracking on about Australia!'

Paul remembered then that Smut's boy was known in the Valley as 'Bonbon', a name derived from his mother's impatient response to all enquiries when she first came here, soon after the Armistice. He recalled also that the two cousins had always been close friends, notwithstanding the eight-year gap in their ages. It was comforting, he thought, to have two Potters at work in the Coombe area again and asked if he could see what sort of job they were making of the inside of the farm. Repairs were obviously rough and ready and Claire must have noticed as much, for she said, 'This is well enough for men who don't mind pigging it, Dick, but you'll have to get a real builder in if you ever think of marrying!' and Dick said, grinning, 'Bless you, Mrs Craddock, I got no time to think o' marrying now, and no one in mind either! I shall have all my work cut out gettin' this place in shape!'

'I've heard you young chaps talk like that before,' Claire said, 'but you all come round to it sooner or later!' and she looked round the big kitchen, adding rather wistfully, 'This is a place for children. Rose and I were happy here and if my brother Hugh had married at your age he would have been poorer but a good deal happier I think.'

She was thoughtful on the way home and it occurred to Paul that she resented seeing the old farm change hands but he was wrong, for when he asked if this was so he said, with a chuckle, 'No, I wasn't brooding on that! I was just thinking it's lucky Father didn't live to see it; if people really do turn in their graves the poor old chap must be positively threshing about to witness a Potter on his land! He feuded with them for years, remember? It was only old Preacher Willoughby who kept them from tearing each other's throats!'

'You can say what you like of the Potters,' he replied, 'but you have to grant them staying power! They were hanging on by their fingertips when I came here thirty-five years ago and look at them now! One grandson farming at Periwinkle and married to our daughter, two other grandsons reclaiming High Coombe and two of the originals still rooted in the Dell! Damn it, they practically dominate the Valley and I daresay it would have astonished old Tamer, bless his heart!'

*   *   *

The Coronation junketings that year were so tame, Paul
thought, as to be hardly worth organising. Everybody
went through the usual motions – public luncheons, a service in
the parish church, some tepid sports in the water-meadows,
and the ritual distribution of mugs to schoolchildren, but the
heart had gone out of the cult of royalty-worship and it seemed
to him that people found it laborious to light fire-crackers and
get drunk in honour of the new King. Victoria had been an
awesome figure, a kind of arch-priestess deputising for the
Almighty and even prompting Him on occasion, whereas her
son, the portly Edward, had been a man licensed to gamble
and womanise and hobnob with bookmakers without losing his
dignity. Then came Squire George, Vicky's solemn grandson,
and everyone respected his rectitude, even though he never
enjoyed the prestige of his father, and after that everyone had
been prepared to welcome the cheerful young man who had
outraged them by running off with a handsome divorcee, but for
George VI, perhaps because of his shyness and slight stammer,
there was little more than tolerance tinged with sympathy and
somehow this did not add up to reverence or even enthusiasm.
In any case, by this time the front of the stage was cluttered
with clowns, the noisiest and most grotesque troop anyone
in the Valley could remember, not excluding the Kaiser, who
had always been seen with an eagle perched on his helmet.
The clamour from across the water grew louder and louder
as more and more grotesques, with sinister-sounding names
and extravagant characters, claimed attention. There was Dr
Goebbels, with his big head and clumping foot, Goering with
his chestful of medals, Himmler, who was said to cause those
who displeased him to disappear in puffs of smoke, The Duce
(whom the Valley folk knew as 'Musso') with a chin that jutted
like a ledge of the Bluff but, dominating all, the ringmaster
himself, with his lank forelock, Charlie Chaplin moustache,
hysterical oratory and extraordinary reputation for gnawing
carpets when thwarted. Altogether an extravagant and totally
ridiculous bunch thought the Valley, and their opinion of Squire
Craddock's good sense dropped a point or two when the word
went round that he thought the nation was threatened by them

and was reported to have spent thousands of pounds on farm machinery and pedigree stock at the County Show, and also (could caution go further?) in digging a huge concrete-lined pit in the dip between the big house paddock and Home Farm rickyard, rumoured by some to be an air-raid shelter and by others a fuel-storage tank against the day when storm-troopers would come goosestepping up from Coombe Bay.

It was a combination of factors that encouraged Paul to prepare for the worst. He had never forgotten Franz Zorndorff's infallibility in these matters, nor the fact that even Franz's nerve had been shaken by his visit to the Continent just before his death. Then there were Simon's letters, full of a kind of desperate bitterness against the democracies for continuing the farce of non-intervention in Spain, when it was obvious to a child that the war was being won for Franco by Germany and Italy. There was also his deep distrust of waffling politicians like Chamberlain, who behaved like startled chickens in the face of any demand for a show-down but perhaps his most unnerving conclusions were those reached after reading books like Koestler's *Spanish Testament*, and other first-hand accounts of life in Spain, Italy and Germany, sedulously fed him by his daughter-in-law Rachel, with whom he had formed a regular postal-link since Simon had sailed away on the coaster, *Hans Voos*. Until then, notwithstanding the war to end wars, Paul's politics had been largely parochial and his overall policy had been to conserve most of his energy for use in a purely local sphere but now, as the months went by, he found his sympathies inclining more and more towards the militant Left and he began to wonder if, after all, there might not be something to be said for Simon's theories. When men he respected, like the dapper Anthony Eden, resigned from the Government in protest against a policy of weakness towards Mussolini, he found himself chafing under the smart of humiliation but he had come to realise that his anxieties were not shared among the Valley people, not even by men whom he would have expected to favour a stronger line at Westminster. Henry Pitts, for instance, openly laughed at his fears and made him feel a little like old Horace Handcock, the ultra-patriotic gardener, when he admitted the true purpose of the new fuel-storage tank.

'Giddon Maister,' Henry had said, 'whatever be thinking of? You dorn honestly reckon Old Fritz wants another basinful, do 'ee? Why, damme, I mind the poor toads I swapped fags with between trenches, the day us stopped popping off at 'em, and I dorn care 'ow much that bliddy Hitler rampages, I'd lay a pound note to a farden 'ee worn't get they into the firing-line again! They got more bliddy zense, I c'n tell 'ee! and as for the Eyeties – Gordamme, you baint zayin' youm scared o' they, be 'ee?'

Smut Potter, it seemed, held similar views but in this case they were fostered by the policy of playing down his French wife's anxieties regarding a resurgence of the hated Boche, who had already robbed her of a husband. Marie Potter was one of the few people in the Valley who shared Paul's disposition to fear the worst, as he discovered when he called at the Coombe Bay bakery on the morning soon after Hitler's invasion of Austria. She was building a pyramid of cakes in her window and emerged thinking his shout from the bakery was that of the representative of a wholesale sugar firm with whom she did business. When he saw, in the adjoining store, mountains of bagged sugar and remarked on it she only said, with a frown, 'It will disappear one morning and then, *poof*! No cakes! No business! No cash to carry to the bank! Today they are glad enough to sell it in bulk. Tomorrow they will sell it by the half-kilo, M'sieur!'

He talked to her of current affairs and was surprised to find that unlike himself, who was no more than uneasy, she was convinced that Germany would invade France within a matter of months.

'There is no doubt in my mind,' she said, 'the Boche will come seeking *revanche*, and my people will be the first to suffer; as always!'

'You've got the Maginot Line, Madame,' he reminded her but she said '*Poof*' again, as if the new fortifications were made of sugar-icing. He said, with a shrug, 'Well then, if they do come I daresay we will give them another thrashing. After all, we managed it well enough the last time.'

'At a cost!' she said, buttoning her heavily moustached lip. She had great respect for him, not because he was her landlord but because he had the Croix de Guerre, and she did not berate him for lack of realism, as she did every other Englishman who came here talking politics.

In the spring of 1938 news came that Simon was a prisoner-of-war, captured at a place called Teruel and Paul, learning of this through Rachel, who got it from a source she would not disclose over the telephone, asked what they could do to help the boy. She said there was only one thing they could do, contact the local Member of Parliament and ask him to make representations to Franco's people at Government level, for she understood some kind of machinery had been established for exchanging non-nationals captured by one side or the other. Paul saw the new MP without much hope but was cheered by the kindness and cordiality of his reception. Major Harries, MC, who had recently taken Sydney's place as Member for Paxtonbury, was a retired gunner and it might have been Ikey's association with the Artillery that helped for they had served together as subalterns in India, and later on the Western Front. Paul said, when he was introduced, 'It's only fair to tell you, Major, that I've been opposing your party all my life but I daresay you're aware of that already.'

'You're one of my constituents whether you like it or not,' said the ex-gunner cheerfully, 'so don't let's hear any more of that! I'll do what I can and be glad to! I've been watching that bloody business closely and frankly, irrespective of any political views your son holds, I think he's right when he says the Italians and Germans are flexing their muscles for something a little more ambitious! I'm in a minority up there, of course, just as anyone is who heeds Churchill's warnings!'

Paul found himself warming towards the man and over lunch at The Mitre repeated Zorndorff's warnings and spoke of his own modest insurances against war. The Major approved wholeheartedly: 'I was in Germany six months ago,' he said, 'and I was scared stiff by what I witnessed. It goes against the grain to be forced, on pain of being rough-housed, to have to salute that little bastard, but that's what happened to me while I was watching a procession in Bremen. I'll do everything I can to get your boy turned loose and if I'm successful I'd like the privilege of hearing a first-hand account of his recent experiences.'

Major Harries was as good as his word or better. He rang Paul within the week saying that contact had been established with the British Consul in Burgos, and that negotiations had already begun. 'Don't expect rapid results,' he warned, 'you know how long it takes a Spaniard to make a decision but we have ways and means of putting some heat on so maybe the boy will be home for Christmas. He's unwounded, I'm told, so that's something to be thankful for!'

Paul thanked him and 'phoned Rachel, inviting her down to await further developments, but before she arrived he had another 'phone call from the Member to say that a batch of about a dozen British prisoners were being sent home via Gibraltar, and that Simon might well be among them.

Rachel arrived the next day, looking close to breaking point Paul thought and Claire packed her off to stay with Mary at Periwinkle. There had always been a close link between Rachel and Rumble Patrick after Rachel had personally delivered the boy in Hazel's cave one summer evening, in 1913. She was still staying there when Simon arrived, weighing about nine stones and suffering from the after-effects of three months in a verminous Spanish gaol in daily expectation of being marched out and shot with batches of Basques and Catalans. He was stunned, Paul thought, by the miracle of his delivery and it was during their wordless drive across the top of the moor from Paxtonbury that Paul said, 'You owe your release to a Tory, Simon. He went to a great deal of trouble and wondered if you could find time to see him and give an account of what happened over there.'

Simon said, with a tired smile, 'Major Harries? I've already seen him. He met us and gave us lunch at Tilbury yesterday!' and when Paul exclaimed Simon added, stifling a yawn, 'Soon it won't be a question of Tories, Socialists and Liberals, Gov'nor, just for and against – those who oppose the clock being put back a thousand years, and those with nothing else in mind! There won't be any neutrals. Everyone here will have to step to one side of the line and that's what I intend to stress when I lecture.'

'Before you dive back into the mill-race you'll damn well get some rest and put on a bit of weight!' Paul said, gruffly. 'Rachel means to see to that and I intend to back her up!'

'Oh, sure, sure,' Simon said, 'I'll get fit first. That's obligatory if I'm to do any good, but I'm not "cured" as you might say, just confirmed! I daresay it sounds vainglorious but I wouldn't have missed it and I don't regret a bloody day of it! At least I've satisfied myself I was on the right tack. How about you?'

'We'll discuss that when you've had a good meal and ten hours' sleep,' Paul said, 'Doctor Maureen is waiting to give you a good going-over. However, just for the record, I'm on your side of the line and so are a minority of thinking people, although not many hereabouts.'

Simon looked across the Sorrel to the watershed as they topped the rise and began the winding descent to the river road. It was a mild spring day and the Valley looked patiently expectant, not yet in its uniform of spring-green but half-dressed, one might have said, in hourly anticipation of its coming-out date.

'I thought about this place a good deal while I was in Spain,' he admitted. 'You mightn't believe me but it exerts its magic on me as powerfully as on you, although maybe I'm too inhibited to make a fetish of it. It must have been a wonderful place to live in the old, carefree days when you came rampaging down from London.'

'They weren't all that carefree. We had our problems, just as your generation has. The main difference was most people were content with three square meals a day, a good night's rest and to leave it at that!'

'Ah! "Bread alone"!' Simon commented. 'Well, it's all the poor devils in Spain ask but there are plenty to deny them even that!'

'No!' Paul countered, almost savagely, 'not "bread alone" Simon! A man who wants to be more than a cabbage needs a dream to spread on his bread! Otherwise one might as well take one's place alongside the cows and wait to be milked night and morning!' And then, seeing Simon looking at him quizzically, 'I'm sorry, I made up my mind on my way over to meet you that I'd talk platitudes for at least a day or so,' and Simon, grinning, said, 'Well, that comes under the heading of a platitude Gov'nor but I'll not quarrel with it and I don't suppose my mother would have done,' and as they turned on to the river road Paul saw him fumble in his inside pocket and pull out a cheap folder containing the two soiled photographs of Grace he had sent to Spain a month or two after their parting in Falmouth. Impulsively he stopped the car and said, 'Let me look at those, Simon!' and Simon handed him the folder and sat silently while he scrutinised the pictures, one a faded snapshot of Grace in the rose garden she had created, the other a formal studio-portrait, taken on their Paris honeymoon, in 1903. He said, handing them back, 'Environment doesn't count for a damned thing! You're as alike as peas in a pod, physically and temperamentally! What's in the blood stays there!' and he let the clutch in and pulled back on to the road. They drove the rest of the way home in silence.

Chapter Nineteen

I

Simon and Rachel remained in the Valley until early summer but Paul was relieved they were gone before the Munich crisis set everybody (including constitutional optimists like Claire, Henry Pitts and Smut Potter) by the ears. They came to him one by one, freely admitting their misjudgments but when it was all over, and Chamberlain had returned waving his piece of paper, they joined the tumultuous acclamation of the man who had 'saved the peace'. Their complacency angered him, although he went out of his way not to show it. Instead he spent long hours in his office, planning, conserving, getting his stock records up-to-date and cautiously adding to his purchases of seed, chemical manures and machinery. His fear was now not so much that there would be a war but that there would not, that he was laying up stock against a day when the Valley lost its identity in an almost bloodless absorption of Western Europe. For that, it would seem, was the alternative that most people preferred, including those he would have classed as rebels in the old society.

He began thinking along these nightmarish lines after a discussion with Smut Potter round about Christmas-time. Smut, carelessly going his rounds, called to him one day as he was crossing Codsall bridge and said, 'Well, Squire, dree months ago I would have bet my favourite twelve-bore to a pound o' tay us would have been keepin' Christmas in they bliddy trenches but it's blown over after all!' and although it was no more than a casual greeting, of the kind that Smut offered to almost everyone he met between Coombe Bay and Periwinkle, Paul was sour enough to challenge him, saying sharply, 'It's a damned pity we aren't while we've still got a few twelve-bores to put to our shoulders!' and Smut at once lowered his van window, apparently to hear the news that had put so much grit into Paul's voice.

'You abben heard nothin' new, 'ave 'ee?' he asked. 'That bliddy Hitler baint jumped the gun, has he?' and Paul, mollified by the anxiety in his voice, replied, 'No, I've heard nothing new, but I daresay we shall soon enough!'

Smut looked relieved then and also a little sheepish. 'Gordamme, you put the fear o' God into me, Squire!' he admitted and then, in a puzzled voice, 'Don't you reckon us is over it? I had the bliddy jitters backalong but it zeems quiet enough now according to the papers and radio.'

Paul was tempted to stay and preach, to use Smut as a captive audience for his forebodings but he changed his mind, saying, ill-humouredly, 'Well that's very reassuring! I'll sleep a lot better for hearing that, Smut!' and went his way hands in pockets so that Smut looked after him with concern, wondering what factors were at work to make Squire so crusty these days, and whether his own wife, Marie, had infected him with her non-stop Jeremiads about *les salles Boches* but he was not left wondering for long. Winter passed and spring followed and with spring came the pounce on Prague, and after that Mussolini's grab at Albania, and in the confused weeks that followed they began to drift back to him, bringing with them what he most needed, a feeling of unity and purpose and comradeship, that made him feel less like a prophet of doom stalking the Valley and muttering of wrath to come.

Henry Pitts was the first of the prodigals, declaring that "Twas time us stopped the rot', and Harold Codsall was the next, sending his boy over with the trailer to buy chemical manure against the arrival of a stock he had ordered in Paxtonbury. Then Smut, holding forth in the bar of The Raven one night, declared that 'only Squire and his boy' had been right about what would follow Munich and word of this reached Paul the next day by Parson Horsey who confessed, sadly, that sooner or later someone would have to do something about Hitler and that whatever it was would be inconsistent with the charters of the Peace Pledge and the

League of Nations. But none of these affirmations brought him as much comfort as Claire's, who said one night, as they sat by the fire, 'Did I tell you I had a word on the 'phone with two of your daughters-in-law while you were out?'

'No,' he said, without displaying much interest, 'You didn't; anything new?'

'Yes there was,' she said, knitting her brows, 'and perhaps you can make sense of it for I can't and neither, it seemed, could Monica or Margaret, both of whom appear convinced that their respective husbands – our sons that is – have gone raving mad! They've joined the Air Force!'

He dropped the book he was reading and stood up with such a jerk that his Boer scar gave him a twinge.

'They've *what*?'

'Well, not joined exactly but put themselves on some kind of Reserve. You remember one of their crazes was gliding or flying? Well, now they go up every Sunday and they're both going on some kind of course for a fortnight. It's all to do with the scare – you know, flying balloons or something.'

'The Balloon Barrage?'

'Yes, that was it, that's what Margaret said.'

'Well I'm damned,' he said, subsiding, 'they are about the last two I would have thought to join that kind of outfit at a time like this!' and suddenly he laughed. 'I'm not laughing at them but at what old Franz would have said. I hope he's where he can't see them wasting their time fiddling about with barrage balloons when the price of scrap is at an all-time high.'

'What exactly *are* barrage balloons?' she asked, mildly, and he told her, adding that the very fact amateurs like The Pair had been enrolled meant that somebody was taking a more serious view than he had supposed.

'You sound very cheerful about it,' she said, and he replied that he was, in spite of all it might mean, for even a war was better than watching Europe taken over piecemeal and half the world enslaved without so much as a whimper on the part of the victims.

'You never used to think like that, Paul. You were always

utterly opposed to war, even when everyone about here was war-crazy in 1914.'

'It was quite different then,' he said, 'and it amazes me that everybody doesn't *see* it's different! I still think that last war was an act of madness on everybody's part – certainly continuing it after 1916 was – but there's simply no other way of containing that bunch of psychopaths. They haven't a damn thing in common with the Kaiser's bunch. Losing to Germany in '14 or '15 would have been bad but if we'd agreed to a patched-up peace after a year or so, it would have all been forgotten by now!' He leaned forward, earnestly, and she was impressed by the note of pleading in his voice. 'Tell me, Claire, tell me honestly, do *you* think I'm a nervous old maid laying in all these stocks and building that fuel-storage tank? If you do, then for God's sake say so and give me a chance to convince you!'

She said, quietly, 'No, I think you know what you're doing, Paul. I think you always know what you're doing if it concerns the Valley.'

'You've been in a minority of two then,' he said, but with relief in his voice. 'Only Smut's wife, old Marie, encouraged me at the time. You didn't! Why didn't you?'

'Why didn't I what?'

'Back me up, tell me I was right. I would have appreciated it.'

She said, levelly, 'You show me any woman about here with sons who is ready to admit, even to herself, to the prospect of seeing them face what you faced last time, or the possibility of suffering what wives and mothers like me and Marian Eveleigh and Elinor Codsall suffered all the time you were out there. No Paul, you don't bring it into the open, you go on pretending it's a bad dream that will fade out as soon as it's light! That's what I've been doing ever since Simon went off to fight in Spain.'

He pondered her confession, finding it not only human but logical. One was so apt to think of war as a man's business whereas, of course, it was not and involved everybody one way or another, not because the methods of waging war had changed with the introduction of bombers but because feather-distributing women of Gloria Pitts' type were rare. The majority, the Claires, the Marians and the Elinors of this world, seldom came forward to claim their fair share of the misery when their menfolk were lying out in mud under a barrage, or were home again, flaunting their medals and heroism. Usually, as in Claire's case, they kept their thoughts and misgivings to themselves, and tried to look interested when they had to listen to stories of blood and privation. This was the first time in twenty years he had ever given a thought to all she must have suffered during the period he had been in France. Was it any different in any other home in the Valley? He said, gently, 'You should have told me that before, Claire, but I'm glad it popped out!' and suddenly she was on the rug beside him with her arms round his knees, as though interposing herself between him and the pointing finger of Kitchener in 1914. 'You won't go again, Paul! You wouldn't? I couldn't face that time again, no matter what!' and he said, stroking her hair, 'Good heavens, no, I shan't go! How could I, at my age? Besides, if it does come there will be more than enough to do right here, I can tell you.' She nodded, eagerly, and he thought it strange that his reassurance, which did not include immunity for Simon, Stevie, Andy or her two sons-in-law, Ian and Rumble, should bring her such immediate comfort. Then he remembered what Maureen had said, what he himself had always suspected. She didn't give a damn about her children now they were grown and dispersed. All her adult life her eggs had been in one basket.

II

There had always been a rhythm to their relationship, a swing and a drift that seemed not to be governed by external pressures, or by their own impulses but rather the chances that struck high and low notes in the harmony of the marriage. A trivial misunderstanding might promote a period of coolness, a casual mental adjustment, such as that resulting from this talk of war, bring them close together again so that for weeks together they would respond to one another far more like lovers than man and woman who had shared a bed for thirty years.

In that final summer of the old world, or rather to world that had tried so unavailingly to resolve itself into the older pattern, they were closer than they had ever been since the long interval between the children growing up and the birth of John, now a chubby, mischievous child of five. They would sometimes take him down to the shanty where Claire would teach him to swim in the rock-pool where she herself had learned and Paul would squat on a rock at the mouth of the goyle and watch them, marvelling a little at her patience and also at the curious sinuosity of her body in the water. The thrust of her American crawl never ceased to surprise him and these days she was unencumbered by the heavy, serge bathing dress she had worn the day he proposed to her within shouting distance of this favourite spot of theirs. Her figure, he thought, had withstood the years and successive pregnancies astonishingly well. It was thickening about the waist but not appreciably so for a woman over fifty. Her long legs were still, in his view at least, the shapeliest in the Valley, her breasts were full but high and her behind, always ample, had for him the pleasing flow of a ripe pear, so that when he saw her stand poised at the deepest end of the pool, flash down into the clear water and forge the entire length of the trough under water he would gloat over her as some sensual memory stirred in him and sometimes he would select a specially bright coin from his hoard of memories and, as it were, hold it momentarily between finger and thumb.

He did not always accompany her there. He had work to do, although it was now confined, in the main, to checking his defences, like a conscientious garrison-commander anticipating a siege but uncertain when the first enemy hull would show over the horizon. There were times, indeed, when he doubted if there would be a siege, and then he would chide himself for a man who had let fancy dominate him but always, via newspapers, radio or the telephone links he had established with Simon,

Rachel and the twins, would come sinister hints and rumours that hardened his sense of purpose and then she would have to spend her afternoons at the pool alone with John, or in the company of the Lee Gibsons, an elderly American couple who had rented the tall Victorian villa once occupied by Celia Lovell and used as a penitentiary for the erring Bruce Lovell.

Cyrus and Myra Lee Gibson were of the select company of expatriates who, from time to time, strayed into the Valley and never found their way out again. The first of them, in Paul's experience, had been the old German professor, and since then Brissot, the French Canadian, and Marie Potter, Smut's wife, had been added to their number. Mrs Lee Gibson had allegedly come to the West to trace ancestors but her husband, a successful portrait artist (who, as a young man had hob-nobbed with the Paris Impressionists) had stayed on to paint landscapes, confessing himself fascinated by the quality of light in and around the Valley which, in high summer, was the nearest British equivalent to his native Arizona and in early autumn reminiscent of the filtered sunlight of Provence. Paul did not take these compliments seriously, recognising Cyrus as a dabbler in everything but portraiture but both he and Claire had become attached to the old couple. They had no family of their own and made favourites of young John and Mary's son, Jerry, who was often dumped on his grandmother for the afternoon.

During a spell of hot May weather Claire was down here every day and one blazing afternoon, when she had ordered the children out of the pool and was standing with her back to the goyle drying her hair, Lee Gibson hailed from beside the shanty, calling 'Hold it! Don't move, gal!' and she thought he was taking a snapshot but when she went up the beach saw he was touching up a series of charcoal sketches, all of herself in various postures in and about that rock-ledge.

'Can't you find a better model than a grandmother playing Nannie to a couple of toddlers?' she joked but he said, adding a touch here and there, 'I think we've hit on something! Myra thinks so, too. If you're interested we could build on it. Come up to the cabin and see for yourself. Myra will watch over the children,' and he led her into the shanty which Paul let him use as a studio whenever he worked west of the Bluff.

She was astonished at what she saw propped against the empty grate – a full-length portrait, two-thirds completed, of herself, seated on a spur of rock casually engaged in drying herself with a blue towel. He had caught her in a moment of abstraction, half-facing the Channel seen in the right background, with her shoulder-length hair tousled and bunched by the upward thrust of her right hand, and the sun playing strongly on her half-exposed breast and loosely braced thigh. The picture had a quality that was rare, a kind of breadth and freedom so often absent from a posed portrait, and it pleased her enormously not only because it was an excellent likeness but because some good fairy had enabled him to bring out her vitality and with it a strong echo of her youth. She said, throwing modesty aside, 'Cyrus, it's wonderful! It makes me look – well – not more than forty! And nobody could say it wasn't me; you've been gallant enough to slant it so that I look ten stone instead of getting on for twelve!' and she was so flattered and excited that she kissed him, saying, 'Does Paul know? Have you shown it to him yet?'

'Certainly not! For one thing it isn't finished and you'll have to pose in here for the final touches; for another I'm not at all sure he'd approve of an uncommissioned semi-nude of his wife. He's old-fashioned enough to hound me out of the Valley for taking such a liberty!'

'He'll love it!' she declared, and then, 'Look here, his birthday is next week. Could you finish it by then?'

'With your co-operation I could,' he said and she could see that he was pleased with her enthusiasm. 'I'll cover it now. If the children see it they'll go running to him and I take it you want to surprise him?'

'Yes, I do and I will!' she said, helping him to drape it with a sheet and told him of a day long ago, when they were lean and young and vain, and Paul had proposed having her painted in oils by a London artist but somehow the project had been shelved and forgotten. 'We've left it rather late,' she said ruefully, 'for I think I was worth painting in those days!'

'You're worth it now in my eyes and his,' he reassured her, 'in mine because your figure is more interesting that it was then – and if you doubt it take a look at Renoir's "Anna" – and in his because you haven't changed at all, my dear! I happened to see him looking down at you when you were streaking across that pool a day or so ago and, quite frankly, it struck me that his mouth was watering! So there you have it!'

It was a thought to cheer her all the way home and prompt her to do something she did infrequently these days which was to change for high tea, wondering if he would notice. To her relief he did, for although he made no comment she heard him telling Mary on the 'phone that 'Mother had got herself up' as a dress-rehearsal, no doubt, for the family reunion on the occasion of his birthday next week when, for the first time in years, they would reassemble at Shallowford and drink champagne sent on in advance by the twins.

On the last day of May, the day prior to his sixtieth birthday, they began to drift in from the North, the Midlands and Camberley, where Whiz and her husband were currently based, and it was after the last of them had arrived, and they had retired bemused by talk and bustle, than she warned him not to expect his birthday present from her until the children had gone. When, unsuspecting, he enquired if it was coming by post she blushed and her moment of confusion intrigued him, so that he said:

'What are you driving at? Do you mean you would prefer the children not to see it?'

'Not exactly,' she stammered, 'I don't mind them seeing it once it's – well – once it's *established* but it would embarrass me very much if they realised it was a birthday gift. You'll understand when you see it.' He sat on the edge of the bed scratching his head and looking so completely baffled that she laughed, saying, 'I'll tell you what! It's past midnight so have it now! But you must give me your word of honour you won't go whooping downstairs with it, won't even refer to it in front of them!'

His curiosity was now so engaged that he would have promised anything, so she went along the passage to the room that had been Jimmy Grenfell's and came back carrying a package measuring about four feet by three carefully tied in brown paper and sacking. He cut the string with her nails scissors and his expression when the canvas was revealed, was worth all the self-doubts she had suffered since entering into the conspiracy with Cyrus. He propped it against the dressing-table and stood back studying it from every angle. Then he moved it so as to catch the beside light and walked cautiously round it, as though he was playing Peeping Tom on a bathing beach. Finally he said, sombrely, 'It's a bloody miracle! He's seen you not only as you *are* but as you always *were*! I've never looked at a picture so alive and exciting! It's got everything I ever saw in you, from the day you took me swimming there over thirty years ago! It's the most wonderful birthday present you've ever given me, that anyone's ever given me!' and he threw his arms round her and kissed her in a way that convinced her that the instinct that had prompted the gift had been as accurate as were most of her instincts concerning him.

'Where are we going to hang it?' he demanded.

'Not downstairs certainly,' she said. 'Everyone who comes into the house will make that awful music-hall joke about dressing mutton to look like lamb. It's – well Paul – it's a very *private* present, and I certainly don't want it on exhibition! It was just an idea I had the moment I saw it half-done and it seems to have worked, so that's all I care. Hang it in your dressing-room.'

He studied it again, so carefully that she said, laughing, 'For heaven's sake, Paul, you've got the original right here! If you look at it much longer with that leery expression I shall begin to think it's idealised and you're reminiscing!'

'It isn't in the least idealised,' he said, seriously, 'it's a melting-pot of everything about you that has made me look at other women objectively rather than subjectively all the years we've been married! And I'll tell you something else too, if it flatters you!'

'It'll flatter me,' she promised.

'I've led a pretty active life and therefore I've always had plenty to do and mostly have enjoyed doing it but every time you walk into a room I find myself wishing everybody else would walk out of it! Every time I touch you I get the impression of physical renewal and that must be a very rare tonic for a man my age! I can't expect it to last into my seventies, so I'm damned if I don't hang this picture over the bed where I hope it'll keep me from flagging as time runs on!'

'When you flag in that respect I'll 'phone Jonas Whiddon, the undertaker,' she said, chuckling, 'for you'll be ready for him! Now get me out of this party dress so that I can breathe freely again!' and she stood while he unhooked her, reflecting that the strictures she had endured to look as slim and young as possible that evening had been largely unnecessary, for she did not really care a curse what the assembled children thought of her figure and, as far as he was concerned, the picture seemed to have provided him with ample excuse to turn the calendar to the wall.

They were awakened early next morning by a stir below the window and Claire, who could slough off morning drowsiness in a matter of seconds, jumped out of bed and took a peep through the curtains, retiring promptly when confronted with Henry Pitts' melon-slice smile. She said, scrambling into her dressing gown, 'Wake up, Paul! Henry and some of his cronies are outside!' and she shook him so that he sat up, rubbing his eyes and grumbling that it was still too early to get up.

'It's twenty minutes to seven,' she told him, seizing a comb and struggling with her hair, 'and maybe you can tell me why half the Valley is milling about outside our front door! I came within an inch of making a Lady Godiva bow to them!'

'They couldn't have noticed or they would have cheered,' he said and went yawning to the window where, seeing Henry's upturned face, he called down, 'What's up, Henry? Trouble somewhere?'

'No trouble, Maister,' Henry called back, 'but the top o' the marning to 'ee, an' the missis too!' Then, turning to Smut Potter close by he called, 'Tell Mark to bring 'un out, Smut! Let the gentleman zee the rabbit!' and there was a prolonged stir behind the rhododendron clump and Claire, joining Paul at the window, recognised Harold Eveleigh, Rumble Patrick, Farmer Brissot, Jumbo Bellchamber, and, standing a little apart, Francis Willoughby and Dick Potter. As they stared down Mark Codsall emerged from behind the shrubbery leading an unsaddled grey some seventeen hands high and of a build that reminded Claire instantly of old Snowdrop, the well-mannered gelding Paul had ridden about the Valley from the day of his arrival until the early 'twenties. Paul must have noticed the resemblance too for he exclaimed, 'My God! It's Snowdrop's ghost! Where do you suppose they got him and why . . . ?' and then the significance of the assembly dawned on him as he saw her laughing and Henry shouted, 'Come on down, just as you be, Squire! Us baint leavin' without drinking your health an' me, Smut an' Mark have been up an' about zince daylight!'

Paul withdrew, lost for words, blundering round the wrong side of the bed in search of his slippers. She found them, pushed him down on the bed and slipped them on his feet as though he had been a boy late for school, saying, 'I'll stay and get dressed but you go right on down! I can't feed that lot at short notice!' and she hustled him out and slammed the door so that he stood bewildered for a moment before going down through the kitchen and into the stable-yard, where the big grey now stood, surrounded by more than a dozen of them with its rope halter held by Mark Codsall, Shallowford's groom-handyman.

Some of them, he thought, looked vaguely embarrassed but this number included neither Henry Pitts nor Smut, who stood close together, clearly enjoying the occasion. Henry said, 'Tiz the nearest us could come to old Snowdrop, Maister! Didden seem right somehow, you ridin' about the Valley on that bottle-nosed skewbald o' yours, so when Smut zeed this one at Bampton Fair us clubbed together and sent Smut to buy 'un! He got ten pound off what they were asking but us knowed he would, the bliddy old thief!'

'He's rising eight,' Smut said, 'but well-mannered. I knows that because I rode 'un all the way home, just to make sure that nagsman at Bampton weren't lying when he said 'er was traffic-broken! On'y think he shied at was a bliddy motor-bike doing nigh on seventy mile an hour! He's been out two seasons with the Eggesford Hunt, so I reckon us have catched a bargain one way and another! He'll go, mind you, and I daresay he can jump too, but seein' you baint so young as you were us zettled for a soft-mouth and easy temperament!'

'You *all* had a hand in it?' Paul said at length. 'Everyone here?'

'Giddon no,' Henry said, 'us baint all here! There was nigh on fifty subscribed and I got a list here if you can read my writing!' and he presented a soiled sheet of foolscap, containing a long list of names, each of them familiar and representing not only the tenants but all the local craftsmen, men like old Aaron Stokes and Abe Tozer's son. Goss, the new sexton, had contributed and so had Willis, the blind wheelwright, and there were a couple of names from outside the Valley, Ben Godbeer, the Paxtonbury seedsman, and ex-Police Sergeant Price, long since retired, from Whinmouth.

He was too moved to make adequate response but they seemed to understand his confusion and silently made way for him as he walked round the gelding, noting a broad back and heavy quarters proclaiming it a stayer who would carry him over rough ground all day and still be good for a turn of speed towards dusk. It was, he thought, one of the best all-rounders he had ever seen and he did not need to be told it had good manners. Even Snowdrop would have stood chafed at standing unsaddled in the midst of such a crowd, all of them strangers.

He said, quietly, 'He's magnificent, and I can't thank you all enough. It's . . . it's quite the kindest thing anyone ever did for me . . .' and he trailed off, feeling that anything he said in the way of acknowledging their loyalty and generosity would sound trite. Henry came to his rescue with — 'Put 'un away in the loose-box, Mark boy! Let's drink Squire's health and get about our buziness!' and they all trooped into the kitchen where Claire was drawing tankards of ale and The Pair and Simon were on hand to serve them, each of his sons displaying a jocularity suitable to the occasion. Then they drank his health, mercifully without speeches and presently, after wishing him Many Happy Returns, they drifted away so that he was left alone with Simon who said, with a smile, 'I wouldn't have missed that, Gov! It was quite something in this day and age!' and Paul, automatically collecting tankards and piling them into the sink, agreed that it was but he could find no words to convey to the most perceptive of his children the warmth of the glow in his heart but went quietly upstairs to shave, glad of an excuse to take his time over dressing. 'Some of the older ones used to say there were compensations in passing the sixty-mark,' he reflected, 'but I never believed them until this moment,' and he paused in the act of scraping his chin with the open razor he had bought in Cape Town on his twenty-first birthday and glanced out of the little window across the fields, already shimmering in the morning heat-haze. 'I've got this place by the tail at last,' he thought, 'and it's taken me close on forty years to do it! They would never have done a thing like that for the Lovells and I'm damned glad all the children were here to see it!' He wiped the lather from his face and looked hard at himself in the glass, noting the mop of iron-grey hair and brown, lined face that now had a permanent 'Tudor look'. He wondered if the marks of the struggle were as obvious to others as they were to him and then, lowering his glance, noted with satisfaction that he had no paunch, that his body looked more youthful than his face. He pulled on boots and breeches and drifted into the bedroom, hearing the babel from below as his family assembled for breakfast but feeling no immediate inclination to join them. He threw wide the window sniffing the air like a pointer, playing his old game of identifying its components – dew-soaked grass, clover, the scent of roses from Grace's sunken garden and the overall tang of the sea. Well, there it was, looking precisely as it had looked when he first came here limping from the effects of a Boer bullet and as it had looked on all his other birthdays. Many of them he had forgotten but he could remember the notches of successive decades – the day he was thirty for instance, when he and Claire had taken the eight-months-old twins to Coombe Bay in the waggonette and the day he was forty, when he had ridden alone up to the spur of Hermitage Wood and picked the spot for the memorial plantation. On his fiftieth birthday, just before the twins' coming-of-age, he had gone the rounds with old John Rudd, bless his heart, and now that he was sixty they roused him from bed to present him with a hunter that reminded them of Snowdrop, thus underlining the fact that they too, in their way, clamoured for continuity. He looked from the rumpled bed to Claire's portrait, still leaning against the dressing-table, and the memory of last night's frolic made him smile. He didn't feel sixty and he didn't act sixty but then, why should he, with a fine woman like her in his arms and the Valley calling to him outside? And as he thought of Claire and the Valley in relation to one another he reminded himself that they were indivisible, that the vitality they fed him sprang from the same source. The knowledge that it was there, would always be there, put a spring in his step as he went along to the head of the stairs listening to the clatter-clatter from the dining-room. A verse occurred to him and he fumbled for it as he went down to the hall – something of Hardy's that he had read recently and had memorised because it seemed to him to epitomise the life he and Claire had shared in this house and would, he supposed, continue to share throughout their remaining years:

> 'When down to dust we glide
> Men will not say askance,
> As now; "How all the countryside
> Rings with their mad romance!"
> But as they graveward glance
> Remark; "In them we lose
> A worthy pair, who helped advance
>   Sound parish views."'

Dullish and perhaps a little pie-faced, he thought, smiling at his vanity, but an apt epitaph for both of them. 'Sound Parish views!' No more and no less. It was about all he had ever striven after.

III

It seemed to him, as he watched them all at supper that night, that the tensions of the world were reproduced round his own dining-table. On the left sat Simon and Rachel and on the right the conventional Whiz and her rather stuffy husband, Ian. Simon would be thinking, perhaps, of pitiful processions of fugitives and refugees trudging ahead of the victorious Fascists in Spain, whereas Whiz and Ian, if they thought of Spain at all, would dismiss it as none of their business. In between were his other children, The Pair, who almost certainly regarded the prospect of a collision with Hitler as a tremendous lark, and Rumble and Mary, who, like himself, would see their contribution to any struggle for survival in efforts to coax the last blade of wheat from Valley soil. Nobody discussed politics, Simon having been briefed by Claire to keep his views to himself lest they should promote strife between him and his brother-in-law, Ian. The atmosphere remained cordial but the tension was there all right, as he could see when they listened to the nine o'clock news-bulletin. When they broke up and went their several ways the next morning he had a brief word with Simon, whose opinions he valued, but he took care to do it out of earshot of the others. It was Simon, in fact, who promoted the conversation while he stood waiting for Rachel to bring their single hand-grip down.

'It will be a long time before we're all here together again, Gov'nor,' he said, watching The Pair stow their wives' luggage in the boot of the big Wolseley. 'Fact is, I doubt if it'll ever happen, for the whole damned lot of us are standing on a fused bomb. I gather, however, that you are one of the few who admits as much.'

'Yes Si, I admit it and have done for some time but I don't think Ian and Whiz do, and I don't think The Pair regard it as anything more than an excuse to play with balloons at weekends. Could you give an approximate date to it?'

'No,' Simon told him, 'and neither could anyone else but it shouldn't be long now. That mad bastard Hitler has to keep moving in the same direction and Franco's triumph will encourage him to prod us that much harder! I never thought of myself as a man who would look forward to flashpoint but delaying it isn't going to help.'

'What will you do when it does come? Have you made any plans?'

'I shall join the foot-sloggers, I suppose,' Simon said, 'the RAF is too jazzy for me, I'm afraid.'

'Could you get a commission?'

'I wouldn't have one as a gift. In any case, my International Brigade associations would put paid to that. They might be compelled to fight Fascists but, taken all round, they prefer them to Bolshies!'

Paul said, without challenging the dubious logic of this, 'If it does happen would you like Rachel to come here for the duration? She grew up on a farm and could make herself very useful, both to me and Rumble Patrick.'

'Yes,' he said, brightening a little, 'I'd like that very much,' and as Rachel appeared with Monica and Margaret he gave Paul a swift grin and added, 'So long, Gov! You're a spry sixty and I doubt if any of us will make it without a bath chair!' It was meant as a joke, Paul thought, but to a man like himself, who had seen thousands of shattered men occupying invalid carriages in two wars, it was singularly unfunny. He watched them drive off, all six of them piled into Stevie's car and the girls squealing as Stevie, ever a madcap driver, careered round the sharp bend of the drive and skidded a couple of feet on the canting gravel. Then Whiz and Ian said their good-byes and after that Mary and Rumble wandered off hand in hand across the orchard, moving slowly like a couple of village lovers.

'Well,' said Claire, and he could not miss the note of thankfulness in her voice, 'That's that until Christmas, I suppose!' and he replied, slipping his arm around her, 'Let's hope so at all events. Glad as I am to have them all under one roof occasionally, a little goes a long way!' but he said this because he knew she needed his corroboration. Secretly he felt a little sad, even frightened, for it occurred to him that although nothing was likely to occur until the harvest was gathered all

over Europe, a lot could happen between the end of August
and the first snow. Harvest-thanksgiving, he recalled, was the
traditional season of war, always providing mountebanks like
Adolf Hitler followed traditions.

Even then he was caught on the hop; not quite as ludicrously
as in August 1914 but ludicrously enough, after all his months
of planning and worrying. Either he had resigned himself to
another Munich, or Simon and Rachel had laid too much stress
upon Hitler's hatred of Communism. Or perhaps, like Henry, he
found it very difficult to believe that a generation of Germans
who had shared the mud of Passchendaele would actually start
another war. He had relaxed during July and early August but
when Hitler began to threaten Poland he called a meeting of the
Valley co-operative and laid his plans before them in detail, a
pooling of resources on a scale not even practised in 1917, and
every farm in the area, tied and freehold, operating as a unit
under a standing committee composed of Brissot, Honeyman,
Harold Codsall, David Pitts, Willoughby and himself. He had
invited Felton, the county agricultural adviser, to attend the
meeting and Felton was impressed, 'phoning later to say that
he would appreciate Paul's co-operation in fostering similar
co-operatives north and east of Paxtonbury. By then, however,
the harvest was upon them and because the weather was
patchy everyone, including himself, was too busy to pay
overmuch attention to the screaming threats from Berlin, or
the cocksure rantings from Rome. In any case, the cacophony
had now continued so long – ever since the autumn of 1935,
when Mussolini had attacked Abyssinia – and everybody had
become so bored with it, that it acted on them like the beat
of surf on the shore throughout an overlong winter. It was
not until the evening of the 23rd August, that the telephone
bell rang and he heard Simon say, 'Well Gov, this is it,
I imagine!' and when Paul admitted that he had been out
helping Rumble Patrick until dusk, that Claire was away
fetching young John from the annual Sunday School treat,
and that he had not heard a news-bulletin for twenty-four
hours, Simon said, with a bitterness the telephone could not

disguise, 'Germany and Russia have signed a non-aggression pact! You'd better listen to the next news and then ring me. Make it tonight, I'll be off tomorrow.'

'For God's sake – off where? There's no war yet, is there?'

'Camp. Local Terriers. We were going anyway but this will almost certainly mean mobilisation.'

'I'll ring,' Paul promised and hung up, hurrying back to the library and switching on just in time to hear the news delivered as though it had been part of a sports commentary. He heard it out and went back to the 'phone, finding that his steps dragged a little and suddenly feeling the tug of tired muscles after twelve hours in the fields.

'When would Rachel like to come?' he asked as soon as Simon answered, 'Will she wait until something actually happens?'

'She's packing now,' Simon said and then, after a slight pause, 'I'd better say good-bye, Gov. God knows where I shall end up or if I'll be able to ring. There's some talk of actually landing chaps on the Continent as a kind of peace force, if you've ever heard anything so bloody silly! Keep an eye on Rachel, as well as the home fires burning!'

'Good luck wherever you go – if anywhere,' Paul said hoarsely and quickly replaced the receiver. He was not given to premonitions but he had one now. In the half-hour or so before he heard the scrape of Claire's car on the gravel he was as sure as he had ever been of anything, that he would never hear Simon's voice again. All the others', possibly, but not the voice of Grace's son.

Chapter Twenty

I

About half-past five, on the last morning of May, 1940, Paul emerged from Crabpot Willie's cabin in time to see his relief, Henry Pitts, top the rise and descend the shallow tail of the goyle on his pony. He looked, Paul thought, exactly like a burgher commando rider moving down into a donga. The pony was far too small for him and his legs swung barely a foot from the ground. Over his shoulder, supported by a length of whipcord, was a 12-bore and the Boer touch was heightened by the shapeless trilby hat he wore, a hat that had weathered the Valley sun, wind and sleet ever since it had been issued as part of Henry's demobilisation togs in the long dry summer of 1919.

It was strange, Paul reflected, that all the important pattern changes of the Valley were signposted by what the locals called 'a praper ole scorcher'. The sun had burned the grass a dark brown in 1902, the season Paul settled in, and the Valley had withered under its non-stop glare in 1914. The first year of the peace had been just as hot and airless but between then and now, a matter of twenty-one years, he could not recall a dry spell lasting more than a fortnight or so. Perhaps they had come and gone without him noticing but now, with the rhythm of the seasons broken more finally than ever before, one took note of the weather. Somehow the brassiness of the sky, and the windlessness of the dunes above the beach, had within them elements of mockery to men condemned to play soldiers when they should have been making the very most of such sunshine.

He called, 'You're ahead of time, Henry, I didn't expect you until six!' and Henry, sliding down without disturbing the creases of his habitual grin, replied, 'I was woke by they bliddy aircraft passing over. Taaken all round 'twas too early to get up but too late to drop off again, zo I slipped out without wakin' Ellie an' brewed meself a cup o' tay!'

'I was just about to put the kettle on,' Paul said, 'but seeing you're here I'll leave it to you. I'm off along the beach to the fort, then over to Bluff to check with Francis. It's been very quiet, nothing but the aircraft. Blenheims I think they were, off bombing somewhere I imagine!'

'They all gives Ellie the jitters!' Henry said, 'and tidden a particle o' use me zayin' they'm ours. She knows bliddy well I can't tell the diff'rence. Who be inside, Maister?'

'Only Robbie Eveleigh. He was relieved by Noah Williams just after three o'clock when I came on but you send them both home at seven. Nothing's likely to happen now!'

He looked down the gully to the sea, as flat and motionless as he had ever seen it, with its eastern edges turning whitish pink as the sun hoisted itself clear of the Bluff. Birds were chirping in the thicket beyond the pines and a solitary gull dipped over the criss-cross of iron stanchions, sown along the outer edge of the sandbanks, a token of discouragement to Wehrmacht landing-parties.

'Tiz a funny thing,' Henry said, passing his hand over his unshaven jowls, 'you remember us always said in France that ole Jerry could pick his own weather. If 'er maade up 'is mind to pay us a call he could get ashore without gettin' 'is veet wet, an' what's more the lass zays it's zet fair, zame as it's been for a month or more a'ready!'

'And a damned good job too,' Paul reminded him. 'If we had had our usual summer Dunkirk would have been a fiasco and I doubt whether we should have fished the half of them off.'

'Arr,' Henry agreed, 'that's true, but then, if us had had the kind o' weather you an' me had to put up with over there, I dorn reckon his bliddy ole panzers would o' crossed our old stamping ground so fast! Not nearly so fast!' he added, emphatically and then seriously, 'I suppose you baint heard nowt o' your boys?'

'No word so far,' Paul told him, 'but as far as I know only Simon was over there. The Pair had switched to Air-Sea Rescue and Ian, Whiz's husband, was still out East last time I heard. Will you be free to take on tonight, same as usual?'

'Ah, I'll do that. Tiz worked well enough zo far baint it?'

'It'll work a damned sight better when the telephone people give us the outside line they've promised,' Paul said. 'Imagine having to rely on word-of-mouth alerts in this day and age! I can't see Jerry doing it if he was in our shoes!' and he went round the cabin to the lean-to shed where his birthday grey was saddled and tethered, Henry following and tethering his pony in its place at the hay net. The animals accepted the routine as though it had begun a year ago instead of a matter of days, dating from the formation of the coastal patrol of Churchill's LDVs, or Lame-Duck-Vagabonds as Henry designated the Local Defence Volunteers. Valley men were responsible for guarding the coast from a mile west of the landslip, where their right-hand man was in contact with the Whinmouth group, to a mile east of the Bluff, where Francis Willoughby's patrols were in touch with the next section. They were thinly stretched, a mere dozen or so, operating over more than four miles of coastline. As Smut Potter said the first night he took station, 'It baint much more than a bluff, be it? If Jerry was minded to come ashore in the dark he'd be eatin' his bliddy breakfast at The Mitre, in Paxtonbury, bevore us knowed he was around!' Yet the group took themselves seriously. At least they were better armed than the majority of the lookouts around the coasts, having, between them, eight shot-guns and three .22 rifles, as well as Paul's Smith & Wesson revolver. They might, as Henry said, blow a few hats off before they ran for it.

Paul turned east directly into the sun, shading his eyes as he walked the grey along the tideline towards Coombe Bay and perhaps because the morning was so sparkling and he had enjoyed two hours' sleep in the cabin after Noah Williams had reported, he felt reasonably encouraged, despite the incredible tale of disasters that had been theirs since the invasion of Norway, in April. To a man who had spent more than eighteen months on the Western Front it was hard to believe France had been overrun in a month, that Poland, Holland and Belgium had thrown in the sponge, that Paris was already occupied by jubilant, jackbooted Nazis, that British ships had fired on the French fleet, and that all that remained of the British Expeditionary Force was about a quarter-million shaken men lacking guns, transport and every kind of material. Already, however, they were calling Dunkirk a triumph, instead of the disaster it undoubtedly was. Already people like Smut Potter and Henry Pitts, who should know better, had slipped into the easy optimism that had swept down the Valley in the first weeks of the 1914–18 war, when everyone scrambled into uniform for fear it would be over by Christmas. Nobody, or nobody he had encountered since the news of the breakthrough, considered defeat by Hitler a possibility, although surely the speed and terrible finality of recent events made even temporary survival unlikely. They might, he supposed, fight some kind of delaying action, that would harden as it was edged northward, but after that, when the men who had frightened Uncle Franz in Munich and Nuremberg, had overrun the entire island, the war could only continue from Canada and how could such a war, even if it resulted in ultimate victory, save the Valley from the bombs of the Luftwaffe and tanks that had carved their way from the Rhine to the Biscay coast in less than a month?

That was the overall picture. What of the personal tragedy, as it affected him and Claire? Of his four sons and two sons-in-law four were already involved, The Pair (tiring of playing balloons, as he knew they would once they realised their role was static) were now sea-based; Ian was flying Gladiators in Egypt, and Simon – it would be poor old Simon – was probably already dead, or a prisoner marching into endless captivity! So far the Valley had not fared too badly. Only one man, a reservist from Coombe Bay, had been certified dead, after a submarine had found its way into Scapa Flow and sunk the *Royal Oak*, but others would soon qualify for another page at the back of the estate record book. Young Eveleigh, Harold's boy, of Four Winds, had his name down for the REs, and Smut's lad, 'Bon-Bon', who had helped farm

the shrunken High Coombe holding, was waiting to be called
into the RAF. Paul Rudd, Maureen's only son, had written from
Scotland to say he was joining the RAMC, and Albert Pascoe,
whose real name was Timberlake, had left a week ago to join
the Devons. 'God knows!' Paul told himself, as he kicked the
grey into a trot, 'I've enough to make me despondent but for
the life of me I don't *feel* despondent! Is it because the entire
bloody shambles has passed beyond the bounds of sanity, or
has the 'miracle of Dunkirk' had the same effect on me as
on all the others, notwithstanding the dictates of ordinary
commonsense?'

The question interested him deeply and he continued to
ponder it as he headed for the harbour slipway and the bizarre
structure beyond that was now known as 'The Fort'. It was
not really a fort but a café, idiotically disguised as a pillbox,
of the kind that had caused the deaths of so many men in the
morasses about Pilckhem Ridge, Passchendaele. Someone had
had the notion of painting it battleship-grey and knocking a
loophole or two in the seaward side, but to anyone with poor
eyesight and second-rate binoculars it still looked like a café
and a gimcrack one at that. As he rode along the last stretch of
beach Paul found himself pondering the curious contradictions
of the British race, indolent to the point of national suicide in
the face of so many stark warnings, and then, given a lead
from Westminster, in such a hurry to make up for lost time
that they became eager victims of ten thousand bureaucrats.
Two months ago, apart from the tiresome (and, to Paul, useless)
blackout, no one could have supposed the country committed
to a war. Today the entire countryside was in an uproar,
with signposts torn down, the names removed from such
tiny stations as Sorrel Halt, tank-traps showing their teeth
all the way to Paxtonbury, sandbars covered by a *chevaux
de frise* of tubular ironwork, and finally, this absurd little
sea-front café disguised as a pillbox! And in a way everyone
seemed to be enjoying themselves hugely, as though it was
a vast relief to face the prospect of meeting heavy tanks and
dive-bombers with a few rabbit-guns and petrol bombs
made out of ginger-beer bottles. It was commendable, perhaps,

this illogical upsurge of defiance, but it was also pitiful. A people who had survived the Somme and Third Ypres should be waging total war with a better prospect of winning it.

The beach looked deserted so he clattered up the slipway along to the fort where he dismounted and tethered the grey to the guard-rail of the sea-wall. Then, hearing the rattle of stones below, he looked over the top into the sunburned face of Rumble Patrick, perhaps the best beloved of all the males in the Valley, and the current freeholder of Periwinkle. Rumble, as usual, wore nothing but singlet and shorts and still, thought Paul, looked more like a boy than the master of a farm and the father of two children.

'Lovely morning, Gov!' he called, cheerily. 'Saw you a mile off but you didn't spot us, did you now?'

'No, I didn't,' admitted Paul. 'Where were you? Playing in a sandpit?'

'Getting warm!' Rumble called back and then, with a knowing grin, 'Okay! Come out Uncle Smut and show the Gov the welcome we've prepared for Jerry!' and Smut Potter suddenly materialised from a rash of pebbles, all about the size of a clenched fist, so that Paul, looking closer, saw that a cunningly constructed tank-trap now protected the approach to the wall under the pillbox, a trench about ten feet deep and two yards wide, screened by a huge boat-tarpaulin strong enough to bear the weight of camouflage shingle.

'That's not bad!' he said, admiring, 'but suppose Jerry resists the invitation and prefers to tackle the slipway?'

'We've got a better one down there,' Rumble said. 'Smut organised local slave-labour yesterday and my guess is that anything leaving a tank-landing craft would either try the slipway or head straight up the beach to bring point-blank fire on the Fort. He'd want to get over the sea-wall in the shortest possible time, wouldn't he?'

'I daresay, and in any case it's better than sitting waiting and playing cards in the café, as Smut was last time I looked in. Are you two the only ones on patrol over here?'

'We were six strong last night,' Smut said. 'Brissot and
Jumbo Bellchamber turned up, as well as Mark Codsall and
Willis.'

'Willis?' Paul queried. 'What the hell is the good of a
blind chap on this sort of job?'

'Just what I thought, Squire,' Smut said, apologetically, 'but
the fact is I didn't have the heart to turn him away. Panse
brought un down, zoon as it was dimpsy, and he said he could
sit inside and relay messages when us got the phone laid on. He
could too, I reckon, and you can't help admiring his pluck!'

No, Paul thought, you couldn't; a man of over fifty, blinded
by mustard gas on the Lys in 1918 but still anxious to prove
to himself that he wasn't utterly useless in an emergency.

'Tell him this is his post from now on,' he said. 'I'm going
to blitz the GPO people the moment I've had breakfast. We
should have the 'phone link-up between here, the Bluff lookout,
and shanty HQ within twenty-four hours.'

Smut waved his hand and disappeared under the shingle
again, Rumble swinging himself up the short rope-ladder that
connected rampart and tank-trap to sit dusting the sand from
his long, dark hair while Paul untethered the grey and swung
himself into the saddle. So often Rumble had reminded him
painfully of his father, Ikey Palfrey, but never more so than
this morning, with his overlong hair, smooth brown skin and
easy good humour that was encouraged, no doubt, by being
early abroad on such a pleasant morning.

'Mary all right?' Paul asked and Rumble said she was
although he had the impression she considered the LDV lark
a male excuse to indulge in children's games and evade serious
work.

'Claire has much the same viewpoint if that's any comfort,'
Paul told him, 'but to my mind it's somebody's job to keep a
close lookout early evenings and early mornings. If a German
aircraft skims over it wouldn't do for the pilot to report that
there was nothing awake but gulls. If I were you I'd slip
back for your breakfast now. He isn't likely to try it in
broad daylight and until we've got a gun here there's no
sense in maintaining day and night patrols. Love to Mary!'

and he trotted on, turning left off the sea-front at the junction of High Street and climbing the steep street to the church.

No one else was astir as yet and he remembered the first time he had ridden along this road in the early morning, the second day he had arrived here, now almost exactly thirty-eight years ago, when he was a lame young man of twenty-three madly in love with a girl he had met by chance in the Shallowford nursery the previous evening. He smiled grimly, recalling the flutter in his breast as he rode past her house on the hill and wondered, not for the first time, if he would have bought the estate at all had it not been for Grace. Probably, although John Rudd always declared she had been the deciding factor, and as he thought of old John and Grace he remembered other old faces and dismounted at the lych-gate of the churchyard, again tethering the horse and making his way between grass-grown graves to the west door, then hard left to the section of the yard where lay most of the men and women of his first decade in the Valley.

They were none of them really dead to him, and never would be so long as there was breath in his body. He glanced across at the granite obelisk marking the grave of Old Tamer that might so easily have been his own. Close by lay Preacher Willoughby who should, by rights, have been buried in the Nonconformist patch but somehow had not been, and remembering the rosy, saintlike face of the former master of Deepdene he thought of Elinor, his daughter, and wondered how she would fare now, an Englishwoman married to a German and living somewhere in the Wurttemberg area. Behind Willoughby's grave was the Codsall family plot, man and wife quiet at last, and beyond them, the grave of Arthur Pitts and that of Edward Derwent, his father-in-law, who had always been gruff and uncommunicative but had proved a trump once his ruffled pride was soothed by his pretty daughter's elevation to Squiress. He grinned, recalling Edward's honest, shamefaced acceptance of him as a prospective son-in-law, the day of old John Rudd's wedding in the fall of 1906. Dear Heaven! It all seemed so long ago and so improbable, like pondering the dynasties of Plantagenets and Tudors. Could any one of the people lying around him have dreamed up this summer, with a raving madman bestriding Europe and Britain the only country between him and a very promising bid for world domination? Perhaps that was just possible. Some of them had known the Kaiser's ambition but surely there was no real comparison, for not even Horace Handcock, the Valley fire-eater who had so hated Germans had envisaged concentration camps and the deliberate destruction of open cities, like Rotterdam and Warsaw.

He stood for a moment over John Rudd's grave, wondering what kind of advice John would have given him this morning. 'Hold on' perhaps; no more and no less for what else was there to do anyway? He circled the church and went past the Rectory, his riding boots striking hard on the asphalt path so that a dormer window opened and the snow-white head of Parson Horsey appeared, like the head of a gnome emerging from a crooked little house in a fairy-tale book illustration.

'You're up and about betimes!' the old man called. 'Coast-watching, I imagine?'

'Doing the rounds,' Paul told him, 'I can't sit waiting for it at home.'

'You never could,' Horsey threw at him, with a chuckle, 'and I envy you! The only good thing about this war is that one doesn't have the obligatory tussle with one's conscience over participating. I don't think my Keith would have been content to be a stretcher-bearer in this flare-up!'

'I don't think so either!' said Paul, and then, 'What's the latest on the evacuee situation?'

'Another batch of thirty due on Saturday to replace some of those who have gone back, pining for fish and chips!' said the rector. 'I imagine this lot will stay, however. It wouldn't surprise me a bit if that dreadful little man didn't start bombing London any day now. I hear there's talk of sending shiploads of children to the States and Canada. Would you consider sending your John and Mary's babies if you get the chance?'

Paul had already made his decision on this and had his answer pat. 'No! Saving your presence, Rector, I'm damned if I would! This is where they were born and this is where they belong. They can take their chance with the rest of us and

faced them if the Nazis did establish a permanent bridgehead. There would, no doubt, be murder and rape and pillage, on a scale that had not been practised in civilised countries since the Thirty Years War. And as he thought this and dropped down the last terrace to the mereside track, the heat went out of the sun and he shivered, finding the entire situation too terrible to contemplate. One would fight, he supposed, fight with shot-gun, Service revolver and pitchfork, with Molotov cocktails and brickbats, but what would it avail in the end? Up in Westminster Churchill was breathing fire and slaughter and undoubtedly people had taken heart from his words, but who among them had heard Winston's ironic aside after making his famous fight-on-the-beaches oration? Paul had, having passed the time of day with the local MP when he went into Paxtonbury to buy ammunition a week since. The Member had been close to Churchill when he sat down and claimed to have heard him say, in that curious, slurred growl of his, 'I don't know what we'll fight with – bloody axes and pick-handles, I imagine!'

About half-way along the track, almost opposite the ruinous Folly and the island, he met Sam Potter, spare, grizzled and well into his sixties but still swinging along with the stride of a man half his age. Sam, he learned, had made an early call on Harold Codsall, also in search of 12-bore ammunition and the sight of him injected Paul with confidence. Sam, he thought, would defend his cottage to the last gasp and it would take more than a squad of stormtroopers to eject him. He said, 'Any news of the family, Sam?' and Sam told him that his daughter's husband, an anti-aircraft gunner, had been among those rescued at Dunkirk the previous week and was due on leave any day. He seemed in need of reassurance himself for he hesitated when Paul was on the point of moving off, saying, half-apologetically, 'What do 'ee maake of it, Squire? Tiz a bliddy ole mix-up, baint it? Do 'ee reckon they'll try their luck at comin' yer?'

'They might,' Paul said, 'but if they do I daresay they'll get more than they bargained for. The Army will need time to reorganise but we've still got a Navy and an Air Force!'

'Arr!' Sam said, brightening, 'a man forgets that, but for once in my life, Squire, I'd welcome grey skies and a choppy sea outalong. If the Channel turned nasty I reckon us'd maake mincemeat o' the bastards. 'Ave 'ee got enough chaps to cover the landslip-Bluff stretch night times?'

'Francis Willoughby will need a partner when young Bon-Bon goes this weekend. Would you take on, until we can get properly organised and the police let us have some rifles?'

'Arr, I'll do that an' glad to,' Sam said, with a sigh. 'I'll walk over an' fix it up with un after Joannie has put up a bit o' breakfast.' Then, looking up at him earnestly, 'Tiz a real bliddy upset at our time o' life, baint it?'

'Yes,' Paul said, 'it certainly is, Sam, but I don't doubt we'll come through it, the same as we did all our other troubles and you and I have seen plenty in the last forty years. My regards to Joannie!' and he rode on, reflecting that, of all the Valley men, his link with Sam Potter was the strongest, for the instalment of Sam, as woodsman-gamekeeper, had been his first independent act as Squire of Shallowford.

He emerged from the woods and rode down the sunken lane to the stile at the top of the orchard. Looking at his watch he saw that it was ten minutes to seven and suddenly he felt both tired and hungry, ready for one of Claire's generous breakfasts and maybe an hour's nap in the study armchair. 'I'm getting too old for this kind of larkabout,' he told himself, 'and so are most of us around here. Surely to God it's time we had leisure to enjoy this kind of weather, without gadding up and down the Valley half the night!' And then, bracing himself, he succumbed to the spur of vanity, putting his grey at the two-rail fence beside the stile, clearing it easily and recalling, as he swung erect in the saddle, a phrase about 'young men skylarking over fences on their way home after a blank day in the hunting field'. It had not been such a blank night. He had seen the tribal spirit of the Valley at work again, with almost every able-bodied man from Blackberry Moor to the far side of the Bluff caught up in a collective task that reached back and back to the days when Celts and Normans had put themselves in a position of defence against French sea-raiders and Napoleon's

flat-bottomed barges. He unsaddled the grey and put ~~~
in the stable, going in through the kitchen and putting ~~~
iron kettle to boil for tea that he would take up to ~~~
he did so, however, he heard the telephone bell shri~~~
heart missed a beat, although he told himself ste~~~
was probably only the Whinmouth police, checki~~~
local organisation. He went into the hall and lifte~~~
and then his heart began to hammer and his ~~~
little, for the voice at the end of the line was Sim~~~ ~~~d within
it was a crackle of cheerfulness that was un~~~ acteristic of
the boy. He said, breathlessly, '*Simon!* It's ~~~ *you!* You're
. . . you're home and dry, lad?'

'Not so dry!' Simon said, 'but home ok~~~. I'm ringing from
near Folkestone. I got in during the nig~~~. Pretty well the last
of 'em I'd say!'

'God, but I'm glad to hear from y~~~ Paul said, fumbling
for a cigarette to steady himself. 'W~~~ at happened? How did
you make it?'

'Too long a yarn to spin from a ~~~ ic call-box but the bare
bones aren't so remarkable. I jus~~~ ~~~lked into the bloody sea
and swam for it!'

'You're joking!'

'No I'm not!' He heard Simon smother a chuckle. 'I could
see 'em mopping up along the beaches, north of Calais, so
as it was every man for himself I stripped off and struck
out. I was damned lucky, mind, I not only found an empty
oil-drum a mile or so out but I was sighted by a destroyer
late in the afternoon. That's why I've been so long getting
in; they only docked last night!'

'You're . . . you're quite fit?'

'Fit as a fiddle! They gave me lashings of Navy rum on
board and I don't think I've sobered up yet. We're getting nine
days survival leave. Tell Rachel I'll be down some time during
the next forty-eight hours. Look, I can't stop, Gov, there's a
queue outside . . . see you soon!' and the line went dead.

He stood holding the receiver to his ear, thinking not so
much of Simon, whom he had half-decided was dead, but of
some of the other times he had stood here being fed with

information from the world outside the Valley; a night in 1914, when Uncle Franz had rung; the day Simon had 'phoned to tell him he was marrying Rachel Eveleigh; all manner of minor milestones through the years, concerning the comings and goings of The Pair, of Whiz, Mary and young Claire. He thought, 'He's luckier than his mother! He survived that Spanish nightmare and he's survived this! He obviously takes some killing, like me and Smut and old Henry Pitts. *Swam* for it, by God!', and he gave a short, barking laugh, catching sight of himself in the cheval mirror hanging on the cloakroom door. The reflection arrested him. Earlier that morning he had compared Henry to a Boer commando but now he himself looked like an ageing bandit, with tousled grey locks and a Smith & Wesson strapped to his side. He cocked his head on one side, wondering if others would agree with him that he did not look sixty-one, nor more than, say, fifty-four or -five, and still good for a rough and tumble if one was waiting him down on the beach. Then he heard the kettle-lid rattling and went back to the kitchen to make the tea, pouring it into the morning ritual mugs, taking one in each hand, and going slowly up the broad, shallow stairs.

He opened the bedroom door with his knee and was surprised and not a little amused, to find Claire was still heavily asleep. Then he remembered she had got up with him at two o'clock to make his coffee before he rode off to the shanty and had probably had some trouble getting off to sleep again after he had gone. He gently set down the mugs and pulled the curtain aside so that dazzling sunshine filled the room and she stirred and heaved herself over without waking. He went across and looked down at her, conscious of a warm current of relief and pleasure that was only partially due to the cheering news of Simon's escape. She was still, he thought, lovely to look at, particularly when she was relaxed as now. Her hair showed evidence of its fortnightly rinse and there was a suggestion of grey about the temples but one had to look for it, it didn't proclaim itself, as it did in most of the Valley women midway through their fifties. Her skin was still very clear and her cheeks, now slightly pendulous, were as fresh and rosy as on the day he had first ridden into High Coombe farmyard on his initial tour of the estate. Her mouth, showing faint traces of lipstick, was just as inviting and slightly parted lips revealed square, white teeth, the product, as she often told him, of her great weakness for cheese, which made calcium. Suddenly she blinked her eyes and when she saw him sat up very suddenly, her pink nightdress slipping over one shoulder and her expression very bemused.

'What is it? What's the time?'

'Time you were up and about,' he said, handing her a mug. 'It's lucky you woke up when you did. Another moment and I should have been in beside you and half the morning wasted. I've just heard from Simon.'

'*Simon!* He's . . . here? He's all right?'

'Near Folkestone and coming on leave. Not even wounded. Sounded as though he subscribes to the general belief that Dunkirk was an even more shattering victory than Waterloo!'

'Oh God, I'm glad, Paul! Glad for you but gladder still for me!' and she set down the mug and hugged herself with a little girl's glee.

He said, sitting on the edge of the bed, 'I knew you would be. He always was rather special for you, wasn't he? Perhaps because you always leaned over backwards in attempts to disprove the wicked stepmother theory! Well, I daresay he owes his survival to you. He tells me he swam for it. No! I mean it! He actually struck out across the Channel and was picked up by a destroyer a mile or so out! It was you who taught him to swim, Claire.'

'Yes, I did,' she said, with enormous satisfaction, 'and he was always the best swimmer of the lot of them. The Pair wouldn't have got beyond the breakwater. Have you told Rachel yet?'

'No, I only heard as I was making the tea ten minutes ago.'

'Then I'll drive over right away!' she said, scrambling out of bed, but he protested. 'No you won't, woman! You'll get me some breakfast first and while it's cooking you can scout around for Mark Codsall. He came off duty more than seven hours ago and he can take her the news!'

He yawned and suddenly she looked contrite. 'You must be tired out! Why don't you pull off your clothes and slip into bed for an hour or so? Tell you what – I'll bring your breakfast up on a tray!'

He could not remember when he had last breakfasted in bed and the idea was appealing. Then he remembered all the things he had to do and stopped in the act of unbuckling his webbing belt. 'Hell no, I can't do that . . . !' but she had gauged his approval and said, sharply, 'You can and you will! Here, give me those things!' and began peeling off his jacket so that he surrendered and quickly undressed, sliding into a bed that was still warm and smelled very pleasantly of her perfume. He lay back watching her struggle into her clothes, smiling to himself as she inched a frivolous and inadequate foundation-garment over her hips and marvelling at the impression of slimness it lent her when it was in position. Then, after a tug or two at her hair, she was gone and he was drifting into a doze when the dressing-room door opened very cautiously and the bullet head of his six-year-old son John appeared round the crack. He said, sleepily, 'All right, either come in or go out, John!' and John came in, his eyes immediately fastening on the discarded holster.

'Can I look at it, Dad?'

'No you can't, it's loaded!'

'Have you shot any Nazis?'

'No, there were none within range unfortunately!'

John looked mildly disappointed and mooched across to the tall window where Paul saw that he was arrayed in the cowboy outfit the doting Thirza Tremlett had made for him at his urgent demand. It consisted of a loud check shirt, fringed corduroys and a gun-belt slung with two beaded and brass-studded holsters, each sporting a cap pistol.

'Uncle Rumble says the sea will be a-wash with their corpses if they try for Coombe Bay!' John said solemnly. 'Was he pulling my leg, do you think?'

'No,' said Paul, judiciously, 'he wasn't! Every one who tries to get ashore will certainly be picked off from the dunes. Everyone's waiting with a gun and the Navy is all set to drive them right into our line of fire. If you want your breakfast your mother's getting it now!'

'Okay!' said the boy and left abruptly, without noticing the reluctant grin that made his father conscious of the night's bristles on his chin. 'Okay!' And dressed as an American cowboy at a time like this! It was a little incongruous to see a six-year-old adopting a role of make-believe violence when there was so much real violence threatening over the Channel and in the skies overhead. He was nodding off when Claire bustled in with his tray and although, just then, he would have preferred to sleep, he made the effort and sat up while she lifted the cover from a plate of bacon and eggs. Then the smell revived his appetite and he began to eat ravenously as she watched with approval.

'Was it all quiet on the Coombe Bay front?'

'Quiet enough,' he told her, describing Henry's arrival, Rumble Patrick's tank-trap and his own casual visit to the churchyard before riding home through the woods. His detour interested her. She said, looking down on him with a smile, 'I'd like to see the German who could run you off this land, Paul! He'd have to be a six-headed monster armed with a death-ray!'

'A company of second-line troops could do it with last-war rifles,' he said. 'We've only got a few sporting guns and an odd revolver or two!'

'You don't have to worry,' she said, with a finality that made him half-ashamed of his fears, 'they won't even try! And we'll win all right, the same as we always do after the initial flutter in the henhouse. You'll finish your days here and so will I. And so will Mary's children and young John and probably their children! And by that time there won't be anything to worry about except jerry-builders for by then you men will have grown up and learned to attend to the serious business!'

He was exasperated in spite of the assurance she brought him and said, petulantly, 'It isn't that kind of war, Claire! Not this time. It's very real war, with all-or-nothing stakes. You ought to get that into your head and keep it there!'

'Oh, it's in my head,' she said, off-handedly, 'but I can't get so worked up about it as you. I can't really believe that anybody as idiotic as Hitler will be tolerated anywhere for long. Too much Derwent commonsense, maybe. Breakfast to your liking, sir?'

'First-rate. You can make a habit of this after the war!'

'You'd be lucky!' and suddenly she laughed, reached out and rumpled his already rumpled hair. 'I'll see to John's breakfast and get the message over to Rachel!' and she turned to go but he steadied the tray with his right hand and shot out his left, catching her by the wrist.

'Steady on!' she warned him, 'you'll have the lot over the bed-clothes!' but when he lifted her plump hand to his mouth and kissed it she smiled, saying, 'An early ride in Shallowford Woods always takes you this way! Did you pass alongside the mere?'

'Yes,' he admitted, 'past the exact spot where you once tried to seduce me, you huzzy. And me a gangling, city-bred boy with money in the bank!'

'I wish I'd succeeded!' she said. 'We would have had nearly five extra years to look back on!'

'And five more children!'

'Without a shadow of doubt. Help yourself to more tea if you want it. I'll give you a call about ten.'

She went out and he disposed of the tray, stretching and luxuriating in the warmth of the bed and the glow of strong, morning sunlight. Suddenly and improbably the war seemed to recede and with it went all thought of Hitler, a stricken Continent, LDV patrols and Rumble Patrick's tank-traps. All that remained, all that mattered on this earth or beyond it was Claire and Shallowford, Claire's children and Claire's children's children, together with all the old originals and their descendants, living their humdrum lives between the railway line and the sea, between the Teazel in the west and the Bluff in the east. Nothing else was worth a moment's anxiety, and, resolving this, he slept.

She returned about ten but she did not disturb him. He was sleeping very peacefully and she thought, briefly, 'To hell with his orders. He'll be out again half the night and he isn't as

young as he likes to pretend!' And then, for the first time
in a long while, she took a dispassionate look at him, not so
much to assess the toil of the years that drove her to study
her own reflection often enough, but in search of the man
himself. What was it, she asked herself, that had held her to
him all these years, had made his business hers, his trickle of
hopes and fears, anxieties and exultations the threads of her
existence and led, one and all, back to this sprawling house
on the southern slope of a valley by-passed by the century?
She looked closely and seriously at the long, narrow face,
hedged with bluish stubble, the thick grey hair tumbled on
her pillow, the long, relaxed form under the white coverlet. His
loins undoubtedly. They had always brought her fulfilment but
outside the bed, in day-to-day life, there was a quality about
him that was astonishingly rare in this age – an enduring faith
and ceaseless endeavour that was utterly divorced from the
besetting pre-occupation of his generation, concerned, in the
main, with greed of one sort or another. He might, she reflected,
have been a very rich man and he was not, had never wanted
to be, for all the money he had ever had had been poured into
these acres and dribbled away without a sigh on his part, and
he was not even rich in kind, for most of it had gone to those
whose lives, in a sense, he had held in trust over the years.
And yet, she decided, it was not his generosity that made him
the acknowledged leader here but his terrible earnestness, his
sense of purpose and dedication that only today was finding
wider expression from one end of the country to the other.
Realising this, identifying his steadfastness with the national
mood in the face of final disaster, she decided something else
about him that was both old and new. He had been right all
the time, every moment of his working life, since he had first
ridden into the Valley when she was a girl of nineteen. He
had, as it were, selected a target that most men of his means
and single-mindedness would have regarded as far too modest,
but whereas the big-game hunters had missed he had scored
a succession of bull's-eyes and was still scoring. It gave her
a queer sense of pride to realise that, over most of the time,
she had been loading for him. He had prescience but also a

kind of innocence. The one had enabled him to evaluate soil and comradeship in excess of everything else that touched his life and the other had matured him as a human being and brother to whom everyone about here turned, in good times and bad, for advice, steadfastness and friendship. In a way he was the antithesis of the spirit of the century, of the dismal trends of laissez-faire, usury and triviality that had led, after all, to another global calamity and yet he had never lost a certain modesty that some mistook for naïvety, forgetting that, under his seeming mildness was a core of proofed steel. Perhaps she was the only person in the world who was fully aware of this, having seen it tempered over the years but there were still plenty who thought of him as an anachronism, a reactionary, a benevolent autocrat or a genial soft touch but she knew otherwise. He was all these things on the surface but primarily he was a man of faith and a romantic, whose fibres were far tougher and more weatherproof than the fibres of professional adventurers and men in counting-houses, if only because, by now, they probed so deeply into Valley soil. There was enormous strength here, and abundant tenderness. There was virility, at sixty-one, that still retained the power to make her wilt and there was also self-assurance equal to all the stresses of peace and war, change and catastrophe. A woman who troubled herself to understand and appreciate this would always be safe with him; safe, satisfied and grateful for the hand she had been dealt.

She went to the window, remembering how she had stood on this same spot through the long afternoons watching him recover from his tremendous exertions after the wreck in the Cove. Thirty-three years with the same man, and she could still feel about him as she had felt the day he rode over that hill where the south-easterly tongue of the woods melted into the tip of the sloping meadow running down the near side of the Coombe. It was something to be thankful for. She went out, softly closing the door, leaving him to whatever dreams he had. They must have been rewarding. He was smiling slightly as he slept.

He appeared, dressed and shaved, just before noon after she

had carried her coffee into the library and entered the bare facts of Simon's survival into the estate diary. He grumbled a little at being left so long, pointing out that the leisurely days were behind them, but she shrugged off his complaint, reminding him that he would be out again half the night and was due to celebrate his sixty-first birthday in the morning. That stopped him dead, as she knew it would, for she was sure that he had forgotten. He said, scratching his head, 'Sixty-one, by God! What an orchestra to play a man into his dotage! Why, they couldn't even ring a peal of bells in the village without having everyone assume that the balloon had gone up!' And then he laughed, recounting how, that same morning, he had put the grey at the orchard rail and cleared it with eighteen inches in hand.

'The grey is only nine!' she said, and closing the diary crossed to the long cupboard under the lowest bookshelf, returning with a carefully wrapped parcel about four feet in length. 'Since you seem determined to go on playing young men's games until you have a seizure you may as well have your newest toy now!' she said.

'I'm more likely to have one playing games with you!' he told her, a joke aimed at concealing his boyish curiosity of the kind he invariably displayed on these occasions. He cut the string very deliberately and threw back the wrappings. On the table lay a brand new .22 deer rifle, together with a worn bandolier weighted with ammunition.

He recognised the bandolier at once as the sole remaining item of kit he had brought home from the Cape, in 1902, and she smiled as he stood staring down at the gift, as genuinely surprised and overwhelmed as he had been a year ago, when she had given him the bathing-pool portrait that now hung over the bed. He looked, she thought, more like sixteen than sixty as he said, sombrely, 'It's magnificent! It's the best vermin gun on the market. It can kill at half-a-mile, did you know that?'

'Smut advised me to handle it carefully,' she said. 'I had to ask him to get it but don't enquire too closely where. It's my belief he bent the law a little!'

'I'll warrant he did!' and he picked it up, balanced it and let his hand glide over the gleaming stock. Then, after breaking it to make sure it was unloaded, he brought it slowly to his shoulder and clicked the trigger. 'Well,' he said, at length, 'let 'em come! Let 'em all come! I'll knock a few gaps in their bloody ranks before they chase me out of the Valley!' and suddenly she realised that what had seemed at first an extravagant notion was, in fact, an inspiration on her part.

'Last year a provocative oil-painting of a grandmother in half a swimsuit, this year a gun to shoot Stormtroopers! I suppose it's me who encourages you never to grow up!' she said but her sigh was thoroughly counterfeit and when he threw his arms round her and kissed her mouth she strained herself towards him, giving expression to the nostalgic yearning she had felt for him in the bedroom an hour or so earlier. He said, seriously, 'I shall enjoy going on patrol tonight. I can lend my shot-gun to Eveleigh's boy until the rifles arrive. Is there any fresh coffee going?'

'I'll get some,' she said and went out, guessing that, boy-like, he wanted a few minutes alone to relish his gift. She was quite right. The moment her back was turned he threw open the garden door and moved out on to the terrace, slipping a round into the breech and looking about for a likely mark. He found one at the angle of the rose garden, a very amateur scarecrow that Mark Codsall had rigged up to guard the freshly-turned vegetable rows in Little Paddock. It was hardly more than a cross of peasticks, hung about with an old sports jacket and a hard hunting hat, thrown aside by one of the children. He brought the gun to his shoulder and fired, almost without sighting. The hat went spinning and the peastick frame lurched to an angle of sixty degrees. 'Well,' he told himself, with the utmost satisfaction, 'I haven't forgotten how to shoot and that must mean there's nothing wrong with my eyesight!' and then, as though the mood of self-satisfaction demanded enlargement, 'And there was nothing wrong with the post-war generation after all! Most of them turned up trumps in the end – young Bon-Bon falling over himself to get into the RAF, The Pair turning their back on money-making for the duration, Rumble

Patrick down there on the beach building his tank-traps, and dear old Simon, bless his suffragette heart, taking a cool look at those bloody Nazis and deciding to swim for it!' He heard Claire call 'Coffee!' from the library and threw the rifle over his forearm, walking slowly back along the baking terrace and raising his nose an inch to sniff the heavy scent of parched grass. He had walked these flags in many moods over the last four decades but never, he told himself, with a more compelling sense of uplift and dedication.

THE HORSEMAN RIDING BY: BOOK THREE

THE GREEN GAUNTLET

R. F. Delderfield

1942-1964
Paul and Claire Craddock have grown older in years – but not in spirit.

The turbulence of war is followed by a penurious peace. Changes are taking place in the countryside, from the way land is farmed to the hopes and expectations of the men and women who live there. Paul Craddock's livelihood, his peace, and his vision of a good and noble way of life in Shallowford are all threatened.

With the help of his children and his children's children, Paul starts to adapt his dreams in order to preserve the farm. To his surprise and pleasure, in doing so he comes to discover deeper, richer ties with those around him – ties that hold a ripe promise for the future.

HODDER